NATHANIEL HAWTHORNE COLLECTION

Twice-Told Tales, The Scarlet Letter, The House of the Seven Gables

NATHANIEL HAWTHORNE

D1525021

CONTENTS

TWICE-TOLD TALES

THE GRAY CHAMPION

THERE WAS ONCE a time when New England groaned under the actual pressure of heavier wrongs than those threatened ones which brought on the Revolution. James II., the bigoted successor of Charles the Voluptuous, had annulled the charters of all the colonies and sent a harsh and unprincipled soldier to take away our liberties and endanger our religion. The administration of Sir Edmund Andros lacked scarcely a single characteristic of tyranny—a governor and council holding office from the king and wholly independent of the country; laws made and taxes levied without concurrence of the people, immediate or by their representatives; the rights of private citizens violated and the titles of all landed property declared void; the voice of complaint stifled by restrictions on the press; and finally, disaffection overawed by the first band of mercenary troops that ever marched on our free soil. For two years our ancestors were kept in sullen submission by that filial love which had invariably secured their allegiance to the mother-country, whether its head chanced to be a Parliament, Protector or popish monarch. Till these evil times, however, such allegiance had been merely nominal, and the colonists had ruled themselves, enjoying far more freedom than is even yet the privilege of the native subjects of Great Britain.

At length a rumor reached our shores that the prince of Orange had ventured on an enterprise the success of which would be the triumph of civil and religious rights and the salvation of New England. It was but a doubtful whisper; it might be false or the attempt might fail, and in either case the man that stirred against King James would lose his head. Still, the intelligence produced a marked effect. The people smiled mysteriously in the streets and threw bold glances at their oppressors, while far and wide there was a subdued and silent agitation, as if the slightest signal would rouse the whole land from its sluggish despondency. Aware of their danger, the rulers resolved to avert it by an imposing display of strength, and perhaps to confirm their despotism by yet harsher measures.

One afternoon in April, 1689, Sir Edmund Andros and his favorite councilors, being warm with wine, assembled the red-coats of the governor's guard and made their appearance in the streets of Boston. The sun was near setting when the march commenced. The roll of the drum at that unquiet crisis seemed to go through the streets less as the martial music of the soldiers than

3

as a muster-call to the inhabitants themselves. A multitude by various avenues assembled in King street, which was destined to be the scene, nearly a century afterward, of another encounter between the troops of Britain and a people struggling against her tyranny.

Though more than sixty years had elapsed since the Pilgrims came, this crowd of their descendants still showed the strong and sombre features of their character perhaps more strikingly in such a stern emergency than on happier occasions. There was the sober garb, the general severity of mien, the gloomy but undismayed expression, the scriptural forms of speech and the confidence in Heaven's blessing on a righteous cause which would have marked a band of the original Puritans when threatened by some peril of the wilderness. Indeed, it was not yet time for the old spirit to be extinct, since there were men in the street that day who had worshipped there beneath the trees before a house was reared to the God for whom they had become exiles. Old soldiers of the Parliament were here, too, smiling grimly at the thought that their aged arms might strike another blow against the house of Stuart. Here, also, were the veterans of King Philip's war, who had burned villages and slaughtered young and old with pious fierceness while the godly souls throughout the land were helping them with prayer. Several ministers were scattered among the crowd, which, unlike all other mobs, regarded them with such reverence as if there were sanctity in their very garments. These holy men exerted their influence to quiet the people, but not to disperse them.

Meantime, the purpose of the governor in disturbing the peace of the town at a period when the slightest commotion might throw the country into a ferment was almost the Universal subject of inquiry, and variously explained.

"Satan will strike his master-stroke presently," cried some, "because he knoweth that his time is short. All our godly pastors are to be dragged to prison. We shall see them at a Smithfield fire in King street."

Hereupon the people of each parish gathered closer round their minister, who looked calmly upward and assumed a more apostolic dignity, as well befitted a candidate for the highest honor of his profession—a crown of martyrdom. It was actually fancied at that period that New England might have a John Rogers of her own to take the place of that worthy in the *Primer*.

"The pope of Rome has given orders for a new St. Bartholomew," cried others. "We are to be massacred, man and male-child."

Neither was this rumor wholly discredited; although the wiser class believed the governor's object somewhat less atrocious. His predecessor under the old charter, Bradstreet, a venerable companion of the first settlers, was known to be in town. There were grounds for conjecturing that Sir Edmund Andros intended at once to strike terror by a parade of military force and to confound the opposite faction by possessing himself of their chief.

"Stand firm for the old charter-governor!" shouted the crowd, seizing upon the idea—"the good old Governor Bradstreet!"

While this cry was at the loudest the people were surprised by the well-known figure of Governor Bradstreet himself, a patriarch of nearly ninety, who appeared on the elevated steps of a door and with characteristic mildness besought them to submit to the constituted authorities.

"My children," concluded this venerable person, "do nothing rashly. Cry not aloud, but pray for the welfare of New England and expect patiently what the Lord will do in this matter."

The event was soon to be decided. All this time the roll of the drum had been approaching through Cornhill, louder and deeper, till with reverberations from house to house and the regular tramp of martial footsteps it burst into the street. A double rank of soldiers made their appearance, occupying the whole breadth of the passage, with shouldered matchlocks and matches burning, so as to present a row of fires in the dusk. Their steady march was like the progress of a machine that would roll irresistibly over everything in its way. Next, moving slowly, with a confused clatter of hoofs on the pavement, rode a party of mounted gentlemen, the central figure being Sir Edmund Andros, elderly, but erect and soldier-like. Those around him were his favorite councilors and the bitterest foes of New England. At his right hand rode Edward Randolph, our arch-enemy, that "blasted wretch," as Cotton Mather calls him, who achieved the downfall of our ancient government and was followed with a sensible curse-through life and to his grave. On the other side was Bullivant, scattering jests and mockery as he rode along. Dudley came behind with a downcast look, dreading, as well he might, to meet the indignant gaze of the people, who beheld him, their only countryman by birth, among the oppressors of his native land. The captain of a frigate in the harbor and two or three civil officers under the Crown were also there. But the figure which most attracted the public eye and stirred up the deepest feeling was the Episcopal clergyman of King's Chapel riding haughtily among the magistrates in his priestly vestments, the fitting representative of prelacy and persecution, the union of Church and State, and all those abominations which had driven the Puritans to the wilderness. Another guard of soldiers, in double rank, brought up the rear.

The whole scene was a picture of the condition of New England, and its moral, the deformity of any government that does not grow out of the nature of things and the character of the people—on one side the religious multitude with their sad visages and dark attire, and on the other the group of despotic rulers with the high churchman in the midst and here and there a crucifix at their bosoms, all magnificently clad, flushed with wine, proud of unjust authority and scoffing at the universal groan. And the mercenary soldiers, waiting but the word to deluge the street with blood, showed the only means by which obedience could be secured.

"O Lord of hosts," cried a voice among the crowd, "provide a champion for thy people!"

This ejaculation was loudly uttered, and served as a herald's cry to introduce a remarkable personage. The crowd had rolled back, and were now huddled together nearly at the extremity of the street, while the soldiers had advanced no more than a third of its length. The intervening space was empty—a paved solitude between lofty edifices which threw almost a twilight shadow over it. Suddenly there was seen the figure of an ancient man who seemed to have emerged from among the people and was walking by himself along the centre of the street to confront the armed band. He wore the old Puritan dress—a dark cloak and a steeple-crowned hat in the fashion of at least fifty years before, with a heavy sword upon his thigh, but a staff in his hand to assist the tremulous gait of age.

When at some distance from the multitude, the old man turned slowly round, displaying a face of antique majesty rendered doubly venerable by the hoary beard that descended on his breast. He made a gesture at once of encouragement and warning, then turned again and resumed his way.

"Who is this gray patriarch?" asked the young men of their sires.

"Who is this venerable brother?" asked the old men among themselves.

But none could make reply. The fathers of the people, those of fourscore years and upward, were disturbed, deeming it strange that they should forget one of such evident authority whom they must have known in their early days, the associate of Winthrop and all the old councilors, giving laws and making prayers and leading them against the savage. The elderly men ought to have remembered him, too, with locks as gray in their youth as their own were now. And the young! How could he have passed so utterly from their memories—that hoary sire, the relic of long-departed times, whose awful benediction had surely been bestowed on their uncovered heads in childhood?

"Whence did he come? What is his purpose? Who can this old man be?" whispered the wondering crowd.

Meanwhile, the venerable stranger, staff in hand, was pursuing his solitary walk along the centre of the street. As he drew near the advancing soldiers, and as the roll of their drum came full upon his ear, the old man raised himself to a loftier mien, while the decrepitude of age seemed to fall from his shoulders, leaving him in gray but unbroken dignity. Now he marched onward with a warrior's step, keeping time to the military music. Thus the aged form advanced on one side and the whole parade of soldiers and magistrates on the other, till, when scarcely twenty yards remained between, the old man grasped his staff by the middle and held it before him like a leader's truncheon.

"Stand!" cried he.

The eye, the face and attitude of command, the solemn yet warlike peal of that voice—fit either to rule a host in the battle-field or be raised to God in prayer—were irresistible. At the old man's word and outstretched arm the roll of the drum was hushed at once and the advancing line stood still. A tremulous enthusiasm seized upon the multitude. That stately form, combining the leader and the saint, so gray, so dimly seen, in such an ancient garb, could only belong to some old champion of the righteous cause whom the oppressor's drum had summoned from his grave. They raised a shout of awe and exultation, and looked for the deliverance of New England.

The governor and the gentlemen of his party, perceiving themselves brought to an unexpected stand, rode hastily forward, as if they would have pressed their snorting and affrighted horses right against the hoary apparition. He, however, blenched not a step, but, glancing his severe eye round the group, which half encompassed him, at last bent it sternly on Sir Edmund Andros. One would have thought that the dark old man was chief ruler there, and that the governor and council with soldiers at their back, representing the whole power and authority of the Crown, had no alternative but obedience.

"What does this old fellow here?" cried Edward Randolph, fiercely.—"On, Sir Edmund! Bid the soldiers forward, and give the dotard the same choice that you give all his countrymen—to stand aside or be trampled on."

"Nay, nay! Let us show respect to the good grandsire," said Bullivant, laughing. "See you not he is some old round-headed dignitary who hath lain asleep these thirty years and knows nothing of the change of times? Doubtless he thinks to put us down with a proclamation in Old Noll's name."

"Are you mad, old man?" demanded Sir Edmund Andros, in loud and harsh tones. "How dare you stay the march of King James's governor?"

"I have stayed the march of a king himself ere now," replied the gray figure, with stern composure. "I am here, Sir Governor, because the cry of an oppressed people hath disturbed me in my secret place, and, beseeching this favor earnestly of the Lord, it was vouchsafed me to appear once again on earth in the good old cause of his saints. And what speak ye of James? There is no longer a popish tyrant on the throne of England, and by to-morrow noon his name shall be a by-word in this very street, where ye would make it a word of terror. Back, thou that wast a governor, back! With this night thy power is ended. To-morrow, the prison! Back, lest I foretell the scaffold!"

The people had been drawing nearer and nearer and drinking in the words of their champion, who spoke in accents long disused, like one unaccustomed to converse except with the dead of many years ago. But his voice stirred their souls. They confronted the soldiers, not wholly without arms and ready to convert the very stones of the street into deadly weapons. Sir Edmund Andros looked at the old man; then he cast his hard and cruel eye over the multitude and beheld them burning with that lurid wrath so difficult to kindle or to quench, and again he fixed his gaze on the aged form which stood obscurely in an open space where neither friend nor foe had thrust himself. What were his thoughts he uttered no word which might discover, but, whether the oppressor were overawed by the Gray Champion's look or perceived his peril in the threatening attitude of the people, it is certain that he gave back and ordered his soldiers to commence a slow and guarded retreat. Before another sunset the governor and all that rode so proudly with him were prisoners, and long ere it was known that James had abdicated King William was proclaimed throughout New England.

But where was the Gray Champion? Some reported that when the troops had gone from King street and the people were thronging tumultuously in their rear, Bradstreet, the aged governor, was seen to embrace a form more aged than his own. Others soberly affirmed that while they marvelled at the venerable grandeur of his aspect the old man had faded from their eyes, melting slowly into the hues of twilight, till where he stood there was an empty space. But all agreed that the hoary shape was gone. The men of that generation watched for his reappearance in sunshine and in twilight, but never saw him more, nor knew when his funeral passed nor where his gravestone was.

And who was the Gray Champion? Perhaps his name might be found in the records of that stern court of justice which passed a sentence too mighty for the age, but glorious in all after-times for its humbling lesson to the monarch and its high example to the subject. I have heard that whenever the descendants of the Puritans are to show the spirit of their sires the old man appears again. When eighty years had passed, he walked once more in King street. Five years later, in the twilight of an April morning, he stood on the green beside the meeting-house at Lexington where now the obelisk of granite with a slab of slate inlaid commemorates the first-fallen of the Revolution. And when our fathers were toiling at the breastwork on Bunker's Hill, all through that night the old warrior walked his rounds. Long, long may it be ere he comes again! His hour is one of darkness and adversity and peril. But should domestic tyranny oppress us or the invader's step pollute our soil, still may the Gray Champion come! for he is the type of New England's hereditary spirit, and his shadowy march on the eve of danger must ever be the pledge that New England's sons will vindicate their ancestry.

SUNDAY AT HOME

EVERY SABBATH MORNING in the summer-time I thrust back the curtain to watch the sunrise stealing down a steeple which stands opposite my chamber window. First the weathercock begins to flash; then a fainter lustre gives the spire an airy aspect; next it encroaches on the tower and causes the index of the dial to glisten like gold as it points to the gilded figure of the hour. Now the loftiest window gleams, and now the lower. The carved framework of the portal is marked strongly out. At length the morning glory in its descent from heaven comes down the stone steps one by one, and there stands the steeple glowing with fresh radiance, while the shades of twilight still hide themselves among the nooks of the adjacent buildings. Methinks though the same sun brightens it every fair morning, yet the steeple has a peculiar robe of brightness for the Sabbath.

By dwelling near a church a person soon contracts an attachment for the edifice. We naturally personify it, and conceive its massy walls and its dim emptiness to be instinct with a calm and meditative and somewhat melancholy spirit. But the steeple stands foremost in our thoughts, as well as locally. It impresses us as a giant with a mind comprehensive and discriminating enough to care for the great and small concerns of all the town. Hourly, while it speaks a moral to the few that think, it reminds thousands of busy individuals of their separate and most secret affairs. It is the steeple, too, that flings abroad the hurried and irregular accents of general alarm; neither have gladness and festivity found a better utterance than by its tongue; and when the dead are slowly passing to their home, the steeple has a melancholy voice to bid them welcome. Yet, in spite of this connection with human interests, what a moral loneliness on week-days broods round about its stately height! It has no kindred with the houses above which it towers; it looks down into the narrow thoroughfare—the lonelier because the crowd are elbowing their passage at its base. A glance at the body of the church deepens this impression. Within, by the light of distant windows, amid refracted shadows we discern the vacant pews and empty galleries, the silent organ, the voiceless pulpit and the clock which tells to solitude how time is passing. Time—where man lives not—what is it but eternity? And in the church, we might suppose, are garnered up throughout the week all thoughts and feelings that have reference to eternity, until the holy day comes round again to let them forth. Might not, then, its more appropriate site be in the outskirts of the town, with space for old trees to wave around it and throw their solemn shadows over a quiet green? We will say more of this hereafter.

But on the Sabbath I watch the earliest sunshine and fancy that a holier brightness marks the day when there shall be no buzz of voices on the Exchange nor traffic in the shops, nor crowd nor business anywhere but at church. Many have fancied so. For my own part, whether I see it scattered down among tangled woods, or beaming broad across the fields, or hemmed in between brick buildings, or tracing out the figure of the casement on my chamber floor, still I recognize the Sabbath sunshine. And ever let me recognize it! Some illusions—and this among them—are the shadows of great truths. Doubts may flit around me or seem to close their evil wings and settle down, but so long as I imagine that the earth is hallowed and the light of heaven retains its sanctity on the Sabbath—while that blessed sunshine lives within me—never can my soul have lost the instinct of its faith. If it have gone astray, it will return again.

I love to spend such pleasant Sabbaths from morning till night behind the curtain of my open window. Are they spent amiss? Every spot so near the church as to be visited by the circling shadow of the steeple should be deemed consecrated ground to-day. With stronger truth be it said that a devout heart may consecrate a den of thieves, as an evil one may convert a temple to the same. My heart, perhaps, has no such holy, nor, I would fain trust, such impious, potency. It must suffice that, though my form be absent, my inner man goes constantly to church, while many whose bodily presence fills the accustomed seats have left their souls at home. But I am there even before my friend the sexton. At length he comes—a man of kindly but sombre aspect, in dark gray clothes, and hair of the same mixture. He comes and applies his key to the wide portal. Now my thoughts may go in among the dusty pews or ascend the pulpit without sacrilege, but soon come forth again to enjoy the music of the bell. How glad, yet solemn too! All the steeples in town are talking together aloft in the sunny air and rejoicing among themselves while their spires point heavenward. Meantime, here are the children assembling to the Sabbath-school, which is kept somewhere within the church. Often, while looking at the arched portal, I have been gladdened by the sight of a score of these little girls and boys in pink, blue, yellow and crimson frocks bursting suddenly forth into the sunshine like a swarm of gay butterflies that had been shut up in the solemn gloom. Or I might compare them to cherubs haunting that holy place.

About a quarter of an hour before the second ringing of the bell individuals of the congregation begin to appear. The earliest is invariably an old woman in black whose bent frame and rounded shoulders are evidently laden with some heavy affliction which she is eager to rest upon the altar. Would that the Sabbath came twice as often, for the sake of that sorrowful old soul! There is an elderly man, also, who arrives in good season and leans against the corner of the tower, just within the line of its shadow, looking downward with a darksome brow. I sometimes fancy that the old woman is the happier of the two. After these, others drop in singly and by twos and threes, either disappearing through the doorway or taking their stand in its vicinity. At last, and always with an unexpected sensation, the bell turns in the steeple overhead and throws out an irregular clangor, jarring the tower to its foundation. As if there were magic in the sound, the sidewalks of the street, both up and down along, are immediately thronged with two long lines of people, all converging hitherward and streaming into the church. Perhaps the far-off roar of a coach draws nearer—a deeper thunder by its contrast with the surrounding stillness—until it sets down the wealthy worshippers at the portal among their humblest brethren. Beyond that entrance—in theory, at least—there are no distinctions of earthly rank; nor, indeed, by the goodly apparel which is flaunting in the sun would there seem to be such on the hither side. Those pretty girls! Why will they disturb my pious meditations?

Of all days in the week, they should strive to look least fascinating on the Sabbath, instead of heightening their mortal loveliness, as if to rival the blessed angels and keep our thoughts from heaven. Were I the minister himself, I must needs look. One girl is white muslin from the waist upward and black silk downward to her slippers; a second blushes from top-knot to shoe-tie, one universal scarlet; another shines of a pervading yellow, as if she had made a garment of the sunshine. The greater part, however, have adopted a milder cheerfulness of hue. Their veils, especially when the wind raises them, give a lightness to the general effect and make them appear like airy phantoms as they flit up the steps and vanish into the sombre doorway. Nearly all—though it is very strange that I should know it—wear white stockings, white as snow, and neat slippers laced crosswise with black ribbon pretty high above the ankles. A white stocking is infinitely more effective than a black one.

Here comes the clergyman, slow and solemn, in severe simplicity, needing no black silk gown to denote his office. His aspect claims my reverence, but cannot win my love. Were I to picture Saint Peter keeping fast the gate of Heaven and frowning, more stern than pitiful, on the wretched applicants, that face should be my study. By middle age, or sooner, the creed has generally wrought upon the heart or been attempered by it. As the minister passes into the church the bell holds its iron tongue and all the low murmur of the congregation dies away. The gray sexton looks up and down the street and then at my window-curtain, where through the small peephole I half fancy that he has caught my eye. Now every loiterer has gone in and the street lies asleep in the quiet sun, while a feeling of loneliness comes over me, and brings also an uneasy sense of neglected privileges and duties. Oh, I ought to have gone to church! The bustle of the rising congregation reaches my ears. They are standing up to pray. Could I bring my heart into unison with those who are praying in yonder church and lift it heavenward with a fervor of supplication, but no distinct request, would not that be the safest kind of prayer? —"Lord, look down upon me in mercy!" With that sentiment gushing from my soul, might I not leave all the rest to him?

Hark! the hymn! This, at least, is a portion of the service which I can enjoy better than if I sat within the walls, where the full choir and the massive melody of the organ would fall with a weight upon me. At this distance it thrills through my frame and plays upon my heart-strings with a pleasure both of the sense and spirit. Heaven be praised! I know nothing of music as a science, and the most elaborate harmonies, if they please me, please as simply as a nurse's lullaby. The strain has ceased, but prolongs itself in my mind with fanciful echoes till I start from my reverie and find that the sermon has commenced. It is my misfortune seldom to fructify in a regular way by any but printed sermons. The first strong idea which the preacher utters gives birth to a train of thought and leads me onward step by step quite out of hearing of the good man's voice unless he be indeed a son of thunder. At my open window, catching now and then a sentence of the "parson's saw," I am as well situated as at the foot of the pulpit stairs. The broken and scattered fragments of this one discourse will be the texts of many sermons preached by those colleague pastors—colleagues, but often disputants—my Mind and Heart. The former pretends to be a scholar and perplexes me with doctrinal points; the latter takes me on the score of feeling; and both, like several other preachers, spend their strength to very little purpose. I, their sole auditor, cannot always understand them.

Suppose that a few hours have passed, and behold me still behind my curtain just before the close of the afternoon service. The hour-hand on the dial has passed beyond four o'clock. The declining sun is hidden behind the steeple and throws its shadow straight across the street; so that my chamber is darkened as with a cloud. Around the church door all is solitude, and an impenetrable obscurity beyond the threshold. A commotion is heard. The seats are slammed down and the pew doors thrown back; a multitude of feet are trampling along the unseen aisles, and the congregation bursts suddenly through the portal. Foremost scampers a rabble of boys, behind whom moves a dense and dark phalanx of grown men, and lastly a crowd of females with young children and a few scattered husbands. This instantaneous outbreak of life into loneliness is one of the pleasantest scenes of the day. Some of the good people are rubbing their eyes, thereby intimating that they have been wrapped, as it were, in a sort of holy trance by the fervor of their devotion. There is a young man, a third-rate coxcomb, whose first care is always to flourish a white handkerchief and brush the seat of a tight pair of black silk pantaloons which shine as if varnished. They must have been made of the stuff called "everlasting," or perhaps of the same piece as Christian's garments in the *Pilgrim's Progress*, for he put them on two summers ago and has not yet worn the gloss off. I have taken a great liking to those black silk pantaloons. But now, with nods and greetings among friends, each matron takes her husband's arm and paces gravely homeward, while the girls also flutter away after arranging sunset walks with their favored bachelors. The Sabbath eve is the eve of love. At length the whole congregation is dispersed. No; here, with faces as glossy as black satin, come two sable ladies and a sable gentleman, and close in their rear the minister, who softens his severe visage and bestows a kind word on each. Poor souls! To them the most captivating picture of bliss in heaven is "There we shall be white!"

All is solitude again. But hark! A broken warbling of voices, and now, attuning its grandeur to their sweetness, a stately peal of the organ. Who are the choristers? Let me dream that the angels who came down from heaven this blessed morn to blend themselves with the worship of the truly good are playing and singing their farewell to the earth. On the wings of that rich melody they were borne upward.

This, gentle reader, is merely a flight of poetry. A few of the singing-men and singing-women had lingered behind their fellows and raised their voices fitfully and blew a careless note upon the organ. Yet it lifted my soul higher than all their former strains. They are gone—the sons and daughters of Music—and the gray sexton is just closing the portal. For six days more there will be no face of man in the pews and aisles and galleries, nor a voice in the pulpit, nor music in the choir. Was it worth while to rear this massive edifice to be a desert in the heart of the town and populous only for a few hours of each seventh day? Oh, but the church is a symbol of religion. May its site, which was consecrated on the day when the first tree was felled, be kept holy for ever, a spot of solitude and peace amid the trouble and vanity of our week-day world! There is a moral, and a religion too, even in the silent walls. And may the steeple still point heavenward and be decked with the hallowed sunshine of the Sabbath morn!

THE WEDDING-KNELL

THERE IS A CERTAIN CHURCH, in the city of New York which I have always regarded with peculiar interest on account of a marriage there solemnized under very singular circumstances in my grandmother's girlhood. That venerable lady chanced to be a spectator of the scene, and ever after made it her favorite narrative. Whether the edifice now standing on the same site be the identical one to which she referred I am not antiquarian enough to know, nor would it be worth while to correct myself, perhaps, of an agreeable error by reading the date of its erection on the tablet over the door. It is a stately church surrounded by an enclosure of the loveliest green, within which appear urns, pillars, obelisks, and other forms of monumental marble, the tributes of private affection or more splendid memorials of historic dust. With such a place, though the tumult of the city rolls beneath its tower, one would be willing to connect some legendary interest.

The marriage might be considered as the result of an early engagement, though there had been two intermediate weddings on the lady's part and forty years of celibacy on that of the gentleman. At sixty-five Mr. Ellenwood was a shy but not quite a secluded man; selfish, like all men who brood over their own hearts, yet manifesting on rare occasions a vein of generous sentiment; a scholar throughout life, though always an indolent one, because his studies had no definite object either of public advantage or personal ambition; a gentleman, high-bred and fastidiously delicate, yet sometimes requiring a considerable relaxation in his behalf of the common rules of society. In truth, there were so many anomalies in his character, and, though shrinking with diseased sensibility from public notice, it had been his fatality so often to become the topic of the day by some wild eccentricity of conduct, that people searched his lineage for a hereditary taint of insanity. But there was no need of this. His caprices had their origin in a mind that lacked the support of an engrossing purpose, and in feelings that preyed upon themselves for want of other food. If he were mad, it was the consequence, and not the cause, of an aimless and abortive life.

The widow was as complete a contrast to her third bridegroom in everything but age as can well be conceived. Compelled to relinquish her first engagement, she had been united to a man of twice her own years, to whom she became an exemplary wife, and by whose death she was left in possession of a splendid fortune. A Southern gentleman considerably younger than herself succeeded to her hand and carried her to Charleston, where after many uncomfortable years she found herself again a widow. It would have been singular if any uncommon delicacy of feeling had survived through such a life as Mrs. Dabney's; it could not but be crushed and killed by her early disappointment, the cold duty of her first marriage, the dislocation of the heart's principles consequent on a second union, and the unkindness of her Southern husband, which had inevitably driven her to connect the idea of his death with that of her comfort. To be brief, she was that wisest but unloveliest variety of woman, a philosopher, bearing troubles of the heart with equanimity, dispensing with all that should have been her happiness and making the best of what remained. Sage in most matters, the widow was perhaps the more amiable for the one frailty that made her ridiculous. Being childless, she could not remain beautiful by proxy in the person of a daughter; she therefore refused to grow old and ugly on any consideration; she struggled with Time, and held fast her roses in spite of him, till the venerable thief appeared to have relinquished the spoil as not worth the trouble of acquiring it.

The approaching marriage of this woman of the world with such an unworldly man as Mr. Ellenwood was announced soon after Mrs. Dabney's return to her native city. Superficial observers, and deeper ones, seemed to concur in supposing that the lady must have borne no inactive part in arranging the affair; there were considerations of expediency which she would be far more likely to appreciate than Mr. Ellenwood, and there was just the specious phantom of sentiment and romance in this late union of two early lovers which sometimes makes a fool of a woman who has lost her true feelings among the accidents of life. All the wonder was how the gentleman, with his lack of worldly wisdom and agonizing consciousness of ridicule, could have been induced to take a measure at once so prudent and so laughable. But while people talked the wedding-day arrived. The ceremony was to be solemnized according to the Episcopalian forms and in open church, with a degree of publicity that attracted many spectators, who occupied the front seats of the galleries and the pews near the altar and along the broad aisle. It had been arranged, or possibly it was the custom of the day, that the parties should proceed separately to church. By some accident the bridegroom was a little less punctual than the widow and her bridal attendants, with whose arrival, after this tedious but necessary preface, the action of our tale may be said to commence.

The clumsy wheels of several old-fashioned coaches were heard, and the gentlemen and ladies composing the bridal-party came through the church door with the sudden and gladsome effect of a burst of sunshine. The whole group, except the principal figure, was made up of youth and gayety. As they streamed up the broad aisle, while the pews and pillars seemed to brighten on either side, their steps were as buoyant as if they mistook the church for a ball-room and were ready to dance hand in hand to the altar. So brilliant was the spectacle that few took notice of a singular phenomenon that had marked its entrance. At the moment when the bride's foot touched the threshold the bell swung heavily in the tower above her and sent forth its deepest knell. The vibrations died away, and returned with prolonged solemnity as she entered the body of the church.

"Good heavens! What an omen!" whispered a young lady to her lover.

"On my honor," replied the gentleman, "I believe the bell has the good taste to toll of its own accord. What has she to do with weddings? If you, dearest Julia, were approaching the altar, the bell would ring out its merriest peal. It has only a funeral-knell for her."

The bride and most of her company had been too much occupied with the bustle of entrance to hear the first boding stroke of the bell—or, at least, to reflect on the singularity of such a welcome to the altar. They therefore continued to advance with undiminished gayety. The gorgeous dresses of the time—the crimson velvet coats, the gold-laced hats, the hoop-petticoats, the silk, satin, brocade and embroidery, the buckles, canes and swords, all displayed to the best advantage on persons suited to such finery—made the group appear more like a bright-colored picture than anything real. But by what perversity of taste had the artist represented his principal figure as so wrinkled and decayed, while yet he had decked her out in the brightest splendor of attire, as if the loveliest maiden had suddenly withered into age and become a moral to the beautiful around her? On they went, however, and had glittered along about a third of the aisle, when another stroke of the bell seemed to fill the church with a visible gloom, dimming and obscuring the bright-pageant till it shone forth again as from a mist.

This time the party wavered, stopped and huddled closer together, while a slight scream was heard from some of the ladies and a confused whispering among the gentlemen. Thus tossing to and fro, they might have been fancifully compared to a splendid bunch of flowers suddenly shaken by a puff of wind which threatened to scatter the leaves of an old brown, withered rose on the same stalk with two dewy buds, such being the emblem of the widow between her fair young bridesmaids. But her heroism was admirable. She had started with an irrepressible shudder, as if the stroke of the bell had fallen directly on her heart; then, recovering herself, while her attendants were yet in dismay, she took the lead and paced calmly up the aisle. The bell continued to swing, strike and vibrate with the same doleful regularity as when a corpse is on its way to the tomb.

"My young friends here have their nerves a little shaken," said the widow, with a smile, to the clergyman at the altar. "But so many weddings have been ushered in with the merriest peal of the bells, and yet turned out unhappily, that I shall hope for better fortune under such different auspices."

"Madam," answered the rector, in great perplexity, "this strange occurrence brings to my mind a marriage-sermon of the famous Bishop Taylor wherein he mingles so many thoughts of mortality and future woe that, to speak somewhat after his own rich style, he seems to hang the bridal-chamber in black and cut the wedding-garment out of a coffin-pall. And it has been the custom of divers nations to infuse something of sadness into their marriage ceremonies, so to keep death in mind while contracting that engagement which is life's chiefest business. Thus we may draw a sad but profitable moral from this funeral-knell."

But, though the clergyman might have given his moral even a keener point, he did not fail to despatch an attendant to inquire into the mystery and stop those sounds so dismally appropriate to such a marriage. A brief space elapsed, during which the silence was broken only by whispers and a few suppressed titterings among the wedding-party and the spectators, who after the first shock were disposed to draw an ill-natured merriment from the affair. The young have less charity for aged follies than the old for those of youth. The widow's glance was observed to wander for an instant toward a window of the church, as if searching for the time-worn marble that she had dedicated to her first husband; then her eyelids dropped over their faded orbs and her thoughts were drawn irresistibly to another grave. Two buried men with a voice at her ear and a cry afar off were calling her to lie down beside them. Perhaps, with momentary truth of feeling, she thought how much happier had been her fate if, after years of bliss, the bell were now tolling for her funeral and she were followed to the grave by the old affection of her earliest lover, long her husband. But why had she returned to him when their cold hearts shrank from each other's embrace?

Still the death-bell tolled so mournfully that the sunshine seemed to fade in the air. A whisper, communicated from those who stood nearest the windows, now spread through the church: a hearse with a train of several coaches was creeping along the street, conveying some dead man to the churchyard, while the bride awaited a living one at the altar. Immediately after, the footsteps of the bridegroom and his friends were heard at the door. The widow looked down the aisle and clenched the arm of one of her bridemaids in her bony hand with such unconscious violence that the fair girl trembled.

"You frighten me, my dear madam," cried she. "For heaven's sake, what is the matter?"

"Nothing, my dear—nothing," said the widow; then, whispering close to her ear, "There is a foolish fancy that I cannot get rid of. I am expecting my bridegroom to come into the church with my two first husbands for groomsmen."

"Look! look!" screamed the bridemaid. "What is here? The funeral!"

As she spoke a dark procession paced into the church. First came an old man and woman, like chief mourners at a funeral, attired from head to foot in the deepest black, all but their pale features and hoary hair, he leaning on a staff and supporting her decrepit form with his nerveless arm. Behind appeared another and another pair, as aged, as black and mournful as the first. As they drew near the widow recognized in every face some trait of former friends long forgotten, but now returning as if from their old graves to warn her to prepare a shroud, or, with purpose almost as unwelcome, to exhibit their wrinkles and infirmity and claim her as their companion by the tokens of her own decay. Many a merry night had she danced with them in youth, and now in joyless age she felt that some withered partner should request her hand and all unite in a dance of death to the music of the funeral-bell.

While these aged mourners were passing up the aisle it was observed that from pew to pew the spectators shuddered with irrepressible awe as some object hitherto concealed by the intervening figures came full in sight. Many turned away their faces; others kept a fixed and rigid stare, and a young girl giggled hysterically and fainted with the laughter on her lips. When the spectral procession approached the altar, each couple separated and slowly diverged, till in the centre appeared a form that had been worthily ushered in with all this gloomy pomp, the death-knell and the funeral. It was the bridegroom in his shroud.

No garb but that of the grave could have befitted such a death-like aspect. The eyes, indeed, had the wild gleam of a sepulchral lamp; all else was fixed in the stern calmness which old men wear in the coffin. The corpse stood motionless, but addressed the widow in accents that seemed to melt into the clang of the bell, which fell heavily on the air while he spoke.

"Come, my bride!" said those pale lips. "The hearse is ready; the sexton stands waiting for us at the door of the tomb. Let us be married, and then to our coffins!"

How shall the widow's horror be represented? It gave her the ghastliness of a dead man's bride. Her youthful friends stood apart, shuddering at the mourners, the shrouded bridegroom and herself; the whole scene expressed by the strongest imagery the vain struggle of the gilded vanities of this world when opposed to age, infirmity, sorrow and death.

The awestruck silence was first broken by the clergyman.

"Mr. Ellenwood," said he, soothingly, yet with somewhat of authority, "you are not well. Your mind has been agitated by the unusual circumstances in which you are placed. The ceremony must be deferred. As an old friend, let me entreat you to return home."

"Home—yes; but not without my bride," answered he, in the same hollow accents. "You deem this mockery—perhaps madness. Had I bedizened my aged and broken frame with scarlet and embroidery, had I forced my withered lips to smile at my dead heart, that might have been mockery or madness; but now let young and old declare which of us has come hither without a wedding-garment—the bridegroom or the bride."

He stepped forward at a ghostly pace and stood beside the widow, contrasting the awful simplicity of his shroud with the glare and glitter in which she had arrayed herself for this unhappy scene. None that beheld them could deny the terrible strength of the moral which his disordered intellect had contrived to draw.

"Cruel! cruel!" groaned the heartstricken bride.

"Cruel?" repeated he; then, losing his deathlike composure in a wild bitterness, "Heaven judge which of us has been cruel to the other! In youth you deprived me of my happiness, my hopes, my aims; you took away all the substance of my life and made it a dream without reality enough even to grieve at—with only a pervading gloom, through which I walked wearily and cared not whither. But after forty years, when I have built my tomb and would not give up the thought of resting there—no, not for such a life as we once pictured—you call me to the altar. At your summons I am here. But other husbands have enjoyed your youth, your beauty, your warmth of heart and all that could be termed your life. What is there for me but your decay and death? And therefore I have bidden these funeral-friends, and bespoken the sexton's deepest knell, and am come in my shroud to wed you as with a burial-service, that we may join our hands at the door of the sepulchre and enter it together."

It was not frenzy, it was not merely the drunkenness of strong emotion in a heart unused to it, that now wrought upon the bride. The stern lesson of the day had done its work; her worldliness was gone. She seized the bridegroom's hand.

"Yes!" cried she; "let us wed even at the door of the sepulchre. My life is gone in vanity and emptiness, but at its close there is one true feeling. It has made me what I was in youth: it makes me worthy of you. Time is no more for both of us. Let us wed for eternity."

With a long and deep regard the bridegroom looked into her eyes, while a tear was gathering in his own. How strange that gush of human feeling from the frozen bosom of a corpse! He wiped away the tear, even with his shroud.

"Beloved of my youth," said he, "I have been wild. The despair of my whole lifetime had returned at once and maddened me. Forgive and be forgiven. Yes; it is evening with us now, and we have realized none of our morning dreams of happiness. But let us join our hands before the altar as lovers whom adverse circumstances have separated through life, yet who meet again as they are leaving it and find their earthly affection changed into something holy as religion. And what is time to the married of eternity?"

Amid the tears of many and a swell of exalted sentiment in those who felt aright was solemnized the union of two immortal souls. The train of withered mourners, the hoary bridegroom in his shroud, the pale features of the aged bride and the death-bell tolling through the whole till its deep voice overpowered the marriage-words,—all marked the funeral of earthly hopes. But as the ceremony proceeded, the organ, as if stirred by the sympathies of this impressive scene, poured forth an anthem, first mingling with the dismal knell, then rising to a loftier strain, till the soul looked down upon its woe. And when the awful rite was finished and with cold hand in cold hand the married of eternity withdrew, the organ's peal of solemn triumph drowned the wedding-knell.

THE MINISTER'S BLACK VEIL

A PARABLE.

THE SEXTON STOOD in the porch of Milford meeting-house pulling lustily at the bell-rope. The old people of the village came stooping along the street. Children with bright faces tripped merrily beside their parents or mimicked a graver gait in the conscious dignity of their Sunday clothes. Spruce bachelors looked sidelong at the pretty maidens, and fancied that the Sabbath sunshine made them prettier than on week-days. When the throng had mostly streamed into the porch, the sexton began to toll the bell, keeping his eye on the Reverend Mr. Hooper's door. The first glimpse of the clergyman's figure was the signal for the bell to cease its summons.

"But what has good Parson Hooper got upon his face?" cried the sexton, in astonishment.

All within hearing immediately turned about and beheld the semblance of Mr. Hooper pacing slowly his meditative way toward the meeting-house. With one accord they started, expressing more wonder than if some strange minister were coming to dust the cushions of Mr. Hooper's pulpit.

"Are you sure it is our parson?" inquired Goodman Gray of the sexton.

"Of a certainty it is good Mr. Hooper," replied the sexton. "He was to have exchanged pulpits with Parson Shute of Westbury, but Parson Shute sent to excuse himself yesterday, being to preach a funeral sermon."

The cause of so much amazement may appear sufficiently slight. Mr. Hooper, a gentlemanly person of about thirty, though still a bachelor, was dressed with due clerical neatness, as if a careful wife had starched his band and brushed the weekly dust from his Sunday's garb. There was but one thing remarkable in his appearance. Swathed about his forehead and hanging down over his face, so low as to be shaken by his breath, Mr. Hooper had on a black veil. On a nearer view it seemed to consist of two folds of crape, which entirely concealed his features except the mouth and chin, but probably did not intercept his sight further than to give a darkened aspect to all living and inanimate things. With this gloomy shade before him good Mr. Hooper walked onward at a slow and quiet pace, stooping somewhat and looking on the ground, as is customary with abstracted men, yet nodding kindly to those of his parishioners who still waited on the meeting-house steps. But so wonder-struck were they that his greeting hardly met with a return.

"I can't really feel as if good Mr. Hooper's face was behind that piece of crape," said the sexton.

"I don't like it," muttered an old woman as she hobbled into the meeting-house. "He has changed himself into something awful only by hiding his face."

"Our parson has gone mad!" cried Goodman Gray, following him across the threshold.

A rumor of some unaccountable phenomenon had preceded Mr. Hooper into the meeting-house and set all the congregation astir. Few could refrain from twisting their heads toward the door; many stood upright and turned directly about; while several little boys clambered upon the seats, and came down again with a terrible racket. There was a general bustle, a rustling of the women's gowns and shuffling of the men's feet, greatly at variance with that hushed repose which should attend the entrance of the minister. But Mr. Hooper appeared not to notice the perturbation of his people. He entered with an almost noiseless step, bent his head mildly to the pews on each side and bowed as he passed his oldest parishioner, a white-haired great-grandsire, who occupied an arm-chair in the centre of the aisle. It was strange to observe how slowly this venerable man became conscious of something singular in the appearance of his pastor. He seemed not fully to partake of the prevailing wonder till Mr. Hooper had ascended the stairs and showed himself in the pulpit, face to face with his congregation except for the black veil. That mysterious emblem was never once withdrawn. It shook with his measured breath as he gave out the psalm, it threw its obscurity between him and the holy page as he read the Scriptures, and while he prayed the veil lay heavily on his uplifted countenance. Did he seek to hide it from the dread Being whom he was addressing?

Such was the effect of this simple piece of crape that more than one woman of delicate nerves was forced to leave the meeting-house. Yet perhaps the pale-faced congregation was almost as fearful a sight to the minister as his black veil to them.

Mr. Hooper had the reputation of a good preacher, but not an energetic one: he strove to win his people heavenward by mild, persuasive influences rather than to drive them thither by the thunders of the word. The sermon which he now delivered was marked by the same characteristics of style and manner as the general series of his pulpit oratory, but there was something either in the sentiment of the discourse itself or in the imagination of the auditors which made it greatly the most powerful effort that they had ever heard from their pastor's lips. It was tinged rather more darkly than usual with the gentle gloom of Mr. Hooper's temperament. The subject had reference to secret sin and those sad mysteries which we hide from our nearest and dearest, and would fain conceal from our own consciousness, even forgetting that the Omniscient can detect them. A subtle power was breathed into his words. Each member of the congregation, the most innocent girl and the man of hardened breast, felt as if the preacher had crept upon them behind his awful veil and discovered their hoarded iniquity of deed or thought. Many spread their clasped hands on their bosoms. There was nothing terrible in what Mr. Hooper said—at least, no violence; and yet with every tremor of his melancholy voice the hearers quaked. An unsought pathos came hand in hand with awe. So sensible were the audience of some unwonted attribute in their minister that they longed for a breath of wind to blow aside the veil, almost believing that a stranger's visage would be discovered, though the form, gesture and voice were those of Mr. Hooper.

At the close of the services the people hurried out with indecorous confusion, eager to communicate their pent-up amazement, and conscious of lighter spirits the moment they lost sight of the black veil. Some gathered in little circles, huddled closely together, with their mouths all whispering in the centre; some went homeward alone, wrapped in silent meditation; some talked loudly and profaned the Sabbath-day with ostentatious laughter. A few shook their sagacious heads, intimating that they could penetrate the mystery, while one or two affirmed that there was no mystery at all, but only that Mr. Hooper's eyes were so weakened by the midnight lamp as to require a shade.

After a brief interval forth came good Mr. Hooper also, in the rear of his flock. Turning his veiled face from one group to another, he paid due reverence to the hoary heads, saluted the middle-aged with kind dignity as their friend and spiritual guide, greeted the young with mingled authority and love, and laid his hands on the little children's heads to bless them. Such was always his custom on the Sabbath-day. Strange and bewildered looks repaid him for his courtesy. None, as on former occasions, aspired to the honor of walking by their pastor's side. Old Squire Saunders—doubtless by an accidental lapse of memory—neglected to invite Mr. Hooper to his table, where the good clergyman had been wont to bless the food almost every Sunday since his settlement. He returned, therefore, to the parsonage, and at the moment of closing the door was observed to look back upon the people, all of whom had their eyes fixed upon the minister. A sad smile gleamed faintly from beneath the black veil and flickered about his mouth, glimmering as he disappeared.

"How strange," said a lady, "that a simple black veil, such as any woman might wear on her bonnet, should become such a terrible thing on Mr. Hooper's face!"

"Something must surely be amiss with Mr. Hooper's intellects," observed her husband, the physician of the village. "But the strangest part of the affair is the effect of this vagary even on a sober-minded man like myself. The black veil, though it covers only our pastor's face, throws its influence over his whole person and makes him ghost-like from head to foot. Do you not feel it so?"

"Truly do I," replied the lady; "and I would not be alone with him for the world. I wonder he is not afraid to be alone with himself."

"Men sometimes are so," said her husband.

The afternoon service was attended with similar circumstances. At its conclusion the bell tolled for the funeral of a young lady. The relatives and friends were assembled in the house and the more distant acquaintances stood about the door, speaking of the good qualities of the deceased, when their talk was interrupted by the appearance of Mr. Hooper, still covered with his black veil. It was now an appropriate emblem. The clergyman stepped into the room where the corpse was laid, and bent over the coffin to take a last farewell of his deceased parishioner. As he stooped the veil hung straight down from his forehead, so that, if her eye-lids had not been closed for ever, the dead maiden might have seen his face. Could Mr. Hooper be fearful of her glance, that he so hastily caught back the black veil? A person who watched the interview between the dead and living scrupled not to affirm that at the instant when the clergyman's features were disclosed the corpse had slightly shuddered, rustling the shroud and muslin cap, though the countenance retained the composure of death. A superstitious old woman was the only witness of this prodigy.

From the coffin Mr. Hooper passed into the chamber of the mourners, and thence to the head of the staircase, to make the funeral prayer. It was a tender and heart-dissolving prayer, full of sorrow, yet so imbued with celestial hopes that the music of a heavenly harp swept by the fingers of the dead seemed faintly to be heard among the saddest accents of the minister. The people trembled, though they but darkly understood him, when he prayed that they and himself, and all of mortal race, might be ready, as he trusted this young maiden had been, for the dreadful hour that should snatch the veil from their faces. The bearers went heavily forth and the mourners followed, saddening all the street, with the dead before them and Mr. Hooper in his black veil behind.

"Why do you look back?" said one in the procession to his partner.

"I had a fancy," replied she, "that the minister and the maiden's spirit were walking hand in hand."

"And so had I at the same moment," said the other.

That night the handsomest couple in Milford village were to be joined in wedlock. Though reckoned a melancholy man, Mr. Hooper had a placid cheerfulness for such occasions which often excited a sympathetic smile where livelier merriment would have been thrown away. There was no quality of his disposition which made him more beloved than this. The company at the wedding awaited his arrival with impatience, trusting that the strange awe which had gathered over him throughout the day would now be dispelled. But such was not the result. When Mr. Hooper came, the first thing that their eyes rested on was the same horrible black veil which had added deeper gloom to the funeral and could portend nothing but evil to the wedding. Such was its immediate effect on the guests that a cloud seemed to have rolled duskily from beneath the black crape and dimmed the light of the candles. The bridal pair stood up before the minister, but the bride's cold fingers quivered in the tremulous hand of the bridegroom, and her death-like paleness caused a whisper that the maiden who had been buried a few hours before was come from her grave to be married. If ever another wedding were so dismal, it was that famous one where they tolled the wedding-knell.

After performing the ceremony Mr. Hooper raised a glass of wine to his lips, wishing happiness to the new-married couple in a strain of mild pleasantry that ought to have brightened the features of the guests like a cheerful gleam from the hearth. At that instant, catching a glimpse of his figure in the looking-glass, the black veil involved his own spirit in the horror with which it overwhelmed all others. His frame shuddered, his lips grew white, he spilt the untasted wine upon the carpet and rushed forth into the darkness, for the Earth too had on her black veil.

The next day the whole village of Milford talked of little else than Parson Hooper's black veil. That, and the mystery concealed behind it, supplied a topic for discussion between acquaintances meeting in the street and good women gossipping at their open windows. It was the first item of news that the tavernkeeper told to his guests. The children babbled of it on their way to school. One imitative little imp covered his face with an old black handkerchief, thereby so affrighting his playmates that the panic seized himself and he wellnigh lost his wits by his own waggery.

It was remarkable that, of all the busybodies and impertinent people in the parish, not one ventured to put the plain question to Mr. Hooper wherefore he did this thing. Hitherto, whenever there appeared the slightest call for such interference, he had never lacked advisers nor shown himself averse to be guided by their judgment. If he erred at all, it was by so painful a degree of self-distrust that even the mildest censure would lead him to consider an indifferent action as a crime. Yet, though so well acquainted with this amiable weakness, no individual among his parishioners chose to make the black veil a subject of friendly remonstrance. There was a feeling of dread, neither plainly confessed nor carefully concealed, which caused each to shift the responsibility upon another, till at length it was found expedient to send a deputation of the church, in order to deal with Mr. Hooper about the mystery before it should grow into a scandal. Never did an embassy so ill discharge its duties. The minister received them with friendly courtesy, but became silent after they were seated, leaving to his visitors the whole burden of introducing their important business. The topic, it might be supposed, was obvious enough. There was the black veil swathed round Mr. Hooper's forehead and concealing every feature above his placid mouth, on which, at times, they could perceive the glimmering of a melancholy smile. But that piece of crape, to their imagination, seemed to hang down before his heart, the symbol of a fearful secret between him and them. Were the veil but cast aside, they might speak freely of it, but not till then. Thus they sat a considerable time, speechless, confused and shrinking uneasily from Mr. Hooper's eye, which they felt to be fixed upon them with an invisible glance. Finally, the deputies returned abashed to their constituents, pronouncing the matter too weighty to be handled except by a council of the churches, if, indeed, it might not require a General Synod.

But there was one person in the village unappalled by the awe with which the black veil had impressed all besides herself. When the deputies returned without an explanation, or even venturing to demand one, she with the calm energy of her character determined to chase away the strange cloud that appeared to be settling round Mr. Hooper every moment more darkly than before. As his plighted wife it should be her privilege to know what the black veil concealed. At the minister's first visit, therefore, she entered upon the subject with a direct simplicity which made the task easier both for him and her. After he had seated himself she fixed her eyes steadfastly upon the veil, but could discern nothing of the dreadful gloom that had so overawed the multitude; it was but a double fold of crape hanging down from his forehead to his mouth and slightly stirring with his breath.

"No," said she, aloud, and smiling, "there is nothing terrible in this piece of crape, except that it hides a face which I am always glad to look upon. Come, good sir; let the sun shine from behind the cloud. First lay aside your black veil, then tell me why you put it on."

Mr. Hooper's smile glimmered faintly.

"There is an hour to come," said he, "when all of us shall cast aside our veils. Take it not amiss, beloved friend, if I wear this piece of crape till then."

"Your words are a mystery too," returned the young lady. "Take away the veil from them, at least."

"Elizabeth, I will," said he, "so far as my vow may suffer me. Know, then, this veil is a type and a symbol, and I am bound to wear it ever, both in light and darkness, in solitude and before the gaze of multitudes, and as with strangers, so with my familiar friends. No mortal eye will see it withdrawn. This dismal shade must separate me from the world; even you, Elizabeth, can never come behind it."

"What grievous affliction hath befallen you," she earnestly inquired, "that you should thus darken your eyes for ever?"

"If it be a sign of mourning," replied Mr. Hooper, "I, perhaps, like most other mortals, have sorrows dark enough to be typified by a black veil."

"But what if the world will not believe that it is the type of an innocent sorrow?" urged Elizabeth. "Beloved and respected as you are, there may be whispers that you hide your face under the consciousness of secret sin. For the sake of your holy office do away this scandal."

The color rose into her cheeks as she intimated the nature of the rumors that were already abroad in the village. But Mr. Hooper's mildness did not forsake him. He even smiled again— that same sad smile which always appeared like a faint glimmering of light proceeding from the obscurity beneath the veil.

"If I hide my face for sorrow, there is cause enough," he merely replied; "and if I cover it for secret sin, what mortal might not do the same?" And with this gentle but unconquerable obstinacy did he resist all her entreaties.

At length Elizabeth sat silent. For a few moments she appeared lost in thought, considering, probably, what new methods might be tried to withdraw her lover from so dark a fantasy, which, if it had no other meaning, was perhaps a symptom of mental disease. Though of a firmer character than his own, the tears rolled down her cheeks. But in an instant, as it were, a new feeling took the place of sorrow: her eyes were fixed insensibly on the black veil, when like a sudden twilight in the air its terrors fell around her. She arose and stood trembling before him.

"And do you feel it, then, at last?" said he, mournfully.

She made no reply, but covered her eyes with her hand and turned to leave the room. He rushed forward and caught her arm.

"Have patience with me, Elizabeth!" cried he, passionately. "Do not desert me though this veil must be between us here on earth. Be mine, and hereafter there shall be no veil over my face, no darkness between our souls. It is but a mortal veil; it is not for eternity. Oh, you know not how lonely I am, and how frightened to be alone behind my black veil! Do not leave me in this miserable obscurity for ever."

"Lift the veil but once and look me in the face," said she.

"Never! It cannot be!" replied Mr. Hooper.

"Then farewell!" said Elizabeth.

She withdrew her arm from his grasp and slowly departed, pausing at the door to give one long, shuddering gaze that seemed almost to penetrate the mystery of the black veil. But even amid his grief Mr. Hooper smiled to think that only a material emblem had separated him from happiness, though the horrors which it shadowed forth must be drawn darkly between the fondest of lovers.

From that time no attempts were made to remove Mr. Hooper's black veil or by a direct appeal to discover the secret which it was supposed to hide. By persons who claimed a superiority to popular prejudice it was reckoned merely an eccentric whim, such as often mingles with the sober actions of men otherwise rational and tinges them all with its own semblance of insanity. But with the multitude good Mr. Hooper was irreparably a bugbear. He could not walk the street with any peace of mind, so conscious was he that the gentle and timid would turn aside to avoid him, and that others would make it a point of hardihood to throw themselves in his way. The impertinence of the latter class compelled him to give up his customary walk at sunset to the burial-ground; for when he leaned pensively over the gate, there would always be faces behind the gravestones peeping at his black veil. A fable went the rounds that the stare of the dead people drove him thence. It grieved him to the very depth of his kind heart to observe how the children fled from his approach, breaking up their merriest sports while his melancholy figure was yet afar off. Their instinctive dread caused him to feel more strongly than aught else that a preternatural horror was interwoven with the threads of the black crape. In truth, his own antipathy to the veil was known to be so great that he never willingly passed before a mirror nor stooped to drink at a still fountain lest in its peaceful bosom he should be affrighted by himself. This was what gave plausibility to the whispers that Mr. Hooper's conscience tortured him for some great crime too horrible to be entirely concealed or otherwise than so obscurely intimated. Thus from beneath the black veil there rolled a cloud into the sunshine, an ambiguity of sin or sorrow, which enveloped the poor minister, so that love or sympathy could never reach him. It was said that ghost and fiend consorted with him there. With self-shudderings and outward terrors he walked continually in its shadow, groping darkly within his own soul or gazing through a medium that saddened the whole world. Even the lawless wind, it was believed, respected his dreadful secret and never blew aside the veil. But still good Mr. Hooper sadly smiled at the pale visages of the worldly throng as he passed by.

Among all its bad influences, the black veil had the one desirable effect of making its wearer a very efficient clergyman. By the aid of his mysterious emblem—for there was no other apparent cause—he became a man of awful power over souls that were in agony for sin. His converts always regarded him with a dread peculiar to themselves, affirming, though but figuratively, that before he brought them to celestial light they had been with him behind the black veil. Its gloom, indeed, enabled him to sympathize with all dark affections. Dying sinners cried aloud for Mr. Hooper and would not yield their breath till he appeared, though ever, as he stooped to whisper consolation, they shuddered at the veiled face so near their own. Such were the terrors of the black veil even when Death had bared his visage. Strangers came long distances to attend service at his church with the mere idle purpose of gazing at his figure because it was forbidden them to behold his face. But many were made to quake ere they departed. Once, during Governor Belcher's administration, Mr. Hooper was appointed to preach the election sermon. Covered with his black veil, he stood before the chief magistrate, the council and the representatives, and wrought so deep an impression that the legislative measures of that year were characterized by all the gloom and piety of our earliest ancestral sway.

In this manner Mr. Hooper spent a long life, irreproachable in outward act, yet shrouded in dismal suspicions; kind and loving, though unloved and dimly feared; a man apart from men, shunned in their health and joy, but ever summoned to their aid in mortal anguish. As years wore on, shedding their snows above his sable veil, he acquired a name throughout the New England churches, and they called him Father Hooper. Nearly all his parishioners who were of mature age when he was settled had been borne away by many a funeral: he had one congregation in the church and a more crowded one in the churchyard; and, having wrought so late into the evening and done his work so well, it was now good Father Hooper's turn to rest.

Several persons were visible by the shaded candlelight in the death-chamber of the old clergyman. Natural connections he had none. But there was the decorously grave though unmoved physician, seeking only to mitigate the last pangs of the patient whom he could not save. There were the deacons and other eminently pious members of his church. There, also, was the Reverend Mr. Clark of Westbury, a young and zealous divine who had ridden in haste to pray by the bedside of the expiring minister. There was the nurse—no hired handmaiden of Death, but one whose calm affection had endured thus long in secrecy, in solitude, amid the chill of age, and would not perish even at the dying-hour. Who but Elizabeth! And there lay the hoary head of good Father Hooper upon the death-pillow with the black veil still swathed about his brow and reaching down over his face, so that each more difficult gasp of his faint breath caused it to stir. All through life that piece of crape had hung between him and the world; it had separated him from cheerful brotherhood and woman's love and kept him in that saddest of all prisons his own heart; and still it lay upon his face, as if to deepen the gloom of his darksome chamber and shade him from the sunshine of eternity.

For some time previous his mind had been confused, wavering doubtfully between the past and the present, and hovering forward, as it were, at intervals, into the indistinctness of the world to come. There had been feverish turns which tossed him from side to side and wore away what little strength he had. But in his most convulsive struggles and in the wildest vagaries of his intellect, when no other thought retained its sober influence, he still showed an awful solicitude lest the black veil should slip aside. Even if his bewildered soul could have forgotten, there was a faithful woman at his pillow who with averted eyes would have covered that aged face which she had last beheld in the comeliness of manhood.

At length the death-stricken old man lay quietly in the torpor of mental and bodily exhaustion, with an imperceptible pulse and breath that grew fainter and fainter except when a long, deep and irregular inspiration seemed to prelude the flight of his spirit.

The minister of Westbury approached the bedside.

"Venerable Father Hooper," said he, "the moment of your release is at hand. Are you ready for the lifting of the veil that shuts in time from eternity?"

Father Hooper at first replied merely by a feeble motion of his head; then—apprehensive, perhaps, that his meaning might be doubtful—he exerted himself to speak.

"Yea," said he, in faint accents; "my soul hath a patient weariness until that veil be lifted."

"And is it fitting," resumed the Reverend Mr. Clark, "that a man so given to prayer, of such a blameless example, holy in deed and thought, so far as mortal judgment may pronounce,—is it fitting that a father in the Church should leave a shadow on his memory that may seem to blacken a life so pure? I pray you, my venerable brother, let not this thing be! Suffer us to be gladdened by your triumphant aspect as you go to your reward. Before the veil of eternity be lifted let me cast aside this black veil from your face;" and, thus speaking, the Reverend Mr. Clark bent forward to reveal the mystery of so many years.

But, exerting a sudden energy that made all the beholders stand aghast, Father Hooper snatched both his hands from beneath the bedclothes and pressed them strongly on the black veil, resolute to struggle if the minister of Westbury would contend with a dying man.

"Never!" cried the veiled clergyman. "On earth, never!"

"Dark old man," exclaimed the affrighted minister, "with what horrible crime upon your soul are you now passing to the judgment?"

Father Hooper's breath heaved: it rattled in his throat; but, with a mighty effort grasping forward with his hands, he caught hold of life and held it back till he should speak. He even raised himself in bed, and there he sat shivering with the arms of Death around him, while the black veil hung down, awful at that last moment in the gathered terrors of a lifetime. And yet the faint, sad smile so often there now seemed to glimmer from its obscurity and linger on Father Hooper's lips.

"Why do you tremble at me alone?" cried he, turning his veiled face round the circle of pale spectators. "Tremble also at each other. Have men avoided me and women shown no pity and children screamed and fled only for my black veil? What but the mystery which it obscurely typifies has made this piece of crape so awful? When the friend shows his inmost heart to his friend, the lover to his best-beloved; when man does not vainly shrink from the eye of his Creator, loathsomely treasuring up the secret of his sin,—then deem me a monster for the symbol beneath which I have lived and die. I look around me, and, lo! on every visage a black veil!"

While his auditors shrank from one another in mutual affright, Father Hooper fell back upon his pillow, a veiled corpse with a faint smile lingering on the lips. Still veiled, they laid him in his coffin, and a veiled corpse they bore him to the grave. The grass of many years has sprung up and withered on that grave, the burial-stone is moss-grown, and good Mr. Hooper's face is dust; but awful is still the thought that it mouldered beneath the black veil.

THE MAYPOLE OF MERRY MOUNT

THERE IS an admirable foundation for a philosophic romance in the curious history of the early settlement of Mount Wollaston, or Merry Mount. In the slight sketch here attempted the facts recorded on the grave pages of our New England annalists have wrought themselves almost spontaneously into a sort of allegory. The masques, mummeries and festive customs described in the text are in accordance with the manners of the age. Authority on these points may be found in Strutt's *Book of English Sports and Pastimes*.

Bright were the days at Merry Mount when the Maypole was the banner-staff of that gay colony. They who reared it, should their banner be triumphant, were to pour sunshine over New England's rugged hills and scatter flower-seeds throughout the soil. Jollity and gloom were contending for an empire. Midsummer eve had come, bringing deep verdure to the forest, and roses in her lap of a more vivid hue than the tender buds of spring. But May, or her mirthful spirit, dwelt all the year round at Merry Mount, sporting with the summer months and revelling with autumn and basking in the glow of winter's fireside. Through a world of toil and care she flitted with a dream-like smile, and came hither to find a home among the lightsome hearts of Merry Mount.

Never had the Maypole been so gayly decked as at sunset on Midsummer eve. This venerated emblem was a pine tree which had preserved the slender grace of youth, while it equalled the loftiest height of the old wood-monarchs. From its top streamed a silken banner colored like the rainbow. Down nearly to the ground the pole was dressed with birchen boughs, and others of the liveliest green, and some with silvery leaves fastened by ribbons that fluttered in fantastic knots of twenty different colors, but no sad ones. Garden-flowers and blossoms of the wilderness laughed gladly forth amid the verdure, so fresh and dewy that they must have grown by magic on that happy pine tree. Where this green and flowery splendor terminated the shaft of the Maypole was stained with the seven brilliant hues of the banner at its top. On the lowest green bough hung an abundant wreath of roses—some that had been gathered in the sunniest spots of the forest, and others, of still richer blush, which the colonists had reared from English seed. O people of the Golden Age, the chief of your husbandry was to raise flowers!

But what was the wild throng that stood hand in hand about the Maypole? It could not be that the fauns and nymphs, when driven from their classic groves and homes of ancient fable, had sought refuge, as all the persecuted did, in the fresh woods of the West. These were Gothic monsters, though perhaps of Grecian ancestry. On the shoulders of a comely youth uprose the head and branching antlers of a stag; a second, human in all other points, had the grim visage of a wolf; a third, still with the trunk and limbs of a mortal man, showed the beard and horns of a venerable he-goat. There was the likeness of a bear erect, brute in all but his hind legs, which were adorned with pink silk stockings. And here, again, almost as wondrous, stood a real bear of the dark forest, lending each of his forepaws to the grasp of a human hand and as ready for the dance as any in that circle. His inferior nature rose halfway to meet his companions as they stooped. Other faces wore the similitude of man or woman, but distorted or extravagant, with red noses pendulous before their mouths, which seemed of awful depth and stretched from ear to ear in an eternal fit of laughter. Here might be seen the salvage man—well known in heraldry—hairy as a baboon and girdled with green leaves. By his side—a nobler figure, but still a counterfeit—appeared an Indian hunter with feathery crest and wampum-belt. Many of this strange company wore foolscaps and had little bells appended to their garments, tinkling with a silvery sound responsive to the inaudible music of their gleesome spirits. Some youths and maidens were of soberer garb, yet well maintained their places in the irregular throng by the expression of wild revelry upon their features.

Such were the colonists of Merry Mount as they stood in the broad smile of sunset round their venerated Maypole. Had a wanderer bewildered in the melancholy forest heard their mirth and stolen a half-affrighted glance, he might have fancied them the crew of Comus, some already transformed to brutes, some midway between man and beast, and the others rioting in the flow of tipsy jollity that foreran the change; but a band of Puritans who watched the scene, invisible themselves, compared the masques to those devils and ruined souls with whom their superstition peopled the black wilderness.

Within the ring of monsters appeared the two airiest forms that had ever trodden on any more solid footing than a purple-and-golden cloud. One was a youth in glistening apparel with a scarf of the rainbow pattern crosswise on his breast. His right hand held a gilded staff—the ensign of high dignity among the revellers—and his left grasped the slender fingers of a fair maiden not less gayly decorated than himself. Bright roses glowed in contrast with the dark and glossy curls of each, and were scattered round their feet or had sprung up spontaneously there. Behind this lightsome couple, so close to the Maypole that its boughs shaded his jovial face, stood the figure of an English priest, canonically dressed, yet decked with flowers, in heathen fashion, and wearing a chaplet of the native vine leaves. By the riot of his rolling eye and the pagan decorations of his holy garb, he seemed the wildest monster there, and the very Comus of the crew.

"Votaries of the Maypole," cried the flower-decked priest, "merrily all day long have the woods echoed to your mirth. But be this your merriest hour, my hearts! Lo! here stand the Lord and Lady of the May, whom I, a clerk of Oxford and high priest of Merry Mount, am presently to join in holy matrimony.—Up with your nimble spirits, ye morrice-dancers, green men and glee-maidens, bears and wolves and horned gentlemen! Come! a chorus now rich with the old mirth of Merry England and the wilder glee of this fresh forest, and then a dance, to show the youthful pair what life is made of and how airily they should go through it!—All ye that love the Maypole, lend your voices to the nuptial song of the Lord and Lady of the May!"

This wedlock was more serious than most affairs of Merry Mount, where jest and delusion, trick and fantasy, kept up a continual carnival. The Lord and Lady of the May, though their titles must be laid down at sunset, were really and truly to be partners for the dance of life, beginning the measure that same bright eve. The wreath of roses that hung from the lowest green bough of the Maypole had been twined for them, and would be thrown over both their heads in symbol of their flowery union. When the priest had spoken, therefore, a riotous uproar burst from the rout of monstrous figures.

"Begin you the stave, reverend sir," cried they all, "and never did the woods ring to such a merry peal as we of the Maypole shall send up."

Immediately a prelude of pipe, cittern and viol, touched with practised minstrelsy, began to play from a neighboring thicket in such a mirthful cadence that the boughs of the Maypole quivered to the sound. But the May-lord—he of the gilded staff—chancing to look into his lady's eyes, was wonder-struck at the almost pensive glance that met his own.

"Edith, sweet Lady of the May," whispered he, reproachfully, "is yon wreath of roses a garland to hang above our graves that you look so sad? Oh, Edith, this is our golden time. Tarnish it not by any pensive shadow of the mind, for it may be that nothing of futurity will be brighter than the mere remembrance of what is now passing."

"That was the very thought that saddened me. How came it in your mind too?" said Edith, in a still lower tone than he; for it was high treason to be sad at Merry Mount. "Therefore do I sigh amid this festive music. And besides, dear Edgar, I struggle as with a dream, and fancy that these shapes of our jovial friends are visionary and their mirth unreal, and that we are no true lord and lady of the May. What is the mystery in my heart?"

Just then, as if a spell had loosened them, down came a little shower of withering rose-leaves from the Maypole. Alas for the young lovers! No sooner had their hearts glowed with real passion than they were sensible of something vague and unsubstantial in their former pleasures, and felt a dreary presentiment of inevitable change. From the moment that they truly loved they had subjected themselves to earth's doom of care and sorrow and troubled joy, and had no more a home at Merry Mount. That was Edith's mystery. Now leave we the priest to marry them, and the masquers to sport round the Maypole till the last sunbeam be withdrawn from its summit and the shadows of the forest mingle gloomily in the dance. Meanwhile, we may discover who these gay people were.

Two hundred years ago, and more, the Old World and its inhabitants became mutually weary of each other. Men voyaged by thousands to the West—some to barter glass and such like jewels for the furs of the Indian hunter, some to conquer virgin empires, and one stern band to pray. But none of these motives had much weight with the colonists of Merry Mount. Their leaders were men who had sported so long with life, that when Thought and Wisdom came, even these unwelcome guests were led astray by the crowd of vanities which they should have put to flight. Erring Thought and perverted Wisdom were made to put on masques, and play the fool. The men of whom we speak, after losing the heart's fresh gayety, imagined a wild philosophy of pleasure, and came hither to act out their latest day-dream. They gathered followers from all that giddy tribe whose whole life is like the festal days of soberer men. In their train were minstrels, not unknown in London streets; wandering players, whose theatres had been the halls of noblemen; mummers, rope-dancers, and mountebanks, who would long be missed at wakes, church ales, and fairs; in a word, mirth makers of every sort, such as abounded in that age, but now began to be discountenanced by the rapid growth of Puritanism. Light had their footsteps been on land, and as lightly they came across the sea. Many had been maddened by their previous troubles into a gay despair; others were as madly gay in the flush of youth, like the May Lord and his Lady; but whatever might be the quality of their mirth, old and young were gay at Merry Mount. The young deemed themselves happy. The elder spirits, if they knew that mirth was but the counterfeit of happiness, yet followed the false shadow wilfully, because at least her garments glittered brightest. Sworn triflers of a lifetime, they would not venture among the sober truths of life not even to be truly blest.

All the hereditary pastimes of Old England were transplanted hither. The King of Christmas was duly crowned, and the Lord of Misrule bore potent sway. On the Eve of St. John, they felled whole acres of the forest to make bonfires, and danced by the blaze all night, crowned with garlands, and throwing flowers into the flame. At harvest time, though their crop was of the smallest, they made an image with the sheaves of Indian corn, and wreathed it with autumnal garlands, and bore it home triumphantly. But what chiefly characterized the colonists of Merry Mount was their veneration for the Maypole. It has made their true history a poet's tale. Spring decked the hallowed emblem with young blossoms and fresh green boughs; Summer brought roses of the deepest blush, and the perfected foliage of the forest; Autumn enriched it with that red and yellow gorgeousness which converts each wildwood leaf into a painted flower; and Winter silvered it with sleet, and hung it round with icicles, till it flashed in the cold sunshine, itself a frozen sunbeam. Thus each alternate season did homage to the Maypole, and paid it a tribute of its own richest splendor. Its votaries danced round it, once, at least, in every month; sometimes they called it their religion, or their altar; but always, it was the banner staff of Merry Mount.

Unfortunately, there were men in the new world of a sterner faith than those Maypole worshippers. Not far from Merry Mount was a settlement of Puritans, most dismal wretches, who said their prayers before daylight, and then wrought in the forest or the cornfield till evening made it prayer time again. Their weapons were always at hand to shoot down the straggling savage. When they met in conclave, it was never to keep up the old English mirth, but to hear sermons three hours long, or to proclaim bounties on the heads of wolves and the scalps of Indians. Their festivals were fast days, and their chief pastime the singing of psalms. Woe to the youth or maiden who did but dream of a dance! The selectman nodded to the constable; and there sat the light-heeled reprobate in the stocks; or if he danced, it was round the whipping-post, which might be termed the Puritan Maypole.

A party of these grim Puritans, toiling through the difficult woods, each with a horseload of iron armor to burden his footsteps, would sometimes draw near the sunny precincts of Merry Mount. There were the silken colonists, sporting round their Maypole; perhaps teaching a bear to dance, or striving to communicate their mirth to the grave Indian, or masquerading in the skins of deer and wolves which they had hunted for that especial purpose. Often the whole colony were playing at Blindman's Buff, magistrates and all with their eyes bandaged, except a single scapegoat, whom the blinded sinners pursued by the tinkling of the bells at his garments. Once, it is said, they were seen following a flower-decked corpse with merriment and festive music to his grave. But did the dead man laugh? In their quietest times they sang ballads and told tales for the edification of their pious visitors, or perplexed them with juggling tricks, or grinned at them through horse-collars; and when sport itself grew wearisome, they made game of their own stupidity and began a yawning-match. At the very least of these enormities the men of iron shook their heads and frowned so darkly that the revellers looked up, imagining that a momentary cloud had overcast the sunshine which was to be perpetual there. On the other hand, the Puritans affirmed that when a psalm was pealing from their place of worship the echo which the forest sent them back seemed often like the chorus of a jolly catch, closing with a roar of laughter. Who but the fiend and his bond-slaves the crew of Merry Mount had thus disturbed them? In due time a feud arose, stern and bitter on one side, and as serious on the other as anything could be among such light spirits as had sworn allegiance to the Maypole. The future complexion of New England was involved in this important quarrel. Should the grisly saints establish their jurisdiction over the gay sinners, then would their spirits darken all the clime and make it a land of clouded visages, of hard toil, of sermon and psalm for ever; but should the banner-staff of Merry Mount be fortunate, sunshine would break upon the hills, and flowers would beautify the forest and late posterity do homage to the Maypole.

After these authentic passages from history we return to the nuptials of the Lord and Lady of the May. Alas! we have delayed too long, and must darken our tale too suddenly. As we glance again at the Maypole a solitary sunbeam is fading from the summit, and leaves only a faint golden tinge blended with the hues of the rainbow banner. Even that dim light is now withdrawn, relinquishing the whole domain of Merry Mount to the evening gloom which has rushed so instantaneously from the black surrounding woods. But some of these black shadows have rushed forth in human shape.

Yes, with the setting sun the last day of mirth had passed from Merry Mount. The ring of gay masquers was disordered and broken; the stag lowered his antlers in dismay; the wolf grew weaker than a lamb; the bells of the morrice-dancers tinkled with tremulous affright. The Puritans had played a characteristic part in the Maypole mummeries. Their darksome figures were intermixed with the wild shapes of their foes, and made the scene a picture of the moment when waking thoughts start up amid the scattered fantasies of a dream. The leader of the hostile party stood in the centre of the circle, while the rout of monsters cowered around him like evil spirits in the presence of a dread magician. No fantastic foolery could look him in the face. So stern was the energy of his aspect that the whole man, visage, frame and soul, seemed wrought of iron gifted with life and thought, yet all of one substance with his headpiece and breastplate. It was the Puritan of Puritans: it was Endicott himself.

"Stand off, priest of Baal!" said he, with a grim frown and laying no reverent hand upon the surplice. "I know thee, Blackstone! Thou art the man who couldst not abide the rule even of thine own corrupted Church, and hast come hither to preach iniquity and to give example of it in thy life. But now shall it be seen that the Lord hath sanctified this wilderness for his peculiar people. Woe unto them that would defile it! And first for this flower-decked abomination, the altar of thy worship!"

And with his keen sword Endicott assaulted the hallowed Maypole. Nor long did it resist his arm. It groaned with a dismal sound, it showered leaves and rosebuds upon the remorseless enthusiast, and finally, with all its green boughs and ribbons and flowers, symbolic of departed pleasures, down fell the banner-staff of Merry Mount. As it sank, tradition says, the evening sky grew darker and the woods threw forth a more sombre shadow.

"There!" cried Endicott, looking triumphantly on his work; "there lies the only Maypole in New England. The thought is strong within me that by its fall is shadowed forth the fate of light and idle mirthmakers amongst us and our posterity. Amen, saith John Endicott!"

"Amen!" echoed his followers.

But the votaries of the Maypole gave one groan for their idol. At the sound the Puritan leader glanced at the crew of Comus, each a figure of broad mirth, yet at this moment strangely expressive of sorrow and dismay.

"Valiant captain," quoth Peter Palfrey, the ancient of the band, "what order shall be taken with the prisoners?"

"I thought not to repent me of cutting down a Maypole," replied Endicott, "yet now I could find in my heart to plant it again and give each of these bestial pagans one other dance round their idol. It would have served rarely for a whipping-post."

"But there are pine trees enow," suggested the lieutenant.

"True, good ancient," said the leader. "Wherefore bind the heathen crew and bestow on them a small matter of stripes apiece as earnest of our future justice. Set some of the rogues in the stocks to rest themselves so soon as Providence shall bring us to one of our own well-ordered settlements where such accommodations may be found. Further penalties, such as branding and cropping of ears, shall be thought of hereafter."

"How many stripes for the priest?" inquired Ancient Palfrey.

"None as yet," answered Endicott, bending his iron frown upon the culprit. "It must be for the Great and General Court to determine whether stripes and long imprisonment, and other grievous penalty, may atone for his transgressions. Let him look to himself. For such as violate our civil order it may be permitted us to show mercy, but woe to the wretch that troubleth our religion!"

"And this dancing bear?" resumed the officer. "Must he share the stripes of his fellows?"

"Shoot him through the head!" said the energetic Puritan. "I suspect witchcraft in the beast."

"Here be a couple of shining ones," continued Peter Palfrey, pointing his weapon at the Lord and Lady of the May. "They seem to be of high station among these misdoers. Methinks their dignity will not be fitted with less than a double share of stripes."

Endicott rested on his sword and closely surveyed the dress and aspect of the hapless pair. There they stood, pale, downcast and apprehensive, yet there was an air of mutual support and of pure affection seeking aid and giving it that showed them to be man and wife with the sanction of a priest upon their love. The youth in the peril of the moment, had dropped his gilded staff and thrown his arm about the Lady of the May, who leaned against his breast too lightly to burden him, but with weight enough to express that their destinies were linked together for good or evil. They looked first at each other and then into the grim captain's face. There they stood in the first hour of wedlock, while the idle pleasures of which their companions were the emblems had given place to the sternest cares of life, personified by the dark Puritans. But never had their youthful beauty seemed so pure and high as when its glow was chastened by adversity.

"Youth," said Endicott, "ye stand in an evil case—thou and thy maiden-wife. Make ready presently, for I am minded that ye shall both have a token to remember your wedding-day."

"Stern man," cried the May-lord, "how can I move thee? Were the means at hand, I would resist to the death; being powerless, I entreat. Do with me as thou wilt, but let Edith go untouched."

"Not so," replied the immitigable zealot. "We are not wont to show an idle courtesy to that sex which requireth the stricter discipline.—What sayest thou, maid? Shall thy silken bridegroom suffer thy share of the penalty besides his own?"

"Be it death," said Edith, "and lay it all on me."

Truly, as Endicott had said, the poor lovers stood in a woeful case. Their foes were triumphant, their friends captive and abased, their home desolate, the benighted wilderness around them, and a rigorous destiny in the shape of the Puritan leader their only guide. Yet the deepening twilight could not altogether conceal that the iron man was softened. He smiled at the fair spectacle of early love; he almost sighed for the inevitable blight of early hopes.

"The troubles of life have come hastily on this young couple," observed Endicott. "We will see how they comport themselves under their present trials ere we burden them with greater. If among the spoil there be any garments of a more decent fashion, let them be put upon this May-lord and his Lady instead of their glistening vanities. Look to it, some of you."

"And shall not the youth's hair be cut?" asked Peter Palfrey, looking with abhorrence at the lovelock and long glossy curls of the young man.

"Crop it forthwith, and that in the true pumpkin-shell fashion," answered the captain. "Then bring them along with us, but more gently than their fellows. There be qualities in the youth which may make him valiant to fight and sober to toil and pious to pray, and in the maiden that may fit her to become a mother in our Israel, bringing up babes in better nurture than her own hath been.—Nor think ye, young ones, that they are the happiest, even in our lifetime of a moment, who misspend it in dancing round a Maypole."

And Endicott, the severest Puritan of all who laid the rock-foundation of New England, lifted the wreath of roses from the ruin of the Maypole and threw it with his own gauntleted hand over the heads of the Lord and Lady of the May. It was a deed of prophecy. As the moral gloom of the world overpowers all systematic gayety, even so was their home of wild mirth made desolate amid the sad forest. They returned to it no more. But as their flowery garland was wreathed of the brightest roses that had grown there, so in the tie that united them were intertwined all the purest and best of their early joys. They went heavenward supporting each other along the difficult path which it was their lot to tread, and never wasted one regretful thought on the vanities of Merry Mount.

THE GENTLE BOY

In the course of the year 1656 several of the people called Quakers—led, as they professed, by the inward movement of the spirit—made their appearance in New England. Their reputation as holders of mystic and pernicious principles having spread before them, the Puritans early endeavored to banish and to prevent the further intrusion of the rising sect. But the measures by which it was intended to purge the land of heresy, though more than sufficiently vigorous, were entirely unsuccessful. The Quakers, esteeming persecution as a divine call to the post of danger, laid claim to a holy courage unknown to the Puritans themselves, who had shunned the cross by providing for the peaceable exercise of their religion in a distant wilderness. Though it was the singular fact that every nation of the earth rejected the wandering enthusiasts who practised peace toward all men, the place of greatest uneasiness and peril, and therefore in their eyes the most eligible, was the province of Massachusetts Bay.

The fines, imprisonments and stripes liberally distributed by our pious forefathers, the popular antipathy, so strong that it endured nearly a hundred years after actual persecution had ceased, were attractions as powerful for the Quakers as peace, honor and reward would have been for the worldly-minded. Every European vessel brought new cargoes of the sect, eager to testify against the oppression which they hoped to share; and when shipmasters were restrained by heavy fines from affording them passage, they made long and circuitous journeys through the Indian country, and appeared in the province as if conveyed by a supernatural power. Their enthusiasm, heightened almost to madness by the treatment which they received, produced actions contrary to the rules of decency as well as of rational religion, and presented a singular contrast to the calm and staid deportment of their sectarian successors of the present day. The command of the Spirit, inaudible except to the soul and not to be controverted on grounds of human wisdom, was made a plea for most indecorous exhibitions which, abstractedly considered, well deserved the moderate chastisement of the rod. These extravagances, and the persecution which was at once their cause and consequence, continued to increase, till in the year 1659 the government of Massachusetts Bay indulged two members of the Quaker sect with the crown of martyrdom.

An indelible stain of blood is upon the hands of all who consented to this act, but a large share of the awful responsibility must rest upon the person then at the head of the government. He was a man of narrow mind and imperfect education, and his uncompromising bigotry was made hot and mischievous by violent and hasty passions; he exerted his influence indecorously and unjustifiably to compass the death of the enthusiasts, and his whole conduct in respect to them was marked by brutal cruelty. The Quakers, whose revengeful feelings were not less deep because they were inactive, remembered this man and his associates in after-times. The historian of the sect affirms that by the wrath of Heaven a blight fell upon the land in the vicinity of the "bloody town" of Boston, so that no wheat would grow there; and he takes his stand, as it were, among the graves of the ancient persecutors, and triumphantly recounts the judgments that overtook them in old age or at the parting-hour. He tells us that they died suddenly and violently and in madness, but nothing can exceed the bitter mockery with which he records the loathsome disease and "death by rottenness" of the fierce and cruel governor.

On the evening of the autumn day that had witnessed the martyrdom of two men of the Quaker persuasion, a Puritan settler was returning from the metropolis to the neighboring country-town in which he resided. The air was cool, the sky clear, and the lingering twilight was made brighter by the rays of a young moon which had now nearly reached the verge of the horizon. The traveller, a man of middle age, wrapped in a gray frieze cloak, quickened his pace when he had reached the outskirts of the town, for a gloomy extent of nearly four miles lay between him and his home. The low straw-thatched houses were scattered at considerable intervals along the road, and, the country having been settled but about thirty years, the tracts of original forest still bore no small proportion to the cultivated ground. The autumn wind wandered among the branches, whirling away the leaves from all except the pine trees and moaning as if it lamented the desolation of which it was the instrument. The road had penetrated the mass of woods that lay nearest to the town, and was just emerging into an open space, when the traveller's ears were saluted by a sound more mournful than even that of the wind. It was like the wailing of some one in distress, and it seemed to proceed from beneath a tall and lonely fir tree in the centre of a cleared but unenclosed and uncultivated field. The Puritan could not but remember that this was the very spot which had been made accursed a few hours before by the execution of the Quakers, whose bodies had been thrown together into one hasty grave beneath the tree on which they suffered. He struggled, however, against the superstitious fears which belonged to the age, and compelled himself to pause and listen.

"The voice is most likely mortal, nor have I cause to tremble if it be otherwise," thought he, straining his eyes through the dim moonlight. "Methinks it is like the wailing of a child—some infant, it may be, which has strayed from its mother and chanced upon this place of death. For the ease of mine own conscience I must search this matter out." He therefore left the path and walked somewhat fearfully across the field. Though now so desolate, its soil was pressed down and trampled by the thousand footsteps of those who had witnessed the spectacle of that day, all of whom had now retired, leaving the dead to their loneliness.

The traveller at length reached the fir tree, which from the middle upward was covered with living branches, although a scaffold had been erected beneath, and other preparations made for the work of death. Under this unhappy tree—which in after-times was believed to drop poison with its dew—sat the one solitary mourner for innocent blood. It was a slender and light-clad little boy who leaned his face upon a hillock of fresh-turned and half-frozen earth and wailed bitterly, yet in a suppressed tone, as if his grief might receive the punishment of crime. The

Puritan, whose approach had been unperceived, laid his hand upon the child's shoulder and addressed him compassionately.

"You have chosen a dreary lodging, my poor boy, and no wonder that you weep," said he. "But dry your eyes and tell me where your mother dwells; I promise you, if the journey be not too far, I will leave you in her arms tonight."

The boy had hushed his wailing at once, and turned his face upward to the stranger. It was a pale, bright-eyed countenance, certainly not more than six years old, but sorrow, fear and want had destroyed much of its infantile expression. The Puritan, seeing the boy's frightened gaze and feeling that he trembled under his hand, endeavored to reassure him:

"Nay, if I intended to do you harm, little lad, the readiest way were to leave you here. What! you do not fear to sit beneath the gallows on a new-made grave, and yet you tremble at a friend's touch? Take heart, child, and tell me what is your name and where is your home."

"Friend," replied the little boy, in a sweet though faltering voice, "they call me Ilbrahim, and my home is here."

The pale, spiritual face, the eyes that seemed to mingle with the moonlight, the sweet, airy voice and the outlandish name almost made the Puritan believe that the boy was in truth a being which had sprung up out of the grave on which he sat; but perceiving that the apparition stood the test of a short mental prayer, and remembering that the arm which he had touched was lifelike, he adopted a more rational supposition. "The poor child is stricken in his intellect," thought he, "but verily his words are fearful in a place like this." He then spoke soothingly, intending to humor the boy's fantasy:

"Your home will scarce be comfortable, Ilbrahim, this cold autumn night, and I fear you are ill-provided with food. I am hastening to a warm supper and bed; and if you will go with me, you shall share them."

"I thank thee, friend, but, though I be hungry and shivering with cold, thou wilt not give me food nor lodging," replied the boy, in the quiet tone which despair had taught him even so young. "My father was of the people whom all men hate; they have laid him under this heap of earth, and here is my home."

The Puritan, who had laid hold of little Ilbrahim's hand, relinquished it as if he were touching a loathsome reptile. But he possessed a compassionate heart which not even religious prejudice could harden into stone. "God forbid that I should leave this child to perish, though he comes of the accursed sect," said he to himself. "Do we not all spring from an evil root? Are we not all in darkness till the light doth shine upon us? He shall not perish, neither in body nor, if prayer and instruction may avail for him, in soul." He then spoke aloud and kindly to Ilbrahim, who had again hid his face in the cold earth of the grave:

"Was every door in the land shut against you, my child, that you have wandered to this unhallowed spot?"

"They drove me forth from the prison when they took my father thence," said the boy, "and I stood afar off watching the crowd of people; and when they were gone, I came hither, and found only this grave. I knew that my father was sleeping here, and I said, 'This shall be my home.'"

"No, child, no, not while I have a roof over my head or a morsel to share with you," exclaimed the Puritan, whose sympathies were now fully excited. "Rise up and come with me, and fear not any harm."

The boy wept afresh, and clung to the heap of earth as if the cold heart beneath it were warmer to him than any in a living breast. The traveller, however, continued to entreat him tenderly, and, seeming to acquire some degree of confidence, he at length arose; but his slender limbs tottered with weakness, his little head grew dizzy, and he leaned against the tree of death for support.

"My poor boy, are you so feeble?" said the Puritan. "When did you taste food last?"

"I ate of bread and water with my father in the prison," replied Ilbrahim, "but they brought him none neither yesterday nor to-day, saying that he had eaten enough to bear him to his journey's end. Trouble not thyself for my hunger, kind friend, for I have lacked food many times ere now."

The traveller took the child in his arms and wrapped his cloak about him, while his heart stirred with shame and anger against the gratuitous cruelty of the instruments in this persecution. In the awakened warmth of his feelings he resolved that at whatever risk he would not forsake the poor little defenceless being whom Heaven had confided to his care. With this determination he left the accursed field and resumed the homeward path from which the wailing of the boy had called him. The light and motionless burden scarcely impeded his progress, and he soon beheld the fire-rays from the windows of the cottage which he, a native of a distant clime, had built in the Western wilderness. It was surrounded by a considerable extent of cultivated ground, and the dwelling was situated in the nook of a wood-covered hill, whither it seemed to have crept for protection.

"Look up, child," said the Puritan to Ilbrahim, whose faint head had sunk upon his shoulder; "there is our home."

At the word "home" a thrill passed through the child's frame, but he continued silent. A few moments brought them to the cottage door, at which the owner knocked; for at that early period, when savages were wandering everywhere among the settlers, bolt and bar were indispensable to the security of a dwelling. The summons was answered by a bond-servant, a coarse-clad and dull-featured piece of humanity, who, after ascertaining that his master was the applicant, undid the door and held a flaring pine-knot torch to light him in. Farther back in the passageway the red blaze discovered a matronly woman, but no little crowd of children came bounding forth to greet their father's return.

As the Puritan entered he thrust aside his cloak and displayed Ilbrahim's face to the female.

"Dorothy, here is a little outcast whom Providence hath put into our hands," observed he. "Be kind to him, even as if he were of those dear ones who have departed from us."

"What pale and bright-eyed little boy is this, Tobias?" she inquired. "Is he one whom the wilderness-folk have ravished from some Christian mother?"

"No, Dorothy; this poor child is no captive from the wilderness," he replied. "The heathen savage would have given him to eat of his scanty morsel and to drink of his birchen cup, but Christian men, alas! had cast him out to die." Then he told her how he had found him beneath the gallows, upon his father's grave, and how his heart had prompted him like the speaking of an inward voice to take the little outcast home and be kind unto him. He acknowledged his resolution to feed and clothe him as if he were his own child, and to afford him the instruction which should counteract the pernicious errors hitherto instilled into his infant mind.

Dorothy was gifted with even a quicker tenderness than her husband, and she approved of all his doings and intentions.

"Have you a mother, dear child?" she inquired.

The tears burst forth from his full heart as he attempted to reply, but Dorothy at length understood that he had a mother, who like the rest of her sect was a persecuted wanderer. She had been taken from the prison a short time before, carried into the uninhabited wilderness and left to perish there by hunger or wild beasts. This was no uncommon method of disposing of the Quakers, and they were accustomed to boast that the inhabitants of the desert were more hospitable to them than civilized man.

35

"Fear not, little boy; you shall not need a mother, and a kind one," said Dorothy, when she had gathered this information. "Dry your tears, Ilbrahim, and be my child, as I will be your mother."

The good woman prepared the little bed from which her own children had successively been borne to another resting-place. Before Ilbrahim would consent to occupy it he knelt down, and as Dorothy listed to his simple and affecting prayer she marvelled how the parents that had taught it to him could have been judged worthy of death. When the boy had fallen asleep, she bent over his pale and spiritual countenance, pressed a kiss upon his white brow, drew the bedclothes up about his neck, and went away with a pensive gladness in her heart.

Tobias Pearson was not among the earliest emigrants from the old country. He had remained in England during the first years of the Civil War, in which he had borne some share as a cornet of dragoons under Cromwell. But when the ambitious designs of his leader began to develop themselves, he quitted the army of the Parliament and sought a refuge from the strife which was no longer holy among the people of his persuasion in the colony of Massachusetts. A more worldly consideration had perhaps an influence in drawing him thither, for New England offered advantages to men of unprosperous fortunes as well as to dissatisfied religionists, and Pearson had hitherto found it difficult to provide for a wife and increasing family. To this supposed impurity of motive the more bigoted Puritans were inclined to impute the removal by death of all the children for whose earthly good the father had been over-thoughtful. They had left their native country blooming like roses, and like roses they had perished in a foreign soil. Those expounders of the ways of Providence, who had thus judged their brother and attributed his domestic sorrows to his sin, were not more charitable when they saw him and Dorothy endeavoring to fill up the void in their hearts by the adoption of an infant of the accursed sect. Nor did they fail to communicate their disapprobation to Tobias, but the latter in reply merely pointed at the little quiet, lovely boy, whose appearance and deportment were indeed as powerful arguments as could possibly have been adduced in his own favor. Even his beauty, however, and his winning manners sometimes produced an effect ultimately unfavorable; for the bigots, when the outer surfaces of their iron hearts had been softened and again grew hard, affirmed that no merely natural cause could have so worked upon them. Their antipathy to the poor infant was also increased by the ill-success of divers theological discussions in which it was attempted to convince him of the errors of his sect. Ilbrahim, it is true, was not a skilful controversialist, but the feeling of his religion was strong as instinct in him, and he could neither be enticed nor driven from the faith which his father had died for.

The odium of this stubbornness was shared in a great measure by the child's protectors, insomuch that Tobias and Dorothy very shortly began to experience a most bitter species of persecution in the cold regards of many a friend whom they had valued. The common people manifested their opinions more openly. Pearson was a man of some consideration, being a representative to the General Court and an approved lieutenant in the train-bands, yet within a week after his adoption of Ilbrahim he had been both hissed and hooted. Once, also, when walking through a solitary piece of woods, he heard a loud voice from some invisible speaker, and it cried, "What shall be done to the backslider? Lo! the scourge is knotted for him, even the whip of nine cords, and every cord three knots." These insults irritated Pearson's temper for the moment; they entered also into his heart, and became imperceptible but powerful workers toward an end which his most secret thought had not yet whispered.

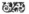

On the second Sabbath after Ilbrahim became a member of their family, Pearson and his wife deemed it proper that he should appear with them at public worship. They had anticipated some opposition to this measure from the boy, but he prepared himself in silence, and at the appointed hour was clad in the new mourning-suit which Dorothy had wrought for him. As the parish was then, and during many subsequent years, unprovided with a bell, the signal for the commencement of religious exercises was the beat of a drum. At the first sound of that martial call to the place of holy and quiet thoughts Tobias and Dorothy set forth, each holding a hand of little Ilbrahim, like two parents linked together by the infant of their love. On their path through the leafless woods they were overtaken by many persons of their acquaintance, all of whom avoided them and passed by on the other side; but a severer trial awaited their constancy when they had descended the hill and drew near the pine-built and undecorated house of prayer. Around the door, from which the drummer still sent forth his thundering summons, was drawn up a formidable phalanx, including several of the oldest members of the congregation, many of the middle-aged and nearly all the younger males. Pearson found it difficult to sustain their united and disapproving gaze, but Dorothy, whose mind was differently circumstanced, merely drew the boy closer to her and faltered not in her approach. As they entered the door they overheard the muttered sentiments of the assemblage; and when the reviling voices of the little children smote Ilbrahim's ear, he wept.

The interior aspect of the meeting-house was rude. The low ceiling, the unplastered walls, the naked woodwork and the undrapeied pulpit offered nothing to excite the devotion which without such external aids often remains latent in the heart. The floor of the building was occupied by rows of long cushionless benches, supplying the place of pews, and the broad aisle formed a sexual division impassable except by children beneath a certain age.

Pearson and Dorothy separated at the door of the meeting-house, and Ilbrahim, being within the years of infancy, was retained under the care of the latter. The wrinkled beldams involved themselves in their rusty cloaks as he passed by; even the mild-featured maidens seemed to dread contamination; and many a stern old man arose and turned his repulsive and unheavenly countenance upon the gentle boy, as if the sanctuary were polluted by his presence. He was a sweet infant of the skies that had strayed away from his home, and all the inhabitants of this miserable world closed up their impure hearts against him, drew back their earth-soiled garments from his touch and said, "We are holier than thou."

Ilbrahim, seated by the side of his adopted mother and retaining fast hold of her hand, assumed a grave and decorous demeanor such as might befit a person of matured taste and understanding who should find himself in a temple dedicated to some worship which he did not recognize, but felt himself bound to respect. The exercises had not yet commenced, however, when the boy's attention was arrested by an event apparently of trifling interest. A woman having her face muffled in a hood and a cloak drawn completely about her form advanced slowly up the broad aisle and took place upon the foremost bench. Ilbrahim's faint color varied, his nerves fluttered; he was unable to turn his eyes from the muffled female.

When the preliminary prayer and hymn were over, the minister arose, and, having turned the hour-glass which stood by the great Bible, commenced his discourse. He was now well stricken in years, a man of pale, thin countenance, and his gray hairs were closely covered by a black velvet skull-cap. In his younger days he had practically learned the meaning of persecution from Archbishop Laud, and he was not now disposed to forget the lesson against which he had murmured then. Introducing the often-discussed subject of the Quakers, he gave a history of that sect and a description of their tenets in which error predominated and prejudice distorted the aspect of what was true. He adverted to the recent measures in the province, and cautioned his hearers of weaker parts against calling in question the just severity which God-fearing magistrates had at length been compelled to exercise. He spoke of the danger of pity—in some cases a commendable and Christian virtue, but inapplicable to this pernicious sect. He observed that such was their devilish obstinacy in error that even the little children, the sucking babes, were hardened and desperate heretics. He affirmed that no man without Heaven's especial warrant should attempt their conversion lest while he lent his hand to draw them from the slough he should himself be precipitated into its lowest depths.

The sands of the second hour were principally in the lower half of the glass when the sermon concluded. An approving murmur followed, and the clergyman, having given out a hymn, took his seat with much self-congratulation, and endeavored to read the effect of his eloquence in the visages of the people. But while voices from all parts of the house were tuning themselves to sing a scene occurred which, though not very unusual at that period in the province, happened to be without precedent in this parish.

The muffled female, who had hitherto sat motionless in the front rank of the audience, now arose and with slow, stately and unwavering step ascended the pulpit stairs. The quaverings of incipient harmony were hushed and the divine sat in speechless and almost terrified astonishment while she undid the door and stood up in the sacred desk from which his maledictions had just been thundered. She then divested herself of the cloak and hood, and appeared in a most singular array. A shapeless robe of sackcloth was girded about her waist with a knotted cord; her raven hair fell down upon her shoulders, and its blackness was defiled by pale streaks of ashes, which she had strewn upon her head. Her eyebrows, dark and strongly defined, added to the deathly whiteness of a countenance which, emaciated with want and wild with enthusiasm and strange sorrows, retained no trace of earlier beauty. This figure stood gazing earnestly on the audience, and there was no sound nor any movement except a faint shuddering which every man observed in his neighbor, but was scarcely conscious of in himself. At length, when her fit of inspiration came, she spoke for the first few moments in a low voice and not invariably distinct utterance. Her discourse gave evidence of an imagination hopelessly entangled with her reason; it was a vague and incomprehensible rhapsody, which, however, seemed to spread its own atmosphere round the hearer's soul, and to move his feelings by some influence unconnected with the words. As she proceeded beautiful but shadowy images would sometimes be seen like bright things moving in a turbid river, or a strong and singularly shaped idea leapt forth and seized at once on the understanding or the heart. But the course of her unearthly eloquence soon led her to the persecutions of her sect, and from thence the step was short to her own peculiar sorrows. She was naturally a woman of mighty passions, and hatred and revenge now wrapped themselves in the garb of piety. The character of her speech was changed; her images became distinct though wild, and her denunciations had an almost hellish bitterness.

"The governor and his mighty men," she said, "have gathered together, taking counsel among themselves and saying, 'What shall we do unto this people—even unto the people that have come into this land to put our iniquity to the blush?' And, lo! the devil entereth into the council-chamber like a lame man of low stature and gravely apparelled, with a dark and twisted countenance and a bright, downcast eye. And he standeth up among the rulers; yea, he goeth to and fro, whispering to each; and every man lends his ear, for his word is 'Slay! Slay!' But I say unto ye, Woe to them that slay! Woe to them that shed the blood of saints! Woe to them that have slain the husband and cast forth the child, the tender infant, to wander homeless and hungry and cold till he die, and have saved the mother alive in the cruelty of their tender mercies! Woe to them in their lifetime! Cursed are they in the delight and pleasure of their hearts! Woe to them in their death-hour, whether it come swiftly with blood and violence or after long and lingering pain! Woe in the dark house, in the rottenness of the grave, when the children's children shall revile the ashes of the fathers! Woe, woe, woe, at the judgment, when all the persecuted and all the slain in this bloody land, and the father, the mother and the child, shall await them in a day that they cannot escape! Seed of the faith, seed of the faith, ye whose hearts are moving with a power that ye know not, arise, wash your hands of this innocent blood! Lift your voices, chosen ones, cry aloud, and call down a woe and a judgment with me!"

Having thus given vent to the flood of malignity which she mistook for inspiration, the speaker was silent. Her voice was succeeded by the hysteric shrieks of several women, but the feelings of the audience generally had not been drawn onward in the current with her own. They remained stupefied, stranded, as it were, in the midst of a torrent which deafened them by its roaring, but might not move them by its violence. The clergyman, who could not hitherto have ejected the usurper of his pulpit otherwise than by bodily force, now addressed her in the tone of just indignation and legitimate authority.

"Get you down, woman, from the holy place which you profane," he said, "Is it to the Lord's house that you come to pour forth the foulness of your heart and the inspiration of the devil? Get you down, and remember that the sentence of death is on you—yea, and shall be executed, were it but for this day's work."

"I go, friend, I go, for the voice hath had its utterance," replied she, in a depressed, and even mild, tone. "I have done my mission unto thee and to thy people; reward me with stripes, imprisonment or death, as ye shall be permitted." The weakness of exhausted passion caused her steps to totter as she descended the pulpit stairs.

The people, in the mean while, were stirring to and fro on the floor of the house, whispering among themselves and glancing toward the intruder. Many of them now recognized her as the woman who had assaulted the governor with frightful language as he passed by the window of her prison; they knew, also, that she was adjudged to suffer death, and had been preserved only by an involuntary banishment into the wilderness. The new outrage by which she had provoked her fate seemed to render further lenity impossible, and a gentleman in military dress, with a stout man of inferior rank, drew toward the door of the meetinghouse and awaited her approach. Scarcely did her feet press the floor, however, when an unexpected scene occurred. In that moment of her peril, when every eye frowned with death, a little timid boy threw his arms round his mother.

"I am here, mother; it is I, and I will go with thee to prison," he exclaimed.

She gazed at him with a doubtful and almost frightened expression, for she knew that the boy had been cast out to perish, and she had not hoped to see his face again. She feared, perhaps, that it was but one of the happy visions with which her excited fancy had often deceived her in the solitude of the desert or in prison; but when she felt his hand warm within her own and heard his little eloquence of childish love, she began to know that she was yet a mother.

"Blessed art thou, my son!" she sobbed. "My heart was withered—yea, dead with thee and with thy father—and now it leaps as in the first moment when I pressed thee to my bosom."

She knelt down and embraced him again and again, while the joy that could find no words expressed itself in broken accents, like the bubbles gushing up to vanish at the surface of a deep fountain. The sorrows of past years and the darker peril that was nigh cast not a shadow on the brightness of that fleeting moment. Soon, however, the spectators saw a change upon her face as the consciousness of her sad estate returned, and grief supplied the fount of tears which joy had opened. By the words she uttered it would seem that the indulgence of natural love had given her mind a momentary sense of its errors, and made her know how far she had strayed from duty in following the dictates of a wild fanaticism.

"In a doleful hour art thou returned to me, poor boy," she said, "for thy mother's path has gone darkening onward, till now the end is death. Son, son, I have borne thee in my arms when my limbs were tottering, and I have fed thee with the food that I was fainting for; yet I have ill-performed a mother's part by thee in life, and now I leave thee no inheritance but woe and shame. Thou wilt go seeking through the world, and find all hearts closed against thee and their sweet affections turned to bitterness for my sake. My child, my child, how many a pang awaits thy gentle spirit, and I the cause of all!"

She hid her face on Ilbrahim's head, and her long raven hair, discolored with the ashes of her mourning, fell down about him like a veil. A low and interrupted moan was the voice of her heart's anguish, and it did not fail to move the sympathies of many who mistook their involuntary virtue for a sin. Sobs were audible in the female section of the house, and every man who was a father drew his hand across his eyes.

Tobias Pearson was agitated and uneasy, but a certain feeling like the consciousness of guilt oppressed him; so that he could not go forth and offer himself as the protector of the child. Dorothy, however, had watched her husband's eye. Her mind was free from the influence that had begun to work on his, and she drew near the Quaker woman and addressed her in the hearing of all the congregation.

"Stranger, trust this boy to me, and I will be his mother," she said, taking Ilbrahim's hand. "Providence has signally marked out my husband to protect him, and he has fed at our table and lodged under our roof now many days, till our hearts have grown very strongly unto him. Leave the tender child with us, and be at ease concerning his welfare."

The Quaker rose from the ground, but drew the boy closer to her, while she gazed earnestly in Dorothy's face. Her mild but saddened features and neat matronly attire harmonized together and were like a verse of fireside poetry. Her very aspect proved that she was blameless, so far as mortal could be so, in respect to God and man, while the enthusiast, in her robe of sackcloth and girdle of knotted cord, had as evidently violated the duties of the present life and the future by fixing her attention wholly on the latter. The two females, as they held each a hand of Ilbrahim, formed a practical allegory: it was rational piety and unbridled fanaticism contending for the empire of a young heart.

"Thou art not of our people," said the Quaker, mournfully.

"No, we are not of your people," replied Dorothy, with mildness, "but we are Christians looking upward to the same heaven with you. Doubt not that your boy shall meet you there, if there be a blessing on our tender and prayerful guidance of him. Thither, I trust, my own children have gone before me, for I also have been a mother. I am no longer so," she added, in a faltering tone, "and your son will have all my care."

"But will ye lead him in the path which his parents have trodden?" demanded the Quaker. "Can ye teach him the enlightened faith which his father has died for, and for which I—even I —am soon to become an unworthy martyr? The boy has been baptized in blood; will ye keep the mark fresh and ruddy upon his forehead?"

"I will not deceive you," answered Dorothy. "If your child become our child, we must breed him up in the instruction which Heaven has imparted to us; we must pray for him the prayers of our own faith; we must do toward him according to the dictates of our own consciences, and not of yours. Were we to act otherwise, we should abuse your trust, even in complying with your wishes."

The mother looked down upon her boy with a troubled countenance, and then turned her eyes upward to heaven. She seemed to pray internally, and the contention of her soul was evident.

"Friend," she said, at length, to Dorothy, "I doubt not that my son shall receive all earthly tenderness at thy hands. Nay, I will believe that even thy imperfect lights may guide him to a better world, for surely thou art on the path thither. But thou hast spoken of a husband. Doth he stand here among this multitude of people? Let him come forth, for I must know to whom I commit this most precious trust."

She turned her face upon the male auditors, and after a momentary delay Tobias Pearson came forth from among them. The Quaker saw the dress which marked his military rank, and shook her head; but then she noted the hesitating air, the eyes that struggled with her own and were vanquished, the color that went and came and could find no resting-place. As she gazed an unmirthful smile spread over her features, like sunshine that grows melancholy in some desolate spot. Her lips moved inaudibly, but at length she spake:

"I hear it, I hear it! The voice speaketh within me and saith, 'Leave thy child, Catharine, for his place is here, and go hence, for I have other work for thee. Break the bonds of natural affection, martyr thy love, and know that in all these things eternal wisdom hath its ends.' I go, friends, I go. Take ye my boy, my precious jewel. I go hence trusting that all shall be well, and that even for his infant hands there is a labor in the vineyard."

She knelt down and whispered to Ilbrahim, who at first struggled and clung to his mother with sobs and tears, but remained passive when she had kissed his cheek and arisen from the ground. Having held her hands over his head in mental prayer, she was ready to depart.

"Farewell, friends in mine extremity," she said to Pearson and his wife; "the good deed ye have done me is a treasure laid up in heaven, to be returned a thousandfold hereafter.—And farewell, ye mine enemies, to whom it is not permitted to harm so much as a hair of my head, nor to stay my footsteps even for a moment. The day is coming when ye shall call upon me to witness for ye to this one sin uncommitted, and I will rise up and answer."

She turned her steps toward the door, and the men who had stationed themselves to guard it withdrew and suffered her to pass. A general sentiment of pity overcame the virulence of religious hatred. Sanctified by her love and her affliction, she went forth, and all the people gazed after her till she had journeyed up the hill and was lost behind its brow. She went, the apostle of her own unquiet heart, to renew the wanderings of past years. For her voice had been already heard in many lands of Christendom, and she had pined in the cells of a Catholic Inquisition before she felt the lash and lay in the dungeons of the Puritans. Her mission had extended also to the followers of the Prophet, and from them she had received the courtesy and kindness which all the contending sects of our purer religion united to deny her. Her husband and herself had resided many months in Turkey, where even the sultan's countenance was gracious to them; in that pagan land, too, was Ilbrahim's birthplace, and his Oriental name was a mark of gratitude for the good deeds of an unbeliever.

When Pearson and his wife had thus acquired all the rights over Ilbrahim that could be delegated, their affection for him became, like the memory of their native land or their mild sorrow for the dead, a piece of the immovable furniture of their hearts. The boy, also, after a week or two of mental disquiet, began to gratify his protectors by many inadvertent proofs that he considered them as parents and their house as home. Before the winter snows were melted the persecuted infant, the little wanderer from a remote and heathen country, seemed native in the New England cottage and inseparable from the warmth and security of its hearth. Under the influence of kind treatment, and in the consciousness that he was loved, Ilbrahim's demeanor lost a premature manliness which had resulted from his earlier situation; he became more childlike and his natural character displayed itself with freedom. It was in many respects a beautiful one, yet the disordered imaginations of both his father and mother had perhaps propagated a certain unhealthiness in the mind of the boy. In his general state Ilbrahim would derive enjoyment from the most trifling events and from every object about him; he seemed to discover rich treasures of happiness by a faculty analogous to that of the witch-hazel, which points to hidden gold where all is barren to the eye. His airy gayety, coming to him from a thousand sources, communicated itself to the family, and Ilbrahim was like a domesticated sunbeam, brightening moody countenances and chasing away the gloom from the dark corners of the cottage.

On the other hand, as the susceptibility of pleasure is also that of pain, the exuberant cheerfulness of the boy's prevailing temper sometimes yielded to moments of deep depression. His sorrows could not always be followed up to their original source, but most frequently they appeared to flow—though Ilbrahim was young to be sad for such a cause—from wounded love. The flightiness of his mirth rendered him often guilty of offences against the decorum of a Puritan household, and on these occasions he did not invariably escape rebuke. But the slightest word of real bitterness, which he was infallible in distinguishing from pretended anger, seemed to sink into his heart and poison all his enjoyments till he became sensible that he was entirely forgiven. Of the malice which generally accompanies a superfluity of sensitiveness Ilbrahim was altogether destitute. When trodden upon, he would not turn; when wounded, he could but die. His mind was wanting in the stamina of self-support. It was a plant that would twine beautifully round something stronger than itself; but if repulsed or torn away, it had no choice but to wither on the ground. Dorothy's acuteness taught her that severity would crush the spirit of the child, and she nurtured him with the gentle care of one who handles a butterfly. Her husband manifested an equal affection, although it grew daily less productive of familiar caresses.

The feelings of the neighboring people in regard to the Quaker infant and his protectors had not undergone a favorable change, in spite of the momentary triumph which the desolate mother had obtained over their sympathies. The scorn and bitterness of which he was the object were very grievous to Ilbrahim, especially when any circumstance made him sensible that the children his equals in age partook of the enmity of their parents. His tender and social nature had already overflowed in attachments to everything about him, and still there was a residue of unappropriated love which he yearned to bestow upon the little ones who were taught to hate him. As the warm days of spring came on Ilbrahim was accustomed to remain for hours silent and inactive within hearing of the children's voices at their play, yet with his usual delicacy of feeling he avoided their notice, and would flee and hide himself from the smallest individual among them. Chance, however, at length seemed to open a medium of communication between his heart and theirs; it was by means of a boy about two years older than Ilbrahim, who was injured by a fall from a tree in the vicinity of Pearson's habitation. As the sufferer's own home was at some distance, Dorothy willingly received him under her roof and became his tender and careful nurse.

Ilbrahim was the unconscious possessor of much skill in physiognomy, and it would have deterred him in other circumstances from attempting to make a friend of this boy. The countenance of the latter immediately impressed a beholder disagreeably, but it required some examination to discover that the cause was a very slight distortion of the mouth and the irregular, broken line and near approach of the eyebrows. Analogous, perhaps, to these trifling deformities was an almost imperceptible twist of every joint and the uneven prominence of the breast, forming a body regular in its general outline, but faulty in almost all its details. The disposition of the boy was sullen and reserved, and the village schoolmaster stigmatized him as obtuse in intellect, although at a later period of life he evinced ambition and very peculiar talents. But, whatever might be his personal or moral irregularities, Ilbrahim's heart seized upon and clung to him from the moment that he was brought wounded into the cottage; the child of persecution seemed to compare his own fate with that of the sufferer, and to feel that even different modes of misfortune had created a sort of relationship between them. Food, rest and the fresh air for which he languished were neglected; he nestled continually by the bedside of the little stranger and with a fond jealousy endeavored to be the medium of all the cares that were bestowed upon him. As the boy became convalescent Ilbrahim contrived games suitable to his situation or amused him by a faculty which he had perhaps breathed in with the air of his barbaric birthplace. It was that of reciting imaginary adventures on the spur of the moment, and apparently in inexhaustible succession. His tales were, of course, monstrous, disjointed and without aim, but they were curious on account of a vein of human tenderness which ran through them all and was like a sweet familiar face encountered in the midst of wild and unearthly scenery. The auditor paid much attention to these romances and sometimes interrupted them by brief remarks upon the incidents, displaying shrewdness above his years, mingled with a moral obliquity which grated very harshly against Ilbrahim's instinctive rectitude. Nothing, however, could arrest the progress of the latter's affection, and there were many proofs that it met with a response from the dark and stubborn nature on which it was lavished. The boy's parents at length removed him to complete his cure under their own roof.

Ilbrahim did not visit his new friend after his departure, but he made anxious and continual inquiries respecting him and informed himself of the day when he was to reappear among his playmates. On a pleasant summer afternoon the children of the neighborhood had assembled in the little forest-crowned amphitheatre behind the meeting-house, and the recovering invalid was there, leaning on a staff. The glee of a score of untainted bosoms was heard in light and airy voices, which danced among the trees like sunshine become audible; the grown men of this weary world as they journeyed by the spot marvelled why life, beginning in such brightness, should proceed in gloom, and their hearts or their imaginations answered them and said that the bliss of childhood gushes from its innocence. But it happened that an unexpected addition was made to the heavenly little band. It was Ilbrahim, who came toward the children with a look of sweet confidence on his fair and spiritual face, as if, having manifested his love to one of them, he had no longer to fear a repulse from their society. A hush came over their mirth the moment they beheld him, and they stood whispering to each other while he drew nigh; but all at once the devil of their fathers entered into the unbreeched fanatics, and, sending up a fierce, shrill cry, they rushed upon the poor Quaker child. In an instant he was the centre of a brood of baby-fiends, who lifted sticks against him, pelted him with stones and displayed an instinct of destruction far more loathsome than the bloodthirstiness of manhood.

The invalid, in the mean while, stood apart from the tumult, crying out with a loud voice, "Fear not, Ilbrahim; come hither and take my hand," and his unhappy friend endeavored to obey him. After watching the victim's struggling approach with a calm smile and unabashed eye, the foul-hearted little villain lifted his staff and struck Ilbrahim on the mouth so forcibly that the blood issued in a stream. The poor child's arms had been raised to guard his head from the storm of blows, but now he dropped them at once. His persecutors beat him down, trampled upon him, dragged him by his long fair locks, and Ilbrahim was on the point of becoming as veritable a martyr as ever entered bleeding into heaven. The uproar, however, attracted the notice of a few neighbors, who put themselves to the trouble of rescuing the little heretic, and of conveying him to Pearson's door.

Ilbrahim's bodily harm was severe, but long and careful nursing accomplished his recovery; the injury done to his sensitive spirit was more serious, though not so visible. Its signs were principally of a negative character, and to be discovered only by those who had previously known him. His gait was thenceforth slow, even and unvaried by the sudden bursts of sprightlier motion which had once corresponded to his overflowing gladness; his countenance was heavier, and its former play of expression—the dance of sunshine reflected from moving water—was destroyed by the cloud over his existence; his notice was attracted in a far less degree by passing events, and he appeared to find greater difficulty in comprehending what was new to him than at a happier period. A stranger founding his judgment upon these circumstances would have said that the dulness of the child's intellect widely contradicted the promise of his features, but the secret was in the direction of Ilbrahim's thoughts, which were brooding within him when they should naturally have been wandering abroad. An attempt of Dorothy to revive his former sportiveness was the single occasion on which his quiet demeanor yielded to a violent display of grief; he burst into passionate weeping and ran and hid himself, for his heart had become so miserably sore that even the hand of kindness tortured it like fire. Sometimes at night, and probably in his dreams, he was heard to cry, "Mother! Mother!" as if her place, which a stranger had supplied while Ilbrahim was happy, admitted of no substitute in his extreme affliction. Perhaps among the many life-weary wretches then upon the earth there was not one who combined innocence and misery like this poor broken-hearted infant so soon the victim of his own heavenly nature.

While this melancholy change had taken place in Ilbrahim, one of an earlier origin and of different character had come to its perfection in his adopted father. The incident with which this tale commences found Pearson in a state of religious dulness, yet mentally disquieted and longing for a more fervid faith than he possessed. The first effect of his kindness to Ilbrahim was to produce a softened feeling, an incipient love for the child's whole sect, but joined to this, and resulting, perhaps, from self-suspicion, was a proud and ostentatious contempt of their tenets and practical extravagances. In the course of much thought, however—for the subject struggled irresistibly into his mind—the foolishness of the doctrine began to be less evident, and the points which had particularly offended his reason assumed another aspect or vanished entirely away. The work within him appeared to go on even while he slept, and that which had been a doubt when he laid down to rest would often hold the place of a truth confirmed by some forgotten demonstration when he recalled his thoughts in the morning. But, while he was thus becoming assimilated to the enthusiasts, his contempt, in nowise decreasing toward them, grew very fierce against himself; he imagined, also, that every face of his acquaintance wore a sneer, and that every word addressed to him was a gibe. Such was his state of mind at the period of Ilbrahim's misfortune, and the emotions consequent upon that event completed the change of which the child had been the original instrument.

In the mean time, neither the fierceness of the persecutors nor the infatuation of their victims had decreased. The dungeons were never empty; the streets of almost every village echoed daily with the lash; the life of a woman whose mild and Christian spirit no cruelty could embitter had been sacrificed, and more innocent blood was yet to pollute the hands that were so often raised in prayer. Early after the Restoration the English Quakers represented to Charles II. that a "vein of blood was open in his dominions," but, though the displeasure of the voluptuous king was roused, his interference was not prompt. And now the tale must stride forward over many months, leaving Pearson to encounter ignominy and misfortune; his wife, to a firm endurance of a thousand sorrows; poor Ilbrahim, to pine and droop like a cankered rose-bud; his mother, to wander on a mistaken errand, neglectful of the holiest trust which can be committed to a woman.

A winter evening, a night of storm, had darkened over Pearson's habitation, and there were no cheerful faces to drive the gloom from his broad hearth. The fire, it is true, sent forth a glowing heat and a ruddy light, and large logs dripping with half-melted snow lay ready to cast upon the embers. But the apartment was saddened in its aspect by the absence of much of the homely wealth which had once adorned it, for the exaction of repeated fines and his own neglect of temporal affairs had greatly impoverished the owner. And with the furniture of peace the implements of war had likewise disappeared; the sword was broken, the helm and cuirass were cast away for ever: the soldier had done with battles, and might not lift so much as his naked hand to guard his head. But the Holy Book remained, and the table on which it rested was drawn before the fire, while two of the persecuted sect sought comfort from its pages.

He who listened while the other read was the master of the house, now emaciated in form and altered as to the expression and healthiness of his countenance, for his mind had dwelt too long among visionary thoughts and his body had been worn by imprisonment and stripes. The hale and weatherbeaten old man who sat beside him had sustained less injury from a far longer course of the same mode of life. In person he was tall and dignified, and, which alone would have made him hateful to the Puritans, his gray locks fell from beneath the broad-brimmed hat and rested on his shoulders. As the old man read the sacred page the snow drifted against the windows or eddied in at the crevices of the door, while a blast kept laughing in the chimney and the blaze leaped fiercely up to seek it. And sometimes, when the wind struck the hill at a certain angle and swept down by the cottage across the wintry plain, its voice was the most doleful that can be conceived; it came as if the past were speaking, as if the dead had contributed each a whisper, as if the desolation of ages were breathed in that one lamenting sound.

The Quaker at length closed the book, retaining, however, his hand between the pages which he had been reading, while he looked steadfastly at Pearson. The attitude and features of the latter might have indicated the endurance of bodily pain; he leaned his forehead on his hands, his teeth were firmly closed and his frame was tremulous at intervals with a nervous agitation.

"Friend Tobias," inquired the old man, compassionately, "hast thou found no comfort in these many blessed passages of Scripture?"

"Thy voice has fallen on my ear like a sound afar off and indistinct," replied Pearson, without lifting his eyes. "Yea; and when I have hearkened carefully, the words seemed cold and lifeless and intended for another and a lesser grief than mine. Remove the book," he added, in a tone of sullen bitterness; "I have no part in its consolations, and they do but fret my sorrow the more."

"Nay, feeble brother; be not as one who hath never known the light," said the elder Quaker, earnestly, but with mildness. "Art thou he that wouldst be content to give all and endure all for conscience' sake, desiring even peculiar trials that thy faith might be purified and thy heart weaned from worldly desires? And wilt thou sink beneath an affliction which happens alike to them that have their portion here below and to them that lay up treasure in heaven? Faint not, for thy burden is yet light."

"It is heavy! It is heavier than I can bear!" exclaimed Pearson, with the impatience of a variable spirit. "From my youth upward I have been a man marked out for wrath, and year by year—yea, day after day—I have endured sorrows such as others know not in their lifetime. And now I speak not of the love that has been turned to hatred, the honor to ignominy, the ease and plentifulness of all things to danger, want and nakedness. All this I could have borne and counted myself blessed. But when my heart was desolate with many losses, I fixed it upon the child of a stranger, and he became dearer to me than all my buried ones; and now he too must die as if my love were poison. Verily, I am an accursed man, and I will lay me down in the dust and lift up my head no more."

"Thou sinnest, brother, but it is not for me to rebuke thee, for I also have had my hours of darkness wherein I have murmured against the cross," said the old Quaker. He continued, perhaps in the hope of distracting his companion's thoughts from his own sorrows: "Even of late was the light obscured within me, when the men of blood had banished me on pain of death and the constables led me onward from village to village toward the wilderness. A strong and cruel hand was wielding the knotted cords; they sunk deep into the flesh, and thou mightst have tracked every reel and totter of my footsteps by the blood that followed. As we went on—"

"Have I not borne all this, and have I murmured?" interrupted Pearson, impatiently.

"Nay, friend, but hear me," continued the other. "As we journeyed on night darkened on our path, so that no man could see the rage of the persecutors or the constancy of my endurance, though Heaven forbid that I should glory therein. The lights began to glimmer in the cottage windows, and I could discern the inmates as they gathered in comfort and security, every man with his wife and children by their own evening hearth. At length we came to a tract of fertile land. In the dim light the forest was not visible around it, and, behold, there was a straw-thatched dwelling which bore the very aspect of my home far over the wild ocean—far in our own England. Then came bitter thoughts upon me—yea, remembrances that were like death to my soul. The happiness of my early days was painted to me, the disquiet of my manhood, the altered faith of my declining years. I remembered how I had been moved to go forth a wanderer when my daughter, the youngest, the dearest of my flock, lay on her dying-bed, and—"

"Couldst thou obey the command at such a moment?" exclaimed Pearson, shuddering.

"Yea! yea!" replied the old man, hurriedly. "I was kneeling by her bedside when the voice spoke loud within me, but immediately I rose and took my staff and gat me gone. Oh that it were permitted me to forget her woeful look when I thus withdrew my arm and left her journeying through the dark valley alone! for her soul was faint and she had leaned upon my prayers. Now in that night of horror I was assailed by the thought that I had been an erring Christian and a cruel parent; yea, even my daughter with her pale dying features seemed to stand by me and whisper, 'Father, you are deceived; go home and shelter your gray head.'—O Thou to whom I have looked in my furthest wanderings," continued the Quaker, raising his agitated eyes to heaven, "inflict not upon the bloodiest of our persecutors the unmitigated agony of my soul when I believed that all I had done and suffered for thee was at the instigation of a mocking fiend!—But I yielded not; I knelt down and wrestled with the tempter, while the scourge bit more fiercely into the flesh. My prayer was heard, and I went on in peace and joy toward the wilderness."

The old man, though his fanaticism had generally all the calmness of reason, was deeply moved while reciting this tale, and his unwonted emotion seemed to rebuke and keep down that of his companion. They sat in silence, with their faces to the fire, imagining, perhaps, in its red embers new scenes of persecution yet to be encountered. The snow still drifted hard against the windows, and sometimes, as the blaze of the logs had gradually sunk, came down the spacious chimney and hissed upon the hearth. A cautious footstep might now and then be heard in a neighboring apartment, and the sound invariably drew the eyes of both Quakers to the door which led thither. When a fierce and riotous gust of wind had led his thoughts by a natural association to homeless travellers on such a night, Pearson resumed the conversation.

"I have wellnigh sunk under my own share of this trial," observed he, sighing heavily; "yet

I would that it might be doubled to me, if so the child's mother could be spared. Her wounds have been deep and many, but this will be the sorest of all."

"Fear not for Catharine," replied the old Quaker, "for I know that valiant woman and have seen how she can bear the cross. A mother's heart, indeed, is strong in her, and may seem to contend mightily with her faith; but soon she will stand up and give thanks that her son has been thus early an accepted sacrifice. The boy hath done his work, and she will feel that he is taken hence in kindness both to him and her. Blessed, blessed are they that with so little suffering can enter into peace!"

The fitful rush of the wind was now disturbed by a portentous sound: it was a quick and heavy knocking at the outer door. Pearson's wan countenance grew paler, for many a visit of persecution had taught him what to dread; the old man, on the other hand, stood up erect, and his glance was firm as that of the tried soldier who awaits his enemy.

"The men of blood have come to seek me," he observed, with calmness. "They have heard how I was moved to return from banishment, and now am I to be led to prison, and thence to death. It is an end I have long looked for. I will open unto them lest they say, 'Lo, he feareth!'"

"Nay; I will present myself before them," said Pearson, with recovered fortitude. "It may be that they seek me alone and know not that thou abidest with me."

"Let us go boldly, both one and the other," rejoined his companion. "It is not fitting that thou or I should shrink."

They therefore proceeded through the entry to the door, which they opened, bidding the applicant "Come in, in God's name!" A furious blast of wind drove the storm into their faces and extinguished the lamp; they had barely time to discern a figure so white from head to foot with the drifted snow that it seemed like Winter's self come in human shape to seek refuge from its own desolation.

"Enter, friend, and do thy errand, be it what it may," said Pearson. "It must needs be pressing, since thou comest on such a bitter night."

"Peace be with this household!" said the stranger, when they stood on the floor of the inner apartment.

Pearson started; the elder Quaker stirred the slumbering embers of the fire till they sent up a clear and lofty blaze. It was a female voice that had spoken; it was a female form that shone out, cold and wintry, in that comfortable light.

"Catharine, blessed woman," exclaimed the old man, "art thou come to this darkened land again? Art thou come to bear a valiant testimony as in former years? The scourge hath not prevailed against thee, and from the dungeon hast thou come forth triumphant, but strengthen, strengthen now thy heart, Catharine, for Heaven will prove thee yet this once ere thou go to thy reward."

"Rejoice, friends!" she replied. "Thou who hast long been of our people, and thou whom a little child hath led to us, rejoice! Lo, I come, the messenger of glad tidings, for the day of persecution is over-past. The heart of the king, even Charles, hath been moved in gentleness toward us, and he hath sent forth his letters to stay the hands of the men of blood. A ship's company of our friends hath arrived at yonder town, and I also sailed joyfully among them."

As Catharine spoke her eyes were roaming about the room in search of him for whose sake security was dear to her. Pearson made a silent appeal to the old man, nor did the latter shrink from the painful task assigned him.

"Sister," he began, in a softened yet perfectly calm tone, "thou tellest us of his love manifested in temporal good, and now must we speak to thee of that selfsame love displayed in chastenings. Hitherto, Catharine, thou hast been as one journeying in a darksome and difficult path and leading an infant by the hand; fain wouldst thou have looked heavenward

47

continually, but still the cares of that little child have drawn thine eyes and thy affections to the earth. Sister, go on rejoicing, for his tottering footsteps shall impede thine own no more."

But the unhappy mother was not thus to be consoled. She shook like a leaf; she turned white as the very snow that hung drifted into her hair. The firm old man extended his hand and held her up, keeping his eye upon hers as if to repress any outbreak of passion.

"I am a woman—I am but a woman; will He try me above my strength?" said Catharine, very quickly and almost in a whisper. "I have been wounded sore; I have suffered much— many things in the body, many in the mind; crucified in myself and in them that were dearest to me. Surely," added she, with a long shudder, "he hath spared me in this one thing." She broke forth with sudden and irrepressible violence: "Tell me, man of cold heart, what has God done to me? Hath he cast me down never to rise again? Hath he crushed my very heart in his hand?—And thou to whom I committed my child, how hast thou fulfilled thy trust? Give me back the boy well, sound, alive—alive—or earth and heaven shall avenge me!"

The agonized shriek of Catharine was answered by the faint—the very faint—voice of a child.

On this day it had become evident to Pearson, to his aged guest and to Dorothy that Ilbrahim's brief and troubled pilgrimage drew near its close. The two former would willingly have remained by him to make use of the prayers and pious discourses which they deemed appropriate to the time, and which, if they be impotent as to the departing traveller's reception in the world whither he goes, may at least sustain him in bidding adieu to earth. But, though Ilbrahim uttered no complaint, he was disturbed by the faces that looked upon him; so that Dorothy's entreaties and their own conviction that the child's feet might tread heaven's pavement and not soil it had induced the two Quakers to remove. Ilbrahim then closed his eyes and grew calm, and, except for now and then a kind and low word to his nurse, might have been thought to slumber. As nightfall came on, however, and the storm began to rise, something seemed to trouble the repose of the boy's mind and to render his sense of hearing active and acute. If a passing wind lingered to shake the casement, he strove to turn his head toward it; if the door jarred to and fro upon its hinges, he looked long and anxiously thitherward; if the heavy voice of the old man as he read the Scriptures rose but a little higher, the child almost held his dying-breath to listen; if a snowdrift swept by the cottage with a sound like the trailing of a garment, Ilbrahim seemed to watch that some visitant should enter. But after a little time he relinquished whatever secret hope had agitated him and with one low complaining whisper turned his cheek upon the pillow. He then addressed Dorothy with his usual sweetness and besought her to draw near him; she did so, and Ilbrahim took her hand in both of his, grasping it with a gentle pressure, as if to assure himself that he retained it. At intervals, and without disturbing the repose of his countenance, a very faint trembling passed over him from head to foot, as if a mild but somewhat cool wind had breathed upon him and made him shiver.

As the boy thus led her by the hand in his quiet progress over the borders of eternity, Dorothy almost imagined that she could discern the near though dim delightfulness of the home he was about to reach; she would not have enticed the little wanderer back, though she bemoaned herself that she must leave him and return. But just when Ilbrahim's feet were pressing on the soil of Paradise he heard a voice behind him, and it recalled him a few, few paces of the weary path which he had travelled. As Dorothy looked upon his features she perceived that their placid expression was again disturbed. Her own thoughts had been so wrapped in him that all sounds of the storm and of human speech were lost to her; but when Catharine's shriek pierced through the room, the boy strove to raise himself.

"Friend, she is come! Open unto her!" cried he.

In a moment his mother was kneeling by the bedside; she drew Ilbrahim to her bosom, and he nestled there with no violence of joy, but contentedly as if he were hushing himself to sleep. He looked into her face, and, reading its agony, said with feeble earnestness,

"Mourn not, dearest mother. I am happy now;" and with these words the gentle boy was dead.

The king's mandate to stay the New England persecutors was effectual in preventing further martyrdoms, but the colonial authorities, trusting in the remoteness of their situation, and perhaps in the supposed instability of the royal government, shortly renewed their severities in all other respects. Catharine's fanaticism had become wilder by the sundering of all human ties; and wherever a scourge was lifted, there was she to receive the blow; and whenever a dungeon was unbarred, thither she came to cast herself upon the floor. But in process of time a more Christian spirit—a spirit of forbearance, though not of cordiality or approbation—began to pervade the land in regard to the persecuted sect. And then, when the rigid old Pilgrims eyed her rather in pity than in wrath, when the matrons fed her with the fragments of their children's food and offered her a lodging on a hard and lowly bed, when no little crowd of schoolboys left their sports to cast stones after the roving enthusiast,—then did Catharine return to Pearson's dwelling, and made that her home.

As if Ilbrahim's sweetness yet lingered round his ashes, as if his gentle spirit came down from heaven to teach his parent a true religion, her fierce and vindictive nature was softened by the same griefs which had once irritated it. When the course of years had made the features of the unobtrusive mourner familiar in the settlement, she became a subject of not deep but general interest—a being on whom the otherwise superfluous sympathies of all might be bestowed. Every one spoke of her with that degree of pity which it is pleasant to experience; every one was ready to do her the little kindnesses which are not costly, yet manifest good-will; and when at last she died, a long train of her once bitter persecutors followed her with decent sadness and tears that were not painful to her place by Ilbrahim's green and sunken grave.

MR. HIGGINBOTHAM'S CATASTROPHE

A YOUNG FELLOW, a tobacco-pedler by trade, was on his way from Morristown, where he had dealt largely with the deacon of the Shaker settlement, to the village of Parker's Falls, on Salmon River. He had a neat little cart painted green, with a box of cigars depicted on each side-panel, and an Indian chief holding a pipe and a golden tobacco-stalk on the rear. The pedler drove a smart little mare and was a young man of excellent character, keen at a bargain, but none the worse liked by the Yankees, who, as I have heard them say, would rather be shaved with a sharp razor than a dull one. Especially was he beloved by the pretty girls along the Connecticut, whose favor he used to court by presents of the best smoking-tobacco in his stock, knowing well that the country-lasses of New England are generally great performers on pipes. Moreover, as will be seen in the course of my story, the pedler was inquisitive and something of a tattler, always itching to hear the news and anxious to tell it again.

After an early breakfast at Morristown the tobacco-pedler—whose name was Dominicus Pike—had travelled seven miles through a solitary piece of woods without speaking a word to anybody but himself and his little gray mare. It being nearly seven o'clock, he was as eager to hold a morning gossip as a city shopkeeper to read the morning paper. An opportunity seemed at hand when, after lighting a cigar with a sun-glass, he looked up and perceived a man coming over the brow of the hill at the foot of which the pedler had stopped his green cart. Dominicus watched him as he descended, and noticed that he carried a bundle over his shoulder on the end of a stick and travelled with a weary yet determined pace. He did not look as if he had started in the freshness of the morning, but had footed it all night, and meant to do the same all day.

"Good-morning, mister," said Dominicus, when within speaking-distance. "You go a pretty good jog. What's the latest news at Parker's Falls?"

The man pulled the broad brim of a gray hat over his eyes, and answered, rather sullenly, that he did not come from Parker's Falls, which, as being the limit of his own day's journey, the pedler had naturally mentioned in his inquiry.

"Well, then," rejoined Dominicus Pike, "let's have the latest news where you did come from. I'm not particular about Parker's Falls. Any place will answer."

Being thus importuned, the traveller—who was as ill-looking a fellow as one would desire to meet in a solitary piece of woods—appeared to hesitate a little, as if he was either searching his memory for news or weighing the expediency of telling it. At last, mounting on the step of the cart, he whispered in the ear of Dominicus, though he might have shouted aloud and no other mortal would have heard him.

"I do remember one little trifle of news," said he. "Old Mr. Higginbotham of Kimballton was murdered in his orchard at eight o'clock last night by an Irishman and a nigger. They strung him up to the branch of a St. Michael's pear tree where nobody would find him till the morning."

As soon as this horrible intelligence was communicated the stranger betook himself to his journey again with more speed than ever, not even turning his head when Dominicus invited him to smoke a Spanish cigar and relate all the particulars. The pedler whistled to his mare and went up the hill, pondering on the doleful fate of Mr. Higginbotham, whom he had known in the way of trade, having sold him many a bunch of long nines and a great deal of pig-tail, lady's twist and fig tobacco. He was rather astonished at the rapidity with which the news had spread. Kimballton was nearly sixty miles distant in a straight line; the murder had been perpetrated only at eight o'clock the preceding night, yet Dominicus had heard of it at seven in the morning, when, in all probability, poor Mr. Higginbotham's own family had but just discovered his corpse hanging on the St. Michael's pear tree. The stranger on foot must have worn seven-league boots, to travel at such a rate.

"Ill-news flies fast, they say," thought Dominicus Pike, "but this beats railroads. The fellow ought to be hired to go express with the President's message."

The difficulty was solved by supposing that the narrator had made a mistake of one day in the date of the occurrence; so that our friend did not hesitate to introduce the story at every tavern and country-store along the road, expending a whole bunch of Spanish wrappers among at least twenty horrified audiences. He found himself invariably the first bearer of the intelligence, and was so pestered with questions that he could not avoid filling up the outline till it became quite a respectable narrative. He met with one piece of corroborative evidence. Mr. Higginbotham was a trader, and a former clerk of his to whom Dominicus related the facts testified that the old gentleman was accustomed to return home through the orchard about nightfall with the money and valuable papers of the store in his pocket. The clerk manifested but little grief at Mr. Higginbotham's catastrophe, hinting— what the pedler had discovered in his own dealings with him—that he was a crusty old fellow as close as a vise. His property would descend to a pretty niece who was now keeping school in Kimballton.

What with telling the news for the public good and driving bargains for his own, Dominicus was so much delayed on the road that he chose to put up at a tavern about five miles short of Parker's Falls. After supper, lighting one of his prime cigars, he seated himself in the bar-room and went through the story of the murder, which had grown so fast that it took him half an hour to tell. There were as many as twenty people in the room, nineteen of whom received it all for gospel. But the twentieth was an elderly farmer who had arrived on horseback a short time before and was now seated in a corner, smoking his pipe. When the story was concluded, he rose up very deliberately, brought his chair right in front of Dominicus and stared him full in the face, puffing out the vilest tobacco-smoke the pedler had ever smelt.

"Will you make affidavit," demanded he, in the tone of a country-justice taking an examination, "that old Squire Higginbotham of Kimballton was murdered in his orchard the night before last and found hanging on his great pear tree yesterday morning?"

"I tell the story as I heard it, mister," answered Dominicus, dropping his half-burnt cigar. "I don't say that I saw the thing done, so I can't take my oath that he was murdered exactly in that way."

"But I can take mine," said the farmer, "that if Squire Higginbotham was murdered night before last I drank a glass of bitters with his ghost this morning. Being a neighbor of mine, he called me into his store as I was riding by, and treated me, and then asked me to do a little business for him on the road. He didn't seem to know any more about his own murder than I did."

"Why, then it can't be a fact!" exclaimed Dominicus Pike.

"I guess he'd have mentioned, if it was," said the old farmer; and he removed his chair back to the corner, leaving Dominicus quite down in the mouth.

Here was a sad resurrection of old Mr. Higginbotham! The pedler had no heart to mingle in the conversation any more, but comforted himself with a glass of gin and water and went to bed, where all night long he dreamed of hanging on the St. Michael's pear tree.

To avoid the old farmer (whom he so detested that his suspension would have pleased him better than Mr. Higginbotham's), Dominicus rose in the gray of the morning, put the little mare into the green cart and trotted swiftly away toward Parker's Falls. The fresh breeze, the dewy road and the pleasant summer dawn revived his spirits, and might have encouraged him to repeat the old story had there been anybody awake to bear it, but he met neither ox-team, light wagon, chaise, horseman nor foot-traveller till, just as he crossed Salmon River, a man came trudging down to the bridge with a bundle over his shoulder, on the end of a stick.

"Good-morning, mister," said the pedler, reining in his mare. "If you come from Kimballton or that neighborhood, maybe you can tell me the real fact about this affair of old Mr. Higginbotham. Was the old fellow actually murdered two or three nights ago by an Irishman and a nigger?"

Dominicus had spoken in too great a hurry to observe at first that the stranger himself had a deep tinge of negro blood. On hearing this sudden question the Ethiopian appeared to change his skin, its yellow hue becoming a ghastly white, while, shaking and stammering, he thus replied:

"No, no! There was no colored man. It was an Irishman that hanged him last night at eight o'clock; I came away at seven. His folks can't have looked for him in the orchard yet."

Scarcely had the yellow man spoken, when he interrupted himself and, though he seemed weary enough before, continued his journey at a pace which would have kept the pedler's mare on a smart trot. Dominicus stared after him in great perplexity. If the murder had not been committed till Tuesday night, who was the prophet that had foretold it in all its circumstances on Tuesday morning? If Mr. Higginbotham's corpse were not yet discovered by his own family, how came the mulatto, at above thirty miles' distance, to know that he was hanging in the orchard, especially as he had left Kimballton before the unfortunate man was hanged at all? These ambiguous circumstances, with the stranger's surprise and terror, made Dominicus think of raising a hue-and-cry after him as an accomplice in the murder, since a murder, it seemed, had really been perpetrated.

"But let the poor devil go," thought the pedler. "I don't want his black blood on my head, and hanging the nigger wouldn't unhang Mr. Higginbotham. Unhang the old gentleman? It's a sin, I know, but I should hate to have him come to life a second time and give me the lie."

With these meditations Dominicus Pike drove into the street of Parker's Falls, which, as everybody knows, is as thriving a village as three cotton-factories and a slitting-mill can make it. The machinery was not in motion and but a few of the shop doors unbarred when he alighted in the stable-yard of the tavern and made it his first business to order the mare four quarts of oats. His second duty, of course, was to impart Mr. Higginbotham's catastrophe to the hostler. He deemed it advisable, however, not to be too positive as to the date of the direful fact, and also to be uncertain whether it were perpetrated by an Irishman and a mulatto or by the son of Erin alone. Neither did he profess to relate it on his own authority or that of any one person, but mentioned it as a report generally diffused.

The story ran through the town like fire among girdled trees, and became so much the universal talk that nobody could tell whence it had originated. Mr. Higginbotham was as well known at Parker's Falls as any citizen of the place, being part-owner of the slitting-mill and a considerable stockholder in the cotton-factories. The inhabitants felt their own prosperity interested in his fate. Such was the excitement that the Parker's Falls *Gazette* anticipated its regular day of publication, and came out with half a form of blank paper and a column of double pica emphasized with capitals and headed "HORRID MURDER OF MR. HIGGINBOTHAM!" Among other dreadful details, the printed account described the mark of the cord round the dead man's neck and stated the number of thousand dollars of which he had been robbed; there was much pathos, also, about the affliction of his niece, who had gone from one fainting-fit to another ever since her uncle was found hanging on the St. Michael's pear tree with his pockets inside out. The village poet likewise commemorated the young lady's grief in seventeen stanzas of a ballad. The selectmen held a meeting, and in consideration of Mr. Higginbotham's claims on the town determined to issue handbills offering a reward of five hundred dollars for the apprehension of his murderers and the recovery of the stolen property.

Meanwhile, the whole population of Parker's Falls, consisting of shopkeepers, mistresses of boarding-houses, factory-girls, mill-men and schoolboys, rushed into the street and kept up such a terrible loquacity as more than compensated for the silence of the cotton-machines, which refrained from their usual din out of respect to the deceased. Had Mr. Higginbotham cared about posthumous renown, his untimely ghost would have exulted in this tumult.

Our friend Dominicus in his vanity of heart forgot his intended precautions, and, mounting on the town-pump, announced himself as the bearer of the authentic intelligence which had caused so wonderful a sensation. He immediately became the great man of the moment, and had just begun a new edition of the narrative with a voice like a field-preacher when the mail-stage drove into the village street. It had travelled all night, and must have shifted horses at Kimballton at three in the morning.

"Now we shall hear all the particulars!" shouted the crowd.

The coach rumbled up to the piazza of the tavern followed by a thousand people; for if any man had been minding his own business till then, he now left it at sixes and sevens to hear the news. The pedler, foremost in the race, discovered two passengers, both of whom had been startled from a comfortable nap to find themselves in the centre of a mob. Every man assailing them with separate questions, all propounded at once, the couple were struck speechless, though one was a lawyer and the other a young lady.

"Mr. Higginbotham! Mr. Higginbotham! Tell us the particulars about old Mr. Higginbotham!" bawled the mob. "What is the coroner's verdict? Are the murderers apprehended? Is Mr. Higginbotham's niece come out of her fainting-fits? Mr. Higginbotham! Mr. Higginbotham!"

The coachman said not a word except to swear awfully at the hostler for not bringing him a fresh team of horses. The lawyer inside had generally his wits about him even when asleep; the first thing he did after learning the cause of the excitement was to produce a large red pocketbook. Meantime, Dominicus Pike, being an extremely polite young man, and also suspecting that a female tongue would tell the story as glibly as a lawyer's, had handed the lady out of the coach. She was a fine, smart girl, now wide awake and bright as a button, and had such a sweet, pretty mouth that Dominicus would almost as lief have heard a love-tale from it as a tale of murder.

"Gentlemen and ladies," said the lawyer to the shopkeepers, the mill-men and the factory-girls, "I can assure you that some unaccountable mistake—or, more probably, a wilful falsehood maliciously contrived to injure Mr. Higginbotham's credit—has excited this singular uproar. We passed through Kimballton at three o'clock this morning, and most certainly should have been informed of the murder had any been perpetrated. But I have proof nearly as strong as Mr. Higginbotham's own oral testimony in the negative. Here is a note relating to a suit of his in the Connecticut courts which was delivered me from that gentleman himself. I find it dated at ten o'clock last evening."

So saying, the lawyer exhibited the date and signature of the note, which irrefragably proved either that this perverse Mr. Higginbotham was alive when he wrote it, or, as some deemed the more probable case of two doubtful ones, that he was so absorbed in worldly business as to continue to transact it even after his death. But unexpected evidence was forthcoming. The young lady, after listening to the pedler's explanation, merely seized a moment to smooth her gown and put her curls in order, and then appeared at the tavern door, making a modest signal to be heard.

"Good people," said she, "I am Mr. Higginbotham's niece."

A wondering murmur passed through the crowd on beholding her so rosy and bright—that same unhappy niece whom they had supposed, on the authority of the Parker's Falls *Gazette*, to be lying at death's door in a fainting-fit. But some shrewd fellows had doubted all along whether a young lady would be quite so desperate at the hanging of a rich old uncle.

"You see," continued Miss Higginbotham, with a smile, "that this strange story is quite unfounded as to myself, and I believe I may affirm it to be equally so in regard to my dear uncle Higginbotham. He has the kindness to give me a home in his house, though I contribute to my own support by teaching a school. I left Kimballton this morning to spend the vacation of commencement-week with a friend about five miles from Parker's Falls. My generous uncle, when he heard me on the stairs, called me to his bedside and gave me two dollars and fifty cents to pay my stage-fare, and another dollar for my extra expenses. He then laid his pocketbook under his pillow, shook hands with me, and advised me to take some biscuit in my bag instead of breakfasting on the road. I feel confident, therefore, that I left my beloved relative alive, and trust that I shall find him so on my return."

The young lady courtesied at the close of her speech, which was so sensible and well worded, and delivered with such grace and propriety, that everybody thought her fit to be preceptress of the best academy in the State. But a stranger would have supposed that Mr. Higginbotham was an object of abhorrence at Parker's Falls and that a thanksgiving had been proclaimed for his murder, so excessive was the wrath of the inhabitants on learning their mistake. The mill-men resolved to bestow public honors on Dominicus Pike, only hesitating whether to tar and feather him, ride him on a rail or refresh him with an ablution at the town-pump, on the top of which he had declared himself the bearer of the news. The selectmen, by advice of the lawyer, spoke of prosecuting him for a misdemeanor in circulating unfounded reports, to the great disturbance of the peace of the commonwealth. Nothing saved Dominicus either from mob-law or a court of justice but an eloquent appeal made by the young lady in his behalf. Addressing a few words of heartfelt gratitude to his benefactress, he mounted the green cart and rode out of town under a discharge of artillery from the schoolboys, who found plenty of ammunition in the neighboring clay-pits and mud-holes. As he turned his head to exchange a farewell glance with Mr. Higginbotham's niece a ball of the consistence of hasty-pudding hit him slap in the mouth, giving him a most grim aspect. His whole person was so bespattered with the like filthy missiles that he had almost a mind to ride back and supplicate for the threatened ablution at the town-pump; for, though not meant in kindness, it would now have been a deed of charity.

However, the sun shone bright on poor Dominicus, and the mud—an emblem of all stains of undeserved opprobrium—was easily brushed off when dry. Being a funny rogue, his heart soon cheered up; nor could he refrain from a hearty laugh at the uproar which his story had excited. The handbills of the selectmen would cause the commitment of all the vagabonds in the State, the paragraph in the Parker's Falls *Gazette* would be reprinted from Maine to Florida, and perhaps form an item in the London newspapers, and many a miser would tremble for his moneybags and life on learning the catastrophe of Mr. Higginbotham. The pedler meditated with much fervor on the charms of the young schoolmistress, and swore that Daniel Webster never spoke nor looked so like an angel as Miss Higginbotham while defending him from the wrathful populace at Parker's Falls.

Dominicus was now on the Kimballton turnpike, having all along determined to visit that place, though business had drawn, him out of the most direct road from Morristown. As he approached the scene of the supposed murder he continued to revolve the circumstances in his mind, and was astonished at the aspect which the whole case assumed. Had nothing occurred to corroborate the story of the first traveller, it might now have been considered as a hoax; but the yellow man was evidently acquainted either with the report or the fact, and there was a mystery in his dismayed and guilty look on being abruptly questioned. When to this singular combination of incidents it was added that the rumor tallied exactly with Mr. Higginbotham's character and habits of life, and that he had an orchard and a St. Michael's pear tree, near which he always passed at nightfall, the circumstantial evidence appeared so strong that Dominicus doubted whether the autograph produced by the lawyer, or even the niece's direct testimony, ought to be equivalent. Making cautious inquiries along the road, the pedler further learned that Mr. Higginbotham had in his service an Irishman of doubtful character whom he had hired without a recommendation, on the score of economy.

"May I be hanged myself," exclaimed Dominicus Pike, aloud, on reaching the top of a lonely hill, "if I'll believe old Higginbotham is unhanged till I see him with my own eyes and hear it from his own mouth. And, as he's a real shaver, I'll have the minister, or some other responsible man, for an endorser."

It was growing dusk when he reached the toll-house on Kimballton turnpike, about a quarter of a mile from the village of this name. His little mare was fast bringing him up with a man on horseback who trotted through the gate a few rods in advance of him, nodded to the toll-gatherer and kept on towards the village. Dominicus was acquainted with the toll-man, and while making change the usual remarks on the weather passed between them.

"I suppose," said the pedler, throwing back his whiplash to bring it down like a feather on the mare's flank, "you have not seen anything of old Mr. Higginbotham within a day or two?"

"Yes," answered the toll-gatherer; "he passed the gate just before you drove up, and yonder he rides now, if you can see him through the dusk. He's been to Woodfield this afternoon, attending a sheriff's sale there. The old man generally shakes hands and has a little chat with me, but to-night he nodded, as if to say, 'Charge my toll,' and jogged on; for, wherever he goes, he must always be at home by eight o'clock."

"So they tell me," said Dominicus.

"I never saw a man look so yellow and thin as the squire does," continued the toll-gatherer. "Says I to myself tonight, 'He's more like a ghost or an old mummy than good flesh and blood.'"

The pedler strained his eyes through the twilight, and could just discern the horseman now far ahead on the village road. He seemed to recognize the rear of Mr. Higginbotham, but through the evening shadows and amid the dust from the horse's feet the figure appeared dim and unsubstantial, as if the shape of the mysterious old man were faintly moulded of darkness and gray light.

Dominicus shivered. "Mr. Higginbotham has come back from the other world by way of the Kimballton turnpike," thought he. He shook the reins and rode forward, keeping about the same distance in the rear of the gray old shadow till the latter was concealed by a bend of the road. On reaching this point the pedler no longer saw the man on horseback, but found himself at the head of the village street, not far from a number of stores and two taverns clustered round the meeting-house steeple. On his left was a stone wall and a gate, the boundary of a wood-lot beyond which lay an orchard, farther still a mowing-field, and last of all a house. These were the premises of Mr. Higginbotham, whose dwelling stood beside the old highway, but had been left in the background by the Kimballton turnpike.

Dominicus knew the place, and the little mare stopped short by instinct, for he was not conscious of tightening the reins. "For the soul of me, I cannot get by this gate!" said he, trembling. "I never shall be my own man again till I see whether Mr. Higginbotham is hanging on the St. Michael's pear tree." He leaped from the cart, gave the rein a turn round the gate-post, and ran along the green path of the wood-lot as if Old Nick were chasing behind. Just then the village clock tolled eight, and as each deep stroke fell Dominicus gave a fresh bound and flew faster than before, till, dim in the solitary centre of the orchard, he saw the fated pear tree. One great branch stretched from the old contorted trunk across the path and threw the darkest shadow on that one spot. But something seemed to struggle beneath the branch.

The pedler had never pretended to more courage than befits a man of peaceable occupation, nor could he account for his valor on this awful emergency. Certain it is, however, that he rushed forward, prostrated a sturdy Irishman with the butt-end of his whip, and found—not, indeed, hanging on the St. Michael's pear tree, but trembling beneath it with a halter round his neck—the old identical Mr. Higginbotham.

"Mr. Higginbotham," said Dominicus, tremulously, "you're an honest man, and I'll take your word for it. Have you been hanged, or not?"

If the riddle be not already guessed, a few words will explain the simple machinery by which this "coming event" was made to cast its "shadow before." Three men had plotted the robbery and murder of Mr. Higginbotham; two of them successively lost courage and fled, each delaying the crime one night by their disappearance; the third was in the act of perpetration, when a champion, blindly obeying the call of fate, like the heroes of old romance, appeared in the person of Dominicus Pike.

It only remains to say that Mr. Higginbotham took the pedler into high favor, sanctioned his addresses to the pretty schoolmistress and settled his whole property on their children, allowing themselves the interest. In due time the old gentleman capped the climax of his favors by dying a Christian death in bed; since which melancholy event, Dominicus Pike has removed from Kimballton and established a large tobacco-manufactory in my native village.

LITTLE ANNIE'S RAMBLE

DING-DONG! Ding-dong! Ding-dong!

The town-crier has rung his bell at a distant corner, and little Annie stands on her father's doorsteps trying to hear what the man with the loud voice is talking about. Let me listen too. Oh, he is telling the people that an elephant and a lion and a royal tiger and a horse with horns, and other strange beasts from foreign countries, have come to town and will receive all visitors who choose to wait upon them. Perhaps little Annie would like to go? Yes, and I can see that the pretty child is weary of this wide and pleasant street with the green trees flinging their shade across the quiet sunshine and the pavements and the sidewalks all as clean as if the housemaid had just swept them with her broom. She feels that impulse to go strolling away— that longing after the mystery of the great world—which many children feel, and which I felt in my childhood. Little Annie shall take a ramble with me. See! I do but hold out my hand, and like some bright bird in the sunny air, with her blue silk frock fluttering upward from her white pantalets, she comes bounding on tiptoe across the street.

Smooth back your brown curls, Annie, and let me tie on your bonnet, and we will set forth. What a strange couple to go on their rambles together! One walks in black attire, with a measured step and a heavy brow and his thoughtful eyes bent down, while the gay little girl trips lightly along as if she were forced to keep hold of my hand lest her feet should dance away from the earth. Yet there is sympathy between us. If I pride myself on anything, it is because I have a smile that children love; and, on the other hand, there are few grown ladies that could entice me from the side of little Annie, for I delight to let my mind go hand in hand with the mind of a sinless child. So come, Annie; but if I moralize as we go, do not listen to me: only look about you and be merry.

Now we turn the corner. Here are hacks with two horses and stage-coaches with four thundering to meet each other, and trucks and carts moving at a slower pace, being heavily laden with barrels from the wharves; and here are rattling gigs which perhaps will be smashed to pieces before our eyes. Hitherward, also, comes a man trundling a wheelbarrow along the pavement. Is not little Annie afraid of such a tumult? No; she does not even shrink closer to my side, but passes on with fearless confidence, a happy child amidst a great throng of grown people who pay the same reverence to her infancy that they would to extreme old age. Nobody jostles her: all turn aside to make way for little Annie; and, what is most singular, she appears conscious of her claim to such respect. Now her eyes brighten with pleasure. A street-musician has seated himself on the steps of yonder church and pours forth his strains to the busy town— a melody that has gone astray among the tramp of footsteps, the buzz of voices and the war of passing wheels. Who heeds the poor organ-grinder? None but myself and little Annie, whose feet begin to move in unison with the lively tune, as if she were loth that music should be wasted without a dance. But where would Annie find a partner? Some have the gout in their toes or the rheumatism in their joints; some are stiff with age, some feeble with disease; some are so lean that their bones would rattle, and others of such ponderous size that their agility would crack the flagstones; but many, many have leaden feet because their hearts are far heavier than lead. It is a sad thought that I have chanced upon. What a company of dancers should we be! For I too am a gentleman of sober footsteps, and therefore, little Annie, let us walk sedately on.

It is a question with me whether this giddy child or my sage self have most pleasure in looking at the shop-windows. We love the silks of sunny hue that glow within the darkened premises of the spruce dry-goods men; we are pleasantly dazzled by the burnished silver and the chased gold, the rings of wedlock and the costly love-ornaments, glistening at the window of the jeweller; but Annie, more than I, seeks for a glimpse of her passing figure in the dusty looking-glasses at the hardware-stores. All that is bright and gay attracts us both.

Here is a shop to which the recollections of my boyhood as well as present partialities give a peculiar magic. How delightful to let the fancy revel on the dainties of a confectioner—those pies with such white and flaky paste, their contents being a mystery, whether rich mince with whole plums intermixed, or piquant apple delicately rose-flavored; those cakes, heart-shaped or round, piled in a lofty pyramid; those sweet little circlets sweetly named kisses; those dark majestic masses fit to be bridal-loaves at the wedding of an heiress, mountains in size, their summits deeply snow-covered with sugar! Then the mighty treasures of sugarplums, white and crimson and yellow, in large glass vases, and candy of all varieties, and those little cockles—or whatever they are called—much prized by children for their sweetness, and more for the mottoes which they enclose, by love-sick maids and bachelors! Oh, my mouth waters, little Annie, and so doth yours, but we will not be tempted except to an imaginary feast; so let us hasten onward devouring the vision of a plum-cake.

Here are pleasures, as some people would say, of a more exalted kind, in the window of a bookseller. Is Annie a literary lady? Yes; she is deeply read in Peter Parley's tomes and has an increasing love for fairy-tales, though seldom met with nowadays, and she will subscribe next year to the *Juvenile Miscellany*. But, truth to tell, she is apt to turn away from the printed page and keep gazing at the pretty pictures, such as the gay-colored ones which make this shop-window the continual loitering-place of children. What would Annie think if, in the book which I mean to send her on New Year's day, she should find her sweet little self bound up in silk or morocco with gilt edges, there to remain till she become a woman grown with children of her own to read about their mother's childhood? That would be very queer.

Little Annie is weary of pictures and pulls me onward by the hand, till suddenly we pause at the most wondrous shop in all the town. Oh, my stars! Is this a toyshop, or is it fairy-land? For here are gilded chariots in which the king and queen of the fairies might ride side by side, while their courtiers on these small horses should gallop in triumphal procession before and behind the royal pair. Here, too, are dishes of chinaware fit to be the dining-set of those same princely personages when they make a regal banquet in the stateliest hall of their palace—full five feet high—and behold their nobles feasting adown the long perspective of the table.

Betwixt the king and queen should sit my little Annie, the prettiest fairy of them all. Here stands a turbaned Turk threatening us with his sabre, like an ugly heathen as he is, and next a Chinese mandarin who nods his head at Annie and myself. Here we may review a whole army of horse and foot in red-and-blue uniforms, with drums, fifes, trumpets, and all kinds of noiseless music; they have halted on the shelf of this window after their weary march from Liliput. But what cares Annie for soldiers? No conquering queen is she—neither a Semiramis nor a Catharine; her whole heart is set upon that doll who gazes at us with such a fashionable stare. This is the little girl's true plaything. Though made of wood, a doll is a visionary and ethereal personage endowed by childish fancy with a peculiar life; the mimic lady is a heroine of romance, an actor and a sufferer in a thousand shadowy scenes, the chief inhabitant of that wild world with which children ape the real one. Little Annie does not understand what I am saying, but looks wishfully at the proud lady in the window. We will invite her home with us as we return.—Meantime, good-bye, Dame Doll! A toy yourself, you look forth from your window upon many ladies that are also toys, though they walk and speak, and upon a crowd in pursuit of toys, though they wear grave visages. Oh, with your never-closing eyes, had you but an intellect to moralize on all that flits before them, what a wise doll would you be!—Come, little Annie, we shall find toys enough, go where we may.

Now we elbow our way among the throng again. It is curious in the most crowded part of a town to meet with living creatures that had their birthplace in some far solitude, but have acquired a second nature in the wilderness of men. Look up, Annie, at that canary-bird hanging out of the window in his cage. Poor little fellow! His golden feathers are all tarnished in this smoky sunshine; he would have glistened twice as brightly among the summer islands, but still he has become a citizen in all his tastes and habits, and would not sing half so well without the uproar that drowns his music. What a pity that he does not know how miserable he is! There is a parrot, too, calling out, "Pretty Poll! Pretty Poll!" as we pass by. Foolish bird, to be talking about her prettiness to strangers, especially as she is not a pretty Poll, though gaudily dressed in green and yellow! If she had said "Pretty Annie!" there would have been some sense in it. See that gray squirrel at the door of the fruit-shop whirling round and round so merrily within his wire wheel! Being condemned to the treadmill, he makes it an amusement. Admirable philosophy!

Here comes a big, rough dog—a countryman's dog—in search of his master, smelling at everybody's heels and touching little Annie's hand with his cold nose, but hurrying away, though she would fain have patted him.—Success to your search, Fidelity!—And there sits a great yellow cat upon a window-sill, a very corpulent and comfortable cat, gazing at this transitory world with owl's eyes, and making pithy comments, doubtless, or what appear such, to the silly beast.—Oh, sage puss, make room for me beside you, and we will be a pair of philosophers.

Here we see something to remind us of the town-crier and his ding-dong-bell. Look! look at that great cloth spread out in the air, pictured all over with wild beasts, as if they had met together to choose a king, according to their custom in the days of Æsop. But they are choosing neither a king nor a President, else we should hear a most horrible snarling! They have come from the deep woods and the wild mountains and the desert sands and the polar snows only to do homage to my little Annie. As we enter among them the great elephant makes us a bow in the best style of elephantine courtesy, bending lowly down his mountain bulk, with trunk abased and leg thrust out behind. Annie returns the salute, much to the gratification of the elephant, who is certainly the best-bred monster in the caravan. The lion and the lioness are busy with two beef-bones. The royal tiger, the beautiful, the untamable, keeps pacing his narrow cage with a haughty step, unmindful of the spectators or recalling the fierce deeds of his former life, when he was wont to leap forth upon such inferior animals from the jungles of Bengal.

Here we see the very same wolf—do not go near him, Annie!—the selfsame wolf that devoured little Red Riding-Hood and her grandmother. In the next cage a hyena from Egypt who has doubtless howled around the pyramids and a black bear from our own forests are fellow-prisoners and most excellent friends. Are there any two living creatures who have so few sympathies that they cannot possibly be friends? Here sits a great white bear whom common observers would call a very stupid beast, though I perceive him to be only absorbed in contemplation; he is thinking of his voyages on an iceberg, and of his comfortable home in the vicinity of the north pole, and of the little cubs whom he left rolling in the eternal snows. In fact, he is a bear of sentiment. But oh those unsentimental monkeys! The ugly, grinning, aping, chattering, ill-natured, mischievous and queer little brutes! Annie does not love the monkeys; their ugliness shocks her pure, instinctive delicacy of taste and makes her mind unquiet because it bears a wild and dark resemblance to humanity. But here is a little pony just big enough for Annie to ride, and round and round he gallops in a circle, keeping time with his trampling hoofs to a band of music. And here, with a laced coat and a cocked hat, and a riding-whip in his hand—here comes a little gentleman small enough to be king of the fairies and ugly enough to be king of the gnomes, and takes a flying leap into the saddle. Merrily, merrily plays the music, and merrily gallops the pony, and merrily rides the little old gentleman.—Come, Annie, into the street again; perchance we may see monkeys on horseback there.

Mercy on us! What a noisy world we quiet people live in! Did Annie ever read the cries of London city? With what lusty lungs doth yonder man proclaim that his wheelbarrow is full of lobsters! Here comes another, mounted on a cart and blowing a hoarse and dreadful blast from a tin horn, as much as to say, "Fresh fish!" And hark! a voice on high, like that of a muezzin from the summit of a mosque, announcing that some chimney-sweeper has emerged from smoke and soot and darksome caverns into the upper air. What cares the world for that? But, well-a-day, we hear a shrill voice of affliction—the scream of a little child, rising louder with every repetition of that smart, sharp, slapping sound produced by an open hand on tender flesh. Annie sympathizes, though without experience of such direful woe.

Lo! the town-crier again, with some new secret for the public ear. Will he tell us of an auction, or of a lost pocket-book or a show of beautiful wax figures, or of some monstrous beast more horrible than any in the caravan? I guess the latter. See how he uplifts the bell in his right hand and shakes it slowly at first, then with a hurried motion, till the clapper seems to strike both sides at once, and the sounds are scattered forth in quick succession far and near.

Ding-dong! Ding-dong! Ding-dong!

Now he raises his clear loud voice above all the din of the town. It drowns the buzzing talk of many tongues and draws each man's mind from his own business; it rolls up and down the echoing street, and ascends to the hushed chamber of the sick, and penetrates downward to the cellar kitchen where the hot cook turns from the fire to listen. Who of all that address the public ear, whether in church or court-house or hall of state, has such an attentive audience as the town-crier! What saith the people's orator?

"Strayed from her home, a LITTLE GIRL of five years old, in a blue silk frock and white pantalets, with brown curling hair and hazel eyes. Whoever will bring her back to her afflicted mother—"

Stop, stop, town-crier! The lost is found.—Oh, my pretty Annie, we forgot to tell your mother of our ramble, and she is in despair and has sent the town-crier to bellow up and down the streets, affrighting old and young, for the loss of a little girl who has not once let go my hand? Well, let us hasten homeward; and as we go forget not to thank Heaven, my Annie, that after wandering a little way into the world you may return at the first summons with an untainted and unwearied heart, and be a happy child again. But I have gone too far astray for the town-crier to call me back.

Sweet has been the charm of childhood on my spirit throughout my ramble with little Annie. Say not that it has been a waste of precious moments, an idle matter, a babble of childish talk and a reverie of childish imaginations about topics unworthy of a grown man's notice. Has it been merely this? Not so—not so. They are not truly wise who would affirm it. As the pure breath of children revives the life of aged men, so is our moral nature revived by their free and simple thoughts, their native feeling, their airy mirth for little cause or none, their grief soon roused and soon allayed. Their influence on us is at least reciprocal with ours on them. When our infancy is almost forgotten and our boyhood long departed, though it seems but as yesterday, when life settles darkly down upon us and we doubt whether to call ourselves young any more,—then it is good to steal away from the society of bearded men, and even of gentler woman, and spend an hour or two with children. After drinking from those fountains of still fresh existence we shall return into the crowd, as I do now, to struggle onward and do our part in life—perhaps as fervently as ever, but for a time with a kinder and purer heart and a spirit more lightly wise. All this by thy sweet magic, dear little Annie!

WAKEFIELD

In some old magazine or newspaper I recollect a story, told as truth, of a man—let us call him Wakefield—who absented himself for a long time from his wife. The fact, thus abstractedly stated, is not very uncommon, nor, without a proper distinction of circumstances, to be condemned either as naughty or nonsensical. Howbeit, this, though far from the most aggravated, is perhaps the strangest instance on record of marital delinquency, and, moreover, as remarkable a freak as may be found in the whole list of human oddities. The wedded couple lived in London. The man, under pretence of going a journey, took lodgings in the next street to his own house, and there, unheard of by his wife or friends and without the shadow of a reason for such self-banishment, dwelt upward of twenty years. During that period he beheld his home every day, and frequently the forlorn Mrs. Wakefield. And after so great a gap in his matrimonial felicity—when his death was reckoned certain, his estate settled, his name dismissed from memory and his wife long, long ago resigned to her autumnal widowhood—he entered the door one evening quietly as from a day's absence, and became a loving spouse till death.

This outline is all that I remember. But the incident, though of the purest originality, unexampled, and probably never to be repeated, is one, I think, which appeals to the general sympathies of mankind. We know, each for himself, that none of us would perpetrate such a folly, yet feel as if some other might. To my own contemplations, at least, it has often recurred, always exciting wonder, but with a sense that the story must be true and a conception of its hero's character. Whenever any subject so forcibly affects the mind, time is well spent in thinking of it. If the reader choose, let him do his own meditation; or if he prefer to ramble with me through the twenty years of Wakefield's vagary, I bid him welcome, trusting that there will be a pervading spirit and a moral, even should we fail to find them, done up neatly and condensed into the final sentence. Thought has always its efficacy and every striking incident its moral.

What sort of a man was Wakefield? We are free to shape out our own idea and call it by his name. He was now in the meridian of life; his matrimonial affections, never violent, were sobered into a calm, habitual sentiment; of all husbands, he was likely to be the most constant, because a certain sluggishness would keep his heart at rest wherever it might be placed. He was intellectual, but not actively so; his mind occupied itself in long and lazy musings that tended to no purpose or had not vigor to attain it; his thoughts were seldom so energetic as to seize hold of words. Imagination, in the proper meaning of the term, made no part of Wakefield's gifts. With a cold but not depraved nor wandering heart, and a mind never feverish with riotous thoughts nor perplexed with originality, who could have anticipated that our friend would entitle himself to a foremost place among the doers of eccentric deeds? Had his acquaintances been asked who was the man in London the surest to perform nothing to-day which should be remembered on the morrow, they would have thought of Wakefield. Only the wife of his bosom might have hesitated. She, without having analyzed his character, was partly aware of a quiet selfishness that had rusted into his inactive mind; of a peculiar sort of vanity, the most uneasy attribute about him; of a disposition to craft which had seldom produced more positive effects than the keeping of petty secrets hardly worth revealing; and, lastly, of what she called a little strangeness sometimes in the good man. This latter quality is indefinable, and perhaps non-existent.

Let us now imagine Wakefield bidding adieu to his wife. It is the dusk of an October evening. His equipment is a drab greatcoat, a hat covered with an oil-cloth, top-boots, an umbrella in one hand and a small portmanteau in the other. He has informed Mrs. Wakefield that he is to take the night-coach into the country. She would fain inquire the length of his journey, its object and the probable time of his return, but, indulgent to his harmless love of mystery, interrogates him only by a look. He tells her not to expect him positively by the return-coach nor to be alarmed should he tarry three or four days, but, at all events, to look for him at supper on Friday evening. Wakefield, himself, be it considered, has no suspicion of what is before him. He holds out his hand; she gives her own and meets his parting kiss in the matter-of-course way of a ten years' matrimony, and forth goes the middle-aged Mr. Wakefield, almost resolved to perplex his good lady by a whole week's absence. After the door has closed behind him, she perceives it thrust partly open and a vision of her husband's face through the aperture, smiling on her and gone in a moment. For the time this little incident is dismissed without a thought, but long afterward, when she has been more years a widow than a wife, that smile recurs and flickers across all her reminiscences of Wakefield's visage. In her many musings she surrounds the original smile with a multitude of fantasies which make it strange and awful; as, for instance, if she imagines him in a coffin, that parting look is frozen on his pale features; or if she dreams of him in heaven, still his blessed spirit wears a quiet and crafty smile. Yet for its sake, when all others have given him up for dead, she sometimes doubts whether she is a widow.

But our business is with the husband. We must hurry after him along the street ere he lose his individuality and melt into the great mass of London life. It would be vain searching for him there. Let us follow close at his heels, therefore, until, after several superfluous turns and doublings, we find him comfortably established by the fireside of a small apartment previously bespoken. He is in the next street to his own and at his journey's end. He can scarcely trust his good-fortune in having got thither unperceived, recollecting that at one time he was delayed by the throng in the very focus of a lighted lantern, and again there were footsteps that seemed to tread behind his own, distinct from the multitudinous tramp around him, and anon he heard a voice shouting afar and fancied that it called his name. Doubtless a dozen busybodies had been watching him and told his wife the whole affair.

Poor Wakefield! little knowest thou thine own insignificance in this great world. No mortal eye but mine has traced thee. Go quietly to thy bed, foolish man, and on the morrow, if thou wilt be wise, get thee home to good Mrs. Wakefield and tell her the truth. Remove not thyself even for a little week from thy place in her chaste bosom. Were she for a single moment to deem thee dead or lost or lastingly divided from her, thou wouldst be woefully conscious of a change in thy true wife for ever after. It is perilous to make a chasm in human affections—not that they gape so long and wide, but so quickly close again.

Almost repenting of his frolic, or whatever it may be termed, Wakefield lies down betimes, and, starting from his first nap, spreads forth his arms into the wide and solitary waste of the unaccustomed bed, "No," thinks he, gathering the bedclothes about him; "I will not sleep alone another night." In the morning he rises earlier than usual and sets himself to consider what he really means to do. Such are his loose and rambling modes of thought that he has taken this very singular step with the consciousness of a purpose, indeed, but without being able to define it sufficiently for his own contemplation. The vagueness of the project and the convulsive effort with which he plunges into the execution of it are equally characteristic of a feeble-minded man. Wakefield sifts his ideas, however, as minutely as he may, and finds himself curious to know the progress of matters at home—how his exemplary wife will endure her widowhood of a week, and, briefly, how the little sphere of creatures and circumstances in which he was a central object will be affected by his removal. A morbid vanity, therefore, lies nearest the bottom of the affair. But how is he to attain his ends? Not, certainly, by keeping close in this comfortable lodging, where, though he slept and awoke in the next street to his home, he is as effectually abroad as if the stage-coach had been whirling him away all night. Yet should he reappear, the whole project is knocked in the head. His poor brains being hopelessly puzzled with this dilemma, he at length ventures out, partly resolving to cross the head of the street and send one hasty glance toward his forsaken domicile. Habit—for he is a man of habits—takes him by the hand and guides him, wholly unaware, to his own door, where, just at the critical moment, he is aroused by the scraping of his foot upon the step.—Wakefield, whither are you going?

At that instant his fate was turning on the pivot. Little dreaming of the doom to which his first backward step devotes him, he hurries away, breathless with agitation hitherto unfelt, and hardly dares turn his head at the distant corner. Can it be that nobody caught sight of him? Will not the whole household—the decent Mrs. Wakefield, the smart maid-servant and the dirty little footboy—raise a hue-and-cry through London streets in pursuit of their fugitive lord and master? Wonderful escape! He gathers courage to pause and look homeward, but is perplexed with a sense of change about the familiar edifice such as affects us all when, after a separation of months or years, we again see some hill or lake or work of art with which we were friends of old. In ordinary cases this indescribable impression is caused by the comparison and contrast between our imperfect reminiscences and the reality. In Wakefield the magic of a single night has wrought a similar transformation, because in that brief period a great moral change has been effected. But this is a secret from himself. Before leaving the spot he catches a far and momentary glimpse of his wife passing athwart the front window with her face turned toward the head of the street. The crafty nincompoop takes to his heels, scared with the idea that among a thousand such atoms of mortality her eye must have detected him. Right glad is his heart, though his brain be somewhat dizzy, when he finds himself by the coal-fire of his lodgings.

So much for the commencement of this long whim-wham. After the initial conception and the stirring up of the man's sluggish temperament to put it in practice, the whole matter evolves itself in a natural train. We may suppose him, as the result of deep deliberation, buying a new wig of reddish hair and selecting sundry garments, in a fashion unlike his customary suit of brown, from a Jew's old-clothes bag. It is accomplished: Wakefield is another man. The new system being now established, a retrograde movement to the old would be almost as difficult as the step that placed him in his unparalleled position. Furthermore, he is rendered obstinate by a sulkiness occasionally incident to his temper and brought on at present by the inadequate sensation which he conceives to have been produced in the bosom of Mrs. Wakefield. He will not go back until she be frightened half to death. Well, twice or thrice has she passed before his sight, each time with a heavier step, a paler cheek and more anxious brow, and in the third week of his non-appearance he detects a portent of evil entering the house in the guise of an apothecary. Next day the knocker is muffled. Toward nightfall comes the chariot of a physician and deposits its big-wigged and solemn burden at Wakefield's door, whence after a quarter of an hour's visit he emerges, perchance the herald of a funeral. Dear woman! will she die?

By this time Wakefield is excited to something like energy of feeling, but still lingers away from his wife's bedside, pleading with his conscience that she must not be disturbed at such a juncture. If aught else restrains him, he does not know it. In the course of a few weeks she gradually recovers. The crisis is over; her heart is sad, perhaps, but quiet, and, let him return soon or late, it will never be feverish for him again. Such ideas glimmer through the mist of Wakefield's mind and render him indistinctly conscious that an almost impassable gulf divides his hired apartment from his former home. "It is but in the next street," he sometimes says. Fool! it is in another world. Hitherto he has put off' his return from one particular day to another; henceforward he leaves the precise time undetermined—not to-morrow; probably next week; pretty soon. Poor man! The dead have nearly as much chance of revisiting their earthly homes as the self-banished Wakefield.

Would that I had a folio to write, instead of an article of a dozen pages! Then might I exemplify how an influence beyond our control lays its strong hand on every deed which we do and weaves its consequences into an iron tissue of necessity.

Wakefield is spellbound. We must leave him for ten years or so to haunt around his house without once crossing the threshold, and to be faithful to his wife with all the affection of which his heart is capable, while he is slowly fading out of hers. Long since, it must be remarked, he has lost the perception of singularity in his conduct.

Now for a scene. Amid the throng of a London street we distinguish a man, now waxing elderly, with few characteristics to attract careless observers, yet bearing in his whole aspect the handwriting of no common fate for such as have the skill to read it. He is meagre; his low and narrow forehead is deeply wrinkled; his eyes, small and lustreless, sometimes wander apprehensively about him, but oftener seem to look inward. He bends his head and moves with an indescribable obliquity of gait, as if unwilling to display his full front to the world. Watch him long enough to see what we have described, and you will allow that circumstances—which often produce remarkable men from Nature's ordinary handiwork—have produced one such here. Next, leaving him to sidle along the footwalk, cast your eyes in the opposite direction, where a portly female considerably in the wane of life, with a prayer-book in her hand, is proceeding to yonder church. She has the placid mien of settled widowhood. Her regrets have either died away or have become so essential to her heart that they would be poorly exchanged for joy. Just as the lean man and well-conditioned woman are passing a slight obstruction occurs and brings these two figures directly in contact. Their hands touch; the pressure of the crowd forces her bosom against his shoulder; they stand face to face, staring into each other's eyes. After a ten years' separation thus Wakefield meets his wife. The throng eddies away and carries them asunder. The sober widow, resuming her former pace, proceeds to church, but pauses in the portal and throws a perplexed glance along the street. She passes in, however, opening her prayer-book as she goes.

And the man? With so wild a face that busy and selfish London stands to gaze after him he hurries to his lodgings, bolts the door and throws himself upon the bed. The latent feelings of years break out; his feeble mind acquires a brief energy from their strength; all the miserable strangeness of his life is revealed to him at a glance, and he cries out passionately, "Wakefield, Wakefield! You are mad!" Perhaps he was so. The singularity of his situation must have so moulded him to itself that, considered in regard to his fellow-creatures and the business of life, he could not be said to possess his right mind. He had contrived—or, rather, he had happened—to dissever himself from the world, to vanish, to give up his place and privileges with living men without being admitted among the dead. The life of a hermit is nowise parallel to his. He was in the bustle of the city as of old, but the crowd swept by and saw him not; he was, we may figuratively say, always beside his wife and at his hearth, yet must never feel the warmth of the one nor the affection of the other. It was Wakefield's unprecedented fate to retain his original share of human sympathies and to be still involved in human interests, while he had lost his reciprocal influence on them. It would be a most curious speculation to trace out the effect of such circumstances on his heart and intellect separately and in unison. Yet, changed as he was, he would seldom be conscious of it, but deem himself the same man as ever; glimpses of the truth, indeed, would come, but only for the moment, and still he would keep saying, "I shall soon go back," nor reflect that he had been saying so for twenty years.

I conceive, also, that these twenty years would appear in the retrospect scarcely longer than the week to which Wakefield had at first limited his absence. He would look on the affair as no more than an interlude in the main business of his life. When, after a little while more, he should deem it time to re-enter his parlor, his wife would clap her hands for joy on beholding the middle-aged Mr. Wakefield. Alas, what a mistake! Would Time but await the close of our favorite follies, we should be young men—all of us—and till Doomsday.

One evening, in the twentieth year since he vanished, Wakefield is taking his customary walk toward the dwelling which he still calls his own. It is a gusty night of autumn, with frequent showers that patter down upon the pavement and are gone before a man can put up his umbrella. Pausing near the house, Wakefield discerns through the parlor-windows of the second floor the red glow and the glimmer and fitful flash of a comfortable fire. On the ceiling appears a grotesque shadow of good Mrs. Wakefield. The cap, the nose and chin and the broad waist form an admirable caricature, which dances, moreover, with the up-flickering and down-sinking blaze almost too merrily for the shade of an elderly widow. At this instant a shower chances to fall, and is driven by the unmannerly gust full into Wakefield's face and bosom. He is quite penetrated with its autumnal chill. Shall he stand wet and shivering here, when his own hearth has a good fire to warm him and his own wife will run to fetch the gray coat and small-clothes which doubtless she has kept carefully in the closet of their bedchamber? No; Wakefield is no such fool. He ascends the steps—heavily, for twenty years have stiffened his legs since he came down, but he knows it not.—Stay, Wakefield! Would you go to the sole home that is left you? Then step into your grave.—The door opens. As he passes in we have a parting glimpse of his visage, and recognize the crafty smile which was the precursor of the little joke that he has ever since been playing off at his wife's expense. How unmercifully has he quizzed the poor woman! Well, a good night's rest to Wakefield!

This happy event—supposing it to be such—could only have occurred at an unpremeditated moment. We will not follow our friend across the threshold. He has left us much food for thought, a portion of which shall lend its wisdom to a moral and be shaped into a figure. Amid the seeming confusion of our mysterious world individuals are so nicely adjusted to a system, and systems to one another and to a whole, that by stepping aside for a moment a man exposes himself to a fearful risk of losing his place for ever. Like Wakefield, he may become, as it were, the outcast of the universe.

A RILL FROM THE TOWN-PUMP

(SCENE, THE CORNER OF TWO PRINCIPAL STREETS, THE TOWN-PUMP TALKING THROUGH ITS NOSE.)

NOON BY THE NORTH CLOCK! Noon by the east! High noon, too, by these hot sunbeams, which full, scarcely aslope, upon my head and almost make the water bubble and smoke in the trough under my nose. Truly, we public characters have a tough time of it! And among all the town-officers chosen at March meeting, where is he that sustains for a single year the burden of such manifold duties as are imposed in perpetuity upon the town-pump? The title of "town-treasurer" is rightfully mine, as guardian of the best treasure that the town has. The overseers of the poor ought to make me their chairman, since I provide bountifully for the pauper without expense to him that pays taxes. I am at the head of the fire department and one of the physicians to the board of health. As a keeper of the peace all water-drinkers will confess me equal to the constable. I perform some of the duties of the town-clerk by promulgating public notices when they are posted on my front. To speak within bounds, I am the chief person of the municipality, and exhibit, moreover, an admirable pattern to my brother-officers by the cool, steady, upright, downright and impartial discharge of my business and the constancy with which I stand to my post. Summer or winter, nobody seeks me in vain, for all day long I am seen at the busiest corner, just above the market, stretching out my arms to rich and poor alike, and at night I hold a lantern over my head both to show where I am and keep people out of the gutters. At this sultry noontide I am cupbearer to the parched populace, for whose benefit an iron goblet is chained to my waist. Like a dramseller on the mall at muster-day, I cry aloud to all and sundry in my plainest accents and at the very tiptop of my voice.

Here it is, gentlemen! Here is the good liquor! Walk up, walk up, gentlemen! Walk up, walk up! Here is the superior stuff! Here is the unadulterated ale of Father Adam—better than Cognac, Hollands, Jamaica, strong beer or wine of any price; here it is by the hogshead or the single glass, and not a cent to pay! Walk up, gentlemen, walk up, and help yourselves!

It were a pity if all this outcry should draw no customers. Here they come.—A hot day, gentlemen! Quaff and away again, so as to keep yourselves in a nice cool sweat.—You, my friend, will need another cupful to wash the dust out of your throat, if it be as thick there as it is on your cowhide shoes. I see that you have trudged half a score of miles to-day, and like a wise man have passed by the taverns and stopped at the running brooks and well-curbs. Otherwise,

67

betwixt heat without and fire within, you would have been burnt to a cinder or melted down to nothing at all, in the fashion of a jelly-fish. Drink and make room for that other fellow, who seeks my aid to quench the fiery fever of last night's potations, which he drained from no cup of mine.—Welcome, most rubicund sir! You and I have been great strangers hitherto; nor, to confess the truth, will my nose be anxious for a closer intimacy till the fumes of your breath be a little less potent. Mercy on you, man! the water absolutely hisses down your red-hot gullet and is converted quite to steam in the miniature Tophet which you mistake for a stomach. Fill again, and tell me, on the word of an honest toper, did you ever, in cellar, tavern, or any kind of a dram-shop, spend the price of your children's food for a swig half so delicious? Now, for the first time these ten years, you know the flavor of cold water. Good-bye; and whenever you are thirsty, remember that I keep a constant supply at the old stand.—Who next?—Oh, my little friend, you are let loose from school and come hither to scrub your blooming face and drown the memory of certain taps of the ferule, and other schoolboy troubles, in a draught from the town-pump? Take it, pure as the current of your young life. Take it, and may your heart and tongue never be scorched with a fiercer thirst than now! There, my dear child! put down the cup and yield your place to this elderly gentleman who treads so tenderly over the paving-stones that I suspect he is afraid of breaking them. What! he limps by without so much as thanking me, as if my hospitable offers were meant only for people who have no wine-cellars. —Well, well, sir, no harm done, I hope? Go draw the cork, tip the decanter; but when your great toe shall set you a-roaring, it will be no affair of mine. If gentlemen love the pleasant titillation of the gout, it is all one to the town-pump. This thirsty dog with his red tongue lolling out does not scorn my hospitality, but stands on his hind legs and laps eagerly out of the trough. See how lightly he capers away again!—Jowler, did your worship ever have the gout?

Are you all satisfied? Then wipe your mouths, my good friends, and while my spout has a moment's leisure I will delight the town with a few historical reminiscences. In far antiquity, beneath a darksome shadow of venerable boughs, a spring bubbled out of the leaf-strewn earth in the very spot where you now behold me on the sunny pavement. The water was as bright and clear and deemed as precious as liquid diamonds. The Indian sagamores drank of it from time immemorial till the fatal deluge of the firewater burst upon the red men and swept their whole race away from the cold fountains. Endicott and his followers came next, and often knelt down to drink, dipping their long beards in the spring. The richest goblet then was of birch-bark. Governor Winthrop, after a journey afoot from Boston, drank here out of the hollow of his hand. The elder Higginson here wet his palm and laid it on the brow of the first town-born child. For many years it was the watering-place, and, as it were, the washbowl, of the vicinity, whither all decent folks resorted to purify their visages and gaze at them afterward—at least, the pretty maidens did—in the mirror which it made. On Sabbath-days, whenever a babe was to be baptized, the sexton filled his basin here and placed it on the communion-table of the humble meeting-house, which partly covered the site of yonder stately brick one. Thus one generation after another was consecrated to Heaven by its waters, and cast their waxing and waning shadows into its glassy bosom, and vanished from the earth, as if mortal life were but a flitting image in a fountain. Finally the fountain vanished also. Cellars were dug on all sides and cart-loads of gravel flung upon its source, whence oozed a turbid stream, forming a mud-puddle at the corner of two streets. In the hot months, when its refreshment was most needed, the dust flew in clouds over the forgotten birthplace of the waters, now their grave. But in the course of time a town-pump was sunk into the source of the ancient spring; and when the first decayed, another took its place, and then another, and still another, till here stand I, gentlemen and ladies, to serve you with my iron goblet. Drink and be refreshed. The water is as pure and cold as that which slaked the thirst of the red sagamore beneath the aged boughs, though now the gem of the wilderness is treasured under these hot stones, where no shadow falls but from the brick buildings. And be it the moral of my story that, as this wasted and long-lost fountain is now known and prized again, so shall the virtues of cold water—too little valued since your fathers' days—be recognized by all.

Your pardon, good people! I must interrupt my stream of eloquence and spout forth a stream of water to replenish the trough for this teamster and his two yoke of oxen, who have come from Topsfield, or somewhere along that way. No part of my business is pleasanter than the watering of cattle. Look! how rapidly they lower the water-mark on the sides of the trough, till their capacious stomachs are moistened with a gallon or two apiece and they can afford time to breathe it in with sighs of calm enjoyment. Now they roll their quiet eyes around the brim of their monstrous drinking-vessel. An ox is your true toper.

But I perceive, my dear auditors, that you are impatient for the remainder of my discourse. Impute it, I beseech you, to no defect of modesty if I insist a little longer on so fruitful a topic as my own multifarious merits. It is altogether for your good. The better you think of me, the better men and women you will find yourselves. I shall say nothing of my all-important aid on washing-days, though on that account alone I might call myself the household god of a hundred families. Far be it from me, also, to hint, my respectable friends, at the show of dirty faces which you would present without my pains to keep you clean. Nor will I remind you how often, when the midnight bells make you tremble for your combustible town, you have fled to the town-pump and found me always at my post firm amid the confusion and ready to drain my vital current in your behalf. Neither is it worth while to lay much stress on my claims to a medical diploma as the physician whose simple rule of practice is preferable to all the nauseous lore which has found men sick, or left them so, since the days of Hippocrates. Let us take a broader view of my beneficial influence on mankind.

No; these are trifles, compared with the merits which wise men concede to me—if not in my single self, yet as the representative of a class—of being the grand reformer of the age. From my spout, and such spouts as mine, must flow the stream that shall cleanse our earth of the vast portion of its crime and anguish which has gushed from the fiery fountains of the still. In this mighty enterprise the cow shall be my great confederate. Milk and water—the TOWN-PUMP and the Cow! Such is the glorious copartnership that shall tear down the distilleries and brewhouses, uproot the vineyards, shatter the cider-presses, ruin the tea and coffee trade, and finally monopolize the whole business of quenching thirst. Blessed consummation! Then Poverty shall pass away from the land, finding no hovel so wretched where her squalid form may shelter herself. Then Disease, for lack of other victims, shall gnaw its own heart and die. Then Sin, if she do not die, shall lose half her strength. Until now the frenzy of hereditary fever has raged in the human blood, transmitted from sire to son and rekindled in every generation by fresh draughts of liquid flame. When that inward fire shall be extinguished, the heat of passion cannot but grow cool, and war—the drunkenness of nations—perhaps will cease. At least, there will be no war of households. The husband and wife, drinking deep of peaceful joy —a calm bliss of temperate affections—shall pass hand in hand through life and lie down not reluctantly at its protracted close. To them the past will be no turmoil of mad dreams, nor the future an eternity of such moments as follow the delirium of the drunkard. Their dead faces shall express what their spirits were and are to be by a lingering smile of memory and hope.

Ahem! Dry work, this speechifying, especially to an unpractised orator. I never conceived till now what toil the temperance lecturers undergo for my sake; hereafter they shall have the business to themselves.—Do, some kind Christian, pump a stroke or two, just to wet my whistle.—Thank you, sir!—My dear hearers, when the world shall have been regenerated by my instrumentality, you will collect your useless vats and liquor-casks into one great pile and make a bonfire in honor of the town-pump. And when I shall have decayed like my predecessors, then, if you revere my memory, let a marble fountain richly sculptured take my place upon this spot. Such monuments should be erected everywhere and inscribed with the names of the distinguished champions of my cause. Now, listen, for something very important is to come next.

There are two or three honest friends of mine—and true friends I know they are—who nevertheless by their fiery pugnacity in my behalf do put me in fearful hazard of a broken nose, or even a total overthrow upon the pavement and the loss of the treasure which I guard.—I pray you, gentlemen, let this fault be amended. Is it decent, think you, to get tipsy with zeal for temperance and take up the honorable cause of the town-pump in the style of a toper fighting for his brandy-bottle? Or can the excellent qualities of cold water be no otherwise exemplified than by plunging slapdash into hot water and woefully scalding yourselves and other people? Trust me, they may. In the moral warfare which you are to wage—and, indeed, in the whole conduct of your lives—you cannot choose a better example than myself, who have never permitted the dust and sultry atmosphere, the turbulence and manifold disquietudes, of the world around me to reach that deep, calm well of purity which may be called my soul. And whenever I pour out that soul, it is to cool earth's fever or cleanse its stains.

One o'clock! Nay, then, if the dinner-bell begins to speak, I may as well hold my peace. Here comes a pretty young girl of my acquaintance with a large stone pitcher for me to fill. May she draw a husband while drawing her water, as Rachel did of old!—Hold out your vessel, my dear! There it is, full to the brim; so now run home, peeping at your sweet image in the pitcher as you go, and forget not in a glass of my own liquor to drink "SUCCESS TO THE TOWN-PUMP."

THE GREAT CARBUNCLE.

A MYSTERY OF THE WHITE MOUNTAINS.

AT NIGHTFALL once in the olden time, on the rugged side of one of the Crystal Hills, a party of adventurers were refreshing themselves after a toilsome and fruitless quest for the Great Carbuncle. They had come thither, not as friends nor partners in the enterprise, but each, save one youthful pair, impelled by his own selfish and solitary longing for this wondrous gem. Their feeling of brotherhood, however, was strong enough to induce them to contribute a mutual aid in building a rude hut of branches and kindling a great fire of shattered pines that had drifted down the headlong current of the Amonoosuck, on the lower bank of which they were to pass the night. There was but one of their number, perhaps, who had become so estranged from natural sympathies by the absorbing spell of the pursuit as to acknowledge no satisfaction at the sight of human faces in the remote and solitary region whither they had ascended. A vast extent of wilderness lay between them and the nearest settlement, while scant a mile above their heads was that bleak verge where the hills throw off their shaggy mantle of forest-trees and either robe themselves in clouds or tower naked into the sky. The roar of the Amonoosuck would have been too awful for endurance if only a solitary man had listened while the mountain-stream talked with the wind.

The adventurers, therefore, exchanged hospitable greetings and welcomed one another to the hut where each man was the host and all were the guests of the whole company. They spread their individual supplies of food on the flat surface of a rock and partook of a general repast; at the close of which a sentiment of good-fellowship was perceptible among the party, though repressed by the idea that the renewed search for the Great Carbuncle must make them strangers again in the morning. Seven men and one young woman, they warmed themselves together at the fire, which extended its bright wall along the whole front of their wigwam. As they observed the various and contrasted figures that made up the assemblage, each man looking like a caricature of himself in the unsteady light that flickered over him, they came mutually to the conclusion that an odder society had never met in city or wilderness, on mountain or plain.

The eldest of the group—a tall, lean, weatherbeaten man some sixty years of age—was clad in the skins of wild animals whose fashion of dress he did well to imitate, since the deer, the wolf and the bear had long been his most intimate companions. He was one of those ill-fated mortals, such as the Indians told of, whom in their early youth the Great Carbuncle smote with a peculiar madness and became the passionate dream of their existence. All who visited that region knew him as "the Seeker," and by no other name. As none could remember when he first took up the search, there went a fable in the valley of the Saco that for his inordinate lust after the Great Carbuncle he had been condemned to wander among the mountains till the end of time, still with the same feverish hopes at sunrise, the same despair at eve. Near this miserable Seeker sat a little elderly personage wearing a high-crowned hat shaped somewhat like a crucible. He was from beyond the sea—a Doctor Cacaphodel, who had wilted and dried himself into a mummy by continually stooping over charcoal-furnaces and inhaling unwholesome fumes during his researches in chemistry and alchemy. It was told of him— whether truly or not—that at the commencement of his studies he had drained his body of all its richest blood and wasted it, with other inestimable ingredients, in an unsuccessful experiment, and had never been a well man since. Another of the adventurers was Master Ichabod Pigsnort, a weighty merchant and selectman of Boston, and an elder of the famous Mr. Norton's church. His enemies had a ridiculous story that Master Pigsnort was accustomed to spend a whole hour after prayer-time every morning and evening in wallowing naked among an immense quantity of pine-tree shillings, which were the earliest silver coinage of Massachusetts. The fourth whom we shall notice had no name that his companions knew of, and was chiefly distinguished by a sneer that always contorted his thin visage, and by a prodigious pair of spectacles which were supposed to deform and discolor the whole face of nature to this gentleman's perception. The fifth adventurer likewise lacked a name, which was the greater pity, as he appeared to be a poet. He was a bright-eyed man, but woefully pined away, which was no more than natural if, as some people affirmed, his ordinary diet was fog, morning mist and a slice of the densest cloud within his reach, sauced with moonshine whenever he could get it. Certain it is that the poetry which flowed from him had a smack of all these dainties. The sixth of the party was a young man of haughty mien and sat somewhat apart from the rest, wearing his plumed hat loftily among his elders, while the fire glittered on the rich embroidery of his dress and gleamed intensely on the jewelled pommel of his sword. This was the lord De Vere, who when at home was said to spend much of his time in the burial-vault of his dead progenitors rummaging their mouldy coffins in search of all the earthly pride and vainglory that was hidden among bones and dust; so that, besides his own share, he had the collected haughtiness of his whole line of ancestry. Lastly, there was a handsome youth in rustic garb, and by his side a blooming little person in whom a delicate shade of maiden reserve was just melting into the rich glow of a young wife's affection. Her name was Hannah, and her husband's Matthew—two homely names, yet well enough adapted to the simple pair who seemed strangely out of place among the whimsical fraternity whose wits had been set agog by the Great Carbuncle.

Beneath the shelter of one hut, in the bright blaze of the same fire, sat this varied group of adventurers, all so intent upon a single object that of whatever else they began to speak their closing words were sure to be illuminated with the Great Carbuncle. Several related the circumstances that brought them thither. One had listened to a traveller's tale of this marvellous stone in his own distant country, and had immediately been seized with such a thirst for beholding it as could only be quenched in its intensest lustre. Another, so long ago as when the famous Captain Smith visited these coasts, had seen it blazing far at sea, and had felt no rest in all the intervening years till now that he took up the search. A third, being encamped on a hunting-expedition full forty miles south of the White Mountains, awoke at midnight and beheld the Great Carbuncle gleaming like a meteor, so that the shadows of the trees fell backward from it. They spoke of the innumerable attempts which had been made to reach the spot, and of the singular fatality which had hitherto withheld success from all adventurers, though it might seem so easy to follow to its source a light that overpowered the moon and almost matched the sun. It was observable that each smiled scornfully at the madness of every other in anticipating better fortune than the past, yet nourished a scarcely-hidden conviction that he would himself be the favored one. As if to allay their too sanguine hopes, they recurred to the Indian traditions that a spirit kept watch about the gem and bewildered those who sought it either by removing it from peak to peak of the higher hills or by calling up a mist from the enchanted lake over which it hung. But these tales were deemed unworthy of credit, all professing to believe that the search had been baffled by want of sagacity or perseverance in the adventurers, or such other causes as might naturally obstruct the passage to any given point among the intricacies of forest, valley and mountain.

In a pause of the conversation the wearer of the prodigious spectacles looked round upon the party, making each individual in turn the object of the sneer which invariably dwelt upon his countenance.

"So, fellow-pilgrims," said he, "here we are, seven wise men and one fair damsel, who doubtless is as wise as any graybeard of the company. Here we are, I say, all bound on the same goodly enterprise. Methinks, now, it were not amiss that each of us declare what he proposes to do with the Great Carbuncle, provided he have the good hap to clutch it.—What says our friend in the bearskin? How mean you, good sir, to enjoy the prize which you have been seeking the Lord knows how long among the Crystal Hills?"

"How enjoy it!" exclaimed the aged Seeker, bitterly. "I hope for no enjoyment from it--that folly has past, long ago! I keep up the search for this accursed stone, because the vain ambition of my youth has become a fate upon me, in old age. The pursuit alone is my strength--the energy of my soul--the warmth of my blood, and the pith and marrow of my bones! Were I to turn my back upon it, I should fall down dead, on the hither side of the Notch, which is the gate-way of this mountain region. Yet, not to have my wasted life time back again, would I give up my hopes of the Great Carbuncle! Having found it, I shall bear it to a certain cavern that I wot of, and there, grasping it in my arms, lie down and die, and keep it buried with me for ever."

"Oh, wretch, regardless of the interests of science!" cried Doctor Cacaphodel, with philosophic indignation. "Thou art not worthy to behold, even from afar off, the lustre of this most precious gem that ever was concocted in the laboratory of Nature. Mine is the sole purpose for which a wise man may desire the possession of the Great Carbuncle. Immediately on obtaining it--for I have a presentiment, good people, that the prize is reserved to crown my scientific reputation--I shall return to Europe, and employ my remaining years in reducing it to its first elements. A portion of the stone will I grind to impalpable powder; other parts shall be dissolved in acids, or whatever solvents will act upon so admirable a composition; and the remainder I design to melt in the crucible, or set on fire with the blow-pipe. By these various methods, I shall gain an accurate analysis, and finally bestow the result of my labours upon the world, in a folio volume."

"Excellent!" quoth the man with the spectacles. "Nor need you hesitate, learned Sir, on account of the necessary destruction of the gem; since the perusal of your folio may teach every mother's son of us to concoct a Great Carbuncle of his own."

"But, verily," said Master Ichabod Pigsnort, "for mine own part, I object to the making of these counterfeits, as being calculated to reduce the marketable value of the true gem. I tell ye frankly, Sirs, I have an interest in keeping up the price. Here have I quitted my regular traffic, leaving my warehouse in the care of my clerks, and putting my credit to great hazard, and furthermore, have put myself to peril of death or captivity by the accursed heathen savages-- and all this without daring to ask the prayers of the congregation, because the quest for the Great Carbuncle is deemed little better than a traffic with the evil one. Now think ye that I would have done this grievous wrong to my soul, body, reputation and estate, without a reasonable chance of profit?"

"Not I, pious Master Pigsnort," said the man with the spectacles. "I never laid such a great folly to thy charge."

"Truly, I hope not," said the merchant. "Now, as touching this Great Carbuncle, I am free to own that I have never had a glimpse of it, but, be it only the hundredth part so bright as people tell, it will surely outvalue the Great Mogul's best diamond, which he holds at an incalculable sum; wherefore I am minded to put the Great Carbuncle on shipboard and voyage with it to England, France, Spain, Italy, or into heathendom if Providence should send me thither, and, in a word, dispose of the gem to the best bidder among the potentates of the earth, that he may place it among his crown-jewels. If any of ye have a wiser plan, let him expound it."

"That have I, thou sordid man!" exclaimed the poet. "Dost thou desire nothing brighter than gold, that thou wouldst transmute all this ethereal lustre into such dross as thou wallowest in already? For myself, hiding the jewel under my cloak, I shall hie me back to my attic-chamber in one of the darksome alleys of London. There night and day will I gaze upon it. My soul shall drink its radiance; it shall be diffused throughout my intellectual powers and gleam brightly in every line of poesy that I indite. Thus long ages after I am gone the splendor of the Great Carbuncle will blaze around my name."

"Well said, Master Poet!" cried he of the spectacles. "Hide it under thy cloak, sayest thou? Why, it will gleam through the holes and make thee look like a jack-o'-lantern!"

"To think," ejaculated the lord De Vere, rather to himself than his companions, the best of whom he held utterly unworthy of his intercourse—"to think that a fellow in a tattered cloak should talk of conveying the Great Carbuncle to a garret in Grubb street! Have not I resolved within myself that the whole earth contains no fitter ornament for the great hall of my ancestral castle? There shall it flame for ages, making a noonday of midnight, glittering on the suits of armor, the banners and escutcheons, that hang around the wall, and keeping bright the memory of heroes. Wherefore have all other adventurers sought the prize in vain but that I might win it and make it a symbol of the glories of our lofty line? And never on the diadem of the White Mountains did the Great Carbuncle hold a place half so honored as is reserved for it in the hall of the De Veres."

"It is a noble thought," said the cynic, with an obsequious sneer. "Yet, might I presume to say so, the gem would make a rare sepulchral lamp, and would display the glories of Your Lordship's progenitors more truly in the ancestral vault than in the castle-hall."

"Nay, forsooth," observed Matthew, the young rustic, who sat hand in hand with his bride, "the gentleman has bethought himself of a profitable use for this bright stone. Hannah here and I are seeking it for a like purpose."

"How, fellow?" exclaimed His Lordship, in surprise. "What castle-hall hast thou to hang it in?"

"No castle," replied Matthew, "but as neat a cottage as any within sight of the Crystal Hills. Ye must know, friends, that Hannah and I, being wedded the last week, have taken up the search of the Great Carbuncle because we shall need its light in the long winter evenings and it will be such a pretty thing to show the neighbors when they visit us! It will shine through the house, so that we may pick up a pin in any corner, and will set all the windows a-glowing as if there were a great fire of pine-knots in the chimney. And then how pleasant, when we awake in the night, to be able to see one another's faces!"

There was a general smile among the adventurers at the simplicity of the young couple's project in regard to this wondrous and invaluable stone, with which the greatest monarch on earth might have been proud to adorn his palace. Especially the man with spectacles, who had sneered at all the company in turn, now twisted his visage into such an expression of ill-natured mirth that Matthew asked him rather peevishly what he himself meant to do with the Great Carbuncle.

"The Great Carbuncle!" answered the cynic, with ineffable scorn. "Why, you blockhead, there is no such thing in *rerum naturâ*. I have come three thousand miles, and am resolved to set my foot on every peak of these mountains and poke my head into every chasm for the sole purpose of demonstrating to the satisfaction of any man one whit less an ass than thyself that the Great Carbuncle is all a humbug."

Vain and foolish were the motives that had brought most of the adventurers to the Crystal Hills, but none so vain, so foolish, and so impious too, as that of the scoffer with the prodigious spectacles. He was one of those wretched and evil men whose yearnings are downward to the darkness instead of heavenward, and who, could they but extinguish the lights which God hath kindled for us, would count the midnight gloom their chiefest glory.

As the cynic spoke several of the party were startled by a gleam of red splendor that showed the huge shapes of the surrounding mountains and the rock-bestrewn bed of the turbulent river, with an illumination unlike that of their fire, on the trunks and black boughs of the forest-trees. They listened for the roll of thunder, but heard nothing, and were glad that the tempest came not near them. The stars—those dial-points of heaven—now warned the adventurers to close their eyes on the blazing logs and open them in dreams to the glow of the Great Carbuncle.

The young married couple had taken their lodgings in the farthest corner of the wigwam, and were separated from the rest of the party by a curtain of curiously-woven twigs such as might have hung in deep festoons around the bridal-bower of Eve. The modest little wife had wrought this piece of tapestry while the other guests were talking. She and her husband fell asleep with hands tenderly clasped, and awoke from visions of unearthly radiance to meet the more blessed light of one another's eyes. They awoke at the same instant and with one happy smile beaming over their two faces, which grew brighter with their consciousness of the reality of life and love. But no sooner did she recollect where they were than the bride peeped through the interstices of the leafy curtain and saw that the outer room of the hut was deserted.

"Up, dear Matthew!" cried she, in haste. "The strange folk are all gone. Up this very minute, or we shall lose the Great Carbuncle!"

In truth, so little did these poor young people deserve the mighty prize which had lured them thither that they had slept peacefully all night and till the summits of the hills were glittering with sunshine, while the other adventurers had tossed their limbs in feverish wakefulness or dreamed of climbing precipices, and set off to realize their dreams with the curliest peep of dawn. But Matthew and Hannah after their calm rest were as light as two young deer, and merely stopped to say their prayers and wash themselves in a cold pool of the Amonoosuck, and then to taste a morsel of food ere they turned their faces to the mountain-side. It was a sweet emblem of conjugal affection as they toiled up the difficult ascent gathering strength from the mutual aid which they afforded.

After several little accidents, such as a torn robe, a lost shoe and the entanglement of Hannah's hair in a bough, they reached the upper verge of the forest and were now to pursue a more adventurous course. The innumerable trunks and heavy foliage of the trees had hitherto shut in their thoughts, which now shrank affrighted from the region of wind and cloud and naked rocks and desolate sunshine that rose immeasurably above them. They gazed back at the obscure wilderness which they had traversed, and longed to be buried again in its depths rather than trust themselves to so vast and visible a solitude.

"Shall we go on?" said Matthew, throwing his arm round Hannah's waist both to protect her and to comfort his heart by drawing her close to it.

But the little bride, simple as she was, had a woman's love of jewels, and could not forego the hope of possessing the very brightest in the world, in spite of the perils with which it must be won.

"Let us climb a little higher," whispered she, yet tremulously, as she turned her face upward to the lonely sky.

"Come, then," said Matthew, mustering his manly courage and drawing her along with him; for she became timid again the moment that he grew bold.

And upward, accordingly, went the pilgrims of the Great Carbuncle, now treading upon the tops and thickly-interwoven branches of dwarf pines which by the growth of centuries, though mossy with age, had barely reached three feet in altitude. Next they came to masses and fragments of naked rock heaped confusedly together like a cairn reared by giants in memory of a giant chief. In this bleak realm of upper air nothing breathed, nothing grew; there was no life but what was concentred in their two hearts; they had climbed so high that Nature herself seemed no longer to keep them company. She lingered beneath them within the verge of the forest-trees, and sent a farewell glance after her children as they strayed where her own green footprints had never been. But soon they were to be hidden from her eye. Densely and dark the mists began to gather below, casting black spots of shadow on the vast landscape and sailing heavily to one centre, as if the loftiest mountain-peak had summoned a council of its kindred clouds. Finally the vapors welded themselves, as it were, into a mass, presenting the appearance of a pavement over which the wanderers might have trodden, but where they would vainly have sought an avenue to the blessed earth which they had lost. And the lovers yearned to behold that green earth again—more intensely, alas! than beneath a clouded sky they had ever desired a glimpse of heaven. They even felt it a relief to their desolation when the mists, creeping gradually up the mountain, concealed its lonely peak, and thus annihilated—at least, for them—the whole region of visible space. But they drew closer together with a fond and melancholy gaze, dreading lest the universal cloud should snatch them from each other's sight. Still, perhaps, they would have been resolute to climb as far and as high between earth and heaven as they could find foothold if Hannah's strength had not begun to fail, and with that her courage also. Her breath grew short. She refused to burden her husband with her weight, but often tottered against his side, and recovered herself each time by a feebler effort. At last she sank down on one of the rocky steps of the acclivity.

"We are lost, dear Matthew," said she, mournfully; "we shall never find our way to the earth again. And oh how happy we might have been in our cottage!"

"Dear heart, we will yet be happy there," answered Matthew. "Look! In this direction the sunshine penetrates the dismal mist; by its aid I can direct our course to the passage of the Notch. Let us go back, love, and dream no more of the Great Carbuncle."

"The sun cannot be yonder," said Hannah, with despondence. "By this time it must be noon; if there could ever be any sunshine here, it would come from above our heads."

"But look!" repeated Matthew, in a somewhat altered tone. "It is brightening every moment. If not sunshine, what can it be?"

Nor could the young bride any longer deny that a radiance was breaking through the mist and changing its dim hue to a dusky red, which continually grew more vivid, as if brilliant particles were interfused with the gloom. Now, also, the cloud began to roll away from the mountain, while, as it heavily withdrew, one object after another started out of its impenetrable obscurity into sight with precisely the effect of a new creation before the indistinctness of the old chaos had been completely swallowed up. As the process went on they saw the gleaming of water close at their feet, and found themselves on the very border of a mountain-lake, deep, bright, clear and calmly beautiful, spreading from brim to brim of a basin that had been scooped out of the solid rock. A ray of glory flashed across its surface. The pilgrims looked whence it should proceed, but closed their eyes, with a thrill of awful admiration, to exclude the fervid splendor that glowed from the brow of a cliff impending over the enchanted lake.

For the simple pair had reached that lake of mystery and found the long-sought shrine of the Great Carbuncle. They threw their arms around each other and trembled at their own success, for as the legends of this wondrous gem rushed thick upon their memory they felt themselves marked out by fate, and the consciousness was fearful. Often from childhood upward they had seen it shining like a distant star, and now that star was throwing its intensest lustre on their hearts. They seemed changed to one another's eyes in the red brilliancy that flamed upon their cheeks, while it lent the same fire to the lake, the rocks and sky, and to the mists which had rolled back before its power. But with their next glance they beheld an object that drew their attention even from the mighty stone. At the base of the cliff, directly beneath the Great Carbuncle, appeared the figure of a man with his arms extended in the act of climbing and his face turned upward as if to drink the full gush of splendor. But he stirred not, no more than if changed to marble.

"It is the Seeker," whispered Hannah, convulsively grasping her husband's arm. "Matthew, he is dead."

"The joy of success has killed him," replied Matthew, trembling violently. "Or perhaps the very light of the Great Carbuncle was death."

"'The Great Carbuncle'!" cried a peevish voice behind them. "The great humbug! If you have found it, prithee point it out to me."

They turned their heads, and there was the cynic with his prodigious spectacles set carefully on his nose, staring now at the lake, now at the rocks, now at the distant masses of vapor, now right at the Great Carbuncle itself, yet seemingly as unconscious of its light as if all the scattered clouds were condensed about his person. Though its radiance actually threw the shadow of the unbeliever at his own feet as he turned his back upon the glorious jewel, he would not be convinced that there was the least glimmer there.

"Where is your great humbug?" he repeated. "I challenge you to make me see it."

"There!" said Matthew, incensed at such perverse blindness, and turning the cynic round toward the illuminated cliff. "Take off those abominable spectacles, and you cannot help seeing it."

Now, these colored spectacles probably darkened the cynic's sight in at least as great a degree as the smoked glasses through which people gaze at an eclipse. With resolute bravado, however, he snatched them from his nose and fixed a bold stare full upon the ruddy blaze of the Great Carbuncle. But scarcely had he encountered it when, with a deep, shuddering groan, he dropped his head and pressed both hands across his miserable eyes. Thenceforth there was in very truth no light of the Great Carbuncle, nor any other light on earth, nor light of heaven itself, for the poor cynic. So long accustomed to view all objects through a medium that deprived them of every glimpse of brightness, a single flash of so glorious a phenomenon, striking upon his naked vision, had blinded him for ever.

"Matthew," said Hannah, clinging to him, "let us go hence."

Matthew saw that she was faint, and, kneeling down, supported her in his arms while he threw some of the thrillingly-cold water of the enchanted lake upon her face and bosom. It revived her, but could not renovate her courage.

"Yes, dearest," cried Matthew, pressing her tremulous form to his breast; "we will go hence and return to our humble cottage. The blessed sunshine and the quiet moonlight shall come through our window. We will kindle the cheerful glow of our hearth at eventide and be happy in its light. But never again will we desire more light than all the world may share with us."

"No," said his bride, "for how could we live by day or sleep by night in this awful blaze of the Great Carbuncle?"

Out of the hollow of their hands they drank each a draught from the lake, which presented them its waters uncontaminated by an earthly lip. Then, lending their guidance to the blinded cynic, who uttered not a word, and even stifled his groans in his own most wretched heart, they began to descend the mountain. Yet as they left the shore, till then untrodden, of the spirit's lake, they threw a farewell glance toward the cliff and beheld the vapors gathering in dense volumes, through which the gem burned duskily.

As touching the other pilgrims of the Great Carbuncle, the legend goes on to tell that the worshipful Master Ichabod Pigsnort soon gave up the quest as a desperate speculation, and wisely resolved to betake himself again to his warehouse, near the town-dock, in Boston. But as he passed through the Notch of the mountains a war-party of Indians captured our unlucky merchant and carried him to Montreal, there holding him in bondage till by the payment of a heavy ransom he had woefully subtracted from his hoard of pine-tree shillings. By his long absence, moreover, his affairs had become so disordered that for the rest of his life, instead of wallowing in silver, he had seldom a sixpence-worth of copper. Doctor Cacaphodel, the alchemist, returned to his laboratory with a prodigious fragment of granite, which he ground to powder, dissolved in acids, melted in the crucible and burnt with the blowpipe, and published the result of his experiments in one of the heaviest folios of the day. And for all these purposes the gem itself could not have answered better than the granite. The poet, by a somewhat similar mistake, made prize of a great piece of ice which he found in a sunless chasm of the mountains, and swore that it corresponded in all points with his idea of the Great Carbuncle. The critics say that, if his poetry lacked the splendor of the gem, it retained all the coldness of the ice. The lord De Vere went back to his ancestral hall, where he contented himself with a wax-lighted chandelier, and filled in due course of time another coffin in the ancestral vault. As the funeral torches gleamed within that dark receptacle, there was no need of the Great Carbuncle to show the vanity of earthly pomp.

The cynic, having cast aside his spectacles, wandered about the world a miserable object, and was punished with an agonizing desire of light for the wilful blindness of his former life. The whole night long he would lift his splendor-blasted orbs to the moon and stars; he turned his face eastward at sunrise as duly as a Persian idolater; he made a pilgrimage to Rome to witness the magnificent illumination of Saint Peter's church, and finally perished in the Great Fire of London, into the midst of which he had thrust himself with the desperate idea of catching one feeble ray from the blaze that was kindling earth and heaven.

Matthew and his bride spent many peaceful years and were fond of telling the legend of the Great Carbuncle. The tale, however, toward the close of their lengthened lives, did not meet with the full credence that had been accorded to it by those who remembered the ancient lustre of the gem. For it is affirmed that from the hour when two mortals had shown themselves so simply wise as to reject a jewel which would have dimmed all earthly things its splendor waned. When our pilgrims reached the cliff, they found only an opaque stone with particles of mica glittering on its surface. There is also a tradition that as the youthful pair departed the gem was loosened from the forehead of the cliff and fell into the enchanted lake, and that at noontide the Seeker's form may still be seen to bend over its quenchless gleam.

Some few believe that this inestimable stone is blazing as of old, and say that they have caught its radiance, like a flash of summer lightning, far down the valley of the Saco. And be it owned that many a mile from the Crystal Hills I saw a wondrous light around their summits, and was lured by the faith of poesy to be the latest pilgrim of the Great Carbuncle.

THE PROPHETIC PICTURES.

"But this painter!" cried Walter Ludlow, with animation. "He not only excels in his peculiar art, but possesses vast acquirements in all other learning and science. He talks Hebrew with Dr. Mather and gives lectures in anatomy to Dr. Boylston. In a word, he will meet the best-instructed man among us on his own ground. Moreover, he is a polished gentleman, a citizen of the world—yes, a true cosmopolite; for he will speak like a native of each clime and country on the globe, except our own forests, whither he is now going. Nor is all this what I most admire in him."

"Indeed!" said Elinor, who had listened with a women's interest to the description of such a man. "Yet this is admirable enough."

"Surely it is," replied her lover, "but far less so than his natural gift of adapting himself to every variety of character, insomuch that all men—and all women too, Elinor—shall find a mirror of themselves in this wonderful painter. But the greatest wonder is yet to be told."

"Nay, if he have more wonderful attributes than these," said Elinor, laughing, "Boston is a perilous abode for the poor gentleman. Are you telling me of a painter, or a wizard?"

"In truth," answered he, "that question might be asked much more seriously than you suppose. They say that he paints not merely a man's features, but his mind and heart. He catches the secret sentiments and passions and throws them upon the canvas like sunshine, or perhaps, in the portraits of dark-souled men, like a gleam of infernal fire. It is an awful gift," added Walter, lowering his voice from its tone of enthusiasm. "I shall be almost afraid to sit to him."

"Walter, are you in earnest?" exclaimed Elinor.

"For Heaven's sake, dearest Elinor, do not let him paint the look which you now wear," said her lover, smiling, though rather perplexed. "There! it is passing away now; but when you spoke, you seemed frightened to death, and very sad besides. What were you thinking of?"

"Nothing, nothing!" answered Elinor, hastily. "You paint my face with your own fantasies. Well, come for me tomorrow, and we will visit this wonderful artist."

But when the young man had departed, it cannot be denied that a remarkable expression was again visible on the fair and youthful face of his mistress. It was a sad and anxious look, little in accordance with what should have been the feelings of a maiden on the eve of wedlock. Yet Walter Ludlow was the chosen of her heart.

"A look!" said Elinor to herself. "No wonder that it startled him if it expressed what I sometimes feel. I know by my own experience how frightful a look may be. But it was all fancy. I thought nothing of it at the time; I have seen nothing of it since; I did but dream it;" and she busied herself about the embroidery of a ruff in which she meant that her portrait should be taken.

The painter of whom they had been speaking was not one of those native artists who at a later period than this borrowed their colors from the Indians and manufactured their pencils of the furs of wild beasts. Perhaps, if he could have revoked his life and prearranged his destiny, he might have chosen to belong to that school without a master in the hope of being at least original, since there were no works of art to imitate nor rules to follow. But he had been born and educated in Europe. People said that he had studied the grandeur or beauty of conception and every touch of the master-hand in all the most famous pictures in cabinets and galleries and on the walls of churches till there was nothing more for his powerful mind to learn. Art could add nothing to its lessons, but Nature might. He had, therefore, visited a world whither none of his professional brethren had preceded him, to feast his eyes on visible images that were noble and picturesque, yet had never been transferred to canvas. America was too poor to afford other temptations to an artist of eminence, though many of the colonial gentry on the painter's arrival had expressed a wish to transmit their lineaments to posterity by moans of his skill. Whenever such proposals were made, he fixed his piercing eyes on the applicant and seemed to look him through and through. If he beheld only a sleek and comfortable visage, though there were a gold-laced coat to adorn the picture and golden guineas to pay for it, he civilly rejected the task and the reward; but if the face were the index of anything uncommon in thought, sentiment or experience, or if he met a beggar in the street with a white beard and a furrowed brow, or if sometimes a child happened to look up and smile, he would exhaust all the art on them that he denied to wealth.

Pictorial skill being so rare in the colonies, the painter became an object of general curiosity. If few or none could appreciate the technical merit of his productions, yet there were points in regard to which the opinion of the crowd was as valuable as the refined judgment of the amateur. He watched the effect that each picture produced on such untutored beholders, and derived profit from their remarks, while they would as soon have thought of instructing Nature herself as him who seemed to rival her. Their admiration, it must be owned, was tinctured with the prejudices of the age and country. Some deemed it an offence against the Mosaic law, and even a presumptuous mockery of the Creator, to bring into existence such lively images of his creatures. Others, frightened at the art which could raise phantoms at will and keep the form of the dead among the living, were inclined to consider the painter as a magician, or perhaps the famous Black Man of old witch-times plotting mischief in a new guise. These foolish fancies were more than half believed among the mob. Even in superior circles his character was invested with a vague awe, partly rising like smoke-wreaths from the popular superstitions, but chiefly caused by the varied knowledge and talents which he made subservient to his profession.

Being on the eve of marriage, Walter Ludlow and Elinor were eager to obtain their portraits as the first of what, they doubtless hoped, would be a long series of family pictures. The day after the conversation above recorded they visited the painter's rooms. A servant ushered them into an apartment where, though the artist himself was not visible, there were personages whom they could hardly forbear greeting with reverence. They knew, indeed, that the whole assembly were but pictures, yet felt it impossible to separate the idea of life and intellect from such striking counterfeits. Several of the portraits were known to them either as distinguished characters of the day or their private acquaintances. There was Governor Burnett, looking as if he had just received an undutiful communication from the House of Representatives and were inditing a most sharp response. Mr. Cooke hung beside the ruler whom he opposed, sturdy and somewhat puritanical, as befitted a popular leader. The ancient lady of Sir William Phipps eyed them from the wall in ruff and farthingale, an imperious old dame not unsuspected of witchcraft. John Winslow, then a very young man, wore the expression of warlike enterprise which long afterward made him a distinguished general. Their personal friends were recognized at a glance. In most of the pictures the whole mind and character were brought out on the countenance and concentrated into a single look; so that, to speak paradoxically, the originals hardly resembled themselves so strikingly as the portraits did.

Among these modern worthies there were two old bearded saints who had almost vanished into the darkening canvas. There was also a pale but unfaded Madonna who had perhaps been worshipped in Rome, and now regarded the lovers with such a mild and holy look that they longed to worship too.

"How singular a thought," observed Walter Ludlow, "that this beautiful face has been beautiful for above two hundred years! Oh, if all beauty would endure so well! Do you not envy her, Elinor?"

"If earth were heaven, I might," she replied. "But, where all things fade, how miserable to be the one that could not fade!"

"This dark old St. Peter has a fierce and ugly scowl, saint though he be," continued Walter; "he troubles me. But the Virgin looks kindly at us."

"Yes, but very sorrowfully, methinks," said Elinor.

The easel stood beneath these three old pictures, sustaining one that had been recently commenced. After a little inspection they began to recognize the features of their own minister, the Rev. Dr. Colman, growing into shape and life, as it were, out of a cloud.

"Kind old man!" exclaimed Elinor. "He gazes at me as if he were about to utter a word of paternal advice."

"And at me," said Walter, "as if he were about to shake his head and rebuke me for some suspected iniquity. But so does the original. I shall never feel quite comfortable under his eye till we stand before him to be married."

They now heard a footstep on the floor, and, turning, beheld the painter, who had been some moments in the room and had listened to a few of their remarks. He was a middle-aged man with a countenance well worthy of his own pencil. Indeed, by the picturesque though careless arrangement of his rich dress, and perhaps because his soul dwelt always among painted shapes, he looked somewhat like a portrait himself. His visitors were sensible of a kindred between the artist and his works, and felt as if one of the pictures had stepped from the canvas to salute them.

Walter Ludlow, who was slightly known to the painter, explained the object of their visit. While he spoke a sunbeam was falling athwart his figure and Elinor's with so happy an effect that they also seemed living pictures of youth and beauty gladdened by bright fortune. The artist was evidently struck.

"My easel is occupied for several ensuing days, and my stay in Boston must be brief," said he, thoughtfully; then, after an observant glance, he added, "But your wishes shall be gratified though I disappoint the chief-justice and Madame Oliver. I must not lose this opportunity for the sake of painting a few ells of broadcloth and brocade."

The painter expressed a desire to introduce both their portraits into one picture and represent them engaged in some appropriate action. This plan would have delighted the lovers, but was necessarily rejected because so large a space of canvas would have been unfit for the room which it was intended to decorate. Two half-length portraits were therefore fixed upon. After they had taken leave, Walter Ludlow asked Elinor, with a smile, whether she knew what an influence over their fates the painter was about to acquire.

"The old women of Boston affirm," continued he, "that after he has once got possession of a person's face and figure he may paint him in any act or situation whatever, and the picture will be prophetic. Do you believe it?"

"Not quite," said Elinor, smiling. "Yet if he has such magic, there is something so gentle in his manner that I am sure he will use it well."

It was the painter's choice to proceed with both the portraits at the same time, assigning as a reason, in the mystical language which he sometimes used, that the faces threw light upon each other. Accordingly, he gave now a touch to Walter and now to Elinor, and the features of one and the other began to start forth so vividly that it appeared as if his triumphant art would actually disengage them from the canvas. Amid the rich light and deep shade they beheld their phantom selves, but, though the likeness promised to be perfect, they were not quite satisfied with the expression: it seemed more vague than in most of the painter's works. He, however, was satisfied with the prospect of success, and, being much interested in the lovers, employed his leisure moments, unknown to them, in making a crayon sketch of their two figures. During their sittings he engaged them in conversation and kindled up their faces with characteristic traits, which, though continually varying, it was his purpose to combine and fix. At length he announced that at their next visit both the portraits would be ready for delivery.

"If my pencil will but be true to my conception in the few last touches which I meditate," observed he, "these two pictures will be my very best performances. Seldom indeed has an artist such subjects." While speaking he still bent his penetrative eye upon them, nor withdrew it till they had reached the bottom of the stairs.

Nothing in the whole circle of human vanities takes stronger hold of the imagination than this affair of having a portrait painted. Yet why should it be so? The looking-glass, the polished globes of the andirons, the mirror-like water, and all other reflecting surfaces, continually present us with portraits—or, rather, ghosts—of ourselves which we glance at and straightway forget them. But we forget them only because they vanish. It is the idea of duration—of earthly immortality—that gives such a mysterious interest to our own portraits.

Walter and Elinor were not insensible to this feeling, and hastened to the painter's room punctually at the appointed hour to meet those pictured shapes which were to be their representatives with posterity. The sunshine flashed after them into the apartment, but left it somewhat gloomy as they closed the door. Their eyes were immediately attracted to their portraits, which rested against the farthest wall of the room. At the first glance through the dim light and the distance, seeing themselves in precisely their natural attitudes and with all the air that they recognized so well, they uttered a simultaneous exclamation of delight.

"There we stand," cried Walter, enthusiastically, "fixed in sunshine for ever. No dark passions can gather on our faces."

"No," said Elinor, more calmly; "no dreary change can sadden us."

This was said while they were approaching and had yet gained only an imperfect view of the pictures. The painter, after saluting them, busied himself at a table in completing a crayon sketch, leaving his visitors to form their own judgment as to his perfected labors. At intervals he sent a glance from beneath his deep eyebrows, watching their countenances in profile with his pencil suspended over the sketch. They had now stood some moments, each in front of the other's picture, contemplating it with entranced attention, but without uttering a word. At

83

length Walter stepped forward, then back, viewing Elinor's portrait in various lights, and finally spoke.

"Is there not a change?" said he, in a doubtful and meditative tone. "Yes; the perception of it grows more vivid the longer I look. It is certainly the same picture that I saw yesterday; the dress, the features, all are the same, and yet something is altered."

"Is, then, the picture less like than it was yesterday?" inquired the painter, now drawing near with irrepressible interest.

"The features are perfect Elinor," answered Walter, "and at the first glance the expression seemed also hers; but I could fancy that the portrait has changed countenance while I have been looking at it. The eyes are fixed on mine with a strangely sad and anxious expression. Nay, it is grief and terror. Is this like Elinor?"

"Compare the living face with the pictured one," said the painter.

Walter glanced sidelong at his mistress, and started. Motionless and absorbed, fascinated, as it were, in contemplation of Walter's portrait, Elinor's face had assumed precisely the expression of which he had just been complaining. Had she practised for whole hours before a mirror, she could not have caught the look so successfully. Had the picture itself been a mirror, it could not have thrown back her present aspect with stronger and more melancholy truth. She appeared quite unconscious of the dialogue between the artist and her lover.

"Elinor," exclaimed Walter, in amazement, "what change has come over you?"

She did not hear him nor desist from her fixed gaze till he seized her hand, and thus attracted her notice; then with a sudden tremor she looked from the picture to the face of the original.

"Do you see no change in your portrait?" asked she.

"In mine? None," replied Walter, examining it. "But let me see. Yes; there is a slight change —an improvement, I think, in the picture, though none in the likeness. It has a livelier expression than yesterday, as if some bright thought were flashing from the eyes and about to be uttered from the lips. Now that I have caught the look, it becomes very decided."

While he was intent on these observations Elinor turned to the painter. She regarded him with grief and awe, and felt that he repaid her with sympathy and commiseration, though wherefore she could but vaguely guess.

"That look!" whispered she, and shuddered. "How came it there?"

"Madam," said the painter, sadly, taking her hand and leading her apart, "in both these pictures I have painted what I saw. The artist—the true artist—must look beneath the exterior. It is his gift—his proudest, but often a melancholy one—to see the inmost soul, and by a power indefinable even to himself to make it glow or darken upon the canvas in glances that express the thought and sentiment of years. Would that I might convince myself of error in the present instance!"

They had now approached the table, on which were heads in chalk, hands almost as expressive as ordinary faces, ivied church-towers, thatched cottages, old thunder-stricken trees, Oriental and antique costume, and all such picturesque vagaries of an artist's idle moments. Turning them over with seeming carelessness, a crayon sketch of two figures was disclosed.

"If I have failed," continued he—"if your heart does not see itself reflected in your own portrait, if you have no secret cause to trust my delineation of the other—it is not yet too late to alter them. I might change the action of these figures too. But would it influence the event?" He directed her notice to the sketch.

A thrill ran through Elinor's frame; a shriek was upon her lips, but she stifled it with the self-command that becomes habitual to all who hide thoughts of fear and anguish within their bosoms. Turning from the table, she perceived that Walter had advanced near enough to have seen the sketch, though she could not determine whether it had caught his eye.

"We will not have the pictures altered," said she, hastily. "If mine is sad, I shall but look the gayer for the contrast."

"Be it so," answered the painter, bowing. "May your griefs be such fanciful ones that only your pictures may mourn for them! For your joys, may they be true and deep, and paint themselves upon this lovely face till it quite belie my art!"

After the marriage of Walter and Elinor the pictures formed the two most splendid ornaments of their abode. They hung side by side, separated by a narrow panel, appearing to eye each other constantly, yet always returning the gaze of the spectator. Travelled gentlemen who professed a knowledge of such subjects reckoned these among the most admirable specimens of modern portraiture, while common observers compared them with the originals, feature by feature, and were rapturous in praise of the likeness. But it was on a third class—neither travelled connoisseurs nor common observers, but people of natural sensibility—that the pictures wrought their strongest effect. Such persons might gaze carelessly at first, but, becoming interested, would return day after day and study these painted faces like the pages of a mystic volume. Walter Ludlow's portrait attracted their earliest notice. In the absence of himself and his bride they sometimes disputed as to the expression which the painter had intended to throw upon the features, all agreeing that there was a look of earnest import, though no two explained it alike. There was less diversity of opinion in regard to Elinor's picture. They differed, indeed, in their attempts to estimate the nature and depth of the gloom that dwelt upon her face, but agreed that it was gloom and alien from the natural temperament of their youthful friend. A certain fanciful person announced as the result of much scrutiny that both these pictures were parts of one design, and that the melancholy strength of feeling in Elinor's countenance bore reference to the more vivid emotion—or, as he termed it, the wild passion—in that of Walter. Though unskilled in the art, he even began a sketch in which the action of the two figures was to correspond with their mutual expression.

It was whispered among friends that day by day Elinor's face was assuming a deeper shade of pensiveness which threatened soon to render her too true a counterpart of her melancholy picture. Walter, on the other hand, instead of acquiring the vivid look which the painter had given him on the canvas, became reserved and downcast, with no outward flashes of emotion, however it might be smouldering within. In course of time Elinor hung a gorgeous curtain of purple silk wrought with flowers and fringed with heavy golden tassels before the pictures, under pretence that the dust would tarnish their hues or the light dim them. It was enough. Her visitors felt that the massive folds of the silk must never be withdrawn nor the portraits mentioned in her presence.

Time wore on, and the painter came again. He had been far enough to the north to see the silver cascade of the Crystal Hills, and to look over the vast round of cloud and forest from the summit of New England's loftiest mountain. But he did not profane that scene by the mockery of his art. He had also lain in a canoe on the bosom of Lake George, making his soul the mirror of its loveliness and grandeur till not a picture in the Vatican was more vivid than his recollection. He had gone with the Indian hunters to Niagara, and there, again, had flung his hopeless pencil down the precipice, feeling that he could as soon paint the roar as aught else that goes to make up the wondrous cataract. In truth, it was seldom his impulse to copy natural scenery except as a framework for the delineations of the human form and face, instinct with thought, passion or suffering. With store of such his adventurous ramble had enriched him. The stern dignity of Indian chiefs, the dusky loveliness of Indian girls, the domestic life of wigwams, the stealthy march, the battle beneath gloomy pine trees, the frontier fortress with its garrison, the anomaly of the old French partisan bred in courts, but grown gray in shaggy deserts,—such were the scenes and portraits that he had sketched. The glow of perilous moments, flashes of wild feeling, struggles of fierce power, love, hate, grief, frenzy—in a word, all the worn-out heart of the old earth—had been revealed to him under a new form. His portfolio was filled with graphic illustrations of the volume of his memory which genius would transmute into its own substance and imbue with immortality. He felt that the deep wisdom in his art which he had sought so far was found.

But amid stern or lovely nature, in the perils of the forest or its overwhelming peacefulness, still there had been two phantoms, the companions of his way. Like all other men around whom an engrossing purpose wreathes itself, he was insulated from the mass of humankind. He had no aim, no pleasure, no sympathies, but what were ultimately connected with his art. Though gentle in manner and upright in intent and action, he did not possess kindly feelings; his heart was cold: no living creature could be brought near enough to keep him warm. For these two beings, however, he had felt in its greatest intensity the sort of interest which always allied him to the subjects of his pencil. He had pried into their souls with his keenest insight and pictured the result upon their features with his utmost skill, so as barely to fall short of that standard which no genius ever reached, his own severe conception. He had caught from the duskiness of the future—at least, so he fancied—a fearful secret, and had obscurely revealed it on the portraits. So much of himself—of his imagination and all other powers—had been lavished on the study of Walter and Elinor that he almost regarded them as creations of his own, like the thousands with which he had peopled the realms of Picture. Therefore did they flit through the twilight of the woods, hover on the mist of waterfalls, look forth from the mirror of the lake, nor melt away in the noontide sun. They haunted his pictorial fancy, not as mockeries of life nor pale goblins of the dead, but in the guise of portraits, each with an unalterable expression which his magic had evoked from the caverns of the soul. He could not recross the Atlantic till he had again beheld the originals of those airy pictures.

"O glorious Art!" Thus mused the enthusiastic painter as he trod the street. "Thou art the image of the Creator's own. The innumerable forms that wander in nothingness start into being at thy beck. The dead live again; thou recallest them to their old scenes and givest their gray shadows the lustre of a better life, at once earthly and immortal. Thou snatchest back the fleeting moments of history. With thee there is no past, for at thy touch all that is great becomes for ever present, and illustrious men live through long ages in the visible performance of the very deeds which made them what they are. O potent Art! as thou bringest the faintly-revealed past to stand in that narrow strip of sunlight which we call 'now,' canst thou summon the shrouded future to meet her there? Have I not achieved it? Am I not thy prophet?"

Thus with a proud yet melancholy fervor did he almost cry aloud as he passed through the toilsome street among people that knew not of his reveries nor could understand nor care for them. It is not good for man to cherish a solitary ambition. Unless there be those around him by whose example he may regulate himself, his thoughts, desires and hopes will become extravagant and he the semblance—perhaps the reality—of a madman. Reading other bosoms with an acuteness almost preternatural, the painter failed to see the disorder of his own.

"And this should be the house," said he, looking up and down the front before he knocked. "Heaven help my brains! That picture! Methinks it will never vanish. Whether I look at the windows or the door, there it is framed within them, painted strongly and glowing in the richest tints—the faces of the portraits, the figures and action of the sketch!"

He knocked.

"The portraits—are they within?" inquired he of the domestic; then, recollecting himself, "Your master and mistress—are they at home?"

"They are, sir," said the servant, adding, as he noticed that picturesque aspect of which the painter could never divest himself, "and the portraits too."

The guest was admitted into a parlor communicating by a central door with an interior room of the same size. As the first apartment was empty, he passed to the entrance of the second, within which his eyes were greeted by those living personages, as well as their pictured representatives, who had long been the objects of so singular an interest. He involuntarily paused on the threshold.

They had not perceived his approach. Walter and Elinor were standing before the portraits, whence the former had just flung back the rich and voluminous folds of the silken curtain, holding its golden tassel with one hand, while the other grasped that of his bride. The pictures, concealed for months, gleamed forth again in undiminished splendor, appearing to throw a sombre light across the room rather than to be disclosed by a borrowed radiance. That of Elinor had been almost prophetic. A pensiveness, and next a gentle sorrow, had successively dwelt upon her countenance, deepening with the lapse of time into a quiet anguish. A mixture of affright would now have made it the very expression of the portrait. Walter's face was moody and dull or animated only by fitful flashes which left a heavier darkness for their momentary illumination. He looked from Elinor to her portrait, and thence to his own, in the contemplation of which he finally stood absorbed.

The painter seemed to hear the step of Destiny approaching behind him on its progress toward its victims. A strange thought darted into his mind. Was not his own the form in which that Destiny had embodied itself, and he a chief agent of the coming evil which he had foreshadowed?

Still, Walter remained silent before the picture, communing with it as with his own heart and abandoning himself to the spell of evil influence that the painter had cast upon the features. Gradually his eyes kindled, while as Elinor watched the increasing wildness of his face her own assumed a look of terror; and when, at last, he turned upon her, the resemblance of both to their portraits was complete.

"Our fate is upon us!" howled Walter. "Die!"

Drawing a knife, he sustained her as she was sinking to the ground, and aimed it at her bosom. In the action and in the look and attitude of each the painter beheld the figures of his sketch. The picture, with all its tremendous coloring, was finished.

"Hold, madman!" cried he, sternly.

He had advanced from the door and interposed himself between the wretched beings with the same sense of power to regulate their destiny as to alter a scene upon the canvas. He stood like a magician controlling the phantoms which he had evoked.

"What!" muttered Walter Ludlow as he relapsed from fierce excitement into sullen gloom. "Does Fate impede its own decree?"

"Wretched lady," said the painter, "did I not warn you?"

"You did," replied Elinor, calmly, as her terror gave place to the quiet grief which it had disturbed. "But I loved him."

Is there not a deep moral in the tale? Could the result of one or all our deeds be shadowed forth and set before us, some would call it fate and hurry onward, others be swept along by their passionate desires, and none be turned aside by the prophetic pictures.

DAVID SWAN

A FANTASY.

WE CAN BE but partially acquainted even with the events which actually influence our course through life and our final destiny. There are innumerable other events, if such they may be called, which come close upon us, yet pass away without actual results or even betraying their near approach by the reflection of any light or shadow across our minds. Could we know all the vicissitudes of our fortunes, life would be too full of hope and fear, exultation or disappointment, to afford us a single hour of true serenity. This idea may be illustrated by a page from the secret history of David Swan.

We have nothing to do with David until we find him, at the age of twenty, on the high road from his native place to the city of Boston, where his uncle, a small dealer in the grocery line, was to take him behind the counter. Be it enough to say that he was a native of New Hampshire, born of respectable parents, and had received an ordinary school education with a classic finish by a year at Gilmanton Academy. After journeying on foot from sunrise till nearly noon of a summer's day, his weariness and the increasing heat determined him to sit down in the first convenient shade and await the coming up of the stage-coach. As if planted on purpose for him, there soon appeared a little tuft of maples with a delightful recess in the midst, and such a fresh bubbling spring that it seemed never to have sparkled for any wayfarer but David Swan. Virgin or not, he kissed it with his thirsty lips and then flung himself along the brink, pillowing his head upon some shirts and a pair of pantaloons tied up in a striped cotton handkerchief. The sunbeams could not reach him; the dust did not yet rise from the road after the heavy rain of yesterday, and his grassy lair suited the young man better than a bed of down. The spring murmured drowsily beside him; the branches waved dreamily across the blue sky overhead, and a deep sleep, perchance hiding dreams within its depths, fell upon David Swan. But we are to relate events which he did not dream of.

While he lay sound asleep in the shade other people were wide awake, and passed to and fro, afoot, on horseback and in all sorts of vehicles, along the sunny road by his bedchamber. Some looked neither to the right hand nor the left and knew not that he was there; some merely glanced that way without admitting the slumberer among their busy thoughts; some laughed to see how soundly he slept, and several whose hearts were brimming full of scorn ejected their venomous superfluity on David Swan. A middle-aged widow, when nobody else was near, thrust her head a little way into the recess, and vowed that the young fellow looked charming in his sleep. A temperance lecturer saw him, and wrought poor David into the texture of his evening's discourse as an awful instance of dead drunkenness by the roadside.

But censure, praise, merriment, scorn and indifference were all one—or, rather, all nothing—to David Swan. He had slept only a few moments when a brown carriage drawn by a handsome pair of horses bowled easily along and was brought to a standstill nearly in front of David's resting-place. A linch-pin had fallen out and permitted one of the wheels to slide off. The damage was slight and occasioned merely a momentary alarm to an elderly merchant and his wife, who were returning to Boston in the carriage. While the coachman and a servant were replacing the wheel the lady and gentleman sheltered themselves beneath the maple trees, and there espied the bubbling fountain and David Swan asleep beside it. Impressed with the awe which the humblest sleeper usually sheds around him, the merchant trod as lightly as the gout would allow, and his spouse took good heed not to rustle her silk gown lest David should start up all of a sudden.

"How soundly he sleeps!" whispered the old gentleman. "From what a depth he draws that easy breath! Such sleep as that, brought on without an opiate, would be worth more to me than half my income, for it would suppose health and an untroubled mind."

"And youth besides," said the lady. "Healthy and quiet age does not sleep thus. Our slumber is no more like his than our wakefulness."

The longer they looked, the more did this elderly couple feel interested in the unknown youth to whom the wayside and the maple shade were as a secret chamber with the rich gloom of damask curtains brooding over him. Perceiving that a stray sunbeam glimmered down upon his face, the lady contrived to twist a branch aside so as to intercept it, and, having done this little act of kindness, she began to feel like a mother to him.

"Providence seems to have laid him here," whispered she to her husband, "and to have brought us hither to find him, after our disappointment in our cousin's son. Methinks I can see a likeness to our departed Henry. Shall we waken him?"

"To what purpose?" said the merchant, hesitating. "We know nothing of the youth's character."

"That open countenance!" replied his wife, in the same hushed voice, yet earnestly. "This innocent sleep!"

While these whispers were passing, the sleeper's heart did not throb, nor his breath become agitated, nor his features betray the least token of interest. Yet Fortune was bending over him, just ready to let fall a burden of gold. The old merchant had lost his only son, and had no heir to his wealth except a distant relative with whose conduct he was dissatisfied. In such cases people sometimes do stranger things than to act the magician and awaken a young man to splendor who fell asleep in poverty.

"Shall we not waken him?" repeated the lady, persuasively.

"The coach is ready, sir," said the servant, behind.

The old couple started, reddened and hurried away, mutually wondering that they should ever have dreamed of doing anything so very ridiculous. The merchant threw himself back in the carriage and occupied his mind with the plan of a magnificent asylum for unfortunate men of business. Meanwhile, David Swan enjoyed his nap.

The carriage could not have gone above a mile or two when a pretty young girl came along with a tripping pace which showed precisely how her little heart was dancing in her bosom. Perhaps it was this merry kind of motion that caused—is there any harm in saying it?—her garter to slip its knot. Conscious that the silken girth—if silk it were—was relaxing its hold, she turned aside into the shelter of the maple trees, and there found a young man asleep by the spring. Blushing as red as any rose that she should have intruded into a gentleman's bedchamber, and for such a purpose too, she was about to make her escape on tiptoe. But there was peril near the sleeper. A monster of a bee had been wandering overhead—buzz, buzz, buzz —now among the leaves, now flashing through the strips of sunshine, and now lost in the dark shade, till finally he appeared to be settling on the eyelid of David Swan. The sting of a bee is sometimes deadly. As free-hearted as she was innocent, the girl attacked the intruder with her handkerchief, brushed him soundly and drove him from beneath the maple shade. How sweet a picture! This good deed accomplished, with quickened breath and a deeper blush she stole a glance at the youthful stranger for whom she had been battling with a dragon in the air.

"He is handsome!" thought she, and blushed redder yet.

How could it be that no dream of bliss grew so strong within him that, shattered by its very strength, it should part asunder and allow him to perceive the girl among its phantoms? Why, at least, did no smile of welcome brighten upon his face? She was come, the maid whose soul, according to the old and beautiful idea, had been severed from his own, and whom in all his vague but passionate desires he yearned to meet. Her only could he love with a perfect love, him only could she receive into the depths of her heart, and now her image was faintly blushing in the fountain by his side; should it pass away, its happy lustre would never gleam upon his life again.

"How sound he sleeps!" murmured the girl. She departed, but did not trip along the road so lightly as when she came.

Now, this girl's father was a thriving country merchant in the neighborhood, and happened at that identical time to be looking out for just such a young man as David Swan. Had David formed a wayside acquaintance with the daughter, he would have become the father's clerk, and all else in natural succession. So here, again, had good fortune—the best of fortunes— stolen so near that her garments brushed against him, and he knew nothing of the matter.

The girl was hardly out of sight when two men turned aside beneath the maple shade. Both had dark faces set off by cloth caps, which were drawn down aslant over their brows. Their dresses were shabby, yet had a certain smartness. These were a couple of rascals who got their living by whatever the devil sent them, and now, in the interim of other business, had staked the joint profits of their next piece of villainy on a game of cards which was to have been decided here under the trees. But, finding David asleep by the spring, one of the rogues whispered to his fellow:

"Hist! Do you see that bundle under his head?"

The other villain nodded, winked and leered.

"I'll bet you a horn of brandy," said the first, "that the chap has either a pocketbook or a snug little hoard of small change stowed away amongst his shirts. And if not there, we will find it in his pantaloons pocket."

"But how if he wakes?" said the other.

His companion thrust aside his waistcoat, pointed to the handle of a dirk and nodded.

"So be it!" muttered the second villain.

They approached the unconscious David, and, while one pointed the dagger toward his heart, the other began to search the bundle beneath his head. Their two faces, grim, wrinkled and ghastly with guilt and fear, bent over their victim, looking horrible enough to be mistaken for fiends should he suddenly awake. Nay, had the villains glanced aside into the spring, even they would hardly have known themselves as reflected there. But David Swan had never worn a more tranquil aspect, even when asleep on his mother's breast.

"I must take away the bundle," whispered one.

"If he stirs, I'll strike," muttered the other.

But at this moment a dog scenting along the ground came in beneath the maple trees and gazed alternately at each of these wicked men and then at the quiet sleeper. He then lapped out of the fountain.

"Pshaw!" said one villain. "We can do nothing now. The dog's master must be close behind."

"Let's take a drink and be off," said the other.

The man with the dagger thrust back the weapon into his bosom and drew forth a pocket-pistol, but not of that kind which kills by a single discharge. It was a flask of liquor with a block-tin tumbler screwed upon the mouth. Each drank a comfortable dram, and left the spot with so many jests and such laughter at their unaccomplished wickedness that they might be said to have gone on their way rejoicing. In a few hours they had forgotten the whole affair, nor once imagined that the recording angel had written down the crime of murder against their souls in letters as durable as eternity. As for David Swan, he still slept quietly, neither conscious of the shadow of death when it hung over him nor of the glow of renewed life when that shadow was withdrawn. He slept, but no longer so quietly as at first. An hour's repose had snatched from his elastic frame the weariness with which many hours of toil had burdened it. Now he stirred, now moved his lips without a sound, now talked in an inward tone to the noonday spectres of his dream. But a noise of wheels came rattling louder and louder along the road, until it dashed through the dispersing mist of David's slumber; and there was the stagecoach. He started up with all his ideas about him.

"Halloo, driver! Take a passenger?" shouted he.

"Room on top!" answered the driver.

Up mounted David, and bowled away merrily toward Boston without so much as a parting glance at that fountain of dreamlike vicissitude. He knew not that a phantom of Wealth had thrown a golden hue upon its waters, nor that one of Love had sighed softly to their murmur, nor that one of Death had threatened to crimson them with his blood, all in the brief hour since he lay down to sleep. Sleeping or waking, we hear not the airy footsteps of the strange things that almost happen. Does it not argue a superintending Providence that, while viewless and unexpected events thrust themselves continually athwart our path, there should still be regularity enough in mortal life to render foresight even partially available?

SIGHTS FROM A STEEPLE

So! I have climbed high, and my reward is small. Here I stand with wearied knees—earth, indeed, at a dizzy depth below, but heaven far, far beyond me still. Oh that I could soar up into the very zenith, where man never breathed nor eagle ever flew, and where the ethereal azure melts away from the eye and appears only a deepened shade of nothingness! And yet I shiver at that cold and solitary thought. What clouds are gathering in the golden west with direful intent against the brightness and the warmth of this summer afternoon? They are ponderous air-ships, black as death and freighted with the tempest, and at intervals their thunder—the signal-guns of that unearthly squadron—rolls distant along the deep of heaven. These nearer heaps of fleecy vapor—methinks I could roll and toss upon them the whole day long—seem scattered here and there for the repose of tired pilgrims through the sky. Perhaps—for who can tell?—beautiful spirits are disporting themselves there, and will bless my mortal eye with the brief appearance of their curly locks of golden light and laughing faces fair and faint as the people of a rosy dream. Or where the floating mass so imperfectly obstructs the color of the firmament a slender foot and fairy limb resting too heavily upon the frail support may be thrust through and suddenly withdrawn, while longing fancy follows them in vain. Yonder, again, is an airy archipelago where the sunbeams love to linger in their journeyings through space. Every one of those little clouds has been dipped and steeped in radiance which the slightest pressure might disengage in silvery profusion like water wrung from a sea-maid's hair. Bright they are as a young man's visions, and, like them, would be realized in dullness, obscurity and tears. I will look on them no more.

In three parts of the visible circle whose centre is this spire I discern cultivated fields, villages, white country-seats, the waving lines of rivulets, little placid lakes, and here and there a rising ground that would fain be termed a hill. On the fourth side is the sea, stretching away toward a viewless boundary, blue and calm except where the passing anger of a shadow flits across its surface and is gone. Hitherward a broad inlet penetrates far into the land; on the verge of the harbor formed by its extremity is a town, and over it am I, a watchman, all-heeding and unheeded. Oh that the multitude of chimneys could speak, like those of Madrid, and betray in smoky whispers the secrets of all who since their first foundation have assembled at the hearths within! Oh that the Limping Devil of Le Sage would perch beside me here, extend his wand over this contiguity of roofs, uncover every chamber and make me familiar with their inhabitants! The most desirable mode of existence might be that of a spiritualized Paul Pry hovering invisible round man and woman, witnessing their deeds, searching into their hearts, borrowing brightness from their felicity and shade from their sorrow, and retaining no emotion peculiar to himself. But none of these things are possible; and if I would know the interior of brick walls or the mystery of human bosoms, I can but guess.

Yonder is a fair street extending north and south. The stately mansions are placed each on its carpet of verdant grass, and a long flight of steps descends from every door to the pavement. Ornamental trees—the broadleafed horse-chestnut, the elm so lofty and bending, the graceful but infrequent willow, and others whereof I know not the names—grow thrivingly among brick and stone. The oblique rays of the sun are intercepted by these green citizens and by the houses, so that one side of the street is a shaded and pleasant walk. On its whole extent there is now but a single passenger, advancing from the upper end, and he, unless distance and the medium of a pocket spyglass do him more than justice, is a fine young man of twenty. He saunters slowly forward, slapping his left hand with his folded gloves, bending his eyes upon the pavement, and sometimes raising them to throw a glance before him. Certainly he has a pensive air. Is he in doubt or in debt? Is he—if the question be allowable—in love? Does he strive to be melancholy and gentlemanlike, or is he merely overcome by the heat? But I bid him farewell for the present. The door of one of the houses— an aristocratic edifice with curtains of purple and gold waving from the windows—is now opened, and down the steps come two ladies swinging their parasols and lightly arrayed for a summer ramble. Both are young, both are pretty; but methinks the left-hand lass is the fairer of the twain, and, though she be so serious at this moment, I could swear that there is a treasure of gentle fun within her. They stand talking a little while upon the steps, and finally proceed up the street. Meantime, as their faces are now turned from me, I may look elsewhere.

Upon that wharf and down the corresponding street is a busy contrast to the quiet scene which I have just noticed. Business evidently has its centre there, and many a man is wasting the summer afternoon in labor and anxiety, in losing riches or in gaining them, when he would be wiser to flee away to some pleasant country village or shaded lake in the forest or wild and cool sea-beach. I see vessels unlading at the wharf and precious merchandise strown upon the ground abundantly as at the bottom of the sea—that market whence no goods return, and where there is no captain nor supercargo to render an account of sales. Here the clerks are diligent with their paper and pencils and sailors ply the block and tackle that hang over the hold, accompanying their toil with cries long-drawn and roughly melodious till the bales and puncheons ascend to upper air. At a little distance a group of gentlemen are assembled round the door of a warehouse. Grave seniors be they, and I would wager—if it were safe, in these times, to be responsible for any one—that the least eminent among them might vie with old Vincentio, that incomparable trafficker of Pisa. I can even select the wealthiest of the company. It is the elderly personage in somewhat rusty black, with powdered hair the superfluous whiteness of which is visible upon the cape of his coat. His twenty ships are wafted on some of their many courses by every breeze that blows, and his name, I will venture to say, though I know it not, is a familiar sound among the far-separated merchants of Europe and the Indies.

But I bestow too much of my attention in this quarter. On looking again to the long and shady walk I perceive that the two fair girls have encountered the young man. After a sort of shyness in the recognition, he turns back with them. Moreover, he has sanctioned my taste in regard to his companions by placing himself on the inner side of the pavement, nearest the

Venus to whom I, enacting on a steeple-top the part of Paris on the top of Ida, adjudged the golden apple.

In two streets converging at right angles toward my watch-tower I distinguish three different processions. One is a proud array of voluntary soldiers in bright uniform, resembling, from the height whence I look down, the painted veterans that garrison the windows of a toy-shop. And yet it stirs my heart. Their regular advance, their nodding plumes, the sun-flash on their bayonets and musket-barrels, the roll of their drums ascending past me, and the fife ever and anon piercing through,—these things have wakened a warlike fire, peaceful though I be. Close to their rear marches a battalion of schoolboys ranged in crooked and irregular platoons, shouldering sticks, thumping a harsh and unripe clatter from an instrument of tin and ridiculously aping the intricate manoeuvres of the foremost band. Nevertheless, as slight differences are scarcely perceptible from a church-spire, one might be tempted to ask, "Which are the boys?" or, rather, "Which the men?" But, leaving these, let us turn to the third procession, which, though sadder in outward show, may excite identical reflections in the thoughtful mind. It is a funeral—a hearse drawn by a black and bony steed and covered by a dusty pall, two or three coaches rumbling over the stones, their drivers half asleep, a dozen couple of careless mourners in their every-day attire. Such was not the fashion of our fathers when they carried a friend to his grave. There is now no doleful clang of the bell to proclaim sorrow to the town. Was the King of Terrors more awful in those days than in our own, that wisdom and philosophy have been able to produce this change? Not so. Here is a proof that he retains his proper majesty. The military men and the military boys are wheeling round the corner, and meet the funeral full in the face. Immediately the drum is silent, all but the tap that regulates each simultaneous footfall. The soldiers yield the path to the dusty hearse and unpretending train, and the children quit their ranks and cluster on the sidewalks with timorous and instinctive curiosity. The mourners enter the churchyard at the base of the steeple and pause by an open grave among the burial-stones; the lightning glimmers on them as they lower down the coffin, and the thunder rattles heavily while they throw the earth upon its lid. Verily, the shower is near, and I tremble for the young man and the girls, who have now disappeared from the long and shady street.

How various are the situations of the people covered by the roofs beneath me, and how diversified are the events at this moment befalling them! The new-born, the aged, the dying, the strong in life and the recent dead are in the chambers of these many mansions. The full of hope, the happy, the miserable and the desperate dwell together within the circle of my glance. In some of the houses over which my eyes roam so coldly guilt is entering into hearts that are still tenanted by a debased and trodden virtue; guilt is on the very edge of commission, and the impending deed might be averted; guilt is done, and the criminal wonders if it be irrevocable. There are broad thoughts struggling in my mind, and, were I able to give them distinctness, they would make their way in eloquence. Lo! the raindrops are descending.

The clouds within a little time have gathered over all the sky, hanging heavily, as if about to drop in one unbroken mass upon the earth. At intervals the lightning flashes from their brooding hearts, quivers, disappears, and then comes the thunder, travelling slowly after its twin-born flame. A strong wind has sprung up, howls through the darkened streets, and raises the dust in dense bodies to rebel against the approaching storm. The disbanded soldiers fly, the funeral has already vanished like its dead, and all people hurry homeward—all that have a home—while a few lounge by the corners or trudge on desperately at their leisure. In a narrow lane which communicates with the shady street I discern the rich old merchant putting himself to the top of his speed lest the rain should convert his hair-powder to a paste. Unhappy gentleman! By the slow vehemence and painful moderation wherewith he journeys, it is but too evident that Podagra has left its thrilling tenderness in his great toe. But yonder, at a far more rapid pace, come three other of my acquaintance, the two pretty girls and the young man unseasonably interrupted in their walk. Their footsteps are supported by the risen dust, the wind lends them its velocity, they fly like three sea-birds driven landward by the tempestuous breeze. The ladies would not thus rival Atalanta if they but knew that any one were at leisure to observe them. Ah! as they hasten onward, laughing in the angry face of nature, a sudden catastrophe has chanced. At the corner where the narrow lane enters into the street they come plump against the old merchant, whose tortoise-motion has just brought him to that point. He likes not the sweet encounter; the darkness of the whole air gathers speedily upon his visage, and there is a pause on both sides. Finally he thrusts aside the youth with little courtesy, seizes an arm of each of the two girls, and plods onward like a magician with a prize of captive fairies. All this is easy to be understood. How disconsolate the poor lover stands, regardless of the rain that threatens an exceeding damage to his well-fashioned habiliments, till he catches a backward glance of mirth from a bright eye, and turns away with whatever comfort it conveys!

The old man and his daughters are safely housed, and now the storm lets loose its fury. In every dwelling I perceive the faces of the chambermaids as they shut down the windows, excluding the impetuous shower and shrinking away from the quick fiery glare. The large drops descend with force upon the slated roofs and rise again in smoke. There is a rush and roar as of a river through the air, and muddy streams bubble majestically along the pavement, whirl their dusky foam into the kennel, and disappear beneath iron grates. Thus did Arethusa sink. I love not my station here aloft in the midst of the tumult which I am powerless to direct or quell, with the blue lightning wrinkling on my brow and the thunder muttering its first awful syllables in my ear. I will descend. Yet let me give another glance to the sea, where the foam breaks out in long white lines upon a broad expanse of blackness or boils up in far-distant points like snowy mountain-tops in the eddies of a flood; and let me look once more at the green plain and little hills of the country, over which the giant of the storm is striding in robes of mist, and at the town whose obscured and desolate streets might beseem a city of the dead; and, turning a single moment to the sky, now gloomy as an author's prospects, I prepare to resume my station on lower earth. But stay! A little speck of azure has widened in the western heavens; the sunbeams find a passage and go rejoicing through the tempest, and on yonder darkest cloud, born like hallowed hopes of the glory of another world and the trouble and tears of this, brightens forth the rainbow.

THE HOLLOW OF THE THREE HILLS

IN THOSE STRANGE old times when fantastic dreams and madmen's reveries were realized among the actual circumstances of life, two persons met together at an appointed hour and place. One was a lady graceful in form and fair of feature, though pale and troubled and smitten with an untimely blight in what should have been the fullest bloom of her years; the other was an ancient and meanly-dressed woman of ill-favored aspect, and so withered, shrunken and decrepit that even the space since she began to decay must have exceeded the ordinary term of human existence. In the spot where they encountered no mortal could observe them. Three little hills stood near each other, and down in the midst of them sunk a hollow basin almost mathematically circular, two or three hundred feet in breadth and of such depth that a stately cedar might but just be visible above the sides. Dwarf pines were numerous upon the hills and partly fringed the outer verge of the intermediate hollow, within which there was nothing but the brown grass of October and here and there a tree-trunk that had fallen long ago and lay mouldering with no green successor from its roots. One of these masses of decaying wood, formerly a majestic oak, rested close beside a pool of green and sluggish water at the bottom of the basin. Such scenes as this (so gray tradition tells) were once the resort of a power of evil and his plighted subjects, and here at midnight or on the dim verge of evening they were said to stand round the mantling pool disturbing its putrid waters in the performance of an impious baptismal rite. The chill beauty of an autumnal sunset was now gilding the three hill-tops, whence a paler tint stole down their sides into the hollow.

"Here is our pleasant meeting come to pass," said the aged crone, "according as thou hast desired. Say quickly what thou wouldst have of me, for there is but a short hour that we may tarry here."

As the old withered woman spoke a smile glimmered on her countenance like lamplight on the wall of a sepulchre. The lady trembled and cast her eyes upward to the verge of the basin, as if meditating to return with her purpose unaccomplished. But it was not so ordained.

"I am stranger in this land, as you know," said she, at length. "Whence I come it matters not, but I have left those behind me with whom my fate was intimately bound, and from whom I

96

am cut off for ever. There is a weight in my bosom that I cannot away with, and I have come hither to inquire of their welfare."

"And who is there by this green pool that can bring thee news from the ends of the earth?" cried the old woman, peering into the lady's face. "Not from my lips mayst thou hear these tidings; yet be thou bold, and the daylight shall not pass away from yonder hilltop before thy wish be granted."

"I will do your bidding though I die," replied the lady, desperately.

The old woman seated herself on the trunk of the fallen tree, threw aside the hood that shrouded her gray locks and beckoned her companion to draw near.

"Kneel down," she said, "and lay your forehead on my knees."

She hesitated a moment, but the anxiety that had long been kindling burned fiercely up within her. As she knelt down the border of her garment was dipped into the pool; she laid her forehead on the old woman's knees, and the latter drew a cloak about the lady's face, so that she was in darkness. Then she heard the muttered words of prayer, in the midst of which she started and would have arisen.

"Let me flee! Let me flee and hide myself, that they may not look upon me!" she cried. But, with returning recollection, she hushed herself and was still as death, for it seemed as if other voices, familiar in infancy and unforgotten through many wanderings and in all the vicissitudes of her heart and fortune, were mingling with the accents of the prayer. At first the words were faint and indistinct—not rendered so by distance, but rather resembling the dim pages of a book which we strive to read by an imperfect and gradually brightening light. In such a manner, as the prayer proceeded, did those voices strengthen upon the ear, till at length the petition ended, and the conversation of an aged man and of a woman broken and decayed like himself became distinctly audible to the lady as she knelt. But those strangers appeared not to stand in the hollow depth between the three hills. Their voices were encompassed and re-echoed by the walls of a chamber the windows of which were rattling in the breeze; the regular vibration of a clock, the crackling of a fire and the tinkling of the embers as they fell among the ashes rendered the scene almost as vivid as if painted to the eye. By a melancholy hearth sat these two old people, the man calmly despondent, the woman querulous and tearful, and their words were all of sorrow. They spoke of a daughter, a wanderer they knew not where, bearing dishonor along with her and leaving shame and affliction to bring their gray heads to the grave. They alluded also to other and more recent woe, but in the midst of their talk their voices seemed to melt into the sound of the wind sweeping mournfully among the autumn leaves; and when the lady lifted her eyes, there was she kneeling in the hollow between three hills.

"A weary and lonesome time yonder old couple have of it," remarked the old woman, smiling in the lady's face.

"And did you also hear them?" exclaimed she, a sense of intolerable humiliation triumphing over her agony and fear.

"Yea, and we have yet more to hear," replied the old woman, "wherefore cover thy face quickly."

Again the withered hag poured forth the monotonous words of a prayer that was not meant to be acceptable in heaven, and soon in the pauses of her breath strange murmurings began to thicken, gradually increasing, so as to drown and overpower the charm by which they grew. Shrieks pierced through the obscurity of sound and were succeeded by the singing of sweet female voices, which in their turn gave way to a wild roar of laughter broken suddenly by groanings and sobs, forming altogether a ghastly confusion of terror and mourning and mirth. Chains were rattling, fierce and stern voices uttered threats and the scourge resounded at their command. All these noises deepened and became substantial to the listener's ear, till she could distinguish every soft and dreamy accent of the love-songs that died causelessly into funeral-hymns. She shuddered at the unprovoked wrath which blazed up like the spontaneous kindling of flume, and she grew faint at the fearful merriment raging miserably around her. In the midst of this wild scene, where unbound passions jostled each other in a drunken career, there was one solemn voice of a man, and a manly and melodious voice it might once have been. He went to and fro continually, and his feet sounded upon the floor. In each member of that frenzied company whose own burning thoughts had become their exclusive world he sought an auditor for the story of his individual wrong, and interpreted their laughter and tears as his reward of scorn or pity. He spoke of woman's perfidy, of a wife who had broken her holiest vows, of a home and heart made desolate. Even as he went on, the shout, the laugh, the shriek, the sob, rose up in unison, till they changed into the hollow, fitful and uneven sound of the wind as it fought among the pine trees on those three lonely hills.

The lady looked up, and there was the withered woman smiling in her face.

"Couldst thou have thought there were such merry times in a mad-house?" inquired the latter.

"True, true!" said the lady to herself; "there is mirth within its walls, but misery, misery without."

"Wouldst thou hear more?" demanded the old woman.

"There is one other voice I would fain listen to again," replied the lady, faintly.

"Then lay down thy head speedily upon my knees, that thou mayst get thee hence before the hour be past."

The golden skirts of day were yet lingering upon the hills, but deep shades obscured the hollow and the pool, as if sombre night were rising thence to overspread the world. Again that evil woman began to weave her spell. Long did it proceed unanswered, till the knolling of a bell stole in among the intervals of her words like a clang that had travelled far over valley and rising ground and was just ready to die in the air. The lady shook upon her companion's knees as she heard that boding sound. Stronger it grew, and sadder, and deepened into the tone of a death-bell, knolling dolefully from some ivy-mantled tower and bearing tidings of mortality and woe to the cottage, to the hall and to the solitary wayfarer, that all might weep for the doom appointed in turn to them. Then came a measured tread, passing slowly, slowly on, as of mourners with a coffin, their garments trailing on the ground, so that the ear could measure the length of their melancholy array. Before them went the priest, reading the burial-service, while the leaves of his book were rustling in the breeze. And though no voice but his was heard to speak aloud, still there were revilings and anathemas, whispered but distinct, from women and from men, breathed against the daughter who had wrung the aged hearts of her parents, the wife who had betrayed the trusting fondness of her husband, the mother who had sinned against natural affection and left her child to die. The sweeping sound of the funeral train faded away like a thin vapor, and the wind, that just before had seemed to shake the coffin-pall, moaned sadly round the verge of the hollow between three hills. But when the old woman stirred the kneeling lady, she lifted not her head.

"Here has been a sweet hour's sport!" said the withered crone, chuckling to herself.

THE TOLL-GATHERER'S DAY

A SKETCH OF TRANSITORY LIFE.

METHINKS, for a person whose instinct bids him rather to pore over the current of life than to plunge into its tumultuous waves, no undesirable retreat were a toll-house beside some thronged thoroughfare of the land. In youth, perhaps, it is good for the observer to run about the earth, to leave the track of his footsteps far and wide, to mingle himself with the action of numberless vicissitudes, and, finally, in some calm solitude to feed a musing spirit on all that he has seen and felt. But there are natures too indolent or too sensitive to endure the dust, the sunshine or the rain, the turmoil of moral and physical elements, to which all the wayfarers of the world expose themselves. For such a man how pleasant a miracle could life be made to roll its variegated length by the threshold of his own hermitage, and the great globe, as it were, perform its revolutions and shift its thousand scenes before his eyes without whirling him onward in its course! If any mortal be favored with a lot analogous to this, it is the toll-gatherer. So, at least, have I often fancied while lounging on a bench at the door of a small square edifice which stands between shore and shore in the midst of a long bridge. Beneath the timbers ebbs and flows an arm of the sea, while above, like the life-blood through a great artery, the travel of the north and east is continually throbbing. Sitting on the aforesaid bench, I amuse myself with a conception, illustrated by numerous pencil-sketches in the air, of the toll-gatherer's day.

In the morning—dim, gray, dewy summer's morn—the distant roll of ponderous wheels begins to mingle with my old friend's slumbers, creaking more and more harshly through the midst of his dream and gradually replacing it with realities. Hardly conscious of the change from sleep to wakefulness, he finds himself partly clad and throwing wide the toll-gates for the passage of a fragrant load of hay. The timbers groan beneath the slow-revolving wheels; one sturdy yeoman stalks beside the oxen, and, peering from the summit of the hay, by the glimmer of the half-extinguished lantern over the toll-house is seen the drowsy visage of his comrade, who has enjoyed a nap some ten miles long. The toll is paid; creak, creak, again go the wheels, and the huge hay-mow vanishes into the morning mist. As yet nature is but half awake, and familiar objects appear visionary. But yonder, dashing from the shore with a rattling thunder of the wheels and a confused clatter of hoofs, comes the never-tiring mail, which has hurried onward at the same headlong, restless rate all through the quiet night. The bridge resounds in one continued peal as the coach rolls on without a pause, merely affording the toll-gatherer a glimpse at the sleepy passengers, who now bestir their torpid limbs and snuff a cordial in the briny air. The morn breathes upon them and blushes, and they forget how wearily the darkness toiled away. And behold now the fervid day in his bright chariot, glittering aslant over the waves, nor scorning to throw a tribute of his golden beams on the toll-gatherer's little hermitage. The old man looks eastward, and (for he is a moralizer) frames a simile of the stage-coach and the sun.

While the world is rousing itself we may glance slightly at the scene of our sketch. It sits above the bosom of the broad flood—a spot not of earth, but in the midst of waters which rush with a murmuring sound among the massive beams beneath. Over the door is a weatherbeaten board inscribed with the rates of toll in letters so nearly effaced that the gilding of the sunshine can hardly make them legible. Beneath the window is a wooden bench on which a long succession of weary wayfarers have reposed themselves. Peeping within-doors, we perceive the whitewashed walls bedecked with sundry lithographic prints and advertisements of various import and the immense show-bill of a wandering caravan. And there sits our good old toll-gatherer, glorified by the early sunbeams. He is a man, as his aspect may announce, of quiet soul and thoughtful, shrewd, yet simple mind, who of the wisdom which the passing world scatters along the wayside has gathered a reasonable store.

Now the sun smiles upon the landscape and earth smiles back again upon the sky. Frequent now are the travellers. The toll-gatherer's practised ear can distinguish the weight of every vehicle, the number of its wheels and how many horses beat the resounding timbers with their iron tramp. Here, in a substantial family chaise, setting forth betimes to take advantage of the dewy road, come a gentleman and his wife with their rosy-cheeked little girl sitting gladsomely between them. The bottom of the chaise is heaped with multifarious bandboxes and carpet-bags, and beneath the axle swings a leathern trunk dusty with yesterday's journey. Next appears a four-wheeled carryall peopled with a round half dozen of pretty girls, all drawn by a single horse and driven by a single gentleman. Luckless wight doomed through a whole summer day to be the butt of mirth and mischief among the frolicsome maidens! Bolt upright in a sulky rides a thin, sour-visaged man who as he pays his toll hands the toll-gatherer a printed card to stick upon the wall. The vinegar-faced traveller proves to be a manufacturer of pickles. Now paces slowly from timber to timber a horseman clad in black, with a meditative brow, as of one who, whithersoever his steed might bear him, would still journey through a mist of brooding thought. He is a country preacher going to labor at a protracted meeting. The next object passing townward is a butcher's cart canopied with its arch of snow-white cotton. Behind comes a "sauceman" driving a wagon full of new potatoes, green ears of corn, beets, carrots, turnips and summer squashes, and next two wrinkled, withered witch-looking old gossips in an antediluvian chaise drawn by a horse of former generations and going to peddle out a lot of huckleberries. See, there, a man trundling a wheelbarrow-load of lobsters. And now a milk-cart rattles briskly onward, covered with green canvas and conveying the contributions of a whole herd of cows, in large tin canisters.

But let all these pay their toll and pass. Here comes a spectacle that causes the old toll-gatherer to smile benignantly, as if the travellers brought sunshine with them and lavished its gladsome influence all along the road. It is a barouche of the newest style, the varnished panels of which reflect the whole moving panorama of the landscape, and show a picture, likewise, of our friend with his visage broadened, so that his meditative smile is transformed to grotesque merriment. Within sits a youth fresh as the summer morn, and beside him a young lady in white with white gloves upon her slender hands and a white veil flowing down over her face. But methinks her blushing cheek burns through the snowy veil. Another white-robed virgin sits in front. And who are these on whom, and on all that appertains to them, the dust of earth seems never to have settled? Two lovers whom the priest has blessed this blessed morn and sent them forth, with one of the bride-maids, on the matrimonial tour.—Take my blessing too, ye happy ones! May the sky not frown upon you nor clouds bedew you with their chill and sullen rain! May the hot sun kindle no fever in your hearts! May your whole life's pilgrimage be as blissful as this first day's journey, and its close be gladdened with even brighter anticipations than those which hallow your bridal-night! They pass, and ere the reflection of their joy has faded from his face another spectacle throws a melancholy shadow over the spirit of the observing man. In a close carriage sits a fragile figure muffled carefully and shrinking even from the mild breath of summer. She leans against a manly form, and his arm enfolds her as if to guard his treasure from some enemy. Let but a few weeks pass, and when he shall strive to embrace that loved one, he will press only desolation to his heart.

And now has Morning gathered up her dewy pearls and fled away. The sun rolls blazing through the sky, and cannot find a cloud to cool his face with. The horses toil sluggishly along the bridge, and heave their glistening sides in short quick pantings when the reins are tightened at the toll-house. Glisten, too, the faces of the travellers. Their garments are thickly bestrewn with dust; their whiskers and hair look hoary; their throats are choked with the dusty atmosphere which they have left behind them. No air is stirring on the road. Nature dares draw no breath lest she should inhale a stifling cloud of dust. "A hot and dusty day!" cry the poor pilgrims as they wipe their begrimed foreheads and woo the doubtful breeze which the river bears along with it.—"Awful hot! Dreadful dusty!" answers the sympathetic toll-gatherer. They start again to pass through the fiery furnace, while he re-enters his cool hermitage and besprinkles it with a pail of briny water from the stream beneath. He thinks within himself that the sun is not so fierce here as elsewhere, and that the gentle air doth not forget him in these sultry days. Yes, old friend, and a quiet heart will make a dog-day temperate. He hears a weary footstep, and perceives a traveller with pack and staff, who sits down upon the hospitable bench and removes the hat from his wet brow. The toll-gatherer administers a cup of cold water, and, discovering his guest to be a man of homely sense, he engages him in profitable talk, uttering the maxims of a philosophy which he has found in his own soul, but knows not how it came there. And as the wayfarer makes ready to resume his journey he tells him a sovereign remedy for blistered feet.

Now comes the noontide hour—of all the hours, nearest akin to midnight, for each has its own calmness and repose. Soon, however, the world begins to turn again upon its axis, and it seems the busiest epoch of the day, when an accident impedes the march of sublunary things. The draw being lifted to permit the passage of a schooner laden with wood from the Eastern forests, she sticks immovably right athwart the bridge. Meanwhile, on both sides of the chasm a throng of impatient travellers fret and fume. Here are two sailors in a gig with the top thrown back, both puffing cigars and swearing all sorts of forecastle oaths; there, in a smart chaise, a dashingly-dressed gentleman and lady, he from a tailor's shop-board and she from a milliner's back room—the aristocrats of a summer afternoon. And what are the haughtiest of us but the ephemeral aristocrats of a summer's day? Here is a tin-pedler whose glittering ware bedazzles all beholders like a travelling meteor or opposition sun, and on the other side a seller of spruce beer, which brisk liquor is confined in several dozen of stone bottles. Here conic a party of ladies on horseback, in green ridings habits, and gentlemen attendant, and there a flock of sheep for the market, pattering over the bridge with a multitude nous clatter of their little hoofs; here a Frenchman with a hand-organ on his shoulder, and there an itinerant Swiss jeweller. On this side, heralded by a blast of clarions and bugles, appears a train of wagons conveying all the wild beasts of a caravan; and on that a company of summer soldiers marching from village to village on a festival campaign, attended by the "brass band." Now look at the scene, and it presents an emblem of the mysterious confusion, the apparently insolvable riddle, in which individuals, or the great world itself, seem often to be involved. What miracle shall set all things right again?

But see! the schooner has thrust her bulky carcase through the chasm; the draw descends; horse and foot pass onward and leave the bridge vacant from end to end. "And thus," muses the toll-gatherer, "have I found it with all stoppages, even though the universe seemed to be at a stand." The sage old man!

Far westward now the reddening sun throws a broad sheet of splendor across the flood, and to the eyes of distant boatmen gleams brightly among the timbers of the bridge. Strollers come from the town to quaff the freshening breeze. One or two let down long lines and haul up flapping flounders or cunners or small cod, or perhaps an eel. Others, and fair girls among them, with the flush of the hot day still on their cheeks, bend over the railing and watch the heaps of seaweed floating upward with the flowing tide. The horses now tramp heavily along the bridge and wistfully bethink them of their stables.—Rest, rest, thou weary world! for to-morrow's round of toil and pleasure will be as wearisome as to-day's has been, yet both shall bear thee onward a day's march of eternity.—Now the old toll-gatherer looks seaward and discerns the lighthouse kindling on a far island, and the stars, too, kindling in the sky, as if but a little way beyond; and, mingling reveries of heaven with remembrances of earth, the whole procession of mortal travellers, all the dusty pilgrimage which he has witnessed, seems like a flitting show of phantoms for his thoughtful soul to muse upon.

THE VISION OF THE FOUNTAIN

At fifteen I became a resident in a country village more than a hundred miles from home. The morning after my arrival—a September morning, but warm and bright as any in July—I rambled into a wood of oaks with a few walnut trees intermixed, forming the closest shade above my head. The ground was rocky, uneven, overgrown with bushes and clumps of young saplings and traversed only by cattle-paths. The track which I chanced to follow led me to a crystal spring with a border of grass as freshly green as on May morning, and overshadowed by the limb of a great oak. One solitary sunbeam found its way down and played like a goldfish in the water.

From my childhood I have loved to gaze into a spring. The water filled a circular basin, small but deep and set round with stones, some of which were covered with slimy moss, the others naked and of variegated hue—reddish, white and brown. The bottom was covered with coarse sand, which sparkled in the lonely sunbeam and seemed to illuminate the spring with an unborrowed light. In one spot the gush of the water violently agitated the sand, but without obscuring the fountain or breaking the glassiness of its surface. It appeared as if some living creature were about to emerge—the naiad of the spring, perhaps, in the shape of a beautiful young woman with a gown of filmy water-moss, a belt of rainbow-drops and a cold, pure, passionless countenance. How would the beholder shiver, pleasantly yet fearfully, to see her sitting on one of the stones, paddling her white feet in the ripples and throwing up water to sparkle in the sun! Wherever she laid her hands on grass and flowers, they would immediately be moist, as with morning dew. Then would she set about her labors, like a careful housewife, to clear the fountain of withered leaves, and bits of slimy wood, and old acorns from the oaks above, and grains of corn left by cattle in drinking, till the bright sand in the bright water were like a treasury of diamonds. But, should the intruder approach too near, he would find only the drops of a summer shower glistening about the spot where he had seen her.

Reclining on the border of grass where the dewy goddess should have been, I bent forward, and a pair of eyes met mine within the watery mirror. They were the reflection of my own. I looked again, and, lo! another face, deeper in the fountain than my own image, more distinct in all the features, yet faint as thought. The vision had the aspect of a fair young girl with locks of paly gold. A mirthful expression laughed in the eyes and dimpled over the whole shadowy countenance, till it seemed just what a fountain would be if, while dancing merrily into the sunshine, it should assume the shape of woman. Through the dim rosiness of the cheeks I could see the brown leaves, the slimy twigs, the acorns and the sparkling sand. The solitary sunbeam was diffused among the golden hair, which melted into its faint brightness and became a glory round that head so beautiful.

My description can give no idea how suddenly the fountain was thus tenanted and how soon it was left desolate. I breathed, and there was the face; I held my breath, and it was gone. Had it passed away or faded into nothing? I doubted whether it had ever been.

My sweet readers, what a dreamy and delicious hour did I spend where that vision found and left me! For a long time I sat perfectly still, waiting till it should reappear, and fearful that the slightest motion, or even the flutter of my breath, might frighten it away. Thus have I often started from a pleasant dream, and then kept quiet in hopes to wile it back. Deep were my musings as to the race and attributes of that ethereal being. Had I created her? Was she the daughter of my fancy, akin to those strange shapes which peep under the lids of children's eyes? And did her beauty gladden me for that one moment and then die? Or was she a water-nymph within the fountain, or fairy or woodland goddess peeping over my shoulder, or the ghost of some forsaken maid who had drowned herself for love? Or, in good truth, had a lovely girl with a warm heart and lips that would bear pressure stolen softly behind me and thrown her image into the spring?

I watched and waited, but no vision came again. I departed, but with a spell upon me which drew me back that same afternoon to the haunted spring. There was the water gushing, the sand sparkling and the sunbeam glimmering. There the vision was not, but only a great frog, the hermit of that solitude, who immediately withdrew his speckled snout and made himself invisible—all except a pair of long legs—beneath a stone. Methought he had a devilish look. I could have slain him as an enchanter who kept the mysterious beauty imprisoned in the fountain.

Sad and heavy, I was returning to the village. Between me and the church-spire rose a little hill, and on its summit a group of trees insulated from all the rest of the wood, with their own share of radiance hovering on them from the west and their own solitary shadow falling to the east. The afternoon being far declined, the sunshine was almost pensive and the shade almost cheerful; glory and gloom were mingled in the placid light, as if the spirits of the Day and Evening had met in friendship under those trees and found themselves akin. I was admiring the picture when the shape of a young girl emerged from behind the clump of oaks. My heart knew her: it was the vision, but so distant and ethereal did she seem, so unmixed with earth, so imbued with the pensive glory of the spot where she was standing, that my spirit sunk within me, sadder than before. How could I ever reach her?

While I gazed a sudden shower came pattering down upon the leaves. In a moment the air was full of brightness, each raindrop catching a portion of sunlight as it fell, and the whole gentle shower appearing like a mist, just substantial enough to bear the burden of radiance. A rainbow vivid as Niagara's was painted in the air. Its southern limb came down before the group of trees and enveloped the fair vision as if the hues of heaven were the only garment for her beauty. When the rainbow vanished, she who had seemed a part of it was no longer there. Was her existence absorbed in nature's loveliest phenomenon, and did her pure frame dissolve away in the varied light? Yet I would not despair of her return, for, robed in the rainbow, she was the emblem of Hope.

Thus did the vision leave me, and many a doleful day succeeded to the parting moment. By the spring and in the wood and on the hill and through the village, at dewy sunrise, burning noon, and at that magic hour of sunset, when she had vanished from my sight, I sought her, but in vain. Weeks came and went, months rolled away, and she appeared not in them. I imparted my mystery to none, but wandered to and fro or sat in solitude like one that had caught a glimpse of heaven and could take no more joy on earth. I withdrew into an inner world where my thoughts lived and breathed, and the vision in the midst of them. Without intending it, I became at once the author and hero of a romance, conjuring up rivals, imagining events, the actions of others and my own, and experiencing every change of passion, till jealousy and despair had their end in bliss. Oh, had I the burning fancy of my early youth with manhood's colder gift, the power of expression, your hearts, sweet ladies, should flutter at my tale.

In the middle of January I was summoned home. The day before my departure, visiting the spots which had been hallowed by the vision, I found that the spring had a frozen bosom, and nothing but the snow and a glare of winter sunshine on the hill of the rainbow. "Let me hope," thought I, "or my heart will be as icy as the fountain and the whole world as desolate as this snowy hill." Most of the day was spent in preparing for the journey, which was to commence at four o'clock the next morning. About an hour after supper, when all was in readiness, I descended from my chamber to the sitting-room to take leave of the old clergyman and his family with whom I had been an inmate. A gust of wind blew out my lamp as I passed through the entry.

According to their invariable custom—so pleasant a one when the fire blazes cheerfully— the family were sitting in the parlor with no other light than what came from the hearth. As the good clergyman's scanty stipend compelled him to use all sorts of economy, the foundation of his fires was always a large heap of tan, or ground bark, which would smoulder away from morning till night with a dull warmth and no flame. This evening the heap of tan was newly put on and surmounted with three sticks of red oak full of moisture, and a few pieces of dry pine that had not yet kindled. There was no light except the little that came sullenly from two half-burnt brands, without even glimmering on the andirons. But I knew the position of the old minister's arm-chair, and also where his wife sat with her knitting-work, and how to avoid his two daughters—one a stout country lass, and the other a consumptive girl. Groping through the gloom, I found my own place next to that of the son, a learned collegian who had come home to keep school in the village during the winter vacation. I noticed that there was less room than usual to-night between the collegian's chair and mine.

As people are always taciturn in the dark, not a word was said for some time after my entrance. Nothing broke the stillness but the regular click of the matron's knitting-needles. At times the fire threw out a brief and dusky gleam which twinkled on the old man's glasses and hovered doubtfully round our circle, but was far too faint to portray the individuals who composed it. Were we not like ghosts? Dreamy as the scene was, might it not be a type of the mode in which departed people who had known and loved each other here would hold communion in eternity? We were aware of each other's presence, not by sight nor sound nor touch, but by an inward consciousness. Would it not be so among the dead?

The silence was interrupted by the consumptive daughter addressing a remark to some one in the circle whom she called Rachel. Her tremulous and decayed accents were answered by a single word, but in a voice that made me start and bend toward the spot whence it had proceeded. Had I ever heard that sweet, low tone? If not, why did it rouse up so many old recollections, or mockeries of such, the shadows of things familiar yet unknown, and fill my mind with confused images of her features who had spoken, though buried in the gloom of the parlor? Whom had my heart recognized, that it throbbed so? I listened to catch her gentle breathing, and strove by the intensity of my gaze to picture forth a shape where none was visible.

Suddenly the dry pine caught; the fire blazed up with a ruddy glow, and where the darkness had been, there was she—the vision of the fountain. A spirit of radiance only, she had vanished with the rainbow and appeared again in the firelight, perhaps to flicker with the blaze and be gone. Yet her cheek was rosy and lifelike, and her features, in the bright warmth of the room, were even sweeter and tenderer than my recollection of them. She knew me. The mirthful expression that had laughed in her eyes and dimpled over her countenance when I beheld her faint beauty in the fountain was laughing and dimpling there now. One moment our glance mingled; the next, down rolled the heap of tan upon the kindled wood, and darkness snatched away that daughter of the light, and gave her back to me no more!

Fair ladies, there is nothing more to tell. Must the simple mystery be revealed, then, that Rachel was the daughter of the village squire and had left home for a boarding-school the morning after I arrived and returned the day before my departure? If I transformed her to an angel, it is what every youthful lover does for his mistress. Therein consists the essence of my story. But slight the change, sweet maids, to make angels of yourselves.

FANCY'S SHOW-BOX

A MORALITY.

WHAT IS GUILT? A stain upon the soul. And it is a point of vast interest whether the soul may contract such stains in all their depth and flagrancy from deeds which may have been plotted and resolved upon, but which physically have never had existence. Must the fleshly hand and visible frame of man set its seal to the evil designs of the soul, in order to give them their entire validity against the sinner? Or, while none but crimes perpetrated are cognizable before an earthly tribunal, will guilty thoughts—of which guilty deeds are no more than shadows,—will these draw down the full weight of a condemning sentence in the supreme court of eternity? In the solitude of a midnight chamber or in a desert afar from men or in a church while the body is kneeling the soul may pollute itself even with those crimes which we are accustomed to deem altogether carnal. If this be true, it is a fearful truth.

Let us illustrate the subject by an imaginary example. A venerable gentleman—one Mr. Smith—who had long been regarded as a pattern of moral excellence was warming his aged blood with a glass or two of generous wine. His children being gone forth about their worldly business and his grandchildren at school, he sat alone in a deep luxurious arm-chair with his feet beneath a richly-carved mahogany table. Some old people have a dread of solitude, and when better company may not be had rejoice even to hear the quiet breathing of a babe asleep upon the carpet. But Mr. Smith, whose silver hair was the bright symbol of a life unstained except by such spots as are inseparable from human nature—he had no need of a babe to protect him by its purity, nor of a grown person to stand between him and his own soul. Nevertheless, either manhood must converse with age, or womanhood must soothe him with gentle cares, or infancy must sport around his chair, or his thoughts will stray into the misty region of the past and the old man be chill and sad. Wine will not always cheer him.

Such might have been the case with Mr. Smith, when, through the brilliant medium of his glass of old Madeira, he beheld three figures entering the room. These were Fancy, who had assumed the garb and aspect of an itinerant showman, with a box of pictures on her back; and Memory, in the likeness of a clerk, with a pen behind her ear, an inkhorn at her buttonhole and a huge manuscript volume beneath her arm; and lastly, behind the other two, a person shrouded in a dusky mantle which concealed both face and form. But Mr. Smith had a shrewd idea that it was Conscience. How kind of Fancy, Memory and Conscience to visit the old gentleman just as he was beginning to imagine that the wine had neither so bright a sparkle nor so excellent a flavor as when himself and the liquor were less aged! Through the dim length of the apartment, where crimson curtains muffled the glare of sunshine and created a rich obscurity, the three guests drew near the silver-haired old man. Memory, with a finger between the leaves of her huge volume, placed herself at his right hand; Conscience, with her face still hidden in the dusky mantle, took her station on the left, so as to be next his heart; while Fancy set down her picture-box upon the table with the magnifying-glass convenient to his eye.

We can sketch merely the outlines of two or three out of the many pictures which at the pulling of a string successively peopled the box with the semblances of living scenes. One was a moonlight picture, in the background a lowly dwelling, and in front, partly shadowed by a tree, yet besprinkled with flakes of radiance, two youthful figures, male and female. The young man stood with folded arms, a haughty smile upon his lip and a gleam of triumph in his eye as he glanced downward at the kneeling girl. She was almost prostrate at his feet, evidently sinking under a weight of shame and anguish which hardly allowed her to lift her clasped hands in supplication. Her eyes she could not lift. But neither her agony, nor the lovely features on which it was depicted, nor the slender grace of the form which it convulsed, appeared to soften the obduracy of the young man. He was the personification of triumphant scorn.

Now, strange to say, as old Mr. Smith peeped through the magnifying-glass, which made the objects start out from the canvas with magical deception, he began to recognize the farmhouse, the tree and both the figures of the picture. The young man in times long past had often met his gaze within the looking-glass; the girl was the very image of his first love—his cottage-love, his Martha Burroughs. Mr. Smith was scandalized. "Oh, vile and slanderous picture!" he exclaims. "When have I triumphed over ruined innocence? Was not Martha wedded in her teens to David Tomkins, who won her girlish love and long enjoyed her affection as a wife? And ever since his death she has lived a reputable widow!"

Meantime, Memory was turning over the leaves of her volume, rustling them to and fro with uncertain fingers, until among the earlier pages she found one which had reference to this picture. She reads it close to the old gentleman's ear: it is a record merely of sinful thought which never was embodied in an act, but, while Memory is reading, Conscience unveils her face and strikes a dagger to the heart of Mr. Smith. Though not a death-blow, the torture was extreme.

The exhibition proceeded. One after another Fancy displayed her pictures, all of which appeared to have been painted by some malicious artist on purpose to vex Mr. Smith. Not a shadow of proof could have been adduced in any earthly court that he was guilty of the slightest of those sins which were thus made to stare him in the face. In one scene there was a table set out, with several bottles and glasses half filled with wine, which threw back the dull ray of an expiring lamp. There had been mirth and revelry until the hand of the clock stood just at midnight, when Murder stepped between the boon-companions. A young man had fallen on the floor, and lay stone dead with a ghastly wound crushed into his temple, while over him, with a delirium of mingled rage and horror in his countenance, stood the youthful likeness of Mr. Smith. The murdered youth wore the features of Edward Spencer. "What does this rascal of a painter mean?" cries Mr. Smith, provoked beyond all patience. "Edward Spencer was my earliest and dearest friend, true to me as I to him through more than half a century. Neither I nor any other ever murdered him. Was he not alive within five years, and did he not, in token of our long friendship, bequeath me his gold-headed cane and a mourning-ring?"

Again had Memory been turning over her volume, and fixed at length upon so confused a page that she surely must have scribbled it when she was tipsy. The purport was, however, that while Mr. Smith and Edward Spencer were heating their young blood with wine a quarrel had flashed up between them, and Mr. Smith, in deadly wrath, had flung a bottle at Spencer's head. True, it missed its aim and merely smashed a looking-glass; and the next morning, when the incident was imperfectly remembered, they had shaken hands with a hearty laugh. Yet, again, while Memory was reading, Conscience unveiled her face, struck a dagger to the heart of Mr. Smith and quelled his remonstrance with her iron frown. The pain was quite excruciating.

Some of the pictures had been painted with so doubtful a touch, and in colors so faint and pale, that the subjects could barely be conjectured. A dull, semi-transparent mist had been thrown over the surface of the canvas, into which the figures seemed to vanish while the eye sought most earnestly to fix them. But in every scene, however dubiously portrayed, Mr. Smith was invariably haunted by his own lineaments at various ages as in a dusty mirror. After poring several minutes over one of these blurred and almost indistinguishable pictures, he began to see that the painter had intended to represent him, now in the decline of life, as stripping the clothes from the backs of three half-starved children. "Really, this puzzles me!" quoth Mr. Smith, with the irony of conscious rectitude. "Asking pardon of the painter, I pronounce him a fool as well as a scandalous knave. A man of my standing in the world to be robbing little children of their clothes! Ridiculous!"

But while he spoke Memory had searched her fatal volume and found a page which with her sad calm voice she poured into his ear. It was not altogether inapplicable to the misty scene. It told how Mr. Smith had been grievously tempted by many devilish sophistries, on the ground of a legal quibble, to commence a lawsuit against three orphan-children, joint-heirs to a considerable estate. Fortunately, before he was quite decided, his claims had turned out nearly as devoid of law as justice. As Memory ceased to read Conscience again thrust aside her mantle, and would have struck her victim with the envenomed dagger only that he struggled and clasped his hands before his heart. Even then, however, he sustained an ugly gash.

Why should we follow Fancy through the whole series of those awful pictures? Painted by an artist of wondrous power and terrible acquaintance with the secret soul, they embodied the ghosts of all the never-perpetrated sins that had glided through the lifetime of Mr. Smith. And could such beings of cloudy fantasy, so near akin to nothingness, give valid evidence against him at the day of judgment? Be that the case or not, there is reason to believe that one truly penitential tear would have washed away each hateful picture and left the canvas white as snow. But Mr. Smith, at a prick of Conscience too keen to be endured, bellowed aloud with impatient agony, and suddenly discovered that his three guests were gone. There he sat alone, a silver-haired and highly-venerated old man, in the rich gloom of the crimsoned-curtained room, with no box of pictures on the table, but only a decanter of most excellent Madeira. Yet his heart still seemed to fester with the venom of the dagger.

Nevertheless, the unfortunate old gentleman might have argued the matter with Conscience and alleged many reasons wherefore she should not smite him so pitilessly. Were we to take up his cause, it should be somewhat in the following fashion. A scheme of guilt, till it be put in execution, greatly resembles a train of incidents in a projected tale. The latter, in order to produce a sense of reality in the reader's mind, must be conceived with such proportionate strength by the author as to seem in the glow of fancy more like truth, past, present or to come, than purely fiction. The prospective sinner, on the other hand, weaves his plot of crime, but seldom or never feels a perfect certainty that it will be executed. There is a dreaminess diffused about his thoughts; in a dream, as it were, he strikes the death-blow into his victim's heart and starts to find an indelible blood-stain on his hand. Thus a novel-writer or a dramatist, in creating a villain of romance and fitting him with evil deeds, and the villain of actual life in projecting crimes that will be perpetrated, may almost meet each other halfway between reality and fancy. It is not until the crime is accomplished that Guilt clenches its gripe upon the guilty heart and claims it for his own. Then, and not before, sin is actually felt and acknowledged, and, if unaccompanied by repentance, grows a thousandfold more virulent by its self-consciousness. Be it considered, also, that men often overestimate their capacity for evil. At a distance, while its attendant circumstances do not press upon their notice and its results are dimly seen, they can bear to contemplate it. They may take the steps which lead to crime, impelled by the same sort of mental action as in working out a mathematical problem, yet be powerless with compunction at the final moment. They knew not what deed it was that they deemed themselves resolved to do. In truth, there is no such thing in man's nature as a settled and full resolve, either for good or evil, except at the very moment of execution. Let us hope, therefore, that all the dreadful consequences of sin will not be incurred unless the act have set its seal upon the thought.

Yet, with the slight fancy-work which we have framed, some sad and awful truths are interwoven. Man must not disclaim his brotherhood even with the guiltiest, since, though his hand be clean, his heart has surely been polluted by the flitting phantoms of iniquity. He must feel that when he shall knock at the gate of heaven no semblance of an unspotted life can entitle him to entrance there. Penitence must kneel and Mercy come from the footstool of the throne, or that golden gate will never open.

DR. HEIDEGGER'S EXPERIMENT

THAT VERY SINGULAR man old Dr. Heidegger once invited four venerable friends to meet him in his study. There were three white-bearded gentlemen—Mr. Medbourne, Colonel Killigrew and Mr. Gascoigne—and a withered gentlewoman whose name was the widow Wycherly. They were all melancholy old creatures who had been unfortunate in life, and whose greatest misfortune it was that they were not long ago in their graves. Mr. Medbourne, in the vigor of his age, had been a prosperous merchant, but had lost his all by a frantic speculation, and was now little better than a mendicant. Colonel Killigrew had wasted his best years and his health and substance in the pursuit of sinful pleasures which had given birth to a brood of pains, such as the gout and divers other torments of soul and body. Mr. Gascoigne was a ruined politician, a man of evil fame—or, at least, had been so till time had buried him from the knowledge of the present generation and made him obscure instead of infamous. As for the widow Wycherly, tradition tells us that she was a great beauty in her day, but for a long while past she had lived in deep seclusion on account of certain scandalous stories which had prejudiced the gentry of the town against her. It is a circumstance worth mentioning that each of these three old gentlemen—Mr. Medbourne, Colonel Killigrew and Mr. Gascoigne—were early lovers of the widow Wycherly, and had once been on the point of cutting each other's throats for her sake. And before proceeding farther I will merely hint that Dr. Heidegger and all his four guests were sometimes thought to be a little beside themselves, as is not infrequently the case with old people when worried either by present troubles or woeful recollections.

"My dear old friends," said Dr. Heidegger, motioning them to be seated, "I am desirous of your assistance in one of those little experiments with which I amuse myself here in my study."

If all stories were true, Dr. Heidegger's study must have been a very curious place. It was a dim, old-fashioned chamber festooned with cobwebs and besprinkled with antique dust. Around the walls stood several oaken bookcases, the lower shelves of which were filled with rows of gigantic folios and black-letter quartos, and the upper with little parchment-covered duodecimos. Over the central bookcase was a bronze bust of Hippocrates, with which, according to some authorities, Dr. Heidegger was accustomed to hold consultations in all difficult cases of his practice. In the obscurest corner of the room stood a tall and narrow oaken closet with its door ajar, within which doubtfully appeared a skeleton. Between two of the bookcases hung a looking-glass, presenting its high and dusty plate within a tarnished gilt frame. Among many wonderful stories related of this mirror, it was fabled that the spirits of all the doctor's deceased patients dwelt within its verge and would stare him in the face whenever he looked thitherward. The opposite side of the chamber was ornamented with the full-length portrait of a young lady arrayed in the faded magnificence of silk, satin and brocade, and with a visage as faded as her dress. Above half a century ago Dr. Heidegger had been on the point of marriage with this young lady, but, being affected with some slight disorder, she had swallowed one of her lover's prescriptions and died on the bridal-evening. The greatest curiosity of the study remains to be mentioned: it was a ponderous folio volume bound in black leather, with massive silver clasps. There were no letters on the back, and nobody could tell the title of the book. But it was well known to be a book of magic, and once, when a chambermaid had lifted it merely to brush away the dust, the skeleton had rattled in its closet, the picture of the young lady had stepped one foot upon the floor and several ghastly faces had peeped forth from the mirror, while the brazen head of Hippocrates frowned and said, "Forbear!"

Such was Dr. Heidegger's study. On the summer afternoon of our tale a small round table as black as ebony stood in the centre of the room, sustaining a cut-glass vase of beautiful form and elaborate workmanship. The sunshine came through the window between the heavy festoons of two faded damask curtains and fell directly across this vase, so that a mild splendor was reflected from it on the ashen visages of the five old people who sat around. Four champagne-glasses were also on the table.

"My dear old friends," repeated Dr. Heidegger, "may I reckon on your aid in performing an exceedingly curious experiment?"

Now, Dr. Heidegger was a very strange old gentleman whose eccentricity had become the nucleus for a thousand fantastic stories. Some of these fables—to my shame be it spoken— might possibly be traced back to mine own veracious self; and if any passages of the present tale should startle the reader's faith, I must be content to bear the stigma of a fiction-monger.

When the doctor's four guests heard him talk of his proposed experiment, they anticipated nothing more wonderful than the murder of a mouse in an air-pump or the examination of a cobweb by the microscope, or some similar nonsense with which he was constantly in the habit of pestering his intimates. But without waiting for a reply Dr. Heidegger hobbled across the chamber and returned with the same ponderous folio bound in black leather which common report affirmed to be a book of magic. Undoing the silver clasps, he opened the volume and took from among its black-letter pages a rose, or what was once a rose, though now the green leaves and crimson petals had assumed one brownish hue and the ancient flower seemed ready to crumble to dust in the doctor's hands.

"This rose," said Dr. Heidegger, with a sigh—"this same withered and crumbling flower— blossomed five and fifty years ago. It was given me by Sylvia Ward, whose portrait hangs yonder, and I meant to wear it in my bosom at our wedding. Five and fifty years it has been treasured between the leaves of this old volume. Now, would you deem it possible that this rose of half a century could ever bloom again?"

"Nonsense!" said the widow Wycherly, with a peevish toss of her head. "You might as well ask whether an old woman's wrinkled face could ever bloom again."

"See!" answered Dr. Heidegger. He uncovered the vase and threw the faded rose into the water which it contained. At first it lay lightly on the surface of the fluid, appearing to imbibe none of its moisture. Soon, however, a singular change began to be visible. The crushed and dried petals stirred and assumed a deepening tinge of crimson, as if the flower were reviving from a deathlike slumber, the slender stalk and twigs of foliage became green, and there was the rose of half a century, looking as fresh as when Sylvia Ward had first given it to her lover. It was scarcely full-blown, for some of its delicate red leaves curled modestly around its moist bosom, within which two or three dewdrops were sparkling.

"That is certainly a very pretty deception," said the doctor's friends—carelessly, however, for they had witnessed greater miracles at a conjurer's show. "Pray, how was it effected?"

"Did you never hear of the Fountain of Youth?" asked Dr. Heidegger, "which Ponce de Leon, the Spanish adventurer, went in search of two or three centuries ago?"

"But did Ponce de Leon ever find it?" said the widow Wycherly.

"No," answered Dr. Heidegger, "for he never sought it in the right place. The famous Fountain of Youth, if I am rightly informed, is situated in the southern part of the Floridian peninsula, not far from Lake Macaco. Its source is overshadowed by several gigantic magnolias which, though numberless centuries old, have been kept as fresh as violets by the virtues of this wonderful water. An acquaintance of mine, knowing my curiosity in such matters, has sent me what you see in the vase."

"Ahem!" said Colonel Killigrew, who believed not a word of the doctor's story; "and what may be the effect of this fluid on the human frame?"

"You shall judge for yourself, my dear colonel," replied Dr. Heidegger.—"And all of you, my respected friends, are welcome to so much of this admirable fluid as may restore to you the bloom of youth. For my own part, having had much trouble in growing old, I am in no hurry to grow young again. With your permission, therefore, I will merely watch the progress of the experiment."

While he spoke Dr. Heidegger had been filling the four champagne-glasses with the water of the Fountain of Youth. It was apparently impregnated with an effervescent gas, for little bubbles were continually ascending from the depths of the glasses and bursting in silvery spray at the surface. As the liquor diffused a pleasant perfume, the old people doubted not that it possessed cordial and comfortable properties, and, though utter sceptics as to its rejuvenescent power, they were inclined to swallow it at once. But Dr. Heidegger besought them to stay a moment.

"Before you drink, my respectable old friends," said he, "it would be well that, with the experience of a lifetime to direct you, you should draw up a few general rules for your guidance in passing a second time through the perils of youth. Think what a sin and shame it would be if, with your peculiar advantages, you should not become patterns of virtue and wisdom to all the young people of the age!"

The doctor's four venerable friends made him no answer except by a feeble and tremulous laugh, so very ridiculous was the idea that, knowing how closely Repentance treads behind the steps of Error, they should ever go astray again.

"Drink, then," said the doctor, bowing; "I rejoice that I have so well selected the subjects of my experiment."

With palsied hands they raised the glasses to their lips. The liquor, if it really possessed such virtues as Dr. Heidegger imputed to it, could not have been bestowed on four human beings who needed it more woefully. They looked as if they had never known what youth or pleasure was, but had been the offspring of Nature's dotage, and always the gray, decrepit, sapless, miserable creatures who now sat stooping round the doctor's table without life enough in their souls or bodies to be animated even by the prospect of growing young again. They drank off the water and replaced their glasses on the table.

Assuredly, there was an almost immediate improvement in the aspect of the party—not unlike what might have been produced by a glass of generous wine—together with a sudden glow of cheerful sunshine, brightening over all their visages at once. There was a healthful suffusion on their cheeks instead of the ashen hue that had made them look so corpse-like. They gazed at one another, and fancied that some magic power had really begun to smooth away the deep and sad inscriptions which Father Time had been so long engraving on their brows. The widow Wycherly adjusted her cap, for she felt almost like a woman again.

"Give us more of this wondrous water," cried they, eagerly. "We are younger, but we are still too old. Quick! give us more!"

"Patience, patience!" quoth Dr. Heidegger, who sat, watching the experiment with philosophic coolness. "You have been a long time growing old; surely you might be content to grow young in half an hour. But the water is at your service." Again he filled their glasses with the liquor of youth, enough of which still remained in the vase to turn half the old people in the city to the age of their own grandchildren.

While the bubbles were yet sparkling on the brim the doctor's four guests snatched their glasses from the table and swallowed the contents at a single gulp. Was it delusion? Even while the draught was passing down their throats it seemed to have wrought a change on their whole systems. Their eyes grew clear and bright; a dark shade deepened among their silvery locks: they sat around the table three gentlemen of middle age and a woman hardly beyond her buxom prime.

"My dear widow, you are charming!" cried Colonel Killigrew, whose eyes had been fixed upon her face while the shadows of age were flitting from it like darkness from the crimson daybreak.

The fair widow knew of old that Colonel Killigrew's compliments were not always measured by sober truth; so she started up and ran to the mirror, still dreading that the ugly visage of an old woman would meet her gaze.

Meanwhile, the three gentlemen behaved in such a manner as proved that the water of the Fountain of Youth possessed some intoxicating qualities—unless, indeed, their exhilaration of spirits were merely a lightsome dizziness caused by the sudden removal of the weight of years. Mr. Gascoigne's mind seemed to run on political topics, but whether relating to the past, present or future could not easily be determined, since the same ideas and phrases have been in vogue these fifty years. Now he rattled forth full-throated sentences about patriotism, national glory and the people's right; now he muttered some perilous stuff or other in a sly and doubtful whisper, so cautiously that even his own conscience could scarcely catch the secret; and now, again, he spoke in measured accents and a deeply-deferential tone, as if a royal ear were listening to his well-turned periods. Colonel Killigrew all this time had been trolling forth a jolly bottle-song and ringing his glass in symphony with the chorus, while his eyes wandered toward the buxom figure of the widow Wycherly. On the other side of the table, Mr. Medbourne was involved in a calculation of dollars and cents with which was strangely intermingled a project for supplying the East Indies with ice by harnessing a team of whales to the polar icebergs. As for the widow Wycherly, she stood before the mirror courtesying and simpering to her own image and greeting it as the friend whom she loved better than all the world besides. She thrust her face close to the glass to see whether some long-remembered wrinkle or crow's-foot had indeed vanished; she examined whether the snow had so entirely melted from her hair that the venerable cap could be safely thrown aside. At last, turning briskly away, she came with a sort of dancing step to the table.

"My dear old doctor," cried she, "pray favor me with another glass."

"Certainly, my dear madam—certainly," replied the complaisant doctor. "See! I have already filled the glasses."

There, in fact, stood the four glasses brimful of this wonderful water, the delicate spray of which, as it effervesced from the surface, resembled the tremulous glitter of diamonds.

It was now so nearly sunset that the chamber had grown duskier than ever, but a mild and moonlike splendor gleamed from within the vase and rested alike on the four guests and on the doctor's venerable figure. He sat in a high-backed, elaborately-carved oaken arm-chair with a gray dignity of aspect that might have well befitted that very Father Time whose power had never been disputed save by this fortunate company. Even while quaffing the third draught of the Fountain of Youth, they were almost awed by the expression of his mysterious visage. But the next moment the exhilarating gush of young life shot through their veins. They were now in the happy prime of youth. Age, with its miserable train of cares and sorrows and diseases, was remembered only as the trouble of a dream from which they had joyously awoke. The fresh gloss of the soul, so early lost and without which the world's successive scenes had been but a gallery of faded pictures, again threw its enchantment over all their prospects. They felt like new-created beings in a new-created universe.

"We are young! We are young!" they cried, exultingly.

Youth, like the extremity of age, had effaced the strongly-marked characteristics of middle life and mutually assimilated them all. They were a group of merry youngsters almost maddened with the exuberant frolicsomeness of their years. The most singular effect of their gayety was an impulse to mock the infirmity and decrepitude of which they had so lately been the victims. They laughed loudly at their old-fashioned attire—the wide-skirted coats and flapped waistcoats of the young men and the ancient cap and gown of the blooming girl. One limped across the floor like a gouty grandfather; one set a pair of spectacles astride of his nose and pretended to pore over the black-letter pages of the book of magic; a third seated himself in an arm-chair and strove to imitate the venerable dignity of Dr. Heidegger. Then all shouted mirthfully and leaped about the room.

The widow Wycherly—if so fresh a damsel could be called a widow—tripped up to the doctor's chair with a mischievous merriment in her rosy face.

"Doctor, you dear old soul," cried she, "get up and dance with me;" and then the four young people laughed louder than ever to think what a queer figure the poor old doctor would cut.

"Pray excuse me," answered the doctor, quietly. "I am old and rheumatic, and my dancing-days were over long ago. But either of these gay young gentlemen will be glad of so pretty a partner."

"Dance with me, Clara," cried Colonel Killigrew.

"No, no! I will be her partner," shouted Mr. Gascoigne.

"She promised me her hand fifty years ago," exclaimed Mr. Medbourne.

They all gathered round her. One caught both her hands in his passionate grasp, another threw his arm about her waist, the third buried his hand among the glossy curls that clustered beneath the widow's cap. Blushing, panting, struggling, chiding, laughing, her warm breath fanning each of their faces by turns, she strove to disengage herself, yet still remained in their triple embrace. Never was there a livelier picture of youthful rivalship, with bewitching beauty for the prize. Yet, by a strange deception, owing to the duskiness of the chamber and the antique dresses which they still wore, the tall mirror is said to have reflected the figures of the three old, gray, withered grand-sires ridiculously contending for the skinny ugliness of a shrivelled grandam. But they were young: their burning passions proved them so.

Inflamed to madness by the coquetry of the girl-widow, who neither granted nor quite withheld her favors, the three rivals began to interchange threatening glances. Still keeping hold of the fair prize, they grappled fiercely at one another's throats. As they struggled to and fro the table was overturned and the vase dashed into a thousand fragments. The precious Water of Youth flowed in a bright stream across the floor, moistening the wings of a butterfly which, grown old in the decline of summer, had alighted there to die. The insect fluttered lightly through the chamber and settled on the snowy head of Dr. Heidegger.

"Come, come, gentlemen! Come, Madam Wycherly!" exclaimed the doctor. "I really must protest against this riot."

They stood still and shivered, for it seemed as if gray Time were calling them back from their sunny youth far down into the chill and darksome vale of years. They looked at old Dr. Heidegger, who sat in his carved armchair holding the rose of half a century, which he had rescued from among the fragments of the shattered vase. At the motion of his hand the four rioters resumed their seats—the more readily because their violent exertions had wearied them, youthful though they were.

"My poor Sylvia's rose!" ejaculated Dr. Heidegger, holding it in the light of the sunset clouds. "It appears to be fading again."

And so it was. Even while the party were looking at it the flower continued to shrivel up, till it became as dry and fragile as when the doctor had first thrown it into the vase. He shook off the few drops of moisture which clung to its petals.

"I love it as well thus as in its dewy freshness," observed he, pressing the withered rose to his withered lips.

While he spoke the butterfly fluttered down from the doctor's snowy head and fell upon the floor. His guests shivered again. A strange dullness—whether of the body or spirit they could not tell—was creeping gradually over them all. They gazed at one another, and fancied that each fleeting moment snatched away a charm and left a deepening furrow where none had been before. Was it an illusion? Had the changes of a lifetime been crowded into so brief a space, and were they now four aged people sitting with their old friend Dr. Heidegger?

"Are we grown old again so soon?" cried they, dolefully.

In truth, they had. The Water of Youth possessed merely a virtue more transient than that of wine; the delirium which it created had effervesced away. Yes, they were old again. With a shuddering impulse that showed her a woman still, the widow clasped her skinny hands before her face and wished that the coffin-lid were over it, since it could be no longer beautiful.

"Yes, friends, ye are old again," said Dr. Heidegger, "and, lo! the Water of Youth is all lavished on the ground. Well, I bemoan it not; for if the fountain gushed at my very doorstep, I would not stoop to bathe my lips in it—no, though its delirium were for years instead of moments. Such is the lesson ye have taught me."

But the doctor's four friends had taught no such lesson to themselves. They resolved forthwith to make a pilgrimage to Florida and quaff at morning, noon and night from the Fountain of Youth.

LEGENDS OF THE PROVINCE-HOUSE

I. HOWE'S MASQUERADE

ONE AFTERNOON LAST SUMMER, while walking along Washington street, my eye was attracted by a sign-board protruding over a narrow archway nearly opposite the Old South Church. The sign represented the front of a stately edifice which was designated as the "OLD PROVINCE HOUSE, kept by Thomas Waite." I was glad to be thus reminded of a purpose, long entertained, of visiting and rambling over the mansion of the old royal governors of Massachusetts, and, entering the arched passage which penetrated through the middle of a brick row of shops, a few steps transported me from the busy heart of modern Boston into a small and secluded court-yard. One side of this space was occupied by the square front of the Province House, three stories high and surmounted by a cupola, on the top of which a gilded Indian was discernible, with his bow bent and his arrow on the string, as if aiming at the weathercock on the spire of the Old South. The figure has kept this attitude for seventy years or more, ever since good Deacon Drowne, a cunning carver of wood, first stationed him on his long sentinel's watch over the city.

The Province House is constructed of brick, which seems recently to have been overlaid with a coat of light-colored paint. A flight of red freestone steps fenced in by a balustrade of curiously wrought iron ascends from the court-yard to the spacious porch, over which is a balcony with an iron balustrade of similar pattern and workmanship to that beneath. These letters and figures—"16 P.S. 79"—are wrought into the ironwork of the balcony, and probably express the date of the edifice, with the initials of its founder's name.

A wide door with double leaves admitted me into the hall or entry, on the right of which is the entrance to the bar-room. It was in this apartment, I presume, that the ancient governors held their levees with vice-regal pomp, surrounded by the military men, the counsellors, the judges, and other officers of the Crown, while all the loyalty of the province thronged to do them honor. But the room in its present condition cannot boast even of faded magnificence. The panelled wainscot is covered with dingy paint and acquires a duskier hue from the deep shadow into which the Province House is thrown by the brick block that shuts it in from Washington street. A ray of sunshine never visits this apartment any more than the glare of the festal torches which have been extinguished from the era of the Revolution. The most venerable and ornamental object is a chimney-piece set round with Dutch tiles of blue-figured china, representing scenes from Scripture, and, for aught I know, the lady of Pownall or Bernard may have sat beside this fireplace and told her children the story of each blue tile. A bar in modern style, well replenished with decanters, bottles, cigar-boxes and network bags of lemons, and provided with a beer-pump and a soda-fount, extends along one side of the room.

At my entrance an elderly person was smacking his lips with a zest which satisfied me that the cellars of the Province House still hold good liquor, though doubtless of other vintages than were quaffed by the old governors. After sipping a glass of port-sangaree prepared by the skilful hands of Mr. Thomas Waite, I besought that worthy successor and representative of so many historic personages to conduct me over their time-honored mansion. He readily complied, but, to confess the truth, I was forced to draw strenuously upon my imagination in order to find aught that was interesting in a house which, without its historic associations, would have seemed merely such a tavern as is usually favored by the custom of decent city boarders and old-fashioned country gentlemen. The chambers, which were probably spacious in former times, are now cut up by partitions and subdivided into little nooks, each affording scanty room for the narrow bed and chair and dressing-table of a single lodger: The great staircase, however, may be termed, without much hyperbole, a feature of grandeur and magnificence. It winds through the midst of the house by flights of broad steps, each flight terminating in a square landing-place, whence the ascent is continued toward the cupola. A carved balustrade, freshly painted in the lower stories, but growing dingier as we ascend, borders the staircase with its quaintly twisted and intertwined pillars, from top to bottom. Up these stairs the military boots, or perchance the gouty shoes, of many a governor have trodden as the wearers mounted to the cupola which afforded them so wide a view over their metropolis and the surrounding country. The cupola is an octagon with several windows, and a door opening upon the roof. From this station, as I pleased myself with imagining, Gage may have beheld his disastrous victory on Bunker Hill (unless one of the tri-mountains intervened), and Howe have marked the approaches of Washington's besieging army, although the buildings since erected in the vicinity have shut out almost every object save the steeple of the Old South, which seems almost within arm's length. Descending from the cupola, I paused in the garret to observe the ponderous white-oak framework, so much more massive than the frames of modern houses, and thereby resembling an antique skeleton. The brick walls, the materials of which were imported from Holland, and the timbers of the mansion, are still as sound as ever, but, the floors and other interior parts being greatly decayed, it is contemplated to gut the whole and build a new house within the ancient frame-and brickwork. Among other inconveniences of the present edifice, mine host mentioned that any jar or motion was apt to shake down the dust of ages out of the ceiling of one chamber upon the floor of that beneath it.

We stepped forth from the great front window into the balcony where in old times it was doubtless the custom of the king's representative to show himself to a loyal populace, requiting their huzzas and tossed-up hats with stately bendings of his dignified person. In those days the front of the Province House looked upon the street, and the whole site now occupied by the brick range of stores, as well as the present court-yard, was laid out in grass-plats overshadowed by trees and bordered by a wrought-iron fence. Now the old aristocratic edifice hides its time-worn visage behind an upstart modern building; at one of the back windows I observed some pretty tailoresses sewing and chatting and laughing, with now and then a careless glance toward the balcony. Descending thence, we again entered the bar-room, where the elderly gentleman above mentioned—the smack of whose lips had spoken so favorably for Mr. Waite's good liquor—was still lounging in his chair. He seemed to be, if not a lodger, at least a familiar visitor of the house who might be supposed to have his regular score at the bar, his summer seat at the open window and his prescriptive corner at the winter's fireside. Being of a sociable aspect, I ventured to address him with a remark calculated to draw forth his historical reminiscences, if any such were in his mind, and it gratified me to discover that, between memory and tradition, the old gentleman was really possessed of some very pleasant gossip about the Province House. The portion of his talk which chiefly interested me was the outline of the following legend. He professed to have received it at one or two removes from an eye-witness, but this derivation, together with the lapse of time, must have afforded opportunities for many variations of the narrative; so that, despairing of literal and absolute truth, I have not scrupled to make such further changes as seemed conducive to the reader's profit and delight.

⚜

At one of the entertainments given at the province-house during the latter part of the siege of Boston there passed a scene which has never yet been satisfactorily explained. The officers of the British army and the loyal gentry of the province, most of whom were collected within the beleaguered town, had been invited to a masqued ball, for it was the policy for Sir William Howe to hide the distress and danger of the period and the desperate aspect of the siege under an ostentation of festivity. The spectacle of this evening, if the oldest members of the provincial court circle might be believed, was the most gay and gorgeous affair that had occurred in the annals of the government. The brilliantly-lighted apartments were thronged with figures that seemed to have stepped from the dark canvas of historic portraits or to have flitted forth from the magic pages of romance, or at least to have flown hither from one of the London theatres without a change of garments. Steeled knights of the Conquest, bearded statesmen of Queen Elizabeth and high-ruffed ladies of her court were mingled with characters of comedy, such as a parti-colored Merry Andrew jingling his cap and bells, a Falstaff almost as provocative of laughter as his prototype, and a Don Quixote with a bean-pole for a lance and a pot-lid for a shield.

But the broadest merriment was excited by a group of figures ridiculously dressed in old regimentals which seemed to have been purchased at a military rag-fair or pilfered from some receptacle of the cast-off clothes of both the French and British armies. Portions of their attire had probably been worn at the siege of Louisburg, and the coats of most recent cut might have been rent and tattered by sword, ball or bayonet as long ago as Wolfe's victory. One of these worthies—a tall, lank figure brandishing a rusty sword of immense longitude—purported to be no less a personage than General George Washington, and the other principal officers of the American army, such as Gates, Lee, Putnam, Schuyler, Ward and Heath, were represented by similar scarecrows. An interview in the mock-heroic style between the rebel warriors and the British commander-in-chief was received with immense applause, which came loudest of all from the loyalists of the colony.

There was one of the guests, however, who stood apart, eying these antics sternly and scornfully at once with a frown and a bitter smile. It was an old man formerly of high station and great repute in the province, and who had been a very famous soldier in his day. Some surprise had been expressed that a person of Colonel Joliffe's known Whig principles, though

now too old to take an active part in the contest, should have remained in Boston during the siege, and especially that he should consent to show himself in the mansion of Sir William Howe. But thither he had come with a fair granddaughter under his arm, and there, amid all the mirth and buffoonery, stood this stern old figure, the best-sustained character in the masquerade, because so well representing the antique spirit of his native land. The other guests affirmed that Colonel Joliffe's black puritanical scowl threw a shadow round about him, although, in spite of his sombre influence, their gayety continued to blaze higher, like—an ominous comparison—the flickering brilliancy of a lamp which has but a little while to burn.

Eleven strokes full half an hour ago had pealed from the clock of the Old South, when a rumor was circulated among the company that some new spectacle or pageant was about to be exhibited which should put a fitting close to the splendid festivities of the night.

"What new jest has Your Excellency in hand?" asked the Reverend Mather Byles, whose Presbyterian scruples had not kept him from the entertainment. "Trust me, sir, I have already laughed more than beseems my cloth at your Homeric confabulation with yonder ragamuffin general of the rebels. One other such fit of merriment, and I must throw off my clerical wig and band."

"Not so, good Dr. Byles," answered Sir William Howe; "if mirth were a crime, you had never gained your doctorate in divinity. As to this new foolery, I know no more about it than yourself—perhaps not so much. Honestly, now, doctor, have you not stirred up the sober brains of some of your countrymen to enact a scene in our masquerade?"

"Perhaps," slyly remarked the granddaughter of Colonel Joliffe, whose high spirit had been stung by many taunts against New England—"perhaps we are to have a masque of allegorical figures—Victory with trophies from Lexington and Bunker Hill, Plenty with her overflowing horn to typify the present abundance in this good town, and Glory with a wreath for His Excellency's brow."

Sir William Howe smiled at words which he would have answered with one of his darkest frowns had they been uttered by lips that wore a beard. He was spared the necessity of a retort by a singular interruption. A sound of music was heard without the house, as if proceeding from a full band of military instruments stationed in the street, playing, not such a festal strain as was suited to the occasion, but a slow funeral-march. The drums appeared to be muffled, and the trumpets poured forth a wailing breath which at once hushed the merriment of the auditors, filling all with wonder and some with apprehension. The idea occurred to many that either the funeral procession of some great personage had halted in front of the province-house, or that a corpse in a velvet-covered and gorgeously-decorated coffin was about to be borne from the portal. After listening a moment, Sir William Howe called in a stern voice to the leader of the musicians, who had hitherto enlivened the entertainment with gay and lightsome melodies. The man was drum-major to one of the British regiments.

"Dighton," demanded the general, "what means this foolery? Bid your band silence that dead march, or, by my word, they shall have sufficient cause for their lugubrious strains. Silence it, sirrah!"

"Please, Your Honor," answered the drum-major, whose rubicund visage had lost all its color, "the fault is none of mine. I and my band are all here together, and I question whether there be a man of us that could play that march without book. I never heard it but once before, and that was at the funeral of his late Majesty, King George II."

"Well, well!" said Sir William Howe, recovering his composure; "it is the prelude to some masquerading antic. Let it pass."

A figure now presented itself, but among the many fantastic masks that were dispersed through the apartments none could tell precisely from whence it came. It was a man in an old-fashioned dress of black serge and having the aspect of a steward or principal domestic in the household of a nobleman or great English landholder. This figure advanced to the outer door of the mansion, and, throwing both its leaves wide open, withdrew a little to one side and looked back toward the grand staircase, as if expecting some person to descend. At the same time, the music in the street sounded a loud and doleful summons. The eyes of Sir William Howe and his guests being directed to the staircase, there appeared on the uppermost landing-place, that was discernible from the bottom, several personages descending toward the door. The foremost was a man of stern visage, wearing a steeple-crowned hat and a skull-cap beneath it, a dark cloak and huge wrinkled boots that came halfway up his legs. Under his arm was a rolled-up banner which seemed to be the banner of England, but strangely rent and torn; he had a sword in his right hand and grasped a Bible in his left. The next figure was of milder aspect, yet full of dignity, wearing a broad ruff, over which descended a beard, a gown of wrought velvet and a doublet and hose of black satin; he carried a roll of manuscript in his hand. Close behind these two came a young man of very striking countenance and demeanor with deep thought and contemplation on his brow, and perhaps a flash of enthusiasm in his eye; his garb, like that of his predecessors, was of an antique fashion, and there was a stain of blood upon his ruff. In the same group with these were three or four others, all men of dignity and evident command, and bearing themselves like personages who were accustomed to the gaze of the multitude. It was the idea of the beholders that these figures went to join the mysterious funeral that had halted in front of the province-house, yet that supposition seemed to be contradicted by the air of triumph with which they waved their hands as they crossed the threshold and vanished through the portal.

"In the devil's name, what is this?" muttered Sir William Howe to a gentleman beside him. "A procession of the regicide judges of King Charles the martyr?"

"These," said Colonel Joliffe, breaking silence almost for the first time that evening—"these, if I interpret them aright, are the Puritan governors, the rulers of the old original democracy of Massachusetts—Endicott with the banner from which he had torn the symbol of subjection, and Winthrop and Sir Henry Vane and Dudley, Haynes, Bellingham and Leverett."

"Why had that young man a stain of blood upon his ruff?" asked Miss Joliffe.

"Because in after-years," answered her grandfather, "he laid down the wisest head in England upon the block for the principles of liberty."

"Will not Your Excellency order out the guard?" whispered Lord Percy, who, with other British officers, had now assembled round the general. "There may be a plot under this mummery."

"Tush! we have nothing to fear," carelessly replied Sir William Howe. "There can be no worse treason in the matter than a jest, and that somewhat of the dullest. Even were it a sharp and bitter one, our best policy would be to laugh it off. See! here come more of these gentry."

Another group of characters had now partly descended the staircase. The first was a venerable and white-bearded patriarch who cautiously felt his way downward with a staff. Treading hastily behind him, and stretching forth his gauntleted hand as if to grasp the old man's shoulder, came a tall soldier-like figure equipped with a plumed cap of steel, a bright breastplate and a long sword, which rattled against the stairs. Next was seen a stout man dressed in rich and courtly attire, but not of courtly demeanor; his gait had the swinging motion of a seaman's walk, and, chancing to stumble on the staircase, he suddenly grew wrathful and was heard to mutter an oath. He was followed by a noble-looking personage in a curled wig such as are represented in the portraits of Queen Anne's time and earlier, and the breast of his coat was decorated with an embroidered star. While advancing to the door he bowed to the right hand and to the left in a very gracious and insinuating style, but as he crossed the threshold, unlike the early Puritan governors, he seemed to wring his hands with sorrow.

"Prithee, play the part of a chorus, good Dr. Byles," said Sir William Howe. "What worthies are these?"

"If it please Your Excellency, they lived somewhat before my day," answered the doctor; "but doubtless our friend the colonel has been hand and glove with them."

"Their living faces I never looked upon," said Colonel Joliffe, gravely; "although I have spoken face to face with many rulers of this land, and shall greet yet another with an old man's blessing ere I die. But we talk of these figures. I take the venerable patriarch to be Bradstreet, the last of the Puritans, who was governor at ninety or thereabouts. The next is Sir Edmund Andros, a tyrant, as any New England schoolboy will tell you, and therefore the people cast him down from his high seat into a dungeon. Then comes Sir William Phipps, shepherd, cooper, sea-captain and governor. May many of his countrymen rise as high from as low an origin! Lastly, you saw the gracious earl of Bellamont, who ruled us under King William."

"But what is the meaning of it all?" asked Lord Percy.

"Now, were I a rebel," said Miss Joliffe, half aloud, "I might fancy that the ghosts of these ancient governors had been summoned to form the funeral procession of royal authority in New England."

Several other figures were now seen at the turn of the staircase. The one in advance had a thoughtful, anxious and somewhat crafty expression of face, and in spite of his loftiness of manner, which was evidently the result both of an ambitious spirit and of long continuance in high stations, he seemed not incapable of cringing to a greater than himself. A few steps behind came an officer in a scarlet and embroidered uniform cut in a fashion old enough to have been worn by the duke of Marlborough. His nose had a rubicund tinge, which, together with the twinkle of his eye, might have marked him as a lover of the wine-cup and good-fellowship; notwithstanding which tokens, he appeared ill at ease, and often glanced around him as if apprehensive of some secret mischief. Next came a portly gentleman wearing a coat of shaggy cloth lined with silken velvet; he had sense, shrewdness and humor in his face and a folio volume under his arm, but his aspect was that of a man vexed and tormented beyond all patience and harassed almost to death. He went hastily down, and was followed by a dignified person dressed in a purple velvet suit with very rich embroidery; his demeanor would have possessed much stateliness, only that a grievous fit of the gout compelled him to hobble from stair to stair with contortions of face and body. When Dr. Byles beheld this figure on the staircase, he shivered as with an ague, but continued to watch him steadfastly until the gouty gentleman had reached the threshold, made a gesture of anguish and despair and vanished into the outer gloom, whither the funeral music summoned him.

"Governor Belcher—my old patron—in his very shape and dress!" gasped Dr. Byles. "This is an awful mockery."

"A tedious foolery, rather," said Sir William Howe, with an air of indifference. "But who were the three that preceded him?"

"Governor Dudley, a cunning politician; yet his craft once brought him to a prison," replied Colonel Joliffe. "Governor Shute, formerly a colonel under Marlborough, and whom the people frightened out of the province, and learned Governor Burnett, whom the legislature tormented into a mortal fever."

"Methinks they were miserable men—these royal governors of Massachusetts," observed Miss Joliffe. "Heavens! how dim the light grows!"

It was certainly a fact that the large lamp which illuminated the staircase now burned dim and duskily; so that several figures which passed hastily down the stairs and went forth from the porch appeared rather like shadows than persons of fleshly substance.

Sir William Howe and his guests stood at the doors of the contiguous apartments watching the progress of this singular pageant with various emotions of anger, contempt or half-acknowledged fear, but still with an anxious curiosity. The shapes which now seemed hastening to join the mysterious procession were recognized rather by striking peculiarities of dress or broad characteristics of manner than by any perceptible resemblance of features to their prototypes. Their faces, indeed, were invariably kept in deep shadow, but Dr. Byles and other gentlemen who had long been familiar with the successive rulers of the province were heard to whisper the names of Shirley, of Pownall, of Sir Francis Bernard and of the well-remembered Hutchinson, thereby confessing that the actors, whoever they might be, in this spectral march of governors had succeeded in putting on some distant portraiture of the real personages. As they vanished from the door, still did these shadows toss their arms into the gloom of night with a dread expression of woe. Following the mimic representative of Hutchinson came a military figure holding before his face the cocked hat which he had taken from his powdered head, but his epaulettes and other insignia of rank were those of a general officer, and something in his mien reminded the beholders of one who had recently been master of the province-house and chief of all the land.

"The shape of Gage, as true as in a looking-glass!" exclaimed Lord Percy, turning pale.

"No, surely," cried Miss Joliffe, laughing hysterically; "it could not be Gage, or Sir William would have greeted his old comrade in arms. Perhaps he will not suffer the next to pass unchallenged."

"Of that be assured, young lady," answered Sir William Howe, fixing his eyes with a very marked expression upon the immovable visage of her grandfather. "I have long enough delayed to pay the ceremonies of a host to these departing guests; the next that takes his leave shall receive due courtesy."

A wild and dreary burst of music came through the open door. It seemed as it the procession, which had been gradually filling up its ranks, were now about to move, and that this loud peal of the wailing trumpets and roll of the muffled drums were a call to some loiterer to make haste. Many eyes, by an irresistible impulse, were turned upon Sir William Howe, as if it were he whom the dreary music summoned to the funeral of departed power.

"See! here comes the last," whispered Miss Joliffe, pointing her tremulous finger to the staircase.

A figure had come into view as if descending the stairs, although so dusky was the region whence it emerged some of the spectators fancied that they had seen this human shape suddenly moulding itself amid the gloom. Downward the figure came with a stately and martial tread, and, reaching the lowest stair, was observed to be a tall man booted and wrapped in a military cloak, which was drawn up around the face so as to meet the napped brim of a laced hat; the features, therefore, were completely hidden. But the British officers deemed that they had seen that military cloak before, and even recognized the frayed embroidery on the collar, as well as the gilded scabbard of a sword which protruded from the folds of the cloak and glittered in a vivid gleam of light. Apart from these trifling particulars there were characteristics of gait and bearing which impelled the wondering guests to glance from the shrouded figure to Sir William Howe, as if to satisfy themselves that their host had not suddenly vanished from the midst of them. With a dark flush of wrath upon his brow, they saw the general draw his sword and advance to meet the figure in the cloak before the latter had stepped one pace upon the floor.

"Villain, unmuffle yourself!" cried he. "You pass no farther."

The figure, without blenching a hair's-breadth from the sword which was pointed at his breast, made a solemn pause and lowered the cape of the cloak from about his face, yet not sufficiently for the spectators to catch a glimpse of it. But Sir William Howe had evidently seen enough. The sternness of his countenance gave place to a look of wild amazement, if not horror, while he recoiled several steps from the figure and let fall his sword upon the floor. The martial shape again drew the cloak about his features and passed on, but, reaching the threshold with his back toward the spectators, he was seen to stamp his foot and shake his clenched hands in the air. It was afterward affirmed that Sir William Howe had repeated that selfsame gesture of rage and sorrow when for the last time, and as the last royal governor, he passed through the portal of the province-house.

"Hark! The procession moves," said Miss Joliffe.

The music was dying away along the street, and its dismal strains were mingled with the knell of midnight from the steeple of the Old South and with the roar of artillery which announced that the beleaguered army of Washington had intrenched itself upon a nearer height than before. As the deep boom of the cannon smote upon his ear Colonel Joliffe raised himself to the full height of his aged form and smiled sternly on the British general.

"Would Your Excellency inquire further into the mystery of the pageant?" said he.

"Take care of your gray head!" cried Sir William Howe, fiercely, though with a quivering lip. "It has stood too long on a traitor's shoulders."

"You must make haste to chop it off, then," calmly replied the colonel, "for a few hours longer, and not all the power of Sir William Howe, nor of his master, shall cause one of these gray hairs to fall. The empire of Britain in this ancient province is at its last gasp to-night; almost while I speak it is a dead corpse, and methinks the shadows of the old governors are fit mourners at its funeral."

With these words Colonel Joliffe threw on his cloak, and, drawing his granddaughter's arm within his own, retired from the last festival that a British ruler ever held in the old province of Massachusetts Bay. It was supposed that the colonel and the young lady possessed some secret intelligence in regard to the mysterious pageant of that night. However this might be, such knowledge has never become general. The actors in the scene have vanished into deeper obscurity than even that wild Indian band who scattered the cargoes of the tea-ships on the waves and gained a place in history, yet left no names. But superstition, among other legends of this mansion, repeats the wondrous tale that on the anniversary night of Britain's discomfiture the ghosts of the ancient governors of Massachusetts still glide through the portal of the Province House. And last of all comes a figure shrouded in a military cloak, tossing his clenched hands into the air and stamping his iron-shod boots upon the broad freestone steps with a semblance of feverish despair, but without the sound of a foot-tramp.

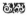

When the truth-telling accents of the elderly gentleman were hushed, I drew a long breath and looked round the room, striving with the best energy of my imagination to throw a tinge of romance and historic grandeur over the realities of the scene. But my nostrils snuffed up a scent of cigar-smoke, clouds of which the narrator had emitted by way of visible emblem, I suppose, of the nebulous obscurity of his tale. Moreover, my gorgeous fantasies were woefully disturbed by the rattling of the spoon in a tumbler of whiskey-punch which Mr. Thomas Waite was mingling for a customer. Nor did it add to the picturesque appearance of the panelled walls that the slate of the Brookline stage was suspended against them, instead of the armorial escutcheon of some far-descended governor. A stage-driver sat at one of the windows reading a penny paper of the day—the Boston *Times*—and presenting a figure which could nowise be brought into any picture of "Times in Boston" seventy or a hundred years ago. On the window-seat lay a bundle neatly done up in brown paper, the direction of which I had the idle curiosity to read: "MISS SUSAN HUGGINS, at the PROVINCE HOUSE." A pretty chambermaid, no doubt. In truth, it is desperately hard work when we attempt to throw the spell of hoar antiquity over localities with which the living world and the day that is passing over us have aught to do. Yet, as I glanced at the stately staircase down which the procession of the old governors had descended, and as I emerged through the venerable portal whence their figures had preceded me, it gladdened me to be conscious of a thrill of awe. Then, diving through the narrow archway, a few strides transported me into the densest throng of Washington street.

II. EDWARD RANDOLPH'S PORTRAIT

The old legendary guest of the Province House abode in my remembrance from midsummer till January. One idle evening last winter, confident that he would be found in the snuggest corner of the bar-room, I resolved to pay him another visit, hoping to deserve well of my country by snatching from oblivion some else unheard-of fact of history. The night was chill and raw, and rendered boisterous by almost a gale of wind which whistled along Washington street, causing the gaslights to flare and flicker within the lamps.

As I hurried onward my fancy was busy with a comparison between the present aspect of the street and that which it probably wore when the British governors inhabited the mansion whither I was now going. Brick edifices in those times were few till a succession of destructive fires had swept, and swept again, the wooden dwellings and warehouses from the most populous quarters of the town. The buildings stood insulated and independent, not, as now, merging their separate existences into connected ranges with a front of tiresome identity, but each possessing features of its own, as if the owner's individual taste had shaped it, and the whole presenting a picturesque irregularity the absence of which is hardly compensated by any beauties of our modern architecture. Such a scene, dimly vanishing from the eye by the ray of here and there a tallow candle glimmering through the small panes of scattered windows, would form a sombre contrast to the street as I beheld it with the gaslights blazing from corner to corner, flaming within the shops and throwing a noonday brightness through the huge plates of glass. But the black, lowering sky, as I turned my eyes upward, wore, doubtless, the same visage as when it frowned upon the ante-Revolutionary New Englanders. The wintry blast had the same shriek that was familiar to their ears. The Old South Church, too, still pointed its antique spire into the darkness and was lost between earth and heaven, and, as I passed, its clock, which had warned so many generations how transitory was their lifetime, spoke heavily and slow the same unregarded moral to myself. "Only seven o'clock!" thought I. "My old friend's legends will scarcely kill the hours 'twixt this and bedtime."

Passing through the narrow arch, I crossed the courtyard, the confined precincts of which were made visible by a lantern over the portal of the Province House. On entering the bar-room, I found, as I expected, the old tradition-monger seated by a special good fire of anthracite, compelling clouds of smoke from a corpulent cigar. He recognized me with evident pleasure, for my rare properties as a patient listener invariably make me a favorite with elderly gentlemen and ladies of narrative propensities. Drawing a chair to the fire, I desired mine host to favor us with a glass apiece of whiskey-punch, which was speedily prepared, steaming hot, with a slice of lemon at the bottom, a dark-red stratum of port wine upon the surface and a sprinkling of nutmeg strewn over all. As we touched our glasses together, my legendary friend made himself known to me as Mr. Bela Tiffany, and I rejoiced at the oddity of the name, because it gave his image and character a sort of individuality in my conception. The old gentleman's draught acted as a solvent upon his memory, so that it overflowed with tales, traditions, anecdotes of famous dead people and traits of ancient manners, some of which were childish as a nurse's lullaby, while others might have been worth the notice of the grave historian. Nothing impressed me more than a story of a black mysterious picture which used to hang in one of the chambers of the Province House, directly above the room where we were now sitting. The following is as correct a version of the fact as the reader would be likely to obtain from any other source, although, assuredly, it has a tinge of romance approaching to the marvellous.

In one of the apartments of the province-house there was long preserved an ancient picture the frame of which was as black as ebony, and the canvas itself so dark with age, damp and smoke that not a touch of the painter's art could be discerned. Time had thrown an impenetrable veil over it and left to tradition and fable and conjecture to say what had once been there portrayed. During the rule of many successive governors it had hung, by prescriptive and undisputed right, over the mantel piece of the same chamber, and it still kept its place when Lieutenant-governor Hutchinson assumed the administration of the province on the departure of Sir Francis Bernard.

The lieutenant-governor sat one afternoon resting his head against the carved back of his stately arm-chair and gazing up thoughtfully at the void blackness of the picture. It was scarcely a time for such inactive musing, when affairs of the deepest moment required the ruler's decision; for within that very hour Hutchinson had received intelligence of the arrival of a British fleet bringing three regiments from Halifax to overawe the insubordination of the people. These troops awaited his permission to occupy the fortress of Castle William and the town itself, yet, instead of affixing his signature to an official order, there sat the lieutenant-governor so carefully scrutinizing the black waste of canvas that his demeanor attracted the notice of two young persons who attended him. One, wearing a military dress of buff, was his kinsman, Francis Lincoln, the provincial captain of Castle William; the other, who sat on a low stool beside his chair, was Alice Vane, his favorite niece. She was clad entirely in white— a pale, ethereal creature who, though a native of New England, had been educated abroad and seemed not merely a stranger from another clime, but almost a being from another world. For several years, until left an orphan, she had dwelt with her father in sunny Italy, and there had acquired a taste and enthusiasm for sculpture and painting which she found few opportunities of gratifying in the undecorated dwellings of the colonial gentry. It was said that the early productions of her own pencil exhibited no inferior genius, though perhaps the rude atmosphere of New England had cramped her hand and dimmed the glowing colors of her fancy. But, observing her uncle's steadfast gaze, which appeared to search through the mist of years to discover the subject of the picture, her curiosity was excited.

"Is it known, my dear uncle," inquired she, "what this old picture once represented? Possibly, could it be made visible, it might prove a masterpiece of some great artist; else why has it so long held such a conspicuous place?"

As her uncle, contrary to his usual custom—for he was as attentive to all the humors and caprices of Alice as if she had been his own best-beloved child—did not immediately reply, the young captain of Castle William took that office upon himself.

"This dark old square of canvas, my fair cousin," said he, "has been an heirloom in the province-house from time immemorial. As to the painter, I can tell you nothing; but if half the stories told of it be true, not one of the great Italian masters has ever produced so marvellous a piece of work as that before you."

Captain Lincoln proceeded to relate some of the strange fables and fantasies which, as it was impossible to refute them by ocular demonstration, had grown to be articles of popular belief in reference to this old picture. One of the wildest, and at the same time the best-accredited, accounts stated it to be an original and authentic portrait of the evil one, taken at a witch-meeting near Salem, and that its strong and terrible resemblance had been confirmed by several of the confessing wizards and witches at their trial in open court. It was likewise affirmed that a familiar spirit or demon abode behind the blackness of the picture, and had shown himself at seasons of public calamity to more than one of the royal governors. Shirley, for instance, had beheld this ominous apparition on the eve of General Abercrombie's shameful and bloody defeat under the walls of Ticonderoga. Many of the servants of the province-house had caught glimpses of a visage frowning down upon them at morning or evening twilight, or in the depths of night while raking up the fire that glimmered on the hearth beneath, although, if any were, bold enough to hold a torch before the picture, it would appear as black and undistinguishable as ever. The oldest inhabitant of Boston recollected that his father—in whose days the portrait had not wholly faded out of sight—had once looked upon it, but would never suffer himself to be questioned as to the face which was there represented. In connection with such stories, it was remarkable that over the top of the frame there were some ragged remnants of black silk, indicating that a veil had formerly hung down before the picture until the duskiness of time had so effectually concealed it. But, after all, it was the most singular part of the affair that so many of the pompous governors of Massachusetts had allowed the obliterated picture to remain in the state-chamber of the province-house.

"Some of these fables are really awful," observed Alice Vane, who had occasionally shuddered as well as smiled while her cousin spoke. "It would be almost worth while to wipe away the black surface of the canvas, since the original picture can hardly be so formidable as those which fancy paints instead of it."

"But would it be possible," inquired her cousin," to restore this dark picture to its pristine hues?"

"Such arts are known in Italy," said Alice.

The lieutenant-governor had roused himself from his abstracted mood, and listened with a smile to the conversation of his young relatives. Yet his voice had something peculiar in its tones when he undertook the explanation of the mystery.

"I am sorry, Alice, to destroy your faith in the legends of which you are so fond," remarked he, "but my antiquarian researches have long since made me acquainted with the subject of this picture—if picture it can be called—which is no more visible, nor ever will be, than the face of the long-buried man whom it once represented. It was the portrait of Edward Randolph, the founder of this house, a person famous in the history of New England."

"Of that Edward Randolph," exclaimed Captain Lincoln, "who obtained the repeal of the first provincial charter, under which our forefathers had enjoyed almost democratic privileges —he that was styled the arch-enemy of New England, and whose memory is still held in detestation as the destroyer of our liberties?"

"It was the same Randolph," answered Hutchinson, moving uneasily in his chair. "It was his lot to taste the bitterness of popular odium."

"Our annals tell us," continued the captain of Castle William, "that the curse of the people followed this Randolph where he went and wrought evil in all the subsequent events of his life, and that its effect was seen, likewise, in the manner of his death. They say, too, that the inward misery of that curse worked itself outward and was visible on the wretched man's countenance, making it too horrible to be looked upon. If so, and if this picture truly represented his aspect, it was in mercy that the cloud of blackness has gathered over it."

"These traditions are folly to one who has proved, as I have, how little of historic truth lies at the bottom," said the lieutenant-governor. "As regards the life and character of Edward Randolph, too implicit credence has been given to Dr. Cotton Mather, who—I must say it, though some of his blood runs in my veins—has filled our early history with old women's tales as fanciful and extravagant as those of Greece or Rome."

"And yet," whispered Alice Vane, "may not such fables have a moral? And methinks, if the visage of this portrait be so dreadful, it is not without a cause that it has hung so long in a chamber of the province-house. When the rulers feel themselves irresponsible, it were well that they should be reminded of the awful weight of a people's curse."

The lieutenant-governor started and gazed for a moment at his niece, as if her girlish fantasies had struck upon some feeling in his own breast which all his policy or principles could not entirely subdue. He knew, indeed, that Alice, in spite of her foreign education, retained the native sympathies of a New England girl.

"Peace, silly child!" cried he, at last, more harshly than he had ever before addressed the gentle Alice. "The rebuke of a king; is more to be dreaded than the clamor of a wild, misguided multitude.—Captain Lincoln, it is decided: the fortress of Castle William must be occupied by the royal troops. The two remaining regiments shall be billeted in the town or encamped upon the Common. It is time, after years of tumult, and almost rebellion, that His Majesty's government should have a wall of strength about it."

"Trust, sir—trust yet a while to the loyalty of the people," said Captain Lincoln, "nor teach them that they can ever be on other terms with British soldiers than those of brotherhood, as when they fought side by side through the French war. Do not convert the streets of your native town into a camp. Think twice before you give up old Castle William, the key of the province, into other keeping than that of true-born New Englanders."

"Young man, it is decided," repeated Hutchinson, rising from his chair. "A British officer will be in attendance this evening to receive the necessary instructions for the disposal of the troops. Your presence also will be required. Till then, farewell."

With these words the lieutenant-governor hastily left the room, while Alice and her cousin more slowly followed, whispering together, and once pausing to glance back at the mysterious picture. The captain of Castle William fancied that the girl's air and mien were such as might have belonged to one of those spirits of fable—fairies or creatures of a more antique mythology—who sometimes mingled their agency with mortal affairs, half in caprice, yet with a sensibility to human weal or woe. As he held the door for her to pass Alice beckoned to the picture and smiled.

"Come forth, dark and evil shape!" cried she. "It is thine hour."

In the evening Lieutenant-governor Hutchinson sat in the same chamber where the foregoing scene had occurred, surrounded by several persons whose various interests had summoned them together. There were the selectmen of Boston—plain patriarchal fathers of the people, excellent representatives of the old puritanical founders whose sombre strength had stamped so deep an impress upon the New England character. Contrasting with these were one or two members of council, richly dressed in the white wigs, the embroidered waistcoats and other magnificence of the time, and making a somewhat ostentatious display of courtier-like ceremonial. In attendance, likewise, was a major of the British army, awaiting the lieutenant-governor's orders for the landing of the troops, which still remained on board the transports. The captain of Castle William stood beside Hutchinson's chair, with folded arms, glancing rather haughtily at the British officer by whom he was soon to be superseded in his command.

On a table in the centre of the chamber stood a branched silver candlestick, throwing down the glow of half a dozen waxlights upon a paper apparently ready for the lieutenant-governor's signature.

Partly shrouded in the voluminous folds of one of the window-curtains, which fell from the ceiling to the floor, was seen the white drapery of a lady's robe. It may appear strange that Alice Vane should have been there at such a time, but there was something so childlike, so wayward, in her singular character, so apart from ordinary rules, that her presence did not surprise the few who noticed it. Meantime, the chairman of the selectmen was addressing to the lieutenant-governor a long and solemn protest against the reception of the British troops into the town.

"And if Your Honor," concluded this excellent but somewhat prosy old gentleman, "shall see fit to persist in bringing these mercenary sworders and musketeers into our quiet streets, not on our heads be the responsibility. Think, sir, while there is yet time, that if one drop of blood be shed, that blood shall be an eternal stain upon Your Honor's memory. You, sir, have written with an able pen the deeds of our forefathers; the more to be desired is it, therefore, that yourself should deserve honorable mention as a true patriot and upright ruler when your own doings shall be written down in history."

"I am not insensible, my good sir, to the natural desire to stand well in the annals of my country," replied Hutchinson, controlling his impatience into courtesy, "nor know I any better method of attaining that end than by withstanding the merely temporary spirit of mischief which, with your pardon, seems to have infected older men than myself. Would you have me wait till the mob shall sack the province-house as they did my private mansion? Trust me, sir, the time may come when you will be glad to flee for protection to the king's banner, the raising of which is now so distasteful to you."

"Yes," said the British major, who was impatiently expecting the lieutenant-governor's orders. "The demagogues of this province have raised the devil, and cannot lay him again. We will exorcise him in God's name and the king's."

"If you meddle with the devil, take care of his claws," answered the captain of Castle William, stirred by the taunt against his countrymen.

"Craving your pardon, young sir," said the venerable selectman, "let not an evil spirit enter into your words. We will strive against the oppressor with prayer and fasting, as our forefathers would have done. Like them, moreover, we will submit to whatever lot a wise Providence may send us—always after our own best exertions to amend it."

"And there peep forth the devil's claws!" muttered Hutchinson, who well understood the nature of Puritan submission. "This matter shall be expedited forthwith. When there shall be a sentinel at every corner and a court of guard before the town-house, a loyal gentleman may venture to walk abroad. What to me is the outcry of a mob in this remote province of the realm? The king is my master, and England is my country; upheld by their armed strength, I set my foot upon the rabble and defy them."

He snatched a pen and was about to affix his signature to the paper that lay on the table, when the captain of Castle William placed his hand upon his shoulder. The freedom of the action, so contrary to the ceremonious respect which was then considered due to rank and dignity, awakened general surprise, and in none more than in the lieutenant-governor himself. Looking angrily up, he perceived that his young relative was pointing his finger to the opposite wall. Hutchinson's eye followed the signal, and he saw what had hitherto been unobserved—that a black silk curtain was suspended before the mysterious picture, so as completely to conceal it. His thoughts immediately recurred to the scene of the preceding afternoon, and in his surprise, confused by indistinct emotions, yet sensible that his niece must have had an agency in this phenomenon, he called loudly upon her:

"Alice! Come hither, Alice!"

No sooner had he spoken than Alice Vane glided from her station, and, pressing one hand across her eyes, with the other snatched away the sable curtain that concealed the portrait. An exclamation of surprise burst from every beholder, but the lieutenant-governor's voice had a tone of horror.

"By Heaven!" said he, in a low inward murmur, speaking rather to himself than to those around him; "if the spirit of Edward Randolph were to appear among us from the place of torment, he could not wear more of the terrors of hell upon his face."

"For some wise end," said the aged selectman, solemnly, "hath Providence scattered away the mist of years that had so long hid this dreadful effigy. Until this hour no living man hath seen what we behold."

Within the antique frame which so recently had enclosed a sable waste of canvas now appeared a visible picture-still dark, indeed, in its hues and shadings, but thrown forward in strong relief. It was a half-length figure of a gentleman in a rich but very old-fashioned dress of embroidered velvet, with a broad ruff and a beard, and wearing a hat the brim of which overshadowed his forehead. Beneath this cloud the eyes had a peculiar glare which was almost lifelike. The whole portrait started so distinctly out of the background that it had the effect of a person looking down from the wall at the astonished and awe-stricken spectators. The expression of the face, if any words can convey an idea of it, was that of a wretch detected in some hideous guilt and exposed to the bitter hatred and laughter and withering scorn of a vast surrounding multitude. There was the struggle of defiance, beaten down and overwhelmed by the crushing weight of ignominy. The torture of the soul had come forth upon the countenance. It seemed as if the picture, while hidden behind the cloud of immemorial years, had been all the time acquiring an intenser depth and darkness of expression, till now it gloomed forth again and threw its evil omen over the present hour. Such, if the wild legend may be credited, was the portrait of Edward Randolph as he appeared when a people's curse had wrought its influence upon his nature.

"'Twould drive me mad, that awful face," said Hutchinson, who seemed fascinated by the contemplation of it.

"Be warned, then," whispered Alice. "He trampled on a people's rights. Behold his punishment, and avoid a crime like his."

The lieutenant-governor actually trembled for an instant, but, exerting his energy—which was not, however, his most characteristic feature—he strove to shake off the spell of Randolph's countenance.

"Girl," cried he, laughing bitterly, as he turned to Alice, "have you brought hither your painter's art, your Italian spirit of intrigue, your tricks of stage-effect, and think to influence the councils of rulers and the affairs of nations by such shallow contrivances? See here!"

"Stay yet a while," said the selectman as Hutchinson again snatched the pen; "for if ever mortal man received a warning from a tormented soul, Your Honor is that man."

"Away!" answered Hutchinson, fiercely. "Though yonder senseless picture cried 'Forbear!' it should not move me!"

Casting a scowl of defiance at the pictured face—which seemed at that moment to intensify the horror of its miserable and wicked look—he scrawled on the paper, in characters that betokened it a deed of desperation, the name of Thomas Hutchinson. Then, it is said, he shuddered, as if that signature had granted away his salvation.

"It is done," said he, and placed his hand upon his brow.

"May Heaven forgive the deed!" said the soft, sad accents of Alice Vane, like the voice of a good spirit flitting away.

When morning came, there was a stifled whisper through the household, and spreading thence about the town, that the dark mysterious picture had started from the wall and spoken face to face with Lieutenant-governor Hutchinson. If such a miracle had been wrought, however, no traces of it remained behind; for within the antique frame nothing could be discerned save the impenetrable cloud which had covered the canvas since the memory of man. If the figure had, indeed, stepped forth, it had fled back, spirit-like, at the day-dawn, and hidden itself behind a century's obscurity. The truth probably was that Alice Vane's secret for restoring the hues of the picture had merely effected a temporary renovation. But those who in that brief interval had beheld the awful visage of Edward Randolph desired no second glance, and ever afterward trembled at the recollection of the scene, as if an evil spirit had appeared visibly among them. And, as for Hutchinson, when, far over the ocean, his dying-hour drew on, he gasped for breath and complained that he was choking with the blood of the Boston Massacre, and Francis Lincoln, the former captain of Castle William, who was standing at his bedside, perceived a likeness in his frenzied look to that of Edward Randolph. Did his broken spirit feel at that dread hour the tremendous burden of a people's curse?

At the conclusion of this miraculous legend I inquired of mine host whether the picture still remained in the chamber over our heads, but Mr. Tiffany informed me that it had long since been removed, and was supposed to be hidden in some out-of-the-way corner of the New England Museum. Perchance some curious antiquary may light upon it there, and, with the assistance of Mr. Howorth, the picture-cleaner, may supply a not unnecessary proof of the authenticity of the facts here set down.

During the progress of the story a storm had been gathering abroad and raging and rattling so loudly in the upper regions of the Province House that it seemed as if all the old governors and great men were running riot above stairs while Mr. Bela Tiffany babbled of them below. In the course of generations, when many people have lived and died in an ancient house, the whistling of the wind through its crannies and the creaking of its beams and rafters become strangely like the tones of the human voice, or thundering laughter, or heavy footsteps treading the deserted chambers. It is as if the echoes of half a century were revived. Such were the ghostly sounds that roared and murmured in our ears when I took leave of the circle round the fireside of the Province House and, plunging down the doorsteps, fought my way homeward against a drifting snow-storm.

III. LADY ELEANORE'S MANTLE

Mine excellent friend the landlord of the Province House was pleased the other evening to invite Mr. Tiffany and myself to an oyster-supper. This slight mark of respect and gratitude, as he handsomely observed, was far less than the ingenious tale-teller, and I, the humble note-taker of his narratives, had fairly earned by the public notice which our joint lucubrations had attracted to his establishment. Many a cigar had been smoked within his premises, many a glass of wine or more potent *aqua vitæ* had been quaffed, many a dinner had been eaten, by curious strangers who, save for the fortunate conjunction of Mr. Tiffany and me, would never have ventured through that darksome avenue which gives access to the historic precincts of the Province House. In short, if any credit be due to the courteous assurances of Mr. Thomas Waite, we had brought his forgotten mansion almost as effectually into public view as if we had thrown down the vulgar range of shoe-shops and dry-good stores which hides its aristocratic front from Washington street. It may be unadvisable, however, to speak too loudly of the increased custom of the house, lest Mr. Waite should find it difficult to renew the lease on so favorable terms as heretofore.

Being thus welcomed as benefactors, neither Mr. Tiffany nor myself felt any scruple in doing full justice to the good things that were set before us. If the feast were less magnificent than those same panelled walls had witnessed in a bygone century; if mine host presided with somewhat less of state than might have befitted a successor of the royal governors; if the guests made a less imposing show than the bewigged and powdered and embroidered dignitaries who erst banqueted at the gubernatorial table and now sleep within their armorial tombs on Copp's Hill or round King's Chapel,—yet never, I may boldly say, did a more comfortable little party assemble in the province-house from Queen Anne's days to the Revolution. The occasion was rendered more interesting by the presence of a venerable personage whose own actual reminiscences went back to the epoch of Gage and Howe, and even supplied him with a doubtful anecdote or two of Hutchinson. He was one of that small, and now all but extinguished, class whose attachment to royalty, and to the colonial institutions and customs that were connected with it, had never yielded to the democratic heresies of after-times. The young queen of Britain has not a more loyal subject in her realm—perhaps not one who would kneel before her throne with such reverential love—as this old grandsire whose head has whitened beneath the mild sway of the republic which still in his mellower moments he terms a usurpation. Yet prejudices so obstinate have not made him an ungentle or impracticable companion. If the truth must be told, the life of the aged loyalist has been of such a scrambling and unsettled character—he has had so little choice of friends and been so often destitute of any —that I doubt whether he would refuse a cup of kindness with either Oliver Cromwell or John Hancock, to say nothing of any democrat now upon the stage. In another paper of this series I may perhaps give the reader a closer glimpse of his portrait.

Our host in due season uncorked a bottle of Madeira of such exquisite perfume and admirable flavor that he surely must have discovered it in an ancient bin down deep beneath the deepest cellar where some jolly old butler stored away the governor's choicest wine and forgot to reveal the secret on his death-bed. Peace to his red-nosed ghost and a libation to his memory! This precious liquor was imbibed by Mr. Tiffany with peculiar zest, and after sipping the third glass it was his pleasure to give us one of the oddest legends which he had yet raked from the storehouse where he keeps such matters. With some suitable adornments from my own fancy, it ran pretty much as follows.

Not long after Colonel Shute had assumed the government of Massachusetts Bay—now nearly a hundred and twenty years ago—a young lady of rank and fortune arrived from England to claim his protection as her guardian. He was her distant relative, but the nearest who had survived the gradual extinction of her family; so that no more eligible shelter could be found for the rich and high-born Lady Eleanore Rochcliffe than within the province-house of a Transatlantic colony. The consort of Governor Shute, moreover, had been as a mother to her childhood, and was now anxious to receive her in the hope that a beautiful young woman would be exposed to infinitely less peril from the primitive society of New England than amid the artifices and corruptions of a court. If either the governor or his lady had especially consulted their own comfort, they would probably have sought to devolve the responsibility on other hands, since with some noble and splendid traits of character Lady Eleanore was remarkable for a harsh, unyielding pride, a haughty consciousness of her hereditary and personal advantages, which made her almost incapable of control. Judging from many traditionary anecdotes, this peculiar temper was hardly less than a monomania; or if the acts which it inspired were those of a sane person, it seemed due from Providence that pride so sinful should be followed by as severe a retribution. That tinge of the marvellous which is thrown over so many of these half-forgotten legends has probably imparted an additional wildness to the strange story of Lady Eleanore Rochcliffe.

The ship in which she came passenger had arrived at Newport, whence Lady Eleanore was conveyed to Boston in the governor's coach, attended by a small escort of gentlemen on horseback. The ponderous equipage, with its four black horses, attracted much notice as it rumbled through Cornhill surrounded by the prancing steeds of half a dozen cavaliers with swords dangling to their stirrups and pistols at their holsters. Through the large glass windows of the coach, as it rolled along, the people could discern the figure of Lady Eleanore, strangely combining an almost queenly stateliness with the grace and beauty of a maiden in her teens. A singular tale had gone abroad among the ladies of the province that their fair rival was indebted for much of the irresistible charm of her appearance to a certain article of dress—an embroidered mantle—which had been wrought by the most skilful artist in London, and possessed even magical properties of adornment. On the present occasion, however, she owed nothing to the witchery of dress, being clad in a riding-habit of velvet which would have appeared stiff and ungraceful on any other form.

The coachman reined in his four black steeds, and the whole cavalcade came to a pause in front of the contorted iron balustrade that fenced the province-house from the public street. It was an awkward coincidence that the bell of the Old South was just then tolling for a funeral; so that, instead of a gladsome peal with which it was customary to announce the arrival of distinguished strangers, Lady Eleanore Rochcliffe was ushered by a doleful clang, as if calamity had come embodied in her beautiful person.

"A very great disrespect!" exclaimed Captain Langford, an English officer who had recently brought despatches to Governor Shute. "The funeral should have been deferred lest Lady Eleanore's spirits be affected by such a dismal welcome."

"With your pardon, sir," replied Dr. Clarke, a physician and a famous champion of the popular party, "whatever the heralds may pretend, a dead beggar must have precedence of a living queen. King Death confers high privileges."

These remarks were interchanged while the speakers waited a passage through the crowd which had gathered on each side of the gateway, leaving an open avenue to the portal of the province-house. A black slave in livery now leaped from behind the coach and threw open the door, while at the same moment Governor Shute descended the flight of steps from his mansion to assist Lady Eleanore in alighting. But the governor's stately approach was anticipated in a manner that excited general astonishment. A pale young man with his black hair all in disorder rushed from the throng and prostrated himself beside the coach, thus offering his person as a footstool for Lady Eleanore Rochcliffe to tread upon. She held back an instant, yet with an expression as if doubting whether the young man were worthy to bear the weight of her footstep rather than dissatisfied to receive such awful reverence from a fellow-mortal.

"Up, sir!" said the governor, sternly, at the same time lifting his cane over the intruder. "What means the Bedlamite by this freak?"

"Nay," answered Lady Eleanore, playfully, but with more scorn than pity in her tone; "Your Excellency shall not strike him. When men seek only to be trampled upon, it were a pity to deny them a favor so easily granted—and so well deserved!" Then, though as lightly as a sunbeam on a cloud, she placed her foot upon the cowering form and extended her hand to meet that of the governor.

There was a brief interval during which Lady Eleanore retained this attitude, and never, surely, was there an apter emblem of aristocracy and hereditary pride trampling on human sympathies and the kindred of nature than these two figures presented at that moment. Yet the spectators were so smitten with her beauty, and so essential did pride seem to the existence of such a creature, that they gave a simultaneous acclamation of applause.

"Who is this insolent young fellow?" inquired Captain Langford, who still remained beside Dr. Clarke. "If he be in his senses, his impertinence demands the bastinado; if mad, Lady Eleanore should be secured from further inconvenience by his confinement."

"His name is Jervase Helwyse," answered the doctor—"a youth of no birth or fortune, or other advantages save the mind and soul that nature gave him; and, being secretary to our colonial agent in London, it was his misfortune to meet this Lady Eleanore Rochcliffe. He loved her, and her scorn has driven him mad."

"He was mad so to aspire," observed the English officer.

"It may be so," said Dr. Clarke, frowning as he spoke; "but I tell you, sir, I could wellnigh doubt the justice of the Heaven above us if no signal humiliation overtake this lady who now treads so haughtily into yonder mansion. She seeks to place herself above the sympathies of our common nature, which envelops all human souls; see if that nature do not assert its claim over her in some mode that shall bring her level with the lowest."

"Never!" cried Captain Langford, indignantly—"neither in life nor when they lay her with her ancestors."

Not many days afterward the governor gave a ball in honor of Lady Eleanore Rochcliffe. The principal gentry of the colony received invitations, which were distributed to their residences far and near by messengers on horseback bearing missives sealed with all the formality of official despatches. In obedience to the summons, there was a general gathering of rank, wealth and beauty, and the wide door of the province-house had seldom given admittance to more numerous and honorable guests than on the evening of Lady Eleanore's ball. Without much extravagance of eulogy, the spectacle might even be termed splendid, for, according to the fashion of the times, the ladies shone in rich silks and satins outspread over wide-projecting hoops, and the gentlemen glittered in gold embroidery laid unsparingly upon the purple or scarlet or sky-blue velvet which was the material of their coats and waistcoats. The latter article of dress was of great importance, since it enveloped the wearer's body nearly to the knees and was perhaps bedizened with the amount of his whole year's income in golden flowers and foliage. The altered taste of the present day—a taste symbolic of a deep change in the whole system of society—would look upon almost any of those gorgeous figures as ridiculous, although that evening the guests sought their reflections in the pier-glasses and rejoiced to catch their own glitter amid the glittering crowd. What a pity that one of the stately mirrors has not preserved a picture of the scene which by the very traits that were so transitory might have taught us much that would be worth knowing and remembering!

Would, at least, that either painter or mirror could convey to us some faint idea of a garment already noticed in this legend—the Lady Eleanore's embroidered mantle, which the gossips whispered was invested with magic properties, so as to lend a new and untried grace to her figure each time that she put it on! Idle fancy as it is, this mysterious mantle has thrown an awe around my image of her, partly from its fabled virtues and partly because it was the handiwork of a dying woman, and perchance owed the fantastic grace of its conception to the delirium of approaching death.

After the ceremonial greetings had been paid, Lady Eleanore Rochcliffe stood apart from the mob of guests, insulating herself within a small and distinguished circle to whom she accorded a more cordial favor than to the general throng. The waxen torches threw their radiance vividly over the scene, bringing out its brilliant points in strong relief, but she gazed carelessly, and with now and then an expression of weariness or scorn tempered with such feminine grace that her auditors scarcely perceived the moral deformity of which it was the utterance. She beheld the spectacle not with vulgar ridicule, as disdaining to be pleased with the provincial mockery of a court-festival, but with the deeper scorn of one whose spirit held itself too high to participate in the enjoyment of other human souls. Whether or no the recollections of those who saw her that evening were influenced by the strange events with which she was subsequently connected, so it was that her figure ever after recurred to them as marked by something wild and unnatural, although at the time the general whisper was of her exceeding beauty and of the indescribable charm which her mantle threw around her. Some close observers, indeed, detected a feverish flush and alternate paleness of countenance, with a corresponding flow and revulsion of spirits, and once or twice a painful and helpless betrayal of lassitude, as if she were on the point of sinking to the ground. Then, with a nervous shudder, she seemed to arouse her energies, and threw some bright and playful yet half-wicked sarcasm into the conversation. There was so strange a characteristic in her manners and sentiments that it astonished every right-minded listener, till, looking in her face, a lurking and incomprehensible glance and smile perplexed them with doubts both as to her seriousness and sanity. Gradually, Lady Eleanore Rochcliffe's circle grew smaller, till only four gentlemen remained in it. These were Captain Langford, the English officer before mentioned; a Virginian planter who had come to Massachusetts on some political errand; a young Episcopal clergyman, the grandson of a British earl; and, lastly, the private secretary of Governor Shute, whose obsequiousness had won a sort of tolerance from Lady Eleanore.

At different periods of the evening the liveried servants of the province-house passed among the guests bearing huge trays of refreshments and French and Spanish wines. Lady Eleanore Rochcliffe, who refused to wet her beautiful lips even with a bubble of champagne, had sunk back into a large damask chair, apparently overwearied either with the excitement of the scene or its tedium; and while, for an instant, she was unconscious of voices, laughter and music, a young man stole forward and knelt down at her feet. He bore a salver in his hand on which was a chased silver goblet filled to the brim with wine, which he offered as reverentially as to a crowned queen—or, rather, with the awful devotion of a priest doing sacrifice to his idol. Conscious that some one touched her robe, Lady Eleanore started, and unclosed her eyes upon the pale, wild features and dishevelled hair of Jervase Helwyse.

"Why do you haunt me thus?" said she, in a languid tone, but with a kindlier feeling than she ordinarily permitted herself to express. "They tell me that I have done you harm."

"Heaven knows if that be so," replied the young man, solemnly. "But, Lady Eleanore, in requital of that harm, if such there be, and for your own earthly and heavenly welfare, I pray you to take one sip of this holy wine and then to pass the goblet round among the guests. And this shall be a symbol that you have not sought to withdraw yourself from the chain of human sympathies, which whoso would shake off must keep company with fallen angels."

"Where has this mad fellow stolen that sacramental vessel?" exclaimed the Episcopal clergyman.

This question drew the notice of the guests to the silver cup, which was recognized as appertaining to the communion-plate of the Old South Church, and, for aught that could be known, it was brimming over with the consecrated wine.

"Perhaps it is poisoned," half whispered the governor's secretary.

"Pour it down the villain's throat!" cried the Virginian, fiercely.

"Turn him out of the house!" cried Captain Langford, seizing Jervase Helwyse so roughly by the shoulder that the sacramental cup was overturned and its contents sprinkled upon Lady

Eleanore's mantle. "Whether knave, fool or Bedlamite, it is intolerable that the fellow should go at large."

"Pray, gentlemen, do my poor admirer no harm," said Lady Eleanore, with a faint and weary smile. "Take him out of my sight, if such be your pleasure, for I can find in my heart to do nothing but laugh at him, whereas, in all decency and conscience, it would become me to weep for the mischief I have wrought."

But while the bystanders were attempting to lead away the unfortunate young man he broke from them and with a wild, impassioned earnestness offered a new and equally strange petition to Lady Eleanore. It was no other than that she should throw off the mantle, which while he pressed the silver cup of wine upon her she had drawn more closely around her form, so as almost to shroud herself within it.

"Cast it from you," exclaimed Jervase Helwyse, clasping his hands in an agony of entreaty. "It may not yet be too late. Give the accursed garment to the flames."

But Lady Eleanore, with a laugh of scorn, drew the rich folds of the embroidered mantle over her head in such a fashion as to give a completely new aspect to her beautiful face, which, half hidden, half revealed, seemed to belong to some being of mysterious character and purposes.

"Farewell, Jervase Helwyse!" said she. "Keep my image in your remembrance as you behold it now."

"Alas, lady!" he replied, in a tone no longer wild, but sad as a funeral-bell; "we must meet shortly when your face may wear another aspect, and that shall be the image that must abide within me." He made no more resistance to the violent efforts of the gentlemen and servants who almost dragged him out of the apartment and dismissed him roughly from the iron gate of the province-house.

Captain Langford, who had been very active in this affair, was returning to the presence of Lady Eleanore Rochcliffe, when he encountered the physician, Dr. Clarke, with whom he had held some casual talk on the day of her arrival. The doctor stood apart, separated from Lady Eleanore by the width of the room, but eying her with such keen sagacity that Captain Langford involuntarily gave him credit for the discovery of some deep secret.

"You appear to be smitten, after all, with the charms of this queenly maiden," said he, hoping thus to draw forth the physician's hidden knowledge.

"God forbid!" answered Dr. Clarke, with a grave smile; "and if you be wise, you will put up the same prayer for yourself. Woe to those who shall be smitten by this beautiful Lady Eleanore! But yonder stands the governor, and I have a word or two for his private ear. Good-night!" He accordingly advanced to Governor Shute and addressed him in so low a tone that none of the bystanders could catch a word of what he said, although the sudden change of His Excellency's hitherto cheerful visage betokened that the communication could be of no agreeable import. A very few moments afterward it was announced to the guests that an unforeseen circumstance rendered it necessary to put a premature close to the festival.

The ball at the province-house supplied a topic of conversation for the colonial metropolis for some days after its occurrence, and might still longer have been the general theme, only that a subject of all-engrossing interest thrust it for a time from the public recollection. This was the appearance of a dreadful epidemic which in that age, and long before and afterward, was wont to slay its hundreds and thousands on both sides of the Atlantic. On the occasion of which we speak it was distinguished by a peculiar virulence, insomuch that it has left its traces—its pitmarks, to use an appropriate figure—on the history of the country, the affairs of which were thrown into confusion by its ravages. At first, unlike its ordinary course, the disease seemed to confine itself to the higher circles of society, selecting its victims from among the proud, the well-born and the wealthy, entering unabashed into stately chambers and lying down with the slumberers in silken beds. Some of the most distinguished guests of the province-house—even those whom the haughty Lady Eleanore Rochcliffe had deemed not unworthy of her favor— were stricken by this fatal scourge. It was noticed with an ungenerous bitterness of feeling that the four gentlemen—the Virginian, the British officer, the young clergyman and the governor's secretary—who had been her most devoted attendants on the evening of the ball were the foremost on whom the plague-stroke fell. But the disease, pursuing its onward progress, soon ceased to be exclusively a prerogative of aristocracy. Its red brand was no longer conferred like a noble's star or an order of knighthood. It threaded its way through the narrow and crooked streets, and entered the low, mean, darksome dwellings and laid its hand of death upon the artisans and laboring classes of the town. It compelled rich and poor to feel themselves brethren then, and stalking to and fro across the Three Hills with a fierceness which made it almost a new pestilence, there was that mighty conqueror—that scourge and horror of our forefathers— the small-pox.

We cannot estimate the affright which this plague inspired of yore by contemplating it as the fangless monster of the present day. We must remember, rather, with what awe we watched the gigantic footsteps of the Asiatic cholera striding from shore to shore of the Atlantic and marching like Destiny upon cities far remote which flight had already half depopulated. There is no other fear so horrible and unhumanizing as that which makes man dread to breathe heaven's vital air lest it be poison, or to grasp the hand of a brother or friend lest the grip of the pestilence should clutch him. Such was the dismay that now followed in the track of the disease or ran before it throughout the town. Graves were hastily dug and the pestilential relics as hastily covered, because the dead were enemies of the living and strove to draw them headlong, as it were, into their own dismal pit. The public councils were suspended, as if mortal wisdom might relinquish its devices now that an unearthly usurper had found his way into the ruler's mansion. Had an enemy's fleet been hovering on the coast or his armies trampling on our soil, the people would probably have committed their defence to that same direful conqueror who had wrought their own calamity and would permit no interference with his sway. This conqueror had a symbol of his triumphs: it was a blood-red flag that fluttered in the tainted air over the door of every dwelling into which the small-pox had entered.

Such a banner was long since waving over the portal of the province-house, for thence, as was proved by tracking its footsteps back, had all this dreadful mischief issued. It had been traced back to a lady's luxurious chamber, to the proudest of the proud, to her that was so delicate and hardly owned herself of earthly mould, to the haughty one who took her stand above human sympathies—to Lady Eleanore. There remained no room for doubt that the contagion had lurked in that gorgeous mantle which threw so strange a grace around her at the festival. Its fantastic splendor had been conceived in the delirious brain of a woman on her death-bed and was the last toil of her stiffening fingers, which had interwoven fate and misery with its golden threads. This dark tale, whispered at first, was now bruited far and wide. The people raved against the Lady Eleanore and cried out that her pride and scorn had evoked a fiend, and that between them both this monstrous evil had been born. At times their rage and despair took the semblance of grinning mirth; and whenever the red flag of the pestilence was hoisted over another and yet another door, they clapped their hands and shouted through the streets in bitter mockery: "Behold a new triumph for the Lady Eleanore!"

One day in the midst of these dismal times a wild figure approached the portal of the province-house, and, folding his arms, stood contemplating the scarlet banner, which a passing breeze shook fitfully, as if to fling abroad the contagion that it typified. At length, climbing one of the pillars by means of the iron balustrade, he took down the flag, and entered the mansion waving it above his head. At the foot of the staircase he met the governor, booted and spurred, with his cloak drawn around him, evidently on the point of setting forth upon a journey.

"Wretched lunatic, what do you seek here?" exclaimed Shute, extending his cane to guard himself from contact. "There is nothing here but Death; back, or you will meet him."

"Death will not touch me, the banner-bearer of the pestilence," cried Jervase Helwyse, shaking the red flag aloft. "Death and the pestilence, who wears the aspect of the Lady Eleanore, will walk through the streets to-night, and I must march before them with this banner."

"Why do I waste words on the fellow?" muttered the governor, drawing his cloak across his mouth. "What matters his miserable life, when none of us are sure of twelve hours' breath?— On, fool, to your own destruction!"

He made way for Jervase Helwyse, who immediately ascended the staircase, but on the first landing-place was arrested by the firm grasp of a hand upon his shoulder. Looking fiercely up with a madman's impulse to struggle with and rend asunder his opponent, he found himself powerless beneath a calm, stern eye which possessed the mysterious property of quelling frenzy at its height. The person whom he had now encountered was the physician, Dr. Clarke, the duties of whose sad profession had led him to the province-house, where he was an infrequent guest in more prosperous times.

"Young man, what is your purpose?" demanded he.

"I seek the Lady Eleanore," answered Jervase Helwyse, submissively.

"All have fled from her," said the physician. "Why do you seek her now? I tell you, youth, her nurse fell death-stricken on the threshold of that fatal chamber. Know ye not that never came such a curse to our shores as this lovely Lady Eleanore, that her breath has filled the air with poison, that she has shaken pestilence and death upon the land from the folds of her accursed mantle?"

"Let me look upon her," rejoined the mad youth, more wildly. "Let me behold her in her awful beauty, clad in the regal garments of the pestilence. She and Death sit on a throne together; let me kneel down before them."

"Poor youth!" said Dr. Clarke, and, moved by a deep sense of human weakness, a smile of caustic humor curled his lip even then. "Wilt thou still worship the destroyer and surround her image with fantasies the more magnificent the more evil she has wrought? Thus man doth ever to his tyrants. Approach, then. Madness, as I have noted, has that good efficacy that it will guard you from contagion, and perhaps its own cure may be found in yonder chamber." Ascending another flight of stairs, he threw open a door and signed to Jervase Helwyse that he should enter.

The poor lunatic, it seems probable, had cherished a delusion that his haughty mistress sat in state, unharmed herself by the pestilential influence which as by enchantment she scattered round about her. He dreamed, no doubt, that her beauty was not dimmed, but brightened into superhuman splendor. With such anticipations he stole reverentially to the door at which the physician stood, but paused upon the threshold, gazing fearfully into the gloom of the darkened chamber.

"Where is the Lady Eleanore?" whispered he.

"Call her," replied the physician.

"Lady Eleanore! princess! queen of Death!" cried Jervase Helwyse, advancing three steps into the chamber. "She is not here. There, on yonder table, I behold the sparkle of a diamond which once she wore upon her bosom. There"—and he shuddered—"there hangs her mantle, on which a dead woman embroidered a spell of dreadful potency. But where is the Lady Eleanore?"

Something stirred within the silken curtains of a canopied bed and a low moan was uttered, which, listening intently, Jervase Helwyse began to distinguish as a woman's voice complaining dolefully of thirst. He fancied, even, that he recognized its tones.

"My throat! My throat is scorched," murmured the voice. "A drop of water!"

"What thing art thou?" said the brain-stricken youth, drawing near the bed and tearing asunder its curtains. "Whose voice hast thou stolen for thy murmurs and miserable petitions, as if Lady Eleanore could be conscious of mortal infirmity? Fie! Heap of diseased mortality, why lurkest thou in my lady's chamber?"

"Oh, Jervase Helwyse," said the voice—and as it spoke the figure contorted itself, struggling to hide its blasted face—"look not now on the woman you once loved. The curse of Heaven hath stricken me because I would not call man my brother nor woman sister. I wrapped myself in pride as in a mantle and scorned the sympathies of nature, and therefore has Nature made this wretched body the medium of a dreadful sympathy. You are avenged, they are all avenged, Nature is avenged; for I am Eleanore Rochcliffe."

The malice of his mental disease, the bitterness lurking at the bottom of his heart, mad as he was, for a blighted and ruined life and love that had been paid with cruel scorn, awoke within the breast of Jervase Helwyse. He shook his finger at the wretched girl, and the chamber echoed, the curtains of the bed were shaken, with his outburst of insane merriment.

"Another triumph for the Lady Eleanore!" he cried. "All have been her victims; who so worthy to be the final victim as herself?" Impelled by some new fantasy of his crazed intellect, he snatched the fatal mantle and rushed from the chamber and the house.

That night a procession passed by torchlight through the streets, bearing in the midst the figure of a woman enveloped with a richly-embroidered mantle, while in advance stalked Jervase Helwyse waving the red flag of the pestilence. Arriving opposite the province-house, the mob burned the effigy, and a strong wind came and swept away the ashes. It was said that from that very hour the pestilence abated, as if its sway had some mysterious connection, from the first plague-stroke to the last, with Lady Elcanore's mantle. A remarkable uncertainty broods over that unhappy lady's fate. There is a belief, however, that in a certain chamber of this mansion a female form may sometimes be duskily discerned shrinking into the darkest corner and muffling her face within an embroidered mantle. Supposing the legend true, can this be other than the once proud Lady Eleanore?

Mine host and the old loyalist and I bestowed no little Warmth of applause upon this narrative, in which we had all been deeply interested; for the reader can scarcely conceive how unspeakably the effect of such a tale is heightened when, as in the present case, we may repose perfect confidence in the veracity of him who tells it. For my own part, knowing how scrupulous is Mr. Tiffany to settle the foundation of his facts, I could not have believed him one whit the more faithfully had he professed himself an eyewitness of the doings and sufferings of poor Lady Eleanore. Some sceptics, it is true, might demand documentary evidence, or even require him to produce the embroidered mantle, forgetting that—Heaven be praised!—it was consumed to ashes.

But now the old loyalist, whose blood was warmed by the good cheer, began to talk, in his turn, about the traditions of the Province House, and hinted that he, if it were agreeable, might add a few reminiscences to our legendary stock. Mr. Tiffany, having no cause to dread a rival, immediately besought him to favor us with a specimen; my own entreaties, of course, were urged to the same effect; and our venerable guest, well pleased to find willing auditors, awaited only the return of Mr. Thomas Waite, who had been summoned forth to provide accommodations for several new arrivals. Perchance the public—but be this as its own caprice and ours shall settle the matter—may read the result in another tale of the Province House.

IV. OLD ESTHER DUDLEY

Our host having resumed the chair, he as well as Mr. Tiffany and myself expressed much eagerness to be made acquainted with the story to which the loyalist had alluded. That venerable man first of all saw lit to moisten his throat with another glass of wine, and then, turning his face toward our coal-fire, looked steadfastly for a few moments into the depths of its cheerful glow. Finally he poured forth a great fluency of speech. The generous liquid that he had imbibed, while it warmed his age-chilled blood, likewise took off the chill from his heart and mind, and gave him an energy to think and feel which we could hardly have expected to find beneath the snows of fourscore winters. His feelings, indeed, appeared to me more excitable than those of a younger man—or, at least, the same degree of feeling manifested itself by more visible effects than if his judgment and will had possessed the potency of meridian life. At the pathetic passages of his narrative he readily melted into tears. When a breath of indignation swept across his spirit, the blood flushed his withered visage even to the roots of his white hair, and he shook his clinched fist at the trio of peaceful auditors, seeming to fancy enemies in those who felt very kindly toward the desolate old soul. But ever and anon, sometimes in the midst of his most earnest talk, this ancient person's intellect would wander vaguely, losing its hold of the matter in hand and groping for it amid misty shadows. Then would he cackle forth a feeble laugh and express a doubt whether his wits—for by that phrase it pleased our ancient friend to signify his mental powers—were not getting a little the worse for wear.

Under these disadvantages, the old loyalist's story required more revision to render it fit for the public eye than those of the series which have preceded it; nor should it be concealed that the sentiment and tone of the affair may have undergone some slight—or perchance more than slight—metamorphosis in its transmission to the reader through the medium of a thoroughgoing democrat. The tale itself is a mere sketch with no involution of plot nor any great interest of events, yet possessing, if I have rehearsed it aright, that pensive influence over the mind which the shadow of the old Province House flings upon the loiterer in its court-yard.

The hour had come—the hour of defeat and humiliation—when Sir William Howe was to pass over the threshold of the province-house and embark, with no such triumphal ceremonies as he once promised himself, on board the British fleet. He bade his servants and military attendants go before him, and lingered a moment in the loneliness of the mansion to quell the fierce emotions that struggled in his bosom as with a death-throb. Preferable then would he have deemed his fate had a warrior's death left him a claim to the narrow territory of a grave within the soil which the king had given him to defend. With an ominous perception that as his departing footsteps echoed adown the staircase the sway of Britain was passing for ever from New England, he smote his clenched hand on his brow and cursed the destiny that had flung the shame of a dismembered empire upon him.

"Would to God," cried he, hardly repressing his tears of rage, "that the rebels were even now at the doorstep! A blood-stain upon the floor should then bear testimony that the last British ruler was faithful to his trust."

The tremulous voice of a woman replied to his exclamation.

"Heaven's cause and the king's are one," it said. "Go forth, Sir William Howe, and trust in Heaven to bring back a royal governor in triumph."

Subduing at once the passion to which he had yielded only in the faith that it was unwitnessed, Sir William Howe became conscious that an aged woman leaning on a gold-headed staff was standing betwixt him and the door. It was old Esther Dudley, who had dwelt almost immemorial years in this mansion, until her presence seemed as inseparable from it as the recollections of its history. She was the daughter of an ancient and once eminent family which had fallen into poverty and decay and left its last descendant no resource save the bounty of the king, nor any shelter except within the walls of the province-house. An office in the household with merely nominal duties had been assigned to her as a pretext for the payment of a small pension, the greater part of which she expended in adorning herself with an antique magnificence of attire. The claims of Esther Dudley's gentle blood were acknowledged by all the successive governors, and they treated her with the punctilious courtesy which it was her foible to demand, not always with success, from a neglectful world. The only actual share which she assumed in the business of the mansion was to glide through its passages and public chambers late at night to see that the servants had dropped no fire from their flaring torches nor left embers crackling and blazing on the hearths. Perhaps it was this invariable custom of walking her rounds in the hush of midnight that caused the superstition of the times to invest the old woman with attributes of awe and mystery, fabling that she had entered the portal of the province-house—none knew whence—in the train of the first royal governor, and that it was her fate to dwell there till the last should have departed.

But Sir William Howe, if he ever heard this legend, had forgotten it.

"Mistress Dudley, why are you loitering here?" asked he, with some severity of tone. "It is my pleasure to be the last in this mansion of the king."

"Not so, if it please Your Excellency," answered the time-stricken woman. "This roof has sheltered me long; I will not pass from it until they bear me to the tomb of my forefathers. What other shelter is there for old Esther Dudley save the province-house or the grave?"

"Now, Heaven forgive me!" said Sir William Howe to himself. "I was about to leave this wretched old creature to starve or beg.—Take this, good Mistress Dudley," he added, putting a purse into her hands. "King George's head on these golden guineas is sterling yet, and will continue so, I warrant you, even should the rebels crown John Hancock their king. That purse will buy a better shelter than the province-house can now afford."

"While the burden of life remains upon me I will have no other shelter than this roof," persisted Esther Dudley, striking her staff upon the floor with a gesture that expressed immovable resolve; "and when Your Excellency returns in triumph, I will totter into the porch to welcome you."

"My poor old friend!" answered the British general, and all his manly and martial pride could no longer restrain a gush of bitter tears. "This is an evil hour for you and me. The province which the king entrusted to my charge is lost. I go hence in misfortune—perchance in disgrace—to return no more. And you, whose present being is incorporated with the past, who have seen governor after governor in stately pageantry ascend these steps, whose whole life has been an observance of majestic ceremonies and a worship of the king,—how will you endure the change? Come with us; bid farewell to a land that has shaken off its allegiance, and live still under a royal government at Halifax."

"Never! never!" said the pertinacious old dame. "Here will I abide, and King George shall still have one true subject in his disloyal province."

"Beshrew the old fool!" muttered Sir William Howe, growing impatient of her obstinacy and ashamed of the emotion into which he had been betrayed. "She is the very moral of old-fashioned prejudice, and could exist nowhere but in this musty edifice.—Well, then, Mistress Dudley, since you will needs tarry, I give the province-house in charge to you. Take this key, and keep it safe until myself or some other royal governor shall demand it of you." Smiling bitterly at himself and her, he took the heavy key of the province-house, and, delivering it into the old lady's hands, drew his cloak around him for departure.

As the general glanced back at Esther Dudley's antique figure he deemed her well fitted for such a charge, as being so perfect a representative of the decayed past—of an age gone by, with its manners, opinions, faith and feelings all fallen into oblivion or scorn, of what had once been a reality, but was now merely a vision of faded magnificence. Then Sir William Howe strode forth, smiting his clenched hands together in the fierce anguish of his spirit, and old Esther Dudley was left to keep watch in the lonely province-house, dwelling there with Memory; and if Hope ever seemed to flit around her, still it was Memory in disguise.

The total change of affairs that ensued on the departure of the British troops did not drive the venerable lady from her stronghold. There was not for many years afterward a governor of Massachusetts, and the magistrates who had charge of such matters saw no objection to Esther Dudley's residence in the province-house, especially as they must otherwise have paid a hireling for taking care of the premises, which with her was a labor of love; and so they left her the undisturbed mistress of the old historic edifice. Many and strange were the fables which the gossips whispered about her in all the chimney-corners of the town.

Among the time-worn articles of furniture that had been left in the mansion, there was a tall antique mirror which was well worthy of a tale by itself, and perhaps may hereafter be the theme of one. The gold of its heavily-wrought frame was tarnished, and its surface so blurred that the old woman's figure, whenever she paused before it, looked indistinct and ghostlike. But it was the general belief that Esther could cause the governors of the overthrown dynasty, with the beautiful ladies who had once adorned their festivals, the Indian chiefs who had come up to the province-house to hold council or swear allegiance, the grim provincial warriors, the severe clergymen—in short, all the pageantry of gone days, all the figures that ever swept across the broad-plate of glass in former times,—she could cause the whole to reappear and people the inner world of the mirror with shadows of old life. Such legends as these, together with the singularity of her isolated existence, her age and the infirmity that each added winter flung upon her, made Mistress Dudley the object both of fear and pity, and it was partly the result of either sentiment that, amid all the angry license of the times, neither wrong nor insult ever fell upon her unprotected head. Indeed, there was so much haughtiness in her demeanor toward intruders—among whom she reckoned all persons acting under the new authorities—that it was really an affair of no small nerve to look her in the face. And, to do the people justice, stern republicans as they had now become, they were well content that the old gentlewoman, in her hoop-petticoat and faded embroidery, should still haunt the palace of ruined pride and overthrown power, the symbol of a departed system, embodying a history in her person. So Esther Dudley dwelt year after year in the province-house, still reverencing all that others had flung aside, still faithful to her king, who, so long as the venerable dame yet held her post, might be said to retain one true subject in New England and one spot of the empire that had been wrested from him.

And did she dwell there in utter loneliness? Rumor said, "Not so." Whenever her chill and withered heart desired warmth, she was wont to summon a black slave of Governor Shirley's from the blurred mirror and send him in search of guests who had long ago been familiar in those deserted chambers. Forth went the sable messenger, with the starlight or the moonshine gleaming through him, and did his errand in the burial-grounds, knocking at the iron doors of tombs or upon the marble slabs that covered them, and whispering to those within, "My mistress, old Esther Dudley, bids you to the province-house at midnight;" and punctually as the clock of the Old South told twelve came the shadows of the Olivers, the Hutchinsons, the Dudleys—all the grandees of a bygone generation—gliding beneath the portal into the well-known mansion, where Esther mingled with them as if she likewise were a shade. Without vouching for the truth of such traditions, it is certain that Mistress Dudley sometimes assembled a few of the stanch though crestfallen old Tories who had lingered in the rebel town during those days of wrath and tribulation. Out of a cobwebbed bottle containing liquor that a royal governor might have smacked his lips over they quaffed healths to the king and babbled treason to the republic, feeling as if the protecting shadow of the throne were still flung around them. But, draining the last drops of their liquor, they stole timorously homeward, and answered not again if the rude mob reviled them in the street.

Yet Esther Dudley's most frequent and favored guests were the children of the town. Toward them she was never stern. A kindly and loving nature hindered elsewhere from its free course by a thousand rocky prejudices lavished itself upon these little ones. By bribes of gingerbread of her own making, stamped with a royal crown, she tempted their sunny sportiveness beneath the gloomy portal of the province-house, and would often beguile them to spend a whole play-day there, sitting in a circle round the verge of her hoop-petticoat, greedily attentive to her stories of a dead world. And when these little boys and girls stole forth again from the dark, mysterious mansion, they went bewildered, full of old feelings that graver people had long ago forgotten, rubbing their eyes at the world around them as if they had gone astray into ancient times and become children of the past. At home, when their parents asked where they had loitered such a weary while and with whom they had been at play, the children would talk of all the departed worthies of the province as far back as Governor Belcher and the haughty dame of Sir William Phipps. It would seem as though they had been sitting on the knees of these famous personages, whom the grave had hidden for half a century, and had toyed with the embroidery of their rich waistcoats or roguishly pulled the long curls of their flowing wigs. "But Governor Belcher has been dead this many a year," would the mother say to her little boy. "And did you really see him at the province-house?"—"Oh yes, dear mother—yes!" the half-dreaming child would answer. "But when old Esther had done speaking about him, he faded away out of his chair." Thus, without affrighting her little guests, she led them by the hand into the chambers of her own desolate heart and made childhood's fancy discern the ghosts that haunted there.

Living so continually in her own circle of ideas, and never regulating her mind by a proper reference to present things, Esther Dudley appears to have grown partially crazed. It was found that she had no right sense of the progress and true state of the Revolutionary war, but held a constant faith that the armies of Britain were victorious on every field and destined to be ultimately triumphant. Whenever the town rejoiced for a battle won by Washington or Gates or Morgan or Greene, the news, in passing through the door of the province-house as through the ivory gate of dreams, became metamorphosed into a strange tale of the prowess of Howe, Clinton or Cornwallis. Sooner or later, it was her invincible belief, the colonies would be prostrate at the footstool of the king. Sometimes she seemed to take for granted that such was already the case. On one occasion she startled the townspeople by a brilliant illumination of the province-house with candles at every pane of glass and a transparency of the king's initials and a crown of light in the great balcony-window. The figure of the aged woman in the most gorgeous of her mildewed velvets and brocades was seen passing from casement to casement, until she paused before the balcony and flourished a huge key above her head. Her wrinkled visage actually gleamed with triumph, as if the soul within her were a festal lamp.

"What means this blaze of light? What does old Esther's joy portend?" whispered a spectator. "It is frightful to see her gliding about the chambers and rejoicing there without a soul to bear her company."

"It is as if she were making merry in a tomb," said another.

"Pshaw! It is no such mystery," observed an old man, after some brief exercise of memory. "Mistress Dudley is keeping jubilee for the king of England's birthday."

Then the people laughed aloud, and would have thrown mud against the blazing transparency of the king's crown and initials, only that they pitied the poor old dame who was so dismally triumphant amid the wreck and ruin of the system to which she appertained.

Oftentimes it was her custom to climb the weary staircase that wound upward to the cupola, and thence strain her dimmed eyesight seaward and countryward, watching for a British fleet or for the march of a grand procession with the king's banner floating over it. The passengers in the street below would discern her anxious visage and send up a shout: "When the golden Indian on the province-house shall shoot his arrow, and when the cock on the Old South spire shall crow, then look for a royal governor again!" for this had grown a by-word through the town. And at last, after long, long years, old Esther Dudley knew—or perchance she only dreamed—that a royal governor was on the eve of returning to the province-house to receive the heavy key which Sir William Howe had committed to her charge. Now, it was the fact that intelligence bearing some faint analogy to Esther's version of it was current among the townspeople. She set the mansion in the best order that her means allowed, and, arraying herself in silks and tarnished gold, stood long before the blurred mirror to admire her own magnificence. As she gazed the gray and withered lady moved her ashen lips, murmuring half aloud, talking to shapes that she saw within the mirror, to shadows of her own fantasies, to the household friends of memory, and bidding them rejoice with her and come forth to meet the governor. And while absorbed in this communion Mistress Dudley heard the tramp of many footsteps in the street, and, looking out at the window, beheld what she construed as the royal governor's arrival.

"Oh, happy day! Oh, blessed, blessed hour!" she exclaimed. "Let me but bid him welcome within the portal, and my task in the province-house and on earth is done." Then, with tottering feet which age and tremulous joy caused to tread amiss, she hurried down the grand staircase, her silks sweeping and rustling as she went; so that the sound was as if a train of special courtiers were thronging from the dim mirror.

And Esther Dudley fancied that as soon as the wide door should be flung open all the pomp and splendor of bygone times would pace majestically into the province-house and the gilded tapestry of the past would be brightened by the sunshine of the present. She turned the key, withdrew it from the lock, unclosed the door and stepped across the threshold. Advancing up the court-yard appeared a person of most dignified mien, with tokens, as Esther interpreted them, of gentle blood, high rank and long-accustomed authority even in his walk and every gesture. He was richly dressed, but wore a gouty shoe, which, however, did not lessen the stateliness of his gait. Around and behind him were people in plain civic dresses and two or three war-worn veterans—evidently officers of rank—arrayed in a uniform of blue and buff. But Esther Dudley, firm in the belief that had fastened its roots about her heart, beheld only the principal personage, and never doubted that this was the long-looked-for governor to whom she was to surrender up her charge. As he approached she involuntarily sank down on her knees and tremblingly held forth the heavy key.

"Receive my trust! Take it quickly," cried she, "for methinks Death is striving to snatch away my triumph. But he comes too late. Thank Heaven for this blessed hour! God save King George!"

"That, madam, is a strange prayer to be offered up at such a moment," replied the unknown guest of the province-house, and, courteously removing his hat, he offered his arm to raise the aged woman. "Yet, in reverence for your gray hairs and long-kept faith, Heaven forbid that any here should say you nay. Over the realms which still acknowledge his sceptre, God save King George!"

Esther Dudley started to her feet, and, hastily clutching back the key, gazed with fearful earnestness at the stranger, and dimly and doubtfully, as if suddenly awakened from a dream, her bewildered eyes half recognized his face. Years ago she had known him among the gentry of the province, but the ban of the king had fallen upon him. How, then, came the doomed victim here? Proscribed, excluded from mercy, the monarch's most dreaded and hated foe, this New England merchant had stood triumphantly against a kingdom's strength, and his foot now trod upon humbled royalty as he ascended the steps of the province-house, the people's chosen governor of Massachusetts.

"Wretch, wretch that I am!" muttered the old woman, with such a heartbroken expression that the tears gushed from the stranger's eyes. "Have I bidden a traitor welcome?—Come, Death! come quickly!"

"Alas, venerable lady!" said Governor Hancock, lending her his support with all the reverence that a courtier would have shown to a queen, "your life has been prolonged until the world has changed around you. You have treasured up all that time has rendered worthless— the principles, feelings, manners, modes of being and acting which another generation has flung aside—and you are a symbol of the past. And I and these around me—we represent a new race of men, living no longer in the past, scarcely in the present, but projecting our lives forward into the future. Ceasing to model ourselves on ancestral superstitions, it is our faith and principle to press onward—onward.—Yet," continued he, turning to his attendants, "let us reverence for the last time the stately and gorgeous prejudices of the tottering past."

While the republican governor spoke he had continued to support the helpless form of Esther Dudley; her weight grew heavier against his arm, but at last, with a sudden effort to free herself, the ancient woman sank down beside one of the pillars of the portal. The key of the province-house fell from her grasp and clanked against the stone.

"I have been faithful unto death," murmured she. "God save the king!"

"She hath done her office," said Hancock, solemnly. "We will follow her reverently to the tomb of her ancestors, and then, my fellow-citizens, onward—onward. We are no longer children of the past."

As the old loyalist concluded his narrative the enthusiasm which had been fitfully flashing within his sunken eyes and quivering across his wrinkled visage faded away, as if all the lingering fire of his soul were extinguished. Just then, too, a lamp upon the mantelpiece threw out a dying gleam, which vanished as speedily as it shot upward, compelling our eyes to grope for one another's features by the dim glow of the hearth. With such a lingering fire, methought, with such a dying gleam, had the glory of the ancient system vanished from the province-house when the spirit of old Esther Dudley took its flight. And now, again, the clock of the Old South threw its voice of ages on the breeze, knolling the hourly knell of the past, crying out far and wide through the multitudinous city, and filling our ears, as we sat in the dusky chamber, with its reverberating depth of tone. In that same mansion—in that very chamber—what a volume of history had been told off into hours by the same voice that was now trembling in the air! Many a governor had heard those midnight accents and longed to exchange his stately cares for slumber. And, as for mine host and Mr. Bela Tiffany and the old loyalist and me, we had babbled about dreams of the past until we almost fancied that the clock was still striking in a bygone century. Neither of us would have wondered had a hoop-petticoated phantom of Esther

Dudley tottered into the chamber, walking her rounds in the hush of midnight as of yore, and motioned us to quench the fading embers of the fire and leave the historic precincts to herself and her kindred shades. But, as no such vision was vouchsafed, I retired unbidden, and would advise Mr. Tiffany to lay hold of another auditor, being resolved not to show my face in the Province House for a good while hence—if ever.

THE HAUNTED MIND

WHAT A SINGULAR MOMENT is the first one, when you have hardly begun to recollect yourself, after starting from midnight slumber! By unclosing your eyes so suddenly you seem to have surprised the personages of your dream in full convocation round your bed, and catch one broad glance at them before they can flit into obscurity. Or, to vary the metaphor, you find yourself for a single instant wide awake in that realm of illusions whither sleep has been the passport, and behold its ghostly inhabitants and wondrous scenery with a perception of their strangeness such as you never attain while the dream is undisturbed. The distant sound of a church-clock is borne faintly on the wind. You question with yourself, half seriously, whether it has stolen to your waking ear from some gray tower that stood within the precincts of your dream. While yet in suspense another clock flings its heavy clang over the slumbering town with so full and distinct a sound, and such a long murmur in the neighboring air, that you are certain it must proceed from the steeple at the nearest corner; You count the strokes—one, two; and there they cease with a booming sound like the gathering of a third stroke within the bell.

If you could choose an hour of wakefulness out of the whole night, it would be this. Since your sober bedtime, at eleven, you have had rest enough to take off the pressure of yesterday's fatigue, while before you, till the sun comes from "Far Cathay" to brighten your window, there is almost the space of a summer night—one hour to be spent in thought with the mind's eye half shut, and two in pleasant dreams, and two in that strangest of enjoyments the forgetfulness alike of joy and woe. The moment of rising belongs to another period of time, and appears so distant that the plunge out of a warm bed into the frosty air cannot yet be anticipated with dismay. Yesterday has already vanished among the shadows of the past; to-morrow has not yet emerged from the future. You have found an intermediate space where the business of life does not intrude, where the passing moment lingers and becomes truly the present; a spot where Father Time, when he thinks nobody is watching him, sits down by the wayside to take breath. Oh that he would fall asleep and let mortals live on without growing older!

Hitherto you have lain perfectly still, because the slightest motion would dissipate the fragments of your slumber. Now, being irrevocably awake, you peep through the half-drawn window-curtain, and observe that the glass is ornamented with fanciful devices in frost-work, and that each pane presents something like a frozen dream. There will be time enough to trace out the analogy while waiting the summons to breakfast. Seen through the clear portion of the glass where the silvery mountain-peaks of the frost-scenery do not ascend, the most conspicuous object is the steeple, the white spire of which directs you to the wintry lustre of the firmament. You may almost distinguish the figures on the clock that has just told the hour. Such a frosty sky and the snow-covered roofs and the long vista of the frozen street, all white, and the distant water hardened into rock, might make you shiver even under four blankets and a woollen comforter. Yet look at that one glorious star! Its beams are distinguishable from all the rest, and actually cast the shadow of the casement on the bed with a radiance of deeper hue than moonlight, though not so accurate an outline.

You sink down and muffle your head in the clothes, shivering all the while, but less from bodily chill than the bare idea of a polar atmosphere. It is too cold even for the thoughts to venture abroad. You speculate on the luxury of wearing out a whole existence in bed like an oyster in its shell, content with the sluggish ecstasy of inaction, and drowsily conscious of nothing but delicious warmth such as you now feel again. Ah! that idea has brought a hideous one in its train. You think how the dead are lying in their cold shrouds and narrow coffins through the drear winter of the grave, and cannot persuade your fancy that they neither shrink nor shiver when the snow is drifting over their little hillocks and the bitter blast howls against the door of the tomb. That gloomy thought will collect a gloomy multitude and throw its complexion over your wakeful hour.

In the depths of every heart there is a tomb and a dungeon, though the lights, the music and revelry, above may cause us to forget their existence and the buried ones or prisoners whom they hide. But sometimes, and oftenest at midnight, those dark receptacles are flung wide open. In an hour like this, when the mind has a passive sensibility, but no active strength—when the imagination is a mirror imparting vividness to all ideas without the power of selecting or controlling them—then pray that your griefs may slumber and the brotherhood of remorse not break their chain. It is too late. A funeral train comes gliding by your bed in which passion and feeling assume bodily shape and things of the mind become dim spectres to the eye. There is your earliest sorrow, a pale young mourner wearing a sister's likeness to first love, sadly beautiful, with a hallowed sweetness in her melancholy features and grace in the flow of her sable robe. Next appears a shade of ruined loveliness with dust among her golden hair and her bright garments all faded and defaced, stealing from your glance with drooping head, as fearful of reproach: she was your fondest hope, but a delusive one; so call her Disappointment now. A sterner form succeeds, with a brow of wrinkles, a look and gesture of iron authority; there is no name for him unless it be Fatality—an emblem of the evil influence that rules your fortunes, a demon to whom you subjected yourself by some error at the outset of life, and were bound his slave for ever by once obeying him. See those fiendish lineaments graven on the darkness, the writhed lip of scorn, the mockery of that living eye, the pointed finger touching the sore place in your heart! Do you remember any act of enormous folly at which you would blush even in the remotest cavern of the earth? Then recognize your shame.

Pass, wretched band! Well for the wakeful one if, riotously miserable, a fiercer tribe do not surround him—the devils of a guilty heart that holds its hell within itself. What if Remorse should assume the features of an injured friend? What if the fiend should come in woman's garments with a pale beauty amid sin and desolation, and lie down by your side? What if he should stand at your bed's foot in the likeness of a corpse with a bloody stain upon the shroud? Sufficient without such guilt is this nightmare of the soul, this heavy, heavy sinking of the spirits, this wintry gloom about the heart, this indistinct horror of the mind blending itself with the darkness of the chamber.

By a desperate effort you start upright, breaking from a sort of conscious sleep and gazing wildly round the bed, as if the fiends were anywhere but in your haunted mind. At the same moment the slumbering embers on the hearth send forth a gleam which palely illuminates the whole outer room and flickers through the door of the bedchamber, but cannot quite dispel its obscurity. Your eye searches for whatever may remind you of the living world. With eager minuteness you take note of the table near the fireplace, the book with an ivory knife between its leaves, the unfolded letter, the hat and the fallen glove. Soon the flame vanishes, and with it the whole scene is gone, though its image remains an instant in your mind's eye when darkness has swallowed the reality. Throughout the chamber there is the same obscurity as before, but not the same gloom within your breast.

As your head falls back upon the pillow you think—in a whisper be it spoken—how pleasant in these night solitudes would be the rise and fall of a softer breathing than your own, the slight pressure of a tenderer bosom, the quiet throb of a purer heart, imparting its peacefulness to your troubled one, as if the fond sleeper were involving you in her dream. Her influence is over you, though she have no existence but in that momentary image. You sink down in a flowery spot on the borders of sleep and wakefulness, while your thoughts rise before you in pictures, all disconnected, yet all assimilated by a pervading gladsomeness and beauty. The wheeling of gorgeous squadrons that glitter in the sun is succeeded by the merriment of children round the door of a schoolhouse beneath the glimmering shadow of old trees at the corner of a rustic lane. You stand in the sunny rain of a summer shower, and wander among the sunny trees of an autumnal wood, and look upward at the brightest of all rainbows overarching the unbroken sheet of snow on the American side of Niagara. Your mind struggles pleasantly between the dancing radiance round the hearth of a young man and his recent bride and the twittering flight of birds in spring about their new-made nest. You feel the merry bounding of a ship before the breeze, and watch the tuneful feet of rosy girls as they twine their last and merriest dance in a splendid ball-room, and find yourself in the brilliant circle of a crowded theatre as the curtain falls over a light and airy scene.

With an involuntary start you seize hold on consciousness, and prove yourself but half awake by running a doubtful parallel between human life and the hour which has now elapsed. In both you emerge from mystery, pass through a vicissitude that you can but imperfectly control, and are borne onward to another mystery. Now comes the peal of the distant clock with fainter and fainter strokes as you plunge farther into the wilderness of sleep. It is the knell of a temporary death. Your spirit has departed, and strays like a free citizen among the people of a shadowy world, beholding strange sights, yet without wonder or dismay. So calm, perhaps, will be the final change—so undisturbed, as if among familiar things, the entrance of the soul to its eternal home.

THE VILLAGE UNCLE

AN IMAGINARY RETROSPECT.

COME! another log upon the hearth. True, our little parlor is comfortable, especially here where the old man sits in his old arm-chair; but on Thanksgiving-night the blaze should dance higher up the chimney and send a shower of sparks into the outer darkness. Toss on an armful of those dry oak chips, the last relics of the Mermaid's knee-timbers—the bones of your namesake, Susan. Higher yet, and clearer, be the blaze, till our cottage windows glow the ruddiest in the village and the light of our household mirth flash far across the bay to Nahant.

And now come, Susan; come, my children. Draw your chairs round me, all of you. There is a dimness over your figures. You sit quivering indistinctly with each motion of the blaze, which eddies about you like a flood; so that you all have the look of visions or people that dwell only in the firelight, and will vanish from existence as completely as your own shadows when the flame shall sink among the embers.

Hark! let me listen for the swell of the surf; it should be audible a mile inland on a night like this. Yes; there I catch the sound, but only an uncertain murmur, as if a good way down over the beach, though by the almanac it is high tide at eight o'clock, and the billows must now be dashing within thirty yards of our door. Ah! the old man's ears are failing him, and so is his eyesight, and perhaps his mind, else you would not all be so shadowy in the blaze of his Thanksgiving fire.

How strangely the past is peeping over the shoulders of the present! To judge by my recollections, it is but a few moments since I sat in another room. Yonder model of a vessel was not there, nor the old chest of drawers, nor Susan's profile and mine in that gilt frame—nothing, in short, except this same fire, which glimmered on books, papers and a picture, and half discovered my solitary figure in a looking-glass. But it was paler than my rugged old self, and younger, too, by almost half a century.

Speak to me, Susan; speak, my beloved ones; for the scene is glimmering on my sight again, and as it brightens you fade away. Oh, I should be loth to lose my treasure of past happiness and become once more what I was then—a hermit in the depths of my own mind, sometimes yawning over drowsy volumes and anon a scribbler of wearier trash than what I read; a man who had wandered out of the real world and got into its shadow, where his troubles, joys and vicissitudes were of such slight stuff that he hardly knew whether he lived or only dreamed of living. Thank Heaven I am an old man now and have done with all such vanities!

Still this dimness of mine eyes!—Come nearer, Susan, and stand before the fullest blaze of the hearth. Now I behold you illuminated from head to foot, in your clean cap and decent gown, with the dear lock of gray hair across your forehead and a quiet smile about your mouth, while the eyes alone are concealed by the red gleam of the fire upon your spectacles. There! you made me tremble again. When the flame quivered, my sweet Susan, you quivered with it and grew indistinct, as if melting into the warm light, that my last glimpse of you might be as visionary as the first was, full many a year since. Do you remember it? You stood on the little bridge over the brook that runs across King's Beach into the sea. It was twilight, the waves rolling in, the wind sweeping by, the crimson clouds fading in the west and the silver moon brightening above the hill; and on the bridge were you, fluttering in the breeze like a sea-bird that might skim away at your pleasure. You seemed a daughter of the viewless wind, a creature of the ocean-foam and the crimson light, whose merry life was spent in dancing on the crests of the billows that threw up their spray to support your footsteps. As I drew nearer I fancied you akin to the race of mermaids, and thought how pleasant it would be to dwell with you among the quiet coves in the shadow of the cliffs, and to roam along secluded beaches of the purest sand, and, when our Northern shores grew bleak, to haunt the islands, green and lonely, far amid summer seas. And yet it gladdened me, after all this nonsense, to find you nothing but a pretty young girl sadly perplexed with the rude behavior of the wind about your petticoats. Thus I did with Susan as with most other things in my earlier days, dipping her image into my mind and coloring it of a thousand fantastic hues before I could see her as she really was.

Now, Susan, for a sober picture of our village. It was a small collection of dwellings that seemed to have been cast up by the sea with the rock-weed and marine plants that it vomits after a storm, or to have come ashore among the pipe-staves and other lumber which had been washed from the deck of an Eastern schooner. There was just space for the narrow and sandy street between the beach in front and a precipitous hill that lifted its rocky forehead in the rear among a waste of juniper-bushes and the wild growth of a broken pasture. The village was picturesque in the variety of its edifices, though all were rude. Here stood a little old hovel, built, perhaps, of driftwood, there a row of boat-houses, and beyond them a two-story dwelling of dark and weatherbeaten aspect, the whole intermixed with one or two snug cottages painted white, a sufficiency of pig-styes and a shoemaker's shop. Two grocery stores stood opposite each other in the centre of the village. These were the places of resort at their idle hours of a hardy throng of fishermen in red baize shirts, oilcloth trousers and boots of brown leather covering the whole leg—true seven-league boots, but fitter to wade the ocean than walk the earth. The wearers seemed amphibious, as if they did but creep out of salt water to sun themselves; nor would it have been wonderful to see their lower limbs covered with clusters of little shellfish such as cling to rocks and old ship-timber over which the tide ebbs and flows. When their fleet of boats was weather-bound, the butchers raised their price, and the spit was busier than the frying-pan; for this was a place of fish, and known as such to all the country round about. The very air was fishy, being perfumed with dead sculpins, hard-heads and dogfish strewn plentifully on the beach.—You see, children, the village is but little changed since your mother and I were young.

How like a dream it was when I bent over a pool of water one pleasant morning and saw that the ocean had dashed its spray over me and made me a fisherman! There was the tarpaulin, the baize shirt, the oilcloth trousers and seven-league boots, and there my own features, but so reddened with sunburn and sea-breezes that methought I had another face, and on other shoulders too. The seagulls and the loons and I had now all one trade: we skimmed the crested waves and sought our prey beneath them, the man with as keen enjoyment as the birds. Always when the east grew purple I launched my dory, my little flat-bottomed skiff, and rowed cross-handed to Point Ledge, the Middle Ledge, or perhaps beyond Egg Rock; often, too, did I anchor off Dread Ledge—a spot of peril to ships unpiloted—and sometimes spread an adventurous sail and tracked across the bay to South Shore, casting my lines in sight of Scituate. Ere nightfall I hauled my skiff high and dry on the beach, laden with red rock-cod or the white-bellied ones of deep water, haddock bearing the black marks of St. Peter's fingers near the gills, the long-bearded hake whose liver holds oil enough for a midnight lamp, and now and then a mighty halibut with a back broad as my boat. In the autumn I toled and caught those lovely fish the mackerel. When the wind was high, when the whale-boats anchored off the Point nodded their slender masts at each other and the dories pitched and tossed in the surf, when Nahant Beach was thundering three miles off and the spray broke a hundred feet in the air round the distant base of Egg Rock, when the brimful and boisterous sea threatened to tumble over the street of our village,—then I made a holiday on shore.

Many such a day did I sit snugly in Mr. Bartlett's store, attentive to the yarns of Uncle Parker—uncle to the whole village by right of seniority, but of Southern blood, with no kindred in New England. His figure is before me now enthroned upon a mackerel-barrel—a lean old man of great height, but bent with years and twisted into an uncouth shape by seven broken limbs; furrowed, also, and weatherworn, as if every gale for the better part of a century had caught him somewhere on the sea. He looked like a harbinger of tempest—a shipmate of the Flying Dutchman. After innumerable voyages aboard men-of-war and merchantmen, fishing-schooners and chebacco-boats, the old salt had become master of a hand-cart, which he daily trundled about the vicinity, and sometimes blew his fish-horn through the streets of Salem. One of Uncle Parker's eyes had been blown out with gunpowder, and the other did but glimmer in its socket. Turning it upward as he spoke, it was his delight to tell of cruises against the French and battles with his own shipmates, when he and an antagonist used to be seated astride of a sailor's chest, each fastened down by a spike-nail through his trousers, and there to fight it out. Sometimes he expatiated on the delicious flavor of the hagden, a greasy and goose-like fowl which the sailors catch with hook and line on the Grand Banks. He dwelt with rapture on an interminable winter at the Isle of Sables, where he had gladdened himself amid polar snows with the rum and sugar saved from the wreck of a West India schooner. And wrathfully did he shake his fist as he related how a party of Cape Cod men had robbed him and his companions of their lawful spoils and sailed away with every keg of old Jamaica, leaving him not a drop to drown his sorrow. Villains they were, and of that wicked brotherhood who are said to tie lanterns to horses' tails to mislead the mariner along the dangerous shores of the Cape.

Even now I seem to see the group of fishermen with that old salt in the midst. One fellow sits on the counter, a second bestrides an oil-barrel, a third lolls at his length on a parcel of new cod-lines, and another has planted the tarry seat of his trousers on a heap of salt which will shortly be sprinkled over a lot of fish. They are a likely set of men. Some have voyaged to the East Indies or the Pacific, and most of them have sailed in Marblehead schooners to Newfoundland; a few have been no farther than the Middle Banks, and one or two have always fished along the shore; but, as Uncle Parker used to say, they have all been christened in salt water and know more than men ever learn in the bushes. A curious figure, by way of contrast, is a fish-dealer from far up-country listening with eyes wide open to narratives that might startle Sinbad the Sailor.—Be it well with you, my brethren! Ye are all gone—some to your graves ashore and others to the depths of ocean—but my faith is strong that ye are happy; for whenever I behold your forms, whether in dream or vision, each departed friend is puffing his long nine, and a mug of the right blackstrap goes round from lip to lip.

But where was the mermaid in those delightful times? At a certain window near the centre of the village appeared a pretty display of gingerbread men and horses, picture-books and ballads, small fish-hooks, pins, needles, sugarplums and brass thimbles—articles on which the young fishermen used to expend their money from pure gallantry. What a picture was Susan behind the counter! A slender maiden, though the child of rugged parents, she had the slimmest of all waists, brown hair curling on her neck, and a complexion rather pale except when the sea-breeze flushed it. A few freckles became beauty-spots beneath her eyelids.—How was it, Susan, that you talked and acted so carelessly, yet always for the best, doing whatever was right in your own eyes, and never once doing wrong in mine, nor shocked a taste that had been morbidly sensitive till now? And whence had you that happiest gift of brightening every topic with an unsought gayety, quiet but irresistible, so that even gloomy spirits felt your sunshine and did not shrink from it? Nature wrought the charm. She made you a frank, simple, kind-hearted, sensible and mirthful girl. Obeying Nature, you did free things without indelicacy, displayed a maiden's thoughts to every eye, and proved yourself as innocent as naked Eve.—It was beautiful to observe how her simple and happy nature mingled itself with mine. She kindled a domestic fire within my heart and took up her dwelling there, even in that chill and lonesome cavern hung round with glittering icicles of fancy. She gave me warmth of feeling, while the influence of my mind made her contemplative. I taught her to love the moonlight hour, when the expanse of the encircled bay was smooth as a great mirror and slept in a transparent shadow, while beyond Nahant the wind rippled the dim ocean into a dreamy brightness which grew faint afar off without becoming gloomier. I held her hand and pointed to the long surf-wave as it rolled calmly on the beach in an unbroken line of silver; we were silent together till its deep and peaceful murmur had swept by us. When the Sabbath sun shone down into the recesses of the cliffs, I led the mermaid thither and told her that those huge gray, shattered rocks, and her native sea that raged for ever like a storm against them, and her own slender beauty in so stern a scene, were all combined into a strain of poetry. But on the Sabbath-eve, when her mother had gone early to bed and her gentle sister had smiled and left us, as we sat alone by the quiet hearth with household things around, it was her turn to make me feel that here was a deeper poetry, and that this was the dearest hour of all. Thus went on our wooing, till I had shot wild-fowl enough to feather our bridal-bed, and the daughter of the sea was mine.

I built a cottage for Susan and myself, and made a gateway in the form of a Gothic arch by setting up a whale's jaw-bones. We bought a heifer with her first calf, and had a little garden on the hillside to supply us with potatoes and green sauce for our fish. Our parlor, small and neat, was ornamented with our two profiles in one gilt frame, and with shells and pretty pebbles on the mantelpiece, selected from the sea's treasury of such things on Nahant Beach. On the desk, beneath the looking-glass, lay the Bible, which I had begun to read aloud at the book of Genesis, and the singing-book that Susan used for her evening psalm. Except the almanac, we had no other literature. All that I heard of books was when an Indian history or tale of shipwreck was sold by a pedler or wandering subscription-man to some one in the village, and read through its owner's nose to a slumbrous auditory.

Like my brother-fishermen, I grew into the belief that all human erudition was collected in our pedagogue, whose green spectacles and solemn phiz as he passed to his little schoolhouse amid a waste of sand might have gained him a diploma from any college in New England. In truth, I dreaded him.—When our children were old enough to claim his care, you remember, Susan, how I frowned, though you were pleased at this learned man's encomiums on their proficiency. I feared to trust them even with the alphabet: it was the key to a fatal treasure. But I loved to lead them by their little hands along the beach and point to nature in the vast and the minute—the sky, the sea, the green earth, the pebbles and the shells. Then did I discourse of the mighty works and coextensive goodness of the Deity with the simple wisdom of a man whose mind had profited by lonely days upon the deep and his heart by the strong and pure affections of his evening home. Sometimes my voice lost itself in a tremulous depth, for I felt his eye upon me as I spoke. Once, while my wife and all of us were gazing at ourselves in the mirror left by the tide in a hollow of the sand, I pointed to the pictured heaven below and bade her observe how religion was strewn everywhere in our path, since even a casual pool of water recalled the idea of that home whither we were travelling to rest for ever with our children. Suddenly your image, Susan, and all the little faces made up of yours and mine, seemed to fade away and vanish around me, leaving a pale visage like my own of former days within the frame of a large looking-glass. Strange illusion!

My life glided on, the past appearing to mingle with the present and absorb the future, till the whole lies before me at a glance. My manhood has long been waning with a stanch decay; my earlier contemporaries, after lives of unbroken health, are all at rest without having known the weariness of later age; and now with a wrinkled forehead and thin white hair as badges of my dignity I have become the patriarch—the uncle—of the village. I love that name: it widens the circle of my sympathies; it joins all the youthful to my household in the kindred of affection.

Like Uncle Parker, whose rheumatic bones were dashed against Egg Rock full forty years ago, I am a spinner of long yarns. Seated on the gunnel of a dory or on the sunny side of a boat-house, where the warmth is grateful to my limbs, or by my own hearth when a friend or two are there, I overflow with talk, and yet am never tedious. With a broken voice I give utterance to much wisdom. Such, Heaven be praised! is the vigor of my faculties that many a forgotten usage, and traditions ancient in my youth, and early adventures of myself or others hitherto effaced by things more recent, acquire new distinctness in my memory. I remember the happy days when the haddock were more numerous on all the fishing-grounds than sculpins in the surf—when the deep-water cod swam close in-shore, and the dogfish, with his poisonous horn, had not learnt to take the hook. I can number every equinoctial storm in which the sea has overwhelmed the street, flooded the cellars of the village and hissed upon our kitchen hearth. I give the history of the great whale that was landed on Whale Beach, and whose jaws, being now my gateway, will last for ages after my coffin shall have passed beneath them. Thence it is an easy digression to the halibut—scarcely smaller than the whale—which ran out six codlines and hauled my dory to the mouth of Boston harbor before I could touch him with the gaff.

If melancholy accidents be the theme of conversation, I tell how a friend of mine was taken out of his boat by an enormous shark, and the sad, true tale of a young man on the eve of marriage who had been nine days missing, when his drowned body floated into the very pathway on Marble-head Neck that had often led him to the dwelling of his bride, as if the dripping corpse would have come where the mourner was. With such awful fidelity did that lover return to fulfil his vows! Another favorite story is of a crazy maiden who conversed with angels and had the gift of prophecy, and whom all the village loved and pitied, though she went from door to door accusing us of sin, exhorting to repentance and foretelling our destruction by flood or earthquake. If the young men boast their knowledge of the ledges and sunken rocks, I speak of pilots who knew the wind by its scent and the wave by its taste, and could have steered blindfold to any port between Boston and Mount Desert guided only by the rote of the shore—the peculiar sound of the surf on each island, beach and line of rocks along the coast. Thus do I talk, and all my auditors grow wise while they deem it pastime.

I recollect no happier portion of my life than this my calm old age. It is like the sunny and sheltered slope of a valley where late in the autumn the grass is greener than in August, and intermixed with golden dandelions that had not been seen till now since the first warmth of the year. But with me the verdure and the flowers are not frost-bitten in the midst of winter. A playfulness has revisited my mind—a sympathy with the young and gay, an unpainful interest in the business of others, a light and wandering curiosity—arising, perhaps, from the sense that my toil on earth is ended and the brief hour till bedtime may be spent in play. Still, I have fancied that there is a depth of feeling and reflection under this superficial levity peculiar to one who has lived long and is soon to die.

Show me anything that would make an infant smile, and you shall behold a gleam of mirth over the hoary ruin of my visage. I can spend a pleasant hour in the sun watching the sports of the village children on the edge of the surf. Now they chase the retreating wave far down over the wet sand; now it steals softly up to kiss their naked feet; now it comes onward with threatening front, and roars after the laughing crew as they scamper beyond its reach. Why should not an old man be merry too, when the great sea is at play with those little children? I delight, also, to follow in the wake of a pleasure-party of young men and girls strolling along the beach after an early supper at the Point. Here, with handkerchiefs at nose, they bend over a heap of eel-grass entangled in which is a dead skate so oddly accoutred with two legs and a long tail that they mistake him for a drowned animal. A few steps farther the ladies scream, and the gentlemen make ready to protect them against a young shark of the dogfish kind rolling with a lifelike motion in the tide that has thrown him up. Next they are smit with wonder at the black shells of a wagon-load of live lobsters packed in rock-weed for the country-market. And when they reach the fleet of dories just hauled ashore after the day's fishing, how do I laugh in my sleeve, and sometimes roar outright, at the simplicity of these young folks and the sly humor of the fishermen! In winter, when our village is thrown into a bustle by the arrival of perhaps a score of country dealers bargaining for frozen fish to be transported hundreds of miles and eaten fresh in Vermont or Canada, I am a pleased but idle spectator in the throng. For I launch my boat no more.

When the shore was solitary, I have found a pleasure that seemed even to exalt my mind in observing the sports or contentions of two gulls as they wheeled and hovered about each other with hoarse screams, one moment flapping on the foam of the wave, and then soaring aloft till their white bosoms melted into the upper sunshine. In the calm of the summer sunset I drag my aged limbs with a little ostentation of activity, because I am so old, up to the rocky brow of the hill. There I see the white sails of many a vessel outward bound or homeward from afar, and the black trail of a vapor behind the Eastern steamboat; there, too, is the sun, going down, but not in gloom, and there the illimitable ocean mingling with the sky, to remind me of eternity.

But sweetest of all is the hour of cheerful musing and pleasant talk that comes between the dusk and the lighted candle by my glowing fireside. And never, even on the first Thanksgiving-night, when Susan and I sat alone with our hopes, nor the second, when a stranger had been sent to gladden us and be the visible image of our affection, did I feel such joy as now. All that belongs to me are here: Death has taken none, nor Disease kept them away, nor Strife divided them from their parents or each other; with neither poverty nor riches to disturb them, nor the misery of desires beyond their lot, they have kept New England's festival round the patriarch's board. For I am a patriarch. Here I sit among my descendants, in my old arm-chair and immemorial corner, while the firelight throws an appropriate glory round my venerable frame.—Susan! My children! Something whispers me that this happiest hour must be the final one, and that nothing remains but to bless you all and depart with a treasure of recollected joys to heaven. Will you meet me there? Alas! your figures grow indistinct, fading into pictures on the air, and now to fainter outlines, while the fire is glimmering on the walls of a familiar room, and shows the book that I flung down and the sheet that I left half written some fifty years ago. I lift my eyes to the looking-glass, and perceive myself alone, unless those be the mermaid's features retiring into the depths of the mirror with a tender and melancholy smile.

Ah! One feels a chilliness—not bodily, but about the heart—and, moreover, a foolish dread of looking behind him, after these pastimes. I can imagine precisely how a magician would sit down in gloom and terror after dismissing the shadows that had personated dead or distant people and stripping his cavern of the unreal splendor which had changed it to a palace.

And now for a moral to my reverie. Shall it be that, since fancy can create so bright a dream of happiness, it were better to dream on from youth to age than to awake and strive doubtfully for something real? Oh, the slight tissue of a dream can no more preserve us from the stern reality of misfortune than a robe of cobweb could repel the wintry blast. Be this the moral, then: In chaste and warm affections, humble wishes and honest toil for some useful end there is health for the mind and quiet for the heart, the prospect of a happy life and the fairest hope of heaven.

THE AMBITIOUS GUEST

ONE SEPTEMBER NIGHT a family had gathered round their hearth and piled it high with the driftwood of mountain-streams, the dry cones of the pine, and the splintered ruins of great trees that had come crashing down the precipice. Up the chimney roared the fire, and brightened the room with its broad blaze. The faces of the father and mother had a sober gladness; the children laughed. The eldest daughter was the image of Happiness at seventeen, and the aged grandmother, who sat knitting in the warmest place, was the image of Happiness grown old. They had found the "herb heart's-ease" in the bleakest spot of all New England. This family were situated in the Notch of the White Hills, where the wind was sharp throughout the year and pitilessly cold in the winter, giving their cottage all its fresh inclemency before it descended on the valley of the Saco. They dwelt in a cold spot and a dangerous one, for a mountain towered above their heads so steep that the stones would often rumble down its sides and startle them at midnight.

The daughter had just uttered some simple jest that filled them all with mirth, when the wind came through the Notch and seemed to pause before their cottage, rattling the door with a sound of wailing and lamentation before it passed into the valley. For a moment it saddened them, though there was nothing unusual in the tones. But the family were glad again when they perceived that the latch was lifted by some traveller whose footsteps had been unheard amid the dreary blast which heralded his approach and wailed as he was entering and went moaning away from the door.

Though they dwelt in such a solitude, these people held daily converse with the world. The romantic pass of the Notch is a great artery through which the life-blood of internal commerce is continually throbbing between Maine on one side and the Green Mountains and the shores of the St. Lawrence on the other. The stage-coach always drew up before the door of the cottage. The wayfarer with no companion but his staff paused here to exchange a word, that the sense of loneliness might not utterly overcome him ere he could pass through the cleft of the mountain or reach the first house in the valley. And here the teamster on his way to Portland market would put up for the night, and, if a bachelor, might sit an hour beyond the usual bedtime and steal a kiss from the mountain-maid at parting. It was one of those primitive taverns where the traveller pays only for food and lodging, but meets with a homely kindness beyond all price. When the footsteps were heard, therefore, between the outer door and the inner one, the whole family rose up, grandmother, children and all, as if about to welcome some one who belonged to them, and whose fate was linked with theirs.

The door was opened by a young man. His face at first wore the melancholy expression, almost despondency, of one who travels a wild and bleak road at nightfall and alone, but soon brightened up when he saw the kindly warmth of his reception. He felt his heart spring forward to meet them all, from the old woman who wiped a chair with her apron to the little child that held out its arms to him. One glance and smile placed the stranger on a footing of innocent familiarity with the eldest daughter.

"Ah! this fire is the right thing," cried he, "especially when there is such a pleasant circle round it. I am quite benumbed, for the Notch is just like the pipe of a great pair of bellows; it has blown a terrible blast in my face all the way from Bartlett."

"Then you are going toward Vermont?" said the master of the house as he helped to take a light knapsack off the young man's shoulders.

"Yes, to Burlington, and far enough beyond," replied he. "I meant to have been at Ethan Crawford's to-night, but a pedestrian lingers along such a road as this. It is no matter; for when I saw this good fire and all your cheerful faces, I felt as if you had kindled it on purpose for me and were waiting my arrival. So I shall sit down among you and make myself at home."

The frank-hearted stranger had just drawn his chair to the fire when something like a heavy footstep was heard without, rushing down the steep side of the mountain as with long and rapid strides, and taking such a leap in passing the cottage as to strike the opposite precipice. The family held their breath, because they knew the sound, and their guest held his by instinct.

"The old mountain has thrown a stone at us for fear we should forget him," said the landlord, recovering himself. "He sometimes nods his head and threatens to come down, but we are old neighbors, and agree together pretty well, upon the whole. Besides, we have a sure place of refuge hard by if he should be coming in good earnest."

Let us now suppose the stranger to have finished his supper of bear's meat, and by his natural felicity of manner to have placed himself on a footing of kindness with the whole family; so that they talked as freely together as if he belonged to their mountain-brood. He was of a proud yet gentle spirit, haughty and reserved among the rich and great, but ever ready to stoop his head to the lowly cottage door and be like a brother or a son at the poor man's fireside. In the household of the Notch he found warmth and simplicity of feeling, the pervading intelligence of New England, and a poetry of native growth which they had gathered when they little thought of it from the mountain-peaks and chasms, and at the very threshold of their romantic and dangerous abode. He had travelled far and alone; his whole life, indeed, had been a solitary path, for, with the lofty caution of his nature, he had kept himself apart from those who might otherwise have been his companions. The family, too, though so kind and hospitable, had that consciousness of unity among themselves and separation from the world at large which in every domestic circle should still keep a holy place where no stranger may intrude. But this evening a prophetic sympathy impelled the refined and educated youth to pour out his heart before the simple mountaineers, and constrained them to answer him with the same free confidence. And thus it should have been. Is not the kindred of a common fate a closer tie than that of birth?

The secret of the young man's character was a high and abstracted ambition. He could have borne to live an undistinguished life, but not to be forgotten in the grave. Yearning desire had been transformed to hope, and hope, long cherished, had become like certainty that, obscurely as he journeyed now, a glory was to beam on all his pathway, though not, perhaps, while he was treading it. But when posterity should gaze back into the gloom of what was now the present, they would trace the brightness of his footsteps, brightening as meaner glories faded, and confess that a gifted one had passed from his cradle to his tomb with none to recognize him.

"As yet," cried the stranger, his cheek glowing and his eye flashing with enthusiasm—"as yet I have done nothing. Were I to vanish from the earth to-morrow, none would know so much of me as you—that a nameless youth came up at nightfall from the valley of the Saco, and opened his heart to you in the evening, and passed through the Notch by sunrise, and was seen no more. Not a soul would ask, 'Who was he? Whither did the wanderer go?' But I cannot die till I have achieved my destiny. Then let Death come: I shall have built my monument."

There was a continual flow of natural emotion gushing forth amid abstracted reverie which enabled the family to understand this young man's sentiments, though so foreign from their own. With quick sensibility of the ludicrous, he blushed at the ardor into which he had been betrayed.

"You laugh at me," said he, taking the eldest daughter's hand and laughing himself. "You think my ambition as nonsensical as if I were to freeze myself to death on the top of Mount Washington only that people might spy at me from the country roundabout. And truly that would be a noble pedestal for a man's statue."

"It is better to sit here by this fire," answered the girl, blushing, "and be comfortable and contented, though nobody thinks about us."

"I suppose," said her father, after a fit of musing, "there is something natural in what the young man says; and if my mind had been turned that way, I might have felt just the same.—It is strange, wife, how his talk has set my head running on things that are pretty certain never to come to pass."

"Perhaps they may," observed the wife. "Is the man thinking what he will do when he is a widower?"

"No, no!" cried he, repelling the idea with reproachful kindness. "When I think of your death, Esther, I think of mine too. But I was wishing we had a good farm in Bartlett or Bethlehem or Littleton, or some other township round the White Mountains, but not where they could tumble on our heads. I should want to stand well with my neighbors and be called squire and sent to General Court for a term or two; for a plain, honest man may do as much good there as a lawyer. And when I should be grown quite an old man, and you an old woman, so as not to be long apart, I might die happy enough in my bed, and leave you all crying around me. A slate gravestone would suit me as well as a marble one, with just my name and age, and a verse of a hymn, and something to let people know that I lived an honest man and died a Christian."

"There, now!" exclaimed the stranger; "it is our nature to desire a monument, be it slate or marble, or a pillar of granite, or a glorious memory in the universal heart of man."

"We're in a strange way to-night," said the wife, with tears in her eyes. "They say it's a sign of something when folks' minds go a-wandering so. Hark to the children!"

They listened accordingly. The younger children had been put to bed in another room, but with an open door between; so that they could be heard talking busily among themselves. One and all seemed to have caught the infection from the fireside circle, and were outvying each other in wild wishes and childish projects of what they would do when they came to be men and women. At length a little boy, instead of addressing his brothers and sisters, called out to his mother.

"I'll tell you what I wish, mother," cried he: "I want you and father and grandma'm, and all of us, and the stranger too, to start right away and go and take a drink out of the basin of the Flume."

Nobody could help laughing at the child's notion of leaving a warm bed and dragging them from a cheerful fire to visit the basin of the Flume—a brook which tumbles over the precipice deep within the Notch.

The boy had hardly spoken, when a wagon rattled along the road and stopped a moment before the door. It appeared to contain two or three men who were cheering their hearts with the rough chorus of a song which resounded in broken notes between the cliffs, while the singers hesitated whether to continue their journey or put up here for the night.

"Father," said the girl, "they are calling you by name."

But the good man doubted whether they had really called him, and was unwilling to show himself too solicitous of gain by inviting people to patronize his house. He therefore did not hurry to the door, and, the lash being soon applied, the travellers plunged into the Notch, still singing and laughing, though their music and mirth came back drearily from the heart of the mountain.

"There, mother!" cried the boy, again; "they'd have given us a ride to the Flume."

Again they laughed at the child's pertinacious fancy for a night-ramble. But it happened that a light cloud passed over the daughter's spirit; she looked gravely into the fire and drew a breath that was almost a sigh. It forced its way, in spite of a little struggle to repress it. Then, starting and blushing, she looked quickly around the circle, as if they had caught a glimpse into her bosom. The stranger asked what she had been thinking of.

"Nothing," answered she, with a downcast smile; "only I felt lonesome just then."

"Oh, I have always had a gift of feeling what is in other people's hearts," said he, half seriously. "Shall I tell the secrets of yours? For I know what to think when a young girl shivers by a warm hearth and complains of lonesomeness at her mother's side. Shall I put these feelings into words?"

"They would not be a girl's feelings any longer if they could be put into words," replied the mountain-nymph, laughing, but avoiding his eye.

All this was said apart. Perhaps a germ of love was springing in their hearts so pure that it might blossom in Paradise, since it could not be matured on earth; for women worship such gentle dignity as his, and the proud, contemplative, yet kindly, soul is oftenest captivated by simplicity like hers. But while they spoke softly, and he was watching the happy sadness, the lightsome shadows, the shy yearnings, of a maiden's nature, the wind through the Notch took a deeper and drearier sound. It seemed, as the fanciful stranger said, like the choral strain of the spirits of the blast who in old Indian times had their dwelling among these mountains and made their heights and recesses a sacred region. There was a wail along the road as if a funeral were passing. To chase away the gloom, the family threw pine-branches on their fire till the dry leaves crackled and the flame arose, discovering once again a scene of peace and humble happiness. The light hovered about them fondly and caressed them all. There were the little faces of the children peeping from their bed apart, and here the father's frame of strength, the mother's subdued and careful mien, the high-browed youth, the budding girl and the good old grandam, still knitting in the warmest place.

The aged woman looked up from her task, and with fingers ever busy was the next to speak.

"Old folks have their notions," said she, "as well as young ones. You've been wishing and planning and letting your heads run on one thing and another till you've set my mind a-wandering too. Now, what should an old woman wish for, when she can go but a step or two before she comes to her grave? Children, it will haunt me night and day till I tell you."

"What is it, mother?" cried the husband and wife at once.

Then the old woman, with an air of mystery which drew the circle closer round the fire, informed them that she had provided her grave-clothes some years before—a nice linen shroud, a cap with a muslin ruff, and everything of a finer sort than she had worn since her wedding-day. But this evening an old superstition had strangely recurred to her. It used to be said in her younger days that if anything were amiss with a corpse—if only the ruff were not smooth or the cap did not set right—the corpse, in the coffin and beneath the clods, would strive to put up its cold hands and arrange it. The bare thought made her nervous.

"Don't talk so, grandmother," said the girl, shuddering.

"Now," continued the old woman, with singular earnestness, yet smiling strangely at her own folly, "I want one of you, my children, when your mother is dressed and in the coffin,—I want one of you to hold a looking-glass over my face. Who knows but I may take a glimpse at myself and see whether all's right?"

"Old and young, we dream of graves and monuments," murmured the stranger-youth. "I wonder how mariners feel when the ship is sinking and they, unknown and undistinguished, are to be buried together in the ocean, that wide and nameless sepulchre?"

For a moment the old woman's ghastly conception so engrossed the minds of her hearers that a sound abroad in the night, rising like the roar of a blast, had grown broad, deep and terrible before the fated group were conscious of it. The house and all within it trembled; the foundations of the earth seemed to be shaken, as if this awful sound were the peal of the last trump. Young and old exchanged one wild glance and remained an instant pale, affrighted, without utterance or power to move. Then the same shriek burst simultaneously from all their lips:

"The slide! The slide!"

The simplest words must intimate, but not portray, the unutterable horror of the catastrophe. The victims rushed from their cottage and sought refuge in what they deemed a safer spot, where, in contemplation of such an emergency, a sort of barrier had been reared. Alas! they had quitted their security and fled right into the pathway of destruction. Down came the whole side of the mountain in a cataract of ruin. Just before it reached the house the stream broke into two branches, shivered not a window there, but overwhelmed the whole vicinity, blocked up the road and annihilated everything in its dreadful course. Long ere the thunder of that great slide had ceased to roar among the mountains the mortal agony had been endured and the victims were at peace. Their bodies were never found.

The next morning the light smoke was seen stealing from the cottage chimney up the mountain-side. Within, the fire was yet smouldering on the hearth, and the chairs in a circle round it, as if the inhabitants had but gone forth to view the devastation of the slide and would shortly return to thank Heaven for their miraculous escape. All had left separate tokens by which those who had known the family were made to shed a tear for each. Who has not heard their name? The story has been told far and wide, and will for ever be a legend of these mountains. Poets have sung their fate.

There were circumstances which led some to suppose that a stranger had been received into the cottage on this awful night, and had shared the catastrophe of all its inmates; others denied that there were sufficient grounds for such a conjecture. Woe for the high-souled youth with his dream of earthly immortality! His name and person utterly unknown, his history, his way of life, his plans, a mystery never to be solved, his death and his existence equally a doubt,— whose was the agony of that death-moment?

THE SISTER-YEARS

LAST NIGHT, between eleven and twelve o'clock, when the Old Year was leaving her final footprints on the borders of Time's empire, she found herself in possession of a few spare moments, and sat down—of all places in the world—on the steps of our new city-hall. The wintry moonlight showed that she looked weary of body and sad of heart, like many another wayfarer of earth. Her garments, having been exposed to much foul weather and rough usage, were in very ill condition, and, as the hurry of her journey had never before allowed her to take an instant's rest, her shoes were so worn as to be scarcely worth the mending. But after trudging only a little distance farther this poor Old Year was destined to enjoy a long, long sleep. I forgot to mention that when she seated herself on the steps she deposited by her side a very capacious bandbox in which, as is the custom among travellers of her sex, she carried a great deal of valuable property. Besides this luggage, there was a folio book under her arm very much resembling the annual volume of a newspaper. Placing this volume across her knees and resting her elbows upon it, with her forehead in her hands, the weary, bedraggled, world-worn Old Year heaved a heavy sigh and appeared to be taking no very pleasant retrospect of her past existence.

While she thus awaited the midnight knell that was to summon her to the innumerable sisterhood of departed years, there came a young maiden treading lightsomely on tip-toe along the street from the direction of the railroad dépôt. She was evidently a stranger, and perhaps had come to town by the evening train of cars. There was a smiling cheerfulness in this fair maiden's face which bespoke her fully confident of a kind reception from the multitude of people with whom she was soon to form acquaintance. Her dress was rather too airy for the season, and was bedizened with fluttering ribbons and other vanities which were likely soon to be rent away by the fierce storms or to fade in the hot sunshine amid which she was to pursue her changeful course. But still she was a wonderfully pleasant-looking figure, and had so much promise and such an indescribable hopefulness in her aspect that hardly anybody could meet her without anticipating some very desirable thing—the consummation of some long-sought good—from her kind offices. A few dismal characters there may be here and there about the world who have so often been trifled with by young maidens as promising as she that they have now ceased to pin any faith upon the skirts of the New Year. But, for my own part, I have great faith in her, and, should I live to see fifty more such, still from each of those successive sisters I shall reckon upon receiving something that will be worth living for.

The New Year—for this young maiden was no less a personage—carried all her goods and chattels in a basket of no great size or weight, which hung upon her arm. She greeted the disconsolate Old Year with great affection, and sat down beside her on the steps of the city-hall, waiting for the signal to begin her rambles through the world. The two were own sisters, being both granddaughters of Time, and, though one looked so much older than the other, it was rather owing to hardships and trouble than to age, since there was but a twelvemonth's difference between them.

"Well, my dear sister," said the New Year, after the first salutations, "you look almost tired to death. What have you been about during your sojourn in this part of infinite space?"

"Oh, I have it all recorded here in my book of chronicles," answered the Old Year, in a heavy tone. "There is nothing that would amuse you, and you will soon get sufficient knowledge of such matters from your own personal experience. It is but tiresome reading."

Nevertheless, she turned over the leaves of the folio and glanced at them by the light of the moon, feeling an irresistible spell of interest in her own biography, although its incidents were remembered without pleasure. The volume, though she termed it her book of chronicles, seemed to be neither more nor less than the Salem *Gazette* for 1838; in the accuracy of which journal this sagacious Old Year had so much confidence that she deemed it needless to record her history with her own pen.

"What have you been doing in the political way?" asked the New Year.

"Why, my course here in the United States," said the Old Year—"though perhaps I ought to blush at the confession—my political course, I must acknowledge, has been rather vacillatory, sometimes inclining toward the Whigs, then causing the administration party to shout for triumph, and now again uplifting what seemed the almost prostrate banner of the opposition; so that historians will hardly know what to make of me in this respect. But the Loco-Focos—"

"I do not like these party nicknames," interrupted her sister, who seemed remarkably touchy about some points. "Perhaps we shall part in better humor if we avoid any political discussion."

"With all my heart," replied the Old Year, who had already been tormented half to death with squabbles of this kind. "I care not if the name of Whig or Tory, with their interminable brawls about banks and the sub-treasury, abolition, Texas, the Florida war, and a million of other topics which you will learn soon enough for your own comfort,—I care not, I say, if no whisper of these matters ever reaches my ears again. Yet they have occupied so large a share of my attention that I scarcely know what else to tell you. There has, indeed been a curious sort of war on the Canada border, where blood has streamed in the names of liberty and patriotism; but it must remain for some future, perhaps far-distant, year to tell whether or no those holy names have been rightfully invoked. Nothing so much depresses me in my view of mortal affairs as to see high energies wasted and human life and happiness thrown away for ends that appear oftentimes unwise, and still oftener remain unaccomplished. But the wisest people and the best keep a steadfast faith that the progress of mankind is onward and upward, and that the toil and anguish of the path serve to wear away the imperfections of the immortal pilgrim, and will be felt no more when they have done their office."

"Perhaps," cried the hopeful New Year—"perhaps I shall see that happy day."

"I doubt whether it be so close at hand," answered the Old Year, gravely smiling. "You will soon grow weary of looking for that blessed consummation, and will turn for amusement—as has frequently been my own practice—to the affairs of some sober little city like this of Salem.

NATHANIEL HAWTHORNE

Here we sit on the steps of the new city-hall which has been completed under my administration, and it would make you laugh to see how the game of politics of which the Capitol at Washington is the great chess-board is here played in miniature. Burning Ambition finds its fuel here; here patriotism speaks boldly in the people's behalf and virtuous economy demands retrenchment in the emoluments of a lamplighter; here the aldermen range their senatorial dignity around the mayor's chair of state and the common council feel that they have liberty in charge. In short, human weakness and strength, passion and policy, man's tendencies, his aims and modes of pursuing them, his individual character and his character in the mass, may be studied almost as well here as on the theatre of nations, and with this great advantage—that, be the lesson ever so disastrous, its Liliputian scope still makes the beholder smile."

"Have you done much for the improvement of the city?" asked the New Year. "Judging from what little I have seen, it appears to be ancient and time-worn."

"I have opened the railroad," said the elder Year, "and half a dozen times a day you will hear the bell which once summoned the monks of a Spanish convent to their devotions announcing the arrival or departure of the cars. Old Salem now wears a much livelier expression than when I first beheld her. Strangers rumble down from Boston by hundreds at a time. New faces throng in Essex street. Railroad-hacks and omnibuses rattle over the pavements. There is a perceptible increase of oyster-shops and other establishments for the accommodation of a transitory diurnal multitude. But a more important change awaits the venerable town. An immense accumulation of musty prejudices will be carried off by the free circulation of society. A peculiarity of character of which the inhabitants themselves are hardly sensible will be rubbed down and worn away by the attrition of foreign substances. Much of the result will be good; there will likewise be a few things not so good. Whether for better or worse, there will be a probable diminution of the moral influence of wealth, and the sway of an aristocratic class which from an era far beyond my memory has held firmer dominion here than in any other New England town."

The Old Year, having talked away nearly all of her little remaining breath, now closed her book of chronicles, and was about to take her departure, but her sister detained her a while longer by inquiring the contents of the huge bandbox which she was so painfully lugging along with her.

"These are merely a few trifles," replied the Old Year, "which I have picked up in my rambles and am going to deposit in the receptacle of things past and forgotten. We sisterhood of years never carry anything really valuable out of the world with us. Here are patterns of most of the fashions which I brought into vogue, and which have already lived out their allotted term; you will supply their place with others equally ephemeral. Here, put up in little china pots, like rouge, is a considerable lot of beautiful women's bloom which the disconsolate fair ones owe me a bitter grudge for stealing. I have likewise a quantity of men's dark hair, instead of which I have left gray locks or none at all. The tears of widows and other afflicted mortals who have received comfort during the last twelve months are preserved in some dozens of essence-bottles well corked and sealed. I have several bundles of love-letters eloquently breathing an eternity of burning passion which grew cold and perished almost before the ink was dry. Moreover, here is an assortment of many thousand broken promises and other broken ware, all very light and packed into little space. The heaviest articles in my possession are a large parcel of disappointed hopes which a little while ago were buoyant enough to have inflated Mr. Lauriat's balloon."

"I have a fine lot of hopes here in my basket," remarked the New Year. "They are a sweet-smelling flower—a species of rose."

"They soon lose their perfume," replied the sombre Old Year. "What else have you brought to insure a welcome from the discontented race of mortals?"

"Why, to say the truth, little or nothing else," said her sister, with a smile, "save a few new *Annuals* and almanacs, and some New Year's gifts for the children. But I heartily wish well to poor mortals, and mean to do all I can for their improvement and happiness."

"It is a good resolution," rejoined the Old Year. "And, by the way, I have a plentiful assortment of good resolutions which have now grown so stale and musty that I am ashamed to carry them any farther. Only for fear that the city authorities would send Constable Mansfield with a warrant after me, I should toss them into the street at once. Many other matters go to make up the contents of my bandbox, but the whole lot would not fetch a single bid even at an auction of worn-out furniture; and as they are worth nothing either to you or anybody else, I need not trouble you with a longer catalogue."

"And must I also pick up such worthless luggage in my travels?" asked the New Year.

"Most certainly, and well if you have no heavier load to bear," replied the other. "And now, my dear sister, I must bid you farewell, earnestly advising and exhorting you to expect no gratitude nor good-will from this peevish, unreasonable, inconsiderate, ill-intending and worse-behaving world. However warmly its inhabitants may seem to welcome you, yet, do what you may and lavish on them what means of happiness you please, they will still be complaining, still craving what it is not in your power to give, still looking forward to some other year for the accomplishment of projects which ought never to have been formed, and which, if successful, would only provide new occasions of discontent. If these ridiculous people ever see anything tolerable in you, it will be after you are gone for ever."

"But I," cried the fresh-hearted New Year—"I shall try to leave men wiser than I find them. I will offer them freely whatever good gifts Providence permits me to distribute, and will tell them to be thankful for what they have and humbly hopeful for more; and surely, if they are not absolute fools, they will condescend to be happy, and will allow me to be a happy year. For my happiness must depend on them."

"Alas for you, then, my poor sister!" said the Old Year, sighing, as she uplifted her burden. "We grandchildren of Time are born to trouble. Happiness, they say, dwells in the mansions of eternity, but we can only lead mortals thither step by step with reluctant murmurings, and ourselves must perish on the threshold. But hark! my task is done."

The clock in the tall steeple of Dr. Emerson's church struck twelve; there was a response from Dr. Flint's, in the opposite quarter of the city; and while the strokes were yet dropping into the air the Old Year either flitted or faded away, and not the wisdom and might of angels, to say nothing of the remorseful yearnings of the millions who had used her ill, could have prevailed with that departed year to return one step. But she, in the company of Time and all her kindred, must hereafter hold a reckoning with mankind. So shall it be, likewise, with the maidenly New Year, who, as the clock ceased to strike, arose from the steps of the city-hall and set out rather timorously on her earthly course.

"A happy New Year!" cried a watchman, eying her figure very questionably, but without the least suspicion that he was addressing the New Year in person.

"Thank you kindly," said the New Year; and she gave the watchman one of the roses of hope from her basket. "May this flower keep a sweet smell long after I have bidden you good-bye!"

Then she stepped on more briskly through the silent streets, and such as were awake at the moment heard her footfall and said, "The New Year is come!" Wherever there was a knot of midnight roisterers, they quaffed her health. She sighed, however, to perceive that the air was tainted—as the atmosphere of this world must continually be—with the dying breaths of mortals who had lingered just long enough for her to bury them. But there were millions left alive to rejoice at her coming, and so she pursued her way with confidence, strewing emblematic flowers on the doorstep of almost every dwelling, which some persons will gather up and wear in their bosoms, and others will trample under foot. The carrier-boy can only say further that early this morning she filled his basket with New Year's addresses, assuring him that the whole city, with our new mayor and the aldermen and common council at its head, would make a general rush to secure copies. Kind patrons, will not you redeem the pledge of the New Year?

SNOWFLAKES

THERE IS snow in yonder cold gray sky of the morning, and through the partially-frosted window-panes I love to watch the gradual beginning of the storm. A few feathery flakes are scattered widely through the air and hover downward with uncertain flight, now almost alighting on the earth, now whirled again aloft into remote regions of the atmosphere. These are not the big flakes heavy with moisture which melt as they touch the ground and are portentous of a soaking rain. It is to be in good earnest a wintry storm. The two or three people visible on the sidewalks have an aspect of endurance, a blue-nosed, frosty fortitude, which is evidently assumed in anticipation of a comfortless and blustering day. By nightfall—or, at least, before the sun sheds another glimmering smile upon us—the street and our little garden will be heaped with mountain snowdrifts. The soil, already frozen for weeks past, is prepared to sustain whatever burden may be laid upon it, and to a Northern eye the landscape will lose its melancholy bleakness and acquire a beauty of its own when Mother Earth, like her children, shall have put on the fleecy garb of her winter's wear. The cloud-spirits are slowly weaving her white mantle. As yet, indeed, there is barely a rime like hoar-frost over the brown surface of the street; the withered green of the grass-plat is still discernible, and the slated roofs of the houses do but begin to look gray instead of black. All the snow that has yet fallen within the circumference of my view, were it heaped up together, would hardly equal the hillock of a grave. Thus gradually by silent and stealthy influences are great changes wrought. These little snow-particles which the storm-spirit flings by handfuls through the air will bury the great Earth under their accumulated mass, nor permit her to behold her sister Sky again for dreary months. We likewise shall lose sight of our mother's familiar visage, and must content ourselves with looking heavenward the oftener.

Now, leaving the Storm to do his appointed office, let us sit down, pen in hand, by our fireside. Gloomy as it may seem, there is an influence productive of cheerfulness and favorable to imaginative thought in the atmosphere of a snowy day. The native of a Southern clime may woo the Muse beneath the heavy shade of summer foliage reclining on banks of turf, while the sound of singing-birds and warbling rivulets chimes in with the music of his soul. In our brief summer I do not think, but only exist in the vague enjoyment of a dream. My hour of inspiration—if that hour ever comes—is when the green log hisses upon the hearth, and the bright flame, brighter for the gloom of the chamber, rustles high up the chimney, and the coals drop tinkling down among the growing heaps of ashes. When the casement rattles in the gust and the snowflakes or the sleety raindrops pelt hard against the window-panes, then I spread out my sheet of paper with the certainty that thoughts and fancies will gleam forth upon it like stars at twilight or like violets in May, perhaps to fade as soon. However transitory their glow, they at least shine amid the darksome shadow which the clouds of the outward sky fling through the room. Blessed, therefore, and reverently welcomed by me, her true-born son, be New England's winter, which makes us one and all the nurslings of the storm and sings a familiar lullaby even in the wildest shriek of the December blast. Now look we forth again and see how much of his task the storm-spirit has done.

Slow and sure! He has the day—perchance the week—before him, and may take his own time to accomplish Nature's burial in snow. A smooth mantle is scarcely yet thrown over the withered grass-plat, and the dry stalks of annuals still thrust themselves through the white surface in all parts of the garden. The leafless rose-bushes stand shivering in a shallow snowdrift, looking, poor things! as disconsolate as if they possessed a human consciousness of the dreary scene. This is a sad time for the shrubs that do not perish with the summer. They neither live nor die; what they retain of life seems but the chilling sense of death. Very sad are the flower-shrubs in midwinter. The roofs of the houses are now all white, save where the eddying wind has kept them bare at the bleak corners. To discern the real intensity of the storm, we must fix upon some distant object—as yonder spire—and observe how the riotous gust fights with the descending snow throughout the intervening space. Sometimes the entire prospect is obscured; then, again, we have a distinct but transient glimpse of the tall steeple, like a giant's ghost; and now the dense wreaths sweep between, as if demons were flinging snowdrifts at each other in mid-air. Look next into the street, where we have an amusing parallel to the combat of those fancied demons in the upper regions. It is a snow-battle of schoolboys. What a pretty satire on war and military glory might be written in the form of a child's story by describing the snow-ball fights of two rival schools, the alternate defeats and victories of each, and the final triumph of one party, or perhaps of neither! What pitched battles worthy to be chanted in Homeric strains! What storming of fortresses built all of massive snow-blocks! What feats of individual prowess and embodied onsets of martial enthusiasm! And when some well-contested and decisive victory had put a period to the war, both armies should unite to build a lofty monument of snow upon the battlefield and crown it with the victor's statue hewn of the same frozen marble. In a few days or weeks thereafter the passer-by would observe a shapeless mound upon the level common, and, unmindful of the famous victory, would ask, "How came it there? Who reared it? And what means it?" The shattered pedestal of many a battle-monument has provoked these questions when none could answer.

Turn we again to the fireside and sit musing there, lending our ears to the wind till perhaps it shall seem like an articulate voice and dictate wild and airy matter for the pen. Would it might inspire me to sketch out the personification of a New England winter! And that idea, if I can seize the snow-wreathed figures that flit before my fancy, shall be the theme of the next page.

How does Winter herald his approach? By the shrieking blast of latter autumn which is Nature's cry of lamentation as the destroyer rushes among the shivering groves where she has lingered and scatters the sear leaves upon the tempest. When that cry is heard, the people wrap themselves in cloaks and shake their heads disconsolately, saying, "Winter is at hand." Then the axe of the woodcutter echoes sharp and diligently in the forest; then the coal-merchants rejoice because each shriek of Nature in her agony adds something to the price of coal per ton; then the peat-smoke spreads its aromatic fragrance through the atmosphere. A few days more, and at eventide the children look out of the window and dimly perceive the flaunting of a snowy mantle in the air. It is stern Winter's vesture. They crowd around the hearth and cling to their mother's gown or press between their father's knees, affrighted by the hollow roaring voice that bellows adown the wide flue of the chimney.

It is the voice of Winter; and when parents and children hear it, they shudder and exclaim, "Winter is come. Cold Winter has begun his reign already." Now throughout New England each hearth becomes an altar sending up the smoke of a continued sacrifice to the immitigable deity who tyrannizes over forest, country-side and town. Wrapped in his white mantle, his staff a huge icicle, his beard and hair a wind-tossed snowdrift, he travels over the land in the midst of the northern blast, and woe to the homeless wanderer whom he finds upon his path! There he lies stark and stiff, a human shape of ice, on the spot where Winter overtook him. On strides the tyrant over the rushing rivers and broad lakes, which turn to rock beneath his footsteps. His dreary empire is established; all around stretches the desolation of the pole. Yet not ungrateful be his New England children (for Winter is our sire, though a stern and rough one)—not ungrateful even for the severities which have nourished our unyielding strength of character. And let us thank him, too, for the sleigh-rides cheered by the music of merry bells; for the crackling and rustling hearth when the ruddy firelight gleams on hardy manhood and the blooming cheek of woman: for all the home-enjoyments and the kindred virtues which flourish in a frozen soil. Not that we grieve when, after some seven months of storm and bitter frost, Spring, in the guise of a flower-crowned virgin, is seen driving away the hoary despot, pelting him with violets by the handful and strewing green grass on the path behind him. Often ere he will give up his empire old Winter rushes fiercely buck and hurls a snowdrift at the shrinking form of Spring, yet step by step he is compelled to retreat northward, and spends the summer month within the Arctic circle.

Such fantasies, intermixed among graver toils of mind, have made the winter's day pass pleasantly. Meanwhile, the storm has raged without abatement, and now, as the brief afternoon declines, is tossing denser volumes to and fro about the atmosphere. On the window-sill there is a layer of snow reaching halfway up the lowest pane of glass. The garden is one unbroken bed. Along the street are two or three spots of uncovered earth where the gust has whirled away the snow, heaping it elsewhere to the fence-tops or piling huge banks against the doors of houses. A solitary passenger is seen, now striding mid-leg deep across a drift, now scudding over the bare ground, while his cloak is swollen with the wind. And now the jingling of bells— a sluggish sound responsive to the horse's toilsome progress through the unbroken drifts— announces the passage of a sleigh with a boy clinging behind and ducking his head to escape detection by the driver. Next comes a sledge laden with wood for some unthrifty housekeeper whom winter has surprised at a cold hearth. But what dismal equipage now struggles along the uneven street? A sable hearse bestrewn with snow is bearing a dead man through the storm to his frozen bed. Oh how dreary is a burial in winter, when the bosom of Mother Earth has no warmth for her poor child!

Evening—the early eve of December—begins to spread its deepening veil over the comfortless scene. The firelight gradually brightens and throws my flickering shadow upon the walls and ceiling of the chamber, but still the storm rages and rattles against the windows. Alas! I shiver and think it time to be disconsolate, but, taking a farewell glance at dead Nature in her shroud, I perceive a flock of snowbirds skimming lightsomely through the tempest and flitting from drift to drift as sportively as swallows in the delightful prime of summer. Whence come they? Where do they build their nests and seek their food? Why, having airy wings, do they not follow summer around the earth, instead of making themselves the playmates of the storm and fluttering on the dreary verge of the winter's eve? I know not whence they come, nor why; yet my spirit has been cheered by that wandering flock of snow-birds.

THE SEVEN VAGABONDS

RAMBLING on foot in the spring of my life and the summer of the year, I came one afternoon to a point which gave me the choice of three directions. Straight before me the main road extended its dusty length to Boston; on the left a branch went toward the sea, and would have lengthened my journey a trifle of twenty or thirty miles, while by the right-hand path I might have gone over hills and lakes to Canada, visiting in my way the celebrated town of Stamford. On a level spot of grass at the foot of the guide-post appeared an object which, though locomotive on a different principle, reminded me of Gulliver's portable mansion among the Brobdignags. It was a huge covered wagon—or, more properly, a small house on wheels—with a door on one side and a window shaded by green blinds on the other. Two horses munching provender out of the baskets which muzzled them were fastened near the vehicle. A delectable sound of music proceeded from the interior, and I immediately conjectured that this was some itinerant show halting at the confluence of the roads to intercept such idle travellers as myself. A shower had long been climbing up the western sky, and now hung so blackly over my onward path that it was a point of wisdom to seek shelter here.

"Halloo! Who stands guard here? Is the doorkeeper asleep?" cried I, approaching a ladder of two or three steps which was let down from the wagon.

The music ceased at my summons, and there appeared at the door, not the sort of figure that I had mentally assigned to the wandering showman, but a most respectable old personage whom I was sorry to have addressed in so free a style. He wore a snuff-colored coat and small-clothes, with white top-boots, and exhibited the mild dignity of aspect and manner which may often be noticed in aged schoolmasters, and sometimes in deacons, selectmen or other potentates of that kind. A small piece of silver was my passport within his premises, where I found only one other person, hereafter to be described.

"This is a dull day for business," said the old gentleman as he ushered me in; "but I merely tarry here to refresh the cattle, being bound for the camp-meeting at Stamford."

Perhaps the movable scene of this narrative is still peregrinating New England, and may enable the reader to test the accuracy of my description. The spectacle—for I will not use the unworthy term of "puppet-show"—consisted of a multitude of little people assembled on a miniature stage. Among them were artisans of every kind in the attitudes of their toil, and a group of fair ladies and gay gentlemen standing ready for the dance; a company of foot-soldiers formed a line across the stage, looking stern, grim and terrible enough to make it a pleasant consideration that they were but three inches high; and conspicuous above the whole was seen a Merry Andrew in the pointed cap and motley coat of his profession. All the inhabitants of this mimic world were motionless, like the figures in a picture, or like that people who one moment were alive in the midst of their business and delights and the next were transformed to statues, preserving an eternal semblance of labor that was ended and pleasure that could be felt no more. Anon, however, the old gentleman turned the handle of a barrel-organ, the first note of which produced a most enlivening effect upon the figures and awoke them all to their proper occupations and amusements. By the selfsame impulse the tailor plied his needle, the blacksmith's hammer descended upon the anvil and the dancers whirled away on feathery tiptoes; the company of soldiers broke into platoons, retreated from the stage, and were succeeded by a troop of horse, who came prancing onward with such a sound of trumpets and trampling of hoofs as might have startled Don Quixote himself; while an old toper of inveterate ill-habits uplifted his black bottle and took off a hearty swig. Meantime, the Merry Andrew began to caper and turn somersets, shaking his sides, nodding his head and winking his eyes in as lifelike a manner as if he were ridiculing the nonsense of all human affairs and making fun of the whole multitude beneath him. At length the old magician (for I compared the showman to Prospero entertaining his guests with a masque of shadows) paused that I might give utterance to my wonder.

"What an admirable piece of work is this!" exclaimed I, lifting up my hands in astonishment.

Indeed, I liked the spectacle and was tickled with the old man's gravity as he presided at it, for I had none of that foolish wisdom which reproves every occupation that is not useful in this world of vanities. If there be a faculty which I possess more perfectly than most men, it is that of throwing myself mentally into situations foreign to my own and detecting with a cheerful eye the desirable circumstances of each. I could have envied the life of this gray-headed showman, spent as it had been in a course of safe and pleasurable adventure in driving his huge vehicle sometimes through the sands of Cape Cod and sometimes over the rough forest-roads of the north and east, and halting now on the green before a village meeting-house and now in a paved square of the metropolis. How often must his heart have been gladdened by the delight of children as they viewed these animated figures, or his pride indulged by haranguing learnedly to grown men on the mechanical powers which produced such wonderful effects, or his gallantry brought into play—for this is an attribute which such grave men do not lack—by the visits of pretty maidens! And then with how fresh a feeling must he return at intervals to his own peculiar home! "I would I were assured of as happy a life as his," thought I.

Though the showman's wagon might have accommodated fifteen or twenty spectators, it now contained only himself and me and a third person, at whom I threw a glance on entering. He was a neat and trim young man of two or three and twenty; his drab hat and green frock-coat with velvet collar were smart, though no longer new, while a pair of green spectacles that seemed needless to his brisk little eyes gave him something of a scholar-like and literary air. After allowing me a sufficient time to inspect the puppets, he advanced with a bow and drew my attention to some books in a corner of the wagon. These he forthwith began to extol with an amazing volubility of well-sounding words and an ingenuity of praise that won him my heart as being myself one of the most merciful of critics. Indeed, his stock required some considerable powers of commendation in the salesman. There were several ancient friends of mine—the novels of those happy days when my affections wavered between the *Scottish Chiefs* and *Thomas*

Thumb—besides a few of later date whose merits had not been acknowledged by the public. I was glad to find that dear little venerable volume the *New England Primer*, looking as antique as ever, though in its thousandth new edition; a bundle of superannuated gilt picture-books made such a child of me that, partly for the glittering covers and partly for the fairy-tales within, I bought the whole, and an assortment of ballads and popular theatrical songs drew largely on my purse. To balance these expenditures, I meddled neither with sermons nor science nor morality, though volumes of each were there, nor with a *Life of Franklin* in the coarsest of paper, but so showily bound that it was emblematical of the doctor himself in the court-dress which he refused to wear at Paris, nor with Webster's spelling-book, nor some of Byron's minor poems, nor half a dozen little Testaments at twenty-five cents each. Thus far the collection might have been swept from some great bookstore or picked up at an evening auction-room, but there was one small blue-covered pamphlet which the pedler handed me with so peculiar an air that I purchased it immediately at his own price; and then for the first time the thought struck me that I had spoken face to face with the veritable author of a printed book.

The literary-man now evinced a great kindness for me, and I ventured to inquire which way he was travelling.

"Oh," said he, "I keep company with this old gentlemen here, and we are moving now toward the camp-meeting at Stamford."

He then explained to me that for the present season he had rented a corner of the wagon as a book-store, which, as he wittily observed, was a true circulating library, since there were few parts of the country where it had not gone its rounds. I approved of the plan exceedingly, and began to sum up within my mind the many uncommon felicities in the life of a book-pedler, especially when his character resembled that of the individual before me. At a high rate was to be reckoned the daily and hourly enjoyment of such interviews as the present, in which he seized upon the admiration of a passing stranger and made him aware that a man of literary taste, and even of literary achievement, was travelling the country in a showman's wagon. A more valuable yet not infrequent triumph might be won in his conversations with some elderly clergyman long vegetating in a rocky, woody, watery back-settlement of New England, who as he recruited his library from the pedler's stock of sermons would exhort him to seek a college education and become the first scholar in his class. Sweeter and prouder yet would be his sensations when, talking poetry while he sold spelling-books, he should charm the mind, and haply touch the heart, of a fair country schoolmistress, herself an unhonored poetess, a wearer of blue stockings which none but himself took pains to look at. But the scene of his completest glory would be when the wagon had halted for the night and his stock of books was transferred to some crowded bar-room. Then would he recommend to the multifarious company, whether traveller from the city, or teamster from the hills, or neighboring squire, or the landlord himself, or his loutish hostler, works suited to each particular taste and capacity, proving, all the while, by acute criticism and profound remark, that the lore in his books was even exceeded by that in his brain. Thus happily would he traverse the land, sometimes a herald before the march of Mind, sometimes walking arm in arm with awful Literature, and reaping everywhere a harvest of real and sensible popularity which the secluded bookworms by whose toil he lived could never hope for.

"If ever I meddle with literature," thought I, fixing myself in adamantine resolution, "it shall be as a travelling bookseller."

Though it was still mid-afternoon, the air had now grown dark about us, and a few drops of rain came down upon the roof of our vehicle, pattering like the feet of birds that had flown thither to rest. A sound of pleasant voices made us listen, and there soon appeared halfway up the ladder the pretty person of a young damsel whose rosy face was so cheerful that even amid the gloomy light it seemed as if the sunbeams were peeping under her bonnet. We next saw the dark and handsome features of a young man who, with easier gallantry than might have been expected in the heart of Yankee-land, was assisting her into the wagon. It became immediately evident to us, when the two strangers stood within the door, that they were of a profession kindred to those of my companions, and I was delighted with the more than hospitable—the even paternal—kindness of the old showman's manner as he welcomed them, while the man of literature hastened to lead the merry-eyed girl to a seat on the long bench.

"You are housed but just in time, my young friends," said the master of the wagon; "the sky would have been down upon you within five minutes."

The young man's reply marked him as a foreigner—not by any variation from the idiom and accent of good English, but because he spoke with more caution and accuracy than if perfectly familiar with the language.

"We knew that a shower was hanging over us," said he, "and consulted whether it were best to enter the house on the top of yonder hill, but, seeing your wagon in the road—"

"We agreed to come hither," interrupted the girl, with a smile, "because we should be more at home in a wandering house like this."

I, meanwhile, with many a wild and undetermined fantasy was narrowly inspecting these two doves that had flown into our ark. The young man, tall, agile and athletic, wore a mass of black shining curls clustering round a dark and vivacious countenance which, if it had not greater expression, was at least more active and attracted readier notice, than the quiet faces of our countrymen. At his first appearance he had been laden with a neat mahogany box of about two feet square, but very light in proportion to its size, which he had immediately unstrapped from his shoulders and deposited on the floor of the wagon.

The girl had nearly as fair a complexion as our own beauties, and a brighter one than most of them; the lightness of her figure, which seemed calculated to traverse the whole world without weariness, suited well with the glowing cheerfulness of her face, and her gay attire, combining the rainbow hues of crimson, green and a deep orange, was as proper to her lightsome aspect as if she had been born in it. This gay stranger was appropriately burdened with that mirth-inspiring instrument the fiddle, which her companion took from her hands, and shortly began the process of tuning. Neither of us the previous company of the wagon needed to inquire their trade, for this could be no mystery to frequenters of brigade-musters, ordinations, cattle-shows, commencements, and other festal meetings in our sober land; and there is a dear friend of mine who will smile when this page recalls to his memory a chivalrous deed performed by us in rescuing the show-box of such a couple from a mob of great double-fisted countrymen.

"Come," said I to the damsel of gay attire; "shall we visit all the wonders of the world together?"

She understood the metaphor at once, though, indeed, it would not much have troubled me if she had assented to the literal meaning of my words. The mahogany box was placed in a proper position, and I peeped in through its small round magnifying-window while the girl sat by my side and gave short descriptive sketches as one after another the pictures were unfolded to my view. We visited together—at least, our imaginations did—full many a famous city in the streets of which I had long yearned to tread. Once, I remember, we were in the harbor of Barcelona, gazing townward; next, she bore me through the air to Sicily and bade me look up at blazing Ætna; then we took wing to Venice and sat in a gondola beneath the arch of the Rialto, and anon she set me down among the thronged spectators at the coronation of Napoleon. But there was one scene—its locality she could not tell—which charmed my attention longer than all those gorgeous palaces and churches, because the fancy haunted me that I myself the preceding summer had beheld just such a humble meeting-house, in just such a pine-surrounded nook, among our own green mountains. All these pictures were tolerably executed, though far inferior to the girl's touches of description; nor was it easy to comprehend how in so few sentences, and these, as I supposed, in a language foreign to her, she contrived to present an airy copy of each varied scene.

When we had travelled through the vast extent of the mahogany box, I looked into my guide's face.

"'Where are you going, my pretty maid?'" inquired I, in the words of an old song.

"Ah!" said the gay damsel; "you might as well ask where the summer wind is going. We are wanderers here and there and everywhere. Wherever there is mirth our merry hearts are drawn to it. To-day, indeed, the people have told us of a great frolic and festival in these parts; so perhaps we may be needed at what you call the camp-meeting at Stamford."

Then, in my happy youth, and while her pleasant voice yet sounded in my ears, I sighed; for none but myself, I thought, should have been her companion in a life which seemed to realize my own wild fancies cherished all through visionary boyhood to that hour. To these two strangers the world was in its Golden Age—not that, indeed, it was less dark and sad than ever, but because its weariness and sorrow had no community with their ethereal nature. Wherever they might appear in their pilgrimage of bliss, Youth would echo back their gladness, care-stricken Maturity would rest a moment from its toil, and Age, tottering among the graves, would smile in withered joy for their sakes. The lonely cot, the narrow and gloomy street, the sombre shade, would catch a passing gleam like that now shining on ourselves as these bright spirits wandered by. Blessed pair, whose happy home was throughout all the earth! I looked at my shoulders, and thought them broad enough to sustain those pictured towns and mountains; mine, too, was an elastic foot as tireless as the wing of the bird of Paradise; mine was then an untroubled heart that would have gone singing on its delightful way.

"Oh, maiden," said I aloud, "why did you not come hither alone?"

While the merry girl and myself were busy with the show-box the unceasing rain had driven another wayfarer into the wagon. He seemed pretty nearly of the old showman's age, but much smaller, leaner and more withered than he, and less respectably clad in a patched suit of gray; withal, he had a thin, shrewd countenance and a pair of diminutive gray eyes, which peeped rather too keenly out of their puckered sockets. This old fellow had been joking with the showman in a manner which intimated previous acquaintance, but, perceiving that the damsel and I had terminated our affairs, he drew forth a folded document and presented it to me. As I had anticipated, it proved to be a circular, written in a very fair and legible hand and signed by several distinguished gentlemen whom I had never heard of, stating that the bearer had encountered every variety of misfortune and recommending him to the notice of all charitable people. Previous disbursements had left me no more than a five-dollar bill, out of which, however, I offered to make the beggar a donation provided he would give me change for it. The object of my beneficence looked keenly in my face, and discerned that I had none of that abominable spirit, characteristic though it be, of a full-blooded Yankee, which takes pleasure in detecting every little harmless piece of knavery.

"Why, perhaps," said the ragged old mendicant, "if the bank is in good standing, I can't say but I may have enough about me to change your bill."

"It is a bill of the Suffolk Bank," said I, "and better than the specie."

As the beggar had nothing to object, he now produced a small buff leather bag tied up carefully with a shoe-string. When this was opened, there appeared a very comfortable treasure of silver coins of all sorts and sizes, and I even fancied that I saw gleaming among them the golden plumage of that rare bird in our currency the American eagle. In this precious heap was my bank-note deposited, the rate of exchange being considerably against me.

His wants being thus relieved, the destitute man pulled out of his pocket an old pack of greasy cards which had probably contributed to fill the buff leather bag in more ways than one.

"Come!" said he; "I spy a rare fortune in your face, and for twenty-five cents more I'll tell you what it is."

I never refuse to take a glimpse into futurity; so, after shuffling the cards and when the fair damsel had cut them, I dealt a portion to the prophetic beggar. Like others of his profession, before predicting the shadowy events that were moving on to meet me he gave proof of his preternatural science by describing scenes through which I had already passed.

Here let me have credit for a sober fact. When the old man had read a page in his book of fate, he bent his keen gray eyes on mine and proceeded to relate in all its minute particulars what was then the most singular event of my life. It was one which I had no purpose to disclose till the general unfolding of all secrets, nor would it be a much stranger instance of inscrutable knowledge or fortunate conjecture if the beggar were to meet me in the street today and repeat word for word the page which I have here written.

The fortune-teller, after predicting a destiny which time seems loth to make good, put up his cards, secreted his treasure-bag and began to converse with the other occupants of the wagon.

"Well, old friend," said the showman, "you have not yet told us which way your face is turned this afternoon."

"I am taking a trip northward this warm weather," replied the conjurer, "across the Connecticut first, and then up through Vermont, and maybe into Canada before the fall. But I must stop and see the breaking up of the camp-meeting at Stamford."

I began to think that all the vagrants in New England were converging to the camp-meeting and had made this wagon, their rendezvous by the way.

The showman now proposed that when the shower was over they should pursue the road to Stamford together, it being sometimes the policy of these people to form a sort of league and confederacy.

"And the young lady too," observed the gallant bibliopolist, bowing to her profoundly, "and this foreign gentleman, as I understand, are on a jaunt of pleasure to the same spot. It would add incalculably to my own enjoyment, and I presume to that of my colleague and his friend, if they could be prevailed upon to join our party."

This arrangement met with approbation on all hands, nor were any of those concerned more sensible of its advantages than myself, who had no title to be included in it.

Having already satisfied myself as to the several modes in which the four others attained felicity, I next set my mind at work to discover what enjoyments were peculiar to the old "straggler," as the people of the country would have termed the wandering mendicant and prophet. As he pretended to familiarity with the devil, so I fancied that he was fitted to pursue and take delight in his way of life by possessing some of the mental and moral characteristics— the lighter and more comic ones—of the devil in popular stories. Among them might be reckoned a love of deception for its own sake, a shrewd eye and keen relish for human weakness and ridiculous infirmity, and the talent of petty fraud. Thus to this old man there would be pleasure even in the consciousness—so insupportable to some minds—that his whole life was a cheat upon the world, and that, so far as he was concerned with the public, his little cunning had the upper hand of its united wisdom. Every day would furnish him with a succession of minute and pungent triumphs—as when, for instance, his importunity wrung a pittance out of the heart of a miser, or when my silly good-nature transferred a part of my slender purse to his plump leather bag, or when some ostentatious gentleman should throw a coin to the ragged beggar who was richer than himself, or when—though he would not always be so decidedly diabolical—his pretended wants should make him a sharer in the scanty living of real indigence. And then what an inexhaustible field of enjoyment, both as enabling him to discern so much folly and achieve such quantities of minor mischief, was opened to his sneering spirit by his pretensions to prophetic knowledge.

All this was a sort of happiness which I could conceive of, though I had little sympathy with it. Perhaps, had I been then inclined to admit it, I might have found that the roving life was more proper to him than to either of his companions; for Satan, to whom I had compared the poor man, has delighted, ever since the time of Job, in "wandering up and down upon the earth," and, indeed, a crafty disposition which operates not in deep-laid plans, but in disconnected tricks, could not have an adequate scope, unless naturally impelled to a continual change of scene and society.

My reflections were here interrupted.

"Another visitor!" exclaimed the old showman.

The door of the wagon had been closed against the tempest, which was roaring and blustering with prodigious fury and commotion and beating violently against our shelter, as if it claimed all those homeless people for its lawful prey, while we, caring little for the displeasure of the elements, sat comfortably talking. There was now an attempt to open the door, succeeded by a voice uttering some strange, unintelligible gibberish which my companions mistook for Greek and I suspected to be thieves' Latin. However, the showman stepped forward and gave admittance to a figure which made me imagine either that our wagon had rolled back two hundred years into past ages or that the forest and its old inhabitants had sprung up around us by enchantment. It was a red Indian armed with his bow and arrow. His dress was a sort of cap adorned with a single feather of some wild bird, and a frock of blue cotton girded tight about him; on his breast, like orders of knighthood, hung a crescent and a circle and other ornaments of silver, while a small crucifix betokened that our father the pope had interposed between the Indian and the Great Spirit whom he had worshipped in his simplicity. This son of the wilderness and pilgrim of the storm took his place silently in the midst of us. When the first surprise was over, I rightly conjectured him to be one of the Penobscot tribe, parties of which I had often seen in their summer excursions down our Eastern rivers. There they paddle their birch canoes among the coasting-schooners, and build their wigwam beside some roaring mill-dam, and drive a little trade in basket-work where their fathers hunted deer. Our new visitor was probably wandering through the country toward Boston, subsisting on the careless charity of the people while he turned his archery to profitable account by shooting at cents which were to be the prize of his successful aim.

The Indian had not long been seated ere our merry damsel sought to draw him into conversation. She, indeed, seemed all made up of sunshine in the month of May, for there was nothing so dark and dismal that her pleasant mind could not cast a glow over it; and the wild man, like a fir tree in his native forest, soon began to brighten into a sort of sombre cheerfulness. At length she inquired whether his journey had any particular end or purpose.

"I go shoot at the camp-meeting at Stamford," replied the Indian.

"And here are five more," said the girl, "all aiming at the camp-meeting too. You shall be one of us, for we travel with light hearts; and, as for me, I sing merry songs and tell merry tales and am full of merry thoughts, and I dance merrily along the road, so that there is never any sadness among them that keep me company. But oh, you would find it very dull indeed to go all the way to Stamford alone."

My ideas of the aboriginal character led me to fear that the Indian would prefer his own solitary musings to the gay society thus offered him; on the contrary, the girl's proposal met with immediate acceptance and seemed to animate him with a misty expectation of enjoyment.

I now gave myself up to a course of thought which, whether it flowed naturally from this combination of events or was drawn forth by a wayward fancy, caused my mind to thrill as if I were listening to deep music. I saw mankind in this weary old age of the world either enduring a sluggish existence amid the smoke and dust of cities, or, if they breathed a purer air, still lying down at night with no hope but to wear out to-morrow, and all the to-morrows which make up life, among the same dull scenes and in the same wretched toil that had darkened the sunshine of today. But there were some full of the primeval instinct who preserved the freshness of youth to their latest years by the continual excitement of new objects, new pursuits and new associates, and cared little, though their birthplace might have been here in New England, if the grave should close over them in Central Asia. Fate was summoning a parliament of these free spirits; unconscious of the impulse which directed them to a common centre, they had come hither from far and near, and last of all appeared the representatives of those mighty vagrants who had chased the deer during thousands of years, and were chasing it now in the spirit-land. Wandering down through the waste of ages, the woods had vanished around his path; his arm had lost somewhat of its strength, his foot of its fleetness, his mien of its wild regality, his heart and mind of their savage virtue and uncultured force, but here, untamable to the routine of artificial life, roving now along the dusty road as of old over the forest-leaves,—here was the Indian still.

"Well," said the old showman, in the midst of my meditations, "here is an honest company of us—one, two, three, four, five, six—all going to the camp-meeting at Stamford. Now, hoping no offence, I should like to know where this young gentleman may be going?"

I started. How came I among these wanderers? The free mind that preferred its own folly to another's wisdom, the open spirit that found companions everywhere—above all, the restless impulse that had so often made me wretched in the midst of enjoyments,—these were my claims to be of their society.

"My friends," cried I, stepping into the centre of the wagon, "I am going with you to the camp-meeting at Stamford."

"But in what capacity?" asked the old showman, after a moment's silence. "All of us here can get our bread in some creditable way. Every honest man should have his livelihood. You, sir, as I take it, are a mere strolling gentleman."

I proceeded to inform the company that when Nature gave me a propensity to their way of life she had not left me altogether destitute of qualifications for it, though I could not deny that my talent was less respectable, and might be less profitable, than the meanest of theirs. My design, in short, was to imitate the story-tellers of whom Oriental travellers have told us, and become an itinerant novelist, reciting my own extemporaneous fictions to such audiences as I could collect.

"Either this," said I, "is my vocation, or I have been born in vain."

The fortune-teller, with a sly wink to the company, proposed to take me as an apprentice to one or other of his professions, either of which undoubtedly would have given full scope to whatever inventive talent I might possess. The bibliopolist spoke a few words in opposition to my plan—influenced partly, I suspect, by the jealousy of authorship, and partly by an apprehension that the *vivâ-voce* practice would become general among novelists, to the infinite detriment of the book trade.

Dreading a rejection, I solicited the interest of the merry damsel.

"'Mirth,'" cried I, most aptly appropriating the words of L'Allegro, "'to thee I sue! Mirth, admit me of thy crew!'"

"Let us indulge the poor youth," said Mirth, with a kindness which made me love her dearly, though I was no such coxcomb as to misinterpret her motives. "I have espied much promise in him. True, a shadow sometimes flits across his brow, but the sunshine is sure to follow in a moment. He is never guilty of a sad thought but a merry one is twin-born with it. We will take him with us, and you shall see that he will set us all a-laughing before we reach the camp-meeting at Stamford." Her voice silenced the scruples of the rest and gained me admittance into the league; according to the terms of which, without a community of goods or profits, we were to lend each other all the aid and avert all the harm that might be in our power.

This affair settled, a marvellous jollity entered into the whole tribe of us, manifesting itself characteristically in each individual. The old showman, sitting down to his barrel-organ, stirred up the souls of the pigmy people with one of the quickest tunes in the music-book; tailors, blacksmiths, gentlemen and ladies all seemed to share in the spirit of the occasion, and the Merry Andrew played his part more facetiously than ever, nodding and winking particularly at me. The young foreigner flourished his fiddle-bow with a master's hand, and gave an inspiring echo to the showman's melody. The bookish man and the merry damsel started up simultaneously to dance, the former enacting the double shuffle in a style which everybody must have witnessed ere election week was blotted out of time, while the girl, setting her arms akimbo with both hands at her slim waist, displayed such light rapidity of foot and harmony of varying attitude and motion that I could not conceive how she ever was to stop, imagining at the moment that Nature had made her, as the old showman had made his puppets, for no earthly purpose but to dance jigs. The Indian bellowed forth a succession of most hideous outcries, somewhat affrighting us till we interpreted them as the war-song with which, in imitation of his ancestors, he was prefacing the assault on Stamford. The conjurer, meanwhile, sat demurely in a corner extracting a sly enjoyment from the whole scene, and, like the facetious Merry Andrew, directing his queer glance particularly at me. As for myself, with great exhilaration of fancy, I began to arrange and color the incidents of a tale wherewith I proposed to amuse an audience that very evening; for I saw that my associates were a little ashamed of me, and that no time was to be lost in obtaining a public acknowledgment of my abilities.

"Come, fellow-laborers," at last said the old showman, whom we had elected president; "the shower is over, and we must be doing our duty by these poor souls at Stamford."

"We'll come among them in procession, with music and dancing," cried the merry damsel.

Accordingly—for it must be understood that our pilgrimage was to be performed on foot— we sallied joyously out of the wagon, each of us, even the old gentleman in his white top-boots, giving a great skip as we came down the ladder. Above our heads there was such a glory of sunshine and splendor of clouds, and such brightness of verdure below, that, as I modestly remarked at the time, Nature seemed to have washed her face and put on the best of her jewelry and a fresh green gown in honor of our confederation. Casting our eyes northward, we beheld a horseman approaching leisurely and splashing through the little puddle on the Stamford road. Onward he came, sticking up in his saddle with rigid perpendicularity, a tall, thin figure in rusty black, whom the showman and the conjurer shortly recognized to be what his aspect sufficiently indicated—a travelling preacher of great fame among the Methodists. What puzzled us was the fact that his face appeared turned from, instead of to, the camp-meeting at Stamford. However, as this new votary of the wandering life drew near the little green space where the guide-post and our wagon were situated, my six fellow-vagabonds and myself rushed forward and surrounded him, crying out with united voices, "What news? What news from the camp-meeting at Stamford?"

The missionary looked down in surprise at as singular a knot of people as could have been selected from all his heterogeneous auditors. Indeed, considering that we might all be classified under the general head of Vagabond, there was great diversity of character among the grave old showman, the sly, prophetic beggar, the fiddling foreigner and his merry damsel, the smart bibliopolist, the sombre Indian and myself, the itinerant novelist, a slender youth of eighteen. I even fancied that a smile was endeavoring to disturb the iron gravity of the preacher's mouth.

"Good people," answered he, "the camp-meeting is broke up."

So saying, the Methodist minister switched his steed and rode westward. Our union being thus nullified by the removal of its object, we were sundered at once to the four winds of heaven. The fortune-teller, giving a nod to all and a peculiar wink to me, departed on his Northern tour, chuckling within himself as he took the Stamford road. The old showman and his literary coadjutor were already tackling their horses to the wagon with a design to peregrinate south-west along the sea-coast. The foreigner and the merry damsel took their laughing leave and pursued the eastern road, which I had that day trodden; as they passed away the young man played a lively strain and the girl's happy spirit broke into a dance, and, thus dissolving, as it were, into sunbeams and gay music, that pleasant pair departed from my view. Finally, with a pensive shadow thrown across my mind, yet emulous of the light philosophy of my late companions, I joined myself to the Penobscot Indian and set forth toward the distant city.

THE WHITE OLD MAID

THE MOONBEAMS CAME through two deep and narrow windows and showed a spacious chamber richly furnished in an antique fashion. From one lattice the shadow of the diamond panes was thrown upon the floor; the ghostly light through the other slept upon a bed, falling between the heavy silken curtains and illuminating the face of a young man. But how quietly the slumberer lay! how pale his features! And how like a shroud the sheet was wound about his frame! Yes, it was a corpse in its burial-clothes.

Suddenly the fixed features seemed to move with dark emotion. Strange fantasy! It was but the shadow of the fringed curtain waving betwixt the dead face and the moonlight as the door of the chamber opened and a girl stole softly to the bedside. Was there delusion in the moonbeams, or did her gesture and her eye betray a gleam of triumph as she bent over the pale corpse, pale as itself, and pressed her living lips to the cold ones of the dead? As she drew back from that long kiss her features writhed as if a proud heart were fighting with its anguish. Again it seemed that the features of the corpse had moved responsive to her own. Still an illusion. The silken curtains had waved a second time betwixt the dead face and the moonlight as another fair young girl unclosed the door and glided ghostlike to the bedside. There the two maidens stood, both beautiful, with the pale beauty of the dead between them. But she who had first entered was proud and stately, and the other a soft and fragile thing.

"Away!" cried the lofty one. "Thou hadst him living; the dead is mine."

"Thine!" returned the other, shuddering. "Well hast thou spoken; the dead is thine."

The proud girl started and stared into her face with a ghastly look, but a wild-and mournful expression passed across the features of the gentle one, and, weak and helpless, she sank down on the bed, her head pillowed beside that of the corpse and her hair mingling with his dark locks. A creature of hope and joy, the first draught of sorrow had bewildered her.

"Edith!" cried her rival.

Edith groaned as with a sudden compression of the heart, and, removing her cheek from the dead youth's pillow, she stood upright, fearfully encountering the eyes of the lofty girl.

"Wilt thou betray me?" said the latter, calmly.

"Till the dead bid me speak I will be silent," answered Edith. "Leave us alone together. Go and live many years, and then return and tell me of thy life. He too will be here. Then, if thou tellest of sufferings more than death, we will both forgive thee."

"And what shall be the token?" asked the proud girl, as if her heart acknowledged a meaning in these wild words.

"This lock of hair," said Edith, lifting one of the dark clustering curls that lay heavily on the dead man's brow.

The two maidens joined their hands over the bosom of the corpse and appointed a day and hour far, far in time to come for their next meeting in that chamber. The statelier girl gave one deep look at the motionless countenance and departed, yet turned again and trembled ere she closed the door, almost believing that her dead lover frowned upon her. And Edith, too! Was not her white form fading into the moonlight? Scorning her own weakness, she went forth and perceived that a negro slave was waiting in the passage with a waxlight, which he held between her face and his own and regarded her, as she thought, with an ugly expression of merriment. Lifting his torch on high, the slave lighted her down the staircase and undid the portal of the mansion. The young clergyman of the town had just ascended the steps, and, bowing to the lady, passed in without a word.

Years—many years—rolled on. The world seemed new again, so much older was it grown since the night when those pale girls had clasped their hands across the bosom of the corpse. In the interval a lonely woman had passed from youth to extreme age, and was known by all the town as the "Old Maid in the Winding-Sheet." A taint of insanity had affected her whole life, but so quiet, sad and gentle, so utterly free from violence, that she was suffered to pursue her harmless fantasies unmolested by the world with whose business or pleasures she had naught to do. She dwelt alone, and never came into the daylight except to follow funerals. Whenever a corpse was borne along the street, in sunshine, rain or snow, whether a pompous train of the rich and proud thronged after it or few and humble were the mourners, behind them came the lonely woman in a long white garment which the people called her shroud. She took no place among the kindred or the friends, but stood at the door to hear the funeral prayer, and walked in the rear of the procession as one whose earthly charge it was to haunt the house of mourning and be the shadow of affliction and see that the dead were duly buried. So long had this been her custom that the inhabitants of the town deemed her a part of every funeral, as much as the coffin-pall or the very corpse itself, and augured ill of the sinner's destiny unless the Old Maid in the Winding-Sheet came gliding like a ghost behind. Once, it is said, she affrighted a bridal-party with her pale presence, appearing suddenly in the illuminated hall just as the priest was uniting a false maid to a wealthy man before her lover had been dead a year. Evil was the omen to that marriage. Sometimes she stole forth by moonlight and visited the graves of venerable integrity and wedded love and virgin innocence, and every spot where the ashes of a kind and faithful heart were mouldering. Over the hillocks of those favored dead would she stretch out her arms with a gesture as if she were scattering seeds, and many believed that she brought them from the garden of Paradise, for the graves which she had visited were green beneath the snow and covered with sweet flowers from April to November. Her blessing was better than a holy verse upon the tombstone. Thus wore away her long, sad, peaceful and fantastic life till few were so old as she, and the people of later generations wondered how the dead had ever been buried or mourners had endured their grief without the Old Maid in the Winding-Sheet. Still years went on, and still she followed funerals and was not yet summoned to her own festival of death.

One afternoon the great street of the town was all alive with business and bustle, though the sun now gilded only the upper half of the church-spire, having left the housetops and loftiest trees in shadow. The scene was cheerful and animated in spite of the sombre shade between the high brick buildings. Here were pompous merchants in white wigs and laced velvet, the bronzed faces of sea-captains, the foreign garb and air of Spanish Creoles, and the disdainful port of natives of Old England, all contrasted with the rough aspect of one or two back-settlers negotiating sales of timber from forests where axe had never sounded. Sometimes a lady passed, swelling roundly forth in an embroidered petticoat, balancing her steps in high-heeled shoes and courtesying with lofty grace to the punctilious obeisances of the gentlemen. The life of the town seemed to have its very centre not far from an old mansion that stood somewhat back from the pavement, surrounded by neglected grass, with a strange air of loneliness rather deepened than dispelled by the throng so near it. Its site would have been suitably occupied by a magnificent Exchange or a brick block lettered all over with various signs, or the large house itself might have made a noble tavern with the "King's Arms" swinging before it and guests in every chamber, instead of the present solitude. But, owing to some dispute about the right of inheritance, the mansion had been long without a tenant, decaying from year to year and throwing the stately gloom of its shadow over the busiest part of the town.

Such was the scene, and such time, when a figure unlike any that have been described was observed at a distance down the street.

"I espy a strange sail yonder," remarked a Liverpool captain—"that woman in the long white garment."

The sailor seemed much struck by the object, as were several others who at the same moment caught a glimpse of the figure that had attracted his notice. Almost immediately the various topics of conversation gave place to speculations in an undertone on this unwonted occurrence.

"Can there be a funeral so late this afternoon?" inquired some.

They looked for the signs of death at every door—the sexton, the hearse, the assemblage of black-clad relatives, all that makes up the woeful pomp of funerals. They raised their eyes, also, to the sun-gilt spire of the church, and wondered that no clang proceeded from its bell, which had always tolled till now when this figure appeared in the light of day. But none had heard that a corpse was to be borne to its home that afternoon, nor was there any token of a funeral except the apparition of the Old Maid in the Winding-Sheet.

"What may this portend?" asked each man of his neighbor.

All smiled as they put the question, yet with a certain trouble in their eyes, as if pestilence, or some other wide calamity, were prognosticated by the untimely intrusion among the living of one whose presence had always been associated with death and woe. What a comet is to the earth was that sad woman to the town. Still she moved on, while the hum of surprise was hushed at her approach, and the proud and the humble stood aside that her white garment might not wave against them. It was a long, loose robe of spotless purity. Its wearer appeared very old, pale, emaciated and feeble, yet glided onward without the unsteady pace of extreme age. At one point of her course a little rosy boy burst forth from a door and ran with open arms toward the ghostly woman, seeming to expect a kiss from her bloodless lips. She made a slight pause, fixing her eye upon him with an expression of no earthly sweetness, so that the child shivered and stood awestruck rather than affrighted while the Old Maid passed on. Perhaps her garment might have been polluted even by an infant's touch; perhaps her kiss would have been death to the sweet boy within the year.

"She is but a shadow," whispered the superstitious. "The child put forth his arms and could not grasp her robe."

The wonder was increased when the Old Maid passed beneath the porch of the deserted mansion, ascended the moss-covered steps, lifted the iron knocker and gave three raps. The people could only conjecture that some old remembrance, troubling her bewildered brain, had impelled the poor woman hither to visit the friends of her youth—all gone from their home long since and for ever unless their ghosts still haunted it, fit company for the Old Maid in the Winding-Sheet.

An elderly man approached the steps, and, reverently uncovering his gray locks, essayed to explain the matter.

"None, madam," said he, "have dwelt in this house these fifteen years agone—no, not since the death of old Colonel Fenwicke, whose funeral you may remember to have followed. His heirs, being ill-agreed among themselves, have let the mansion-house go to ruin."

The Old Maid looked slowly round with a slight gesture of one hand and a finger of the other upon her lip, appearing more shadow-like than ever in the obscurity of the porch. But again she lifted the hammer, and gave, this time, a single rap. Could it be that a footstep was now heard coming down the staircase of the old mansion which all conceived to have been so long untenanted? Slowly, feebly, yet heavily, like the pace of an aged and infirm person, the step approached, more distinct on every downward stair, till it reached the portal. The bar fell on the inside; the door was opened. One upward glance toward the church-spire, whence the sunshine had just faded, was the last that the people saw of the Old Maid in the Winding-Sheet.

"Who undid the door?" asked many.

This question, owing to the depth of shadow beneath the porch, no one could satisfactorily answer. Two or three aged men, while protesting against an inference which might be drawn, affirmed that the person within was a negro and bore a singular resemblance to old Cæsar, formerly a slave in the house, but freed by death some thirty years before.

"Her summons has waked up a servant of the old family," said one, half seriously.

"Let us wait here," replied another; "more guests will knock at the door anon. But the gate of the graveyard should be thrown open."

Twilight had overspread the town before the crowd began to separate or the comments on this incident were exhausted. One after another was wending his way homeward, when a coach—no common spectacle in those days—drove slowly into the street. It was an old-fashioned equipage, hanging close to the ground, with arms on the panels, a footman behind and a grave, corpulent coachman seated high in front, the whole giving an idea of solemn state and dignity. There was something awful in the heavy rumbling of the wheels.

The coach rolled down the street, till, coming to the gateway of the deserted mansion, it drew up, and the footman sprang to the ground.

"Whose grand coach is this?" asked a very inquisitive body.

The footman made no reply, but ascended the steps of the old house, gave three taps with the iron hammer, and returned to open the coach door. An old man possessed of the heraldic lore so common in that day examined the shield of arms on the panel.

"Azure, a lion's head erased, between three flowers de luce," said he, then whispered the name of the family to whom these bearings belonged. The last inheritor of its honors was recently dead, after a long residence amid the splendor of the British court, where his birth and wealth had given him no mean station. "He left no child," continued the herald, "and these arms, being in a lozenge, betoken that the coach appertains to his widow."

Further disclosures, perhaps, might have been made had not the speaker been suddenly struck dumb by the stern eye of an ancient lady who thrust forth her head from the coach, preparing to descend. As she emerged the people saw that her dress was magnificent, and her figure dignified in spite of age and infirmity—a stately ruin, but with a look at once of pride and wretchedness. Her strong and rigid features had an awe about them unlike that of the white Old Maid, but as of something evil. She passed up the steps, leaning on a gold-headed cane. The door swung open as she ascended, and the light of a torch glittered on the embroidery of her dress and gleamed on the pillars of the porch. After a momentary pause, a glance backward and then a desperate effort, she went in.

The decipherer of the coat-of-arms had ventured up the lower step, and, shrinking back immediately, pale and tremulous, affirmed that the torch was held by the very image of old Cæsar.

"But such a hideous grin," added he, "was never seen on the face of mortal man, black or white. It will haunt me till my dying-day."

Meantime, the coach had wheeled round with a prodigious clatter on the pavement and rumbled up the street, disappearing in the twilight, while the ear still tracked its course. Scarcely was it gone when the people began to question whether the coach and attendants, the ancient lady, the spectre of old Cæsar and the Old Maid herself were not all a strangely-combined delusion with some dark purport in its mystery. The whole town was astir, so that, instead of dispersing, the crowd continually increased, and stood gazing up at the windows of the mansion, now silvered by the brightening moon. The elders, glad to indulge the narrative propensity of age, told of the long-faded splendor of the family, the entertainments they had given and the guests, the greatest of the land, and even titled and noble ones from abroad, who had passed beneath that portal. These graphic reminiscences seemed to call up the ghosts of those to whom they referred. So strong was the impression on some of the more imaginative hearers that two or three were seized with trembling fits at one and the same moment, protesting that they had distinctly heard three other raps of the iron knocker.

"Impossible!" exclaimed others. "See! The moon shines beneath the porch, and shows every part of it except in the narrow shade of that pillar. There is no one there."

"Did not the door open?" whispered one of these fanciful persons.

"Didst thou see it too?" said his companion, in a startled tone.

But the general sentiment was opposed to the idea that a third visitant had made application at the door of the deserted house. A few, however, adhered to this new marvel, and even declared that a red gleam like that of a torch had shone through the great front window, as if the negro were lighting a guest up the staircase. This too was pronounced a mere fantasy.

But at once the whole multitude started, and each man beheld his own terror painted in the faces of all the rest.

"What an awful thing is this!" cried they.

A shriek too fearfully distinct for doubt had been heard within the mansion, breaking forth suddenly and succeeded by a deep stillness, as if a heart had burst in giving it utterance. The people knew not whether to fly from the very sight of the house or to rush trembling in and search out the strange mystery. Amid their confusion and affright they were somewhat reassured by the appearance of their clergyman, a venerable patriarch, and equally a saint, who had taught them and their fathers the way to heaven for more than the space of an ordinary lifetime. He was a reverend figure with long white hair upon his shoulders, a white beard upon his breast and a back so bent over his staff that he seemed to be looking downward continually, as if to choose a proper grave for his weary frame. It was some time before the good old man, being deaf and of impaired intellect, could be made to comprehend such portions of the affair as were comprehensible at all. But when possessed of the facts, his energies assumed unexpected vigor.

"Verily," said the old gentleman, "it will be fitting that I enter the mansion-house of the worthy Colonel Fenwicke, lest any harm should have befallen that true Christian woman whom ye call the 'Old Maid in the Winding-Sheet.'"

Behold, then, the venerable clergyman ascending the steps of the mansion with a torch-bearer behind him. It was the elderly man who had spoken to the Old Maid, and the same who had afterward explained the shield of arms and recognized the features of the negro. Like their predecessors, they gave three raps with the iron hammer.

"Old Cæsar cometh not," observed the priest. "Well, I wot he no longer doth service in this mansion."

"Assuredly, then, it was something worse in old Cæsar's likeness," said the other adventurer.

"Be it as God wills," answered the clergyman. "See! my strength, though it be much decayed, hath sufficed to open this heavy door. Let us enter and pass up the staircase."

Here occurred a singular exemplification of the dreamy state of a very old man's mind. As they ascended the wide flight of stairs the aged clergyman appeared to move with caution, occasionally standing aside, and oftener bending his head, as it were in salutation, thus practising all the gestures of one who makes his way through a throng. Reaching the head of the staircase, he looked around with sad and solemn benignity, laid aside his staff, bared his hoary locks, and was evidently on the point of commencing a prayer.

"Reverend sir," said his attendant, who conceived this a very suitable prelude to their further search, "would it not be well that the people join with us in prayer?"

"Well-a-day!" cried the old clergyman, staring strangely around him. "Art thou here with me, and none other? Verily, past times were present to me, and I deemed that I was to make a funeral prayer, as many a time heretofore, from the head of this staircase. Of a truth, I saw the shades of many that are gone. Yea, I have prayed at their burials, one after another, and the Old Maid in the Winding-Sheet hath seen them to their graves."

Being now more thoroughly awake to their present purpose, he took his staff and struck forcibly on the floor, till there came an echo from each deserted chamber, but no menial to answer their summons. They therefore walked along the passage, and again paused, opposite to the great front window, through which was seen the crowd in the shadow and partial moonlight of the street beneath. On their right hand was the open door of a chamber, and a closed one on their left.

The clergyman pointed his cane to the carved oak panel of the latter.

"Within that chamber," observed he, "a whole lifetime since, did I sit by the death-bed of a goodly young man who, being now at the last gasp—" Apparently, there was some powerful excitement in the ideas which had now flashed across his mind. He snatched the torch from his companion's hand, and threw open the door with such sudden violence that the flame was extinguished, leaving them no other light than the moonbeams which fell through two windows into the spacious chamber. It was sufficient to discover all that could be known. In a high-backed oaken arm-chair, upright, with her hands clasped across her breast and her head thrown back, sat the Old Maid in the Winding-Sheet. The stately dame had fallen on her knees with her forehead on the holy knees of the Old Maid, one hand upon the floor and the other pressed convulsively against her heart. It clutched a lock of hair—once sable, now discolored with a greenish mould.

As the priest and layman advanced into the chamber the Old Maid's features assumed such a semblance of shifting expression that they trusted to hear the whole mystery explained by a single word. But it was only the shadow of a tattered curtain waving betwixt the dead face and the moonlight.

"Both dead!" said the venerable man. "Then who shall divulge the secret? Methinks it glimmers to and fro in my mind like the light and shadow across the Old Maid's face. And now 'tis gone!"

PETER GOLDTHWAITE'S TREASURE

"And so, Peter, you won't even consider of the business?" said Mr. John Brown, buttoning his surtout over the snug rotundity of his person and drawing on his gloves. "You positively refuse to let me have this crazy old house, and the land under and adjoining, at the price named?"

"Neither at that, nor treble the sum," responded the gaunt, grizzled and threadbare Peter Goldthwaite. "The fact is, Mr. Brown, you must find another site for your brick block and be content to leave my estate with the present owner. Next summer I intend to put a splendid new mansion over the cellar of the old house."

"Pho, Peter!" cried Mr. Brown as he opened the kitchen door; "content yourself with building castles in the air, where house-lots are cheaper than on earth, to say nothing of the cost of bricks and mortar. Such foundations are solid enough for your edifices, while this underneath us is just the thing for mine; and so we may both be suited. What say you, again?"

"Precisely what I said before, Mr. Brown," answered Peter Goldthwaite. "And, as for castles in the air, mine may not be as magnificent as that sort of architecture, but perhaps as substantial, Mr. Brown, as the very respectable brick block with dry-goods stores, tailors' shops and banking-rooms on the lower floor, and lawyers' offices in the second story, which you are so anxious to substitute."

"And the cost, Peter? Eh?" said Mr. Brown as he withdrew in something of a pet. "That, I suppose, will be provided for off-hand by drawing a check on Bubble Bank?"

John Brown and Peter Goldthwaite had been jointly known to the commercial world between twenty and thirty years before under the firm of Goldthwaite & Brown; which copartnership, however, was speedily dissolved by the natural incongruity of its constituent parts. Since that event, John Brown, with exactly the qualities of a thousand other John Browns, and by just such plodding methods as they used, had prospered wonderfully and become one of the wealthiest John Browns on earth. Peter Goldthwaite, on the contrary, after innumerable schemes which ought to have collected all the coin and paper currency of the country into his coffers, was as needy a gentleman as ever wore a patch upon his elbow. The contrast between him and his former partner may be briefly marked, for Brown never reckoned upon luck, yet always had it, while Peter made luck the main condition of his projects, and always missed it. While the means held out his speculations had been magnificent, but were chiefly confined of late years to such small business as adventures in the lottery. Once he had gone on a gold-gathering expedition somewhere to the South, and ingeniously contrived to empty his pockets more thoroughly than ever, while others, doubtless, were filling theirs with native bullion by the handful. More recently he had expended a legacy of a thousand or two of dollars in purchasing Mexican scrip, and thereby became the proprietor of a province; which, however, so far as Peter could find out, was situated where he might have had an empire for the same money—in the clouds. From a search after this valuable real estate Peter returned so gaunt and threadbare that on reaching New England the scarecrows in the corn-fields beckoned to him as he passed by. "They did but flutter in the wind," quoth Peter Goldthwaite. No, Peter, they beckoned, for the scarecrows knew their brother.

At the period of our story his whole visible income would not have paid the tax of the old mansion in which we find him. It was one of those rusty, moss-grown, many-peaked wooden houses which are scattered about the streets of our elder towns, with a beetle-browed second story projecting over the foundation, as if it frowned at the novelty around it. This old paternal edifice, needy as he was, and though, being centrally situated on the principal street of the town, it would have brought him a handsome sum, the sagacious Peter had his own reasons for never parting with, either by auction or private sale. There seemed, indeed, to be a fatality that connected him with his birthplace; for, often as he had stood on the verge of ruin, and standing there even now, he had not yet taken the step beyond it which would have compelled him to surrender the house to his creditors. So here he dwelt with bad luck till good should come.

Here, then, in his kitchen—the only room where a spark of fire took off the chill of a November evening—poor Peter Goldthwaite had just been visited by his rich old partner. At the close of their interview, Peter, with rather a mortified look, glanced downward at his dress, parts of which appeared as ancient as the days of Goldthwaite & Brown. His upper garment was a mixed surtout, woefully faded, and patched with newer stuff on each elbow; beneath this he wore a threadbare black coat, some of the silk buttons of which had been replaced with others of a different pattern; and, lastly, though he lacked not a pair of gray pantaloons, they were very shabby ones, and had been partially turned brown by the frequent toasting of Peter's shins before a scanty fire. Peter's person was in keeping with his goodly apparel. Gray-headed, hollow-eyed, pale-cheeked and lean-bodied, he was the perfect picture of a man who had fed on windy schemes and empty hopes till he could neither live on such unwholesome trash nor stomach more substantial food. But, withal, this Peter Goldthwaite, crack-brained simpleton as, perhaps, he was, might have cut a very brilliant figure in the world had he employed his imagination in the airy business of poetry instead of making it a demon of mischief in mercantile pursuits. After all, he was no bad fellow, but as harmless as a child, and as honest and honorable, and as much of the gentleman which Nature meant him for, as an irregular life and depressed circumstances will permit any man to be.

As Peter stood on the uneven bricks of his hearth looking round at the disconsolate old kitchen his eyes began to kindle with the illumination of an enthusiasm that never long deserted him. He raised his hand, clenched it and smote it energetically against the smoky panel over the fireplace.

"The time is come," said he; "with such a treasure at command, it were folly to be a poor man any longer. Tomorrow morning I will begin with the garret, nor desist till I have torn the house down."

Deep in the chimney-corner, like a witch in a dark cavern, sat a little old woman mending one of the two pairs of stockings wherewith Peter Goldthwaite kept his toes from being frost-bitten. As the feet were ragged past all darning, she had cut pieces out of a cast-off flannel petticoat to make new soles. Tabitha Porter was an old maid upward of sixty years of age, fifty-five of which she had sat in that same chimney-corner, such being the length of time since Peter's grandfather had taken her from the almshouse. She had no friend but Peter, nor Peter any friend but Tabitha; so long as Peter might have a shelter for his own head, Tabitha would know where to shelter hers, or, being homeless elsewhere, she would take her master by the hand and bring him to her native home, the almshouse. Should it ever be necessary, she loved him well enough to feed him with her last morsel and clothe him with her under-petticoat. But Tabitha was a queer old woman, and, though never infected with Peter's flightiness, had become so accustomed to his freaks and follies that she viewed them all as matters of course. Hearing him threaten to tear the house down, she looked quietly up from her work.

"Best leave the kitchen till the last, Mr. Peter," said she.

"The sooner we have it all down, the better," said Peter Goldthwaite. "I am tired to death of living in this cold, dark, windy, smoky, creaking, groaning, dismal old house. I shall feel like a younger man when we get into my splendid brick mansion, as, please Heaven, we shall by this time next autumn. You shall have a room on the sunny side, old Tabby, finished and furnished as best may suit your own notions."

"I should like it pretty much such a room as this kitchen," answered Tabitha. "It will never be like home to me till the chimney-corner gets as black with smoke as this, and that won't be these hundred years. How much do you mean to lay out on the house, Mr. Peter?"

"What is that to the purpose?" exclaimed Peter, loftily. "Did not my great-grand-uncle, Peter Goldthwaite, who died seventy years ago, and whose namesake I am, leave treasure enough to build twenty such?"

"I can't say but he did, Mr. Peter," said Tabitha, threading her needle.

Tabitha well understood that Peter had reference to an immense hoard of the precious metals which was said to exist somewhere in the cellar or walls, or under the floors, or in some concealed closet or other out-of-the-way nook of the old house. This wealth, according to tradition, had been accumulated by a former Peter Goldthwaite whose character seems to have borne a remarkable similitude to that of the Peter of our story. Like him, he was a wild projector, seeking to heap up gold by the bushel and the cart-load instead of scraping it together coin by coin. Like Peter the second, too, his projects had almost invariably failed, and, but for the magnificent success of the final one, would have left him with hardly a coat and pair of breeches to his gaunt and grizzled person. Reports were various as to the nature of his fortunate speculation, one intimating that the ancient Peter had made the gold by alchemy; another, that he had conjured it out of people's pockets by the black art; and a third—still more unaccountable—that the devil had given him free access to the old provincial treasury. It was affirmed, however, that some secret impediment had debarred him from the enjoyment of his riches, and that he had a motive for concealing them from his heir, or, at any rate, had died without disclosing the place of deposit. The present Peter's father had faith enough in the story to cause the cellar to be dug over. Peter himself chose to consider the legend as an indisputable truth, and amid his many troubles had this one consolation—that, should all other resources fail, he might build up his fortunes by tearing his house down. Yet, unless he felt a lurking distrust of the golden tale, it is difficult to account for his permitting the paternal roof to stand so long, since he had never yet seen the moment when his predecessor's treasure would not have found plenty of room in his own strong-box. But now was the crisis. Should he delay the search a little longer, the house would pass from the lineal heir, and with it the vast heap of gold, to remain in its burial-place till the ruin of the aged walls should discover it to strangers of a future generation.

"Yes," cried Peter Goldthwaite, again; "to-morrow I will set about it."

The deeper he looked at the matter, the more certain of success grew Peter. His spirits were naturally so elastic that even now, in the blasted autumn of his age, he could often compete with the springtime gayety of other people. Enlivened by his brightening prospects, he began to caper about the kitchen like a hobgoblin, with the queerest antics of his lean limbs and gesticulations of his starved features. Nay, in the exuberance of his feelings, he seized both of Tabitha's hands and danced the old lady across the floor till the oddity of her rheumatic motions set him into a roar of laughter, which was echoed back from the rooms and chambers, as if Peter Goldthwaite were laughing in every one. Finally, he bounded upward, almost out of sight, into the smoke that clouded the roof of the kitchen, and, alighting safely on the floor again, endeavored to resume his customary gravity.

"To-morrow, at sunrise," he repeated, taking his lamp to retire to bed, "I'll see whether this treasure be hid in the wall of the garret."

"And, as we're out of wood, Mr. Peter," said Tabitha, puffing and panting with her late gymnastics, "as fast as you tear the house down I'll make a fire with the pieces."

Gorgeous that night were the dreams of Peter Goldthwaite. At one time he was turning a ponderous key in an iron door not unlike the door of a sepulchre, but which, being opened, disclosed a vault heaped up with gold coin as plentifully as golden corn in a granary. There were chased goblets, also, and tureens, salvers, dinner-dishes and dish-covers of gold or silver-gilt, besides chains and other jewels, incalculably rich, though tarnished with the damps of the vault; for, of all the wealth that was irrevocably lost to man, whether buried in the earth or sunken in the sea, Peter Goldthwaite had found it in this one treasure-place. Anon he had returned to the old house as poor as ever, and was received at the door by the gaunt and grizzled figure of a man whom he might have mistaken for himself, only that his garments were of a much elder fashion. But the house, without losing its former aspect, had been changed into a palace of the precious metals. The floors, walls and ceilings were of burnished silver; the doors, the window-frames, the cornices, the balustrades and the steps of the staircase, of pure gold; and silver, with gold bottoms, were the chairs, and gold, standing on silver legs, the high chests of drawers, and silver the bedsteads, with blankets of woven gold and sheets of silver tissue. The house had evidently been transmuted by a single touch, for it retained all the marks that Peter remembered, but in gold or silver instead of wood, and the initials of his name—which when a boy he had cut in the wooden door-post—remained as deep in the pillar of gold. A happy man would have been Peter Goldthwaite except for a certain ocular deception which, whenever he glanced backward, caused the house to darken from its glittering magnificence into the sordid gloom of yesterday.

Up betimes rose Peter, seized an axe, hammer and saw which he had placed by his bedside, and hied him to the garret. It was but scantily lighted up as yet by the frosty fragments of a sunbeam which began to glimmer through the almost opaque bull-eyes of the window. A moralizer might find abundant themes for his speculative and impracticable wisdom in a garret. There is the limbo of departed fashions, aged trifles of a day and whatever was valuable only to one generation of men, and which passed to the garret when that generation passed to the grave—not for safekeeping, but to be out of the way. Peter saw piles of yellow and musty account-books in parchment covers, wherein creditors long dead and buried had written the names of dead and buried debtors in ink now so faded that their moss-grown tombstones were more legible. He found old moth-eaten garments, all in rags and tatters, or Peter would have put them on. Here was a naked and rusty sword—not a sword of service, but a gentleman's small French rapier—which had never left its scabbard till it lost it. Here were canes of twenty different sorts, but no gold-headed ones, and shoebuckles of various pattern and material, but not silver nor set with precious stones. Here was a large box full of shoes with high heels and peaked toes. Here, on a shelf, were a multitude of phials half filled with old apothecary's stuff which, when the other half had done its business on Peter's ancestors, had been brought hither from the death-chamber. Here—not to give a longer inventory of articles that will never be put up at auction—was the fragment of a full-length looking-glass which by the dust and dimness of its surface made the picture of these old things look older than the reality. When Peter, not knowing that there was a mirror there, caught the faint traces of his own figure, he partly imagined that the former Peter Goldthwaite had come back either to assist or impede his search for the hidden wealth. And at that moment a strange notion glimmered through his brain that he was the identical Peter who had concealed the gold, and ought to know whereabout it lay. This, however, he had unaccountably forgotten.

"Well, Mr. Peter!" cried Tabitha, on the garret stairs. "Have you torn the house down enough to heat the teakettle?"

"Not yet, old Tabby," answered Peter, "but that's soon done, as you shall see." With the word in his mouth, he uplifted the axe, and laid about him so vigorously that the dust flew, the boards crashed, and in a twinkling the old woman had an apron full of broken rubbish.

"We shall get our winter's wood cheap," quoth Tabitha.

The good work being thus commenced, Peter beat down all before him, smiting and hewing at the joints and timbers, unclenching spike-nails, ripping and tearing away boards, with a tremendous racket from morning till night. He took care, however, to leave the outside shell of the house untouched, so that the neighbors might not suspect what was going on.

Never, in any of his vagaries, though each had made him happy while it lasted, had Peter been happier than now. Perhaps, after all, there was something in Peter Goldthwaite's turn of mind which brought him an inward recompense for all the external evil that it caused. If he were poor, ill-clad, even hungry and exposed, as it were, to be utterly annihilated by a precipice of impending ruin, yet only his body remained in these miserable circumstances, while his aspiring soul enjoyed the sunshine of a bright futurity. It was his nature to be always young, and the tendency of his mode of life to keep him so. Gray hairs were nothing—no, nor wrinkles nor infirmity; he might look old, indeed, and be somewhat disagreeably connected with a gaunt old figure much the worse for wear, but the true, the essential Peter was a young man of high hopes just entering on the world. At the kindling of each new fire his burnt-out youth rose afresh from the old embers and ashes. It rose exulting now. Having lived thus long—not too long, but just to the right age—a susceptible bachelor with warm and tender dreams, he resolved, so soon as the hidden gold should flash to light, to go a-wooing and win the love of the fairest maid in town. What heart could resist him? Happy Peter Goldthwaite!

Every evening—as Peter had long absented himself from his former lounging-places at insurance offices, news-rooms, and book-stores, and as the honor of his company was seldom requested in private circles—he and Tabitha used to sit down sociably by the kitchen hearth. This was always heaped plentifully with the rubbish of his day's labor. As the foundation of the fire there would be a goodly-sized back-log of red oak, which after being sheltered from rain or damp above a century still hissed with the heat and distilled streams of water from each end, as if the tree had been cut down within a week or two. Next there were large sticks, sound, black and heavy, which had lost the principle of decay and were indestructible except by fire, wherein they glowed like red-hot bars of iron. On this solid basis Tabitha would rear a lighter structure, composed of the splinters of door-panels, ornamented mouldings, and such quick combustibles, which caught like straw and threw a brilliant blaze high up the spacious flue, making its sooty sides visible almost to the chimney-top. Meantime, the gloom of the old kitchen would be chased out of the cobwebbed corners and away from the dusky cross-beams overhead, and driven nobody could tell whither, while Peter smiled like a gladsome man and Tabitha seemed a picture of comfortable age. All this, of course, was but an emblem of the bright fortune which the destruction of the house would shed upon its occupants.

While the dry pine was flaming and crackling like an irregular discharge of fairy-musketry, Peter sat looking and listening in a pleasant state of excitement; but when the brief blaze and uproar were succeeded by the dark-red glow, the substantial heat and the deep singing sound which were to last throughout the evening, his humor became talkative. One night—the hundredth time—he teased Tabitha to tell him something new about his great-granduncle.

"You have been sitting in that chimney-corner fifty-five years, old Tabby, and must have heard many a tradition about him," said Peter. "Did not you tell me that when you first came to the house there was an old woman sitting where you sit now who had been housekeeper to the famous Peter Goldthwaite?"

"So there was, Mr. Peter," answered Tabitha, "and she was near about a hundred years old. She used to say that she and old Peter Goldthwaite had often spent a sociable evening by the kitchen fire—pretty much as you and I are doing now, Mr. Peter."

"The old fellow must have resembled me in more points than one," said Peter, complacently, "or he never would have grown so rich. But methinks he might have invested the money better than he did. No interest! nothing but good security! and the house to be torn down to come at it! What made him hide it so snug, Tabby?"

"Because he could not spend it," said Tabitha, "for as often as he went to unlock the chest the Old Scratch came behind and caught his arm. The money, they say, was paid Peter out of his purse, and he wanted Peter to give him a deed of this house and land, which Peter swore he would not do."

"Just as I swore to John Brown, my old partner," remarked Peter. "But this is all nonsense, Tabby; I don't believe the story."

"Well, it may not be just the truth," said Tabitha, "for some folks say that Peter did make over the house to the Old Scratch, and that's the reason it has always been so unlucky to them that lived in it. And as soon as Peter had given him the deed the chest flew open, and Peter caught up a handful of the gold. But, lo and behold! there was nothing in his fist but a parcel of old rags."

"Hold your tongue, you silly old Tabby!" cried Peter, in great wrath. "They were as good golden guineas as ever bore the effigies of the king of England. It seems as if I could recollect the whole circumstance, and how I, or old Peter, or whoever it was, thrust in my hand, or his hand, and drew it out all of a blaze with gold. Old rags indeed!"

But it was not an old woman's legend that would discourage Peter Goldthwaite. All night long he slept among pleasant dreams, and awoke at daylight with a joyous throb of the heart which few are fortunate enough to feel beyond their boyhood. Day after day he labored hard without wasting a moment except at meal-times, when Tabitha summoned him to the pork and cabbage, or such other sustenance as she had picked up or Providence had sent them. Being a truly pious man, Peter never failed to ask a blessing—if the food were none of the best, then so much the more earnestly, as it was more needed—nor to return thanks, if the dinner had been scanty, yet for the good appetite which was better than a sick stomach at a feast. Then did he hurry back to his toil, and in a moment was lost to sight in a cloud of dust from the old walls, though sufficiently perceptible to the ear by the clatter which he raised in the midst of it.

How enviable is the consciousness of being usefully employed! Nothing troubled Peter, or nothing but those phantoms of the mind which seem like vague recollections, yet have also the aspect of presentiments. He often paused with his axe uplifted in the air, and said to himself, "Peter Goldthwaite, did you never strike this blow before?" or "Peter, what need of tearing the whole house down? Think a little while, and you will remember where the gold is hidden." Days and weeks passed on, however, without any remarkable discovery. Sometimes, indeed, a lean gray rat peeped forth at the lean gray man, wondering what devil had got into the old house, which had always been so peaceable till now. And occasionally Peter sympathized with the sorrows of a female mouse who had brought five or six pretty, little, soft and delicate young ones into the world just in time to see them crushed by its ruin. But as yet no treasure.

By this time, Peter, being as determined as fate and as diligent as time, had made an end with the uppermost regions and got down to the second story, where he was busy in one of the front chambers. It had formerly been the state-bedchamber, and was honored by tradition as the sleeping-apartment of Governor Dudley and many other eminent guests. The furniture was gone. There were remnants of faded and tattered paper-hangings, but larger spaces of bare wall ornamented with charcoal sketches, chiefly of people's heads in profile. These being specimens of Peter's youthful genius, it went more to his heart to obliterate them than if they had been pictures on a church wall by Michael Angelo. One sketch, however, and that the best one, affected him differently. It represented a ragged man partly supporting himself on a spade and bending his lean body over a hole in the earth, with one hand extended to grasp something that he had found. But close behind him, with a fiendish laugh on his features, appeared a figure with horns, a tufted tail and a cloven hoof.

"Avaunt, Satan!" cried Peter. "The man shall have his gold." Uplifting his axe, he hit the horned gentleman such a blow on the head as not only demolished him, but the treasure-seeker also, and caused the whole scene to vanish like magic. Moreover, his axe broke quite through the plaster and laths and discovered a cavity.

"Mercy on us, Mr. Peter! Are you quarrelling with the Old Scratch?" said Tabitha, who was seeking some fuel to put under the dinner-pot.

Without answering the old woman, Peter broke down a further space of the wall, and laid open a small closet or cupboard on one side of the fireplace, about breast-high from the ground. It contained nothing but a brass lamp covered with verdigris, and a dusty piece of parchment. While Peter inspected the latter, Tabitha seized the lamp and began to rub it with her apron.

"There is no use in rubbing it, Tabitha," said Peter. "It is not Aladdin's lamp, though I take it to be a token of as much luck. Look here, Tabby!"

Tabitha took the parchment and held it close to her nose, which was saddled with a pair of iron-bound spectacles. But no sooner had she begun to puzzle over it than she burst into a chuckling laugh, holding both her hands against her sides.

"You can't make a fool of the old woman," cried she. "This is your own handwriting, Mr. Peter, the same as in the letter you sent me from Mexico."

"There is certainly a considerable resemblance," said Peter, again examining the parchment. "But you know yourself, Tabby, that this closet must have been plastered up before you came to the house or I came into the world. No; this is old Peter Goldthwaite's writing. These columns of pounds, shillings and pence are his figures, denoting the amount of the treasure, and this, at the bottom, is doubtless a reference to the place of concealment. But the ink has either faded or peeled off, so that it is absolutely illegible. What a pity!"

"Well, this lamp is as good as new. That's some comfort," said Tabitha.

"A lamp!" thought Peter. "That indicates light on my researches."

For the present Peter felt more inclined to ponder on this discovery than to resume his labors. After Tabitha had gone down stairs he stood poring over the parchment at one of the front windows, which was so obscured with dust that the sun could barely throw an uncertain shadow of the casement across the floor. Peter forced it open and looked out upon the great street of the town, while the sun looked in at his old house. The air, though mild, and even warm, thrilled Peter as with a dash of water.

It was the first day of the January thaw. The snow lay deep upon the housetops, but was rapidly dissolving into millions of water-drops, which sparkled downward through the sunshine with the noise of a summer shower beneath the eaves. Along the street the trodden snow was as hard and solid as a pavement of white marble, and had not yet grown moist in the spring-like temperature. But when Peter thrust forth his head, he saw that the inhabitants, if not the town, were already thawed out by this warm day, after two or three weeks of winter weather. It gladdened him—a gladness with a sigh breathing through it—to see the stream of ladies gliding along the slippery sidewalks with their red cheeks set off by quilted hoods, boas and sable capes like roses amidst a new kind of foliage. The sleigh bells jingled to and fro continually, sometimes announcing the arrival of a sleigh from Vermont laden with the frozen bodies of porkers or sheep, and perhaps a deer or two; sometimes, of a regular marketman with chickens, geese and turkeys, comprising the whole colony of a barn-yard; and sometimes, of a farmer and his dame who had come to town partly for the ride, partly to go a-shopping and partly for the sale of some eggs and butter. This couple rode in an old-fashioned square sleigh which had served them twenty winters and stood twenty summers in the sun beside their door. Now a gentleman and lady skimmed the snow in an elegant car shaped somewhat like a cockle-shell; now a stage-sleigh with its cloth curtains thrust aside to admit the sun dashed rapidly down the street, whirling in and out among the vehicles that obstructed its passage; now came round a corner the similitude of Noah's ark on runners, being an immense open sleigh with seats for fifty people and drawn by a dozen horses. This spacious receptacle was populous with merry maids and merry bachelors, merry girls and boys and merry old folks, all alive with fun and grinning to the full width of their mouths. They kept up a buzz of babbling voices and low laughter, and sometimes burst into a deep, joyous shout which the spectators answered with three cheers, while a gang of roguish boys let drive their snow-balls right among the pleasure-party. The sleigh passed on, and when concealed by a bend of the street was still audible by a distant cry of merriment.

Never had Peter beheld a livelier scene than was constituted by all these accessories—the bright sun, the flashing water-drops, the gleaming snow, the cheerful multitude, the variety of rapid vehicles and the jingle-jangle of merry bells which made the heart dance to their music. Nothing dismal was to be seen except that peaked piece of antiquity Peter Goldthwaite's house, which might well look sad externally, since such a terrible consumption was preying on its insides. And Peter's gaunt figure, half visible in the projecting second story, was worthy of his house.

"Peter! How goes it, friend Peter?" cried a voice across the street as Peter was drawing in his head. "Look out here, Peter!"

Peter looked, and saw his old partner, Mr. John Brown, on the opposite sidewalk, portly and comfortable, with his furred cloak thrown open, disclosing a handsome surtout beneath. His voice had directed the attention of the whole town to Peter Goldthwaite's window, and to the dusty scarecrow which appeared at it.

"I say, Peter!" cried Mr. Brown, again; "what the devil are you about there, that I hear such a racket whenever I pass by? You are repairing the old house, I suppose, making a new one of it? Eh?"

"Too late for that, I am afraid, Mr. Brown," replied Peter. "If I make it new, it will be new inside and out, from the cellar upward."

"Had not you better let me take the job?" said Mr. Brown, significantly.

"Not yet," answered Peter, hastily shutting the window; for ever since he had been in search of the treasure he hated to have people stare at him.

As he drew back, ashamed of his outward poverty, yet proud of the secret wealth within his grasp, a haughty smile shone out on Peter's visage with precisely the effect of the dim sunbeams in the squalid chamber. He endeavored to assume such a mien as his ancestor had probably worn when he gloried in the building of a strong house for a home to many generations of his posterity. But the chamber was very dark to his snow-dazzled eyes, and very dismal, too, in contrast with the living scene that he had just looked upon. His brief glimpse into the street had given him a forcible impression of the manner in which the world kept itself cheerful and prosperous by social pleasures and an intercourse of business, while he in seclusion was pursuing an object that might possibly be a phantasm by a method which most people would call madness. It is one great advantage of a gregarious mode of life that each person rectifies his mind by other minds and squares his conduct to that of his neighbors, so as seldom to be lost in eccentricity. Peter Goldthwaite had exposed himself to this influence by merely looking out of the window. For a while he doubted whether there were any hidden chest of gold, and in that case whether it was so exceedingly wise to tear the house down only to be convinced of its non-existence.

But this was momentary. Peter the Destroyer resumed the task which Fate had assigned him, nor faltered again till it was accomplished. In the course of his search he met with many things that are usually found in the ruins of an old house, and also with some that are not. What seemed most to the purpose was a rusty key which had been thrust into a chink of the wall, with a wooden label appended to the handle, bearing the initials "P.G." Another singular discovery was that of a bottle of wine walled up in an old oven. A tradition ran in the family that Peter's grandfather, a jovial officer in the old French war, had set aside many dozens of the precious liquor for the benefit of topers then unborn. Peter needed no cordial to sustain his hopes, and therefore kept the wine to gladden his success. Many half-pence did he pick up that had been lost through the cracks of the floor, and some few Spanish coins, and the half of a broken sixpence which had doubtless been a love-token. There was likewise a silver coronation medal of George III. But old Peter Goldthwaite's strong-box fled from one dark corner to another, or otherwise eluded the second Peter's clutches till, should he seek much farther, he must burrow into the earth.

We will not follow him in his triumphant progress step by step. Suffice it that Peter worked like a steam-engine and finished in that one winter the job which all the former inhabitants of the house, with time and the elements to aid them, had only half done in a century. Except the kitchen, every room and chamber was now gutted. The house was nothing but a shell, the apparition of a house, as unreal as the painted edifices of a theatre. It was like the perfect rind of a great cheese in which a mouse had dwelt and nibbled till it was a cheese no more. And Peter was the mouse.

What Peter had torn down, Tabitha had burnt up, for she wisely considered that without a house they should need no wood to warm it, and therefore economy was nonsense. Thus the whole house might be said to have dissolved in smoke and flown up among the clouds through the great black flue of the kitchen chimney. It was an admirable parallel to the feat of the man who jumped down his own throat.

On the night between the last day of winter and the first of spring every chink and cranny had been ransacked except within the precincts of the kitchen. This fated evening was an ugly one. A snow-storm had set in some hours before, and was still driven and tossed about the atmosphere by a real hurricane which fought against the house as if the prince of the air in person were putting the final stroke to Peter's labors. The framework being so much weakened and the inward props removed, it would have been no marvel if in some stronger wrestle of the blast the rotten walls of the edifice and all the peaked roofs had come crashing down upon the owner's head. He, however, was careless of the peril, but as wild and restless as the night itself, or as the flame that quivered up the chimney at each roar of the tempestuous wind.

"The wine, Tabitha," he cried—"my grandfather's rich old wine! We will drink it now."

Tabitha arose from her smoke-blackened bench in the chimney-corner and placed the bottle before Peter, close beside the old brass lamp which had likewise been the prize of his researches. Peter held it before his eyes, and, looking through the liquid medium, beheld the kitchen illuminated with a golden glory which also enveloped Tabitha and gilded her silver hair and converted her mean garments into robes of queenly splendor. It reminded him of his golden dream.

"Mr. Peter," remarked Tabitha, "must the wine be drunk before the money is found?"

"The money is found!" exclaimed Peter, with a sort of fierceness. "The chest is within my reach; I will not sleep till I have turned this key in the rusty lock. But first of all let us drink."

There being no corkscrew in the house, he smote the neck of the bottle with old Peter Goldthwaite's rusty key, and decapitated the sealed cork at a single blow. He then filled two little china teacups which Tabitha had brought from the cupboard. So clear and brilliant was this aged wine that it shone within the cups and rendered the sprig of scarlet flowers at the bottom of each more distinctly visible than when there had been no wine there. Its rich and delicate perfume wasted itself round the kitchen.

"Drink, Tabitha!" cried Peter. "Blessings on the honest old fellow who set aside this good liquor for you and me! And here's to Peter Goldthwaite's memory!"

"And good cause have we to remember him," quoth Tabitha as she drank.

How many years, and through what changes of fortune and various calamity, had that bottle hoarded up its effervescent joy, to be quaffed at last by two such boon-companions! A portion of the happiness of a former age had been kept for them, and was now set free in a crowd of rejoicing visions to sport amid the storm and desolation of the present time. Until they have finished the bottle we must turn our eyes elsewhere.

It so chanced that on this stormy night Mr. John Brown found himself ill at ease in his wire-cushioned arm-chair by the glowing grate of anthracite which heated his handsome parlor. He was naturally a good sort of a man, and kind and pitiful whenever the misfortunes of others happened to reach his heart through the padded vest of his own prosperity. This evening he had thought much about his old partner, Peter Goldthwaite, his strange vagaries and continual ill-luck, the poverty of his dwelling at Mr. Brown's last visit, and Peter's crazed and haggard aspect when he had talked with him at the window.

"Poor fellow!" thought Mr. John Brown. "Poor crack-brained Peter Goldthwaite! For old acquaintance' sake I ought to have taken care that he was comfortable this rough winter." These feelings grew so powerful that, in spite of the inclement weather, he resolved to visit Peter Goldthwaite immediately.

The strength of the impulse was really singular. Every shriek of the blast seemed a summons, or would have seemed so had Mr. Brown been accustomed to hear the echoes of his own fancy in the wind. Much amazed at such active benevolence, he huddled himself in his cloak, muffled his throat and ears in comforters and handkerchiefs, and, thus fortified, bade defiance to the tempest. But the powers of the air had rather the best of the battle. Mr. Brown was just weathering the corner by Peter Goldthwaite's house when the hurricane caught him off his feet, tossed him face downward into a snow-bank and proceeded to bury his protuberant part beneath fresh drifts. There seemed little hope of his reappearance earlier than the next thaw. At the same moment his hat was snatched away and whirled aloft into some far-distant region whence no tidings have as yet returned.

Nevertheless Mr. Brown contrived to burrow a passage through the snow-drift, and with his bare head bent against the storm floundered onward to Peter's door. There was such a creaking and groaning and rattling, and such an ominous shaking, throughout the crazy edifice that the loudest rap would have been inaudible to those within. He therefore entered without ceremony, and groped his way to the kitchen. His intrusion even there was unnoticed. Peter and Tabitha stood with their backs to the door, stooping over a large chest which apparently they had just dragged from a cavity or concealed closet on the left side of the chimney. By the lamp in the old woman's hand Mr. Brown saw that the chest was barred and clamped with iron, strengthened with iron plates and studded with iron nails, so as to be a fit receptacle in which the wealth of one century might be hoarded up for the wants of another.

Peter Goldthwaite was inserting a key into the lock.

"Oh, Tabitha," cried he, with tremulous rapture, "how shall I endure the effulgence? The gold!—the bright, bright gold! Methinks I can remember my last glance at it just as the iron-plated lid fell down. And ever since, being seventy years, it has been blazing in secret and gathering its splendor against this glorious moment. It will flash upon us like the noonday sun."

"Then shade your eyes, Mr. Peter!" said Tabitha, with somewhat less patience than usual. "But, for mercy's sake, do turn the key!"

And with a strong effort of both hands Peter did force the rusty key through the intricacies of the rusty lock. Mr. Brown, in the mean time, had drawn near and thrust his eager visage between those of the other two at the instant that Peter threw up the lid. No sudden blaze illuminated the kitchen.

"What's here?" exclaimed Tabitha, adjusting her spectacles and holding the lamp over the open chest. "Old Peter Goldthwaite's hoard of old rags!"

"Pretty much so, Tabby," said Mr. Brown, lifting a handful of the treasure.

Oh what a ghost of dead and buried wealth had Peter Goldthwaite raised to scare himself out of his scanty wits withal! Here was the semblance of an incalculable sum, enough to purchase the whole town and build every street anew, but which, vast as it was, no sane man would have given a solid sixpence for. What, then, in sober earnest, were the delusive treasures of the chest? Why, here were old provincial bills of credit and treasury notes and bills of land-banks, and all other bubbles of the sort, from the first issue—above a century and a half ago—down nearly to the Revolution. Bills of a thousand pounds were intermixed with parchment pennies, and worth no more than they.

"And this, then, is old Peter Goldthwaite's treasure!" said John Brown. "Your namesake, Peter, was something like yourself; and when the provincial currency had depreciated fifty or seventy-five per cent, he bought it up in expectation of a rise. I have heard my grandfather say that old Peter gave his father a mortgage of this very house and land to raise cash for his silly project. But the currency kept sinking till nobody would take it as a gift, and there was old Peter Goldthwaite, like Peter the second, with thousands in his strong-box and hardly a coat to his back. He went mad upon the strength of it. But never mind, Peter; it is just the sort of capital for building castles in the air."

"The house will be down about our ears," cried Tabitha as the wind shook it with increasing violence.

"Let it fall," said Peter, folding his arms, as he seated himself upon the chest.

"No, no, my old friend Peter!" said John Brown. "I have house-room for you and Tabby, and a safe vault for the chest of treasure. To-morrow we will try to come to an agreement about the sale of this old house; real estate is well up, and I could afford you a pretty handsome price."

"And I," observed Peter Goldthwaite, with reviving spirits, "have a plan for laying out the cash to great advantage."

"Why, as to that," muttered John Brown to himself, "we must apply to the next court for a guardian to take care of the solid cash; and if Peter insists upon speculating, he may do it to his heart's content with old Peter Goldthwaite's treasure."

CHIPPINGS WITH A CHISEL

PASSING a summer several years since at Edgartown, on the island of Martha's Vineyard, I became acquainted with a certain carver of tombstones who had travelled and voyaged thither from the interior of Massachusetts in search of professional employment. The speculation had turned out so successful that my friend expected to transmute slate and marble into silver and gold to the amount of at least a thousand dollars during the few months of his sojourn at Nantucket and the Vineyard. The secluded life and the simple and primitive spirit which still characterizes the inhabitants of those islands, especially of Martha's Vineyard, insure their dead friends a longer and dearer remembrance than the daily novelty and revolving bustle of the world can elsewhere afford to beings of the past. Yet, while every family is anxious to erect a memorial to its departed members, the untainted breath of Ocean bestows such health and length of days upon the people of the isles as would cause a melancholy dearth of business to a resident artist in that line. His own monument, recording his decease by starvation, would probably be an early specimen of his skill. Gravestones, therefore, have generally been an article of imported merchandise.

In my walks through the burial-ground of Edgartown—where the dead have lain so long that the soil, once enriched by their decay, has returned to its original barrenness—in that ancient burial-ground I noticed much variety of monumental sculpture. The elder stones, dated a century back or more, have borders elaborately carved with flowers and are adorned with a multiplicity of death's-heads, crossbones, scythes, hour-glasses, and other lugubrious emblems of mortality, with here and there a winged cherub to direct the mourner's spirit upward. These productions of Gothic taste must have been quite beyond the colonial skill of the day, and were probably carved in London and brought across the ocean to commemorate the defunct worthies of this lonely isle. The more recent monuments are mere slabs of slate in the ordinary style, without any superfluous flourishes to set off the bald inscriptions. But others—and those far the most impressive both to my taste and feelings—were roughly hewn from the gray rocks of the island, evidently by the unskilled hands of surviving friends and relatives. On some there were merely the initials of a name; some were inscribed with misspelt prose or rhyme, in deep letters which the moss and wintry rain of many years had not been able to obliterate. These, these were graves where loved ones slept. It is an old theme of satire, the falsehood and vanity of monumental eulogies; but when affection and sorrow grave the letters with their own painful labor, then we may be sure that they copy from the record on their hearts.

My acquaintance the sculptor—he may share that title with Greenough, since the dauber of signs is a painter as well as Raphael—had found a ready market for all his blank slabs of marble and full occupation in lettering and ornamenting them. He was an elderly man, a descendant of the old Puritan family of Wigglesworth, with a certain simplicity and singleness both of heart and mind which, methinks, is more rarely found among us Yankees than in any other community of people. In spite of his gray head and wrinkled brow, he was quite like a child in all matters save what had some reference to his own business; he seemed, unless my fancy misled me, to view mankind in no other relation than as people in want of tombstones, and his literary attainments evidently comprehended very little either of prose or poetry which had not at one time or other been inscribed on slate or marble. His sole task and office among the immortal pilgrims of the tomb—the duty for which Providence had sent the old man into the world, as it were with a chisel in his hand—was to label the dead bodies, lest their names should be forgotten at the resurrection. Yet he had not failed, within a narrow scope, to gather a few sprigs of earthly, and more than earthly, wisdom—the harvest of many a grave. And, lugubrious as his calling might appear, he was as cheerful an old soul as health and integrity and lack of care could make him, and used to set to work upon one sorrowful inscription or another with that sort of spirit which impels a man to sing at his labor. On the whole, I found Mr. Wigglesworth an entertaining, and often instructive, if not an interesting, character; and, partly for the charm of his society, and still more because his work has an invariable attraction for "man that is born of woman," I was accustomed to spend some hours a day at his workshop. The quaintness of his remarks and their not infrequent truth—a truth condensed and pointed by the limited sphere of his view—gave a raciness to his talk which mere worldliness and general cultivation would at once have destroyed.

Sometimes we would discuss the respective merits of the various qualities of marble, numerous slabs of which were resting against the walls of the shop, or sometimes an hour or two would pass quietly without a word on either side while I watched how neatly his chisel struck out letter after letter of the names of the Nortons, the Mayhews, the Luces, the Daggets, and other immemorial families of the Vineyard. Often with an artist's pride the good old sculptor would speak of favorite productions of his skill which were scattered throughout the village graveyards of New England. But my chief and most instructive amusement was to witness his interviews with his customers, who held interminable consultations about the form and fashion of the desired monuments, the buried excellence to be commemorated, the anguish to be expressed, and finally the lowest price in dollars and cents for which a marble transcript of their feelings might be obtained. Really, my mind received many fresh ideas which perhaps may remain in it even longer than Mr. Wigglesworth's hardest marble will retain the deepest strokes of his chisel.

An elderly lady came to bespeak a monument for her first love, who had been killed by a whale in the Pacific Ocean no less than forty years before. It was singular that so strong an impression of early feeling should have survived through the changes of her subsequent life, in the course of which she had been a wife and a mother, and, so far as I could judge, a comfortable and happy woman. Reflecting within myself, it appeared to me that this lifelong sorrow—as, in all good faith, she deemed it—was one of the most fortunate circumstances of her history. It had given an ideality to her mind; it had kept her purer and less earthy than she would otherwise have been by drawing a portion of her sympathies apart from earth. Amid the throng of enjoyments and the pressure of worldly care and all the warm materialism of this life she had communed with a vision, and had been the better for such intercourse. Faithful to the husband of her maturity, and loving him with a far more real affection than she ever could have felt for this dream of her girlhood, there had still been an imaginative faith to the ocean-buried; so that an ordinary character had thus been elevated and refined. Her sighs had been the breath of Heaven to her soul. The good lady earnestly desired that the proposed monument should be ornamented with a carved border of marine plants interwined with twisted sea-shells, such as were probably waving over her lover's skeleton or strewn around it in the far depths of the Pacific. But, Mr. Wigglesworth's chisel being inadequate to the task, she was forced to content herself with a rose hanging its head from a broken stem.

After her departure I remarked that the symbol was none of the most apt.

"And yet," said my friend the sculptor, embodying in this image the thoughts that had been passing through my own mind, "that broken rose has shed its sweet smell through forty years of the good woman's life."

It was seldom that I could find such pleasant food for contemplation as in the above instance. None of the applicants, I think, affected me more disagreeably than an old man who came, with his fourth wife hanging on his arm, to bespeak gravestones for the three former occupants of his marriage-bed. I watched with some anxiety to see whether his remembrance of either were more affectionate than of the other two, but could discover no symptom of the kind. The three monuments were all to be of the same material and form, and each decorated in bas-relief with two weeping willows, one of these sympathetic trees bending over its fellow, which was to be broken in the midst and rest upon a sepulchral urn. This, indeed, was Mr. Wigglesworth's standing emblem of conjugal bereavement. I shuddered at the gray polygamist who had so utterly lost the holy sense of individuality in wedlock that methought he was fain to reckon upon his fingers how many women who had once slept by his side were now sleeping in their graves. There was even—if I wrong him, it is no great matter—a glance sidelong at his living spouse, as if he were inclined to drive a thriftier bargain by bespeaking four gravestones in a lot.

I was better pleased with a rough old whaling-captain who gave directions for a broad marble slab divided into two compartments, one of which was to contain an epitaph on his deceased wife and the other to be left vacant till death should engrave his own name there. As is frequently the case among the whalers of Martha's Vineyard, so much of this storm-beaten widower's life had been tossed away on distant seas that out of twenty years of matrimony he had spent scarce three, and those at scattered intervals, beneath his own roof. Thus the wife of his youth, though she died in his and her declining age, retained the bridal dewdrops fresh around her memory.

My observations gave me the idea, and Mr. Wigglesworth confirmed it, that husbands were more faithful in setting up memorials to their dead wives than widows to their dead husbands. I was not ill-natured enough to fancy that women less than men feel so sure of their own constancy as to be willing to give a pledge of it in marble. It is more probably the fact that, while men are able to reflect upon their lost companions as remembrances apart from themselves, women, on the other hand, are conscious that a portion of their being has gone with the departed whithersoever he has gone. Soul clings to soul, the living dust has a sympathy with the dust of the grave; and by the very strength of that sympathy the wife of the dead shrinks the more sensitively from reminding the world of its existence. The link is already strong enough; it needs no visible symbol. And, though a shadow walks ever by her side and the touch of a chill hand is on her bosom, yet life, and perchance its natural yearnings, may still be warm within her and inspire her with new hopes of happiness. Then would she mark out the grave the scent of which would be perceptible on the pillow of the second bridal? No, but rather level its green mound with the surrounding earth, as if, when she dug up again her buried heart, the spot had ceased to be a grave.

Yet, in spite of these sentimentalities, I was prodigiously amused by an incident of which I had not the good-fortune to be a witness, but which Mr. Wigglesworth related with considerable humor. A gentlewoman of the town, receiving news of her husband's loss at sea, had bespoken a handsome slab of marble, and came daily to watch the progress of my friend's chisel. One afternoon, when the good lady and the sculptor were in the very midst of the epitaph—which the departed spirit might have been greatly comforted to read—who should walk into the workshop but the deceased himself, in substance as well as spirit! He had been picked up at sea, and stood in no present need of tombstone or epitaph.

"And how," inquired I, "did his wife bear the shock of joyful surprise?"

"Why," said the old man, deepening the grin of a death's-head on which his chisel was just then employed, "I really felt for the poor woman; it was one of my best pieces of marble—and to be thrown away on a living man!"

A comely woman with a pretty rosebud of a daughter came to select a gravestone for a twin-daughter, who had died a month before. I was impressed with the different nature of their feelings for the dead. The mother was calm and woefully resigned, fully conscious of her loss, as of a treasure which she had not always possessed, and therefore had been aware that it might be taken from her; but the daughter evidently had no real knowledge of what Death's doings were. Her thoughts knew, but not her heart. It seemed to me that by the print and pressure which the dead sister had left upon the survivor's spirit her feelings were almost the same as if she still stood side by side and arm in arm with the departed, looking at the slabs of marble, and once or twice she glanced around with a sunny smile, which, as its sister-smile had faded for ever, soon grew confusedly overshadowed. Perchance her consciousness was truer than her reflection; perchance her dead sister was a closer companion than in life.

The mother and daughter talked a long while with Mr. Wigglesworth about a suitable epitaph, and finally chose an ordinary verse of ill-matched rhymes which had already been inscribed upon innumerable tombstones. But when we ridicule the triteness of monumental verses, we forget that Sorrow reads far deeper in them than we can, and finds a profound and individual purport in what seems so vague and inexpressive unless interpreted by her. She makes the epitaph anew, though the selfsame words may have served for a thousand graves.

"And yet," said I afterward to Mr. Wigglesworth, "they might have made a better choice than this. While you were discussing the subject I was struck by at least a dozen simple and natural expressions from the lips of both mother and daughter. One of these would have formed an inscription equally original and appropriate."

"No, no!" replied the sculptor, shaking his head; "there is a good deal of comfort to be gathered from these little old scraps of poetry, and so I always recommend them in preference to any new-fangled ones. And somehow they seem to stretch to suit a great grief and shrink to fit a small one."

It was not seldom that ludicrous images were excited by what took place between Mr. Wigglesworth and his customers. A shrewd gentlewoman who kept a tavern in the town was anxious to obtain two or three gravestones for the deceased members of her family, and to pay for these solemn commodities by taking the sculptor to board. Hereupon a fantasy arose in my mind of good Mr. Wigglesworth sitting down to dinner at a broad, flat tombstone carving one of his own plump little marble cherubs, gnawing a pair of crossbones and drinking out of a hollow death's-head or perhaps a lachrymatory vase or sepulchral urn, while his hostess's dead children waited on him at the ghastly banquet. On communicating this nonsensical picture to the old man he laughed heartily and pronounced my humor to be of the right sort.

"I have lived at such a table all my days," said he, "and eaten no small quantity of slate and marble."

"Hard fare," rejoined I, smiling, "but you seemed to have found it excellent of digestion, too."

A man of fifty or thereabouts with a harsh, unpleasant countenance ordered a stone for the grave of his bitter enemy, with whom he had waged warfare half a lifetime, to their mutual misery and ruin. The secret of this phenomenon was that hatred had become the sustenance and enjoyment of the poor wretch's soul; it had supplied the place of all kindly affections; it had been really a bond of sympathy between himself and the man who shared the passion; and when its object died, the unappeasable foe was the only mourner for the dead. He expressed a purpose of being buried side by side with his enemy.

"I doubt whether their dust will mingle," remarked the old sculptor to me; for often there was an earthliness in his conceptions.

"Oh yes," replied I, who had mused long upon the incident; "and when they rise again, these bitter foes may find themselves dear friends. Methinks what they mistook for hatred was but love under a mask."

A gentleman of antiquarian propensities provided a memorial for an Indian of Chabbiquidick—one of the few of untainted blood remaining in that region, and said to be a hereditary chieftain descended from the sachem who welcomed Governor Mayhew to the Vineyard. Mr. Wiggles-worth exerted his best skill to carve a broken bow and scattered sheaf of arrows in memory of the hunters and warriors whose race was ended here, but he likewise sculptured a cherub, to denote that the poor Indian had shared the Christian's hope of immortality.

"Why," observed I, taking a perverse view of the winged boy and the bow and arrows, "it looks more like Cupid's tomb than an Indian chief's."

"You talk nonsense," said the sculptor, with the offended pride of art. He then added with his usual good-nature, "How can Cupid die when there are such pretty maidens in the Vineyard?"

"Very true," answered I; and for the rest of the day I thought of other matters than tombstones.

At our next meeting I found him chiselling an open book upon a marble headstone, and concluded that it was meant to express the erudition of some black-letter clergyman of the Cotton Mather school. It turned out, however, to be emblematical of the scriptural knowledge of an old woman who had never read anything but her Bible, and the monument was a tribute to her piety and good works from the orthodox church of which she had been a member. In strange contrast with this Christian woman's memorial was that of an infidel whose gravestone, by his own direction, bore an avowal of his belief that the spirit within him would be extinguished like a flame, and that the nothingness whence he sprang would receive him again.

Mr. Wigglesworth consulted me as to the propriety of enabling a dead man's dust to utter this dreadful creed.

"If I thought," said he, "that a single mortal would read the inscription without a shudder, my chisel should never cut a letter of it. But when the grave speaks such falsehoods, the soul of man will know the truth by its own horror."

"So it will," said I, struck by the idea. "The poor infidel may strive to preach blasphemies from his grave, but it will be only another method of impressing the soul with a consciousness of immortality."

There was an old man by the name of Norton, noted throughout the island for his great wealth, which he had accumulated by the exercise of strong and shrewd faculties combined with a most penurious disposition. This wretched miser, conscious that he had not a friend to be mindful of him in his grave, had himself taken the needful precautions for posthumous remembrance by bespeaking an immense slab of white marble with a long epitaph in raised letters, the whole to be as magnificent as Mr. Wigglesworth's skill could make it. There was something very characteristic in this contrivance to have his money's worth even from his own tombstone, which, indeed, afforded him more enjoyment in the few months that he lived thereafter than it probably will in a whole century, now that it is laid over his bones.

This incident reminds me of a young girl—a pale, slender, feeble creature most unlike the other rosy and healthful damsels of the Vineyard, amid whose brightness she was fading away. Day after day did the poor maiden come to the sculptor's shop and pass from one piece of marble to another, till at last she pencilled her name upon a slender slab which, I think, was of a more spotless white than all the rest. I saw her no more, but soon afterward found Mr. Wigglesworth cutting her virgin-name into the stone which she had chosen.

"She is dead, poor girl!" said he, interrupting the tune which he was whistling, "and she chose a good piece of stuff for her headstone. Now, which of these slabs would you like best to see your own name upon?"

"Why, to tell you the truth, my good Mr. Wigglesworth," replied I, after a moment's pause, for the abruptness of the question had somewhat startled me—"to be quite sincere with you, I care little or nothing about a stone for my own grave, and am somewhat inclined to scepticism as to the propriety of erecting monuments at all over the dust that once was human. The weight of these heavy marbles, though unfelt by the dead corpse or the enfranchised soul, presses drearily upon the spirit of the survivor and causes him to connect the idea of death with the dungeon-like imprisonment of the tomb, instead of with the freedom of the skies. Every gravestone that you ever made is the visible symbol of a mistaken system. Our thoughts should soar upward with the butterfly, not linger with the exuviæ that confined him. In truth and reason, neither those whom we call the living, and still less the departed, have anything to do with the grave."

"I never heard anything so heathenish," said Mr. Wigglesworth, perplexed and displeased at sentiments which controverted all his notions and feelings and implied the utter waste, and worse, of his whole life's labor. "Would you forget your dead friends the moment they are under the sod?"

"They are not under the sod," I rejoined; "then why should I mark the spot where there is no treasure hidden? Forget them? No; but, to remember them aright, I would forget what they have cast off. And to gain the truer conception of death I would forget the grave."

But still the good old sculptor murmured, and stumbled, as it were, over the gravestones amid which he had walked through life. Whether he were right or wrong, I had grown the wiser from our companionship and from my observations of nature and character as displayed by those who came, with their old griefs or their new ones, to get them recorded upon his slabs of marble. And yet with my gain of wisdom I had likewise gained perplexity; for there was a strange doubt in my mind whether the dark shadowing of this life, the sorrows and regrets, have not as much real comfort in them—leaving religious influences out of the question—as what we term life's joys.

THE SHAKER BRIDAL

ONE DAY, in the sick-chamber of Father Ephraim, who had been forty years the presiding elder over the Shaker settlement at Goshen, there was an assemblage of several of the chief men of the sect. Individuals had come from the rich establishment at Lebanon, from Canterbury, Harvard and Alfred, and from all the other localities where this strange people have fertilized the rugged hills of New England by their systematic industry. An elder was likewise there who had made a pilgrimage of a thousand miles from a village of the faithful in Kentucky to visit his spiritual kindred the children of the sainted Mother Ann. He had partaken of the homely abundance of their tables, had quaffed the far-famed Shaker cider, and had joined in the sacred dance every step of which is believed to alienate the enthusiast from earth and bear him onward to heavenly purity and bliss. His brethren of the North had now courteously invited him to be present on an occasion when the concurrence of every eminent member of their community was peculiarly desirable.

The venerable Father Ephraim sat in his easy-chair, not only hoary-headed and infirm with age, but worn down by a lingering disease which it was evident would very soon transfer his patriarchal staff to other hands. At his footstool stood a man and woman, both clad in the Shaker garb.

"My brethren," said Father Ephraim to the surrounding elders, feebly exerting himself to utter these few words, "here are the son and daughter to whom I would commit the trust of which Providence is about to lighten my weary shoulders. Read their faces, I pray you, and say whether the inward movement of the spirit hath guided my choice aright."

Accordingly, each elder looked at the two candidates with a most scrutinizing gaze. The man—whose name was Adam Colburn—had a face sunburnt with labor in the fields, yet intelligent, thoughtful and traced with cares enough for a whole lifetime, though he had barely reached middle age. There was something severe in his aspect and a rigidity throughout his person—characteristics that caused him generally to be taken for a schoolmaster; which vocation, in fact, he had formerly exercised for several years. The woman, Martha Pierson, was somewhat above thirty, thin and pale, as a Shaker sister almost invariably is, and not entirely

205

free from that corpse-like appearance which the garb of the sisterhood is so well calculated to impart.

"This pair are still in the summer of their years," observed the elder from Harvard, a shrewd old man. "I would like better to see the hoar-frost of autumn on their heads. Methinks, also, they will be exposed to peculiar temptations on account of the carnal desires which have heretofore subsisted between them."

"Nay, brother," said the elder from Canterbury; "the hoar-frost and the black frost hath done its work on Brother Adam and Sister Martha, even as we sometimes discern its traces in our cornfields while they are yet green. And why should we question the wisdom of our venerable Father's purpose, although this pair in their early youth have loved one another as the world's people love? Are there not many brethren and sisters among us who have lived long together in wedlock, yet, adopting our faith, find their hearts purified from all but spiritual affection?"

Whether or no the early loves of Adam and Martha had rendered it inexpedient that they should now preside together over a Shaker village, it was certainly most singular that such should be the final result of many warm and tender hopes. Children of neighboring families, their affection was older even than their school-days; it seemed an innate principle interfused among all their sentiments and feelings, and not so much a distinct remembrance as connected with their whole volume of remembrances. But just as they reached a proper age for their union misfortunes had fallen heavily on both and made it necessary that they should resort to personal labor for a bare subsistence. Even under these circumstances Martha Pierson would probably have consented to unite her fate with Adam Colburn's, and, secure of the bliss of mutual love, would patiently have awaited the less important gifts of Fortune. But Adam, being of a calm and cautious character, was loth to relinquish the advantages which a single man possesses for raising himself in the world. Year after year, therefore, their marriage had been deferred.

Adam Colburn had followed many vocations, had travelled far and seen much of the world and of life. Martha had earned her bread sometimes as a sempstress, sometimes as help to a farmer's wife, sometimes as schoolmistress of the village children, sometimes as a nurse or watcher of the sick, thus acquiring a varied experience the ultimate use of which she little anticipated. But nothing had gone prosperously with either of the lovers; at no subsequent moment would matrimony have been so prudent a measure as when they had first parted, in the opening bloom of life, to seek a better fortune. Still, they had held fast their mutual faith. Martha might have been the wife of a man who sat among the senators of his native State, and Adam could have won the hand, as he had unintentionally won the heart, of a rich and comely widow. But neither of them desired good-fortune save to share it with the other.

At length that calm despair which occurs only in a strong and somewhat stubborn character and yields to no second spring of hope settled down on the spirit of Adam Colburn. He sought an interview with Martha and proposed that they should join the Society of Shakers. The converts of this sect are oftener driven within its hospitable gates by worldly misfortune than drawn thither by fanaticism, and are received without inquisition as to their motives. Martha, faithful still, had placed her hand in that of her lover and accompanied him to the Shaker village. Here the natural capacity of each, cultivated and strengthened by the difficulties of their previous lives, had soon gained them an important rank in the society, whose members are generally below the ordinary standard of intelligence. Their faith and feelings had in some degree become assimilated to those of their fellow-worshippers. Adam Colburn gradually acquired reputation not only in the management of the temporal affairs of the society, but as a clear and efficient preacher of their doctrines. Martha was not less distinguished in the duties proper to her sex. Finally, when the infirmities of Father Ephraim had admonished him to seek a successor in his patriarchal office, he thought of Adam and Martha, and proposed to renew in their persons the primitive form of Shaker government as established by Mother Ann. They were to be the father and mother of the village. The simple ceremony which would constitute them such was now to be performed.

"Son Adam and daughter Martha," said the venerable Father Ephraim, fixing his aged eyes piercingly upon them, "if ye can conscientiously undertake this charge, speak, that the brethren may not doubt of your fitness."

"Father," replied Adam, speaking with the calmness of his character, "I came to your village a disappointed man, weary of the world, worn out with continual trouble, seeking only a security against evil fortune, as I had no hope of good. Even my wishes of worldly success were almost dead within me. I came hither as a man might come to a tomb willing to lie down in its gloom and coldness for the sake of its peace and quiet. There was but one earthly affection in my breast, and it had grown calmer since my youth; so that I was satisfied to bring Martha to be my sister in our new abode. We are brother and sister, nor would I have it otherwise. And in this peaceful village I have found all that I hope for—all that I desire. I will strive with my best strength for the spiritual and temporal good of our community. My conscience is not doubtful in this matter. I am ready to receive the trust."

"Thou hast spoken well, son Adam," said the father. "God will bless thee in the office which I am about to resign."

"But our sister," observed the elder from Harvard. "Hath she not likewise a gift to declare her sentiments?"

Martha started and moved her lips as if she would have made a formal reply to this appeal. But, had she attempted it, perhaps the old recollections, the long-repressed feelings of childhood, youth and womanhood, might have gushed from her heart in words that it would have been profanation to utter there.

"Adam has spoken," said she, hurriedly; "his sentiments are likewise mine."

But while speaking these few words Martha grew so pale that she looked fitter to be laid in her coffin than to stand in the presence of Father Ephraim and the elders; she shuddered, also, as if there were something awful or horrible in her situation and destiny. It required, indeed, a more than feminine strength of nerve to sustain the fixed observance of men so exalted and famous throughout the sect as these were. They had overcome their natural sympathy with human frailties and affections. One, when he joined the society, had brought with him his wife and children, but never from that hour had spoken a fond word to the former or taken his best-loved child upon his knee. Another, whose family refused to follow him, had been enabled—such was his gift of holy fortitude—to leave them to the mercy of the world. The youngest of the elders, a man of about fifty, had been bred from infancy in a Shaker village, and was said never to have clasped a woman's hand in his own, and to have no conception of a closer tie than the cold fraternal one of the sect. Old Father Ephraim was the most awful character of all. In his youth he had been a dissolute libertine, but was converted by Mother Ann herself, and had partaken of the wild fanaticism of the early Shakers. Tradition whispered at the firesides of the village that Mother Ann had been compelled to sear his heart of flesh with a red-hot iron before it could be purified from earthly passions.

However that might be, poor Martha had a woman's heart, and a tender one, and it quailed within her as she looked round at those strange old men, and from them to the calm features of Adam Colburn. But, perceiving that the elders eyed her doubtfully, she gasped for breath and again spoke.

"With what strength is left me by my many troubles," said she, "I am ready to undertake this charge, and to do my best in it."

"My children, join your hands," said Father Ephraim.

They did so. The elders stood up around, and the father feebly raised himself to a more erect position, but continued sitting in his great chair.

"I have bidden you to join your hands," said he, "not in earthly affection, for ye have cast off its chains for ever, but as brother and sister in spiritual love and helpers of one another in your allotted task. Teach unto others the faith which ye have received. Open wide your gates—I deliver you the keys thereof—open them wide to all who will give up the iniquities of the world and come hither to lead lives of purity and peace. Receive the weary ones who have known the vanity of earth; receive the little children, that they may never learn that miserable lesson. And a blessing be upon your labors; so that the time may hasten on when the mission of Mother Ann shall have wrought its full effect, when children shall no more be born and die, and the last survivor of mortal race—some old and weary man like me—shall see the sun go down nevermore to rise on a world of sin and sorrow."

The aged father sank back exhausted, and the surrounding elders deemed, with good reason, that the hour was come when the new heads of the village must enter on their patriarchal duties. In their attention to Father Ephraim their eyes were turned from Martha Pierson, who grew paler and paler, unnoticed even by Adam Colburn. He, indeed, had withdrawn his hand from hers and folded his arms with a sense of satisfied ambition. But paler and paler grew Martha by his side, till, like a corpse in its burial-clothes, she sank down at the feet of her early lover; for, after many trials firmly borne, her heart could endure the weight of its desolate agony no longer.

NIGHT-SKETCHES

BENEATH AN UMBRELLA.

Pleasant is a rainy winter's day within-doors. The best study for such a day—or the best amusement: call it what you will—is a book of travels describing scenes the most unlike that sombre one which is mistily presented through the windows. I have experienced that Fancy is then most successful in imparting distinct shapes and vivid colors to the objects which the author has spread upon his page, and that his words become magic spells to summon up a thousand varied pictures. Strange landscapes glimmer through the familiar walls of the room, and outlandish figures thrust themselves almost within the sacred precincts of the hearth. Small as my chamber is, it has space enough to contain the ocean-like circumference of an Arabian desert, its parched sands tracked by the long line of a caravan with the camels patiently journeying through the heavy sunshine. Though my ceiling be not lofty, yet I can pile up the mountains of Central Asia beneath it till their summits shine far above the clouds of the middle atmosphere. And with my humble means—a wealth that is not taxable—I can transport hither the magnificent merchandise of an Oriental bazaar, and call a crowd of purchasers from distant countries to pay a fair profit for the precious articles which are displayed on all sides. True it is, however, that amid the bustle of traffic, or whatever else may seem to be going on around me, the raindrops will occasionally be heard to patter against my window-panes, which look forth upon one of the quietest streets in a New England town. After a time, too, the visions vanish, and will not appear again at my bidding. Then, it being nightfall, a gloomy sense of unreality depresses my spirits, and impels me to venture out before the clock shall strike bedtime to satisfy myself that the world is not entirely made up of such shadowy materials as have busied me throughout the day. A dreamer may dwell so long among fantasies that the things without him will seem as unreal as those within.

When eve has fairly set in, therefore, I sally forth, tightly buttoning my shaggy overcoat and hoisting my umbrella, the silken dome of which immediately resounds with the heavy drumming of the invisible raindrops. Pausing on the lowest doorstep, I contrast the warmth and cheerfulness of my deserted fireside with the drear obscurity and chill discomfort into which I am about to plunge. Now come fearful auguries innumerable as the drops of rain. Did not my manhood cry shame upon me, I should turn back within-doors, resume my elbow-chair, my slippers and my book, pass such an evening of sluggish enjoyment as the day has been, and go to bed inglorious. The same shivering reluctance, no doubt, has quelled for a moment the adventurous spirit of many a traveller when his feet, which were destined to measure the earth around, were leaving their last tracks in the home-paths.

In my own case poor human nature may be allowed a few misgivings. I look upward and discern no sky, not even an unfathomable void, but only a black, impenetrable nothingness, as though heaven and all its lights were blotted from the system of the universe. It is as if Nature were dead and the world had put on black and the clouds were weeping for her. With their tears upon my cheek I turn my eyes earthward, but find little consolation here below. A lamp is burning dimly at the distant corner, and throws just enough of light along the street to show, and exaggerate by so faintly showing, the perils and difficulties which beset my path. Yonder dingily-white remnant of a huge snowbank, which will yet cumber the sidewalk till the latter days of March, over or through that wintry waste must I stride onward. Beyond lies a certain Slough of Despond, a concoction of mud and liquid filth, ankle-deep, leg-deep, neck-deep—in a word, of unknown bottom—on which the lamplight does not even glimmer, but which I have occasionally watched in the gradual growth of its horrors from morn till nightfall. Should I flounder into its depths, farewell to upper earth! And hark! how roughly resounds the roaring of a stream the turbulent career of which is partially reddened by the gleam of the lamp, but elsewhere brawls noisily through the densest gloom! Oh, should I be swept away in fording that impetuous and unclean torrent, the coroner will have a job with an unfortunate gentleman who would fain end his troubles anywhere but in a mud-puddle.

Pshaw! I will linger not another instant at arm's-length from these dim terrors, which grow more obscurely formidable the longer I delay to grapple with them. Now for the onset, and, lo! with little damage save a dash of rain in the face and breast, a splash of mud high up the pantaloons and the left boot full of ice-cold water, behold me at the corner of the street. The lamp throws down a circle of red light around me, and twinkling onward from corner to corner I discern other beacons, marshalling my way to a brighter scene. But this is a lonesome and dreary spot. The tall edifices bid gloomy defiance to the storm with their blinds all closed, even as a man winks when he faces a spattering gust. How loudly tinkles the collected rain down the tin spouts! The puffs of wind are boisterous, and seem to assail me from various quarters at once. I have often observed that this corner is a haunt and loitering-place for those winds which have no work to do upon the deep dashing ships against our iron-bound shores, nor in the forest tearing up the sylvan giants with half a rood of soil at their vast roots. Here they amuse themselves with lesser freaks of mischief. See, at this moment, how they assail yonder poor woman who is passing just within the verge of the lamplight! One blast struggles for her umbrella and turns it wrong side outward, another whisks the cape of her cloak across her eyes, while a third takes most unwarrantable liberties with the lower part of her attire. Happily, the good dame is no gossamer, but a figure of rotundity and fleshly substance; else would these aerial tormentors whirl her aloft like a witch upon a broomstick, and set her down, doubtless, in the filthiest kennel hereabout.

From hence I tread upon firm pavements into the centre of the town. Here there is almost as brilliant an illumination as when some great victory has been won either on the battlefield or at the polls. Two rows of shops with windows down nearly to the ground cast a glow from side to side, while the black night hangs overhead like a canopy, and thus keeps the splendor from diffusing itself away. The wet sidewalks gleam with a broad sheet of red light. The raindrops glitter as if the sky were pouring down rubies. The spouts gush with fire. Methinks the scene is an emblem of the deceptive glare which mortals throw around their footsteps in the moral world, thus bedazzling themselves till they forget the impenetrable obscurity that hems them in, and that can be dispelled only by radiance from above.

And, after all, it is a cheerless scene, and cheerless are the wanderers in it. Here comes one who has so long been familiar with tempestuous weather that he takes the bluster of the storm for a friendly greeting, as if it should say, "How fare ye, brother?" He is a retired sea-captain wrapped in some nameless garment of the pea-jacket order, and is now laying his course toward the marine-insurance office, there to spin yarns of gale and shipwreck with a crew of old seadogs like himself. The blast will put in its word among their hoarse voices, and be understood by all of them. Next I meet an unhappy slipshod gentleman with a cloak flung hastily over his shoulders, running a race with boisterous winds and striving to glide between the drops of rain. Some domestic emergency or other has blown this miserable man from his warm fireside in quest of a doctor. See that little vagabond! How carelessly he has taken his stand right underneath a spout while staring at some object of curiosity in a shop-window! Surely the rain is his native element; he must have fallen with it from the clouds, as frogs are supposed to do.

Here is a picture, and a pretty one—a young man and a girl, both enveloped in cloaks and huddled beneath the scanty protection of a cotton umbrella. She wears rubber overshoes, but he is in his dancing-pumps, and they are on their way no doubt, to some cotillon-party or subscription-ball at a dollar a head, refreshments included. Thus they struggle against the gloomy tempest, lured onward by a vision of festal splendor. But ah! a most lamentable disaster! Bewildered by the red, blue and yellow meteors in an apothecary's window, they have stepped upon a slippery remnant of ice, and are precipitated into a confluence of swollen floods at the corner of two streets. Luckless lovers! Were it my nature to be other than a looker-on in life, I would attempt your rescue. Since that may not be, I vow, should you be drowned, to weave such a pathetic story of your fate as shall call forth tears enough to drown you both anew. Do ye touch bottom, my young friends? Yes; they emerge like a water-nymph and a river-deity, and paddle hand in hand out of the depths of the dark pool. They hurry homeward, dripping, disconsolate, abashed, but with love too warm to be chilled by the cold water. They have stood a test which proves too strong for many. Faithful though over head and ears in trouble!

Onward I go, deriving a sympathetic joy or sorrow from the varied aspect of mortal affairs even as my figure catches a gleam from the lighted windows or is blackened by an interval of darkness. Not that mine is altogether a chameleon spirit with no hue of its own. Now I pass into a more retired street where the dwellings of wealth and poverty are intermingled, presenting a range of strongly-contrasted pictures. Here, too, may be found the golden mean. Through yonder casement I discern a family circle—the grandmother, the parents and the children—all flickering, shadow-like, in the glow of a wood-fire.—Bluster, fierce blast, and beat, thou wintry rain, against the window-panes! Ye cannot damp the enjoyment of that fireside.— Surely my fate is hard that I should be wandering homeless here, taking to my bosom night and storm and solitude instead of wife and children. Peace, murmurer! Doubt not that darker guests are sitting round the hearth, though the warm blaze hides all but blissful images.

Well, here is still a brighter scene—a stately mansion illuminated for a ball, with cut-glass chandeliers and alabaster lamps in every room, and sunny landscapes hanging round the walls. See! a coach has stopped, whence emerges a slender beauty who, canopied by two umbrellas, glides within the portal and vanishes amid lightsome thrills of music. Will she ever feel the night-wind and the rain? Perhaps—perhaps! And will Death and Sorrow ever enter that proud mansion? As surely as the dancers will be gay within its halls to-night. Such thoughts sadden yet satisfy my heart, for they teach me that the poor man in this mean, weatherbeaten hovel, without a fire to cheer him, may call the rich his brother—brethren by Sorrow, who must be an inmate of both their households; brethren by Death, who will lead them both to other homes.

Onward, still onward, I plunge into the night. Now have I reached the utmost limits of the town, where the last lamp struggles feebly with the darkness like the farthest star that stands sentinel on the borders of uncreated space. It is strange what sensations of sublimity may spring from a very humble source. Such are suggested by this hollow roar of a subterranean cataract where the mighty stream of a kennel precipitates itself beneath an iron grate and is seen no more on earth. Listen a while to its voice of mystery, and Fancy will magnify it till you start and smile at the illusion. And now another sound—the rumbling of wheels as the mail-coach, outward bound, rolls heavily off the pavements and splashes through the mud and water of the road. All night long the poor passengers will be tossed to and fro between drowsy watch and troubled sleep, and will dream of their own quiet beds and awake to find themselves still jolting onward. Happier my lot, who will straightway hie me to my familiar room and toast myself comfortably before the fire, musing and fitfully dozing and fancying a strangeness in such sights as all may see. But first let me gaze at this solitary figure who comes hitherward with a tin lantern which throws the circular pattern of its punched holes on the ground about him. He passes fearlessly into the unknown gloom, whither I will not follow him.

This figure shall supply me with a moral wherewith, for lack of a more appropriate one, I may wind up my sketch. He fears not to tread the dreary path before him, because his lantern, which was kindled at the fireside of his home, will light him back to that same fireside again. And thus we, night-wanderers through a stormy and dismal world, if we bear the lamp of Faith enkindled at a celestial fire, it will surely lead us home to that heaven whence its radiance was borrowed.

ENDICOTT AND THE RED CROSS

AT NOON of an autumnal day more than two centuries ago the English colors were displayed by the standard bearer of the Salem train-band, which had mustered for martial exercise under the orders of John Endicott. It was a period when the religious exiles were accustomed often to buckle on their armor and practise the handling of their weapons of war. Since the first settlement of New England its prospects had never been so dismal. The dissensions between Charles I. and his subjects were then, and for several years afterward, confined to the floor of Parliament. The measures of the king and ministry were rendered more tyrannically violent by an opposition which had not yet acquired sufficient confidence in its own strength to resist royal injustice with the sword. The bigoted and haughty primate Laud, archbishop of Canterbury, controlled the religious affairs of the realm, and was consequently invested with powers which might have wrought the utter ruin of the two Puritan colonies, Plymouth and Massachusetts. There is evidence on record that our forefathers perceived their danger, but were resolved that their infant country should not fall without a struggle, even beneath the giant strength of the king's right arm.

Such was the aspect of the times when the folds of the English banner with the red cross in its field were flung out over a company of Puritans. Their leader, the famous Endicott, was a man of stern and resolute countenance, the effect of which was heightened by a grizzled beard that swept the upper portion of his breastplate. This piece of armor was so highly polished that the whole surrounding scene had its image in the glittering steel. The central object in the mirrored picture was an edifice of humble architecture with neither steeple nor bell to proclaim it—what, nevertheless, it was—the house of prayer. A token of the perils of the wilderness was seen in the grim head of a wolf which had just been slain within the precincts of the town, and, according to the regular mode of claiming the bounty, was nailed on the porch of the meeting-house. The blood was still plashing on the doorstep. There happened to be visible at the same noontide hour so many other characteristics of the times and manners of the Puritans that we must endeavor to represent them in a sketch, though far less vividly than they were reflected in the polished breastplate of John Endicott.

In close vicinity to the sacred edifice appeared that important engine of Puritanic authority the whipping-post, with the soil around it well trodden by the feet of evil-doers who had there been disciplined. At one corner of the meeting-house was the pillory and at the other the stocks, and, by a singular good fortune for our sketch, the head of an Episcopalian and suspected Catholic was grotesquely encased in the former machine, while a fellow-criminal who had boisterously quaffed a health to the king was confined by the legs in the latter. Side by side on the meeting-house steps stood a male and a female figure. The man was a tall, lean, haggard personification of fanaticism, bearing on his breast this label, "A WANTON GOSPELLER," which betokened that he had dared to give interpretations of Holy Writ unsanctioned by the infallible judgment of the civil and religious rulers. His aspect showed no lack of zeal to maintain his heterodoxies even at the stake. The woman wore a cleft stick on her tongue, in appropriate retribution for having wagged that unruly member against the elders of the church, and her countenance and gestures gave much cause to apprehend that the moment the stick should be removed a repetition of the offence would demand new ingenuity in chastising it.

The above-mentioned individuals had been sentenced to undergo their various modes of ignominy for the space of one hour at noonday. But among the crowd were several whose punishment would be lifelong—some whose ears had been cropped like those of puppy-dogs, others whose cheeks had been branded with the initials of their misdemeanors; one with his nostrils slit and seared, and another with a halter about his neck, which he was forbidden ever to take off or to conceal beneath his garments. Methinks he must have been grievously tempted to affix the other end of the rope to some convenient beam or bough. There was likewise a young woman with no mean share of beauty whose doom it was to wear the letter A on the breast of her gown in the eyes of all the world and her own children. And even her own children knew what that initial signified. Sporting with her infamy, the lost and desperate creature had embroidered the fatal token in scarlet cloth with golden thread and the nicest art of needlework; so that the capital A might have been thought to mean "Admirable," or anything rather than "Adulteress."

Let not the reader argue from any of these evidences of iniquity that the times of the Puritans were more vicious than our own, when as we pass along the very street of this sketch we discern no badge of infamy on man or woman. It was the policy of our ancestors to search out even the most secret sins and expose them to shame, without fear or favor, in the broadest light of the noonday sun. Were such the custom now, perchance we might find materials for a no less piquant sketch than the above.

Except the malefactors whom we have described and the diseased or infirm persons, the whole male population of the town, between sixteen years and sixty were seen in the ranks of the train-band. A few stately savages in all the pomp and dignity of the primeval Indian stood gazing at the spectacle. Their flint-headed arrows were but childish weapons, compared with the matchlocks of the Puritans, and would have rattled harmlessly against the steel caps and hammered iron breastplates which enclosed each soldier in an individual fortress. The valiant John Endicott glanced with an eye of pride at his sturdy followers, and prepared to renew the martial toils of the day.

"Come, my stout hearts!" quoth he, drawing his sword. "Let us show these poor heathen that we can handle our weapons like men of might. Well for them if they put us not to prove it in earnest!"

The iron-breasted company straightened their line, and each man drew the heavy butt of his matchlock close to his left foot, thus awaiting the orders of the captain. But as Endicott glanced right and left along the front he discovered a personage at some little distance with whom it behoved him to hold a parley. It was an elderly gentleman wearing a black cloak and band and a high-crowned hat beneath which was a velvet skull-cap, the whole being the garb of a Puritan minister. This reverend person bore a staff which seemed to have been recently cut in the forest, and his shoes were bemired, as if he had been travelling on foot through the swamps of the wilderness. His aspect was perfectly that of a pilgrim, heightened also by an apostolic dignity. Just as Endicott perceived him he laid aside his staff and stooped to drink at a bubbling fountain which gushed into the sunshine about a score of yards from the corner of the meeting-house. But ere the good man drank he turned his face heavenward in thankfulness, and then, holding back his gray beard with one hand, he scooped up his simple draught in the hollow of the other.

"What ho, good Mr. Williams!" shouted Endicott. "You are welcome back again to our town of peace. How does our worthy Governor Winthrop? And what news from Boston?"

"The governor hath his health, worshipful sir," answered Roger Williams, now resuming his staff and drawing near. "And, for the news, here is a letter which, knowing I was to travel hitherward to-day, His Excellency committed to my charge. Belike it contains tidings of much import, for a ship arrived yesterday from England."

Mr. Williams, the minister of Salem, and of course known to all the spectators, had now reached the spot where Endicott was standing under the banner of his company, and put the governor's epistle into his hand. The broad seal was impressed with Winthrop's coat-of-arms. Endicott hastily unclosed the letter and began to read, while, as his eye passed down the page, a wrathful change came over his manly countenance. The blood glowed through it till it seemed to be kindling with an internal heat, nor was it unnatural to suppose that his breastplate would likewise become red hot with the angry fire of the bosom which it covered. Arriving at the conclusion, he shook the letter fiercely in his hand, so that it rustled as loud as the flag above his head.

"Black tidings these, Mr. Williams," said he; "blacker never came to New England. Doubtless you know their purport?"

"Yea, truly," replied Roger Williams, "for the governor consulted respecting this matter with my brethren in the ministry at Boston, and my opinion was likewise asked. And His Excellency entreats you by me that the news be not suddenly noised abroad, lest the people be stirred up unto some outbreak, and thereby give the king and the archbishop a handle against us."

"The governor is a wise man—a wise man, and a meek and moderate," said Endicott, setting his teeth grimly. "Nevertheless, I must do according to my own best judgment. There is neither man, woman nor child in New England but has a concern as dear as life in these tidings; and if John Endicott's voice be loud enough, man, woman and child shall hear them.—Soldiers, wheel into a hollow square.—Ho, good people! Here are news for one and all of you."

The soldiers closed in around their captain, and he and Roger Williams stood together under the banner of the red cross, while the women and the aged men pressed forward and the mothers held up their children to look Endicott in the face. A few taps of the drum gave signal for silence and attention.

"Fellow-soldiers, fellow-exiles," began Endicott, speaking under strong excitement, yet powerfully restraining it, "wherefore did ye leave your native country? Wherefore, I say, have we left the green and fertile fields, the cottages, or, perchance, the old gray halls, where we were born and bred, the churchyards where our forefathers lie buried? Wherefore have we come hither to set up our own tombstones in a wilderness? A howling wilderness it is. The wolf and the bear meet us within halloo of our dwellings. The savage lieth in wait for us in the dismal shadow of the woods. The stubborn roots of the trees break our ploughshares when we would till the earth. Our children cry for bread, and we must dig in the sands of the seashore to satisfy them. Wherefore, I say again, have we sought this country of a rugged soil and wintry sky? Was it not for the enjoyment of our civil rights? Was it not for liberty to worship God according to our conscience?"

"Call you this liberty of conscience?" interrupted a voice on the steps of the meeting-house.

It was the wanton gospeller. A sad and quiet smile flitted across the mild visage of Roger Williams, but Endicott, in the excitement of the moment, shook his sword wrathfully at the culprit—an ominous gesture from a man like him.

"What hast thou to do with conscience, thou knave?" cried he. "I said liberty to worship God, not license to profane and ridicule him. Break not in upon my speech, or I will lay thee neck and heels till this time to-morrow.—Hearken to me, friends, nor heed that accursed rhapsodist. As I was saying, we have sacrificed all things, and have come to a land whereof the Old World hath scarcely heard, that we might make a new world unto ourselves and painfully seek a path from hence to heaven. But what think ye now? This son of a Scotch tyrant—this grandson of a papistical and adulterous Scotch woman whose death proved that a golden crown doth not always save an anointed head from the block—"

"Nay, brother, nay," interposed Mr. Williams; "thy words are not meet for a secret chamber, far less for a public street."

"Hold thy peace, Roger Williams!" answered Endicott, imperiously. "My spirit is wiser than thine for the business now in hand.—I tell ye, fellow-exiles, that Charles of England and Laud, our bitterest persecutor, arch-priest of Canterbury, are resolute to pursue us even hither. They are taking counsel, saith this letter, to send over a governor-general in whose breast shall be deposited all the law and equity of the land. They are minded, also, to establish the idolatrous forms of English episcopacy; so that when Laud shall kiss the pope's toe as cardinal of Rome he may deliver New England, bound hand and foot, into the power of his master."

A deep groan from the auditors—a sound of wrath as well as fear and sorrow—responded to this intelligence.

"Look ye to it, brethren," resumed Endicott, with increasing energy. "If this king and this arch-prelate have their will, we shall briefly behold a cross on the spire of this tabernacle which we have builded, and a high altar within its walls, with wax tapers burning round it at noon-day. We shall hear the sacring-bell and the voices of the Romish priests saying the mass. But think ye, Christian men, that these abominations may be suffered without a sword drawn, without a shot fired, without blood spilt—yea, on the very stairs of the pulpit? No! Be ye strong of hand and stout of heart. Here we stand on our own soil, which we have bought with our goods, which we have won with our swords, which we have cleared with our axes, which we have tilled with the sweat of our brows, which we have sanctified with our prayers to the God that brought us hither! Who shall enslave us here? What have we to do with this mitred prelate —with this crowned king? What have we to do with England?"

Endicott gazed round at the excited countenances of the people, now full of his own spirit, and then turned suddenly to the standard-bearer, who stood close behind him.

"Officer, lower your banner," said he.

The officer obeyed, and, brandishing his sword, Endicott thrust it through the cloth and with his left hand rent the red cross completely out of the banner. He then waved the tattered ensign above his head.

"Sacrilegious wretch!" cried the high-churchman in the pillory, unable longer to restrain himself; "thou hast rejected the symbol of our holy religion."

"Treason! treason!" roared the royalist in the stocks. "He hath defaced the king's banner!"

"Before God and man I will avouch the deed," answered Endicott.—"Beat a flourish, drummer—shout, soldiers and people—in honor of the ensign of New England. Neither pope nor tyrant hath part in it now."

With a cry of triumph the people gave their sanction to one of the boldest exploits which our history records. And for ever honored be the name of Endicott! We look back through the mist of ages, and recognize in the rending of the red cross from New England's banner the first omen of that deliverance which our fathers consummated after the bones of the stern Puritan had lain more than a century in the dust.

THE LILY'S QUEST

AN APOLOGUE.

Two LOVERS once upon a time had planned a little summer-house in the form of an antique temple which it was their purpose to consecrate to all manner of refined and innocent enjoyments. There they would hold pleasant intercourse with one another and the circle of their familiar friends; there they would give festivals of delicious fruit; there they would hear lightsome music intermingled with the strains of pathos which make joy more sweet; there they would read poetry and fiction and permit their own minds to flit away in day-dreams and romance; there, in short—for why should we shape out the vague sunshine of their hopes?— there all pure delights were to cluster like roses among the pillars of the edifice and blossom ever new and spontaneously.

So one breezy and cloudless afternoon Adam Forrester and Lilias Fay set out upon a ramble over the wide estate which they were to possess together, seeking a proper site for their temple of happiness. They were themselves a fair and happy spectacle, fit priest and priestess for such a shrine, although, making poetry of the pretty name of Lilias, Adam Forrester was wont to call her "Lily" because her form was as fragile and her cheek almost as pale. As they passed hand in hand down the avenue of drooping elms that led from the portal of Lilias Fay's paternal mansion they seemed to glance like winged creatures through the strips of sunshine, and to scatter brightness where the deep shadows fell.

But, setting forth at the same time with this youthful pair, there was a dismal figure wrapped in a black velvet cloak that might have been made of a coffin-pall, and with a sombre hat such as mourners wear drooping its broad brim over his heavy brows. Glancing behind them, the lovers well knew who it was that followed, but wished from their hearts that he had been elsewhere, as being a companion so strangely unsuited to their joyous errand. It was a near relative of Lilias Fay, an old man by the name of Walter Gascoigne, who had long labored under the burden of a melancholy spirit which was sometimes maddened into absolute insanity and always had a tinge of it. What a contrast between the young pilgrims of bliss and their unbidden associate! They looked as if moulded of heaven's sunshine and he of earth's gloomiest shade; they flitted along like Hope and Joy roaming hand in hand through life, while his darksome figure stalked behind, a type of all the woeful influences which life could fling upon them.

But the three had not gone far when they reached a spot that pleased the gentle Lily, and she paused.

"What sweeter place shall we find than this?" said she. "Why should we seek farther for the site of our temple?"

It was indeed a delightful spot of earth, though undistinguished by any very prominent beauties, being merely a nook in the shelter of a hill, with the prospect of a distant lake in one direction and of a church-spire in another. There were vistas and pathways leading onward and onward into the green woodlands and vanishing away in the glimmering shade. The temple, if erected here, would look toward the west; so that the lovers could shape all sorts of magnificent dreams out of the purple, violet and gold of the sunset sky, and few of their anticipated pleasures were dearer than this sport of fantasy.

"Yes," said Adam Forrester; "we might seek all day and find no lovelier spot. We will build our temple here."

But their sad old companion, who had taken his stand on the very site which they proposed to cover with a marble floor, shook his head and frowned, and the young man and the Lily deemed it almost enough to blight the spot and desecrate it for their airy temple that his dismal figure had thrown its shadow there. He pointed to some scattered stones, the remnants of a former structure, and to flowers such as young girls delight to nurse in their gardens, but which had now relapsed into the wild simplicity of nature.

"Not here," cried old Walter Gascoigne. "Here, long ago, other mortals built their temple of happiness; seek another site for yours."

"What!" exclaimed Lilias Fay. "Have any ever planned such a temple save ourselves?"

"Poor child!" said her gloomy kinsman. "In one shape or other every mortal has dreamed your dream." Then he told the lovers, how—not, indeed, an antique temple, but a dwelling— had once stood there, and that a dark-clad guest had dwelt among its inmates, sitting for ever at the fireside and poisoning all their household mirth.

Under this type Adam Forrester and Lilias saw that the old man spake of sorrow. He told of nothing that might not be recorded in the history of almost every household, and yet his hearers felt as if no sunshine ought to fall upon a spot where human grief had left so deep a stain—or, at least, that no joyous temple should be built there.

"This is very sad," said the Lily, sighing.

"Well, there are lovelier spots than this," said Adam Forrester, soothingly—"spots which sorrow has not blighted."

So they hastened away, and the melancholy Gascoigne followed them, looking as if he had gathered up all the gloom of the deserted spot and was bearing it as a burden of inestimable treasure. But still they rambled on, and soon found themselves in a rocky dell through the midst of which ran a streamlet with ripple and foam and a continual voice of inarticulate joy. It was a wild retreat walled on either side with gray precipices which would have frowned somewhat too sternly had not a profusion of green shrubbery rooted itself into their crevices and wreathed gladsome foliage around their solemn brows. But the chief joy of the dell was in the little stream which seemed like the presence of a blissful child with nothing earthly to do save to babble merrily and disport itself, and make every living soul its playfellow, and throw the sunny gleams of its spirit upon all.

"Here, here is the spot!" cried the two lovers, with one voice, as they reached a level space on the brink of a small cascade. "This glen was made on purpose for our temple."

"And the glad song of the brook will be always in our ears," said Lilias Fay.

"And its long melody shall sing the bliss of our lifetime," said Adam Forrester.

"Ye must build no temple here," murmured their dismal companion.

And there again was the old lunatic standing just on the spot where they meant to rear their lightsome dome, and looking like the embodied symbol of some great woe that in forgotten days had happened there. And, alas! there had been woe, nor that alone. A young man more than a hundred years before had lured hither a girl that loved him, and on this spot had murdered her and washed his bloody hands in the stream which sang so merrily, and ever since the victim's death-shrieks were often heard to echo between the cliffs.

"And see!" cried old Gascoigne; "is the stream yet pure from the stain of the murderer's hands?"

"Methinks it has a tinge of blood," faintly answered the Lily; and, being as slight as the gossamer, she trembled and clung to her lover's arm, whispering, "Let us flee from this dreadful vale."

"Come, then," said Adam Forrester as cheerily as he could; "we shall soon find a happier spot."

They set forth again, young pilgrims on that quest which millions—which every child of earth—has tried in turn.

And were the Lily and her lover to be more fortunate than all those millions? For a long time it seemed not so. The dismal shape of the old lunatic still glided behind them, and for every spot that looked lovely in their eyes he had some legend of human wrong or suffering so miserably sad that his auditors could never afterward connect the idea of joy with the place where it had happened. Here a heartbroken woman kneeling to her child had been spurned from his feet; here a desolate old creature had prayed to the evil one, and had received a fiendish malignity of soul in answer to her prayer; here a new-born infant, sweet blossom of life, had been found dead with the impress of its mother's fingers round its throat; and here, under a shattered oak, two lovers had been stricken by lightning and fell blackened corpses in each other's arms. The dreary Gascoigne had a gift to know whatever evil and lamentable thing had stained the bosom of Mother Earth; and when his funereal voice had told the tale, it appeared like a prophecy of future woe as well as a tradition of the past. And now, by their sad demeanor, you would have fancied that the pilgrim-lovers were seeking, not a temple of earthly joy, but a tomb for themselves and their posterity.

"Where in this world," exclaimed Adam Forrester, despondingly, "shall we build our temple of happiness?"

"Where in this world, indeed?" repeated Lilias Fay; and, being faint and weary—the more so by the heaviness of her heart—the Lily drooped her head and sat down on the summit of a knoll, repeating, "Where in this world shall we build our temple?"

"Ah! have you already asked yourselves that question?" said their companion, his shaded features growing even gloomier with the smile that dwelt on them. "Yet there is a place even in this world where ye may build it."

While the old man spoke Adam Forrester and Lilias had carelessly thrown their eyes around, and perceived that the spot where they had chanced to pause possessed a quiet charm which was well enough adapted to their present mood of mind. It was a small rise of ground with a certain regularity of shape that had perhaps been bestowed by art, and a group of trees which almost surrounded it threw their pensive shadows across and far beyond, although some softened glory of the sunshine found its way there. The ancestral mansion wherein the lovers would dwell together appeared on one side, and the ivied church where they were to worship on another. Happening to cast their eyes on the ground, they smiled, yet with a sense of wonder, to see that a pale lily was growing at their feet.

"We will build our temple here," said they, simultaneously, and with an indescribable conviction that they had at last found the very spot.

Yet while they uttered this exclamation the young man and the Lily turned an apprehensive glance at their dreary associate, deeming it hardly possible that some tale of earthly affliction should not make those precincts loathsome, as in every former case. The old man stood just behind them, so as to form the chief figure in the group, with his sable cloak muffling the lower part of his visage and his sombre hat overshadowing his brows. But he gave no word of dissent from their purpose, and an inscrutable smile was accepted by the lovers as a token that here had been no footprint of guilt or sorrow to desecrate the site of their temple of happiness.

In a little time longer, while summer was still in its prime, the fairy-structure of the temple arose on the summit of the knoll amid the solemn shadows of the trees, yet often gladdened with bright sunshine. It was built of white marble, with slender and graceful pillars supporting a vaulted dome, and beneath the centre of this dome, upon a pedestal, was a slab of dark-veined marble on which books and music might be strewn. But there was a fantasy among the people of the neighborhood that the edifice was planned after an ancient mausoleum and was intended for a tomb, and that the central slab of dark-veined marble was to be inscribed with the names of buried ones. They doubted, too, whether the form of Lilias Fay could appertain to a creature of this earth, being so very delicate and growing every day more fragile, so that she looked as if the summer breeze should snatch her up and waft her heavenward. But still she watched the daily growth of the temple, and so did old Walter Gascoigne, who now made that spot his continual haunt, leaning whole hours together on his staff and giving as deep attention to the work as though it had been indeed a tomb. In due time it was finished and a day appointed for a simple rite of dedication.

On the preceding evening, after Adam Forrester had taken leave of his mistress, he looked back toward the portal of her dwelling and felt a strange thrill of fear, for he imagined that as the setting sunbeams faded from her figure she was exhaling away, and that something of her ethereal substance was withdrawn with each lessening gleam of light. With his farewell glance a shadow had fallen over the portal, and Lilias was invisible. His foreboding spirit deemed it an omen at the time, and so it proved; for the sweet earthly form by which the Lily had been manifested to the world was found lifeless the next morning in the temple with her head resting on her arms, which were folded upon the slab of dark-veined marble. The chill winds of the earth had long since breathed a blight into this beautiful flower; so that a loving hand had now transplanted it to blossom brightly in the garden of Paradise.

But alas for the temple of happiness! In his unutterable grief Adam Forrester had no purpose more at heart than to convert this temple of many delightful hopes into a tomb and bury his dead mistress there. And, lo! a wonder! Digging a grave beneath the temple's marble floor, the sexton found no virgin earth such as was meet to receive the maiden's dust, but an ancient sepulchre in which were treasured up the bones of generations that had died long ago. Among those forgotten ancestors was the Lily to be laid; and when the funeral procession brought Lilias thither in her coffin, they beheld old Walter Gascoigne standing beneath the dome of the temple with his cloak of pall and face of darkest gloom, and wherever that figure might take its stand the spot would seem a sepulchre. He watched the mourners as they lowered the coffin down.

"And so," said he to Adam Forrester, with the strange smile in which his insanity was wont to gleam forth, "you have found no better foundation for your happiness than on a grave?"

But as the shadow of Affliction spoke a vision of hope and joy had its birth in Adam's mind even from the old man's taunting words, for then he knew what was betokened by the parable in which the Lily and himself had acted, and the mystery of life and death was opened to him.

"Joy! joy!" he cried, throwing his arms toward heaven. "On a grave be the site of our temple, and now our happiness is for eternity."

With those words a ray of sunshine broke through the dismal sky and glimmered down into the sepulchre, while at the same moment the shape of old Walter Gascoigne stalked drearily away, because his gloom, symbolic of all earthly sorrow, might no longer abide there now that the darkest riddle of humanity was read.

FOOTPRINTS ON THE SEASHORE

IT MUST BE a spirit much unlike my own which can keep itself in health and vigor without sometimes stealing from the sultry sunshine of the world to plunge into the cool bath of solitude. At intervals, and not infrequent ones, the forest and the ocean summon me—one with the roar of its waves, the other with the murmur of its boughs—forth from the haunts of men. But I must wander many a mile ere I could stand beneath the shadow of even one primeval tree, much less be lost among the multitude of hoary trunks and hidden from the earth and sky by the mystery of darksome foliage. Nothing is within my daily reach more like a forest than the acre or two of woodland near some suburban farmhouse. When, therefore, the yearning for seclusion becomes a necessity within me, I am drawn to the seashore which extends its line of rude rocks and seldom-trodden sands for leagues around our bay. Setting forth at my last ramble on a September morning, I bound myself with a hermit's vow to interchange no thoughts with man or woman, to share no social pleasure, but to derive all that day's enjoyment from shore and sea and sky, from my soul's communion with these, and from fantasies and recollections or anticipated realities. Surely here is enough to feed a human spirit for a single day.—Farewell, then, busy world! Till your evening lights shall shine along the street—till they gleam upon my sea-flushed face as I tread homeward—free me from your ties and let me be a peaceful outlaw.

Highways and cross-paths are hastily traversed, and, clambering down a crag, I find myself at the extremity of a long beach. How gladly does the spirit leap forth and suddenly enlarge its sense of being to the full extent of the broad blue, sunny deep! A greeting and a homage to the sea! I descend over its margin and dip my hand into the wave that meets me, and bathe my brow. That far-resounding roar is Ocean's voice of welcome. His salt breath brings a blessing along with it. Now let us pace together—the reader's fancy arm in arm with mine—this noble beach, which extends a mile or more from that craggy promontory to yonder rampart of broken rocks. In front, the sea; in the rear, a precipitous bank the grassy verge of which is breaking away year after year, and flings down its tufts of verdure upon the barrenness below. The beach itself is a broad space of sand, brown and sparkling, with hardly any pebbles intermixed. Near the water's edge there is a wet margin which glistens brightly in the sunshine and reflects

223

objects like a mirror, and as we tread along the glistening border a dry spot flashes around each footstep, but grows moist again as we lift our feet. In some spots the sand receives a complete impression of the sole, square toe and all; elsewhere it is of such marble firmness that we must stamp heavily to leave a print even of the iron-shod heel. Along the whole of this extensive beach gambols the surf-wave. Now it makes a feint of dashing onward in a fury, yet dies away with a meek murmur and does but kiss the strand; now, after many such abortive efforts, it rears itself up in an unbroken line, heightening as it advances, without a speck of foam on its green crest. With how fierce a roar it flings itself forward and rushes far up the beach!

As I threw my eyes along the edge of the surf I remember that I was startled, as Robinson Crusoe might have been, by the sense that human life was within the magic circle of my solitude. Afar off in the remote distance of the beach, appearing like sea-nymphs, or some airier things such as might tread upon the feathery spray, was a group of girls. Hardly had I beheld them, when they passed into the shadow of the rocks and vanished. To comfort myself—for truly I would fain have gazed a while longer—I made acquaintance with a flock of beach-birds. These little citizens of the sea and air preceded me by about a stone's-throw along the strand, seeking, I suppose, for food upon its margin. Yet, with a philosophy which mankind would do well to imitate, they drew a continual pleasure from their toil for a subsistence. The sea was each little bird's great playmate. They chased it downward as it swept back, and again ran up swiftly before the impending wave, which sometimes overtook them and bore them off their feet. But they floated as lightly as one of their own feathers on the breaking crest. In their airy flutterings they seemed to rest on the evanescent spray. Their images—long-legged little figures with gray backs and snowy bosoms—were seen as distinctly as the realities in the mirror of the glistening strand. As I advanced they flew a score or two of yards, and, again alighting, recommenced their dalliance with the surf-wave; and thus they bore me company along the beach, the types of pleasant fantasies, till at its extremity they took wing over the ocean and were gone. After forming a friendship with these small surf-spirits, it is really worth a sigh to find no memorial of them save their multitudinous little tracks in the sand.

When we have paced the length of the beach, it is pleasant and not unprofitable to retrace our steps and recall the whole mood and occupation of the mind during the former passage. Our tracks, being all discernible, will guide us with an observing consciousness through every unconscious wandering of thought and fancy. Here we followed the surf in its reflux to pick up a shell which the sea seemed loth to relinquish. Here we found a seaweed with an immense brown leaf, and trailed it behind us by its long snake-like stalk. Here we seized a live horseshoe by the tail, and counted the many claws of that queer monster. Here we dug into the sand for pebbles, and skipped them upon the surface of the water. Here we wet our feet while examining a jelly-fish which the waves, having just tossed it up, now sought to snatch away again. Here we trod along the brink of a fresh-water brooklet which flows across the beach, becoming shallower and more shallow, till at last it sinks into the sand and perishes in the effort to bear its little tribute to the main. Here some vagary appears to have bewildered us, for our tracks go round and round and are confusedly intermingled, as if we had found a labyrinth upon the level beach. And here amid our idle pastime we sat down upon almost the only stone that breaks the surface of the sand, and were lost in an unlooked-for and overpowering conception of the majesty and awfulness of the great deep. Thus by tracking our footprints in the sand we track our own nature in its wayward course, and steal a glance upon it when it never dreams of being so observed. Such glances always make us wiser.

This extensive beach affords room for another pleasant pastime. With your staff you may write verses—love-verses if they please you best—and consecrate them with a woman's name. Here, too, may be inscribed thoughts, feelings, desires, warm outgushings from the heart's secret places, which you would not pour upon the sand without the certainty that almost ere the sky has looked upon them the sea will wash them out. Stir not hence till the record be effaced. Now (for there is room enough on your canvas) draw huge faces—huge as that of the Sphynx on Egyptian sands—and fit them with bodies of corresponding immensity and legs which might stride halfway to yonder island. Child's-play becomes magnificent on so grand a scale. But, after all, the most fascinating employment is simply to write your name in the sand. Draw the letters gigantic, so that two strides may barely measure them, and three for the long strokes; cut deep, that the record may be permanent. Statesmen and warriors and poets have spent their strength in no better cause than this. Is it accomplished? Return, then, in an hour or two, and seek for this mighty record of a name. The sea will have swept over it, even as time rolls its effacing waves over the names of statesmen and warriors and poets. Hark! the surf-wave laughs at you.

Passing from the beach, I begin to clamber over the crags, making my difficult way among the ruins of a rampart shattered and broken by the assaults of a fierce enemy. The rocks rise in every variety of attitude. Some of them have their feet in the foam and are shagged halfway upward with seaweed; some have been hollowed almost into caverns by the unwearied toil of the sea, which can afford to spend centuries in wearing away a rock, or even polishing a pebble. One huge rock ascends in monumental shape, with a face like a giant's tombstone, on which the veins resemble inscriptions, but in an unknown tongue. We will fancy them the forgotten characters of an antediluvian race, or else that Nature's own hand has here recorded a mystery which, could I read her language, would make mankind the wiser and the happier. How many a thing has troubled me with that same idea! Pass on and leave it unexplained. Here is a narrow avenue which might seem to have been hewn through the very heart of an enormous crag, affording passage for the rising sea to thunder back and forth, filling it with tumultuous foam and then leaving its floor of black pebbles bare and glistening. In this chasm there was once an intersecting vein of softer stone, which the waves have gnawed away piecemeal, while the granite walls remain entire on either side. How sharply and with what harsh clamor does the sea rake back the pebbles as it momentarily withdraws into its own depths! At intervals the floor of the chasm is left nearly dry, but anon, at the outlet, two or three great waves are seen struggling to get in at once; two hit the walls athwart, while one rushes straight through, and all three thunder as if with rage and triumph. They heap the chasm with a snow-drift of foam and spray. While watching this scene I can never rid myself of the idea that a monster endowed with life and fierce energy is striving to burst his way through the narrow pass. And what a contrast to look through the stormy chasm and catch a glimpse of the calm bright sea beyond!

Many interesting discoveries may be made among these broken cliffs. Once, for example, I found a dead seal which a recent tempest had tossed into the nook of the rocks, where his shaggy carcase lay rolled in a heap of eel-grass as if the sea-monster sought to hide himself from my eye. Another time a shark seemed on the point of leaping from the surf to swallow me, nor did I wholly without dread approach near enough to ascertain that the man-eater had already met his own death from some fisherman in the bay. In the same ramble I encountered a bird—a large gray bird—but whether a loon or a wild goose or the identical albatross of the Ancient Mariner was beyond my ornithology to decide. It reposed so naturally on a bed of dry seaweed, with its head beside its wing, that I almost fancied it alive, and trod softly lest it should suddenly spread its wings skyward. But the sea-bird would soar among the clouds no more, nor ride upon its native waves; so I drew near and pulled out one of its mottled tail-feathers for a remembrance. Another day I discovered an immense bone wedged into a chasm of the rocks; it was at least ten feet long, curved like a scymitar, bejewelled with barnacles and small shellfish and partly covered with a growth of seaweed. Some leviathan of former ages had used this ponderous mass as a jaw-bone. Curiosities of a minuter order may be observed in a deep reservoir which is replenished with water at every tide, but becomes a lake among the crags save when the sea is at its height. At the bottom of this rocky basin grow marine plants, some of which tower high beneath the water and cast a shadow in the sunshine. Small fishes dart to and fro and hide themselves among the seaweed; there is also a solitary crab who appears to lead the life of a hermit, communing with none of the other denizens of the place, and likewise several five-fingers; for I know no other name than that which children give them. If your imagination be at all accustomed to such freaks, you may look down into the depths of this pool and fancy it the mysterious depth of ocean. But where are the hulks and scattered timbers of sunken ships? where the treasures that old Ocean hoards? where the corroded cannon? where the corpses and skeletons of seamen who went down in storm and battle?

On the day of my last ramble—it was a September day, yet as warm as summer—what should I behold as I approached the above-described basin but three girls sitting on its margin and—yes, it is veritably so—laving their snowy feet in the sunny water? These, these are the warm realities of those three visionary shapes that flitted from me on the beach. Hark their merry voices as they toss up the water with their feet! They have not seen me. I must shrink behind this rock and steal away again.

In honest truth, vowed to solitude as I am, there is something in this encounter that makes the heart flutter with a strangely pleasant sensation. I know these girls to be realities of flesh and blood, yet, glancing at them so briefly, they mingle like kindred creatures with the ideal beings of my mind. It is pleasant, likewise, to gaze down from some high crag and watch a group of children gathering pebbles and pearly shells and playing with the surf as with old Ocean's hoary beard. Nor does it infringe upon my seclusion to see yonder boat at anchor off the shore swinging dreamily to and fro and rising and sinking with the alternate swell, while the crew—four gentlemen in roundabout jackets—are busy with their fishing-lines. But with an inward antipathy and a headlong flight do I eschew the presence of any meditative stroller like myself, known by his pilgrim-staff, his sauntering step, his shy demeanor, his observant yet abstracted eye.

From such a man as if another self had scared me I scramble hastily over the rocks, and take refuge in a nook which many a secret hour has given me a right to call my own. I would do battle for it even with the churl that should produce the title-deeds. Have not my musings melted into its rocky walls and sandy floor and made them a portion of myself? It is a recess in the line of cliffs, walled round by a rough, high precipice which almost encircles and shuts in a little space of sand. In front the sea appears as between the pillars of a portal; in the rear the precipice is broken and intermixed with earth which gives nourishment not only to clinging and twining shrubs, but to trees that grip the rock with their naked roots and seem to struggle hard for footing and for soil enough to live upon. These are fir trees, but oaks hang their heavy branches from above, and throw down acorns on the beach, and shed their withering foliage upon the waves. At this autumnal season the precipice is decked with variegated splendor. Trailing wreaths of scarlet flaunt from the summit downward; tufts of yellow-flowering shrubs and rose-bushes, with their reddened leaves and glossy seed-berries, sprout from each crevice; at every glance I detect some new light or shade of beauty, all contrasting with the stern gray rock. A rill of water trickles down the cliff and fills a little cistern near the base. I drain it at a draught, and find it fresh and pure. This recess shall be my dining-hall. And what the feast? A few biscuits made savory by soaking them in sea-water, a tuft of samphire gathered from the beach, and an apple for the dessert. By this time the little rill has filled its reservoir again, and as I quaff it I thank God more heartily than for a civic banquet that he gives me the healthful appetite to make a feast of bread and water.

Dinner being over, I throw myself at length upon the sand and, basking in the sunshine, let my mind disport itself at will. The walls of this my hermitage have no tongue to tell my follies, though I sometimes fancy that they have ears to hear them and a soul to sympathize. There is a magic in this spot. Dreams haunt its precincts and flit around me in broad sunlight, nor require that sleep shall blindfold me to real objects ere these be visible. Here can I frame a story of two lovers, and make their shadows live before me and be mirrored in the tranquil water as they tread along the sand, leaving no footprints. Here, should I will it, I can summon up a single shade and be myself her lover.—Yes, dreamer, but your lonely heart will be the colder for such fancies.—Sometimes, too, the Past comes back, and finds me here, and in her train come faces which were gladsome when I knew them, yet seem not gladsome now. Would that my hiding-place were lonelier, so that the Past might not find me!—Get ye all gone, old friends, and let me listen to the murmur of the sea—a melancholy voice, but less sad than yours. Of what mysteries is it telling? Of sunken ships and whereabouts they lie? Of islands afar and undiscovered whose tawny children are unconscious of other islands and of continents, and deem the stars of heaven their nearest neighbors? Nothing of all this. What, then? Has it talked for so many ages and meant nothing all the while? No; for those ages find utterance in the sea's unchanging voice, and warn the listener to withdraw his interest from mortal vicissitudes and let the infinite idea of eternity pervade his soul. This is wisdom, and therefore will I spend the next half-hour in shaping little boats of driftwood and launching them on voyages across the cove, with the feather of a sea-gull for a sail. If the voice of ages tell me true, this is as wise an occupation as to build ships of five hundred tons and launch them forth upon the main, bound to "Far Cathay." Yet how would the merchant sneer at me!

And, after all, can such philosophy be true? Methinks I could find a thousand arguments against it. Well, then, let yonder shaggy rock mid-deep in the surf—see! he is somewhat wrathful: he rages and roars and foams,—let that tall rock be my antagonist, and let me exercise my oratory like him of Athens who bandied words with an angry sea and got the victory. My maiden-speech is a triumphant one, for the gentleman in seaweed has nothing to offer in reply save an immitigable roaring. His voice, indeed, will be heard a long while after mine is hushed. Once more I shout and the cliffs reverberate the sound. Oh what joy for a shy man to feel himself so solitary that he may lift his voice to its highest pitch without hazard of a listener!—But hush! Be silent, my good friend! Whence comes that stifled laughter? It was musical, but how should there be such music in my solitude? Looking upward, I catch a glimpse of three faces peeping from the summit of the cliff like angels between me and their native sky.—Ah, fair girls! you may make yourself merry at my eloquence, but it was my turn to smile when I saw your white feet in the pool. Let us keep each other's secrets.

The sunshine has now passed from my hermitage, except a gleam upon the sand just where it meets the sea. A crowd of gloomy fantasies will come and haunt me if I tarry longer here in the darkening twilight of these gray rocks. This is a dismal place in some moods of the mind. Climb we, therefore, the precipice, and pause a moment on the brink gazing down into that hollow chamber by the deep where we have been what few can be—sufficient to our own pastime. Yes, say the word outright: self-sufficient to our own happiness. How lonesome looks the recess now, and dreary too, like all other spots where happiness has been! There lies my shadow in the departing sunshine with its head upon the sea. I will pelt it with pebbles. A hit! a hit! I clap my hands in triumph, and see my shadow clapping its unreal hands and claiming the triumph for itself. What a simpleton must I have been all day, since my own shadow makes a mock of my fooleries!

Homeward! homeward! It is time to hasten home. It is time—it is time; for as the sun sinks over the western wave the sea grows melancholy and the surf has a saddened tone. The distant sails appear astray and not of earth in their remoteness amid the desolate waste. My spirit wanders forth afar, but finds no resting-place and comes shivering back. It is time that I were hence. But grudge me not the day that has been spent in seclusion which yet was not solitude, since the great sea has been my companion, and the little sea-birds my friends, and the wind has told me his secrets, and airy shapes have flitted around me in my hermitage. Such companionship works an effect upon a man's character as if he had been admitted to the society of creatures that are not mortal. And when, at noontide, I tread the crowded streets, the influence of this day will still be felt; so that I shall walk among men kindly and as a brother, with affection and sympathy, but yet shall not melt into the indistinguishable mass of humankind. I shall think my own thoughts and feel my own emotions and possess my individuality unviolated.

But it is good at the eve of such a day to feel and know that there are men and women in the world. That feeling and that knowledge are mine at this moment, for on the shore, far below me, the fishing-party have landed from their skiff and are cooking their scaly prey by a fire of driftwood kindled in the angle of two rude rocks. The three visionary girls are likewise there. In the deepening twilight, while the surf is dashing near their hearth, the ruddy gleam of the fire throws a strange air of comfort over the wild cove, bestrewn as it is with pebbles and seaweed and exposed to the "melancholy main." Moreover, as the smoke climbs up the precipice, it brings with it a savory smell from a pan of fried fish and a black kettle of chowder, and reminds me that my dinner was nothing but bread and water and a tuft of samphire and an apple. Methinks the party might find room for another guest at that flat rock which serves them for a table; and if spoons be scarce, I could pick up a clam-shell on the beach. They see me now; and —the blessing of a hungry man upon him!—one of them sends up a hospitable shout: "Halloo, Sir Solitary! Come down and sup with us!" The ladies wave their handkerchiefs. Can I decline? No; and be it owned, after all my solitary joys, that this is the sweetest moment of a day by the seashore.

EDWARD FANE'S ROSEBUD

THERE IS HARDLY A MORE difficult exercise of fancy than, while gazing at a figure of melancholy age, to recreate its youth, and without entirely obliterating the identity of form and features to restore those graces which Time has snatched away. Some old people—especially women—so age-worn and woeful are they, seem never to have been young and gay. It is easier to conceive that such gloomy phantoms were sent into the world as withered and decrepit as we behold them now, with sympathies only for pain and grief, to watch at death-beds and weep at funerals. Even the sable garments of their widowhood appear essential to their existence; all their attributes combine to render them darksome shadows creeping strangely amid the sunshine of human life. Yet it is no unprofitable task to take one of these doleful creatures and set Fancy resolutely at work to brighten the dim eye, and darken the silvery locks, and paint the ashen cheek with rose-color, and repair the shrunken and crazy form, till a dewy maiden shall be seen in the old matron's elbow-chair. The miracle being wrought, then let the years roll back again, each sadder than the last, and the whole weight of age and sorrow settle down upon the youthful figure. Wrinkles and furrows, the handwriting of Time, may thus be deciphered and found to contain deep lessons of thought and feeling.

Such profit might be derived by a skilful observer from my much-respected friend the Widow Toothaker, a nurse of great repute who has breathed the atmosphere of sick-chambers and dying-breaths these forty years. See! she sits cowering over her lonesome hearth with her gown and upper petticoat drawn upward, gathering thriftily into her person the whole warmth of the fire which now at nightfall begins to dissipate the autumnal chill of her chamber. The blaze quivers capriciously in front, alternately glimmering into the deepest chasms of her wrinkled visage, and then permitting a ghostly dimness to mar the outlines of her venerable figure. And Nurse Toothaker holds a teaspoon in her right hand with which to stir up the contents of a tumbler in her left, whence steams a vapory fragrance abhorred of temperance societies. Now she sips, now stirs, now sips again. Her sad old heart has need to be revived by the rich infusion of Geneva which is mixed half and half with hot water in the tumbler. All day long she has been sitting by a death-pillow, and quitted it for her home only when the spirit of her patient left the clay and went homeward too. But now are her melancholy meditations cheered and her torpid blood warmed and her shoulders lightened of at least twenty ponderous years by a draught from the true fountain of youth in a case-bottle. It is strange that men should deem that fount a fable, when its liquor fills more bottles than the Congress-water. —Sip it again, good nurse, and see whether a second draught will not take off another score of years, and perhaps ten more, and show us in your high-backed chair the blooming damsel who plighted troths with Edward Fane.—Get you gone, Age and Widowhood!—Come back, unwedded Youth!—But, alas! the charm will not work. In spite of Fancy's most potent spell, I can see only an old dame cowering over the fire, a picture of decay and desolation, while the November blast roars at her in the chimney and fitful showers rush suddenly against the window.

Yet there was a time when Rose Grafton—such was the pretty maiden-name of Nurse Toothaker—possessed beauty that would have gladdened this dim and dismal chamber as with sunshine. It won for her the heart of Edward Fane, who has since made so great a figure in the world and is now a grand old gentleman with powdered hair and as gouty as a lord. These early lovers thought to have walked hand in hand through life. They had wept together for Edward's little sister Mary, whom Rose tended in her sickness—partly because she was the sweetest child that ever lived or died, but more for love of him. She was but three years old. Being such an infant, Death could not embody his terrors in her little corpse; nor did Rose fear to touch the dead child's brow, though chill, as she curled the silken hair around it, nor to take her tiny hand and clasp a flower within its fingers. Afterward, when she looked through the pane of glass in the coffin-lid and beheld Mary's face, it seemed not so much like death or life as like a wax-work wrought into the perfect image of a child asleep and dreaming of its mother's smile. Rose thought her too fair a thing to be hidden in the grave, and wondered that an angel did not snatch up little Mary's coffin and bear the slumbering babe to heaven and bid her wake immortal. But when the sods were laid on little Mary, the heart of Rose was troubled. She shuddered at the fantasy that in grasping the child's cold fingers her virgin hand had exchanged a first greeting with mortality and could never lose the earthy taint. How many a greeting since! But as yet she was a fair young girl with the dewdrops of fresh feeling in her bosom, and, instead of "Rose"—which seemed too mature a name for her half-opened beauty— her lover called her "Rosebud."

The rosebud was destined never to bloom for Edward Fane. His mother was a rich and haughty dame with all the aristocratic prejudices of colonial times. She scorned Rose Grafton's humble parentage and caused her son to break his faith, though, had she let him choose, he would have prized his Rosebud above the richest diamond. The lovers parted, and have seldom met again. Both may have visited the same mansions, but not at the same time, for one was bidden to the festal hall and the other to the sick-chamber; he was the guest of Pleasure and Prosperity, and she of Anguish. Rose, after their separation, was long secluded within the dwelling of Mr. Toothaker, whom she married with the revengeful hope of breaking her false lover's heart. She went to her bridegroom's arms with bitterer tears, they say, than young girls ought to shed at the threshold of the bridal-chamber. Yet, though her husband's head was getting gray and his heart had been chilled with an autumnal frost, Rose soon began to love him, and wondered at her own conjugal affection. He was all she had to love; there were no children.

In a year or two poor Mr. Toothaker was visited with a wearisome infirmity which settled in his joints and made him weaker than a child. He crept forth about his business, and came home at dinner-time and eventide, not with the manly tread that gladdens a wife's heart, but slowly, feebly, jotting down each dull footstep with a melancholy dub of his staff. We must pardon his pretty wife if she sometimes blushed to own him. Her visitors, when they heard him coming, looked for the appearance of some old, old man, but he dragged his nerveless limbs into the parlor—and there was Mr. Toothaker! The disease increasing, he never went into the sunshine save with a staff in his right hand and his left on his wife's shoulder, bearing heavily downward like a dead man's hand. Thus, a slender woman still looking maiden-like, she supported his tall, broad-chested frame along the pathway of their little garden, and plucked the roses for her gray-haired husband, and spoke soothingly as to an infant. His mind was palsied with his body; its utmost energy was peevishness. In a few months more she helped him up the staircase with a pause at every step, and a longer one upon the landing-place, and a heavy glance behind as he crossed the threshold of his chamber. He knew, poor man! that the precincts of those four walls would thenceforth be his world—his world, his home, his tomb, at once a dwelling-and a burial-place—till he were borne to a darker and a narrower one. But Rose was with him in the tomb. He leaned upon her in his daily passage from the bed to the chair by the fireside, and back again from the weary chair to the joyless bed—his bed and hers, their marriage-bed—till even this short journey ceased and his head lay all day upon the pillow and hers all night beside it. How long poor Mr. Toothaker was kept in misery! Death seemed to draw near the door, and often to lift the latch, and sometimes to thrust his ugly skull into the chamber, nodding to Rose and pointing at her husband, but still delayed to enter. "This bedridden wretch cannot escape me," quoth Death. "I will go forth and run a race with the swift and fight a battle with the strong, and come back for Toothaker at my leisure." Oh, when the deliverer came so near, in the dull anguish of her worn-out sympathies did she never long to cry, "Death, come in"?

But no; we have no right to ascribe such a wish to our friend Rose. She never failed in a wife's duty to her poor sick husband. She murmured not though a glimpse of the sunny sky was as strange to her as him, nor answered peevishly though his complaining accents roused her from sweetest dream only to share his wretchedness. He knew her faith, yet nourished a cankered jealousy; and when the slow disease had chilled all his heart save one lukewarm spot which Death's frozen fingers were searching for, his last words were, "What would my Rose have done for her first love, if she has been so true and kind to a sick old man like me?" And then his poor soul crept away and left the body lifeless, though hardly more so than for years before, and Rose a widow, though in truth it was the wedding-night that widowed her. She felt glad, it must be owned, when Mr. Toothaker was buried, because his corpse had retained such a likeness to the man half alive that she hearkened for the sad murmur of his voice bidding her shift his pillow. But all through the next winter, though the grave had held him many a month, she fancied him calling from that cold bed, "Rose, Rose! Come put a blanket on my feet!"

So now the Rosebud was the widow Toothaker. Her troubles had come early, and, tedious as they seemed, had passed before all her bloom was fled. She was still fair enough to captivate a bachelor, or with a widow's cheerful gravity she might have won a widower, stealing into his heart in the very guise of his dead wife. But the widow Toothaker had no such projects. By her watchings and continual cares her heart had become knit to her first husband with a constancy which changed its very nature and made her love him for his infirmities, and infirmity for his sake. When the palsied old man was gone, even her early lover could not have supplied his place. She had dwelt in a sick-chamber and been the companion of a half-dead wretch till she could scarcely breathe in a free air and felt ill at ease with the healthy and the happy. She missed the fragrance of the doctor's stuff. She walked the chamber with a noiseless footfall. If visitors came in, she spoke in soft and soothing accents, and was startled and shocked by their loud voices. Often in the lonesome evening she looked timorously from the fireside to the bed, with almost a hope of recognizing a ghastly face upon the pillow. Then went her thoughts sadly to her husband's grave. If one impatient throb had wronged him in his lifetime, if she had secretly repined because her buoyant youth was imprisoned with his torpid age, if ever while slumbering beside him a treacherous dream had admitted another into her heart,—yet the sick man had been preparing a revenge which the dead now claimed. On his painful pillow he had cast a spell around her; his groans and misery had proved more captivating charms than gayety and youthful grace; in his semblance Disease itself had won the Rosebud for a bride, nor could his death dissolve the nuptials. By that indissoluble bond she had gained a home in every sick-chamber, and nowhere else; there were her brethren and sisters; thither her husband summoned her with that voice which had seemed to issue from the grave of Toothaker. At length she recognized her destiny.

We have beheld her as the maid, the wife, the widow; now we see her in a separate and insulated character: she was in all her attributes Nurse Toothaker. And Nurse Toothaker alone, with her own shrivelled lips, could make known her experience in that capacity. What a history might she record of the great sicknesses in which she has gone hand in hand with the exterminating angel! She remembers when the small-pox hoisted a red banner on almost every house along the street. She has witnessed when the typhus fever swept off a whole household, young and old, all but a lonely mother, who vainly shrieked to follow her last loved one. Where would be Death's triumph if none lived to weep? She can speak of strange maladies that have broken out as if spontaneously, but were found to have been imported from foreign lands with rich silks and other merchandise, the costliest portion of the cargo. And once, she recollects, the people died of what was considered a new pestilence, till the doctors traced it to the ancient grave of a young girl who thus caused many deaths a hundred years after her own burial. Strange that such black mischief should lurk in a maiden's grave! She loves to tell how strong men fight with fiery fevers, utterly refusing to give up their breath, and how consumptive virgins fade out of the world, scarcely reluctant, as if their lovers were wooing them to a far country.—Tell us, thou fearful woman; tell us the death-secrets. Fain would I search out the meaning of words faintly gasped with intermingled sobs and broken sentences half-audibly spoken between earth and the judgment-seat.

An awful woman! She is the patron-saint of young physicians and the bosom-friend of old ones. In the mansions where she enters the inmates provide themselves black garments; the coffin-maker follows her, and the bell tolls as she comes away from the threshold. Death himself has met her at so many a bedside that he puts forth his bony hand to greet Nurse Toothaker. She is an awful woman. And oh, is it conceivable that this handmaid of human infirmity and affliction—so darkly stained, so thoroughly imbued with all that is saddest in the doom of mortals—can ever again be bright and gladsome even though bathed in the sunshine of eternity? By her long communion with woe has she not forfeited her inheritance of immortal joy? Does any germ of bliss survive within her?

Hark! an eager knocking st Nurse Toothaker's door. She starts from her drowsy reverie, sets aside the empty tumbler and teaspoon, and lights a lamp at the dim embers of the fire. "Rap, rap, rap!" again, and she hurries adown the staircase, wondering which of her friends can be at death's door now, since there is such an earnest messenger at Nurse Toothaker's. Again the peal resounds just as her hand is on the lock. "Be quick, Nurse Toothaker!" cries a man on the doorstep. "Old General Fane is taken with the gout in his stomach and has sent for you to watch by his death-bed. Make haste, for there is no time to lose."—"Fane! Edward Fane! And has he sent for me at last? I am ready. I will get on my cloak and begone. So," adds the sable-gowned, ashen-visaged, funereal old figure, "Edward Fane remembers his Rosebud."

Our question is answered. There is a germ of bliss within her. Her long-hoarded constancy, her memory of the bliss that was remaining amid the gloom of her after-life like a sweet-smelling flower in a coffin, is a symbol that all may be renewed. In some happier clime the Rosebud may revive again with all the dewdrops in its bosom.

THE THREEFOLD DESTINY

A FAËRY LEGEND.

I HAVE SOMETIMES PRODUCED a singular and not unpleasing effect, so far as my own mind was concerned, by imagining a train of incidents in which the spirit and mechanism of the faëry legend should be combined with the characters and manners of familiar life. In the little tale which follows a subdued tinge of the wild and wonderful is thrown over a sketch of New England personages and scenery, yet, it is hoped, without entirely obliterating the sober hues of nature. Rather than a story of events claiming to be real, it may be considered as an allegory such as the writers of the last century would have expressed in the shape of an Eastern tale, but to which I have endeavored to give a more lifelike warmth than could be infused into those fanciful productions.

In the twilight of a summer eve a tall dark figure over which long and remote travel had thrown an outlandish aspect was entering a village not in "faëry londe," but within our own familiar boundaries. The staff on which this traveller leaned had been his companion from the spot where it grew in the jungles of Hindostan; the hat that overshadowed his sombre brow, had shielded him from the suns of Spain; but his cheek had been blackened by the red-hot wind of an Arabian desert and had felt the frozen breath of an Arctic region. Long sojourning amid wild and dangerous men, he still wore beneath his vest the ataghan which he had once struck into the throat of a Turkish robber. In every foreign clime he had lost something of his New England characteristics, and perhaps from every people he had unconsciously borrowed a new peculiarity; so that when the world-wanderer again trod the street of his native village it is no wonder that he passed unrecognized, though exciting the gaze and curiosity of all. Yet, as his arm casually touched that of a young woman who was wending her way to an evening lecture, she started and almost uttered a cry.

"Ralph Cranfield!" was the name that she half articulated.

"Can that be my old playmate Faith Egerton?" thought the traveller, looking round at her figure, but without pausing.

Ralph Cranfield from his youth upward had felt himself marked out for a high destiny. He had imbibed the idea—we say not whether it were revealed to him by witchcraft or in a dream of prophecy, or that his brooding fancy had palmed its own dictates upon him as the oracles of a sybil, but he had imbibed the idea, and held it firmest among his articles of faith—that three marvellous events of his life were to be confirmed to him by three signs.

The first of these three fatalities, and perhaps the one on which his youthful imagination had dwelt most fondly, was the discovery of the maid who alone of all the maids on earth could make him happy by her love. He was to roam around the world till he should meet a beautiful woman wearing on her bosom a jewel in the shape of a heart—whether of pearl or ruby or emerald or carbuncle or a changeful opal, or perhaps a priceless diamond, Ralph Cranfield little cared, so long as it were a heart of one peculiar shape. On encountering this lovely stranger he was bound to address her thus: "Maiden, I have brought you a heavy heart. May I rest its weight on you?" And if she were his fated bride—if their kindred souls were destined to form a union here below which all eternity should only bind more closely—she would reply, with her finger on the heart-shaped jewel, "This token which I have worn so long is the assurance that you may."

And, secondly, Ralph Cranfield had a firm belief that there was a mighty treasure hidden somewhere in the earth of which the burial-place would be revealed to none but him. When his feet should press upon the mysterious spot, there would be a hand before him pointing downward—whether carved of marble or hewn in gigantic dimensions on the side of a rocky precipice, or perchance a hand of flame in empty air, he could not tell, but at least he would discern a hand, the forefinger pointing downward, and beneath it the Latin word "*Effode*"—"Dig!" And, digging thereabouts, the gold in coin or ingots, the precious stones, or of whatever else the treasure might consist, would be certain to reward his toil.

The third and last of the miraculous events in the life of this high-destined man was to be the attainment of extensive influence and sway over his fellow-creatures. Whether he were to be a king and founder of a hereditary throne, or the victorious leader of a people contending for their freedom, or the apostle of a purified and regenerated faith, was left for futurity to show. As messengers of the sign by which Ralph Cranfield might recognize the summons, three venerable men were to claim audience of him. The chief among them—a dignified and majestic person arrayed, it may be supposed, in the flowing garments of an ancient sage—would be the bearer of a wand or prophet's rod. With this wand or rod or staff the venerable sage would trace a certain figure in the air, and then proceed to make known his Heaven-instructed message, which, if obeyed, must lead to glorious results.

With this proud fate before him, in the flush of his imaginative youth Ralph Cranfield had set forth to seek the maid, the treasure, and the venerable sage with his gift of extended empire. And had he found them? Alas! it was not with the aspect of a triumphant man who had achieved a nobler destiny than all his fellows, but rather with the gloom of one struggling against peculiar and continual adversity, that he now passed homeward to his mother's cottage. He had come back, but only for a time, to lay aside the pilgrim's staff, trusting that his weary manhood would regain somewhat of the elasticity of youth in the spot where his threefold fate had been foreshown him. There had been few changes in the village, for it was not one of those thriving places where a year's prosperity makes more than the havoc of a century's decay, but, like a gray hair in a young man's head, an antiquated little town full of old maids and aged elms and moss-grown dwellings. Few seemed to be the changes here. The drooping elms, indeed, had a more majestic spread, the weather-blackened houses were adorned with a denser thatch of verdant moss, and doubtless there were a few more gravestones in the burial-ground inscribed with names that had once been familiar in the village street; yet, summing up all the mischief that ten years had wrought, it seemed scarcely more than if Ralph Cranfield had gone forth that very morning and dreamed a day-dream till the twilight, and then turned back again. But his heart grew cold because the village did not remember him as he remembered the village.

"Here is the change," sighed he, striking his hand upon his breast. "Who is this man of thought and care, weary with world-wandering and heavy with disappointed hopes? The youth returns not who went forth so joyously."

And now Ralph Cranfield was at his mother's gate, in front of the small house where the old lady, with slender but sufficient means, had kept herself comfortable during her son's long absence. Admitting himself within the enclosure, he leaned against a great old tree, trifling with his own impatience as people often do in those intervals when years are summed into a moment. He took a minute survey of the dwelling—its windows brightened with the sky-gleam, its doorway with the half of a millstone for a step, and the faintly-traced path waving thence to the gate. He made friends again with his childhood's friend—the old tree against which he leaned—and, glancing his eye down its trunk, beheld something that excited a melancholy smile. It was a half-obliterated inscription—the Latin word *"Effode"*—which he remembered to have carved in the bark of the tree with a whole day's toil when he had first begun to muse about his exalted destiny. It might be accounted a rather singular coincidence that the bark just above the inscription had put forth an excrescence shaped not unlike a hand, with the forefinger pointing obliquely at the word of fate. Such, at least, was its appearance in the dusky light.

"Now, a credulous man," said Ralph Cranfield, carelessly, to himself, "might suppose that the treasure which I have sought round the world lies buried, after all, at the very door of my mother's dwelling. That would be a jest indeed."

More he thought not about the matter, for now the door was opened and an elderly woman appeared on the threshold, peering into the dusk to discover who it might be that had intruded on her premises and was standing in the shadow of her tree. It was Ralph Cranfield's mother. Pass we over their greeting, and leave the one to her joy and the other to his rest—if quiet rest he found.

But when morning broke, he arose with a troubled brow, for his sleep and his wakefulness had alike been full of dreams. All the fervor was rekindled with which he had burned of yore to unravel the threefold mystery of his fate. The crowd of his early visions seemed to have awaited him beneath his mother's roof and thronged riotously around to welcome his return. In the well-remembered chamber, on the pillow where his infancy had slumbered, he had passed a wilder night than ever in an Arab tent or when he had reposed his head in the ghastly shades of a haunted forest. A shadowy maid had stolen to his bedside and laid her finger on the scintillating heart; a hand of flame had glowed amid the darkness, pointing downward to a mystery within the earth; a hoary sage had waved his prophetic wand and beckoned the dreamer onward to a chair of state. The same phantoms, though fainter in the daylight, still flitted about the cottage and mingled among the crowd of familiar faces that were drawn thither by the news of Ralph Cranfield's return to bid him welcome for his mother's sake. There they found him, a tall, dark, stately man of foreign aspect, courteous in demeanor and mild of speech, yet with an abstracted eye which seemed often to snatch a glance at the invisible.

Meantime, the widow Cranfield went bustling about the house full of joy that she again had somebody to love and be careful of, and for whom she might vex and tease herself with the petty troubles of daily life. It was nearly noon when she looked forth from the door and descried three personages of note coming along the street through the hot sunshine and the masses of elm-tree shade. At length they reached her gate and undid the latch.

"See, Ralph!" exclaimed she, with maternal pride; "here is Squire Hawkwood and the two other selectmen coming on purpose to see you. Now, do tell them a good long story about what you have seen in foreign parts."

The foremost of the three visitors, Squire Hawkwood, was a very pompous but excellent old gentleman, the head and prime-mover in all the affairs of the village, and universally acknowledged to be one of the sagest men on earth. He wore, according to a fashion even then becoming antiquated, a three-cornered hat, and carried a silver-headed cane the use of which seemed to be rather for flourishing in the air than for assisting the progress of his legs. His two companions were elderly and respectable yeomen who, retaining an ante-Revolutionary reverence for rank and hereditary wealth, kept a little in the squire's rear.

As they approached along the pathway Ralph Cranfield sat in an oaken elbow-chair half unconsciously gazing at the three visitors and enveloping their homely figures in the misty romance that pervaded his mental world. "Here," thought he, smiling at the conceit—"here come three elderly personages, and the first of the three is a venerable sage with a staff. What if this embassy should bring me the message of my fate?"

While Squire Hawkwood and his colleagues entered, Ralph rose from his seat and advanced a few steps to receive them, and his stately figure and dark countenance as he bent courteously toward his guests had a natural dignity contrasting well with the bustling importance of the squire. The old gentleman, according to invariable custom, gave an elaborate preliminary flourish with his cane in the air, then removed his three-cornered hat in order to wipe his brow, and finally proceeded to make known his errand.

"My colleagues and myself," began the squire, "are burdened with momentous duties, being jointly selectmen of this village. Our minds for the space of three days past have been laboriously bent on the selection of a suitable person to fill a most important office and take upon himself a charge and rule which, wisely considered, may be ranked no lower than those of kings and potentates. And whereas you, our native townsman, are of good natural intellect and well cultivated by foreign travel, and that certain vagaries and fantasies of your youth are doubtless long ago corrected,—taking all these matters, I say, into due consideration, we are of opinion that Providence hath sent you hither at this juncture for our very purpose."

During this harangue Cranfield gazed fixedly at the speaker, as if he beheld something mysterious and unearthly in his pompous little figure, and as if the squire had worn the flowing robes of an ancient sage instead of a square-skirted coat, flapped waistcoat, velvet breeches and silk stockings. Nor was his wonder without sufficient cause, for the flourish of the squire's staff, marvellous to relate, had described precisely the signal in the air which was to ratify the message of the prophetic sage whom Cranfield had sought around the world.

"And what," inquired Ralph Cranfield, with a tremor in his voice—"what may this office be which is to equal me with kings and potentates?"

"No less than instructor of our village school," answered Squire Hawkwood, "the office being now vacant by the death of the venerable Master Whitaker after a fifty years' incumbency."

"I will consider of your proposal," replied Ralph Cranfield, hurriedly, "and will make known my decision within three days."

After a few more words the village dignitary and his companions took their leave. But to Cranfield's fancy their images were still present, and became more and more invested with the dim awfulness of figures which had first appeared to him in a dream, and afterward had shown themselves in his waking moments, assuming homely aspects among familiar things. His mind dwelt upon the features of the squire till they grew confused with those of the visionary sage and one appeared but the shadow of the other. The same visage, he now thought, had looked forth upon him from the Pyramid of Cheops; the same form had beckoned to him among the colonnades of the Alhambra; the same figure had mistily revealed itself through the ascending steam of the Great Geyser. At every effort of his memory he recognized some trait of the dreamy messenger of destiny in this pompous, bustling, self-important, little-great man of the village. Amid such musings Ralph Cranfield sat all day in the cottage, scarcely hearing and vaguely answering his mother's thousand questions about his travels and adventures. At sunset he roused himself to take a stroll, and, passing the aged elm tree, his eye was again caught by the semblance of a hand pointing downward at the half-obliterated inscription.

As Cranfield walked down the street of the village the level sunbeams threw his shadow far before him, and he fancied that, as his shadow walked among distant objects, so had there been a presentiment stalking in advance of him throughout his life. And when he drew near each object over which his tall shadow had preceded him, still it proved to be one of the familiar recollections of his infancy and youth. Every crook in the pathway was remembered. Even the more transitory characteristics of the scene were the same as in by-gone days. A company of cows were grazing on the grassy roadside, and refreshed him with their fragrant breath. "It is sweeter," thought he, "than the perfume which was wafted to our ship from the Spice Islands." The round little figure of a child rolled from a doorway and lay laughing almost beneath Cranfield's feet. The dark and stately man stooped down, and, lifting the infant, restored him to his mother's arms. "The children," said he to himself, and sighed and smiled—"the children are to be my charge." And while a flow of natural feeling gushed like a well-spring in his heart he came to a dwelling which he could nowise forbear to enter. A sweet voice which seemed to come from a deep and tender soul was warbling a plaintive little air within. He bent his head and passed through the lowly door. As his foot sounded upon the threshold a young woman advanced from the dusky interior of the house, at first hastily, and then with a more uncertain step, till they met face to face. There was a singular contrast in their two figures—he dark and picturesque, one who had battled with the world, whom all suns had shone upon and whom all winds had blown on a varied course; she neat, comely and quiet—quiet even in her agitation—as if all her emotions had been subdued to the peaceful tenor of her life. Yet their faces, all unlike as they were, had an expression that seemed not so alien—a glow of kindred feeling flashing upward anew from half-extinguished embers.

"You are welcome home," said Faith Egerton.

But Cranfield did not immediately answer, for his eye had, been caught by an ornament in the shape of a heart which Faith wore as a brooch upon her bosom. The material was the ordinary white quartz, and he recollected having himself shaped it out of one of those Indian arrowheads which are so often found in the ancient haunts of the red men. It was precisely on the pattern of that worn by the visionary maid. When Cranfield departed on his shadowy search, he had bestowed this brooch, in a gold setting, as a parting gift to Faith Egerton.

"So, Faith, you have kept the heart?" said he, at length.

"Yes," said she, blushing deeply; then, more gayly, "And what else have you brought me from beyond the sea?"

"Faith," replied Ralph Cranfield, uttering the fated words by an uncontrollable impulse, "I have brought you nothing but a heavy heart. May I rest its weight on you?"

"This token which I have worn so long," said Faith, laying her tremulous finger on the heart, "is the assurance that you may."

"Faith, Faith!" cried Cranfield, clasping her in his arms; "you have interpreted my wild and weary dream!"

Yes, the wild dreamer was awake at last. To find the mysterious treasure he was to till the earth around his mother's dwelling and reap its products; instead of warlike command or regal or religious sway, he was to rule over the village children; and now the visionary maid had faded from his fancy, and in her place he saw the playmate of his childhood.

Would all who cherish such wild wishes but look around them, they would oftenest find their sphere of duty, of prosperity and happiness, within those precincts and in that station where Providence itself has cast their lot. Happy they who read the riddle without a weary world-search or a lifetime spent in vain!

THE SCARLET LETTER

THE CUSTOM-HOUSE

INTRODUCTORY TO "THE SCARLET LETTER"

IT IS A LITTLE REMARKABLE, that—though disinclined to talk overmuch of myself and my affairs at the fireside, and to my personal friends—an autobiographical impulse should twice in my life have taken possession of me, in addressing the public. The first time was three or four years since, when I favoured the reader—inexcusably, and for no earthly reason that either the indulgent reader or the intrusive author could imagine—with a description of my way of life in the deep quietude of an Old Manse. And now—because, beyond my deserts, I was happy enough to find a listener or two on the former occasion—I again seize the public by the button, and talk of my three years' experience in a Custom-House. The example of the famous "P. P., Clerk of this Parish," was never more faithfully followed. The truth seems to be, however, that when he casts his leaves forth upon the wind, the author addresses, not the many who will fling aside his volume, or never take it up, but the few who will understand him better than most of his schoolmates or lifemates. Some authors, indeed, do far more than this, and indulge themselves in such confidential depths of revelation as could fittingly be addressed only and exclusively to the one heart and mind of perfect sympathy; as if the printed book, thrown at large on the wide world, were certain to find out the divided segment of the writer's own nature, and complete his circle of existence by bringing him into communion with it. It is scarcely decorous, however, to speak all, even where we speak impersonally. But, as thoughts are frozen and utterance benumbed, unless the speaker stand in some true relation with his audience, it may be pardonable to imagine that a friend, a kind and apprehensive, though not the closest friend, is listening to our talk; and then, a native reserve being thawed by this genial consciousness, we may prate of the circumstances that lie around us, and even of ourself, but still keep the inmost Me behind its veil. To this extent, and within these limits, an author, methinks, may be autobiographical, without violating either the reader's rights or his own.

It will be seen, likewise, that this Custom-House sketch has a certain propriety, of a kind always recognised in literature, as explaining how a large portion of the following pages came into my possession, and as offering proofs of the authenticity of a narrative therein contained. This, in fact—a desire to put myself in my true position as editor, or very little more, of the most prolix among the tales that make up my volume—this, and no other, is my true reason for assuming a personal relation with the public. In accomplishing the main purpose, it has appeared allowable, by a few extra touches, to give a faint representation of a mode of life not heretofore described, together with some of the characters that move in it, among whom the author happened to make one.

In my native town of Salem, at the head of what, half a century ago, in the days of old King Derby, was a bustling wharf—but which is now burdened with decayed wooden warehouses, and exhibits few or no symptoms of commercial life; except, perhaps, a bark or brig, half-way down its melancholy length, discharging hides; or, nearer at hand, a Nova Scotia schooner, pitching out her cargo of firewood—at the head, I say, of this dilapidated wharf, which the tide often overflows, and along which, at the base and in the rear of the row of buildings, the track of many languid years is seen in a border of unthrifty grass—here, with a view from its front windows adown this not very enlivening prospect, and thence across the harbour, stands a spacious edifice of brick. From the loftiest point of its roof, during precisely three and a half hours of each forenoon, floats or droops, in breeze or calm, the banner of the republic; but with the thirteen stripes turned vertically, instead of horizontally, and thus indicating that a civil, and not a military, post of Uncle Sam's government is here established. Its front is ornamented with a portico of half-a-dozen wooden pillars, supporting a balcony, beneath which a flight of wide granite steps descends towards the street. Over the entrance hovers an enormous specimen of the American eagle, with outspread wings, a shield before her breast, and, if I recollect aright, a bunch of intermingled thunderbolts and barbed arrows in each claw. With the customary infirmity of temper that characterizes this unhappy fowl, she appears by the fierceness of her beak and eye, and the general truculency of her attitude, to threaten mischief to the inoffensive community; and especially to warn all citizens careful of their safety against intruding on the premises which she overshadows with her wings. Nevertheless, vixenly as she looks, many people are seeking at this very moment to shelter themselves under the wing of the federal eagle; imagining, I presume, that her bosom has all the softness and snugness of an eiderdown pillow. But she has no great tenderness even in her best of moods, and, sooner or later—oftener soon than late—is apt to fling off her nestlings with a scratch of her claw, a dab of her beak, or a rankling wound from her barbed arrows.

The pavement round about the above-described edifice—which we may as well name at once as the Custom-House of the port—has grass enough growing in its chinks to show that it has not, of late days, been worn by any multitudinous resort of business. In some months of the year, however, there often chances a forenoon when affairs move onward with a livelier tread. Such occasions might remind the elderly citizen of that period, before the last war with England, when Salem was a port by itself; not scorned, as she is now, by her own merchants and ship-owners, who permit her wharves to crumble to ruin while their ventures go to swell, needlessly and imperceptibly, the mighty flood of commerce at New York or Boston. On some such morning, when three or four vessels happen to have arrived at once usually from Africa or South America—or to be on the verge of their departure thitherward, there is a sound of frequent feet passing briskly up and down the granite steps. Here, before his own wife has greeted him, you may greet the sea-flushed ship-master, just in port, with his vessel's papers under his arm in a tarnished tin box. Here, too, comes his owner, cheerful, sombre, gracious or in the sulks, accordingly as his scheme of the now accomplished voyage has been realized in merchandise that will readily be turned to gold, or has buried him under a bulk of incommodities such as nobody will care to rid him of. Here, likewise—the germ of the wrinkle-browed, grizzly-bearded, careworn merchant—we have the smart young clerk, who gets the taste of traffic as a wolf-cub does of blood, and already sends adventures in his master's ships, when he had better be sailing mimic boats upon a mill-pond. Another figure in the scene is the outward-bound sailor, in quest of a protection; or the recently arrived one, pale and feeble, seeking a passport to the hospital. Nor must we forget the captains of the rusty little schooners that bring firewood from the British provinces; a rough-looking set of tarpaulins, without the alertness of the Yankee aspect, but contributing an item of no slight importance to our decaying trade.

Cluster all these individuals together, as they sometimes were, with other miscellaneous ones to diversify the group, and, for the time being, it made the Custom-House a stirring scene. More frequently, however, on ascending the steps, you would discern— in the entry if it were summer time, or in their appropriate rooms if wintry or inclement weathers—a row of venerable figures, sitting in old-fashioned chairs, which were tipped on their hind legs back against the wall. Oftentimes they were asleep, but occasionally might be heard talking together, in voices between a speech and a snore, and with that lack of energy that distinguishes the occupants of alms-houses, and all other human beings who depend for subsistence on charity, on monopolized labour, or anything else but their own independent exertions. These old gentlemen—seated, like Matthew at the receipt of custom, but not very liable to be summoned thence, like him, for apostolic errands—were Custom-House officers.

Furthermore, on the left hand as you enter the front door, is a certain room or office, about fifteen feet square, and of a lofty height, with two of its arched windows commanding a view of the aforesaid dilapidated wharf, and the third looking across a narrow lane, and along a portion of Derby Street. All three give glimpses of the shops of grocers, block-makers, slop-sellers, and ship-chandlers, around the doors of which are generally to be seen, laughing and gossiping, clusters of old salts, and such other wharf-rats as haunt the Wapping of a seaport. The room itself is cobwebbed, and dingy with old paint; its floor is strewn with grey sand, in a fashion that has elsewhere fallen into long disuse; and it is easy to conclude, from the general slovenliness of the place, that this is a sanctuary into which womankind, with her tools of magic, the broom and mop, has very infrequent access. In the way of furniture, there is a stove with a voluminous funnel; an old pine desk with a three-legged stool beside it; two or three wooden-bottom chairs, exceedingly decrepit and infirm; and—not to forget the library—on some shelves, a score or two of volumes of the Acts of Congress, and a bulky Digest of the Revenue laws. A tin pipe ascends through the ceiling, and forms a medium of vocal communication with other parts of the edifice. And here, some six months ago—pacing from corner to corner, or lounging on the long-legged stool, with his elbow on the desk, and his eyes wandering up and down the columns of the morning newspaper—you might have recognised, honoured reader, the same individual who welcomed you into his cheery little study, where the sunshine glimmered so pleasantly through the willow branches on the western side of the Old Manse. But now, should you go thither to seek him, you would inquire in vain for the Locofoco Surveyor. The besom of reform hath swept him out of office, and a worthier successor wears his dignity and pockets his emoluments.

This old town of Salem—my native place, though I have dwelt much away from it both in boyhood and maturer years—possesses, or did possess, a hold on my affection, the force of which I have never realized during my seasons of actual residence here. Indeed, so far as its physical aspect is concerned, with its flat, unvaried surface, covered chiefly with wooden houses, few or none of which pretend to architectural beauty—its irregularity, which is neither picturesque nor quaint, but only tame—its long and lazy street, lounging wearisomely through the whole extent of the peninsula, with Gallows Hill and New Guinea at one end, and a view of the alms-house at the other—such being the features of my native town, it would be quite as reasonable to form a sentimental attachment to a disarranged checker-board. And yet, though invariably happiest elsewhere, there is within me a feeling for Old Salem, which, in lack of a better phrase, I must be content to call affection. The sentiment is probably assignable to the deep and aged roots which my family has stuck into the soil. It is now nearly two centuries and a quarter since the original Briton, the earliest emigrant of my name, made his appearance in the wild and forest-bordered settlement which has since become a city. And here his descendants have been born and died, and have mingled their earthly substance with the soil, until no small portion of it must necessarily be akin to the mortal frame wherewith, for a little while, I walk the streets. In part, therefore, the attachment which I speak of is the mere sensuous sympathy of dust for dust. Few of my countrymen can know what it is; nor, as frequent transplantation is perhaps better for the stock, need they consider it desirable to know.

But the sentiment has likewise its moral quality. The figure of that first ancestor, invested by family tradition with a dim and dusky grandeur, was present to my boyish imagination as far back as I can remember. It still haunts me, and induces a sort of home-feeling with the past, which I scarcely claim in reference to the present phase of the town. I seem to have a stronger claim to a residence here on account of this grave, bearded, sable-cloaked, and steeple-crowned progenitor—who came so early, with his Bible and his sword, and trode the unworn street with such a stately port, and made so large a figure, as a man of war and peace—a stronger claim than for myself, whose name is seldom heard and my face hardly known. He was a soldier, legislator, judge; he was a ruler in the Church; he had all the Puritanic traits, both good and evil. He was likewise a bitter persecutor; as witness the Quakers, who have remembered him in their histories, and relate an incident of his hard severity towards a woman of their sect, which will last longer, it is to be feared, than any record of his better deeds, although these were many. His son, too, inherited the persecuting spirit, and made himself so conspicuous in the martyrdom of the witches, that their blood may fairly be said to have left a stain upon him. So deep a stain, indeed, that his dry old bones, in the Charter-street burial-ground, must still retain it, if they have not crumbled utterly to dust! I know not whether these ancestors of mine bethought themselves to repent, and ask pardon of Heaven for their cruelties; or whether they are now groaning under the heavy consequences of them in another state of being. At all events, I, the present writer, as their representative, hereby take shame upon myself for their sakes, and pray that any curse incurred by them—as I have heard, and as the dreary and unprosperous condition of the race, for many a long year back, would argue to exist—may be now and henceforth removed.

Doubtless, however, either of these stern and black-browed Puritans would have thought it quite a sufficient retribution for his sins that, after so long a lapse of years, the old trunk of the family tree, with so much venerable moss upon it, should have borne, as its topmost bough, an idler like myself. No aim that I have ever cherished would they recognise as laudable; no success of mine—if my life, beyond its domestic scope, had ever been brightened by success—would they deem otherwise than worthless, if not positively disgraceful. "What is he?" murmurs one grey shadow of my forefathers to the other. "A writer of story books! What kind of business in life—what mode of glorifying God, or being serviceable to mankind in his day and generation—may that be? Why, the degenerate fellow might as well have been a fiddler!" Such are the compliments bandied between my great grandsires and myself, across the gulf of time! And yet, let them scorn me as they will, strong traits of their nature have intertwined themselves with mine.

Planted deep, in the town's earliest infancy and childhood, by these two earnest and energetic men, the race has ever since subsisted here; always, too, in respectability; never, so far as I have known, disgraced by a single unworthy member; but seldom or never, on the other hand, after the first two generations, performing any memorable deed, or so much as putting forward a claim to public notice. Gradually, they have sunk almost out of sight; as old houses, here and there about the streets, get covered half-way to the eaves by the accumulation of new soil. From father to son, for above a hundred years, they followed the sea; a grey-headed shipmaster, in each generation, retiring from the quarter-deck to the homestead, while a boy of fourteen took the hereditary place before the mast, confronting the salt spray and the gale which had blustered against his sire and grandsire. The boy, also in due time, passed from the forecastle to the cabin, spent a tempestuous manhood, and returned from his world-wanderings, to grow old, and die, and mingle his dust with the natal earth. This long connexion of a family with one spot, as its place of birth and burial, creates a kindred between the human being and the locality, quite independent of any charm in the scenery or moral circumstances that surround him. It is not love but instinct. The new inhabitant—who came himself from a foreign land, or whose father or grandfather came—has little claim to be called a Salemite; he has no conception of the oyster-like tenacity with which an old settler, over whom his third century is creeping, clings to the spot where his successive generations have been embedded. It is no matter that the place is joyless for him; that he is weary of the old wooden houses, the mud and dust, the dead level of site and sentiment, the chill east wind, and the chillest of social atmospheres;—all these, and whatever faults besides he may see or imagine, are nothing to the purpose. The spell survives, and just as powerfully as if the natal spot were an earthly paradise. So has it been in my case. I felt it almost as a destiny to make Salem my home; so that the mould of features and cast of character which had all along been familiar here—ever, as one representative of the race lay down in the grave, another assuming, as it were, his sentry-march along the main street—might still in my little day be seen and recognised in the old town. Nevertheless, this very sentiment is an evidence that the connexion, which has become an unhealthy one, should at last be severed. Human nature will not flourish, any more than a potato, if it be planted and re-planted, for too long a series of generations, in the same worn-out soil. My children have had other birth-places, and, so far as their fortunes may be within my control, shall strike their roots into unaccustomed earth.

On emerging from the Old Manse, it was chiefly this strange, indolent, unjoyous attachment for my native town that brought me to fill a place in Uncle Sam's brick edifice, when I might as well, or better, have gone somewhere else. My doom was on me. It was not the first time, nor the second, that I had gone away—as it seemed, permanently—but yet returned, like the bad halfpenny, or as if Salem were for me the inevitable centre of the universe. So, one fine morning I ascended the flight of granite steps, with the President's commission in my pocket, and was introduced to the corps of gentlemen who were to aid me in my weighty responsibility as chief executive officer of the Custom-House.

I doubt greatly—or, rather, I do not doubt at all—whether any public functionary of the United States, either in the civil or military line, has ever had such a patriarchal body of veterans under his orders as myself. The whereabouts of the Oldest Inhabitant was at once settled when I looked at them. For upwards of twenty years before this epoch, the independent position of the Collector had kept the Salem Custom-House out of the whirlpool of political vicissitude, which makes the tenure of office generally so fragile. A soldier—New England's most distinguished soldier—he stood firmly on the pedestal of his gallant services; and, himself secure in the wise liberality of the successive administrations through which he had held office, he had been the safety of his subordinates in many an hour of danger and heart-quake. General Miller was radically conservative; a man over whose kindly nature habit had no slight influence; attaching himself strongly to familiar faces, and with difficulty moved to change, even when change might have brought unquestionable improvement. Thus, on taking charge of my department, I found few but aged men. They were ancient sea-captains, for the most part, who, after being tossed on every sea, and standing up sturdily against life's tempestuous blast, had finally drifted into this quiet nook, where, with little to disturb them, except the periodical terrors of a Presidential election, they one and all acquired a new lease of existence. Though by no means less liable than their fellow-men to age and infirmity, they had evidently some talisman or other that kept death at bay. Two or three of their number, as I was assured, being gouty and rheumatic, or perhaps bed-ridden, never dreamed of making their appearance at the Custom-House during a large part of the year; but, after a torpid winter, would creep out into the warm sunshine of May or June, go lazily about what they termed duty, and, at their own leisure and convenience, betake themselves to bed again. I must plead guilty to the charge of abbreviating the official breath of more than one of these venerable servants of the republic. They were allowed, on my representation, to rest from their arduous labours, and soon afterwards—as if their sole principle of life had been zeal for their country's service—as I verily believe it was—withdrew to a better world. It is a pious consolation to me that, through my interference, a sufficient space was allowed them for repentance of the evil and corrupt practices into which, as a matter of course, every Custom-House officer must be supposed to fall. Neither the front nor the back entrance of the Custom-House opens on the road to Paradise.

The greater part of my officers were Whigs. It was well for their venerable brotherhood that the new Surveyor was not a politician, and though a faithful Democrat in principle, neither received nor held his office with any reference to political services. Had it been otherwise—had an active politician been put into this influential post, to assume the easy task of making head against a Whig Collector, whose infirmities withheld him from the personal administration of his office—hardly a man of the old corps would have drawn the breath of official life within a month after the exterminating angel had come up the Custom-House steps. According to the received code in such matters, it would have been nothing short of duty, in a politician, to bring every one of those white heads under the axe of the guillotine. It was plain enough to discern that the old fellows dreaded some such discourtesy at my hands. It pained, and at the same time amused me, to behold the terrors that attended my advent, to see a furrowed cheek, weather-beaten by half a century of storm, turn ashy pale at the glance of so harmless an individual as myself; to detect, as one or another addressed me, the tremor of a voice which, in long-past days, had been wont to bellow through a speaking-trumpet, hoarsely enough to frighten Boreas himself to silence. They knew, these excellent old persons, that, by all established rule—and, as regarded some of them, weighed by their own lack of efficiency for business—they ought to have given place to younger men, more orthodox in politics, and altogether fitter than themselves to serve our common Uncle. I knew it, too, but could never quite find in my heart to act upon the knowledge. Much and deservedly to my own discredit, therefore, and considerably to the detriment of my official conscience, they continued, during my incumbency, to creep about the wharves, and loiter up and down the Custom-House steps. They spent a good deal of time, also, asleep in their accustomed corners, with their chairs tilted back against the walls; awaking, however, once or twice in the forenoon, to bore one another with the several thousandth repetition of old sea-stories and mouldy jokes, that had grown to be passwords and countersigns among them.

The discovery was soon made, I imagine, that the new Surveyor had no great harm in him. So, with lightsome hearts and the happy consciousness of being usefully employed—in their own behalf at least, if not for our beloved country—these good old gentlemen went through the various formalities of office. Sagaciously under their spectacles, did they peep into the holds of vessels. Mighty was their fuss about little matters, and marvellous, sometimes, the obtuseness that allowed greater ones to slip between their fingers Whenever such a mischance occurred— when a waggon-load of valuable merchandise had been smuggled ashore, at noonday, perhaps, and directly beneath their unsuspicious noses—nothing could exceed the vigilance and alacrity with which they proceeded to lock, and double-lock, and secure with tape and sealing-wax, all the avenues of the delinquent vessel. Instead of a reprimand for their previous negligence, the case seemed rather to require an eulogium on their praiseworthy caution after the mischief had happened; a grateful recognition of the promptitude of their zeal the moment that there was no longer any remedy.

Unless people are more than commonly disagreeable, it is my foolish habit to contract a kindness for them. The better part of my companion's character, if it have a better part, is that which usually comes uppermost in my regard, and forms the type whereby I recognise the man. As most of these old Custom-House officers had good traits, and as my position in reference to them, being paternal and protective, was favourable to the growth of friendly sentiments, I soon grew to like them all. It was pleasant in the summer forenoons—when the fervent heat, that almost liquefied the rest of the human family, merely communicated a genial warmth to their half torpid systems—it was pleasant to hear them chatting in the back entry, a row of them all tipped against the wall, as usual; while the frozen witticisms of past generations were thawed out, and came bubbling with laughter from their lips. Externally, the jollity of aged men has much in common with the mirth of children; the intellect, any more than a deep sense of humour, has little to do with the matter; it is, with both, a gleam that plays upon the surface, and imparts a sunny and cheery aspect alike to the green branch and grey, mouldering trunk. In one case, however, it is real sunshine; in the other, it more resembles the phosphorescent glow of decaying wood.

It would be sad injustice, the reader must understand, to represent all my excellent old friends as in their dotage. In the first place, my coadjutors were not invariably old; there were men among them in their strength and prime, of marked ability and energy, and altogether superior to the sluggish and dependent mode of life on which their evil stars had cast them. Then, moreover, the white locks of age were sometimes found to be the thatch of an intellectual tenement in good repair. But, as respects the majority of my corps of veterans, there will be no wrong done if I characterize them generally as a set of wearisome old souls, who had gathered nothing worth preservation from their varied experience of life. They seemed to have flung away all the golden grain of practical wisdom, which they had enjoyed so many opportunities of harvesting, and most carefully to have stored their memory with the husks. They spoke with far more interest and unction of their morning's breakfast, or yesterday's, to-day's, or tomorrow's dinner, than of the shipwreck of forty or fifty years ago, and all the world's wonders which they had witnessed with their youthful eyes.

The father of the Custom-House—the patriarch, not only of this little squad of officials, but, I am bold to say, of the respectable body of tide-waiters all over the United States—was a certain permanent Inspector. He might truly be termed a legitimate son of the revenue system, dyed in the wool, or rather born in the purple; since his sire, a Revolutionary colonel, and formerly collector of the port, had created an office for him, and appointed him to fill it, at a period of the early ages which few living men can now remember. This Inspector, when I first knew him, was a man of fourscore years, or thereabouts, and certainly one of the most wonderful specimens of winter-green that you would be likely to discover in a lifetime's search. With his florid cheek, his compact figure smartly arrayed in a bright-buttoned blue coat, his brisk and vigorous step, and his hale and hearty aspect, altogether he seemed—not young, indeed—but a kind of new contrivance of Mother Nature in the shape of man, whom age and infirmity had no business to touch. His voice and laugh, which perpetually re-echoed through the Custom-House, had nothing of the tremulous quaver and cackle of an old man's utterance; they came strutting out of his lungs, like the crow of a cock, or the blast of a clarion. Looking at him merely as an animal—and there was very little else to look at—he was a most satisfactory object, from the thorough healthfulness and wholesomeness of his system, and his capacity, at that extreme age, to enjoy all, or nearly all, the delights which he had ever aimed at or conceived of. The careless security of his life in the Custom-House, on a regular income, and with but slight and infrequent apprehensions of removal, had no doubt contributed to make time pass lightly over him. The original and more potent causes, however, lay in the rare perfection of his animal nature, the moderate proportion of intellect, and the very trifling admixture of moral and spiritual ingredients; these latter qualities, indeed, being in barely enough measure to keep the old gentleman from walking on all-fours. He possessed no power of thought, no depth of feeling, no troublesome sensibilities: nothing, in short, but a few commonplace instincts, which, aided by the cheerful temper which grew inevitably out of his physical well-being, did duty very respectably, and to general acceptance, in lieu of a heart. He had been the husband of three wives, all long since dead; the father of twenty children, most of whom, at every age of childhood or maturity, had likewise returned to dust. Here, one would suppose, might have been sorrow enough to imbue the sunniest disposition through and through with a sable tinge. Not so with our old Inspector. One brief sigh sufficed to carry off the entire burden of these dismal reminiscences. The next moment he was as ready for sport as any unbreeched infant: far readier than the Collector's junior clerk, who at nineteen years was much the elder and graver man of the two.

I used to watch and study this patriarchal personage with, I think, livelier curiosity than any other form of humanity there presented to my notice. He was, in truth, a rare phenomenon; so perfect, in one point of view; so shallow, so delusive, so impalpable such an absolute nonentity, in every other. My conclusion was that he had no soul, no heart, no mind; nothing, as I have already said, but instincts; and yet, withal, so cunningly had the few materials of his character been put together that there was no painful perception of deficiency, but, on my part, an entire contentment with what I found in him. It might be difficult—and it was so—to conceive how he should exist hereafter, so earthly and sensuous did he seem; but surely his existence here, admitting that it was to terminate with his last breath, had been not unkindly given; with no higher moral responsibilities than the beasts of the field, but with a larger scope of enjoyment than theirs, and with all their blessed immunity from the dreariness and duskiness of age.

One point in which he had vastly the advantage over his four-footed brethren was his ability to recollect the good dinners which it had made no small portion of the happiness of his life to eat. His gourmandism was a highly agreeable trait; and to hear him talk of roast meat was as appetizing as a pickle or an oyster. As he possessed no higher attribute, and neither sacrificed nor vitiated any spiritual endowment by devoting all his energies and ingenuities to subserve the delight and profit of his maw, it always pleased and satisfied me to hear him expatiate on fish, poultry, and butcher's meat, and the most eligible methods of preparing them for the table. His reminiscences of good cheer, however ancient the date of the actual banquet, seemed to bring the savour of pig or turkey under one's very nostrils. There were flavours on his palate that had lingered there not less than sixty or seventy years, and were still apparently as fresh as that of the mutton chop which he had just devoured for his breakfast. I have heard him smack his lips over dinners, every guest at which, except himself, had long been food for worms. It was marvellous to observe how the ghosts of bygone meals were continually rising up before him—not in anger or retribution, but as if grateful for his former appreciation, and seeking to reduplicate an endless series of enjoyment, at once shadowy and sensual: a tenderloin of beef, a hind-quarter of veal, a spare-rib of pork, a particular chicken, or a remarkably praiseworthy turkey, which had perhaps adorned his board in the days of the elder Adams, would be remembered; while all the subsequent experience of our race, and all the events that brightened or darkened his individual career, had gone over him with as little permanent effect as the passing breeze. The chief tragic event of the old man's life, so far as I could judge, was his mishap with a certain goose, which lived and died some twenty or forty years ago: a goose of most promising figure, but which, at table, proved so inveterately tough, that the carving-knife would make no impression on its carcase, and it could only be divided with an axe and handsaw.

But it is time to quit this sketch; on which, however, I should be glad to dwell at considerably more length, because of all men whom I have ever known, this individual was fittest to be a Custom-House officer. Most persons, owing to causes which I may not have space to hint at, suffer moral detriment from this peculiar mode of life. The old Inspector was incapable of it; and, were he to continue in office to the end of time, would be just as good as he was then, and sit down to dinner with just as good an appetite.

There is one likeness, without which my gallery of Custom-House portraits would be strangely incomplete, but which my comparatively few opportunities for observation enable me to sketch only in the merest outline. It is that of the Collector, our gallant old General, who, after his brilliant military service, subsequently to which he had ruled over a wild Western territory, had come hither, twenty years before, to spend the decline of his varied and honourable life.

The brave soldier had already numbered, nearly or quite, his three-score years and ten, and was pursuing the remainder of his earthly march, burdened with infirmities which even the martial music of his own spirit-stirring recollections could do little towards lightening. The step was palsied now, that had been foremost in the charge. It was only with the assistance of a servant, and by leaning his hand heavily on the iron balustrade, that he could slowly and painfully ascend the Custom-House steps, and, with a toilsome progress across the floor, attain his customary chair beside the fireplace. There he used to sit, gazing with a somewhat dim serenity of aspect at the figures that came and went, amid the rustle of papers, the administering of oaths, the discussion of business, and the casual talk of the office; all which sounds and circumstances seemed but indistinctly to impress his senses, and hardly to make their way into his inner sphere of contemplation. His countenance, in this repose, was mild and kindly. If his notice was sought, an expression of courtesy and interest gleamed out upon his features, proving that there was light within him, and that it was only the outward medium of the intellectual lamp that obstructed the rays in their passage. The closer you penetrated to the substance of his mind, the sounder it appeared. When no longer called upon to speak or listen —either of which operations cost him an evident effort—his face would briefly subside into its former not uncheerful quietude. It was not painful to behold this look; for, though dim, it had not the imbecility of decaying age. The framework of his nature, originally strong and massive, was not yet crumpled into ruin.

To observe and define his character, however, under such disadvantages, was as difficult a task as to trace out and build up anew, in imagination, an old fortress, like Ticonderoga, from a view of its grey and broken ruins. Here and there, perchance, the walls may remain almost complete; but elsewhere may be only a shapeless mound, cumbrous with its very strength, and overgrown, through long years of peace and neglect, with grass and alien weeds.

Nevertheless, looking at the old warrior with affection—for, slight as was the communication between us, my feeling towards him, like that of all bipeds and quadrupeds who knew him, might not improperly be termed so,—I could discern the main points of his portrait. It was marked with the noble and heroic qualities which showed it to be not a mere accident, but of good right, that he had won a distinguished name. His spirit could never, I conceive, have been characterized by an uneasy activity; it must, at any period of his life, have required an impulse to set him in motion; but once stirred up, with obstacles to overcome, and an adequate object to be attained, it was not in the man to give out or fail. The heat that had formerly pervaded his nature, and which was not yet extinct, was never of the kind that flashes and flickers in a blaze; but rather a deep red glow, as of iron in a furnace. Weight, solidity, firmness—this was the expression of his repose, even in such decay as had crept untimely over him at the period of which I speak. But I could imagine, even then, that, under some excitement which should go deeply into his consciousness—roused by a trumpet's peal, loud enough to awaken all of his energies that were not dead, but only slumbering—he was yet capable of flinging off his infirmities like a sick man's gown, dropping the staff of age to seize a battle-sword, and starting up once more a warrior. And, in so intense a moment his demeanour would have still been calm. Such an exhibition, however, was but to be pictured in fancy; not to be anticipated, nor desired. What I saw in him—as evidently as the indestructible ramparts of Old Ticonderoga, already cited as the most appropriate simile—was the features of stubborn and ponderous endurance, which might well have amounted to obstinacy in his earlier days; of integrity, that, like most of his other endowments, lay in a somewhat heavy mass, and was just as unmalleable or unmanageable as a ton of iron ore; and of benevolence which, fiercely as he led the bayonets on at Chippewa or Fort Erie, I take to be of quite as genuine a stamp as what actuates any or all the polemical philanthropists of the age. He had slain men with his own hand, for aught I know—certainly, they had fallen like blades of grass at the sweep of the scythe before the charge to which his spirit imparted its triumphant energy—but, be that as it might, there was never in his heart so much cruelty as would have brushed the down off a butterfly's wing. I have not known the man to whose innate kindliness I would more confidently make an appeal.

Many characteristics—and those, too, which contribute not the least forcibly to impart resemblance in a sketch—must have vanished, or been obscured, before I met the General. All merely graceful attributes are usually the most evanescent; nor does nature adorn the human ruin with blossoms of new beauty, that have their roots and proper nutriment only in the chinks and crevices of decay, as she sows wall-flowers over the ruined fortress of Ticonderoga. Still, even in respect of grace and beauty, there were points well worth noting. A ray of humour, now and then, would make its way through the veil of dim obstruction, and glimmer pleasantly upon our faces. A trait of native elegance, seldom seen in the masculine character after childhood or early youth, was shown in the General's fondness for the sight and fragrance of flowers. An old soldier might be supposed to prize only the bloody laurel on his brow; but here was one who seemed to have a young girl's appreciation of the floral tribe.

There, beside the fireplace, the brave old General used to sit; while the Surveyor—though seldom, when it could be avoided, taking upon himself the difficult task of engaging him in conversation—was fond of standing at a distance, and watching his quiet and almost slumberous countenance. He seemed away from us, although we saw him but a few yards off; remote, though we passed close beside his chair; unattainable, though we might have stretched forth our hands and touched his own. It might be that he lived a more real life within his thoughts than amid the unappropriate environment of the Collector's office. The evolutions of the parade; the tumult of the battle; the flourish of old heroic music, heard thirty years before— such scenes and sounds, perhaps, were all alive before his intellectual sense. Meanwhile, the merchants and ship-masters, the spruce clerks and uncouth sailors, entered and departed; the bustle of his commercial and Custom-House life kept up its little murmur round about him; and neither with the men nor their affairs did the General appear to sustain the most distant relation. He was as much out of place as an old sword—now rusty, but which had flashed once in the battle's front, and showed still a bright gleam along its blade—would have been among the inkstands, paper-folders, and mahogany rulers on the Deputy Collector's desk.

There was one thing that much aided me in renewing and re-creating the stalwart soldier of the Niagara frontier—the man of true and simple energy. It was the recollection of those memorable words of his—"I'll try, Sir"—spoken on the very verge of a desperate and heroic enterprise, and breathing the soul and spirit of New England hardihood, comprehending all perils, and encountering all. If, in our country, valour were rewarded by heraldic honour, this phrase—which it seems so easy to speak, but which only he, with such a task of danger and glory before him, has ever spoken—would be the best and fittest of all mottoes for the General's shield of arms.

It contributes greatly towards a man's moral and intellectual health to be brought into habits of companionship with individuals unlike himself, who care little for his pursuits, and whose sphere and abilities he must go out of himself to appreciate. The accidents of my life have often afforded me this advantage, but never with more fulness and variety than during my continuance in office. There was one man, especially, the observation of whose character gave me a new idea of talent. His gifts were emphatically those of a man of business; prompt, acute, clear-minded; with an eye that saw through all perplexities, and a faculty of arrangement that made them vanish as by the waving of an enchanter's wand. Bred up from boyhood in the Custom-House, it was his proper field of activity; and the many intricacies of business, so harassing to the interloper, presented themselves before him with the regularity of a perfectly comprehended system. In my contemplation, he stood as the ideal of his class. He was, indeed, the Custom-House in himself; or, at all events, the mainspring that kept its variously revolving wheels in motion; for, in an institution like this, where its officers are appointed to subserve their own profit and convenience, and seldom with a leading reference to their fitness for the duty to be performed, they must perforce seek elsewhere the dexterity which is not in them. Thus, by an inevitable necessity, as a magnet attracts steel-filings, so did our man of business draw to himself the difficulties which everybody met with. With an easy condescension, and kind forbearance towards our stupidity—which, to his order of mind, must have seemed little short of crime—would he forth-with, by the merest touch of his finger, make the incomprehensible as clear as daylight. The merchants valued him not less than we, his esoteric friends. His integrity was perfect; it was a law of nature with him, rather than a choice or a principle; nor can it be otherwise than the main condition of an intellect so remarkably clear and accurate as his to be honest and regular in the administration of affairs. A stain on his conscience, as to anything that came within the range of his vocation, would trouble such a man very much in the same way, though to a far greater degree, than an error in the balance of an account, or an ink-blot on the fair page of a book of record. Here, in a word—and it is a rare instance in my life—I had met with a person thoroughly adapted to the situation which he held.

Such were some of the people with whom I now found myself connected. I took it in good part, at the hands of Providence, that I was thrown into a position so little akin to my past habits; and set myself seriously to gather from it whatever profit was to be had. After my fellowship of toil and impracticable schemes with the dreamy brethren of Brook Farm; after living for three years within the subtle influence of an intellect like Emerson's; after those wild, free days on the Assabeth, indulging fantastic speculations, beside our fire of fallen boughs, with Ellery Channing; after talking with Thoreau about pine-trees and Indian relics in his hermitage at Walden; after growing fastidious by sympathy with the classic refinement of Hillard's culture; after becoming imbued with poetic sentiment at Longfellow's hearthstone—it was time, at length, that I should exercise other faculties of my nature, and nourish myself with food for which I had hitherto had little appetite. Even the old Inspector was desirable, as a change of diet, to a man who had known Alcott. I looked upon it as an evidence, in some measure, of a system naturally well balanced, and lacking no essential part of a thorough organization, that, with such associates to remember, I could mingle at once with men of altogether different qualities, and never murmur at the change.

Literature, its exertions and objects, were now of little moment in my regard. I cared not at this period for books; they were apart from me. Nature—except it were human nature—the nature that is developed in earth and sky, was, in one sense, hidden from me; and all the imaginative delight wherewith it had been spiritualized passed away out of my mind. A gift, a faculty, if it had not been departed, was suspended and inanimate within me. There would have been something sad, unutterably dreary, in all this, had I not been conscious that it lay at my own option to recall whatever was valuable in the past. It might be true, indeed, that this was a life which could not, with impunity, be lived too long; else, it might make me permanently other than I had been, without transforming me into any shape which it would be worth my while to take. But I never considered it as other than a transitory life. There was always a prophetic instinct, a low whisper in my ear, that within no long period, and whenever a new change of custom should be essential to my good, change would come.

Meanwhile, there I was, a Surveyor of the Revenue and, so far as I have been able to understand, as good a Surveyor as need be. A man of thought, fancy, and sensibility (had he ten times the Surveyor's proportion of those qualities), may, at any time, be a man of affairs, if he will only choose to give himself the trouble. My fellow-officers, and the merchants and sea-captains with whom my official duties brought me into any manner of connection, viewed me in no other light, and probably knew me in no other character. None of them, I presume, had ever read a page of my inditing, or would have cared a fig the more for me if they had read them all; nor would it have mended the matter, in the least, had those same unprofitable pages been written with a pen like that of Burns or of Chaucer, each of whom was a Custom-House officer in his day, as well as I. It is a good lesson—though it may often be a hard one—for a man who has dreamed of literary fame, and of making for himself a rank among the world's dignitaries by such means, to step aside out of the narrow circle in which his claims are recognized and to find how utterly devoid of significance, beyond that circle, is all that he achieves, and all he aims at. I know not that I especially needed the lesson, either in the way of warning or rebuke; but at any rate, I learned it thoroughly: nor, it gives me pleasure to reflect, did the truth, as it came home to my perception, ever cost me a pang, or require to be thrown off in a sigh. In the way of literary talk, it is true, the Naval Officer—an excellent fellow, who came into the office with me, and went out only a little later—would often engage me in a discussion about one or the other of his favourite topics, Napoleon or Shakespeare. The Collector's junior clerk, too a young gentleman who, it was whispered occasionally covered a sheet of Uncle Sam's letter paper with what (at the distance of a few yards) looked very much like poetry—used now and then to speak to me of books, as matters with which I might possibly be conversant. This was my all of lettered intercourse; and it was quite sufficient for my necessities.

No longer seeking nor caring that my name should be blasoned abroad on title-pages, I smiled to think that it had now another kind of vogue. The Custom-House marker imprinted it, with a stencil and black paint, on pepper-bags, and baskets of anatto, and cigar-boxes, and bales of all kinds of dutiable merchandise, in testimony that these commodities had paid the impost, and gone regularly through the office. Borne on such queer vehicle of fame, a knowledge of my existence, so far as a name conveys it, was carried where it had never been before, and, I hope, will never go again.

But the past was not dead. Once in a great while, the thoughts that had seemed so vital and so active, yet had been put to rest so quietly, revived again. One of the most remarkable occasions, when the habit of bygone days awoke in me, was that which brings it within the law of literary propriety to offer the public the sketch which I am now writing.

In the second storey of the Custom-House there is a large room, in which the brick-work and naked rafters have never been covered with panelling and plaster. The edifice—originally projected on a scale adapted to the old commercial enterprise of the port, and with an idea of subsequent prosperity destined never to be realized—contains far more space than its occupants know what to do with. This airy hall, therefore, over the Collector's apartments, remains unfinished to this day, and, in spite of the aged cobwebs that festoon its dusky beams, appears still to await the labour of the carpenter and mason. At one end of the room, in a recess, were a number of barrels piled one upon another, containing bundles of official documents. Large quantities of similar rubbish lay lumbering the floor. It was sorrowful to think how many days, and weeks, and months, and years of toil had been wasted on these musty papers, which were now only an encumbrance on earth, and were hidden away in this forgotten corner, never more to be glanced at by human eyes. But then, what reams of other manuscripts—filled, not with the dulness of official formalities, but with the thought of inventive brains and the rich effusion of deep hearts—had gone equally to oblivion; and that, moreover, without serving a purpose in their day, as these heaped-up papers had, and—saddest of all—without purchasing for their writers the comfortable livelihood which the clerks of the Custom-House had gained by these worthless scratchings of the pen. Yet not altogether worthless, perhaps, as materials of local history. Here, no doubt, statistics of the former commerce of Salem might be discovered, and memorials of her princely merchants—old King Derby—old Billy Gray—old Simon Forrester—and many another magnate in his day, whose powdered head, however, was scarcely in the tomb before his mountain pile of wealth began to dwindle. The founders of the greater part of the families which now compose the aristocracy of Salem might here be traced, from the petty and obscure beginnings of their traffic, at periods generally much posterior to the Revolution, upward to what their children look upon as long-established rank.

Prior to the Revolution there is a dearth of records; the earlier documents and archives of the Custom-House having, probably, been carried off to Halifax, when all the king's officials accompanied the British army in its flight from Boston. It has often been a matter of regret with me; for, going back, perhaps, to the days of the Protectorate, those papers must have contained many references to forgotten or remembered men, and to antique customs, which would have affected me with the same pleasure as when I used to pick up Indian arrow-heads in the field near the Old Manse.

But, one idle and rainy day, it was my fortune to make a discovery of some little interest. Poking and burrowing into the heaped-up rubbish in the corner, unfolding one and another document, and reading the names of vessels that had long ago foundered at sea or rotted at the wharves, and those of merchants never heard of now on 'Change, nor very readily decipherable on their mossy tombstones; glancing at such matters with the saddened, weary, half-reluctant interest which we bestow on the corpse of dead activity—and exerting my fancy, sluggish with little use, to raise up from these dry bones an image of the old town's brighter aspect, when India was a new region, and only Salem knew the way thither—I chanced to lay my hand on a small package, carefully done up in a piece of ancient yellow parchment. This envelope had the air of an official record of some period long past, when clerks engrossed their stiff and formal chirography on more substantial materials than at present. There was something about it that quickened an instinctive curiosity, and made me undo the faded red tape that tied up the package, with the sense that a treasure would here be brought to light. Unbending the rigid folds of the parchment cover, I found it to be a commission, under the hand and seal of Governor Shirley, in favour of one Jonathan Pue, as Surveyor of His Majesty's Customs for the Port of Salem, in the Province of Massachusetts Bay. I remembered to have read (probably in Felt's "Annals") a notice of the decease of Mr. Surveyor Pue, about fourscore years ago; and likewise, in a newspaper of recent times, an account of the digging up of his remains in the little graveyard of St. Peter's Church, during the renewal of that edifice. Nothing, if I rightly call to mind, was left of my respected predecessor, save an imperfect skeleton, and some fragments of apparel, and a wig of majestic frizzle, which, unlike the head that it once adorned, was in very satisfactory preservation. But, on examining the papers which the parchment commission served to envelop, I found more traces of Mr. Pue's mental part, and the internal operations of his head, than the frizzled wig had contained of the venerable skull itself.

They were documents, in short, not official, but of a private nature, or, at least, written in his private capacity, and apparently with his own hand. I could account for their being included in the heap of Custom-House lumber only by the fact that Mr. Pue's death had happened suddenly, and that these papers, which he probably kept in his official desk, had never come to the knowledge of his heirs, or were supposed to relate to the business of the revenue. On the transfer of the archives to Halifax, this package, proving to be of no public concern, was left behind, and had remained ever since unopened.

The ancient Surveyor—being little molested, I suppose, at that early day with business pertaining to his office—seems to have devoted some of his many leisure hours to researches as a local antiquarian, and other inquisitions of a similar nature. These supplied material for petty activity to a mind that would otherwise have been eaten up with rust.

A portion of his facts, by-the-by, did me good service in the preparation of the article entitled "MAIN STREET," included in the present volume. The remainder may perhaps be applied to purposes equally valuable hereafter, or not impossibly may be worked up, so far as they go, into a regular history of Salem, should my veneration for the natal soil ever impel me to so pious a task. Meanwhile, they shall be at the command of any gentleman, inclined and competent, to take the unprofitable labour off my hands. As a final disposition I contemplate depositing them with the Essex Historical Society. But the object that most drew my attention to the mysterious package was a certain affair of fine red cloth, much worn and faded, There were traces about it of gold embroidery, which, however, was greatly frayed and defaced, so that none, or very little, of the glitter was left. It had been wrought, as was easy to perceive, with wonderful skill of needlework; and the stitch (as I am assured by ladies conversant with such mysteries) gives evidence of a now forgotten art, not to be discovered even by the process of picking out the threads. This rag of scarlet cloth—for time, and wear, and a sacrilegious moth had reduced it to little other than a rag—on careful examination, assumed the shape of a letter.

It was the capital letter A. By an accurate measurement, each limb proved to be precisely three inches and a quarter in length. It had been intended, there could be no doubt, as an ornamental article of dress; but how it was to be worn, or what rank, honour, and dignity, in by-past times, were signified by it, was a riddle which (so evanescent are the fashions of the world in these particulars) I saw little hope of solving. And yet it strangely interested me. My eyes fastened themselves upon the old scarlet letter, and would not be turned aside. Certainly there was some deep meaning in it most worthy of interpretation, and which, as it were, streamed forth from the mystic symbol, subtly communicating itself to my sensibilities, but evading the analysis of my mind.

When thus perplexed—and cogitating, among other hypotheses, whether the letter might not have been one of those decorations which the white men used to contrive in order to take the eyes of Indians—I happened to place it on my breast. It seemed to me—the reader may smile, but must not doubt my word—it seemed to me, then, that I experienced a sensation not altogether physical, yet almost so, as of burning heat, and as if the letter were not of red cloth, but red-hot iron. I shuddered, and involuntarily let it fall upon the floor.

In the absorbing contemplation of the scarlet letter, I had hitherto neglected to examine a small roll of dingy paper, around which it had been twisted. This I now opened, and had the satisfaction to find recorded by the old Surveyor's pen, a reasonably complete explanation of the whole affair. There were several foolscap sheets, containing many particulars respecting the life and conversation of one Hester Prynne, who appeared to have been rather a noteworthy personage in the view of our ancestors. She had flourished during the period between the early days of Massachusetts and the close of the seventeenth century. Aged persons, alive in the time of Mr. Surveyor Pue, and from whose oral testimony he had made up his narrative, remembered her, in their youth, as a very old, but not decrepit woman, of a stately and solemn aspect. It had been her habit, from an almost immemorial date, to go about the country as a kind of voluntary nurse, and doing whatever miscellaneous good she might; taking upon herself, likewise, to give advice in all matters, especially those of the heart, by which means—as a person of such propensities inevitably must—she gained from many people the reverence due to an angel, but, I should imagine, was looked upon by others as an intruder and a nuisance. Prying further into the manuscript, I found the record of other doings and sufferings of this singular woman, for most of which the reader is referred to the story entitled "THE SCARLET LETTER"; and it should be borne carefully in mind that the main facts of that story are authorized and authenticated by the document of Mr. Surveyor Pue. The original papers, together with the scarlet letter itself—a most curious relic—are still in my possession, and shall be freely exhibited to whomsoever, induced by the great interest of the narrative, may desire a sight of them. I must not be understood affirming that, in the dressing up of the tale, and imagining the motives and modes of passion that influenced the characters who figure in it, I have invariably confined myself within the limits of the old Surveyor's half-a-dozen sheets of foolscap. On the contrary, I have allowed myself, as to such points, nearly, or altogether, as much license as if the facts had been entirely of my own invention. What I contend for is the authenticity of the outline.

This incident recalled my mind, in some degree, to its old track. There seemed to be here the groundwork of a tale. It impressed me as if the ancient Surveyor, in his garb of a hundred years gone by, and wearing his immortal wig—which was buried with him, but did not perish in the grave—had met me in the deserted chamber of the Custom-House. In his port was the dignity of one who had borne His Majesty's commission, and who was therefore illuminated by a ray of the splendour that shone so dazzlingly about the throne. How unlike alas the hangdog look of a republican official, who, as the servant of the people, feels himself less than the least, and below the lowest of his masters. With his own ghostly hand, the obscurely seen, but majestic, figure had imparted to me the scarlet symbol and the little roll of explanatory manuscript. With his own ghostly voice he had exhorted me, on the sacred consideration of my filial duty and reverence towards him—who might reasonably regard himself as my official ancestor—to bring his mouldy and moth-eaten lucubrations before the public. "Do this," said the ghost of Mr. Surveyor Pue, emphatically nodding the head that looked so imposing within its memorable wig; "do this, and the profit shall be all your own. You will shortly need it; for it is not in your days as it was in mine, when a man's office was a life-lease, and oftentimes an heirloom. But I charge you, in this matter of old Mistress Prynne, give to your predecessor's memory the credit which will be rightfully due" And I said to the ghost of Mr. Surveyor Pue—"I will".

On Hester Prynne's story, therefore, I bestowed much thought. It was the subject of my meditations for many an hour, while pacing to and fro across my room, or traversing, with a hundredfold repetition, the long extent from the front door of the Custom-House to the side entrance, and back again. Great were the weariness and annoyance of the old Inspector and the Weighers and Gaugers, whose slumbers were disturbed by the unmercifully lengthened tramp of my passing and returning footsteps. Remembering their own former habits, they used to say that the Surveyor was walking the quarter-deck. They probably fancied that my sole object—and, indeed, the sole object for which a sane man could ever put himself into voluntary motion—was to get an appetite for dinner. And, to say the truth, an appetite, sharpened by the east wind that generally blew along the passage, was the only valuable result of so much indefatigable exercise. So little adapted is the atmosphere of a Custom-house to the delicate harvest of fancy and sensibility, that, had I remained there through ten Presidencies yet to come, I doubt whether the tale of "The Scarlet Letter" would ever have been brought before the public eye. My imagination was a tarnished mirror. It would not reflect, or only with miserable dimness, the figures with which I did my best to people it. The characters of the narrative would not be warmed and rendered malleable by any heat that I could kindle at my intellectual forge. They would take neither the glow of passion nor the tenderness of sentiment, but retained all the rigidity of dead corpses, and stared me in the face with a fixed and ghastly grin of contemptuous defiance. "What have you to do with us?" that expression seemed to say. "The little power you might have once possessed over the tribe of unrealities is gone! You have bartered it for a pittance of the public gold. Go then, and earn your wages!" In short, the almost torpid creatures of my own fancy twitted me with imbecility, and not without fair occasion.

It was not merely during the three hours and a half which Uncle Sam claimed as his share of my daily life that this wretched numbness held possession of me. It went with me on my sea-shore walks and rambles into the country, whenever—which was seldom and reluctantly—I bestirred myself to seek that invigorating charm of Nature which used to give me such freshness and activity of thought, the moment that I stepped across the threshold of the Old Manse. The same torpor, as regarded the capacity for intellectual effort, accompanied me home, and weighed upon me in the chamber which I most absurdly termed my study. Nor did it quit me when, late at night, I sat in the deserted parlour, lighted only by the glimmering coal-fire and the moon, striving to picture forth imaginary scenes, which, the next day, might flow out on the brightening page in many-hued description.

If the imaginative faculty refused to act at such an hour, it might well be deemed a hopeless case. Moonlight, in a familiar room, falling so white upon the carpet, and showing all its figures so distinctly—making every object so minutely visible, yet so unlike a morning or noontide visibility—is a medium the most suitable for a romance-writer to get acquainted with his illusive guests. There is the little domestic scenery of the well-known apartment; the chairs, with each its separate individuality; the centre-table, sustaining a work-basket, a volume or two, and an extinguished lamp; the sofa; the book-case; the picture on the wall—all these details, so completely seen, are so spiritualised by the unusual light, that they seem to lose their actual substance, and become things of intellect. Nothing is too small or too trifling to undergo this change, and acquire dignity thereby. A child's shoe; the doll, seated in her little wicker carriage; the hobby-horse—whatever, in a word, has been used or played with during the day is now invested with a quality of strangeness and remoteness, though still almost as vividly present as by daylight. Thus, therefore, the floor of our familiar room has become a neutral territory, somewhere between the real world and fairy-land, where the Actual and the Imaginary may meet, and each imbue itself with the nature of the other. Ghosts might enter here without affrighting us. It would be too much in keeping with the scene to excite surprise, were we to look about us and discover a form, beloved, but gone hence, now sitting quietly in a streak of this magic moonshine, with an aspect that would make us doubt whether it had returned from afar, or had never once stirred from our fireside.

The somewhat dim coal fire has an essential Influence in producing the effect which I would describe. It throws its unobtrusive tinge throughout the room, with a faint ruddiness upon the walls and ceiling, and a reflected gleam upon the polish of the furniture. This warmer light mingles itself with the cold spirituality of the moon-beams, and communicates, as it were, a heart and sensibilities of human tenderness to the forms which fancy summons up. It converts them from snow-images into men and women. Glancing at the looking-glass, we behold—deep within its haunted verge—the smouldering glow of the half-extinguished anthracite, the white moon-beams on the floor, and a repetition of all the gleam and shadow of the picture, with one remove further from the actual, and nearer to the imaginative. Then, at such an hour, and with this scene before him, if a man, sitting all alone, cannot dream strange things, and make them look like truth, he need never try to write romances.

But, for myself, during the whole of my Custom-House experience, moonlight and sunshine, and the glow of firelight, were just alike in my regard; and neither of them was of one whit more avail than the twinkle of a tallow-candle. An entire class of susceptibilities, and a gift connected with them—of no great richness or value, but the best I had—was gone from me.

It is my belief, however, that had I attempted a different order of composition, my faculties would not have been found so pointless and inefficacious. I might, for instance, have contented myself with writing out the narratives of a veteran shipmaster, one of the Inspectors, whom I should be most ungrateful not to mention, since scarcely a day passed that he did not stir me to laughter and admiration by his marvelous gifts as a story-teller. Could I have preserved the picturesque force of his style, and the humourous colouring which nature taught him how to throw over his descriptions, the result, I honestly believe, would have been something new in literature. Or I might readily have found a more serious task. It was a folly, with the materiality of this daily life pressing so intrusively upon me, to attempt to fling myself back into another age, or to insist on creating the semblance of a world out of airy matter, when, at every moment, the impalpable beauty of my soap-bubble was broken by the rude contact of some actual circumstance. The wiser effort would have been to diffuse thought and imagination through the opaque substance of to-day, and thus to make it a bright transparency; to spiritualise the burden that began to weigh so heavily; to seek, resolutely, the true and indestructible value that lay hidden in the petty and wearisome incidents, and ordinary characters with which I was now conversant. The fault was mine. The page of life that was spread out before me seemed dull and commonplace only because I had not fathomed its deeper import. A better book than I shall ever write was there; leaf after leaf presenting itself to me, just as it was written out by the reality of the flitting hour, and vanishing as fast as written, only because my brain wanted the insight, and my hand the cunning, to transcribe it. At some future day, it may be, I shall remember a few scattered fragments and broken paragraphs, and write them down, and find the letters turn to gold upon the page.

These perceptions had come too late. At the Instant, I was only conscious that what would have been a pleasure once was now a hopeless toil. There was no occasion to make much moan about this state of affairs. I had ceased to be a writer of tolerably poor tales and essays, and had become a tolerably good Surveyor of the Customs. That was all. But, nevertheless, it is anything but agreeable to be haunted by a suspicion that one's intellect is dwindling away, or exhaling, without your consciousness, like ether out of a phial; so that, at every glance, you find a smaller and less volatile residuum. Of the fact there could be no doubt and, examining myself and others, I was led to conclusions, in reference to the effect of public office on the character, not very favourable to the mode of life in question. In some other form, perhaps, I may hereafter develop these effects. Suffice it here to say that a Custom-House officer of long continuance can hardly be a very praiseworthy or respectable personage, for many reasons; one of them, the tenure by which he holds his situation, and another, the very nature of his business, which—though, I trust, an honest one—is of such a sort that he does not share in the united effort of mankind.

An effect—which I believe to be observable, more or less, in every individual who has occupied the position—is, that while he leans on the mighty arm of the Republic, his own proper strength departs from him. He loses, in an extent proportioned to the weakness or force of his original nature, the capability of self-support. If he possesses an unusual share of native energy, or the enervating magic of place do not operate too long upon him, his forfeited powers may be redeemable. The ejected officer—fortunate in the unkindly shove that sends him forth betimes, to struggle amid a struggling world—may return to himself, and become all that he has ever been. But this seldom happens. He usually keeps his ground just long enough for his own ruin, and is then thrust out, with sinews all unstrung, to totter along the difficult footpath of life as he best may. Conscious of his own infirmity—that his tempered steel and elasticity are lost—he for ever afterwards looks wistfully about him in quest of support external to himself. His pervading and continual hope—a hallucination, which, in the face of all discouragement, and making light of impossibilities, haunts him while he lives, and, I fancy, like the convulsive throes of the cholera, torments him for a brief space after death—is, that finally, and in no long time, by some happy coincidence of circumstances, he shall be restored to office. This faith, more than anything else, steals the pith and availability out of whatever enterprise he may dream of undertaking. Why should he toil and moil, and be at so much trouble to pick himself up out of the mud, when, in a little while hence, the strong arm of his Uncle will raise and support him? Why should he work for his living here, or go to dig gold in California, when he is so soon to be made happy, at monthly intervals, with a little pile of glittering coin out of his Uncle's pocket? It is sadly curious to observe how slight a taste of office suffices to infect a poor fellow with this singular disease. Uncle Sam's gold—meaning no disrespect to the worthy old gentleman—has, in this respect, a quality of enchantment like that of the devil's wages. Whoever touches it should look well to himself, or he may find the bargain to go hard against him, involving, if not his soul, yet many of its better attributes; its sturdy force, its courage and constancy, its truth, its self-reliance, and all that gives the emphasis to manly character.

Here was a fine prospect in the distance. Not that the Surveyor brought the lesson home to himself, or admitted that he could be so utterly undone, either by continuance in office or ejectment. Yet my reflections were not the most comfortable. I began to grow melancholy and restless; continually prying into my mind, to discover which of its poor properties were gone, and what degree of detriment had already accrued to the remainder. I endeavoured to calculate how much longer I could stay in the Custom-House, and yet go forth a man. To confess the truth, it was my greatest apprehension—as it would never be a measure of policy to turn out so quiet an individual as myself; and it being hardly in the nature of a public officer to resign—it was my chief trouble, therefore, that I was likely to grow grey and decrepit in the Surveyorship, and become much such another animal as the old Inspector. Might it not, in the tedious lapse of official life that lay before me, finally be with me as it was with this venerable friend—to make the dinner-hour the nucleus of the day, and to spend the rest of it, as an old dog spends it, asleep in the sunshine or in the shade? A dreary look-forward, this, for a man who felt it to be the best definition of happiness to live throughout the whole range of his faculties and sensibilities. But, all this while, I was giving myself very unnecessary alarm. Providence had meditated better things for me than I could possibly imagine for myself.

A remarkable event of the third year of my Surveyorship—to adopt the tone of "P. P."—was the election of General Taylor to the Presidency. It is essential, in order to form a complete estimate of the advantages of official life, to view the incumbent at the in-coming of a hostile administration. His position is then one of the most singularly irksome, and, in every contingency, disagreeable, that a wretched mortal can possibly occupy; with seldom an alternative of good on either hand, although what presents itself to him as the worst event may very probably be the best. But it is a strange experience, to a man of pride and sensibility, to know that his interests are within the control of individuals who neither love nor understand him, and by whom, since one or the other must needs happen, he would rather be injured than obliged. Strange, too, for one who has kept his calmness throughout the contest, to observe the bloodthirstiness that is developed in the hour of triumph, and to be conscious that he is himself among its objects! There are few uglier traits of human nature than this tendency—which I now witnessed in men no worse than their neighbours—to grow cruel, merely because they possessed the power of inflicting harm. If the guillotine, as applied to office-holders, were a literal fact, instead of one of the most apt of metaphors, it is my sincere belief that the active members of the victorious party were sufficiently excited to have chopped off all our heads, and have thanked Heaven for the opportunity! It appears to me—who have been a calm and curious observer, as well in victory as defeat—that this fierce and bitter spirit of malice and revenge has never distinguished the many triumphs of my own party as it now did that of the Whigs. The Democrats take the offices, as a general rule, because they need them, and because the practice of many years has made it the law of political warfare, which unless a different system be proclaimed, it was weakness and cowardice to murmur at. But the long habit of victory has made them generous. They know how to spare when they see occasion; and when they strike, the axe may be sharp indeed, but its edge is seldom poisoned with ill-will; nor is it their custom ignominiously to kick the head which they have just struck off.

In short, unpleasant as was my predicament, at best, I saw much reason to congratulate myself that I was on the losing side rather than the triumphant one. If, heretofore, I had been none of the warmest of partisans I began now, at this season of peril and adversity, to be pretty acutely sensible with which party my predilections lay; nor was it without something like regret and shame that, according to a reasonable calculation of chances, I saw my own prospect of retaining office to be better than those of my democratic brethren. But who can see an inch into futurity beyond his nose? My own head was the first that fell.

The moment when a man's head drops off is seldom or never, I am inclined to think, precisely the most agreeable of his life. Nevertheless, like the greater part of our misfortunes, even so serious a contingency brings its remedy and consolation with it, if the sufferer will but make the best rather than the worst, of the accident which has befallen him. In my particular case the consolatory topics were close at hand, and, indeed, had suggested themselves to my meditations a considerable time before it was requisite to use them. In view of my previous weariness of office, and vague thoughts of resignation, my fortune somewhat resembled that of a person who should entertain an idea of committing suicide, and although beyond his hopes, meet with the good hap to be murdered. In the Custom-House, as before in the Old Manse, I had spent three years—a term long enough to rest a weary brain: long enough to break off old intellectual habits, and make room for new ones: long enough, and too long, to have lived in an unnatural state, doing what was really of no advantage nor delight to any human being, and withholding myself from toil that would, at least, have stilled an unquiet impulse in me. Then, moreover, as regarded his unceremonious ejectment, the late Surveyor was not altogether ill-pleased to be recognised by the Whigs as an enemy; since his inactivity in political affairs—his tendency to roam, at will, in that broad and quiet field where all mankind may meet, rather than confine himself to those narrow paths where brethren of the same household must diverge from one another—had sometimes made it questionable with his brother Democrats whether he was a friend. Now, after he had won the crown of martyrdom (though with no longer a head to wear it on), the point might be looked upon as settled. Finally, little heroic as he was, it seemed more decorous to be overthrown in the downfall of the party with which he had been content to stand than to remain a forlorn survivor, when so many worthier men were falling: and at last, after subsisting for four years on the mercy of a hostile administration, to be compelled then to define his position anew, and claim the yet more humiliating mercy of a friendly one.

Meanwhile, the press had taken up my affair, and kept me for a week or two careering through the public prints, in my decapitated state, like Irving's Headless Horseman, ghastly and grim, and longing to be buried, as a political dead man ought. So much for my figurative self. The real human being all this time, with his head safely on his shoulders, had brought himself to the comfortable conclusion that everything was for the best; and making an investment in ink, paper, and steel pens, had opened his long-disused writing desk, and was again a literary man.

Now it was that the lucubrations of my ancient predecessor, Mr. Surveyor Pue, came into play. Rusty through long idleness, some little space was requisite before my intellectual machinery could be brought to work upon the tale with an effect in any degree satisfactory. Even yet, though my thoughts were ultimately much absorbed in the task, it wears, to my eye, a stern and sombre aspect: too much ungladdened by genial sunshine; too little relieved by the tender and familiar influences which soften almost every scene of nature and real life, and undoubtedly should soften every picture of them. This uncaptivating effect is perhaps due to the period of hardly accomplished revolution, and still seething turmoil, in which the story shaped itself. It is no indication, however, of a lack of cheerfulness in the writer's mind: for he was happier while straying through the gloom of these sunless fantasies than at any time since he had quitted the Old Manse. Some of the briefer articles, which contribute to make up the volume, have likewise been written since my involuntary withdrawal from the toils and honours of public life, and the remainder are gleaned from annuals and magazines, of such antique date, that they have gone round the circle, and come back to novelty again. Keeping up the metaphor of the political guillotine, the whole may be considered as the POSTHUMOUS PAPERS OF A DECAPITATED SURVEYOR: and the sketch which I am now bringing to a close, if too autobiographical for a modest person to publish in his lifetime, will readily be excused in a gentleman who writes from beyond the grave. Peace be with all the world! My blessing on my friends! My forgiveness to my enemies! For I am in the realm of quiet!

The life of the Custom-House lies like a dream behind me. The old Inspector—who, by-the-bye, I regret to say, was overthrown and killed by a horse some time ago, else he would certainly have lived for ever—he, and all those other venerable personages who sat with him at the receipt of custom, are but shadows in my view: white-headed and wrinkled images, which my fancy used to sport with, and has now flung aside for ever. The merchants—Pingree, Phillips, Shepard, Upton, Kimball, Bertram, Hunt—these and many other names, which had such classic familiarity for my ear six months ago,—these men of traffic, who seemed to occupy so important a position in the world—how little time has it required to disconnect me from them all, not merely in act, but recollection! It is with an effort that I recall the figures and appellations of these few. Soon, likewise, my old native town will loom upon me through the haze of memory, a mist brooding over and around it; as if it were no portion of the real earth, but an overgrown village in cloud-land, with only imaginary inhabitants to people its wooden houses and walk its homely lanes, and the unpicturesque prolixity of its main street. Henceforth it ceases to be a reality of my life; I am a citizen of somewhere else. My good townspeople will not much regret me, for—though it has been as dear an object as any, in my literary efforts, to be of some importance in their eyes, and to win myself a pleasant memory in this abode and burial-place of so many of my forefathers—there has never been, for me, the genial atmosphere which a literary man requires in order to ripen the best harvest of his mind. I shall do better amongst other faces; and these familiar ones, it need hardly be said, will do just as well without me.

It may be, however—oh, transporting and triumphant thought—that the great-grandchildren of the present race may sometimes think kindly of the scribbler of bygone days, when the antiquary of days to come, among the sites memorable in the town's history, shall point out the locality of THE TOWN PUMP.

❦ I ❦

IN THE PRISON DOOR

A THRONG OF BEARDED MEN, in sad-coloured garments and grey steeple-crowned hats, inter-mixed with women, some wearing hoods, and others bareheaded, was assembled in front of a wooden edifice, the door of which was heavily timbered with oak, and studded with iron spikes.

The founders of a new colony, whatever Utopia of human virtue and happiness they might originally project, have invariably recognised it among their earliest practical necessities to allot a portion of the virgin soil as a cemetery, and another portion as the site of a prison. In accordance with this rule it may safely be assumed that the forefathers of Boston had built the first prison-house somewhere in the Vicinity of Cornhill, almost as seasonally as they marked out the first burial-ground, on Isaac Johnson's lot, and round about his grave, which subsequently became the nucleus of all the congregated sepulchres in the old churchyard of King's Chapel. Certain it is that, some fifteen or twenty years after the settlement of the town, the wooden jail was already marked with weather-stains and other indications of age, which gave a yet darker aspect to its beetle-browed and gloomy front. The rust on the ponderous iron-work of its oaken door looked more antique than anything else in the New World. Like all that pertains to crime, it seemed never to have known a youthful era. Before this ugly edifice, and between it and the wheel-track of the street, was a grass-plot, much overgrown with burdock, pig-weed, apple-pern, and such unsightly vegetation, which evidently found something congenial in the soil that had so early borne the black flower of civilised society, a prison. But on one side of the portal, and rooted almost at the threshold, was a wild rose-bush, covered, in this month of June, with its delicate gems, which might be imagined to offer their fragrance and fragile beauty to the prisoner as he went in, and to the condemned criminal as he came forth to his doom, in token that the deep heart of Nature could pity and be kind to him.

This rose-bush, by a strange chance, has been kept alive in history; but whether it had merely survived out of the stern old wilderness, so long after the fall of the gigantic pines and oaks that originally overshadowed it, or whether, as there is fair authority for believing, it had sprung up under the footsteps of the sainted Ann Hutchinson as she entered the prison-door,

264

we shall not take upon us to determine. Finding it so directly on the threshold of our narrative, which is now about to issue from that inauspicious portal, we could hardly do otherwise than pluck one of its flowers, and present it to the reader. It may serve, let us hope, to symbolise some sweet moral blossom that may be found along the track, or relieve the darkening close of a tale of human frailty and sorrow.

❦ 2 ❦

THE MARKET-PLACE

THE GRASS-PLOT BEFORE THE JAIL, in Prison Lane, on a certain summer morning, not less than two centuries ago, was occupied by a pretty large number of the inhabitants of Boston, all with their eyes intently fastened on the iron-clamped oaken door. Amongst any other population, or at a later period in the history of New England, the grim rigidity that petrified the bearded physiognomies of these good people would have augured some awful business in hand. It could have betokened nothing short of the anticipated execution of some noted culprit, on whom the sentence of a legal tribunal had but confirmed the verdict of public sentiment. But, in that early severity of the Puritan character, an inference of this kind could not so indubitably be drawn. It might be that a sluggish bond-servant, or an undutiful child, whom his parents had given over to the civil authority, was to be corrected at the whipping-post. It might be that an Antinomian, a Quaker, or other heterodox religionist, was to be scourged out of the town, or an idle or vagrant Indian, whom the white man's firewater had made riotous about the streets, was to be driven with stripes into the shadow of the forest. It might be, too, that a witch, like old Mistress Hibbins, the bitter-tempered widow of the magistrate, was to die upon the gallows. In either case, there was very much the same solemnity of demeanour on the part of the spectators, as befitted a people among whom religion and law were almost identical, and in whose character both were so thoroughly interfused, that the mildest and severest acts of public discipline were alike made venerable and awful. Meagre, indeed, and cold, was the sympathy that a transgressor might look for, from such bystanders, at the scaffold. On the other hand, a penalty which, in our days, would infer a degree of mocking infamy and ridicule, might then be invested with almost as stern a dignity as the punishment of death itself.

It was a circumstance to be noted on the summer morning when our story begins its course, that the women, of whom there were several in the crowd, appeared to take a peculiar interest in whatever penal infliction might be expected to ensue. The age had not so much refinement, that any sense of impropriety restrained the wearers of petticoat and farthingale from stepping forth into the public ways, and wedging their not unsubstantial persons, if occasion were, into the throng nearest to the scaffold at an execution. Morally, as well as materially, there was a coarser fibre in those wives and maidens of old English birth and breeding than in their fair descendants, separated from them by a series of six or seven generations; for, throughout that chain of ancestry, every successive mother had transmitted to her child a fainter bloom, a more delicate and briefer beauty, and a slighter physical frame, if not character of less force and solidity than her own. The women who were now standing about the prison-door stood within less than half a century of the period when the man-like Elizabeth had been the not altogether unsuitable representative of the sex. They were her countrywomen: and the beef and ale of their native land, with a moral diet not a whit more refined, entered largely into their composition. The bright morning sun, therefore, shone on broad shoulders and well-developed busts, and on round and ruddy cheeks, that had ripened in the far-off island, and had hardly yet grown paler or thinner in the atmosphere of New England. There was, moreover, a boldness and rotundity of speech among these matrons, as most of them seemed to be, that would startle us at the present day, whether in respect to its purport or its volume of tone.

"Goodwives," said a hard-featured dame of fifty, "I'll tell ye a piece of my mind. It would be greatly for the public behoof if we women, being of mature age and church-members in good repute, should have the handling of such malefactresses as this Hester Prynne. What think ye, gossips? If the hussy stood up for judgment before us five, that are now here in a knot together, would she come off with such a sentence as the worshipful magistrates have awarded? Marry, I trow not."

"People say," said another, "that the Reverend Master Dimmesdale, her godly pastor, takes it very grievously to heart that such a scandal should have come upon his congregation."

"The magistrates are God-fearing gentlemen, but merciful overmuch—that is a truth," added a third autumnal matron. "At the very least, they should have put the brand of a hot iron on Hester Prynne's forehead. Madame Hester would have winced at that, I warrant me. But she —the naughty baggage—little will she care what they put upon the bodice of her gown! Why, look you, she may cover it with a brooch, or such like heathenish adornment, and so walk the streets as brave as ever!"

"Ah, but," interposed, more softly, a young wife, holding a child by the hand, "let her cover the mark as she will, the pang of it will be always in her heart."

"What do we talk of marks and brands, whether on the bodice of her gown or the flesh of her forehead?" cried another female, the ugliest as well as the most pitiless of these self-constituted judges. "This woman has brought shame upon us all, and ought to die; is there not law for it? Truly there is, both in the Scripture and the statute-book. Then let the magistrates, who have made it of no effect, thank themselves if their own wives and daughters go astray."

"Mercy on us, goodwife!" exclaimed a man in the crowd, "is there no virtue in woman, save what springs from a wholesome fear of the gallows? That is the hardest word yet! Hush now, gossips for the lock is turning in the prison-door, and here comes Mistress Prynne herself."

The door of the jail being flung open from within there appeared, in the first place, like a black shadow emerging into sunshine, the grim and grisly presence of the town-beadle, with a sword by his side, and his staff of office in his hand. This personage prefigured and represented in his aspect the whole dismal severity of the Puritanic code of law, which it was his business to administer in its final and closest application to the offender. Stretching forth the official staff in his left hand, he laid his right upon the shoulder of a young woman, whom he thus drew forward, until, on the threshold of the prison-door, she repelled him, by an action marked with natural dignity and force of character, and stepped into the open air as if by her own free will. She bore in her arms a child, a baby of some three months old, who winked and turned aside its little face from the too vivid light of day; because its existence, heretofore, had brought it acquaintance only with the grey twilight of a dungeon, or other darksome apartment of the prison.

When the young woman—the mother of this child—stood fully revealed before the crowd, it seemed to be her first impulse to clasp the infant closely to her bosom; not so much by an impulse of motherly affection, as that she might thereby conceal a certain token, which was wrought or fastened into her dress. In a moment, however, wisely judging that one token of her shame would but poorly serve to hide another, she took the baby on her arm, and with a burning blush, and yet a haughty smile, and a glance that would not be abashed, looked around at her townspeople and neighbours. On the breast of her gown, in fine red cloth, surrounded with an elaborate embroidery and fantastic flourishes of gold thread, appeared the letter A. It was so artistically done, and with so much fertility and gorgeous luxuriance of fancy, that it had all the effect of a last and fitting decoration to the apparel which she wore, and which was of a splendour in accordance with the taste of the age, but greatly beyond what was allowed by the sumptuary regulations of the colony.

The young woman was tall, with a figure of perfect elegance on a large scale. She had dark and abundant hair, so glossy that it threw off the sunshine with a gleam; and a face which, besides being beautiful from regularity of feature and richness of complexion, had the impressiveness belonging to a marked brow and deep black eyes. She was ladylike, too, after the manner of the feminine gentility of those days; characterised by a certain state and dignity, rather than by the delicate, evanescent, and indescribable grace which is now recognised as its indication. And never had Hester Prynne appeared more ladylike, in the antique interpretation of the term, than as she issued from the prison. Those who had before known her, and had expected to behold her dimmed and obscured by a disastrous cloud, were astonished, and even startled, to perceive how her beauty shone out, and made a halo of the misfortune and ignominy in which she was enveloped. It may be true that, to a sensitive observer, there was some thing exquisitely painful in it. Her attire, which indeed, she had wrought for the occasion in prison, and had modelled much after her own fancy, seemed to express the attitude of her spirit, the desperate recklessness of her mood, by its wild and picturesque peculiarity. But the point which drew all eyes, and, as it were, transfigured the wearer—so that both men and women who had been familiarly acquainted with Hester Prynne were now impressed as if they beheld her for the first time—was that SCARLET LETTER, so fantastically embroidered and illuminated upon her bosom. It had the effect of a spell, taking her out of the ordinary relations with humanity, and enclosing her in a sphere by herself.

"She hath good skill at her needle, that's certain," remarked one of her female spectators; "but did ever a woman, before this brazen hussy, contrive such a way of showing it? Why, gossips, what is it but to laugh in the faces of our godly magistrates, and make a pride out of what they, worthy gentlemen, meant for a punishment?"

"It were well," muttered the most iron-visaged of the old dames, "if we stripped Madame Hester's rich gown off her dainty shoulders; and as for the red letter which she hath stitched so curiously, I'll bestow a rag of mine own rheumatic flannel to make a fitter one!"

"Oh, peace, neighbours—peace!" whispered their youngest companion; "do not let her hear you! Not a stitch in that embroidered letter but she has felt it in her heart."

The grim beadle now made a gesture with his staff. "Make way, good people—make way, in the King's name!" cried he. "Open a passage; and I promise ye, Mistress Prynne shall be set where man, woman, and child may have a fair sight of her brave apparel from this time till an hour past meridian. A blessing on the righteous colony of the Massachusetts, where iniquity is dragged out into the sunshine! Come along, Madame Hester, and show your scarlet letter in the market-place!"

A lane was forthwith opened through the crowd of spectators. Preceded by the beadle, and attended by an irregular procession of stern-browed men and unkindly visaged women, Hester

Prynne set forth towards the place appointed for her punishment. A crowd of eager and curious schoolboys, understanding little of the matter in hand, except that it gave them a half-holiday, ran before her progress, turning their heads continually to stare into her face and at the winking baby in her arms, and at the ignominious letter on her breast. It was no great distance, in those days, from the prison door to the market-place. Measured by the prisoner's experience, however, it might be reckoned a journey of some length; for haughty as her demeanour was, she perchance underwent an agony from every footstep of those that thronged to see her, as if her heart had been flung into the street for them all to spurn and trample upon. In our nature, however, there is a provision, alike marvellous and merciful, that the sufferer should never know the intensity of what he endures by its present torture, but chiefly by the pang that rankles after it. With almost a serene deportment, therefore, Hester Prynne passed through this portion of her ordeal, and came to a sort of scaffold, at the western extremity of the market-place. It stood nearly beneath the eaves of Boston's earliest church, and appeared to be a fixture there.

In fact, this scaffold constituted a portion of a penal machine, which now, for two or three generations past, has been merely historical and traditionary among us, but was held, in the old time, to be as effectual an agent, in the promotion of good citizenship, as ever was the guillotine among the terrorists of France. It was, in short, the platform of the pillory; and above it rose the framework of that instrument of discipline, so fashioned as to confine the human head in its tight grasp, and thus hold it up to the public gaze. The very ideal of ignominy was embodied and made manifest in this contrivance of wood and iron. There can be no outrage, methinks, against our common nature—whatever be the delinquencies of the individual—no outrage more flagrant than to forbid the culprit to hide his face for shame; as it was the essence of this punishment to do. In Hester Prynne's instance, however, as not unfrequently in other cases, her sentence bore that she should stand a certain time upon the platform, but without undergoing that gripe about the neck and confinement of the head, the proneness to which was the most devilish characteristic of this ugly engine. Knowing well her part, she ascended a flight of wooden steps, and was thus displayed to the surrounding multitude, at about the height of a man's shoulders above the street.

Had there been a Papist among the crowd of Puritans, he might have seen in this beautiful woman, so picturesque in her attire and mien, and with the infant at her bosom, an object to remind him of the image of Divine Maternity, which so many illustrious painters have vied with one another to represent; something which should remind him, indeed, but only by contrast, of that sacred image of sinless motherhood, whose infant was to redeem the world. Here, there was the taint of deepest sin in the most sacred quality of human life, working such effect, that the world was only the darker for this woman's beauty, and the more lost for the infant that she had borne.

The scene was not without a mixture of awe, such as must always invest the spectacle of guilt and shame in a fellow-creature, before society shall have grown corrupt enough to smile, instead of shuddering at it. The witnesses of Hester Prynne's disgrace had not yet passed beyond their simplicity. They were stern enough to look upon her death, had that been the sentence, without a murmur at its severity, but had none of the heartlessness of another social state, which would find only a theme for jest in an exhibition like the present. Even had there been a disposition to turn the matter into ridicule, it must have been repressed and overpowered by the solemn presence of men no less dignified than the governor, and several of his counsellors, a judge, a general, and the ministers of the town, all of whom sat or stood in a balcony of the meeting-house, looking down upon the platform. When such personages could constitute a part of the spectacle, without risking the majesty, or reverence of rank and office, it was safely to be inferred that the infliction of a legal sentence would have an earnest and effectual meaning. Accordingly, the crowd was sombre and grave. The unhappy culprit sustained herself as best a woman might, under the heavy weight of a thousand unrelenting eyes, all fastened upon her, and concentrated at her bosom. It was almost intolerable to be borne. Of an impulsive and passionate nature, she had fortified herself to encounter the stings and venomous stabs of public contumely, wreaking itself in every variety of insult; but there was a quality so much more terrible in the solemn mood of the popular mind, that she longed rather to behold all those rigid countenances contorted with scornful merriment, and herself the object. Had a roar of laughter burst from the multitude—each man, each woman, each little shrill-voiced child, contributing their individual parts—Hester Prynne might have repaid them all with a bitter and disdainful smile. But, under the leaden infliction which it was her doom to endure, she felt, at moments, as if she must needs shriek out with the full power of her lungs, and cast herself from the scaffold down upon the ground, or else go mad at once.

Yet there were intervals when the whole scene, in which she was the most conspicuous object, seemed to vanish from her eyes, or, at least, glimmered indistinctly before them, like a mass of imperfectly shaped and spectral images. Her mind, and especially her memory, was preternaturally active, and kept bringing up other scenes than this roughly hewn street of a little town, on the edge of the western wilderness: other faces than were lowering upon her from beneath the brims of those steeple-crowned hats. Reminiscences, the most trifling and immaterial, passages of infancy and school-days, sports, childish quarrels, and the little domestic traits of her maiden years, came swarming back upon her, intermingled with recollections of whatever was gravest in her subsequent life; one picture precisely as vivid as another; as if all were of similar importance, or all alike a play. Possibly, it was an instinctive device of her spirit to relieve itself by the exhibition of these phantasmagoric forms, from the cruel weight and hardness of the reality.

Be that as it might, the scaffold of the pillory was a point of view that revealed to Hester Prynne the entire track along which she had been treading, since her happy infancy. Standing on that miserable eminence, she saw again her native village, in Old England, and her paternal home: a decayed house of grey stone, with a poverty-stricken aspect, but retaining a half obliterated shield of arms over the portal, in token of antique gentility. She saw her father's face, with its bold brow, and reverend white beard that flowed over the old-fashioned Elizabethan ruff; her mother's, too, with the look of heedful and anxious love which it always wore in her remembrance, and which, even since her death, had so often laid the impediment of a gentle remonstrance in her daughter's pathway. She saw her own face, glowing with girlish beauty, and illuminating all the interior of the dusky mirror in which she had been wont to gaze at it. There she beheld another countenance, of a man well stricken in years, a pale, thin, scholar-like visage, with eyes dim and bleared by the lamp-light that had served them to pore over many ponderous books. Yet those same bleared optics had a strange, penetrating power, when it was their owner's purpose to read the human soul. This figure of the study and the cloister, as Hester Prynne's womanly fancy failed not to recall, was slightly deformed, with the left shoulder a trifle higher than the right. Next rose before her in memory's picture-gallery, the intricate and narrow thoroughfares, the tall, grey houses, the huge cathedrals, and the public edifices, ancient in date and quaint in architecture, of a continental city; where new life had awaited her, still in connexion with the misshapen scholar: a new life, but feeding itself on time-worn materials, like a tuft of green moss on a crumbling wall. Lastly, in lieu of these shifting scenes, came back the rude market-place of the Puritan settlement, with all the townspeople assembled, and levelling their stern regards at Hester Prynne—yes, at herself—who stood on the scaffold of the pillory, an infant on her arm, and the letter A, in scarlet, fantastically embroidered with gold thread, upon her bosom.

Could it be true? She clutched the child so fiercely to her breast that it sent forth a cry; she turned her eyes downward at the scarlet letter, and even touched it with her finger, to assure herself that the infant and the shame were real. Yes these were her realities—all else had vanished!

✨ 3 ✨

THE RECOGNITION

FROM THIS INTENSE consciousness of being the object of severe and universal observation, the wearer of the scarlet letter was at length relieved, by discerning, on the outskirts of the crowd, a figure which irresistibly took possession of her thoughts. An Indian in his native garb was standing there; but the red men were not so infrequent visitors of the English settlements that one of them would have attracted any notice from Hester Prynne at such a time; much less would he have excluded all other objects and ideas from her mind. By the Indian's side, and evidently sustaining a companionship with him, stood a white man, clad in a strange disarray of civilized and savage costume.

He was small in stature, with a furrowed visage, which as yet could hardly be termed aged. There was a remarkable intelligence in his features, as of a person who had so cultivated his mental part that it could not fail to mould the physical to itself and become manifest by unmistakable tokens. Although, by a seemingly careless arrangement of his heterogeneous garb, he had endeavoured to conceal or abate the peculiarity, it was sufficiently evident to Hester Prynne that one of this man's shoulders rose higher than the other. Again, at the first instant of perceiving that thin visage, and the slight deformity of the figure, she pressed her infant to her bosom with so convulsive a force that the poor babe uttered another cry of pain. But the mother did not seem to hear it.

At his arrival in the market-place, and some time before she saw him, the stranger had bent his eyes on Hester Prynne. It was carelessly at first, like a man chiefly accustomed to look inward, and to whom external matters are of little value and import, unless they bear relation to something within his mind. Very soon, however, his look became keen and penetrative. A writhing horror twisted itself across his features, like a snake gliding swiftly over them, and making one little pause, with all its wreathed intervolutions in open sight. His face darkened with some powerful emotion, which, nevertheless, he so instantaneously controlled by an effort of his will, that, save at a single moment, its expression might have passed for calmness. After a brief space, the convulsion grew almost imperceptible, and finally subsided into the depths of his nature. When he found the eyes of Hester Prynne fastened on his own, and saw that she appeared to recognize him, he slowly and calmly raised his finger, made a gesture with it in the air, and laid it on his lips.

Then touching the shoulder of a townsman who stood near to him, he addressed him in a formal and courteous manner:

"I pray you, good Sir," said he, "who is this woman?—and wherefore is she here set up to public shame?"

"You must needs be a stranger in this region, friend," answered the townsman, looking curiously at the questioner and his savage companion, "else you would surely have heard of Mistress Hester Prynne and her evil doings. She hath raised a great scandal, I promise you, in godly Master Dimmesdale's church."

"You say truly," replied the other; "I am a stranger, and have been a wanderer, sorely against my will. I have met with grievous mishaps by sea and land, and have been long held in bonds among the heathen-folk to the southward; and am now brought hither by this Indian to be redeemed out of my captivity. Will it please you, therefore, to tell me of Hester Prynne's— have I her name rightly?—of this woman's offences, and what has brought her to yonder scaffold?"

"Truly, friend; and methinks it must gladden your heart, after your troubles and sojourn in the wilderness," said the townsman, "to find yourself at length in a land where iniquity is searched out and punished in the sight of rulers and people, as here in our godly New England. Yonder woman, Sir, you must know, was the wife of a certain learned man, English by birth, but who had long ago dwelt in Amsterdam, whence some good time agone he was minded to cross over and cast in his lot with us of the Massachusetts. To this purpose he sent his wife before him, remaining himself to look after some necessary affairs. Marry, good Sir, in some two years, or less, that the woman has been a dweller here in Boston, no tidings have come of this learned gentleman, Master Prynne; and his young wife, look you, being left to her own misguidance—"

"Ah!—aha!—I conceive you," said the stranger with a bitter smile. "So learned a man as you speak of should have learned this too in his books. And who, by your favour, Sir, may be the father of yonder babe—it is some three or four months old, I should judge—which Mistress Prynne is holding in her arms?"

"Of a truth, friend, that matter remaineth a riddle; and the Daniel who shall expound it is yet a-wanting," answered the townsman. "Madame Hester absolutely refuseth to speak, and the magistrates have laid their heads together in vain. Peradventure the guilty one stands looking on at this sad spectacle, unknown of man, and forgetting that God sees him."

"The learned man," observed the stranger with another smile, "should come himself to look into the mystery."

"It behoves him well if he be still in life," responded the townsman. "Now, good Sir, our Massachusetts magistracy, bethinking themselves that this woman is youthful and fair, and doubtless was strongly tempted to her fall, and that, moreover, as is most likely, her husband may be at the bottom of the sea, they have not been bold to put in force the extremity of our righteous law against her. The penalty thereof is death. But in their great mercy and tenderness of heart they have doomed Mistress Prynne to stand only a space of three hours on the platform of the pillory, and then and thereafter, for the remainder of her natural life to wear a mark of shame upon her bosom."

"A wise sentence," remarked the stranger, gravely, bowing his head. "Thus she will be a living sermon against sin, until the ignominious letter be engraved upon her tombstone. It irks me, nevertheless, that the partner of her iniquity should not at least, stand on the scaffold by her side. But he will be known—he will be known!—he will be known!"

He bowed courteously to the communicative townsman, and whispering a few words to his Indian attendant, they both made their way through the crowd.

While this passed, Hester Prynne had been standing on her pedestal, still with a fixed gaze towards the stranger—so fixed a gaze that, at moments of intense absorption, all other objects in the visible world seemed to vanish, leaving only him and her. Such an interview, perhaps, would have been more terrible than even to meet him as she now did, with the hot mid-day sun burning down upon her face, and lighting up its shame; with the scarlet token of infamy on her breast; with the sin-born infant in her arms; with a whole people, drawn forth as to a festival, staring at the features that should have been seen only in the quiet gleam of the fireside, in the happy shadow of a home, or beneath a matronly veil at church. Dreadful as it was, she was conscious of a shelter in the presence of these thousand witnesses. It was better to stand thus, with so many betwixt him and her, than to greet him face to face—they two alone. She fled for refuge, as it were, to the public exposure, and dreaded the moment when its protection should be withdrawn from her. Involved in these thoughts, she scarcely heard a voice behind her until it had repeated her name more than once, in a loud and solemn tone, audible to the whole multitude.

"Hearken unto me, Hester Prynne!" said the voice.

It has already been noticed that directly over the platform on which Hester Prynne stood was a kind of balcony, or open gallery, appended to the meeting-house. It was the place whence proclamations were wont to be made, amidst an assemblage of the magistracy, with all the ceremonial that attended such public observances in those days. Here, to witness the scene which we are describing, sat Governor Bellingham himself with four sergeants about his chair, bearing halberds, as a guard of honour. He wore a dark feather in his hat, a border of embroidery on his cloak, and a black velvet tunic beneath—a gentleman advanced in years, with a hard experience written in his wrinkles. He was not ill-fitted to be the head and representative of a community which owed its origin and progress, and its present state of development, not to the impulses of youth, but to the stern and tempered energies of manhood and the sombre sagacity of age; accomplishing so much, precisely because it imagined and hoped so little. The other eminent characters by whom the chief ruler was surrounded were distinguished by a dignity of mien, belonging to a period when the forms of authority were felt to possess the sacredness of Divine institutions. They were, doubtless, good men, just and sage. But, out of the whole human family, it would not have been easy to select the same number of wise and virtuous persons, who should be less capable of sitting in judgment on an erring woman's heart, and disentangling its mesh of good and evil, than the sages of rigid aspect towards whom Hester Prynne now turned her face. She seemed conscious, indeed, that whatever sympathy she might expect lay in the larger and warmer heart of the multitude; for, as she lifted her eyes towards the balcony, the unhappy woman grew pale, and trembled.

The voice which had called her attention was that of the reverend and famous John Wilson, the eldest clergyman of Boston, a great scholar, like most of his contemporaries in the profession, and withal a man of kind and genial spirit. This last attribute, however, had been less carefully developed than his intellectual gifts, and was, in truth, rather a matter of shame than self-congratulation with him. There he stood, with a border of grizzled locks beneath his skull-cap, while his grey eyes, accustomed to the shaded light of his study, were winking, like those of Hester's infant, in the unadulterated sunshine. He looked like the darkly engraved portraits which we see prefixed to old volumes of sermons, and had no more right than one of those portraits would have to step forth, as he now did, and meddle with a question of human guilt, passion, and anguish.

"Hester Prynne," said the clergyman, "I have striven with my young brother here, under whose preaching of the Word you have been privileged to sit"—here Mr. Wilson laid his hand on the shoulder of a pale young man beside him—"I have sought, I say, to persuade this godly youth, that he should deal with you, here in the face of Heaven, and before these wise and upright rulers, and in hearing of all the people, as touching the vileness and blackness of your sin. Knowing your natural temper better than I, he could the better judge what arguments to use, whether of tenderness or terror, such as might prevail over your hardness and obstinacy, insomuch that you should no longer hide the name of him who tempted you to this grievous fall. But he opposes to me—with a young man's over-softness, albeit wise beyond his years— that it were wronging the very nature of woman to force her to lay open her heart's secrets in such broad daylight, and in presence of so great a multitude. Truly, as I sought to convince him, the shame lay in the commission of the sin, and not in the showing of it forth. What say you to it, once again, brother Dimmesdale? Must it be thou, or I, that shall deal with this poor sinner's soul?"

There was a murmur among the dignified and reverend occupants of the balcony; and Governor Bellingham gave expression to its purport, speaking in an authoritative voice, although tempered with respect towards the youthful clergyman whom he addressed:

"Good Master Dimmesdale," said he, "the responsibility of this woman's soul lies greatly with you. It behoves you; therefore, to exhort her to repentance and to confession, as a proof and consequence thereof."

The directness of this appeal drew the eyes of the whole crowd upon the Reverend Mr. Dimmesdale—young clergyman, who had come from one of the great English universities, bringing all the learning of the age into our wild forest land. His eloquence and religious fervour had already given the earnest of high eminence in his profession. He was a person of very striking aspect, with a white, lofty, and impending brow; large, brown, melancholy eyes, and a mouth which, unless when he forcibly compressed it, was apt to be tremulous, expressing both nervous sensibility and a vast power of self restraint. Notwithstanding his high native gifts and scholar-like attainments, there was an air about this young minister—an apprehensive, a startled, a half-frightened look—as of a being who felt himself quite astray, and at a loss in the pathway of human existence, and could only be at ease in some seclusion of his own. Therefore, so far as his duties would permit, he trod in the shadowy by-paths, and thus kept himself simple and childlike, coming forth, when occasion was, with a freshness, and fragrance, and dewy purity of thought, which, as many people said, affected them like the speech of an angel.

Such was the young man whom the Reverend Mr. Wilson and the Governor had introduced so openly to the public notice, bidding him speak, in the hearing of all men, to that mystery of a woman's soul, so sacred even in its pollution. The trying nature of his position drove the blood from his cheek, and made his lips tremulous.

"Speak to the woman, my brother," said Mr. Wilson. "It is of moment to her soul, and, therefore, as the worshipful Governor says, momentous to thine own, in whose charge hers is. Exhort her to confess the truth!"

The Reverend Mr. Dimmesdale bent his head, in silent prayer, as it seemed, and then came forward.

"Hester Prynne," said he, leaning over the balcony and looking down steadfastly into her eyes, "thou hearest what this good man says, and seest the accountability under which I labour. If thou feelest it to be for thy soul's peace, and that thy earthly punishment will thereby be made more effectual to salvation, I charge thee to speak out the name of thy fellow-sinner and fellow-sufferer! Be not silent from any mistaken pity and tenderness for him; for, believe me, Hester, though he were to step down from a high place, and stand there beside thee, on thy pedestal of shame, yet better were it so than to hide a guilty heart through life. What can thy silence do for him, except it tempt him—yea, compel him, as it were—to add hypocrisy to sin? Heaven hath granted thee an open ignominy, that thereby thou mayest work out an open triumph over the evil within thee and the sorrow without. Take heed how thou deniest to him —who, perchance, hath not the courage to grasp it for himself—the bitter, but wholesome, cup that is now presented to thy lips!"

The young pastor's voice was tremulously sweet, rich, deep, and broken. The feeling that it so evidently manifested, rather than the direct purport of the words, caused it to vibrate within all hearts, and brought the listeners into one accord of sympathy. Even the poor baby at Hester's bosom was affected by the same influence, for it directed its hitherto vacant gaze towards Mr. Dimmesdale, and held up its little arms with a half-pleased, half-plaintive murmur. So powerful seemed the minister's appeal that the people could not believe but that Hester Prynne would speak out the guilty name, or else that the guilty one himself in whatever high or lowly place he stood, would be drawn forth by an inward and inevitable necessity, and compelled to ascend the scaffold.

Hester shook her head.

"Woman, transgress not beyond the limits of Heaven's mercy!" cried the Reverend Mr. Wilson, more harshly than before. "That little babe hath been gifted with a voice, to second and confirm the counsel which thou hast heard. Speak out the name! That, and thy repentance, may avail to take the scarlet letter off thy breast."

"Never," replied Hester Prynne, looking, not at Mr. Wilson, but into the deep and troubled eyes of the younger clergyman. "It is too deeply branded. Ye cannot take it off. And would that I might endure his agony as well as mine!"

"Speak, woman!" said another voice, coldly and sternly, proceeding from the crowd about the scaffold, "Speak; and give your child a father!"

"I will not speak!" answered Hester, turning pale as death, but responding to this voice, which she too surely recognised. "And my child must seek a heavenly father; she shall never know an earthly one!"

"She will not speak!" murmured Mr. Dimmesdale, who, leaning over the balcony, with his hand upon his heart, had awaited the result of his appeal. He now drew back with a long respiration. "Wondrous strength and generosity of a woman's heart! She will not speak!"

Discerning the impracticable state of the poor culprit's mind, the elder clergyman, who had carefully prepared himself for the occasion, addressed to the multitude a discourse on sin, in all its branches, but with continual reference to the ignominious letter. So forcibly did he dwell upon this symbol, for the hour or more during which his periods were rolling over the people's heads, that it assumed new terrors in their imagination, and seemed to derive its scarlet hue from the flames of the infernal pit. Hester Prynne, meanwhile, kept her place upon the pedestal of shame, with glazed eyes, and an air of weary indifference. She had borne that morning all that nature could endure; and as her temperament was not of the order that escapes from too intense suffering by a swoon, her spirit could only shelter itself beneath a stony crust of insensibility, while the faculties of animal life remained entire. In this state, the voice of the preacher thundered remorselessly, but unavailingly, upon her ears. The infant, during the latter portion of her ordeal, pierced the air with its wailings and screams; she strove to hush it mechanically, but seemed scarcely to sympathise with its trouble. With the same hard demeanour, she was led back to prison, and vanished from the public gaze within its iron-clamped portal. It was whispered by those who peered after her that the scarlet letter threw a lurid gleam along the dark passage-way of the interior.

❧ 4 ❧

THE INTERVIEW

AFTER HER RETURN to the prison, Hester Prynne was found to be in a state of nervous excitement, that demanded constant watchfulness, lest she should perpetrate violence on herself, or do some half-frenzied mischief to the poor babe. As night approached, it proving impossible to quell her insubordination by rebuke or threats of punishment, Master Brackett, the jailer, thought fit to introduce a physician. He described him as a man of skill in all Christian modes of physical science, and likewise familiar with whatever the savage people could teach in respect to medicinal herbs and roots that grew in the forest. To say the truth, there was much need of professional assistance, not merely for Hester herself, but still more urgently for the child—who, drawing its sustenance from the maternal bosom, seemed to have drank in with it all the turmoil, the anguish and despair, which pervaded the mother's system. It now writhed in convulsions of pain, and was a forcible type, in its little frame, of the moral agony which Hester Prynne had borne throughout the day.

Closely following the jailer into the dismal apartment, appeared that individual, of singular aspect whose presence in the crowd had been of such deep interest to the wearer of the scarlet letter. He was lodged in the prison, not as suspected of any offence, but as the most convenient and suitable mode of disposing of him, until the magistrates should have conferred with the Indian sagamores respecting his ransom. His name was announced as Roger Chillingworth. The jailer, after ushering him into the room, remained a moment, marvelling at the comparative quiet that followed his entrance; for Hester Prynne had immediately become as still as death, although the child continued to moan.

"Prithee, friend, leave me alone with my patient," said the practitioner. "Trust me, good jailer, you shall briefly have peace in your house; and, I promise you, Mistress Prynne shall hereafter be more amenable to just authority than you may have found her heretofore."

"Nay, if your worship can accomplish that," answered Master Brackett, "I shall own you for a man of skill, indeed! Verily, the woman hath been like a possessed one; and there lacks little that I should take in hand, to drive Satan out of her with stripes."

The stranger had entered the room with the characteristic quietude of the profession to which he announced himself as belonging. Nor did his demeanour change when the withdrawal of the prison keeper left him face to face with the woman, whose absorbed notice of him, in the crowd, had intimated so close a relation between himself and her. His first care was given to the child, whose cries, indeed, as she lay writhing on the trundle-bed, made it of peremptory necessity to postpone all other business to the task of soothing her. He examined the infant carefully, and then proceeded to unclasp a leathern case, which he took from beneath his dress. It appeared to contain medical preparations, one of which he mingled with a cup of water.

"My old studies in alchemy," observed he, "and my sojourn, for above a year past, among a people well versed in the kindly properties of simples, have made a better physician of me than many that claim the medical degree. Here, woman! The child is yours—she is none of mine—neither will she recognise my voice or aspect as a father's. Administer this draught, therefore, with thine own hand."

Hester repelled the offered medicine, at the same time gazing with strongly marked apprehension into his face. "Wouldst thou avenge thyself on the innocent babe?" whispered she.

"Foolish woman!" responded the physician, half coldly, half soothingly. "What should ail me to harm this misbegotten and miserable babe? The medicine is potent for good, and were it my child—yea, mine own, as well as thine! I could do no better for it."

As she still hesitated, being, in fact, in no reasonable state of mind, he took the infant in his arms, and himself administered the draught. It soon proved its efficacy, and redeemed the leech's pledge. The moans of the little patient subsided; its convulsive tossings gradually ceased; and in a few moments, as is the custom of young children after relief from pain, it sank into a profound and dewy slumber. The physician, as he had a fair right to be termed, next bestowed his attention on the mother. With calm and intent scrutiny, he felt her pulse, looked into her eyes—a gaze that made her heart shrink and shudder, because so familiar, and yet so strange and cold—and, finally, satisfied with his investigation, proceeded to mingle another draught.

"I know not Lethe nor Nepenthe," remarked he; "but I have learned many new secrets in the wilderness, and here is one of them—a recipe that an Indian taught me, in requital of some lessons of my own, that were as old as Paracelsus. Drink it! It may be less soothing than a sinless conscience. That I cannot give thee. But it will calm the swell and heaving of thy passion, like oil thrown on the waves of a tempestuous sea."

He presented the cup to Hester, who received it with a slow, earnest look into his face; not precisely a look of fear, yet full of doubt and questioning as to what his purposes might be. She looked also at her slumbering child.

"I have thought of death," said she—"have wished for it—would even have prayed for it, were it fit that such as I should pray for anything. Yet, if death be in this cup, I bid thee think again, ere thou beholdest me quaff it. See! it is even now at my lips."

"Drink, then," replied he, still with the same cold composure. "Dost thou know me so little, Hester Prynne? Are my purposes wont to be so shallow? Even if I imagine a scheme of vengeance, what could I do better for my object than to let thee live—than to give thee medicines against all harm and peril of life—so that this burning shame may still blaze upon thy bosom?" As he spoke, he laid his long fore-finger on the scarlet letter, which forthwith seemed to scorch into Hester's breast, as if it had been red hot. He noticed her involuntary gesture, and smiled. "Live, therefore, and bear about thy doom with thee, in the eyes of men and women—in the eyes of him whom thou didst call thy husband—in the eyes of yonder child! And, that thou mayest live, take off this draught."

Without further expostulation or delay, Hester Prynne drained the cup, and, at the motion of the man of skill, seated herself on the bed, where the child was sleeping; while he drew the only chair which the room afforded, and took his own seat beside her. She could not but tremble at these preparations; for she felt that—having now done all that humanity, or principle, or, if so it were, a refined cruelty, impelled him to do for the relief of physical suffering—he was next to treat with her as the man whom she had most deeply and irreparably injured.

"Hester," said he, "I ask not wherefore, nor how thou hast fallen into the pit, or say, rather, thou hast ascended to the pedestal of infamy on which I found thee. The reason is not far to seek. It was my folly, and thy weakness. I—a man of thought—the book-worm of great libraries —a man already in decay, having given my best years to feed the hungry dream of knowledge —what had I to do with youth and beauty like thine own? Misshapen from my birth-hour, how could I delude myself with the idea that intellectual gifts might veil physical deformity in a young girl's fantasy? Men call me wise. If sages were ever wise in their own behoof, I might have foreseen all this. I might have known that, as I came out of the vast and dismal forest, and entered this settlement of Christian men, the very first object to meet my eyes would be thyself, Hester Prynne, standing up, a statue of ignominy, before the people. Nay, from the moment when we came down the old church-steps together, a married pair, I might have beheld the bale-fire of that scarlet letter blazing at the end of our path!"

"Thou knowest," said Hester—for, depressed as she was, she could not endure this last quiet stab at the token of her shame—"thou knowest that I was frank with thee. I felt no love, nor feigned any."

"True," replied he. "It was my folly! I have said it. But, up to that epoch of my life, I had lived in vain. The world had been so cheerless! My heart was a habitation large enough for many guests, but lonely and chill, and without a household fire. I longed to kindle one! It seemed not so wild a dream—old as I was, and sombre as I was, and misshapen as I was—that the simple bliss, which is scattered far and wide, for all mankind to gather up, might yet be mine. And so, Hester, I drew thee into my heart, into its innermost chamber, and sought to warm thee by the warmth which thy presence made there!"

"I have greatly wronged thee," murmured Hester.

"We have wronged each other," answered he. "Mine was the first wrong, when I betrayed thy budding youth into a false and unnatural relation with my decay. Therefore, as a man who has not thought and philosophised in vain, I seek no vengeance, plot no evil against thee. Between thee and me, the scale hangs fairly balanced. But, Hester, the man lives who has wronged us both! Who is he?"

"Ask me not!" replied Hester Prynne, looking firmly into his face. "That thou shalt never know!"

"Never, sayest thou?" rejoined he, with a smile of dark and self-relying intelligence. "Never know him! Believe me, Hester, there are few things whether in the outward world, or, to a certain depth, in the invisible sphere of thought—few things hidden from the man who devotes himself earnestly and unreservedly to the solution of a mystery. Thou mayest cover up thy secret from the prying multitude. Thou mayest conceal it, too, from the ministers and magistrates, even as thou didst this day, when they sought to wrench the name out of thy heart, and give thee a partner on thy pedestal. But, as for me, I come to the inquest with other senses than they possess. I shall seek this man, as I have sought truth in books: as I have sought gold in alchemy. There is a sympathy that will make me conscious of him. I shall see him tremble. I shall feel myself shudder, suddenly and unawares. Sooner or later, he must needs be mine."

The eyes of the wrinkled scholar glowed so intensely upon her, that Hester Prynne clasped her hand over her heart, dreading lest he should read the secret there at once.

"Thou wilt not reveal his name? Not the less he is mine," resumed he, with a look of confidence, as if destiny were at one with him. "He bears no letter of infamy wrought into his garment, as thou dost, but I shall read it on his heart. Yet fear not for him! Think not that I shall interfere with Heaven's own method of retribution, or, to my own loss, betray him to the gripe of human law. Neither do thou imagine that I shall contrive aught against his life; no, nor against his fame, if as I judge, he be a man of fair repute. Let him live! Let him hide himself in outward honour, if he may! Not the less he shall be mine!"

"Thy acts are like mercy," said Hester, bewildered and appalled; "but thy words interpret thee as a terror!"

"One thing, thou that wast my wife, I would enjoin upon thee," continued the scholar. "Thou hast kept the secret of thy paramour. Keep, likewise, mine! There are none in this land that know me. Breathe not to any human soul that thou didst ever call me husband! Here, on this wild outskirt of the earth, I shall pitch my tent; for, elsewhere a wanderer, and isolated from human interests, I find here a woman, a man, a child, amongst whom and myself there exist the closest ligaments. No matter whether of love or hate: no matter whether of right or wrong! Thou and thine, Hester Prynne, belong to me. My home is where thou art and where he is. But betray me not!"

"Wherefore dost thou desire it?" inquired Hester, shrinking, she hardly knew why, from this secret bond. "Why not announce thyself openly, and cast me off at once?"

"It may be," he replied, "because I will not encounter the dishonour that besmirches the husband of a faithless woman. It may be for other reasons. Enough, it is my purpose to live and die unknown. Let, therefore, thy husband be to the world as one already dead, and of whom no tidings shall ever come. Recognise me not, by word, by sign, by look! Breathe not the secret, above all, to the man thou wottest of. Shouldst thou fail me in this, beware! His fame, his position, his life will be in my hands. Beware!"

"I will keep thy secret, as I have his," said Hester.

"Swear it!" rejoined he.

And she took the oath.

"And now, Mistress Prynne," said old Roger Chillingworth, as he was hereafter to be named, "I leave thee alone: alone with thy infant and the scarlet letter! How is it, Hester? Doth thy sentence bind thee to wear the token in thy sleep? Art thou not afraid of nightmares and hideous dreams?"

"Why dost thou smile so at me?" inquired Hester, troubled at the expression of his eyes. "Art thou like the Black Man that haunts the forest round about us? Hast thou enticed me into a bond that will prove the ruin of my soul?"

"Not thy soul," he answered, with another smile. "No, not thine!"

5

HESTER AT HER NEEDLE

HESTER PRYNNE'S term of confinement was now at an end. Her prison-door was thrown open, and she came forth into the sunshine, which, falling on all alike, seemed, to her sick and morbid heart, as if meant for no other purpose than to reveal the scarlet letter on her breast. Perhaps there was a more real torture in her first unattended footsteps from the threshold of the prison than even in the procession and spectacle that have been described, where she was made the common infamy, at which all mankind was summoned to point its finger. Then, she was supported by an unnatural tension of the nerves, and by all the combative energy of her character, which enabled her to convert the scene into a kind of lurid triumph. It was, moreover, a separate and insulated event, to occur but once in her lifetime, and to meet which, therefore, reckless of economy, she might call up the vital strength that would have sufficed for many quiet years. The very law that condemned her—a giant of stern features but with vigour to support, as well as to annihilate, in his iron arm—had held her up through the terrible ordeal of her ignominy. But now, with this unattended walk from her prison door, began the daily custom; and she must either sustain and carry it forward by the ordinary resources of her nature, or sink beneath it. She could no longer borrow from the future to help her through the present grief. Tomorrow would bring its own trial with it; so would the next day, and so would the next: each its own trial, and yet the very same that was now so unutterably grievous to be borne. The days of the far-off future would toil onward, still with the same burden for her to take up, and bear along with her, but never to fling down; for the accumulating days and added years would pile up their misery upon the heap of shame. Throughout them all, giving up her individuality, she would become the general symbol at which the preacher and moralist might point, and in which they might vivify and embody their images of woman's frailty and sinful passion. Thus the young and pure would be taught to look at her, with the scarlet letter flaming on her breast—at her, the child of honourable parents—at her, the mother of a babe that would hereafter be a woman—at her, who had once been innocent—as the figure, the body, the reality of sin. And over her grave, the infamy that she must carry thither would be her only monument.

It may seem marvellous that, with the world before her—kept by no restrictive clause of her condemnation within the limits of the Puritan settlement, so remote and so obscure—free to return to her birth-place, or to any other European land, and there hide her character and identity under a new exterior, as completely as if emerging into another state of being—and having also the passes of the dark, inscrutable forest open to her, where the wildness of her nature might assimilate itself with a people whose customs and life were alien from the law that had condemned her—it may seem marvellous that this woman should still call that place her home, where, and where only, she must needs be the type of shame. But there is a fatality, a feeling so irresistible and inevitable that it has the force of doom, which almost invariably compels human beings to linger around and haunt, ghost-like, the spot where some great and marked event has given the colour to their lifetime; and, still more irresistibly, the darker the tinge that saddens it. Her sin, her ignominy, were the roots which she had struck into the soil. It was as if a new birth, with stronger assimilations than the first, had converted the forest-land, still so uncongenial to every other pilgrim and wanderer, into Hester Prynne's wild and dreary, but life-long home. All other scenes of earth—even that village of rural England, where happy infancy and stainless maidenhood seemed yet to be in her mother's keeping, like garments put off long ago—were foreign to her, in comparison. The chain that bound her here was of iron links, and galling to her inmost soul, but could never be broken.

It might be, too—doubtless it was so, although she hid the secret from herself, and grew pale whenever it struggled out of her heart, like a serpent from its hole—it might be that another feeling kept her within the scene and pathway that had been so fatal. There dwelt, there trode, the feet of one with whom she deemed herself connected in a union that, unrecognised on earth, would bring them together before the bar of final judgment, and make that their marriage-altar, for a joint futurity of endless retribution. Over and over again, the tempter of souls had thrust this idea upon Hester's contemplation, and laughed at the passionate and desperate joy with which she seized, and then strove to cast it from her. She barely looked the idea in the face, and hastened to bar it in its dungeon. What she compelled herself to believe—what, finally, she reasoned upon as her motive for continuing a resident of New England—was half a truth, and half a self-delusion. Here, she said to herself had been the scene of her guilt, and here should be the scene of her earthly punishment; and so, perchance, the torture of her daily shame would at length purge her soul, and work out another purity than that which she had lost: more saint-like, because the result of martyrdom.

Hester Prynne, therefore, did not flee. On the outskirts of the town, within the verge of the peninsula, but not in close vicinity to any other habitation, there was a small thatched cottage. It had been built by an earlier settler, and abandoned, because the soil about it was too sterile for cultivation, while its comparative remoteness put it out of the sphere of that social activity which already marked the habits of the emigrants. It stood on the shore, looking across a basin of the sea at the forest-covered hills, towards the west. A clump of scrubby trees, such as alone grew on the peninsula, did not so much conceal the cottage from view, as seem to denote that here was some object which would fain have been, or at least ought to be, concealed. In this little lonesome dwelling, with some slender means that she possessed, and by the licence of the magistrates, who still kept an inquisitorial watch over her, Hester established herself, with her infant child. A mystic shadow of suspicion immediately attached itself to the spot. Children, too young to comprehend wherefore this woman should be shut out from the sphere of human charities, would creep nigh enough to behold her plying her needle at the cottage-window, or standing in the doorway, or labouring in her little garden, or coming forth along the pathway that led townward, and, discerning the scarlet letter on her breast, would scamper off with a strange contagious fear.

Lonely as was Hester's situation, and without a friend on earth who dared to show himself, she, however, incurred no risk of want. She possessed an art that sufficed, even in a land that afforded comparatively little scope for its exercise, to supply food for her thriving infant and herself. It was the art, then, as now, almost the only one within a woman's grasp—of needle-work. She bore on her breast, in the curiously embroidered letter, a specimen of her delicate and imaginative skill, of which the dames of a court might gladly have availed themselves, to add the richer and more spiritual adornment of human ingenuity to their fabrics of silk and gold. Here, indeed, in the sable simplicity that generally characterised the Puritanic modes of dress, there might be an infrequent call for the finer productions of her handiwork. Yet the taste of the age, demanding whatever was elaborate in compositions of this kind, did not fail to extend its influence over our stern progenitors, who had cast behind them so many fashions which it might seem harder to dispense with.

Public ceremonies, such as ordinations, the installation of magistrates, and all that could give majesty to the forms in which a new government manifested itself to the people, were, as a matter of policy, marked by a stately and well-conducted ceremonial, and a sombre, but yet a studied magnificence. Deep ruffs, painfully wrought bands, and gorgeously embroidered gloves, were all deemed necessary to the official state of men assuming the reins of power, and were readily allowed to individuals dignified by rank or wealth, even while sumptuary laws forbade these and similar extravagances to the plebeian order. In the array of funerals, too—whether for the apparel of the dead body, or to typify, by manifold emblematic devices of sable cloth and snowy lawn, the sorrow of the survivors—there was a frequent and characteristic demand for such labour as Hester Prynne could supply. Baby-linen—for babies then wore robes of state—afforded still another possibility of toil and emolument.

By degrees, not very slowly, her handiwork became what would now be termed the fashion. Whether from commiseration for a woman of so miserable a destiny; or from the morbid curiosity that gives a fictitious value even to common or worthless things; or by whatever other intangible circumstance was then, as now, sufficient to bestow, on some persons, what others might seek in vain; or because Hester really filled a gap which must otherwise have remained vacant; it is certain that she had ready and fairly requited employment for as many hours as she saw fit to occupy with her needle. Vanity, it may be, chose to mortify itself, by putting on, for ceremonials of pomp and state, the garments that had been wrought by her sinful hands. Her needle-work was seen on the ruff of the Governor; military men wore it on their scarfs, and the minister on his band; it decked the baby's little cap; it was shut up, to be mildewed and moulder away, in the coffins of the dead. But it is not recorded that, in a single instance, her skill was called in to embroider the white veil which was to cover the pure blushes of a bride. The exception indicated the ever relentless vigour with which society frowned upon her sin.

Hester sought not to acquire anything beyond a subsistence, of the plainest and most ascetic description, for herself, and a simple abundance for her child. Her own dress was of the coarsest materials and the most sombre hue, with only that one ornament—the scarlet letter—which it was her doom to wear. The child's attire, on the other hand, was distinguished by a fanciful, or, we may rather say, a fantastic ingenuity, which served, indeed, to heighten the airy charm that early began to develop itself in the little girl, but which appeared to have also a deeper meaning. We may speak further of it hereafter. Except for that small expenditure in the decoration of her infant, Hester bestowed all her superfluous means in charity, on wretches less miserable than herself, and who not unfrequently insulted the hand that fed them. Much of the time, which she might readily have applied to the better efforts of her art, she employed in making coarse garments for the poor. It is probable that there was an idea of penance in this mode of occupation, and that she offered up a real sacrifice of enjoyment in devoting so many hours to such rude handiwork. She had in her nature a rich, voluptuous, Oriental characteristic

—a taste for the gorgeously beautiful, which, save in the exquisite productions of her needle, found nothing else, in all the possibilities of her life, to exercise itself upon. Women derive a pleasure, incomprehensible to the other sex, from the delicate toil of the needle. To Hester Prynne it might have been a mode of expressing, and therefore soothing, the passion of her life. Like all other joys, she rejected it as sin. This morbid meddling of conscience with an immaterial matter betokened, it is to be feared, no genuine and steadfast penitence, but something doubtful, something that might be deeply wrong beneath.

In this manner, Hester Prynne came to have a part to perform in the world. With her native energy of character and rare capacity, it could not entirely cast her off, although it had set a mark upon her, more intolerable to a woman's heart than that which branded the brow of Cain. In all her intercourse with society, however, there was nothing that made her feel as if she belonged to it. Every gesture, every word, and even the silence of those with whom she came in contact, implied, and often expressed, that she was banished, and as much alone as if she inhabited another sphere, or communicated with the common nature by other organs and senses than the rest of human kind. She stood apart from mortal interests, yet close beside them, like a ghost that revisits the familiar fireside, and can no longer make itself seen or felt; no more smile with the household joy, nor mourn with the kindred sorrow; or, should it succeed in manifesting its forbidden sympathy, awakening only terror and horrible repugnance. These emotions, in fact, and its bitterest scorn besides, seemed to be the sole portion that she retained in the universal heart. It was not an age of delicacy; and her position, although she understood it well, and was in little danger of forgetting it, was often brought before her vivid self-perception, like a new anguish, by the rudest touch upon the tenderest spot. The poor, as we have already said, whom she sought out to be the objects of her bounty, often reviled the hand that was stretched forth to succour them. Dames of elevated rank, likewise, whose doors she entered in the way of her occupation, were accustomed to distil drops of bitterness into her heart; sometimes through that alchemy of quiet malice, by which women can concoct a subtle poison from ordinary trifles; and sometimes, also, by a coarser expression, that fell upon the sufferer's defenceless breast like a rough blow upon an ulcerated wound. Hester had schooled herself long and well; and she never responded to these attacks, save by a flush of crimson that rose irrepressibly over her pale cheek, and again subsided into the depths of her bosom. She was patient—a martyr, indeed—but she forebore to pray for enemies, lest, in spite of her forgiving aspirations, the words of the blessing should stubbornly twist themselves into a curse.

Continually, and in a thousand other ways, did she feel the innumerable throbs of anguish that had been so cunningly contrived for her by the undying, the ever-active sentence of the Puritan tribunal. Clergymen paused in the streets, to address words of exhortation, that brought a crowd, with its mingled grin and frown, around the poor, sinful woman. If she entered a church, trusting to share the Sabbath smile of the Universal Father, it was often her mishap to find herself the text of the discourse. She grew to have a dread of children; for they had imbibed from their parents a vague idea of something horrible in this dreary woman gliding silently through the town, with never any companion but one only child. Therefore, first allowing her to pass, they pursued her at a distance with shrill cries, and the utterances of a word that had no distinct purport to their own minds, but was none the less terrible to her, as proceeding from lips that babbled it unconsciously. It seemed to argue so wide a diffusion of her shame, that all nature knew of it; it could have caused her no deeper pang had the leaves of the trees whispered the dark story among themselves—had the summer breeze murmured about it—had the wintry blast shrieked it aloud! Another peculiar torture was felt in the gaze of a new eye. When strangers looked curiously at the scarlet letter—and none ever failed to do so

—they branded it afresh in Hester's soul; so that, oftentimes, she could scarcely refrain, yet always did refrain, from covering the symbol with her hand. But then, again, an accustomed eye had likewise its own anguish to inflict. Its cool stare of familiarity was intolerable. From first to last, in short, Hester Prynne had always this dreadful agony in feeling a human eye upon the token; the spot never grew callous; it seemed, on the contrary, to grow more sensitive with daily torture.

But sometimes, once in many days, or perchance in many months, she felt an eye—a human eye—upon the ignominious brand, that seemed to give a momentary relief, as if half of her agony were shared. The next instant, back it all rushed again, with still a deeper throb of pain; for, in that brief interval, she had sinned anew. (Had Hester sinned alone?)

Her imagination was somewhat affected, and, had she been of a softer moral and intellectual fibre would have been still more so, by the strange and solitary anguish of her life. Walking to and fro, with those lonely footsteps, in the little world with which she was outwardly connected, it now and then appeared to Hester—if altogether fancy, it was nevertheless too potent to be resisted—she felt or fancied, then, that the scarlet letter had endowed her with a new sense. She shuddered to believe, yet could not help believing, that it gave her a sympathetic knowledge of the hidden sin in other hearts. She was terror-stricken by the revelations that were thus made. What were they? Could they be other than the insidious whispers of the bad angel, who would fain have persuaded the struggling woman, as yet only half his victim, that the outward guise of purity was but a lie, and that, if truth were everywhere to be shown, a scarlet letter would blaze forth on many a bosom besides Hester Prynne's? Or, must she receive those intimations—so obscure, yet so distinct—as truth? In all her miserable experience, there was nothing else so awful and so loathsome as this sense. It perplexed, as well as shocked her, by the irreverent inopportuneness of the occasions that brought it into vivid action. Sometimes the red infamy upon her breast would give a sympathetic throb, as she passed near a venerable minister or magistrate, the model of piety and justice, to whom that age of antique reverence looked up, as to a mortal man in fellowship with angels. "What evil thing is at hand?" would Hester say to herself. Lifting her reluctant eyes, there would be nothing human within the scope of view, save the form of this earthly saint! Again a mystic sisterhood would contumaciously assert itself, as she met the sanctified frown of some matron, who, according to the rumour of all tongues, had kept cold snow within her bosom throughout life. That unsunned snow in the matron's bosom, and the burning shame on Hester Prynne's—what had the two in common? Or, once more, the electric thrill would give her warning—"Behold Hester, here is a companion!" and, looking up, she would detect the eyes of a young maiden glancing at the scarlet letter, shyly and aside, and quickly averted, with a faint, chill crimson in her cheeks as if her purity were somewhat sullied by that momentary glance. O Fiend, whose talisman was that fatal symbol, wouldst thou leave nothing, whether in youth or age, for this poor sinner to revere?—such loss of faith is ever one of the saddest results of sin. Be it accepted as a proof that all was not corrupt in this poor victim of her own frailty, and man's hard law, that Hester Prynne yet struggled to believe that no fellow-mortal was guilty like herself.

The vulgar, who, in those dreary old times, were always contributing a grotesque horror to what interested their imaginations, had a story about the scarlet letter which we might readily work up into a terrific legend. They averred that the symbol was not mere scarlet cloth, tinged in an earthly dye-pot, but was red-hot with infernal fire, and could be seen glowing all alight whenever Hester Prynne walked abroad in the night-time. And we must needs say it seared Hester's bosom so deeply, that perhaps there was more truth in the rumour than our modern incredulity may be inclined to admit.

❧ 6 ❧

PEARL

WE HAVE AS YET HARDLY SPOKEN of the infant; that little creature, whose innocent life had sprung, by the inscrutable decree of Providence, a lovely and immortal flower, out of the rank luxuriance of a guilty passion. How strange it seemed to the sad woman, as she watched the growth, and the beauty that became every day more brilliant, and the intelligence that threw its quivering sunshine over the tiny features of this child! Her Pearl—for so had Hester called her; not as a name expressive of her aspect, which had nothing of the calm, white, unimpassioned lustre that would be indicated by the comparison. But she named the infant "Pearl," as being of great price—purchased with all she had—her mother's only treasure! How strange, indeed! Man had marked this woman's sin by a scarlet letter, which had such potent and disastrous efficacy that no human sympathy could reach her, save it were sinful like herself. God, as a direct consequence of the sin which man thus punished, had given her a lovely child, whose place was on that same dishonoured bosom, to connect her parent for ever with the race and descent of mortals, and to be finally a blessed soul in heaven! Yet these thoughts affected Hester Prynne less with hope than apprehension. She knew that her deed had been evil; she could have no faith, therefore, that its result would be good. Day after day she looked fearfully into the child's expanding nature, ever dreading to detect some dark and wild peculiarity that should correspond with the guiltiness to which she owed her being.

Certainly there was no physical defect. By its perfect shape, its vigour, and its natural dexterity in the use of all its untried limbs, the infant was worthy to have been brought forth in Eden: worthy to have been left there to be the plaything of the angels after the world's first parents were driven out. The child had a native grace which does not invariably co-exist with faultless beauty; its attire, however simple, always impressed the beholder as if it were the very garb that precisely became it best. But little Pearl was not clad in rustic weeds. Her mother, with a morbid purpose that may be better understood hereafter, had bought the richest tissues that could be procured, and allowed her imaginative faculty its full play in the arrangement and decoration of the dresses which the child wore before the public eye. So magnificent was the small figure when thus arrayed, and such was the splendour of Pearl's own proper beauty, shining through the gorgeous robes which might have extinguished a paler loveliness, that there was an absolute circle of radiance around her on the darksome cottage floor. And yet a russet gown, torn and soiled with the child's rude play, made a picture of her just as perfect. Pearl's aspect was imbued with a spell of infinite variety; in this one child there were many children, comprehending the full scope between the wild-flower prettiness of a peasant-baby, and the pomp, in little, of an infant princess. Throughout all, however, there was a trait of passion, a certain depth of hue, which she never lost; and if in any of her changes, she had grown fainter or paler, she would have ceased to be herself—it would have been no longer Pearl!

This outward mutability indicated, and did not more than fairly express, the various properties of her inner life. Her nature appeared to possess depth, too, as well as variety; but— or else Hester's fears deceived her—it lacked reference and adaptation to the world into which she was born. The child could not be made amenable to rules. In giving her existence a great law had been broken; and the result was a being whose elements were perhaps beautiful and brilliant, but all in disorder, or with an order peculiar to themselves, amidst which the point of variety and arrangement was difficult or impossible to be discovered. Hester could only account for the child's character—and even then most vaguely and imperfectly—by recalling what she herself had been during that momentous period while Pearl was imbibing her soul from the spiritual world, and her bodily frame from its material of earth. The mother's impassioned state had been the medium through which were transmitted to the unborn infant the rays of its moral life; and, however white and clear originally, they had taken the deep stains of crimson and gold, the fiery lustre, the black shadow, and the untempered light of the intervening substance. Above all, the warfare of Hester's spirit at that epoch was perpetuated in Pearl. She could recognize her wild, desperate, defiant mood, the flightiness of her temper, and even some of the very cloud-shapes of gloom and despondency that had brooded in her heart. They were now illuminated by the morning radiance of a young child's disposition, but, later in the day of earthly existence, might be prolific of the storm and whirlwind.

The discipline of the family in those days was of a far more rigid kind than now. The frown, the harsh rebuke, the frequent application of the rod, enjoined by Scriptural authority, were used, not merely in the way of punishment for actual offences, but as a wholesome regimen for the growth and promotion of all childish virtues. Hester Prynne, nevertheless, the loving mother of this one child, ran little risk of erring on the side of undue severity. Mindful, however, of her own errors and misfortunes, she early sought to impose a tender but strict control over the infant immortality that was committed to her charge. But the task was beyond her skill. After testing both smiles and frowns, and proving that neither mode of treatment possessed any calculable influence, Hester was ultimately compelled to stand aside and permit the child to be swayed by her own impulses. Physical compulsion or restraint was effectual, of course, while it lasted. As to any other kind of discipline, whether addressed to her mind or heart, little Pearl might or might not be within its reach, in accordance with the caprice that ruled the moment. Her mother, while Pearl was yet an infant, grew acquainted with a certain peculiar look, that warned her when it would be labour thrown away to insist, persuade or plead.

It was a look so intelligent, yet inexplicable, perverse, sometimes so malicious, but generally accompanied by a wild flow of spirits, that Hester could not help questioning at such moments whether Pearl was a human child. She seemed rather an airy sprite, which, after playing its fantastic sports for a little while upon the cottage floor, would flit away with a mocking smile. Whenever that look appeared in her wild, bright, deeply black eyes, it invested her with a strange remoteness and intangibility: it was as if she were hovering in the air, and might vanish, like a glimmering light that comes we know not whence and goes we know not whither. Beholding it, Hester was constrained to rush towards the child—to pursue the little elf in the flight which she invariably began—to snatch her to her bosom with a close pressure and earnest kisses—not so much from overflowing love as to assure herself that Pearl was flesh and blood, and not utterly delusive. But Pearl's laugh, when she was caught, though full of merriment and music, made her mother more doubtful than before.

Heart-smitten at this bewildering and baffling spell, that so often came between herself and her sole treasure, whom she had bought so dear, and who was all her world, Hester sometimes burst into passionate tears. Then, perhaps—for there was no foreseeing how it might affect her —Pearl would frown, and clench her little fist, and harden her small features into a stern, unsympathising look of discontent. Not seldom she would laugh anew, and louder than before, like a thing incapable and unintelligent of human sorrow. Or—but this more rarely happened— she would be convulsed with rage of grief and sob out her love for her mother in broken words, and seem intent on proving that she had a heart by breaking it. Yet Hester was hardly safe in confiding herself to that gusty tenderness: it passed as suddenly as it came. Brooding over all these matters, the mother felt like one who has evoked a spirit, but, by some irregularity in the process of conjuration, has failed to win the master-word that should control this new and incomprehensible intelligence. Her only real comfort was when the child lay in the placidity of sleep. Then she was sure of her, and tasted hours of quiet, sad, delicious happiness; until— perhaps with that perverse expression glimmering from beneath her opening lids—little Pearl awoke!

How soon—with what strange rapidity, indeed—did Pearl arrive at an age that was capable of social intercourse beyond the mother's ever-ready smile and nonsense-words! And then what a happiness would it have been could Hester Prynne have heard her clear, bird-like voice mingling with the uproar of other childish voices, and have distinguished and unravelled her own darling's tones, amid all the entangled outcry of a group of sportive children. But this could never be. Pearl was a born outcast of the infantile world. An imp of evil, emblem and product of sin, she had no right among christened infants. Nothing was more remarkable than the instinct, as it seemed, with which the child comprehended her loneliness: the destiny that had drawn an inviolable circle round about her: the whole peculiarity, in short, of her position in respect to other children. Never since her release from prison had Hester met the public gaze without her. In all her walks about the town, Pearl, too, was there: first as the babe in arms, and afterwards as the little girl, small companion of her mother, holding a forefinger with her whole grasp, and tripping along at the rate of three or four footsteps to one of Hester's. She saw the children of the settlement on the grassy margin of the street, or at the domestic thresholds, disporting themselves in such grim fashions as the Puritanic nurture would permit; playing at going to church, perchance, or at scourging Quakers; or taking scalps in a sham fight with the Indians, or scaring one another with freaks of imitative witchcraft. Pearl saw, and gazed intently, but never sought to make acquaintance. If spoken to, she would not speak again. If the children gathered about her, as they sometimes did, Pearl would grow positively terrible in her puny wrath, snatching up stones to fling at them, with shrill, incoherent exclamations, that made her mother tremble, because they had so much the sound of a witch's anathemas in some unknown tongue.

The truth was, that the little Puritans, being of the most intolerant brood that ever lived, had got a vague idea of something outlandish, unearthly, or at variance with ordinary fashions, in the mother and child, and therefore scorned them in their hearts, and not unfrequently reviled them with their tongues. Pearl felt the sentiment, and requited it with the bitterest hatred that can be supposed to rankle in a childish bosom. These outbreaks of a fierce temper had a kind of value, and even comfort for the mother; because there was at least an intelligible earnestness in the mood, instead of the fitful caprice that so often thwarted her in the child's manifestations. It appalled her, nevertheless, to discern here, again, a shadowy reflection of the evil that had existed in herself. All this enmity and passion had Pearl inherited, by inalienable right, out of Hester's heart. Mother and daughter stood together in the same circle of seclusion from human society; and in the nature of the child seemed to be perpetuated those unquiet elements that had distracted Hester Prynne before Pearl's birth, but had since begun to be soothed away by the softening influences of maternity.

At home, within and around her mother's cottage, Pearl wanted not a wide and various circle of acquaintance. The spell of life went forth from her ever-creative spirit, and communicated itself to a thousand objects, as a torch kindles a flame wherever it may be applied. The unlikeliest materials—a stick, a bunch of rags, a flower—were the puppets of Pearl's witchcraft, and, without undergoing any outward change, became spiritually adapted to whatever drama occupied the stage of her inner world. Her one baby-voice served a multitude of imaginary personages, old and young, to talk withal. The pine-trees, aged, black, and solemn, and flinging groans and other melancholy utterances on the breeze, needed little transformation to figure as Puritan elders; the ugliest weeds of the garden were their children, whom Pearl smote down and uprooted most unmercifully. It was wonderful, the vast variety of forms into which she threw her intellect, with no continuity, indeed, but darting up and dancing, always in a state of preternatural activity—soon sinking down, as if exhausted by so rapid and feverish a tide of life—and succeeded by other shapes of a similar wild energy. It was like nothing so much as the phantasmagoric play of the northern lights. In the mere exercise of the fancy, however, and the sportiveness of a growing mind, there might be a little more than was observable in other children of bright faculties; except as Pearl, in the dearth of human playmates, was thrown more upon the visionary throng which she created. The singularity lay in the hostile feelings with which the child regarded all these offsprings of her own heart and mind. She never created a friend, but seemed always to be sowing broadcast the dragon's teeth, whence sprung a harvest of armed enemies, against whom she rushed to battle. It was inexpressibly sad—then what depth of sorrow to a mother, who felt in her own heart the cause —to observe, in one so young, this constant recognition of an adverse world, and so fierce a training of the energies that were to make good her cause in the contest that must ensue.

Gazing at Pearl, Hester Prynne often dropped her work upon her knees, and cried out with an agony which she would fain have hidden, but which made utterance for itself betwixt speech and a groan—"O Father in Heaven—if Thou art still my Father—what is this being which I have brought into the world?" And Pearl, overhearing the ejaculation, or aware through some more subtile channel, of those throbs of anguish, would turn her vivid and beautiful little face upon her mother, smile with sprite-like intelligence, and resume her play.

One peculiarity of the child's deportment remains yet to be told. The very first thing which she had noticed in her life, was—what?—not the mother's smile, responding to it, as other babies do, by that faint, embryo smile of the little mouth, remembered so doubtfully afterwards, and with such fond discussion whether it were indeed a smile. By no means! But that first object of which Pearl seemed to become aware was—shall we say it?—the scarlet letter on Hester's bosom! One day, as her mother stooped over the cradle, the infant's eyes had been caught by the glimmering of the gold embroidery about the letter; and putting up her little hand she grasped at it, smiling, not doubtfully, but with a decided gleam, that gave her face the look of a much older child. Then, gasping for breath, did Hester Prynne clutch the fatal token, instinctively endeavouring to tear it away, so infinite was the torture inflicted by the intelligent touch of Pearl's baby-hand. Again, as if her mother's agonised gesture were meant only to make sport for her, did little Pearl look into her eyes, and smile. From that epoch, except when the child was asleep, Hester had never felt a moment's safety: not a moment's calm enjoyment of her. Weeks, it is true, would sometimes elapse, during which Pearl's gaze might never once be fixed upon the scarlet letter; but then, again, it would come at unawares, like the stroke of sudden death, and always with that peculiar smile and odd expression of the eyes.

Once this freakish, elvish cast came into the child's eyes while Hester was looking at her own image in them, as mothers are fond of doing; and suddenly—for women in solitude, and with troubled hearts, are pestered with unaccountable delusions—she fancied that she beheld, not her own miniature portrait, but another face in the small black mirror of Pearl's eye. It was a face, fiend-like, full of smiling malice, yet bearing the semblance of features that she had known full well, though seldom with a smile, and never with malice in them. It was as if an evil spirit possessed the child, and had just then peeped forth in mockery. Many a time afterwards had Hester been tortured, though less vividly, by the same illusion.

In the afternoon of a certain summer's day, after Pearl grew big enough to run about, she amused herself with gathering handfuls of wild flowers, and flinging them, one by one, at her mother's bosom; dancing up and down like a little elf whenever she hit the scarlet letter. Hester's first motion had been to cover her bosom with her clasped hands. But whether from pride or resignation, or a feeling that her penance might best be wrought out by this unutterable pain, she resisted the impulse, and sat erect, pale as death, looking sadly into little Pearl's wild eyes. Still came the battery of flowers, almost invariably hitting the mark, and covering the mother's breast with hurts for which she could find no balm in this world, nor knew how to seek it in another. At last, her shot being all expended, the child stood still and gazed at Hester, with that little laughing image of a fiend peeping out—or, whether it peeped or no, her mother so imagined it—from the unsearchable abyss of her black eyes.

"Child, what art thou?" cried the mother.

"Oh, I am your little Pearl!" answered the child.

But while she said it, Pearl laughed, and began to dance up and down with the humoursome gesticulation of a little imp, whose next freak might be to fly up the chimney.

"Art thou my child, in very truth?" asked Hester.

Nor did she put the question altogether idly, but, for the moment, with a portion of genuine earnestness; for, such was Pearl's wonderful intelligence, that her mother half doubted whether she were not acquainted with the secret spell of her existence, and might not now reveal herself.

"Yes; I am little Pearl!" repeated the child, continuing her antics.

"Thou art not my child! Thou art no Pearl of mine!" said the mother half playfully; for it was often the case that a sportive impulse came over her in the midst of her deepest suffering. "Tell me, then, what thou art, and who sent thee hither?"

"Tell me, mother!" said the child, seriously, coming up to Hester, and pressing herself close to her knees. "Do thou tell me!"

"Thy Heavenly Father sent thee!" answered Hester Prynne.

But she said it with a hesitation that did not escape the acuteness of the child. Whether moved only by her ordinary freakishness, or because an evil spirit prompted her, she put up her small forefinger and touched the scarlet letter.

"He did not send me!" cried she, positively. "I have no Heavenly Father!"

"Hush, Pearl, hush! Thou must not talk so!" answered the mother, suppressing a groan. "He sent us all into the world. He sent even me, thy mother. Then, much more thee! Or, if not, thou strange and elfish child, whence didst thou come?"

"Tell me! Tell me!" repeated Pearl, no longer seriously, but laughing and capering about the floor. "It is thou that must tell me!"

But Hester could not resolve the query, being herself in a dismal labyrinth of doubt. She remembered—betwixt a smile and a shudder—the talk of the neighbouring townspeople, who, seeking vainly elsewhere for the child's paternity, and observing some of her odd attributes, had given out that poor little Pearl was a demon offspring: such as, ever since old Catholic times, had occasionally been seen on earth, through the agency of their mother's sin, and to promote some foul and wicked purpose. Luther, according to the scandal of his monkish enemies, was a brat of that hellish breed; nor was Pearl the only child to whom this inauspicious origin was assigned among the New England Puritans.

❧ 7 ❧

THE GOVERNOR'S HALL

HESTER PRYNNE WENT one day to the mansion of Governor Bellingham, with a pair of gloves which she had fringed and embroidered to his order, and which were to be worn on some great occasion of state; for, though the chances of a popular election had caused this former ruler to descend a step or two from the highest rank, he still held an honourable and influential place among the colonial magistracy.

Another and far more important reason than the delivery of a pair of embroidered gloves, impelled Hester, at this time, to seek an interview with a personage of so much power and activity in the affairs of the settlement. It had reached her ears that there was a design on the part of some of the leading inhabitants, cherishing the more rigid order of principles in religion and government, to deprive her of her child. On the supposition that Pearl, as already hinted, was of demon origin, these good people not unreasonably argued that a Christian interest in the mother's soul required them to remove such a stumbling-block from her path. If the child, on the other hand, were really capable of moral and religious growth, and possessed the elements of ultimate salvation, then, surely, it would enjoy all the fairer prospect of these advantages by being transferred to wiser and better guardianship than Hester Prynne's. Among those who promoted the design, Governor Bellingham was said to be one of the most busy. It may appear singular, and, indeed, not a little ludicrous, that an affair of this kind, which in later days would have been referred to no higher jurisdiction than that of the select men of the town, should then have been a question publicly discussed, and on which statesmen of eminence took sides. At that epoch of pristine simplicity, however, matters of even slighter public interest, and of far less intrinsic weight than the welfare of Hester and her child, were strangely mixed up with the deliberations of legislators and acts of state. The period was hardly, if at all, earlier than that of our story, when a dispute concerning the right of property in a pig not only caused a fierce and bitter contest in the legislative body of the colony, but resulted in an important modification of the framework itself of the legislature.

Full of concern, therefore—but so conscious of her own right that it seemed scarcely an unequal match between the public on the one side, and a lonely woman, backed by the sympathies of nature, on the other—Hester Prynne set forth from her solitary cottage. Little

Pearl, of course, was her companion. She was now of an age to run lightly along by her mother's side, and, constantly in motion from morn till sunset, could have accomplished a much longer journey than that before her. Often, nevertheless, more from caprice than necessity, she demanded to be taken up in arms; but was soon as imperious to be let down again, and frisked onward before Hester on the grassy pathway, with many a harmless trip and tumble. We have spoken of Pearl's rich and luxuriant beauty—a beauty that shone with deep and vivid tints, a bright complexion, eyes possessing intensity both of depth and glow, and hair already of a deep, glossy brown, and which, in after years, would be nearly akin to black. There was fire in her and throughout her: she seemed the unpremeditated offshoot of a passionate moment. Her mother, in contriving the child's garb, had allowed the gorgeous tendencies of her imagination their full play, arraying her in a crimson velvet tunic of a peculiar cut, abundantly embroidered in fantasies and flourishes of gold thread. So much strength of colouring, which must have given a wan and pallid aspect to cheeks of a fainter bloom, was admirably adapted to Pearl's beauty, and made her the very brightest little jet of flame that ever danced upon the earth.

But it was a remarkable attribute of this garb, and indeed, of the child's whole appearance, that it irresistibly and inevitably reminded the beholder of the token which Hester Prynne was doomed to wear upon her bosom. It was the scarlet letter in another form: the scarlet letter endowed with life! The mother herself—as if the red ignominy were so deeply scorched into her brain that all her conceptions assumed its form—had carefully wrought out the similitude, lavishing many hours of morbid ingenuity to create an analogy between the object of her affection and the emblem of her guilt and torture. But, in truth, Pearl was the one as well as the other; and only in consequence of that identity had Hester contrived so perfectly to represent the scarlet letter in her appearance.

As the two wayfarers came within the precincts of the town, the children of the Puritans looked up from their play,—or what passed for play with those sombre little urchins—and spoke gravely one to another.

"Behold, verily, there is the woman of the scarlet letter: and of a truth, moreover, there is the likeness of the scarlet letter running along by her side! Come, therefore, and let us fling mud at them!"

But Pearl, who was a dauntless child, after frowning, stamping her foot, and shaking her little hand with a variety of threatening gestures, suddenly made a rush at the knot of her enemies, and put them all to flight. She resembled, in her fierce pursuit of them, an infant pestilence—the scarlet fever, or some such half-fledged angel of judgment—whose mission was to punish the sins of the rising generation. She screamed and shouted, too, with a terrific volume of sound, which, doubtless, caused the hearts of the fugitives to quake within them. The victory accomplished, Pearl returned quietly to her mother, and looked up, smiling, into her face.

Without further adventure, they reached the dwelling of Governor Bellingham. This was a large wooden house, built in a fashion of which there are specimens still extant in the streets of our older towns now moss-grown, crumbling to decay, and melancholy at heart with the many sorrowful or joyful occurrences, remembered or forgotten, that have happened and passed away within their dusky chambers. Then, however, there was the freshness of the passing year on its exterior, and the cheerfulness, gleaming forth from the sunny windows, of a human habitation, into which death had never entered. It had, indeed, a very cheery aspect, the walls being overspread with a kind of stucco, in which fragments of broken glass were plentifully intermixed; so that, when the sunshine fell aslant-wise over the front of the edifice, it glittered and sparkled as if diamonds had been flung against it by the double handful. The brilliancy might have be fitted Aladdin's palace rather than the mansion of a grave old Puritan ruler. It was further decorated with strange and seemingly cabalistic figures and diagrams, suitable to the quaint taste of the age which had been drawn in the stucco, when newly laid on, and had now grown hard and durable, for the admiration of after times.

Pearl, looking at this bright wonder of a house began to caper and dance, and imperatively required that the whole breadth of sunshine should be stripped off its front, and given her to play with.

"No, my little Pearl!" said her mother; "thou must gather thine own sunshine. I have none to give thee!"

They approached the door, which was of an arched form, and flanked on each side by a narrow tower or projection of the edifice, in both of which were lattice-windows, the wooden shutters to close over them at need. Lifting the iron hammer that hung at the portal, Hester Prynne gave a summons, which was answered by one of the Governor's bond servant—a free-born Englishman, but now a seven years' slave. During that term he was to be the property of his master, and as much a commodity of bargain and sale as an ox, or a joint-stool. The serf wore the customary garb of serving-men at that period, and long before, in the old hereditary halls of England.

"Is the worshipful Governor Bellingham within?" inquired Hester.

"Yea, forsooth," replied the bond-servant, staring with wide-open eyes at the scarlet letter, which, being a new-comer in the country, he had never before seen. "Yea, his honourable worship is within. But he hath a godly minister or two with him, and likewise a leech. Ye may not see his worship now."

"Nevertheless, I will enter," answered Hester Prynne; and the bond-servant, perhaps judging from the decision of her air, and the glittering symbol in her bosom, that she was a great lady in the land, offered no opposition.

So the mother and little Pearl were admitted into the hall of entrance. With many variations, suggested by the nature of his building materials, diversity of climate, and a different mode of social life, Governor Bellingham had planned his new habitation after the residences of gentlemen of fair estate in his native land. Here, then, was a wide and reasonably lofty hall, extending through the whole depth of the house, and forming a medium of general communication, more or less directly, with all the other apartments. At one extremity, this spacious room was lighted by the windows of the two towers, which formed a small recess on either side of the portal. At the other end, though partly muffled by a curtain, it was more powerfully illuminated by one of those embowed hall windows which we read of in old books, and which was provided with a deep and cushioned seat. Here, on the cushion, lay a folio tome, probably of the Chronicles of England, or other such substantial literature; even as, in our own days, we scatter gilded volumes on the centre table, to be turned over by the casual guest. The furniture of the hall consisted of some ponderous chairs, the backs of which were elaborately carved with wreaths of oaken flowers; and likewise a table in the same taste, the whole being of the Elizabethan age, or perhaps earlier, and heirlooms, transferred hither from the Governor's paternal home. On the table—in token that the sentiment of old English hospitality had not been left behind—stood a large pewter tankard, at the bottom of which, had Hester or Pearl peeped into it, they might have seen the frothy remnant of a recent draught of ale.

On the wall hung a row of portraits, representing the forefathers of the Bellingham lineage, some with armour on their breasts, and others with stately ruffs and robes of peace. All were characterised by the sternness and severity which old portraits so invariably put on, as if they were the ghosts, rather than the pictures, of departed worthies, and were gazing with harsh and intolerant criticism at the pursuits and enjoyments of living men.

At about the centre of the oaken panels that lined the hall was suspended a suit of mail, not, like the pictures, an ancestral relic, but of the most modern date; for it had been manufactured by a skilful armourer in London, the same year in which Governor Bellingham came over to New England. There was a steel head-piece, a cuirass, a gorget and greaves, with a pair of gauntlets and a sword hanging beneath; all, and especially the helmet and breastplate, so highly burnished as to glow with white radiance, and scatter an illumination everywhere about upon the floor. This bright panoply was not meant for mere idle show, but had been worn by the Governor on many a solemn muster and training field, and had glittered, moreover, at the head of a regiment in the Pequod war. For, though bred a lawyer, and accustomed to speak of Bacon, Coke, Noye, and Finch, as his professional associates, the exigencies of this new country had transformed Governor Bellingham into a soldier, as well as a statesman and ruler.

Little Pearl, who was as greatly pleased with the gleaming armour as she had been with the glittering frontispiece of the house, spent some time looking into the polished mirror of the breastplate.

"Mother," cried she, "I see you here. Look! Look!"

Hester looked by way of humouring the child; and she saw that, owing to the peculiar effect of this convex mirror, the scarlet letter was represented in exaggerated and gigantic proportions, so as to be greatly the most prominent feature of her appearance. In truth, she seemed absolutely hidden behind it. Pearl pointed upwards also, at a similar picture in the head-piece; smiling at her mother, with the elfish intelligence that was so familiar an expression on her small physiognomy. That look of naughty merriment was likewise reflected in the mirror, with so much breadth and intensity of effect, that it made Hester Prynne feel as if it could not be the image of her own child, but of an imp who was seeking to mould itself into Pearl's shape.

"Come along, Pearl," said she, drawing her away, "Come and look into this fair garden. It may be we shall see flowers there; more beautiful ones than we find in the woods."

Pearl accordingly ran to the bow-window, at the further end of the hall, and looked along the vista of a garden walk, carpeted with closely-shaven grass, and bordered with some rude and immature attempt at shrubbery. But the proprietor appeared already to have relinquished as hopeless, the effort to perpetuate on this side of the Atlantic, in a hard soil, and amid the close struggle for subsistence, the native English taste for ornamental gardening. Cabbages grew in plain sight; and a pumpkin-vine, rooted at some distance, had run across the intervening space, and deposited one of its gigantic products directly beneath the hall window, as if to warn the Governor that this great lump of vegetable gold was as rich an ornament as New England earth would offer him. There were a few rose-bushes, however, and a number of apple-trees, probably the descendants of those planted by the Reverend Mr. Blackstone, the first settler of the peninsula; that half mythological personage who rides through our early annals, seated on the back of a bull.

Pearl, seeing the rose-bushes, began to cry for a red rose, and would not be pacified.

"Hush, child—hush!" said her mother, earnestly. "Do not cry, dear little Pearl! I hear voices in the garden. The Governor is coming, and gentlemen along with him."

In fact, adown the vista of the garden avenue, a number of persons were seen approaching towards the house. Pearl, in utter scorn of her mother's attempt to quiet her, gave an eldritch scream, and then became silent, not from any notion of obedience, but because the quick and mobile curiosity of her disposition was excited by the appearance of those new personages.

❧ 8 ❧

THE ELF-CHILD AND THE MINISTER

GOVERNOR BELLINGHAM, in a loose gown and easy cap—such as elderly gentlemen loved to endue themselves with, in their domestic privacy—walked foremost, and appeared to be showing off his estate, and expatiating on his projected improvements. The wide circumference of an elaborate ruff, beneath his grey beard, in the antiquated fashion of King James's reign, caused his head to look not a little like that of John the Baptist in a charger. The impression made by his aspect, so rigid and severe, and frost-bitten with more than autumnal age, was hardly in keeping with the appliances of worldly enjoyment wherewith he had evidently done his utmost to surround himself. But it is an error to suppose that our great forefathers—though accustomed to speak and think of human existence as a state merely of trial and warfare, and though unfeignedly prepared to sacrifice goods and life at the behest of duty—made it a matter of conscience to reject such means of comfort, or even luxury, as lay fairly within their grasp. This creed was never taught, for instance, by the venerable pastor, John Wilson, whose beard, white as a snow-drift, was seen over Governor Bellingham's shoulders, while its wearer suggested that pears and peaches might yet be naturalised in the New England climate, and that purple grapes might possibly be compelled to flourish against the sunny garden-wall. The old clergyman, nurtured at the rich bosom of the English Church, had a long established and legitimate taste for all good and comfortable things, and however stern he might show himself in the pulpit, or in his public reproof of such transgressions as that of Hester Prynne, still, the genial benevolence of his private life had won him warmer affection than was accorded to any of his professional contemporaries.

Behind the Governor and Mr. Wilson came two other guests—one, the Reverend Arthur Dimmesdale, whom the reader may remember as having taken a brief and reluctant part in the scene of Hester Prynne's disgrace; and, in close companionship with him, old Roger Chillingworth, a person of great skill in physic, who for two or three years past had been settled in the town. It was understood that this learned man was the physician as well as friend of the young minister, whose health had severely suffered of late by his too unreserved self-sacrifice to the labours and duties of the pastoral relation.

The Governor, in advance of his visitors, ascended one or two steps, and, throwing open the leaves of the great hall window, found himself close to little Pearl. The shadow of the curtain fell on Hester Prynne, and partially concealed her.

"What have we here?" said Governor Bellingham, looking with surprise at the scarlet little figure before him. "I profess, I have never seen the like since my days of vanity, in old King James's time, when I was wont to esteem it a high favour to be admitted to a court mask! There used to be a swarm of these small apparitions in holiday time, and we called them children of the Lord of Misrule. But how gat such a guest into my hall?"

"Ay, indeed!" cried good old Mr. Wilson. "What little bird of scarlet plumage may this be? Methinks I have seen just such figures when the sun has been shining through a richly painted window, and tracing out the golden and crimson images across the floor. But that was in the old land. Prithee, young one, who art thou, and what has ailed thy mother to bedizen thee in this strange fashion? Art thou a Christian child—ha? Dost know thy catechism? Or art thou one of those naughty elfs or fairies whom we thought to have left behind us, with other relics of Papistry, in merry old England?"

"I am mother's child," answered the scarlet vision, "and my name is Pearl!"

"Pearl?—Ruby, rather—or Coral!—or Red Rose, at the very least, judging from thy hue!" responded the old minister, putting forth his hand in a vain attempt to pat little Pearl on the cheek. "But where is this mother of thine? Ah! I see," he added; and, turning to Governor Bellingham, whispered, "This is the selfsame child of whom we have held speech together; and behold here the unhappy woman, Hester Prynne, her mother!"

"Sayest thou so?" cried the Governor. "Nay, we might have judged that such a child's mother must needs be a scarlet woman, and a worthy type of her of Babylon! But she comes at a good time, and we will look into this matter forthwith."

Governor Bellingham stepped through the window into the hall, followed by his three guests.

"Hester Prynne," said he, fixing his naturally stern regard on the wearer of the scarlet letter, "there hath been much question concerning thee of late. The point hath been weightily discussed, whether we, that are of authority and influence, do well discharge our consciences by trusting an immortal soul, such as there is in yonder child, to the guidance of one who hath stumbled and fallen amid the pitfalls of this world. Speak thou, the child's own mother! Were it not, thinkest thou, for thy little one's temporal and eternal welfare that she be taken out of thy charge, and clad soberly, and disciplined strictly, and instructed in the truths of heaven and earth? What canst thou do for the child in this kind?"

"I can teach my little Pearl what I have learned from this!" answered Hester Prynne, laying her finger on the red token.

"Woman, it is thy badge of shame!" replied the stern magistrate. "It is because of the stain which that letter indicates that we would transfer thy child to other hands."

"Nevertheless," said the mother, calmly, though growing more pale, "this badge hath taught me—it daily teaches me—it is teaching me at this moment—lessons whereof my child may be the wiser and better, albeit they can profit nothing to myself."

"We will judge warily," said Bellingham, "and look well what we are about to do. Good Master Wilson, I pray you, examine this Pearl—since that is her name—and see whether she hath had such Christian nurture as befits a child of her age."

The old minister seated himself in an arm-chair and made an effort to draw Pearl betwixt his knees. But the child, unaccustomed to the touch or familiarity of any but her mother, escaped through the open window, and stood on the upper step, looking like a wild tropical bird of rich plumage, ready to take flight into the upper air. Mr. Wilson, not a little astonished at this outbreak—for he was a grandfatherly sort of personage, and usually a vast favourite with children—essayed, however, to proceed with the examination.

"Pearl," said he, with great solemnity, "thou must take heed to instruction, that so, in due season, thou mayest wear in thy bosom the pearl of great price. Canst thou tell me, my child, who made thee?"

Now Pearl knew well enough who made her, for Hester Prynne, the daughter of a pious home, very soon after her talk with the child about her Heavenly Father, had begun to inform her of those truths which the human spirit, at whatever stage of immaturity, imbibes with such eager interest. Pearl, therefore—so large were the attainments of her three years' lifetime—could have borne a fair examination in the New England Primer, or the first column of the Westminster Catechisms, although unacquainted with the outward form of either of those celebrated works. But that perversity, which all children have more or less of, and of which little Pearl had a tenfold portion, now, at the most inopportune moment, took thorough possession of her, and closed her lips, or impelled her to speak words amiss. After putting her finger in her mouth, with many ungracious refusals to answer good Mr. Wilson's question, the child finally announced that she had not been made at all, but had been plucked by her mother off the bush of wild roses that grew by the prison-door.

This phantasy was probably suggested by the near proximity of the Governor's red roses, as Pearl stood outside of the window, together with her recollection of the prison rose-bush, which she had passed in coming hither.

Old Roger Chillingworth, with a smile on his face, whispered something in the young clergyman's ear. Hester Prynne looked at the man of skill, and even then, with her fate hanging in the balance, was startled to perceive what a change had come over his features—how much uglier they were, how his dark complexion seemed to have grown duskier, and his figure more misshapen—since the days when she had familiarly known him. She met his eyes for an instant, but was immediately constrained to give all her attention to the scene now going forward.

"This is awful!" cried the Governor, slowly recovering from the astonishment into which Pearl's response had thrown him. "Here is a child of three years old, and she cannot tell who made her! Without question, she is equally in the dark as to her soul, its present depravity, and future destiny! Methinks, gentlemen, we need inquire no further."

Hester caught hold of Pearl, and drew her forcibly into her arms, confronting the old Puritan magistrate with almost a fierce expression. Alone in the world, cast off by it, and with this sole treasure to keep her heart alive, she felt that she possessed indefeasible rights against the world, and was ready to defend them to the death.

"God gave me the child!" cried she. "He gave her in requital of all things else which ye had taken from me. She is my happiness—she is my torture, none the less! Pearl keeps me here in life! Pearl punishes me, too! See ye not, she is the scarlet letter, only capable of being loved, and so endowed with a millionfold the power of retribution for my sin? Ye shall not take her! I will die first!"

"My poor woman," said the not unkind old minister, "the child shall be well cared for—far better than thou canst do for it."

"God gave her into my keeping!" repeated Hester Prynne, raising her voice almost to a shriek. "I will not give her up!" And here by a sudden impulse, she turned to the young clergyman, Mr. Dimmesdale, at whom, up to this moment, she had seemed hardly so much as once to direct her eyes. "Speak thou for me!" cried she. "Thou wast my pastor, and hadst charge of my soul, and knowest me better than these men can. I will not lose the child! Speak for me! Thou knowest—for thou hast sympathies which these men lack—thou knowest what is in my heart, and what are a mother's rights, and how much the stronger they are when that mother has but her child and the scarlet letter! Look thou to it! I will not lose the child! Look to it!"

At this wild and singular appeal, which indicated that Hester Prynne's situation had provoked her to little less than madness, the young minister at once came forward, pale, and holding his hand over his heart, as was his custom whenever his peculiarly nervous temperament was thrown into agitation. He looked now more careworn and emaciated than as we described him at the scene of Hester's public ignominy; and whether it were his failing health, or whatever the cause might be, his large dark eyes had a world of pain in their troubled and melancholy depth.

"There is truth in what she says," began the minister, with a voice sweet, tremulous, but powerful, insomuch that the hall re-echoed and the hollow armour rang with it—"truth in what Hester says, and in the feeling which inspires her! God gave her the child, and gave her, too, an instinctive knowledge of its nature and requirements—both seemingly so peculiar—which no other mortal being can possess. And, moreover, is there not a quality of awful sacredness in the relation between this mother and this child?"

"Ay—how is that, good Master Dimmesdale?" interrupted the Governor. "Make that plain, I pray you!"

"It must be even so," resumed the minister. "For, if we deem it otherwise, do we not thereby say that the Heavenly Father, the creator of all flesh, hath lightly recognised a deed of sin, and made of no account the distinction between unhallowed lust and holy love? This child of its father's guilt and its mother's shame has come from the hand of God, to work in many ways upon her heart, who pleads so earnestly and with such bitterness of spirit the right to keep her. It was meant for a blessing—for the one blessing of her life! It was meant, doubtless, the mother herself hath told us, for a retribution, too; a torture to be felt at many an unthought-of moment; a pang, a sting, an ever-recurring agony, in the midst of a troubled joy! Hath she not expressed this thought in the garb of the poor child, so forcibly reminding us of that red symbol which sears her bosom?"

"Well said again!" cried good Mr. Wilson. "I feared the woman had no better thought than to make a mountebank of her child!"

"Oh, not so!—not so!" continued Mr. Dimmesdale. "She recognises, believe me, the solemn miracle which God hath wrought in the existence of that child. And may she feel, too—what, methinks, is the very truth—that this boon was meant, above all things else, to keep the mother's soul alive, and to preserve her from blacker depths of sin into which Satan might else have sought to plunge her! Therefore it is good for this poor, sinful woman, that she hath an infant immortality, a being capable of eternal joy or sorrow, confided to her care—to be trained up by her to righteousness, to remind her, at every moment, of her fall, but yet to teach her, as if it were by the Creator's sacred pledge, that, if she bring the child to heaven, the child also will bring its parents thither! Herein is the sinful mother happier than the sinful father. For Hester Prynne's sake, then, and no less for the poor child's sake, let us leave them as Providence hath seen fit to place them!"

"You speak, my friend, with a strange earnestness," said old Roger Chillingworth, smiling at him.

"And there is a weighty import in what my young brother hath spoken," added the Rev. Mr. Wilson.

"What say you, worshipful Master Bellingham? Hath he not pleaded well for the poor woman?"

"Indeed hath he," answered the magistrate; "and hath adduced such arguments, that we will even leave the matter as it now stands; so long, at least, as there shall be no further scandal in the woman. Care must be had nevertheless, to put the child to due and stated examination in the catechism, at thy hands or Master Dimmesdale's. Moreover, at a proper season, the tithing-men must take heed that she go both to school and to meeting."

The young minister, on ceasing to speak had withdrawn a few steps from the group, and stood with his face partially concealed in the heavy folds of the window-curtain; while the shadow of his figure, which the sunlight cast upon the floor, was tremulous with the vehemence of his appeal. Pearl, that wild and flighty little elf stole softly towards him, and taking his hand in the grasp of both her own, laid her cheek against it; a caress so tender, and withal so unobtrusive, that her mother, who was looking on, asked herself—"Is that my Pearl?" Yet she knew that there was love in the child's heart, although it mostly revealed itself in passion, and hardly twice in her lifetime had been softened by such gentleness as now. The minister—for, save the long-sought regards of woman, nothing is sweeter than these marks of childish preference, accorded spontaneously by a spiritual instinct, and therefore seeming to imply in us something truly worthy to be loved—the minister looked round, laid his hand on the child's head, hesitated an instant, and then kissed her brow. Little Pearl's unwonted mood of sentiment lasted no longer; she laughed, and went capering down the hall so airily, that old Mr. Wilson raised a question whether even her tiptoes touched the floor.

"The little baggage hath witchcraft in her, I profess," said he to Mr. Dimmesdale. "She needs no old woman's broomstick to fly withal!"

"A strange child!" remarked old Roger Chillingworth. "It is easy to see the mother's part in her. Would it be beyond a philosopher's research, think ye, gentlemen, to analyse that child's nature, and, from it make a mould, to give a shrewd guess at the father?"

"Nay; it would be sinful, in such a question, to follow the clue of profane philosophy," said Mr. Wilson. "Better to fast and pray upon it; and still better, it may be, to leave the mystery as we find it, unless Providence reveal it of its own accord. Thereby, every good Christian man hath a title to show a father's kindness towards the poor, deserted babe."

The affair being so satisfactorily concluded, Hester Prynne, with Pearl, departed from the house. As they descended the steps, it is averred that the lattice of a chamber-window was thrown open, and forth into the sunny day was thrust the face of Mistress Hibbins, Governor Bellingham's bitter-tempered sister, and the same who, a few years later, was executed as a witch.

"Hist, hist!" said she, while her ill-omened physiognomy seemed to cast a shadow over the cheerful newness of the house. "Wilt thou go with us to-night? There will be a merry company in the forest; and I well-nigh promised the Black Man that comely Hester Prynne should make one."

"Make my excuse to him, so please you!" answered Hester, with a triumphant smile. "I must tarry at home, and keep watch over my little Pearl. Had they taken her from me, I would willingly have gone with thee into the forest, and signed my name in the Black Man's book too, and that with mine own blood!"

"We shall have thee there anon!" said the witch-lady, frowning, as she drew back her head.

But here—if we suppose this interview betwixt Mistress Hibbins and Hester Prynne to be authentic, and not a parable—was already an illustration of the young minister's argument against sundering the relation of a fallen mother to the offspring of her frailty. Even thus early had the child saved her from Satan's snare.

❦ 9 ❧

THE LEECH

UNDER THE APPELLATION of Roger Chillingworth, the reader will remember, was hidden another name, which its former wearer had resolved should never more be spoken. It has been related, how, in the crowd that witnessed Hester Prynne's ignominious exposure, stood a man, elderly, travel-worn, who, just emerging from the perilous wilderness, beheld the woman, in whom he hoped to find embodied the warmth and cheerfulness of home, set up as a type of sin before the people. Her matronly fame was trodden under all men's feet. Infamy was babbling around her in the public market-place. For her kindred, should the tidings ever reach them, and for the companions of her unspotted life, there remained nothing but the contagion of her dishonour; which would not fail to be distributed in strict accordance and proportion with the intimacy and sacredness of their previous relationship. Then why—since the choice was with himself—should the individual, whose connexion with the fallen woman had been the most intimate and sacred of them all, come forward to vindicate his claim to an inheritance so little desirable? He resolved not to be pilloried beside her on her pedestal of shame. Unknown to all but Hester Prynne, and possessing the lock and key of her silence, he chose to withdraw his name from the roll of mankind, and, as regarded his former ties and interest, to vanish out of life as completely as if he indeed lay at the bottom of the ocean, whither rumour had long ago consigned him. This purpose once effected, new interests would immediately spring up, and likewise a new purpose; dark, it is true, if not guilty, but of force enough to engage the full strength of his faculties.

In pursuance of this resolve, he took up his residence in the Puritan town as Roger Chillingworth, without other introduction than the learning and intelligence of which he possessed more than a common measure. As his studies, at a previous period of his life, had made him extensively acquainted with the medical science of the day, it was as a physician that he presented himself and as such was cordially received. Skilful men, of the medical and chirurgical profession, were of rare occurrence in the colony. They seldom, it would appear, partook of the religious zeal that brought other emigrants across the Atlantic. In their researches into the human frame, it may be that the higher and more subtle faculties of such men were materialised, and that they lost the spiritual view of existence amid the intricacies of that wondrous mechanism, which seemed to involve art enough to comprise all of life within itself. At all events, the health of the good town of Boston, so far as medicine had aught to do with it, had hitherto lain in the guardianship of an aged deacon and apothecary, whose piety and godly deportment were stronger testimonials in his favour than any that he could have produced in the shape of a diploma. The only surgeon was one who combined the occasional exercise of that noble art with the daily and habitual flourish of a razor. To such a professional body Roger Chillingworth was a brilliant acquisition. He soon manifested his familiarity with the ponderous and imposing machinery of antique physic; in which every remedy contained a multitude of far-fetched and heterogeneous ingredients, as elaborately compounded as if the proposed result had been the Elixir of Life. In his Indian captivity, moreover, he had gained much knowledge of the properties of native herbs and roots; nor did he conceal from his patients that these simple medicines, Nature's boon to the untutored savage, had quite as large a share of his own confidence as the European Pharmacopoeia, which so many learned doctors had spent centuries in elaborating.

This learned stranger was exemplary as regarded at least the outward forms of a religious life; and early after his arrival, had chosen for his spiritual guide the Reverend Mr. Dimmesdale. The young divine, whose scholar-like renown still lived in Oxford, was considered by his more fervent admirers as little less than a heavenly ordained apostle, destined, should he live and labour for the ordinary term of life, to do as great deeds, for the now feeble New England Church, as the early Fathers had achieved for the infancy of the Christian faith. About this period, however, the health of Mr. Dimmesdale had evidently begun to fail. By those best acquainted with his habits, the paleness of the young minister's cheek was accounted for by his too earnest devotion to study, his scrupulous fulfilment of parochial duty, and more than all, to the fasts and vigils of which he made a frequent practice, in order to keep the grossness of this earthly state from clogging and obscuring his spiritual lamp. Some declared, that if Mr. Dimmesdale were really going to die, it was cause enough that the world was not worthy to be any longer trodden by his feet. He himself, on the other hand, with characteristic humility, avowed his belief that if Providence should see fit to remove him, it would be because of his own unworthiness to perform its humblest mission here on earth. With all this difference of opinion as to the cause of his decline, there could be no question of the fact. His form grew emaciated; his voice, though still rich and sweet, had a certain melancholy prophecy of decay in it; he was often observed, on any slight alarm or other sudden accident, to put his hand over his heart with first a flush and then a paleness, indicative of pain.

Such was the young clergyman's condition, and so imminent the prospect that his dawning light would be extinguished, all untimely, when Roger Chillingworth made his advent to the town. His first entry on the scene, few people could tell whence, dropping down as it were out of the sky or starting from the nether earth, had an aspect of mystery, which was easily heightened to the miraculous. He was now known to be a man of skill; it was observed that he gathered herbs and the blossoms of wild-flowers, and dug up roots and plucked off twigs from the forest-trees like one acquainted with hidden virtues in what was valueless to common eyes. He was heard to speak of Sir Kenelm Digby and other famous men—whose scientific attainments were esteemed hardly less than supernatural—as having been his correspondents or associates. Why, with such rank in the learned world, had he come hither? What, could he, whose sphere was in great cities, be seeking in the wilderness? In answer to this query, a rumour gained ground—and however absurd, was entertained by some very sensible people— that Heaven had wrought an absolute miracle, by transporting an eminent Doctor of Physic from a German university bodily through the air and setting him down at the door of Mr. Dimmesdale's study! Individuals of wiser faith, indeed, who knew that Heaven promotes its purposes without aiming at the stage-effect of what is called miraculous interposition, were inclined to see a providential hand in Roger Chillingworth's so opportune arrival.

This idea was countenanced by the strong interest which the physician ever manifested in the young clergyman; he attached himself to him as a parishioner, and sought to win a friendly regard and confidence from his naturally reserved sensibility. He expressed great alarm at his pastor's state of health, but was anxious to attempt the cure, and, if early undertaken, seemed not despondent of a favourable result. The elders, the deacons, the motherly dames, and the young and fair maidens of Mr. Dimmesdale's flock, were alike importunate that he should make trial of the physician's frankly offered skill. Mr. Dimmesdale gently repelled their entreaties.

"I need no medicine," said he.

But how could the young minister say so, when, with every successive Sabbath, his cheek was paler and thinner, and his voice more tremulous than before—when it had now become a constant habit, rather than a casual gesture, to press his hand over his heart? Was he weary of his labours? Did he wish to die? These questions were solemnly propounded to Mr. Dimmesdale by the elder ministers of Boston, and the deacons of his church, who, to use their own phrase, "dealt with him," on the sin of rejecting the aid which Providence so manifestly held out. He listened in silence, and finally promised to confer with the physician.

"Were it God's will," said the Reverend Mr. Dimmesdale, when, in fulfilment of this pledge, he requested old Roger Chillingworth's professional advice, "I could be well content that my labours, and my sorrows, and my sins, and my pains, should shortly end with me, and what is earthly of them be buried in my grave, and the spiritual go with me to my eternal state, rather than that you should put your skill to the proof in my behalf."

"Ah," replied Roger Chillingworth, with that quietness, which, whether imposed or natural, marked all his deportment, "it is thus that a young clergyman is apt to speak. Youthful men, not having taken a deep root, give up their hold of life so easily! And saintly men, who walk with God on earth, would fain be away, to walk with him on the golden pavements of the New Jerusalem."

"Nay," rejoined the young minister, putting his hand to his heart, with a flush of pain flitting over his brow, "were I worthier to walk there, I could be better content to toil here."

"Good men ever interpret themselves too meanly," said the physician.

In this manner, the mysterious old Roger Chillingworth became the medical adviser of the Reverend Mr. Dimmesdale. As not only the disease interested the physician, but he was strongly moved to look into the character and qualities of the patient, these two men, so different in age, came gradually to spend much time together. For the sake of the minister's health, and to enable the leech to gather plants with healing balm in them, they took long walks on the sea-shore, or in the forest; mingling various walks with the splash and murmur of the waves, and the solemn wind-anthem among the tree-tops. Often, likewise, one was the guest of the other in his place of study and retirement. There was a fascination for the minister in the company of the man of science, in whom he recognised an intellectual cultivation of no moderate depth or scope; together with a range and freedom of ideas, that he would have vainly looked for among the members of his own profession. In truth, he was startled, if not shocked, to find this attribute in the physician. Mr. Dimmesdale was a true priest, a true religionist, with the reverential sentiment largely developed, and an order of mind that impelled itself powerfully along the track of a creed, and wore its passage continually deeper with the lapse of time. In no state of society would he have been what is called a man of liberal views; it would always be essential to his peace to feel the pressure of a faith about him, supporting, while it confined him within its iron framework. Not the less, however, though with a tremulous enjoyment, did he feel the occasional relief of looking at the universe through the medium of another kind of intellect than those with which he habitually held converse. It was as if a window were thrown open, admitting a freer atmosphere into the close and stifled study, where his life was wasting itself away, amid lamp-light, or obstructed day-beams, and the musty fragrance, be it sensual or moral, that exhales from books. But the air was too fresh and chill to be long breathed with comfort. So the minister, and the physician with him, withdrew again within the limits of what their Church defined as orthodox.

Thus Roger Chillingworth scrutinised his patient carefully, both as he saw him in his ordinary life, keeping an accustomed pathway in the range of thoughts familiar to him, and as he appeared when thrown amidst other moral scenery, the novelty of which might call out something new to the surface of his character. He deemed it essential, it would seem, to know the man, before attempting to do him good. Wherever there is a heart and an intellect, the diseases of the physical frame are tinged with the peculiarities of these. In Arthur Dimmesdale, thought and imagination were so active, and sensibility so intense, that the bodily infirmity would be likely to have its groundwork there. So Roger Chillingworth—the man of skill, the kind and friendly physician—strove to go deep into his patient's bosom, delving among his principles, prying into his recollections, and probing everything with a cautious touch, like a treasure-seeker in a dark cavern. Few secrets can escape an investigator, who has opportunity and licence to undertake such a quest, and skill to follow it up. A man burdened with a secret should especially avoid the intimacy of his physician. If the latter possess native sagacity, and a nameless something more,—let us call it intuition; if he show no intrusive egotism, nor disagreeable prominent characteristics of his own; if he have the power, which must be born with him, to bring his mind into such affinity with his patient's, that this last shall unawares have spoken what he imagines himself only to have thought; if such revelations be received without tumult, and acknowledged not so often by an uttered sympathy as by silence, an inarticulate breath, and here and there a word to indicate that all is understood; if to these qualifications of a confidant be joined the advantages afforded by his recognised character as a physician;—then, at some inevitable moment, will the soul of the sufferer be dissolved, and flow forth in a dark but transparent stream, bringing all its mysteries into the daylight.

Roger Chillingworth possessed all, or most, of the attributes above enumerated. Nevertheless, time went on; a kind of intimacy, as we have said, grew up between these two cultivated minds, which had as wide a field as the whole sphere of human thought and study to meet upon; they discussed every topic of ethics and religion, of public affairs, and private character; they talked much, on both sides, of matters that seemed personal to themselves; and yet no secret, such as the physician fancied must exist there, ever stole out of the minister's consciousness into his companion's ear. The latter had his suspicions, indeed, that even the nature of Mr. Dimmesdale's bodily disease had never fairly been revealed to him. It was a strange reserve!

After a time, at a hint from Roger Chillingworth, the friends of Mr. Dimmesdale effected an arrangement by which the two were lodged in the same house; so that every ebb and flow of the minister's life-tide might pass under the eye of his anxious and attached physician. There was much joy throughout the town when this greatly desirable object was attained. It was held to be the best possible measure for the young clergyman's welfare; unless, indeed, as often urged by such as felt authorised to do so, he had selected some one of the many blooming damsels, spiritually devoted to him, to become his devoted wife. This latter step, however, there was no present prospect that Arthur Dimmesdale would be prevailed upon to take; he rejected all suggestions of the kind, as if priestly celibacy were one of his articles of Church discipline. Doomed by his own choice, therefore, as Mr. Dimmesdale so evidently was, to eat his unsavoury morsel always at another's board, and endure the life-long chill which must be his lot who seeks to warm himself only at another's fireside, it truly seemed that this sagacious, experienced, benevolent old physician, with his concord of paternal and reverential love for the young pastor, was the very man, of all mankind, to be constantly within reach of his voice.

The new abode of the two friends was with a pious widow, of good social rank, who dwelt in a house covering pretty nearly the site on which the venerable structure of King's Chapel has since been built. It had the graveyard, originally Isaac Johnson's home-field, on one side, and so was well adapted to call up serious reflections, suited to their respective employments, in both minister and man of physic. The motherly care of the good widow assigned to Mr. Dimmesdale a front apartment, with a sunny exposure, and heavy window-curtains, to create a noontide shadow when desirable. The walls were hung round with tapestry, said to be from the Gobelin looms, and, at all events, representing the Scriptural story of David and Bathsheba, and Nathan the Prophet, in colours still unfaded, but which made the fair woman of the scene almost as grimly picturesque as the woe-denouncing seer. Here the pale clergyman piled up his library, rich with parchment-bound folios of the Fathers, and the lore of Rabbis, and monkish erudition, of which the Protestant divines, even while they vilified and decried that class of writers, were yet constrained often to avail themselves. On the other side of the house, old Roger Chillingworth arranged his study and laboratory: not such as a modern man of science would reckon even tolerably complete, but provided with a distilling apparatus and the means of compounding drugs and chemicals, which the practised alchemist knew well how to turn to purpose. With such commodiousness of situation, these two learned persons sat themselves down, each in his own domain, yet familiarly passing from one apartment to the other, and bestowing a mutual and not incurious inspection into one another's business.

And the Reverend Arthur Dimmesdale's best discerning friends, as we have intimated, very reasonably imagined that the hand of Providence had done all this for the purpose—besought in so many public and domestic and secret prayers—of restoring the young minister to health. But, it must now be said, another portion of the community had latterly begun to take its own view of the relation betwixt Mr. Dimmesdale and the mysterious old physician. When an uninstructed multitude attempts to see with its eyes, it is exceedingly apt to be deceived. When, however, it forms its judgment, as it usually does, on the intuitions of its great and warm heart, the conclusions thus attained are often so profound and so unerring as to possess the character of truth supernaturally revealed. The people, in the case of which we speak, could justify its prejudice against Roger Chillingworth by no fact or argument worthy of serious refutation. There was an aged handicraftsman, it is true, who had been a citizen of London at the period of Sir Thomas Overbury's murder, now some thirty years agone; he testified to having seen the physician, under some other name, which the narrator of the story had now forgotten, in company with Dr. Forman, the famous old conjurer, who was implicated in the affair of Overbury. Two or three individuals hinted that the man of skill, during his Indian captivity, had enlarged his medical attainments by joining in the incantations of the savage priests, who were universally acknowledged to be powerful enchanters, often performing seemingly miraculous cures by their skill in the black art. A large number—and many of these were persons of such sober sense and practical observation that their opinions would have been valuable in other matters—affirmed that Roger Chillingworth's aspect had undergone a remarkable change while he had dwelt in town, and especially since his abode with Mr. Dimmesdale. At first, his expression had been calm, meditative, scholar-like. Now there was something ugly and evil in his face, which they had not previously noticed, and which grew still the more obvious to sight the oftener they looked upon him. According to the vulgar idea, the fire in his laboratory had been brought from the lower regions, and was fed with infernal fuel; and so, as might be expected, his visage was getting sooty with the smoke.

To sum up the matter, it grew to be a widely diffused opinion that the Rev. Arthur Dimmesdale, like many other personages of special sanctity, in all ages of the Christian world, was haunted either by Satan himself or Satan's emissary, in the guise of old Roger Chillingworth. This diabolical agent had the Divine permission, for a season, to burrow into the clergyman's intimacy, and plot against his soul. No sensible man, it was confessed, could doubt on which side the victory would turn. The people looked, with an unshaken hope, to see the minister come forth out of the conflict transfigured with the glory which he would unquestionably win. Meanwhile, nevertheless, it was sad to think of the perchance mortal agony through which he must struggle towards his triumph.

Alas! to judge from the gloom and terror in the depth of the poor minister's eyes, the battle was a sore one, and the victory anything but secure.

✣ 10 ✣

THE LEECH AND HIS PATIENT

OLD ROGER CHILLINGWORTH, throughout life, had been calm in temperament, kindly, though not of warm affections, but ever, and in all his relations with the world, a pure and upright man. He had begun an investigation, as he imagined, with the severe and equal integrity of a judge, desirous only of truth, even as if the question involved no more than the air-drawn lines and figures of a geometrical problem, instead of human passions, and wrongs inflicted on himself. But, as he proceeded, a terrible fascination, a kind of fierce, though still calm, necessity, seized the old man within its gripe, and never set him free again until he had done all its bidding. He now dug into the poor clergyman's heart, like a miner searching for gold; or, rather, like a sexton delving into a grave, possibly in quest of a jewel that had been buried on the dead man's bosom, but likely to find nothing save mortality and corruption. Alas, for his own soul, if these were what he sought!

Sometimes a light glimmered out of the physician's eyes, burning blue and ominous, like the reflection of a furnace, or, let us say, like one of those gleams of ghastly fire that darted from Bunyan's awful doorway in the hillside, and quivered on the pilgrim's face. The soil where this dark miner was working had perchance shown indications that encouraged him.

"This man," said he, at one such moment, to himself, "pure as they deem him—all spiritual as he seems—hath inherited a strong animal nature from his father or his mother. Let us dig a little further in the direction of this vein!"

Then after long search into the minister's dim interior, and turning over many precious materials, in the shape of high aspirations for the welfare of his race, warm love of souls, pure sentiments, natural piety, strengthened by thought and study, and illuminated by revelation—all of which invaluable gold was perhaps no better than rubbish to the seeker—he would turn back, discouraged, and begin his quest towards another point. He groped along as stealthily, with as cautious a tread, and as wary an outlook, as a thief entering a chamber where a man lies only half asleep—or, it may be, broad awake—with purpose to steal the very treasure which this man guards as the apple of his eye. In spite of his premeditated carefulness, the floor would now and then creak; his garments would rustle; the shadow of his presence, in a forbidden proximity, would be thrown across his victim. In other words, Mr. Dimmesdale, whose sensibility of nerve often produced the effect of spiritual intuition, would become vaguely aware that something inimical to his peace had thrust itself into relation with him. But Old Roger Chillingworth, too, had perceptions that were almost intuitive; and when the minister threw his startled eyes towards him, there the physician sat; his kind, watchful, sympathising, but never intrusive friend.

Yet Mr. Dimmesdale would perhaps have seen this individual's character more perfectly, if a certain morbidness, to which sick hearts are liable, had not rendered him suspicious of all mankind. Trusting no man as his friend, he could not recognize his enemy when the latter actually appeared. He therefore still kept up a familiar intercourse with him, daily receiving the old physician in his study, or visiting the laboratory, and, for recreation's sake, watching the processes by which weeds were converted into drugs of potency.

One day, leaning his forehead on his hand, and his elbow on the sill of the open window, that looked towards the grave-yard, he talked with Roger Chillingworth, while the old man was examining a bundle of unsightly plants.

"Where," asked he, with a look askance at them—for it was the clergyman's peculiarity that he seldom, now-a-days, looked straight forth at any object, whether human or inanimate, "where, my kind doctor, did you gather those herbs, with such a dark, flabby leaf?"

"Even in the graveyard here at hand," answered the physician, continuing his employment. "They are new to me. I found them growing on a grave, which bore no tombstone, no other memorial of the dead man, save these ugly weeds, that have taken upon themselves to keep him in remembrance. They grew out of his heart, and typify, it may be, some hideous secret that was buried with him, and which he had done better to confess during his lifetime."

"Perchance," said Mr. Dimmesdale, "he earnestly desired it, but could not."

"And wherefore?" rejoined the physician.

"Wherefore not; since all the powers of nature call so earnestly for the confession of sin, that these black weeds have sprung up out of a buried heart, to make manifest, an outspoken crime?"

"That, good sir, is but a phantasy of yours," replied the minister. "There can be, if I forbode aright, no power, short of the Divine mercy, to disclose, whether by uttered words, or by type or emblem, the secrets that may be buried in the human heart. The heart, making itself guilty of such secrets, must perforce hold them, until the day when all hidden things shall be revealed. Nor have I so read or interpreted Holy Writ, as to understand that the disclosure of human thoughts and deeds, then to be made, is intended as a part of the retribution. That, surely, were a shallow view of it. No; these revelations, unless I greatly err, are meant merely to promote the intellectual satisfaction of all intelligent beings, who will stand waiting, on that day, to see the dark problem of this life made plain. A knowledge of men's hearts will be needful to the completest solution of that problem. And, I conceive moreover, that the hearts holding such miserable secrets as you speak of, will yield them up, at that last day, not with reluctance, but with a joy unutterable."

"Then why not reveal it here?" asked Roger Chillingworth, glancing quietly aside at the minister. "Why should not the guilty ones sooner avail themselves of this unutterable solace?"

"They mostly do," said the clergyman, griping hard at his breast, as if afflicted with an importunate throb of pain. "Many, many a poor soul hath given its confidence to me, not only on the death-bed, but while strong in life, and fair in reputation. And ever, after such an outpouring, oh, what a relief have I witnessed in those sinful brethren! even as in one who at last draws free air, after a long stifling with his own polluted breath. How can it be otherwise? Why should a wretched man—guilty, we will say, of murder—prefer to keep the dead corpse buried in his own heart, rather than fling it forth at once, and let the universe take care of it!"

"Yet some men bury their secrets thus," observed the calm physician.

"True; there are such men," answered Mr. Dimmesdale. "But not to suggest more obvious reasons, it may be that they are kept silent by the very constitution of their nature. Or—can we not suppose it?—guilty as they may be, retaining, nevertheless, a zeal for God's glory and man's welfare, they shrink from displaying themselves black and filthy in the view of men; because, thenceforward, no good can be achieved by them; no evil of the past be redeemed by better service. So, to their own unutterable torment, they go about among their fellow-creatures, looking pure as new-fallen snow, while their hearts are all speckled and spotted with iniquity of which they cannot rid themselves."

"These men deceive themselves," said Roger Chillingworth, with somewhat more emphasis than usual, and making a slight gesture with his forefinger. "They fear to take up the shame that rightfully belongs to them. Their love for man, their zeal for God's service—these holy impulses may or may not coexist in their hearts with the evil inmates to which their guilt has unbarred the door, and which must needs propagate a hellish breed within them. But, if they seek to glorify God, let them not lift heavenward their unclean hands! If they would serve their fellowmen, let them do it by making manifest the power and reality of conscience, in constraining them to penitential self-abasement! Would thou have me to believe, O wise and pious friend, that a false show can be better—can be more for God's glory, or man' welfare—than God's own truth? Trust me, such men deceive themselves!"

"It may be so," said the young clergyman, indifferently, as waiving a discussion that he considered irrelevant or unseasonable. He had a ready faculty, indeed, of escaping from any topic that agitated his too sensitive and nervous temperament.—"But, now, I would ask of my well-skilled physician, whether, in good sooth, he deems me to have profited by his kindly care of this weak frame of mine?"

Before Roger Chillingworth could answer, they heard the clear, wild laughter of a young child's voice, proceeding from the adjacent burial-ground. Looking instinctively from the open window—for it was summer-time—the minister beheld Hester Prynne and little Pearl passing along the footpath that traversed the enclosure. Pearl looked as beautiful as the day, but was in one of those moods of perverse merriment which, whenever they occurred, seemed to remove her entirely out of the sphere of sympathy or human contact. She now skipped irreverently from one grave to another; until coming to the broad, flat, armorial tombstone of a departed worthy—perhaps of Isaac Johnson himself—she began to dance upon it. In reply to her mother's command and entreaty that she would behave more decorously, little Pearl paused to gather the prickly burrs from a tall burdock which grew beside the tomb. Taking a handful of these, she arranged them along the lines of the scarlet letter that decorated the maternal bosom, to which the burrs, as their nature was, tenaciously adhered. Hester did not pluck them off.

Roger Chillingworth had by this time approached the window and smiled grimly down.

"There is no law, nor reverence for authority, no regard for human ordinances or opinions, right or wrong, mixed up with that child's composition," remarked he, as much to himself as to his companion. "I saw her, the other day, bespatter the Governor himself with water at the cattle-trough in Spring Lane. What, in heaven's name, is she? Is the imp altogether evil? Hath she affections? Hath she any discoverable principle of being?"

"None, save the freedom of a broken law," answered Mr. Dimmesdale, in a quiet way, as if he had been discussing the point within himself, "Whether capable of good, I know not."

The child probably overheard their voices, for, looking up to the window with a bright, but naughty smile of mirth and intelligence, she threw one of the prickly burrs at the Rev. Mr.

Dimmesdale. The sensitive clergyman shrank, with nervous dread, from the light missile. Detecting his emotion, Pearl clapped her little hands in the most extravagant ecstacy. Hester Prynne, likewise, had involuntarily looked up, and all these four persons, old and young, regarded one another in silence, till the child laughed aloud, and shouted—"Come away, mother! Come away, or yonder old black man will catch you! He hath got hold of the minister already. Come away, mother or he will catch you! But he cannot catch little Pearl!"

So she drew her mother away, skipping, dancing, and frisking fantastically among the hillocks of the dead people, like a creature that had nothing in common with a bygone and buried generation, nor owned herself akin to it. It was as if she had been made afresh out of new elements, and must perforce be permitted to live her own life, and be a law unto herself without her eccentricities being reckoned to her for a crime.

"There goes a woman," resumed Roger Chillingworth, after a pause, "who, be her demerits what they may, hath none of that mystery of hidden sinfulness which you deem so grievous to be borne. Is Hester Prynne the less miserable, think you, for that scarlet letter on her breast?"

"I do verily believe it," answered the clergyman. "Nevertheless, I cannot answer for her. There was a look of pain in her face which I would gladly have been spared the sight of. But still, methinks, it must needs be better for the sufferer to be free to show his pain, as this poor woman Hester is, than to cover it up in his heart."

There was another pause, and the physician began anew to examine and arrange the plants which he had gathered.

"You inquired of me, a little time agone," said he, at length, "my judgment as touching your health."

"I did," answered the clergyman, "and would gladly learn it. Speak frankly, I pray you, be it for life or death."

"Freely then, and plainly," said the physician, still busy with his plants, but keeping a wary eye on Mr. Dimmesdale, "the disorder is a strange one; not so much in itself nor as outwardly manifested,—in so far, at least as the symptoms have been laid open to my observation. Looking daily at you, my good sir, and watching the tokens of your aspect now for months gone by, I should deem you a man sore sick, it may be, yet not so sick but that an instructed and watchful physician might well hope to cure you. But I know not what to say, the disease is what I seem to know, yet know it not."

"You speak in riddles, learned sir," said the pale minister, glancing aside out of the window.

"Then, to speak more plainly," continued the physician, "and I crave pardon, sir, should it seem to require pardon, for this needful plainness of my speech. Let me ask as your friend, as one having charge, under Providence, of your life and physical well being, hath all the operations of this disorder been fairly laid open and recounted to me?"

"How can you question it?" asked the minister. "Surely it were child's play to call in a physician and then hide the sore!"

"You would tell me, then, that I know all?" said Roger Chillingworth, deliberately, and fixing an eye, bright with intense and concentrated intelligence, on the minister's face. "Be it so! But again! He to whom only the outward and physical evil is laid open, knoweth, oftentimes, but half the evil which he is called upon to cure. A bodily disease, which we look upon as whole and entire within itself, may, after all, be but a symptom of some ailment in the spiritual part. Your pardon once again, good sir, if my speech give the shadow of offence. You, sir, of all men whom I have known, are he whose body is the closest conjoined, and imbued, and identified, so to speak, with the spirit whereof it is the instrument."

"Then I need ask no further," said the clergyman, somewhat hastily rising from his chair. "You deal not, I take it, in medicine for the soul!"

"Thus, a sickness," continued Roger Chillingworth, going on, in an unaltered tone, without heeding the interruption, but standing up and confronting the emaciated and white-cheeked minister, with his low, dark, and misshapen figure,—"a sickness, a sore place, if we may so call it, in your spirit hath immediately its appropriate manifestation in your bodily frame. Would you, therefore, that your physician heal the bodily evil? How may this be unless you first lay open to him the wound or trouble in your soul?"

"No, not to thee! not to an earthly physician!" cried Mr. Dimmesdale, passionately, and turning his eyes, full and bright, and with a kind of fierceness, on old Roger Chillingworth. "Not to thee! But, if it be the soul's disease, then do I commit myself to the one Physician of the soul! He, if it stand with His good pleasure, can cure, or he can kill. Let Him do with me as, in His justice and wisdom, He shall see good. But who art thou, that meddlest in this matter? that dares thrust himself between the sufferer and his God?"

With a frantic gesture he rushed out of the room.

"It is as well to have made this step," said Roger Chillingworth to himself, looking after the minister, with a grave smile. "There is nothing lost. We shall be friends again anon. But see, now, how passion takes hold upon this man, and hurrieth him out of himself! As with one passion so with another. He hath done a wild thing ere now, this pious Master Dimmesdale, in the hot passion of his heart."

It proved not difficult to re-establish the intimacy of the two companions, on the same footing and in the same degree as heretofore. The young clergyman, after a few hours of privacy, was sensible that the disorder of his nerves had hurried him into an unseemly outbreak of temper, which there had been nothing in the physician's words to excuse or palliate. He marvelled, indeed, at the violence with which he had thrust back the kind old man, when merely proffering the advice which it was his duty to bestow, and which the minister himself had expressly sought. With these remorseful feelings, he lost no time in making the amplest apologies, and besought his friend still to continue the care which, if not successful in restoring him to health, had, in all probability, been the means of prolonging his feeble existence to that hour. Roger Chillingworth readily assented, and went on with his medical supervision of the minister; doing his best for him, in all good faith, but always quitting the patient's apartment, at the close of the professional interview, with a mysterious and puzzled smile upon his lips. This expression was invisible in Mr. Dimmesdale's presence, but grew strongly evident as the physician crossed the threshold.

"A rare case," he muttered. "I must needs look deeper into it. A strange sympathy betwixt soul and body! Were it only for the art's sake, I must search this matter to the bottom."

It came to pass, not long after the scene above recorded, that the Reverend Mr. Dimmesdale, noon-day, and entirely unawares, fell into a deep, deep slumber, sitting in his chair, with a large black-letter volume open before him on the table. It must have been a work of vast ability in the somniferous school of literature. The profound depth of the minister's repose was the more remarkable, inasmuch as he was one of those persons whose sleep ordinarily is as light as fitful, and as easily scared away, as a small bird hopping on a twig. To such an unwonted remoteness, however, had his spirit now withdrawn into itself that he stirred not in his chair when old Roger Chillingworth, without any extraordinary precaution, came into the room. The physician advanced directly in front of his patient, laid his hand upon his bosom, and thrust aside the vestment, that hitherto had always covered it even from the professional eye.

Then, indeed, Mr. Dimmesdale shuddered, and slightly stirred.

After a brief pause, the physician turned away.

But with what a wild look of wonder, joy, and horror! With what a ghastly rapture, as it were, too mighty to be expressed only by the eye and features, and therefore bursting forth through the whole ugliness of his figure, and making itself even riotously manifest by the extravagant gestures with which he threw up his arms towards the ceiling, and stamped his foot upon the floor! Had a man seen old Roger Chillingworth, at that moment of his ecstasy, he would have had no need to ask how Satan comports himself when a precious human soul is lost to heaven, and won into his kingdom.

But what distinguished the physician's ecstasy from Satan's was the trait of wonder in it!

❧ 11 ❧

THE INTERIOR OF A HEART

AFTER THE INCIDENT LAST DESCRIBED, the intercourse between the clergyman and the physician, though externally the same, was really of another character than it had previously been. The intellect of Roger Chillingworth had now a sufficiently plain path before it. It was not, indeed, precisely that which he had laid out for himself to tread. Calm, gentle, passionless, as he appeared, there was yet, we fear, a quiet depth of malice, hitherto latent, but active now, in this unfortunate old man, which led him to imagine a more intimate revenge than any mortal had ever wreaked upon an enemy. To make himself the one trusted friend, to whom should be confided all the fear, the remorse, the agony, the ineffectual repentance, the backward rush of sinful thoughts, expelled in vain! All that guilty sorrow, hidden from the world, whose great heart would have pitied and forgiven, to be revealed to him, the Pitiless—to him, the Unforgiving! All that dark treasure to be lavished on the very man, to whom nothing else could so adequately pay the debt of vengeance!

The clergyman's shy and sensitive reserve had balked this scheme. Roger Chillingworth, however, was inclined to be hardly, if at all, less satisfied with the aspect of affairs, which Providence—using the avenger and his victim for its own purposes, and, perchance, pardoning, where it seemed most to punish—had substituted for his black devices. A revelation, he could almost say, had been granted to him. It mattered little for his object, whether celestial or from what other region. By its aid, in all the subsequent relations betwixt him and Mr. Dimmesdale, not merely the external presence, but the very inmost soul of the latter, seemed to be brought out before his eyes, so that he could see and comprehend its every movement. He became, thenceforth, not a spectator only, but a chief actor in the poor minister's interior world. He could play upon him as he chose. Would he arouse him with a throb of agony? The victim was for ever on the rack; it needed only to know the spring that controlled the engine: and the physician knew it well. Would he startle him with sudden fear? As at the waving of a magician's wand, up rose a grisly phantom—up rose a thousand phantoms—in many shapes, of death, or more awful shame, all flocking round about the clergyman, and pointing with their fingers at his breast!

All this was accomplished with a subtlety so perfect, that the minister, though he had constantly a dim perception of some evil influence watching over him, could never gain a knowledge of its actual nature. True, he looked doubtfully, fearfully—even, at times, with horror and the bitterness of hatred—at the deformed figure of the old physician. His gestures, his gait, his grizzled beard, his slightest and most indifferent acts, the very fashion of his garments, were odious in the clergyman's sight; a token implicitly to be relied on of a deeper antipathy in the breast of the latter than he was willing to acknowledge to himself. For, as it was impossible to assign a reason for such distrust and abhorrence, so Mr. Dimmesdale, conscious that the poison of one morbid spot was infecting his heart's entire substance, attributed all his presentiments to no other cause. He took himself to task for his bad sympathies in reference to Roger Chillingworth, disregarded the lesson that he should have drawn from them, and did his best to root them out. Unable to accomplish this, he nevertheless, as a matter of principle, continued his habits of social familiarity with the old man, and thus gave him constant opportunities for perfecting the purpose to which—poor forlorn creature that he was, and more wretched than his victim—the avenger had devoted himself.

While thus suffering under bodily disease, and gnawed and tortured by some black trouble of the soul, and given over to the machinations of his deadliest enemy, the Reverend Mr. Dimmesdale had achieved a brilliant popularity in his sacred office. He won it indeed, in great part, by his sorrows. His intellectual gifts, his moral perceptions, his power of experiencing and communicating emotion, were kept in a state of preternatural activity by the prick and anguish of his daily life. His fame, though still on its upward slope, already overshadowed the soberer reputations of his fellow-clergymen, eminent as several of them were. There are scholars among them, who had spent more years in acquiring abstruse lore, connected with the divine profession, than Mr. Dimmesdale had lived; and who might well, therefore, be more profoundly versed in such solid and valuable attainments than their youthful brother. There were men, too, of a sturdier texture of mind than his, and endowed with a far greater share of shrewd, hard iron, or granite understanding; which, duly mingled with a fair proportion of doctrinal ingredient, constitutes a highly respectable, efficacious, and unamiable variety of the clerical species. There were others again, true saintly fathers, whose faculties had been elaborated by weary toil among their books, and by patient thought, and etherealised, moreover, by spiritual communications with the better world, into which their purity of life had almost introduced these holy personages, with their garments of mortality still clinging to them. All that they lacked was, the gift that descended upon the chosen disciples at Pentecost, in tongues of flame; symbolising, it would seem, not the power of speech in foreign and unknown languages, but that of addressing the whole human brotherhood in the heart's native language. These fathers, otherwise so apostolic, lacked Heaven's last and rarest attestation of their office, the Tongue of Flame. They would have vainly sought—had they ever dreamed of seeking—to express the highest truths through the humblest medium of familiar words and images. Their voices came down, afar and indistinctly, from the upper heights where they habitually dwelt.

Not improbably, it was to this latter class of men that Mr. Dimmesdale, by many of his traits of character, naturally belonged. To the high mountain peaks of faith and sanctity he would have climbed, had not the tendency been thwarted by the burden, whatever it might be, of crime or anguish, beneath which it was his doom to totter. It kept him down on a level with the lowest; him, the man of ethereal attributes, whose voice the angels might else have listened to and answered! But this very burden it was that gave him sympathies so intimate with the sinful brotherhood of mankind; so that his heart vibrated in unison with theirs, and received their pain into itself and sent its own throb of pain through a thousand other hearts, in gushes of sad, persuasive eloquence. Oftenest persuasive, but sometimes terrible! The people knew not the power that moved them thus. They deemed the young clergyman a miracle of holiness. They fancied him the mouth-piece of Heaven's messages of wisdom, and rebuke, and love. In their eyes, the very ground on which he trod was sanctified. The virgins of his church grew pale around him, victims of a passion so imbued with religious sentiment, that they imagined it to be all religion, and brought it openly, in their white bosoms, as their most acceptable sacrifice before the altar. The aged members of his flock, beholding Mr. Dimmesdale's frame so feeble, while they were themselves so rugged in their infirmity, believed that he would go heavenward before them, and enjoined it upon their children that their old bones should be buried close to their young pastor's holy grave. And all this time, perchance, when poor Mr. Dimmesdale was thinking of his grave, he questioned with himself whether the grass would ever grow on it, because an accursed thing must there be buried!

It is inconceivable, the agony with which this public veneration tortured him. It was his genuine impulse to adore the truth, and to reckon all things shadow-like, and utterly devoid of weight or value, that had not its divine essence as the life within their life. Then what was he?— a substance?—or the dimmest of all shadows? He longed to speak out from his own pulpit at the full height of his voice, and tell the people what he was. "I, whom you behold in these black garments of the priesthood—I, who ascend the sacred desk, and turn my pale face heavenward, taking upon myself to hold communion in your behalf with the Most High Omniscience—I, in whose daily life you discern the sanctity of Enoch—I, whose footsteps, as you suppose, leave a gleam along my earthly track, whereby the Pilgrims that shall come after me may be guided to the regions of the blest—I, who have laid the hand of baptism upon your children—I, who have breathed the parting prayer over your dying friends, to whom the Amen sounded faintly from a world which they had quitted—I, your pastor, whom you so reverence and trust, am utterly a pollution and a lie!"

More than once, Mr. Dimmesdale had gone into the pulpit, with a purpose never to come down its steps until he should have spoken words like the above. More than once he had cleared his throat, and drawn in the long, deep, and tremulous breath, which, when sent forth again, would come burdened with the black secret of his soul. More than once—nay, more than a hundred times—he had actually spoken! Spoken! But how? He had told his hearers that he was altogether vile, a viler companion of the vilest, the worst of sinners, an abomination, a thing of unimaginable iniquity, and that the only wonder was that they did not see his wretched body shrivelled up before their eyes by the burning wrath of the Almighty! Could there be plainer speech than this? Would not the people start up in their seats, by a simultaneous impulse, and tear him down out of the pulpit which he defiled? Not so, indeed! They heard it all, and did but reverence him the more. They little guessed what deadly purport lurked in those self-condemning words. "The godly youth!" said they among themselves. "The saint on earth! Alas! if he discern such sinfulness in his own white soul, what horrid spectacle would he behold in thine or mine!" The minister well knew—subtle, but remorseful hypocrite that he was!—the light in which his vague confession would be viewed. He had striven to put a cheat upon himself by making the avowal of a guilty conscience, but had gained only one other sin, and a self-acknowledged shame, without the momentary relief of being self-deceived. He had spoken the very truth, and transformed it into the veriest falsehood. And yet, by the constitution of his nature, he loved the truth, and loathed the lie, as few men ever did. Therefore, above all things else, he loathed his miserable self!

His inward trouble drove him to practices more in accordance with the old, corrupted faith of Rome than with the better light of the church in which he had been born and bred. In Mr. Dimmesdale's secret closet, under lock and key, there was a bloody scourge. Oftentimes, this Protestant and Puritan divine had plied it on his own shoulders, laughing bitterly at himself the while, and smiting so much the more pitilessly because of that bitter laugh. It was his custom, too, as it has been that of many other pious Puritans, to fast—not however, like them, in order to purify the body, and render it the fitter medium of celestial illumination—but rigorously, and until his knees trembled beneath him, as an act of penance. He kept vigils, likewise, night after night, sometimes in utter darkness, sometimes with a glimmering lamp, and sometimes, viewing his own face in a looking-glass, by the most powerful light which he could throw upon it. He thus typified the constant introspection wherewith he tortured, but could not purify himself. In these lengthened vigils, his brain often reeled, and visions seemed to flit before him; perhaps seen doubtfully, and by a faint light of their own, in the remote dimness of the chamber, or more vividly and close beside him, within the looking-glass. Now it was a herd of diabolic shapes, that grinned and mocked at the pale minister, and beckoned him away with them; now a group of shining angels, who flew upward heavily, as sorrow-laden, but grew more ethereal as they rose. Now came the dead friends of his youth, and his white-bearded father, with a saint-like frown, and his mother turning her face away as she passed by. Ghost of a mother—thinnest fantasy of a mother—methinks she might yet have thrown a pitying glance towards her son! And now, through the chamber which these spectral thoughts had made so ghastly, glided Hester Prynne leading along little Pearl, in her scarlet garb, and pointing her forefinger, first at the scarlet letter on her bosom, and then at the clergyman's own breast.

None of these visions ever quite deluded him. At any moment, by an effort of his will, he could discern substances through their misty lack of substance, and convince himself that they were not solid in their nature, like yonder table of carved oak, or that big, square, leather-bound and brazen-clasped volume of divinity. But, for all that, they were, in one sense, the truest and most substantial things which the poor minister now dealt with. It is the unspeakable misery of a life so false as his, that it steals the pith and substance out of whatever realities there are around us, and which were meant by Heaven to be the spirit's joy and nutriment. To the untrue man, the whole universe is false—it is impalpable—it shrinks to nothing within his grasp. And he himself in so far as he shows himself in a false light, becomes a shadow, or, indeed, ceases to exist. The only truth that continued to give Mr. Dimmesdale a real existence on this earth was the anguish in his inmost soul, and the undissembled expression of it in his aspect. Had he once found power to smile, and wear a face of gaiety, there would have been no such man!

On one of those ugly nights, which we have faintly hinted at, but forborne to picture forth, the minister started from his chair. A new thought had struck him. There might be a moment's peace in it. Attiring himself with as much care as if it had been for public worship, and precisely in the same manner, he stole softly down the staircase, undid the door, and issued forth.

❧ 12 ❧

THE MINISTER'S VIGIL

WALKING in the shadow of a dream, as it were, and perhaps actually under the influence of a species of somnambulism, Mr. Dimmesdale reached the spot where, now so long since, Hester Prynne had lived through her first hours of public ignominy. The same platform or scaffold, black and weather-stained with the storm or sunshine of seven long years, and foot-worn, too, with the tread of many culprits who had since ascended it, remained standing beneath the balcony of the meeting-house. The minister went up the steps.

It was an obscure night in early May. An unvaried pall of cloud muffled the whole expanse of sky from zenith to horizon. If the same multitude which had stood as eye-witnesses while Hester Prynne sustained her punishment could now have been summoned forth, they would have discerned no face above the platform nor hardly the outline of a human shape, in the dark grey of the midnight. But the town was all asleep. There was no peril of discovery. The minister might stand there, if it so pleased him, until morning should redden in the east, without other risk than that the dank and chill night air would creep into his frame, and stiffen his joints with rheumatism, and clog his throat with catarrh and cough; thereby defrauding the expectant audience of to-morrow's prayer and sermon. No eye could see him, save that ever-wakeful one which had seen him in his closet, wielding the bloody scourge. Why, then, had he come hither? Was it but the mockery of penitence? A mockery, indeed, but in which his soul trifled with itself! A mockery at which angels blushed and wept, while fiends rejoiced with jeering laughter! He had been driven hither by the impulse of that Remorse which dogged him everywhere, and whose own sister and closely linked companion was that Cowardice which invariably drew him back, with her tremulous gripe, just when the other impulse had hurried him to the verge of a disclosure. Poor, miserable man! what right had infirmity like his to burden itself with crime? Crime is for the iron-nerved, who have their choice either to endure it, or, if it press too hard, to exert their fierce and savage strength for a good purpose, and fling it off at once! This feeble and most sensitive of spirits could do neither, yet continually did one thing or another, which intertwined, in the same inextricable knot, the agony of heaven-defying guilt and vain repentance.

And thus, while standing on the scaffold, in this vain show of expiation, Mr. Dimmesdale

317

was overcome with a great horror of mind, as if the universe were gazing at a scarlet token on his naked breast, right over his heart. On that spot, in very truth, there was, and there had long been, the gnawing and poisonous tooth of bodily pain. Without any effort of his will, or power to restrain himself, he shrieked aloud: an outcry that went pealing through the night, and was beaten back from one house to another, and reverberated from the hills in the background; as if a company of devils, detecting so much misery and terror in it, had made a plaything of the sound, and were bandying it to and fro.

"It is done!" muttered the minister, covering his face with his hands. "The whole town will awake and hurry forth, and find me here!"

But it was not so. The shriek had perhaps sounded with a far greater power, to his own startled ears, than it actually possessed. The town did not awake; or, if it did, the drowsy slumberers mistook the cry either for something frightful in a dream, or for the noise of witches, whose voices, at that period, were often heard to pass over the settlements or lonely cottages, as they rode with Satan through the air. The clergyman, therefore, hearing no symptoms of disturbance, uncovered his eyes and looked about him. At one of the chamber-windows of Governor Bellingham's mansion, which stood at some distance, on the line of another street, he beheld the appearance of the old magistrate himself with a lamp in his hand a white night-cap on his head, and a long white gown enveloping his figure. He looked like a ghost evoked unseasonably from the grave. The cry had evidently startled him. At another window of the same house, moreover appeared old Mistress Hibbins, the Governor's sister, also with a lamp, which even thus far off revealed the expression of her sour and discontented face. She thrust forth her head from the lattice, and looked anxiously upward. Beyond the shadow of a doubt, this venerable witch-lady had heard Mr. Dimmesdale's outcry, and interpreted it, with its multitudinous echoes and reverberations, as the clamour of the fiends and night-hags, with whom she was well known to make excursions in the forest.

Detecting the gleam of Governor Bellingham's lamp, the old lady quickly extinguished her own, and vanished. Possibly, she went up among the clouds. The minister saw nothing further of her motions. The magistrate, after a wary observation of the darkness—into which, nevertheless, he could see but little further than he might into a mill-stone—retired from the window.

The minister grew comparatively calm. His eyes, however, were soon greeted by a little glimmering light, which, at first a long way off was approaching up the street. It threw a gleam of recognition, on here a post, and there a garden fence, and here a latticed window-pane, and there a pump, with its full trough of water, and here again an arched door of oak, with an iron knocker, and a rough log for the door-step. The Reverend Mr. Dimmesdale noted all these minute particulars, even while firmly convinced that the doom of his existence was stealing onward, in the footsteps which he now heard; and that the gleam of the lantern would fall upon him in a few moments more, and reveal his long-hidden secret. As the light drew nearer, he beheld, within its illuminated circle, his brother clergyman—or, to speak more accurately, his professional father, as well as highly valued friend—the Reverend Mr. Wilson, who, as Mr. Dimmesdale now conjectured, had been praying at the bedside of some dying man. And so he had. The good old minister came freshly from the death-chamber of Governor Winthrop, who had passed from earth to heaven within that very hour. And now surrounded, like the saint-like personage of olden times, with a radiant halo, that glorified him amid this gloomy night of sin—as if the departed Governor had left him an inheritance of his glory, or as if he had caught upon himself the distant shine of the celestial city, while looking thitherward to see the triumphant pilgrim pass within its gates—now, in short, good Father Wilson was moving homeward, aiding his footsteps with a lighted lantern! The glimmer of this luminary suggested the above conceits to Mr. Dimmesdale, who smiled—nay, almost laughed at them—and then wondered if he was going mad.

As the Reverend Mr. Wilson passed beside the scaffold, closely muffling his Geneva cloak about him with one arm, and holding the lantern before his breast with the other, the minister could hardly restrain himself from speaking—

"A good evening to you, venerable Father Wilson. Come up hither, I pray you, and pass a pleasant hour with me!"

Good Heavens! Had Mr. Dimmesdale actually spoken? For one instant he believed that these words had passed his lips. But they were uttered only within his imagination. The venerable Father Wilson continued to step slowly onward, looking carefully at the muddy pathway before his feet, and never once turning his head towards the guilty platform. When the light of the glimmering lantern had faded quite away, the minister discovered, by the faintness which came over him, that the last few moments had been a crisis of terrible anxiety, although his mind had made an involuntary effort to relieve itself by a kind of lurid playfulness.

Shortly afterwards, the like grisly sense of the humorous again stole in among the solemn phantoms of his thought. He felt his limbs growing stiff with the unaccustomed chilliness of the night, and doubted whether he should be able to descend the steps of the scaffold. Morning would break and find him there. The neighbourhood would begin to rouse itself. The earliest riser, coming forth in the dim twilight, would perceive a vaguely-defined figure aloft on the place of shame; and half-crazed betwixt alarm and curiosity, would go knocking from door to door, summoning all the people to behold the ghost—as he needs must think it—of some defunct transgressor. A dusky tumult would flap its wings from one house to another. Then— the morning light still waxing stronger—old patriarchs would rise up in great haste, each in his flannel gown, and matronly dames, without pausing to put off their night-gear. The whole tribe of decorous personages, who had never heretofore been seen with a single hair of their heads awry, would start into public view with the disorder of a nightmare in their aspects. Old Governor Bellingham would come grimly forth, with his King James' ruff fastened askew, and Mistress Hibbins, with some twigs of the forest clinging to her skirts, and looking sourer than ever, as having hardly got a wink of sleep after her night ride; and good Father Wilson too, after spending half the night at a death-bed, and liking ill to be disturbed, thus early, out of his dreams about the glorified saints. Hither, likewise, would come the elders and deacons of Mr. Dimmesdale's church, and the young virgins who so idolized their minister, and had made a shrine for him in their white bosoms, which now, by-the-bye, in their hurry and confusion, they would scantly have given themselves time to cover with their kerchiefs. All people, in a word, would come stumbling over their thresholds, and turning up their amazed and horror-stricken visages around the scaffold. Whom would they discern there, with the red eastern light upon his brow? Whom, but the Reverend Arthur Dimmesdale, half-frozen to death, overwhelmed with shame, and standing where Hester Prynne had stood!

Carried away by the grotesque horror of this picture, the minister, unawares, and to his own infinite alarm, burst into a great peal of laughter. It was immediately responded to by a light, airy, childish laugh, in which, with a thrill of the heart—but he knew not whether of exquisite pain, or pleasure as acute—he recognised the tones of little Pearl.

"Pearl! Little Pearl!" cried he, after a moment's pause; then, suppressing his voice—"Hester! Hester Prynne! Are you there?"

"Yes; it is Hester Prynne!" she replied, in a tone of surprise; and the minister heard her footsteps approaching from the side-walk, along which she had been passing. "It is I, and my little Pearl."

"Whence come you, Hester?" asked the minister. "What sent you hither?"

"I have been watching at a death-bed," answered Hester Prynne "at Governor Winthrop's death-bed, and have taken his measure for a robe, and am now going homeward to my dwelling."

"Come up hither, Hester, thou and little Pearl," said the Reverend Mr. Dimmesdale. "Ye have both been here before, but I was not with you. Come up hither once again, and we will stand all three together."

She silently ascended the steps, and stood on the platform, holding little Pearl by the hand. The minister felt for the child's other hand, and took it. The moment that he did so, there came what seemed a tumultuous rush of new life, other life than his own pouring like a torrent into his heart, and hurrying through all his veins, as if the mother and the child were communicating their vital warmth to his half-torpid system. The three formed an electric chain.

"Minister!" whispered little Pearl.

"What wouldst thou say, child?" asked Mr. Dimmesdale.

"Wilt thou stand here with mother and me, to-morrow noontide?" inquired Pearl.

"Nay; not so, my little Pearl," answered the minister; for, with the new energy of the moment, all the dread of public exposure, that had so long been the anguish of his life, had returned upon him; and he was already trembling at the conjunction in which—with a strange joy, nevertheless—he now found himself—"not so, my child. I shall, indeed, stand with thy mother and thee one other day, but not to-morrow."

Pearl laughed, and attempted to pull away her hand. But the minister held it fast.

"A moment longer, my child!" said he.

"But wilt thou promise," asked Pearl, "to take my hand, and mother's hand, to-morrow noontide?"

"Not then, Pearl," said the minister; "but another time."

"And what other time?" persisted the child.

"At the great judgment day," whispered the minister; and, strangely enough, the sense that he was a professional teacher of the truth impelled him to answer the child so. "Then, and there, before the judgment-seat, thy mother, and thou, and I must stand together. But the daylight of this world shall not see our meeting!"

Pearl laughed again.

But before Mr. Dimmesdale had done speaking, a light gleamed far and wide over all the muffled sky. It was doubtless caused by one of those meteors, which the night-watcher may so often observe burning out to waste, in the vacant regions of the atmosphere. So powerful was its radiance, that it thoroughly illuminated the dense medium of cloud betwixt the sky and earth. The great vault brightened, like the dome of an immense lamp. It showed the familiar scene of the street with the distinctness of mid-day, but also with the awfulness that is always imparted to familiar objects by an unaccustomed light. The wooden houses, with their jutting storeys and quaint gable-peaks; the doorsteps and thresholds with the early grass springing up about them; the garden-plots, black with freshly-turned earth; the wheel-track, little worn, and even in the market-place margined with green on either side—all were visible, but with a singularity of aspect that seemed to give another moral interpretation to the things of this world than they had ever borne before. And there stood the minister, with his hand over his heart; and Hester Prynne, with the embroidered letter glimmering on her bosom; and little Pearl, herself a symbol, and the connecting link between those two. They stood in the noon of that strange and solemn splendour, as if it were the light that is to reveal all secrets, and the daybreak that shall unite all who belong to one another.

There was witchcraft in little Pearl's eyes; and her face, as she glanced upward at the minister, wore that naughty smile which made its expression frequently so elvish. She withdrew her hand from Mr. Dimmesdale's, and pointed across the street. But he clasped both his hands over his breast, and cast his eyes towards the zenith.

Nothing was more common, in those days, than to interpret all meteoric appearances, and other natural phenomena that occurred with less regularity than the rise and set of sun and moon, as so many revelations from a supernatural source. Thus, a blazing spear, a sword of flame, a bow, or a sheaf of arrows seen in the midnight sky, prefigured Indian warfare. Pestilence was known to have been foreboded by a shower of crimson light. We doubt whether any marked event, for good or evil, ever befell New England, from its settlement down to revolutionary times, of which the inhabitants had not been previously warned by some spectacle of its nature. Not seldom, it had been seen by multitudes. Oftener, however, its credibility rested on the faith of some lonely eye-witness, who beheld the wonder through the coloured, magnifying, and distorted medium of his imagination, and shaped it more distinctly in his after-thought. It was, indeed, a majestic idea that the destiny of nations should be revealed, in these awful hieroglyphics, on the cope of heaven. A scroll so wide might not be deemed too expensive for Providence to write a people's doom upon. The belief was a favourite one with our forefathers, as betokening that their infant commonwealth was under a celestial guardianship of peculiar intimacy and strictness. But what shall we say, when an individual discovers a revelation addressed to himself alone, on the same vast sheet of record. In such a case, it could only be the symptom of a highly disordered mental state, when a man, rendered morbidly self-contemplative by long, intense, and secret pain, had extended his egotism over the whole expanse of nature, until the firmament itself should appear no more than a fitting page for his soul's history and fate.

We impute it, therefore, solely to the disease in his own eye and heart that the minister, looking upward to the zenith, beheld there the appearance of an immense letter—the letter A—marked out in lines of dull red light. Not but the meteor may have shown itself at that point, burning duskily through a veil of cloud, but with no such shape as his guilty imagination gave it, or, at least, with so little definiteness, that another's guilt might have seen another symbol in it.

There was a singular circumstance that characterised Mr. Dimmesdale's psychological state at this moment. All the time that he gazed upward to the zenith, he was, nevertheless, perfectly aware that little Pearl was pointing her finger towards old Roger Chillingworth, who stood at no great distance from the scaffold. The minister appeared to see him, with the same glance that discerned the miraculous letter. To his feature as to all other objects, the meteoric light imparted a new expression; or it might well be that the physician was not careful then, as at all other times, to hide the malevolence with which he looked upon his victim. Certainly, if the meteor kindled up the sky, and disclosed the earth, with an awfulness that admonished Hester Prynne and the clergyman of the day of judgment, then might Roger Chillingworth have passed with them for the arch-fiend, standing there with a smile and scowl, to claim his own. So vivid was the expression, or so intense the minister's perception of it, that it seemed still to remain painted on the darkness after the meteor had vanished, with an effect as if the street and all things else were at once annihilated.

"Who is that man, Hester?" gasped Mr. Dimmesdale, overcome with terror. "I shiver at him! Dost thou know the man? I hate him, Hester!"

She remembered her oath, and was silent.

"I tell thee, my soul shivers at him!" muttered the minister again. "Who is he? Who is he? Canst thou do nothing for me? I have a nameless horror of the man!"

"Minister," said little Pearl, "I can tell thee who he is!"

"Quickly, then, child!" said the minister, bending his ear close to her lips. "Quickly, and as low as thou canst whisper."

Pearl mumbled something into his ear that sounded, indeed, like human language, but was only such gibberish as children may be heard amusing themselves with by the hour together. At all events, if it involved any secret information in regard to old Roger Chillingworth, it was in a tongue unknown to the erudite clergyman, and did but increase the bewilderment of his mind. The elvish child then laughed aloud.

"Dost thou mock me now?" said the minister.

"Thou wast not bold!—thou wast not true!" answered the child. "Thou wouldst not promise to take my hand, and mother's hand, to-morrow noon-tide!"

"Worthy sir," answered the physician, who had now advanced to the foot of the platform —"pious Master Dimmesdale! can this be you? Well, well, indeed! We men of study, whose heads are in our books, have need to be straitly looked after! We dream in our waking moments, and walk in our sleep. Come, good sir, and my dear friend, I pray you let me lead you home!"

"How knewest thou that I was here?" asked the minister, fearfully.

"Verily, and in good faith," answered Roger Chillingworth, "I knew nothing of the matter. I had spent the better part of the night at the bedside of the worshipful Governor Winthrop, doing what my poor skill might to give him ease. He, going home to a better world, I, likewise, was on my way homeward, when this light shone out. Come with me, I beseech you, Reverend sir, else you will be poorly able to do Sabbath duty to-morrow. Aha! see now how they trouble the brain—these books!—these books! You should study less, good sir, and take a little pastime, or these night whimsies will grow upon you."

"I will go home with you," said Mr. Dimmesdale.

With a chill despondency, like one awakening, all nerveless, from an ugly dream, he yielded himself to the physician, and was led away.

The next day, however, being the Sabbath, he preached a discourse which was held to be the richest and most powerful, and the most replete with heavenly influences, that had ever proceeded from his lips. Souls, it is said, more souls than one, were brought to the truth by the efficacy of that sermon, and vowed within themselves to cherish a holy gratitude towards Mr. Dimmesdale throughout the long hereafter. But as he came down the pulpit steps, the grey-bearded sexton met him, holding up a black glove, which the minister recognised as his own.

"It was found," said the Sexton, "this morning on the scaffold where evil-doers are set up to public shame. Satan dropped it there, I take it, intending a scurrilous jest against your reverence. But, indeed, he was blind and foolish, as he ever and always is. A pure hand needs no glove to cover it!"

"Thank you, my good friend," said the minister, gravely, but startled at heart; for so confused was his remembrance, that he had almost brought himself to look at the events of the past night as visionary.

"Yes, it seems to be my glove, indeed!"

"And, since Satan saw fit to steal it, your reverence must needs handle him without gloves henceforward," remarked the old sexton, grimly smiling. "But did your reverence hear of the portent that was seen last night? a great red letter in the sky—the letter A, which we interpret to stand for Angel. For, as our good Governor Winthrop was made an angel this past night, it was doubtless held fit that there should be some notice thereof!"

"No," answered the minister; "I had not heard of it."

❧ 13 ❧

ANOTHER VIEW OF HESTER

IN HER LATE singular interview with Mr. Dimmesdale, Hester Prynne was shocked at the condition to which she found the clergyman reduced. His nerve seemed absolutely destroyed. His moral force was abased into more than childish weakness. It grovelled helpless on the ground, even while his intellectual faculties retained their pristine strength, or had perhaps acquired a morbid energy, which disease only could have given them. With her knowledge of a train of circumstances hidden from all others, she could readily infer that, besides the legitimate action of his own conscience, a terrible machinery had been brought to bear, and was still operating, on Mr. Dimmesdale's well-being and repose. Knowing what this poor fallen man had once been, her whole soul was moved by the shuddering terror with which he had appealed to her—the outcast woman—for support against his instinctively discovered enemy. She decided, moreover, that he had a right to her utmost aid. Little accustomed, in her long seclusion from society, to measure her ideas of right and wrong by any standard external to herself, Hester saw—or seemed to see—that there lay a responsibility upon her in reference to the clergyman, which she owned to no other, nor to the whole world besides. The links that united her to the rest of humankind—links of flowers, or silk, or gold, or whatever the material —had all been broken. Here was the iron link of mutual crime, which neither he nor she could break. Like all other ties, it brought along with it its obligations.

Hester Prynne did not now occupy precisely the same position in which we beheld her during the earlier periods of her ignominy. Years had come and gone. Pearl was now seven years old. Her mother, with the scarlet letter on her breast, glittering in its fantastic embroidery, had long been a familiar object to the townspeople. As is apt to be the case when a person stands out in any prominence before the community, and, at the same time, interferes neither with public nor individual interests and convenience, a species of general regard had ultimately grown up in reference to Hester Prynne. It is to the credit of human nature that, except where its selfishness is brought into play, it loves more readily than it hates. Hatred, by a gradual and quiet process, will even be transformed to love, unless the change be impeded by a continually new irritation of the original feeling of hostility. In this matter of Hester Prynne there was neither irritation nor irksomeness. She never battled with the public, but submitted uncomplainingly to its worst usage; she made no claim upon it in requital for what she suffered; she did not weigh upon its sympathies. Then, also, the blameless purity of her life during all these years in which she had been set apart to infamy was reckoned largely in her favour. With nothing now to lose, in the sight of mankind, and with no hope, and seemingly no wish, of gaining anything, it could only be a genuine regard for virtue that had brought back the poor wanderer to its paths.

It was perceived, too, that while Hester never put forward even the humblest title to share in the world's privileges—further than to breathe the common air and earn daily bread for little Pearl and herself by the faithful labour of her hands—she was quick to acknowledge her sisterhood with the race of man whenever benefits were to be conferred. None so ready as she to give of her little substance to every demand of poverty, even though the bitter-hearted pauper threw back a gibe in requital of the food brought regularly to his door, or the garments wrought for him by the fingers that could have embroidered a monarch's robe. None so self-devoted as Hester when pestilence stalked through the town. In all seasons of calamity, indeed, whether general or of individuals, the outcast of society at once found her place. She came, not as a guest, but as a rightful inmate, into the household that was darkened by trouble, as if its gloomy twilight were a medium in which she was entitled to hold intercourse with her fellow-creature. There glimmered the embroidered letter, with comfort in its unearthly ray. Elsewhere the token of sin, it was the taper of the sick chamber. It had even thrown its gleam, in the sufferer's hard extremity, across the verge of time. It had shown him where to set his foot, while the light of earth was fast becoming dim, and ere the light of futurity could reach him. In such emergencies Hester's nature showed itself warm and rich—a well-spring of human tenderness, unfailing to every real demand, and inexhaustible by the largest. Her breast, with its badge of shame, was but the softer pillow for the head that needed one. She was self-ordained a Sister of Mercy, or, we may rather say, the world's heavy hand had so ordained her, when neither the world nor she looked forward to this result. The letter was the symbol of her calling. Such helpfulness was found in her—so much power to do, and power to sympathise—that many people refused to interpret the scarlet A by its original signification. They said that it meant Able, so strong was Hester Prynne, with a woman's strength.

It was only the darkened house that could contain her. When sunshine came again, she was not there. Her shadow had faded across the threshold. The helpful inmate had departed, without one backward glance to gather up the meed of gratitude, if any were in the hearts of those whom she had served so zealously. Meeting them in the street, she never raised her head to receive their greeting. If they were resolute to accost her, she laid her finger on the scarlet letter, and passed on. This might be pride, but was so like humility, that it produced all the softening influence of the latter quality on the public mind. The public is despotic in its temper; it is capable of denying common justice when too strenuously demanded as a right; but quite as frequently it awards more than justice, when the appeal is made, as despots love to have it made, entirely to its generosity. Interpreting Hester Prynne's deportment as an appeal of this nature, society was inclined to show its former victim a more benign countenance than she cared to be favoured with, or, perchance, than she deserved.

The rulers, and the wise and learned men of the community, were longer in acknowledging the influence of Hester's good qualities than the people. The prejudices which they shared in common with the latter were fortified in themselves by an iron frame-work of reasoning, that made it a far tougher labour to expel them. Day by day, nevertheless, their sour and rigid wrinkles were relaxing into something which, in the due course of years, might grow to be an expression of almost benevolence. Thus it was with the men of rank, on whom their eminent position imposed the guardianship of the public morals. Individuals in private life, meanwhile, had quite forgiven Hester Prynne for her frailty; nay, more, they had begun to look upon the scarlet letter as the token, not of that one sin for which she had borne so long and dreary a penance, but of her many good deeds since. "Do you see that woman with the embroidered badge?" they would say to strangers. "It is our Hester—the town's own Hester—who is so kind to the poor, so helpful to the sick, so comfortable to the afflicted!" Then, it is true, the propensity of human nature to tell the very worst of itself, when embodied in the person of another, would constrain them to whisper the black scandal of bygone years. It was none the less a fact, however, that in the eyes of the very men who spoke thus, the scarlet letter had the effect of the cross on a nun's bosom. It imparted to the wearer a kind of sacredness, which enabled her to walk securely amid all peril. Had she fallen among thieves, it would have kept her safe. It was reported, and believed by many, that an Indian had drawn his arrow against the badge, and that the missile struck it, and fell harmless to the ground.

The effect of the symbol—or rather, of the position in respect to society that was indicated by it—on the mind of Hester Prynne herself was powerful and peculiar. All the light and graceful foliage of her character had been withered up by this red-hot brand, and had long ago fallen away, leaving a bare and harsh outline, which might have been repulsive had she possessed friends or companions to be repelled by it. Even the attractiveness of her person had undergone a similar change. It might be partly owing to the studied austerity of her dress, and partly to the lack of demonstration in her manners. It was a sad transformation, too, that her rich and luxuriant hair had either been cut off, or was so completely hidden by a cap, that not a shining lock of it ever once gushed into the sunshine. It was due in part to all these causes, but still more to something else, that there seemed to be no longer anything in Hester's face for Love to dwell upon; nothing in Hester's form, though majestic and statue like, that Passion would ever dream of clasping in its embrace; nothing in Hester's bosom to make it ever again the pillow of Affection. Some attribute had departed from her, the permanence of which had been essential to keep her a woman. Such is frequently the fate, and such the stern development, of the feminine character and person, when the woman has encountered, and lived through, an experience of peculiar severity. If she be all tenderness, she will die. If she survive, the tenderness will either be crushed out of her, or—and the outward semblance is the same—crushed so deeply into her heart that it can never show itself more. The latter is perhaps the truest theory. She who has once been a woman, and ceased to be so, might at any moment become a woman again, if there were only the magic touch to effect the transformation. We shall see whether Hester Prynne were ever afterwards so touched and so transfigured.

Much of the marble coldness of Hester's impression was to be attributed to the circumstance that her life had turned, in a great measure, from passion and feeling to thought. Standing alone in the world—alone, as to any dependence on society, and with little Pearl to be guided and protected—alone, and hopeless of retrieving her position, even had she not scorned to consider it desirable—she cast away the fragment of a broken chain. The world's law was no law for her mind. It was an age in which the human intellect, newly emancipated, had taken a more active and a wider range than for many centuries before. Men of the sword had overthrown nobles and kings. Men bolder than these had overthrown and rearranged—not actually, but within the sphere of theory, which was their most real abode—the whole system of ancient prejudice, wherewith was linked much of ancient principle. Hester Prynne imbibed this spirit. She assumed a freedom of speculation, then common enough on the other side of the Atlantic, but which our forefathers, had they known it, would have held to be a deadlier crime than that stigmatised by the scarlet letter. In her lonesome cottage, by the seashore, thoughts visited her such as dared to enter no other dwelling in New England; shadowy guests, that would have been as perilous as demons to their entertainer, could they have been seen so much as knocking at her door.

It is remarkable that persons who speculate the most boldly often conform with the most perfect quietude to the external regulations of society. The thought suffices them, without investing itself in the flesh and blood of action. So it seemed to be with Hester. Yet, had little Pearl never come to her from the spiritual world, it might have been far otherwise. Then she might have come down to us in history, hand in hand with Ann Hutchinson, as the foundress of a religious sect. She might, in one of her phases, have been a prophetess. She might, and not improbably would, have suffered death from the stern tribunals of the period, for attempting to undermine the foundations of the Puritan establishment. But, in the education of her child, the mother's enthusiasm of thought had something to wreak itself upon. Providence, in the person of this little girl, had assigned to Hester's charge, the germ and blossom of womanhood, to be cherished and developed amid a host of difficulties. Everything was against her. The world was hostile. The child's own nature had something wrong in it which continually betokened that she had been born amiss—the effluence of her mother's lawless passion—and often impelled Hester to ask, in bitterness of heart, whether it were for ill or good that the poor little creature had been born at all.

Indeed, the same dark question often rose into her mind with reference to the whole race of womanhood. Was existence worth accepting even to the happiest among them? As concerned her own individual existence, she had long ago decided in the negative, and dismissed the point as settled. A tendency to speculation, though it may keep women quiet, as it does man, yet makes her sad. She discerns, it may be, such a hopeless task before her. As a first step, the whole system of society is to be torn down and built up anew. Then the very nature of the opposite sex, or its long hereditary habit, which has become like nature, is to be essentially modified before woman can be allowed to assume what seems a fair and suitable position. Finally, all other difficulties being obviated, woman cannot take advantage of these preliminary reforms until she herself shall have undergone a still mightier change, in which, perhaps, the ethereal essence, wherein she has her truest life, will be found to have evaporated. A woman never overcomes these problems by any exercise of thought. They are not to be solved, or only in one way. If her heart chance to come uppermost, they vanish. Thus Hester Prynne, whose heart had lost its regular and healthy throb, wandered without a clue in the dark labyrinth of mind; now turned aside by an insurmountable precipice; now starting back from a deep chasm. There was wild and ghastly scenery all around her, and a home and comfort nowhere. At times a fearful doubt strove to possess her soul, whether it were not better to send Pearl at once to Heaven, and go herself to such futurity as Eternal Justice should provide.

The scarlet letter had not done its office. Now, however, her interview with the Reverend Mr. Dimmesdale, on the night of his vigil, had given her a new theme of reflection, and held up to her an object that appeared worthy of any exertion and sacrifice for its attainment. She had witnessed the intense misery beneath which the minister struggled, or, to speak more accurately, had ceased to struggle. She saw that he stood on the verge of lunacy, if he had not already stepped across it. It was impossible to doubt that, whatever painful efficacy there might be in the secret sting of remorse, a deadlier venom had been infused into it by the hand that proffered relief. A secret enemy had been continually by his side, under the semblance of a friend and helper, and had availed himself of the opportunities thus afforded for tampering with the delicate springs of Mr. Dimmesdale's nature. Hester could not but ask herself whether there had not originally been a defect of truth, courage, and loyalty on her own part, in allowing the minister to be thrown into a position where so much evil was to be foreboded and nothing auspicious to be hoped. Her only justification lay in the fact that she had been able to discern no method of rescuing him from a blacker ruin than had overwhelmed herself except by acquiescing in Roger Chillingworth's scheme of disguise. Under that impulse she had made her choice, and had chosen, as it now appeared, the more wretched alternative of the two. She determined to redeem her error so far as it might yet be possible. Strengthened by years of hard and solemn trial, she felt herself no longer so inadequate to cope with Roger Chillingworth as on that night, abased by sin and half-maddened by the ignominy that was still new, when they had talked together in the prison-chamber. She had climbed her way since then to a higher point. The old man, on the other hand, had brought himself nearer to her level, or, perhaps, below it, by the revenge which he had stooped for.

In fine, Hester Prynne resolved to meet her former husband, and do what might be in her power for the rescue of the victim on whom he had so evidently set his gripe. The occasion was not long to seek. One afternoon, walking with Pearl in a retired part of the peninsula, she beheld the old physician with a basket on one arm and a staff in the other hand, stooping along the ground in quest of roots and herbs to concoct his medicine withal.

✿ 14 ✿

HESTER AND THE PHYSICIAN

HESTER BADE little Pearl run down to the margin of the water, and play with the shells and tangled sea-weed, until she should have talked awhile with yonder gatherer of herbs. So the child flew away like a bird, and, making bare her small white feet went pattering along the moist margin of the sea. Here and there she came to a full stop, and peeped curiously into a pool, left by the retiring tide as a mirror for Pearl to see her face in. Forth peeped at her, out of the pool, with dark, glistening curls around her head, and an elf-smile in her eyes, the image of a little maid whom Pearl, having no other playmate, invited to take her hand and run a race with her. But the visionary little maid on her part, beckoned likewise, as if to say—"This is a better place; come thou into the pool." And Pearl, stepping in mid-leg deep, beheld her own white feet at the bottom; while, out of a still lower depth, came the gleam of a kind of fragmentary smile, floating to and fro in the agitated water.

Meanwhile her mother had accosted the physician. "I would speak a word with you," said she—"a word that concerns us much."

"Aha! and is it Mistress Hester that has a word for old Roger Chillingworth?" answered he, raising himself from his stooping posture. "With all my heart! Why, mistress, I hear good tidings of you on all hands! No longer ago than yester-eve, a magistrate, a wise and godly man, was discoursing of your affairs, Mistress Hester, and whispered me that there had been question concerning you in the council. It was debated whether or no, with safety to the commonweal, yonder scarlet letter might be taken off your bosom. On my life, Hester, I made my intreaty to the worshipful magistrate that it might be done forthwith."

"It lies not in the pleasure of the magistrates to take off the badge," calmly replied Hester. "Were I worthy to be quit of it, it would fall away of its own nature, or be transformed into something that should speak a different purport."

"Nay, then, wear it, if it suit you better," rejoined he, "A woman must needs follow her own fancy touching the adornment of her person. The letter is gaily embroidered, and shows right bravely on your bosom!"

All this while Hester had been looking steadily at the old man, and was shocked, as well as wonder-smitten, to discern what a change had been wrought upon him within the past seven years. It was not so much that he had grown older; for though the traces of advancing life were visible he bore his age well, and seemed to retain a wiry vigour and alertness. But the former aspect of an intellectual and studious man, calm and quiet, which was what she best remembered in him, had altogether vanished, and been succeeded by an eager, searching, almost fierce, yet carefully guarded look. It seemed to be his wish and purpose to mask this expression with a smile, but the latter played him false, and flickered over his visage so derisively that the spectator could see his blackness all the better for it. Ever and anon, too, there came a glare of red light out of his eyes, as if the old man's soul were on fire and kept on smouldering duskily within his breast, until by some casual puff of passion it was blown into a momentary flame. This he repressed as speedily as possible, and strove to look as if nothing of the kind had happened.

In a word, old Roger Chillingworth was a striking evidence of man's faculty of transforming himself into a devil, if he will only, for a reasonable space of time, undertake a devil's office. This unhappy person had effected such a transformation by devoting himself for seven years to the constant analysis of a heart full of torture, and deriving his enjoyment thence, and adding fuel to those fiery tortures which he analysed and gloated over.

The scarlet letter burned on Hester Prynne's bosom. Here was another ruin, the responsibility of which came partly home to her.

"What see you in my face," asked the physician, "that you look at it so earnestly?"

"Something that would make me weep, if there were any tears bitter enough for it," answered she. "But let it pass! It is of yonder miserable man that I would speak."

"And what of him?" cried Roger Chillingworth, eagerly, as if he loved the topic, and were glad of an opportunity to discuss it with the only person of whom he could make a confidant. "Not to hide the truth, Mistress Hester, my thoughts happen just now to be busy with the gentleman. So speak freely and I will make answer."

"When we last spake together," said Hester, "now seven years ago, it was your pleasure to extort a promise of secrecy as touching the former relation betwixt yourself and me. As the life and good fame of yonder man were in your hands there seemed no choice to me, save to be silent in accordance with your behest. Yet it was not without heavy misgivings that I thus bound myself, for, having cast off all duty towards other human beings, there remained a duty towards him, and something whispered me that I was betraying it in pledging myself to keep your counsel. Since that day no man is so near to him as you. You tread behind his every footstep. You are beside him, sleeping and waking. You search his thoughts. You burrow and rankle in his heart! Your clutch is on his life, and you cause him to die daily a living death, and still he knows you not. In permitting this I have surely acted a false part by the only man to whom the power was left me to be true!"

"What choice had you?" asked Roger Chillingworth. "My finger, pointed at this man, would have hurled him from his pulpit into a dungeon, thence, peradventure, to the gallows!"

"It had been better so!" said Hester Prynne.

"What evil have I done the man?" asked Roger Chillingworth again. "I tell thee, Hester Prynne, the richest fee that ever physician earned from monarch could not have bought such care as I have wasted on this miserable priest! But for my aid his life would have burned away in torments within the first two years after the perpetration of his crime and thine. For, Hester, his spirit lacked the strength that could have borne up, as thine has, beneath a burden like thy scarlet letter. Oh, I could reveal a goodly secret! But enough. What art can do, I have exhausted on him. That he now breathes and creeps about on earth is owing all to me!"

"Better he had died at once!" said Hester Prynne.

"Yea, woman, thou sayest truly!" cried old Roger Chillingworth, letting the lurid fire of his heart blaze out before her eyes. "Better had he died at once! Never did mortal suffer what this man has suffered. And all, all, in the sight of his worst enemy! He has been conscious of me. He has felt an influence dwelling always upon him like a curse. He knew, by some spiritual sense —for the Creator never made another being so sensitive as this—he knew that no friendly hand was pulling at his heartstrings, and that an eye was looking curiously into him, which sought only evil, and found it. But he knew not that the eye and hand were mine! With the superstition common to his brotherhood, he fancied himself given over to a fiend, to be tortured with frightful dreams and desperate thoughts, the sting of remorse and despair of pardon, as a foretaste of what awaits him beyond the grave. But it was the constant shadow of my presence, the closest propinquity of the man whom he had most vilely wronged, and who had grown to exist only by this perpetual poison of the direst revenge! Yea, indeed, he did not err, there was a fiend at his elbow! A mortal man, with once a human heart, has become a fiend for his especial torment."

The unfortunate physician, while uttering these words, lifted his hands with a look of horror, as if he had beheld some frightful shape, which he could not recognise, usurping the place of his own image in a glass. It was one of those moments—which sometimes occur only at the interval of years—when a man's moral aspect is faithfully revealed to his mind's eye. Not improbably he had never before viewed himself as he did now.

"Hast thou not tortured him enough?" said Hester, noticing the old man's look. "Has he not paid thee all?"

"No, no! He has but increased the debt!" answered the physician, and as he proceeded, his manner lost its fiercer characteristics, and subsided into gloom. "Dost thou remember me, Hester, as I was nine years agone? Even then I was in the autumn of my days, nor was it the early autumn. But all my life had been made up of earnest, studious, thoughtful, quiet years, bestowed faithfully for the increase of mine own knowledge, and faithfully, too, though this latter object was but casual to the other—faithfully for the advancement of human welfare. No life had been more peaceful and innocent than mine; few lives so rich with benefits conferred. Dost thou remember me? Was I not, though you might deem me cold, nevertheless a man thoughtful for others, craving little for himself—kind, true, just and of constant, if not warm affections? Was I not all this?"

"All this, and more," said Hester.

"And what am I now?" demanded he, looking into her face, and permitting the whole evil within him to be written on his features. "I have already told thee what I am—a fiend! Who made me so?"

"It was myself," cried Hester, shuddering. "It was I, not less than he. Why hast thou not avenged thyself on me?"

"I have left thee to the scarlet letter," replied Roger Chillingworth. "If that has not avenged me, I can do no more!"

He laid his finger on it with a smile.

"It has avenged thee," answered Hester Prynne.

"I judged no less," said the physician. "And now what wouldst thou with me touching this man?"

"I must reveal the secret," answered Hester, firmly. "He must discern thee in thy true character. What may be the result I know not. But this long debt of confidence, due from me to him, whose bane and ruin I have been, shall at length be paid. So far as concerns the overthrow or preservation of his fair fame and his earthly state, and perchance his life, he is in my hands. Nor do I—whom the scarlet letter has disciplined to truth, though it be the truth of red-hot iron entering into the soul—nor do I perceive such advantage in his living any longer a life of ghastly emptiness, that I shall stoop to implore thy mercy. Do with him as thou wilt! There is no good for him, no good for me, no good for thee. There is no good for little Pearl. There is no path to guide us out of this dismal maze."

"Woman, I could well-nigh pity thee," said Roger Chillingworth, unable to restrain a thrill of admiration too, for there was a quality almost majestic in the despair which she expressed. "Thou hadst great elements. Peradventure, hadst thou met earlier with a better love than mine, this evil had not been. I pity thee, for the good that has been wasted in thy nature."

"And I thee," answered Hester Prynne, "for the hatred that has transformed a wise and just man to a fiend! Wilt thou yet purge it out of thee, and be once more human? If not for his sake, then doubly for thine own! Forgive, and leave his further retribution to the Power that claims it! I said, but now, that there could be no good event for him, or thee, or me, who are here wandering together in this gloomy maze of evil, and stumbling at every step over the guilt wherewith we have strewn our path. It is not so! There might be good for thee, and thee alone, since thou hast been deeply wronged and hast it at thy will to pardon. Wilt thou give up that only privilege? Wilt thou reject that priceless benefit?"

"Peace, Hester—peace!" replied the old man, with gloomy sternness—"it is not granted me to pardon. I have no such power as thou tellest me of. My old faith, long forgotten, comes back to me, and explains all that we do, and all we suffer. By thy first step awry, thou didst plant the germ of evil; but since that moment it has all been a dark necessity. Ye that have wronged me are not sinful, save in a kind of typical illusion; neither am I fiend-like, who have snatched a fiend's office from his hands. It is our fate. Let the black flower blossom as it may! Now, go thy ways, and deal as thou wilt with yonder man."

He waved his hand, and betook himself again to his employment of gathering herbs.

❧ 15 ❧

HESTER AND PEARL

So Roger Chillingworth—a deformed old figure with a face that haunted men's memories longer than they liked—took leave of Hester Prynne, and went stooping away along the earth. He gathered here and there a herb, or grubbed up a root and put it into the basket on his arm. His gray beard almost touched the ground as he crept onward. Hester gazed after him a little while, looking with a half fantastic curiosity to see whether the tender grass of early spring would not be blighted beneath him and show the wavering track of his footsteps, sere and brown, across its cheerful verdure. She wondered what sort of herbs they were which the old man was so sedulous to gather. Would not the earth, quickened to an evil purpose by the sympathy of his eye, greet him with poisonous shrubs of species hitherto unknown, that would start up under his fingers? Or might it suffice him that every wholesome growth should be converted into something deleterious and malignant at his touch? Did the sun, which shone so brightly everywhere else, really fall upon him? Or was there, as it rather seemed, a circle of ominous shadow moving along with his deformity whichever way he turned himself? And whither was he now going? Would he not suddenly sink into the earth, leaving a barren and blasted spot, where, in due course of time, would be seen deadly nightshade, dogwood, henbane, and whatever else of vegetable wickedness the climate could produce, all flourishing with hideous luxuriance? Or would he spread bat's wings and flee away, looking so much the uglier the higher he rose towards heaven?

"Be it sin or no," said Hester Prynne, bitterly, as still she gazed after him, "I hate the man!"

She upbraided herself for the sentiment, but could not overcome or lessen it. Attempting to do so, she thought of those long-past days in a distant land, when he used to emerge at eventide from the seclusion of his study and sit down in the firelight of their home, and in the light of her nuptial smile. He needed to bask himself in that smile, he said, in order that the chill of so many lonely hours among his books might be taken off the scholar's heart. Such scenes had once appeared not otherwise than happy, but now, as viewed through the dismal medium of her subsequent life, they classed themselves among her ugliest remembrances. She marvelled how such scenes could have been! She marvelled how she could ever have been wrought upon to marry him! She deemed it her crime most to be repented of, that she had ever endured and reciprocated the lukewarm grasp of his hand, and had suffered the smile of her lips and eyes to mingle and melt into his own. And it seemed a fouler offence committed by Roger Chillingworth than any which had since been done him, that, in the time when her heart knew no better, he had persuaded her to fancy herself happy by his side.

"Yes, I hate him!" repeated Hester more bitterly than before.

"He betrayed me! He has done me worse wrong than I did him!"

Let men tremble to win the hand of woman, unless they win along with it the utmost passion of her heart! Else it may be their miserable fortune, as it was Roger Chillingworth's, when some mightier touch than their own may have awakened all her sensibilities, to be reproached even for the calm content, the marble image of happiness, which they will have imposed upon her as the warm reality. But Hester ought long ago to have done with this injustice. What did it betoken? Had seven long years, under the torture of the scarlet letter, inflicted so much of misery and wrought out no repentance?

The emotion of that brief space, while she stood gazing after the crooked figure of old Roger Chillingworth, threw a dark light on Hester's state of mind, revealing much that she might not otherwise have acknowledged to herself.

He being gone, she summoned back her child.

"Pearl! Little Pearl! Where are you?"

Pearl, whose activity of spirit never flagged, had been at no loss for amusement while her mother talked with the old gatherer of herbs. At first, as already told, she had flirted fancifully with her own image in a pool of water, beckoning the phantom forth, and—as it declined to venture—seeking a passage for herself into its sphere of impalpable earth and unattainable sky. Soon finding, however, that either she or the image was unreal, she turned elsewhere for better pastime. She made little boats out of birch-bark, and freighted them with snailshells, and sent out more ventures on the mighty deep than any merchant in New England; but the larger part of them foundered near the shore. She seized a live horse-shoe by the tail, and made prize of several five-fingers, and laid out a jelly-fish to melt in the warm sun. Then she took up the white foam that streaked the line of the advancing tide, and threw it upon the breeze, scampering after it with winged footsteps to catch the great snowflakes ere they fell. Perceiving a flock of beach-birds that fed and fluttered along the shore, the naughty child picked up her apron full of pebbles, and, creeping from rock to rock after these small sea-fowl, displayed remarkable dexterity in pelting them. One little gray bird, with a white breast, Pearl was almost sure had been hit by a pebble, and fluttered away with a broken wing. But then the elf-child sighed, and gave up her sport, because it grieved her to have done harm to a little being that was as wild as the sea-breeze, or as wild as Pearl herself.

Her final employment was to gather seaweed of various kinds, and make herself a scarf or mantle, and a head-dress, and thus assume the aspect of a little mermaid. She inherited her mother's gift for devising drapery and costume. As the last touch to her mermaid's garb, Pearl took some eel-grass and imitated, as best she could, on her own bosom the decoration with which she was so familiar on her mother's. A letter—the letter A—but freshly green instead of scarlet. The child bent her chin upon her breast, and contemplated this device with strange interest, even as if the one only thing for which she had been sent into the world was to make out its hidden import.

"I wonder if mother will ask me what it means?" thought Pearl.

Just then she heard her mother's voice, and, flitting along as lightly as one of the little sea-birds, appeared before Hester Prynne dancing, laughing, and pointing her finger to the ornament upon her bosom.

"My little Pearl," said Hester, after a moment's silence, "the green letter, and on thy childish bosom, has no purport. But dost thou know, my child, what this letter means which thy mother is doomed to wear?"

"Yes, mother," said the child. "It is the great letter A. Thou hast taught me in the horn-book."

Hester looked steadily into her little face; but though there was that singular expression which she had so often remarked in her black eyes, she could not satisfy herself whether Pearl really attached any meaning to the symbol. She felt a morbid desire to ascertain the point.

"Dost thou know, child, wherefore thy mother wears this letter?"

"Truly do I!" answered Pearl, looking brightly into her mother's face. "It is for the same reason that the minister keeps his hand over his heart!"

"And what reason is that?" asked Hester, half smiling at the absurd incongruity of the child's observation; but on second thoughts turning pale.

"What has the letter to do with any heart save mine?"

"Nay, mother, I have told all I know," said Pearl, more seriously than she was wont to speak. "Ask yonder old man whom thou hast been talking with,—it may be he can tell. But in good earnest now, mother dear, what does this scarlet letter mean?—and why dost thou wear it on thy bosom?—and why does the minister keep his hand over his heart?"

She took her mother's hand in both her own, and gazed into her eyes with an earnestness that was seldom seen in her wild and capricious character. The thought occurred to Hester, that the child might really be seeking to approach her with childlike confidence, and doing what she could, and as intelligently as she knew how, to establish a meeting-point of sympathy. It showed Pearl in an unwonted aspect. Heretofore, the mother, while loving her child with the intensity of a sole affection, had schooled herself to hope for little other return than the waywardness of an April breeze, which spends its time in airy sport, and has its gusts of inexplicable passion, and is petulant in its best of moods, and chills oftener than caresses you, when you take it to your bosom; in requital of which misdemeanours it will sometimes, of its own vague purpose, kiss your cheek with a kind of doubtful tenderness, and play gently with your hair, and then be gone about its other idle business, leaving a dreamy pleasure at your heart. And this, moreover, was a mother's estimate of the child's disposition. Any other observer might have seen few but unamiable traits, and have given them a far darker colouring. But now the idea came strongly into Hester's mind, that Pearl, with her remarkable precocity and acuteness, might already have approached the age when she could have been made a friend, and intrusted with as much of her mother's sorrows as could be imparted, without irreverence either to the parent or the child. In the little chaos of Pearl's character there might be seen emerging and could have been from the very first—the steadfast principles of an unflinching courage—an uncontrollable will—sturdy pride, which might be disciplined into self-respect—and a bitter scorn of many things which, when examined, might be found to have the taint of falsehood in them. She possessed affections, too, though hitherto acrid and disagreeable, as are the richest flavours of unripe fruit. With all these sterling attributes, thought Hester, the evil which she inherited from her mother must be great indeed, if a noble woman do not grow out of this elfish child.

Pearl's inevitable tendency to hover about the enigma of the scarlet letter seemed an innate quality of her being. From the earliest epoch of her conscious life, she had entered upon this as her appointed mission. Hester had often fancied that Providence had a design of justice and retribution, in endowing the child with this marked propensity; but never, until now, had she bethought herself to ask, whether, linked with that design, there might not likewise be a purpose of mercy and beneficence. If little Pearl were entertained with faith and trust, as a spirit messenger no less than an earthly child, might it not be her errand to soothe away the sorrow that lay cold in her mother's heart, and converted it into a tomb?—and to help her to overcome the passion, once so wild, and even yet neither dead nor asleep, but only imprisoned within the same tomb-like heart?

Such were some of the thoughts that now stirred in Hester's mind, with as much vivacity of impression as if they had actually been whispered into her ear. And there was little Pearl, all this while, holding her mother's hand in both her own, and turning her face upward, while she put these searching questions, once and again, and still a third time.

"What does the letter mean, mother? and why dost thou wear it? and why does the minister keep his hand over his heart?"

"What shall I say?" thought Hester to herself. "No! if this be the price of the child's sympathy, I cannot pay it."

Then she spoke aloud—

"Silly Pearl," said she, "what questions are these? There are many things in this world that a child must not ask about. What know I of the minister's heart? And as for the scarlet letter, I wear it for the sake of its gold thread."

In all the seven bygone years, Hester Prynne had never before been false to the symbol on her bosom. It may be that it was the talisman of a stern and severe, but yet a guardian spirit, who now forsook her; as recognising that, in spite of his strict watch over her heart, some new evil had crept into it, or some old one had never been expelled. As for little Pearl, the earnestness soon passed out of her face.

But the child did not see fit to let the matter drop. Two or three times, as her mother and she went homeward, and as often at supper-time, and while Hester was putting her to bed, and once after she seemed to be fairly asleep, Pearl looked up, with mischief gleaming in her black eyes.

"Mother," said she, "what does the scarlet letter mean?"

And the next morning, the first indication the child gave of being awake was by popping up her head from the pillow, and making that other enquiry, which she had so unaccountably connected with her investigations about the scarlet letter—

"Mother!—Mother!—Why does the minister keep his hand over his heart?"

"Hold thy tongue, naughty child!" answered her mother, with an asperity that she had never permitted to herself before. "Do not tease me; else I shall put thee into the dark closet!"

❦ 16 ❦

A FOREST WALK

HESTER PRYNNE REMAINED constant in her resolve to make known to Mr. Dimmesdale, at whatever risk of present pain or ulterior consequences, the true character of the man who had crept into his intimacy. For several days, however, she vainly sought an opportunity of addressing him in some of the meditative walks which she knew him to be in the habit of taking along the shores of the Peninsula, or on the wooded hills of the neighbouring country. There would have been no scandal, indeed, nor peril to the holy whiteness of the clergyman's good fame, had she visited him in his own study, where many a penitent, ere now, had confessed sins of perhaps as deep a dye as the one betokened by the scarlet letter. But, partly that she dreaded the secret or undisguised interference of old Roger Chillingworth, and partly that her conscious heart imparted suspicion where none could have been felt, and partly that both the minister and she would need the whole wide world to breathe in, while they talked together—for all these reasons Hester never thought of meeting him in any narrower privacy than beneath the open sky.

At last, while attending a sick chamber, whither the Rev. Mr. Dimmesdale had been summoned to make a prayer, she learnt that he had gone, the day before, to visit the Apostle Eliot, among his Indian converts. He would probably return by a certain hour in the afternoon of the morrow. Betimes, therefore, the next day, Hester took little Pearl—who was necessarily the companion of all her mother's expeditions, however inconvenient her presence—and set forth.

The road, after the two wayfarers had crossed from the Peninsula to the mainland, was no other than a foot-path. It straggled onward into the mystery of the primeval forest. This hemmed it in so narrowly, and stood so black and dense on either side, and disclosed such imperfect glimpses of the sky above, that, to Hester's mind, it imaged not amiss the moral wilderness in which she had so long been wandering. The day was chill and sombre. Overhead was a gray expanse of cloud, slightly stirred, however, by a breeze; so that a gleam of flickering sunshine might now and then be seen at its solitary play along the path. This flitting cheerfulness was always at the further extremity of some long vista through the forest. The sportive sunlight—feebly sportive, at best, in the predominant pensiveness of the day and scene—withdrew itself as they came nigh, and left the spots where it had danced the drearier, because they had hoped to find them bright.

"Mother," said little Pearl, "the sunshine does not love you.
It runs away and hides itself, because it is afraid of something
on your bosom. Now, see! There it is, playing a good way off.
Stand you here, and let me run and catch it. I am but a child.
It will not flee from me—for I wear nothing on my bosom yet!"

"Nor ever will, my child, I hope," said Hester.

"And why not, mother?" asked Pearl, stopping short, just at the beginning of her race. "Will not it come of its own accord when I am a woman grown?"

"Run away, child," answered her mother, "and catch the sunshine.
It will soon be gone."

Pearl set forth at a great pace, and as Hester smiled to perceive, did actually catch the sunshine, and stood laughing in the midst of it, all brightened by its splendour, and scintillating with the vivacity excited by rapid motion. The light lingered about the lonely child, as if glad of such a playmate, until her mother had drawn almost nigh enough to step into the magic circle too.

"It will go now," said Pearl, shaking her head.

"See!" answered Hester, smiling; "now I can stretch out my hand and grasp some of it."

As she attempted to do so, the sunshine vanished; or, to judge from the bright expression that was dancing on Pearl's features, her mother could have fancied that the child had absorbed it into herself, and would give it forth again, with a gleam about her path, as they should plunge into some gloomier shade. There was no other attribute that so much impressed her with a sense of new and untransmitted vigour in Pearl's nature, as this never failing vivacity of spirits: she had not the disease of sadness, which almost all children, in these latter days, inherit, with the scrofula, from the troubles of their ancestors. Perhaps this, too, was a disease, and but the reflex of the wild energy with which Hester had fought against her sorrows before Pearl's birth. It was certainly a doubtful charm, imparting a hard, metallic lustre to the child's character. She wanted—what some people want throughout life—a grief that should deeply touch her, and thus humanise and make her capable of sympathy. But there was time enough yet for little Pearl.

"Come, my child!" said Hester, looking about her from the spot where Pearl had stood still in the sunshine—"we will sit down a little way within the wood, and rest ourselves."

"I am not aweary, mother," replied the little girl. "But you may sit down, if you will tell me a story meanwhile."

"A story, child!" said Hester. "And about what?"

"Oh, a story about the Black Man," answered Pearl, taking hold of her mother's gown, and looking up, half earnestly, half mischievously, into her face.

"How he haunts this forest, and carries a book with him a big, heavy book, with iron clasps; and how this ugly Black Man offers his book and an iron pen to everybody that meets him here among the trees; and they are to write their names with their own blood; and then he sets his mark on their bosoms. Didst thou ever meet the Black Man, mother?"

"And who told you this story, Pearl," asked her mother, recognising a common superstition of the period.

"It was the old dame in the chimney corner, at the house where you watched last night," said the child. "But she fancied me asleep while she was talking of it. She said that a thousand and a thousand people had met him here, and had written in his book, and have his mark on them. And that ugly tempered lady, old Mistress Hibbins, was one. And, mother, the old dame said that this scarlet letter was the Black Man's mark on thee, and that it glows like a red flame when thou meetest him at midnight, here in the dark wood. Is it true, mother? And dost thou go to meet him in the nighttime?"

"Didst thou ever awake and find thy mother gone?" asked Hester. "Not that I remember," said the child. "If thou fearest to leave me in our cottage, thou mightest take me along with thee. I would very gladly go! But, mother, tell me now! Is there such a Black Man? And didst thou ever meet him? And is this his mark?"

"Wilt thou let me be at peace, if I once tell thee?" asked her mother.

"Yes, if thou tellest me all," answered Pearl.

"Once in my life I met the Black Man!" said her mother. "This scarlet letter is his mark!"

Thus conversing, they entered sufficiently deep into the wood to secure themselves from the observation of any casual passenger along the forest track. Here they sat down on a luxuriant heap of moss; which at some epoch of the preceding century, had been a gigantic pine, with its roots and trunk in the darksome shade, and its head aloft in the upper atmosphere. It was a little dell where they had seated themselves, with a leaf-strewn bank rising gently on either side, and a brook flowing through the midst, over a bed of fallen and drowned leaves. The trees impending over it had flung down great branches from time to time, which choked up the current, and compelled it to form eddies and black depths at some points; while, in its swifter and livelier passages there appeared a channel-way of pebbles, and brown, sparkling sand. Letting the eyes follow along the course of the stream, they could catch the reflected light from its water, at some short distance within the forest, but soon lost all traces of it amid the bewilderment of tree-trunks and underbrush, and here and there a huge rock covered over with gray lichens. All these giant trees and boulders of granite seemed intent on making a mystery of the course of this small brook; fearing, perhaps, that, with its never-ceasing loquacity, it should whisper tales out of the heart of the old forest whence it flowed, or mirror its revelations on the smooth surface of a pool. Continually, indeed, as it stole onward, the streamlet kept up a babble, kind, quiet, soothing, but melancholy, like the voice of a young child that was spending its infancy without playfulness, and knew not how to be merry among sad acquaintance and events of sombre hue.

"Oh, brook! Oh, foolish and tiresome little brook!" cried
Pearl, after listening awhile to its talk, "Why art thou so sad?
Pluck up a spirit, and do not be all the time sighing and
murmuring!"

But the brook, in the course of its little lifetime among the forest trees, had gone through so solemn an experience that it could not help talking about it, and seemed to have nothing else to say. Pearl resembled the brook, inasmuch as the current of her life gushed from a well-spring as mysterious, and had flowed through scenes shadowed as heavily with gloom. But, unlike the little stream, she danced and sparkled, and prattled airily along her course.

"What does this sad little brook say, mother?" inquired she.

"If thou hadst a sorrow of thine own, the brook might tell thee of it," answered her mother, "even as it is telling me of mine. But now, Pearl, I hear a footstep along the path, and the noise of one putting aside the branches. I would have thee betake thyself to play, and leave me to speak with him that comes yonder."

"Is it the Black Man?" asked Pearl.

"Wilt thou go and play, child?" repeated her mother, "But do not stray far into the wood. And take heed that thou come at my first call."

"Yes, mother," answered Pearl, "But if it be the Black Man, wilt thou not let me stay a moment, and look at him, with his big book under his arm?"

"Go, silly child!" said her mother impatiently. "It is no Black Man! Thou canst see him now, through the trees. It is the minister!"

"And so it is!" said the child. "And, mother, he has his hand over his heart! Is it because, when the minister wrote his name in the book, the Black Man set his mark in that place? But why does he not wear it outside his bosom, as thou dost, mother?"

"Go now, child, and thou shalt tease me as thou wilt another time," cried Hester Prynne. "But do not stray far. Keep where thou canst hear the babble of the brook."

The child went singing away, following up the current of the brook, and striving to mingle a more lightsome cadence with its melancholy voice. But the little stream would not be comforted, and still kept telling its unintelligible secret of some very mournful mystery that had happened—or making a prophetic lamentation about something that was yet to happen—within the verge of the dismal forest. So Pearl, who had enough of shadow in her own little life, chose to break off all acquaintance with this repining brook. She set herself, therefore, to gathering violets and wood-anemones, and some scarlet columbines that she found growing in the crevice of a high rock.

When her elf-child had departed, Hester Prynne made a step or two towards the track that led through the forest, but still remained under the deep shadow of the trees. She beheld the minister advancing along the path entirely alone, and leaning on a staff which he had cut by the wayside. He looked haggard and feeble, and betrayed a nerveless despondency in his air, which had never so remarkably characterised him in his walks about the settlement, nor in any other situation where he deemed himself liable to notice. Here it was wofully visible, in this intense seclusion of the forest, which of itself would have been a heavy trial to the spirits. There was a listlessness in his gait, as if he saw no reason for taking one step further, nor felt any desire to do so, but would have been glad, could he be glad of anything, to fling himself down at the root of the nearest tree, and lie there passive for evermore. The leaves might bestrew him, and the soil gradually accumulate and form a little hillock over his frame, no matter whether there were life in it or no. Death was too definite an object to be wished for or avoided.

To Hester's eye, the Reverend Mr. Dimmesdale exhibited no symptom of positive and vivacious suffering, except that, as little Pearl had remarked, he kept his hand over his heart.

❦ 17 ❦

THE PASTOR AND HIS PARISHIONER

SLOWLY AS THE MINISTER WALKED, he had almost gone by before Hester Prynne could gather voice enough to attract his observation. At length she succeeded.

"Arthur Dimmesdale!" she said, faintly at first, then louder, but hoarsely—"Arthur Dimmesdale!"

"Who speaks?" answered the minister. Gathering himself quickly up, he stood more erect, like a man taken by surprise in a mood to which he was reluctant to have witnesses. Throwing his eyes anxiously in the direction of the voice, he indistinctly beheld a form under the trees, clad in garments so sombre, and so little relieved from the gray twilight into which the clouded sky and the heavy foliage had darkened the noontide, that he knew not whether it were a woman or a shadow. It may be that his pathway through life was haunted thus by a spectre that had stolen out from among his thoughts.

He made a step nigher, and discovered the scarlet letter.

"Hester! Hester Prynne!", said he; "is it thou? Art thou in life?"

"Even so." she answered. "In such life as has been mine these seven years past! And thou, Arthur Dimmesdale, dost thou yet live?"

It was no wonder that they thus questioned one another's actual and bodily existence, and even doubted of their own. So strangely did they meet in the dim wood that it was like the first encounter in the world beyond the grave of two spirits who had been intimately connected in their former life, but now stood coldly shuddering in mutual dread, as not yet familiar with their state, nor wonted to the companionship of disembodied beings. Each a ghost, and awe-stricken at the other ghost. They were awe-stricken likewise at themselves, because the crisis flung back to them their consciousness, and revealed to each heart its history and experience, as life never does, except at such breathless epochs. The soul beheld its features in the mirror of the passing moment. It was with fear, and tremulously, and, as it were, by a slow, reluctant necessity, that Arthur Dimmesdale put forth his hand, chill as death, and touched the chill hand of Hester Prynne. The grasp, cold as it was, took away what was dreariest in the interview. They now felt themselves, at least, inhabitants of the same sphere.

Without a word more spoken—neither he nor she assuming the guidance, but with an unexpressed consent—they glided back into the shadow of the woods whence Hester had emerged, and sat down on the heap of moss where she and Pearl had before been sitting. When they found voice to speak, it was at first only to utter remarks and inquiries such as any two acquaintances might have made, about the gloomy sky, the threatening storm, and, next, the health of each. Thus they went onward, not boldly, but step by step, into the themes that were brooding deepest in their hearts. So long estranged by fate and circumstances, they needed something slight and casual to run before and throw open the doors of intercourse, so that their real thoughts might be led across the threshold.

After awhile, the minister fixed his eyes on Hester Prynne's.

"Hester," said he, "hast thou found peace?"

She smiled drearily, looking down upon her bosom.

"Hast thou?" she asked.

"None—nothing but despair!" he answered. "What else could I look for, being what I am, and leading such a life as mine? Were I an atheist—a man devoid of conscience—a wretch with coarse and brutal instincts—I might have found peace long ere now. Nay, I never should have lost it. But, as matters stand with my soul, whatever of good capacity there originally was in me, all of God's gifts that were the choicest have become the ministers of spiritual torment. Hester, I am most miserable!"

"The people reverence thee," said Hester. "And surely thou workest good among them! Doth this bring thee no comfort?"

"More misery, Hester!—Only the more misery!" answered the clergyman with a bitter smile. "As concerns the good which I may appear to do, I have no faith in it. It must needs be a delusion. What can a ruined soul like mine effect towards the redemption of other souls?—or a polluted soul towards their purification? And as for the people's reverence, would that it were turned to scorn and hatred! Canst thou deem it, Hester, a consolation that I must stand up in my pulpit, and meet so many eyes turned upward to my face, as if the light of heaven were beaming from it!—must see my flock hungry for the truth, and listening to my words as if a tongue of Pentecost were speaking!—and then look inward, and discern the black reality of what they idolise? I have laughed, in bitterness and agony of heart, at the contrast between what I seem and what I am! And Satan laughs at it!"

"You wrong yourself in this," said Hester gently. "You have deeply and sorely repented. Your sin is left behind you in the days long past. Your present life is not less holy, in very truth, than it seems in people's eyes. Is there no reality in the penitence thus sealed and witnessed by good works? And wherefore should it not bring you peace?"

"No, Hester—no!" replied the clergyman. "There is no substance in it! It is cold and dead, and can do nothing for me! Of penance, I have had enough! Of penitence, there has been none! Else, I should long ago have thrown off these garments of mock holiness, and have shown myself to mankind as they will see me at the judgment-seat. Happy are you, Hester, that wear the scarlet letter openly upon your bosom! Mine burns in secret! Thou little knowest what a relief it is, after the torment of a seven years' cheat, to look into an eye that recognises me for what I am! Had I one friend—or were it my worst enemy!—to whom, when sickened with the praises of all other men, I could daily betake myself, and be known as the vilest of all sinners, methinks my soul might keep itself alive thereby. Even thus much of truth would save me! But now, it is all falsehood!—all emptiness!—all death!"

Hester Prynne looked into his face, but hesitated to speak. Yet, uttering his long-restrained emotions so vehemently as he did, his words here offered her the very point of circumstances in which to interpose what she came to say. She conquered her fears, and spoke:

"Such a friend as thou hast even now wished for," said she, "with whom to weep over thy sin, thou hast in me, the partner of it!" Again she hesitated, but brought out the words with an effort.—"Thou hast long had such an enemy, and dwellest with him, under the same roof!"

The minister started to his feet, gasping for breath, and clutching at his heart, as if he would have torn it out of his bosom.

"Ha! What sayest thou?" cried he. "An enemy! And under mine own roof! What mean you?"

Hester Prynne was now fully sensible of the deep injury for which she was responsible to this unhappy man, in permitting him to lie for so many years, or, indeed, for a single moment, at the mercy of one whose purposes could not be other than malevolent. The very contiguity of his enemy, beneath whatever mask the latter might conceal himself, was enough to disturb the magnetic sphere of a being so sensitive as Arthur Dimmesdale. There had been a period when Hester was less alive to this consideration; or, perhaps, in the misanthropy of her own trouble, she left the minister to bear what she might picture to herself as a more tolerable doom. But of late, since the night of his vigil, all her sympathies towards him had been both softened and invigorated. She now read his heart more accurately. She doubted not that the continual presence of Roger Chillingworth—the secret poison of his malignity, infecting all the air about him—and his authorised interference, as a physician, with the minister's physical and spiritual infirmities—that these bad opportunities had been turned to a cruel purpose. By means of them, the sufferer's conscience had been kept in an irritated state, the tendency of which was, not to cure by wholesome pain, but to disorganize and corrupt his spiritual being. Its result, on earth, could hardly fail to be insanity, and hereafter, that eternal alienation from the Good and True, of which madness is perhaps the earthly type.

Such was the ruin to which she had brought the man, once—nay, why should we not speak it?—still so passionately loved! Hester felt that the sacrifice of the clergyman's good name, and death itself, as she had already told Roger Chillingworth, would have been infinitely preferable to the alternative which she had taken upon herself to choose. And now, rather than have had this grievous wrong to confess, she would gladly have laid down on the forest leaves, and died there, at Arthur Dimmesdale's feet.

"Oh, Arthur!" cried she, "forgive me! In all things else, I have striven to be true! Truth was the one virtue which I might have held fast, and did hold fast, through all extremity; save when thy good—thy life—thy fame—were put in question! Then I consented to a deception. But a lie is never good, even though death threaten on the other side! Dost thou not see what I would say? That old man!—the physician!—he whom they call Roger Chillingworth!—he was my husband!"

The minister looked at her for an instant, with all that violence of passion, which—intermixed in more shapes than one with his higher, purer, softer qualities—was, in fact, the portion of him which the devil claimed, and through which he sought to win the rest. Never was there a blacker or a fiercer frown than Hester now encountered. For the brief space that it lasted, it was a dark transfiguration. But his character had been so much enfeebled by suffering, that even its lower energies were incapable of more than a temporary struggle. He sank down on the ground, and buried his face in his hands.

"I might have known it," murmured he—"I did know it! Was not the secret told me, in the natural recoil of my heart at the first sight of him, and as often as I have seen him since? Why did I not understand? Oh, Hester Prynne, thou little, little knowest all the horror of this thing! And the shame!—the indelicacy!—the horrible ugliness of this exposure of a sick and guilty heart to the very eye that would gloat over it! Woman, woman, thou art accountable for this!—I cannot forgive thee!"

"Thou shalt forgive me!" cried Hester, flinging herself on the fallen leaves beside him. "Let God punish! Thou shalt forgive!"

With sudden and desperate tenderness she threw her arms around him, and pressed his head against her bosom, little caring though his cheek rested on the scarlet letter. He would have released himself, but strove in vain to do so. Hester would not set him free, lest he should look her sternly in the face. All the world had frowned on her—for seven long years had it frowned upon this lonely woman—and still she bore it all, nor ever once turned away her firm, sad eyes. Heaven, likewise, had frowned upon her, and she had not died. But the frown of this pale, weak, sinful, and sorrow-stricken man was what Hester could not bear, and live!

"Wilt thou yet forgive me?" she repeated, over and over again.

"Wilt thou not frown? Wilt thou forgive?"

"I do forgive you, Hester," replied the minister at length, with a deep utterance, out of an abyss of sadness, but no anger. "I freely forgive you now. May God forgive us both. We are not, Hester, the worst sinners in the world. There is one worse than even the polluted priest! That old man's revenge has been blacker than my sin. He has violated, in cold blood, the sanctity of a human heart. Thou and I, Hester, never did so!"

"Never, never!" whispered she. "What we did had a consecration of its own. We felt it so! We said so to each other. Hast thou forgotten it?"

"Hush, Hester!" said Arthur Dimmesdale, rising from the ground.

"No; I have not forgotten!"

They sat down again, side by side, and hand clasped in hand, on the mossy trunk of the fallen tree. Life had never brought them a gloomier hour; it was the point whither their pathway had so long been tending, and darkening ever, as it stole along—and yet it unclosed a charm that made them linger upon it, and claim another, and another, and, after all, another moment. The forest was obscure around them, and creaked with a blast that was passing through it. The boughs were tossing heavily above their heads; while one solemn old tree groaned dolefully to another, as if telling the sad story of the pair that sat beneath, or constrained to forbode evil to come.

And yet they lingered. How dreary looked the forest-track that led backward to the settlement, where Hester Prynne must take up again the burden of her ignominy and the minister the hollow mockery of his good name! So they lingered an instant longer. No golden light had ever been so precious as the gloom of this dark forest. Here seen only by his eyes, the scarlet letter need not burn into the bosom of the fallen woman! Here seen only by her eyes, Arthur Dimmesdale, false to God and man, might be, for one moment true!

He started at a thought that suddenly occurred to him.

"Hester!" cried he, "here is a new horror! Roger Chillingworth knows your purpose to reveal his true character. Will he continue, then, to keep our secret? What will now be the course of his revenge?"

"There is a strange secrecy in his nature," replied Hester, thoughtfully; "and it has grown upon him by the hidden practices of his revenge. I deem it not likely that he will betray the secret. He will doubtless seek other means of satiating his dark passion."

"And I!—how am I to live longer, breathing the same air with this deadly enemy?" exclaimed Arthur Dimmesdale, shrinking within himself, and pressing his hand nervously against his heart—a gesture that had grown involuntary with him. "Think for me, Hester! Thou art strong. Resolve for me!"

"Thou must dwell no longer with this man," said Hester, slowly and firmly. "Thy heart must be no longer under his evil eye!"

"It were far worse than death!" replied the minister. "But how to avoid it? What choice remains to me? Shall I lie down again on these withered leaves, where I cast myself when thou didst tell me what he was? Must I sink down there, and die at once?"

"Alas! what a ruin has befallen thee!" said Hester, with the tears gushing into her eyes. "Wilt thou die for very weakness? There is no other cause!"

"The judgment of God is on me," answered the conscience-stricken priest. "It is too mighty for me to struggle with!"

"Heaven would show mercy," rejoined Hester, "hadst thou but the strength to take advantage of it."

"Be thou strong for me!" answered he. "Advise me what to do."

"Is the world, then, so narrow?" exclaimed Hester Prynne, fixing her deep eyes on the minister's, and instinctively exercising a magnetic power over a spirit so shattered and subdued that it could hardly hold itself erect. "Doth the universe lie within the compass of yonder town, which only a little time ago was but a leaf-strewn desert, as lonely as this around us? Whither leads yonder forest-track? Backward to the settlement, thou sayest! Yes; but, onward, too! Deeper it goes, and deeper into the wilderness, less plainly to be seen at every step; until some few miles hence the yellow leaves will show no vestige of the white man's tread. There thou art free! So brief a journey would bring thee from a world where thou hast been most wretched, to one where thou mayest still be happy! Is there not shade enough in all this boundless forest to hide thy heart from the gaze of Roger Chillingworth?"

"Yes, Hester; but only under the fallen leaves!" replied the minister, with a sad smile.

"Then there is the broad pathway of the sea!" continued Hester. "It brought thee hither. If thou so choose, it will bear thee back again. In our native land, whether in some remote rural village, or in vast London—or, surely, in Germany, in France, in pleasant Italy—thou wouldst be beyond his power and knowledge! And what hast thou to do with all these iron men, and their opinions? They have kept thy better part in bondage too long already!"

"It cannot be!" answered the minister, listening as if he were called upon to realise a dream. "I am powerless to go. Wretched and sinful as I am, I have had no other thought than to drag on my earthly existence in the sphere where Providence hath placed me. Lost as my own soul is, I would still do what I may for other human souls! I dare not quit my post, though an unfaithful sentinel, whose sure reward is death and dishonour, when his dreary watch shall come to an end!"

"Thou art crushed under this seven years' weight of misery," replied Hester, fervently resolved to buoy him up with her own energy. "But thou shalt leave it all behind thee! It shall not cumber thy steps, as thou treadest along the forest-path: neither shalt thou freight the ship with it, if thou prefer to cross the sea. Leave this wreck and ruin here where it hath happened. Meddle no more with it! Begin all anew! Hast thou exhausted possibility in the failure of this one trial? Not so! The future is yet full of trial and success. There is happiness to be enjoyed! There is good to be done! Exchange this false life of thine for a true one. Be, if thy spirit summon thee to such a mission, the teacher and apostle of the red men. Or, as is more thy nature, be a scholar and a sage among the wisest and the most renowned of the cultivated world. Preach! Write! Act! Do anything, save to lie down and die! Give up this name of Arthur Dimmesdale, and make thyself another, and a high one, such as thou canst wear without fear or shame. Why shouldst thou tarry so much as one other day in the torments that have so gnawed into thy life? that have made thee feeble to will and to do? that will leave thee powerless even to repent? Up, and away!"

"Oh, Hester!" cried Arthur Dimmesdale, in whose eyes a fitful light, kindled by her enthusiasm, flashed up and died away, "thou tellest of running a race to a man whose knees are tottering beneath him! I must die here! There is not the strength or courage left me to venture into the wide, strange, difficult world alone!"

It was the last expression of the despondency of a broken spirit. He lacked energy to grasp the better fortune that seemed within his reach.

He repeated the word—"Alone, Hester!"

"Thou shall not go alone!" answered she, in a deep whisper.

Then, all was spoken!

᪥ 18 ᪥

A FLOOD OF SUNSHINE

ARTHUR DIMMESDALE GAZED into Hester's face with a look in which hope and joy shone out, indeed, but with fear betwixt them, and a kind of horror at her boldness, who had spoken what he vaguely hinted at, but dared not speak.

But Hester Prynne, with a mind of native courage and activity, and for so long a period not merely estranged, but outlawed from society, had habituated herself to such latitude of speculation as was altogether foreign to the clergyman. She had wandered, without rule or guidance, in a moral wilderness, as vast, as intricate, and shadowy as the untamed forest, amid the gloom of which they were now holding a colloquy that was to decide their fate. Her intellect and heart had their home, as it were, in desert places, where she roamed as freely as the wild Indian in his woods. For years past she had looked from this estranged point of view at human institutions, and whatever priests or legislators had established; criticising all with hardly more reverence than the Indian would feel for the clerical band, the judicial robe, the pillory, the gallows, the fireside, or the church. The tendency of her fate and fortunes had been to set her free. The scarlet letter was her passport into regions where other women dared not tread. Shame, Despair, Solitude! These had been her teachers—stern and wild ones—and they had made her strong, but taught her much amiss.

The minister, on the other hand, had never gone through an experience calculated to lead him beyond the scope of generally received laws; although, in a single instance, he had so fearfully transgressed one of the most sacred of them. But this had been a sin of passion, not of principle, nor even purpose. Since that wretched epoch, he had watched with morbid zeal and minuteness, not his acts—for those it was easy to arrange—but each breath of emotion, and his every thought. At the head of the social system, as the clergymen of that day stood, he was only the more trammelled by its regulations, its principles, and even its prejudices. As a priest, the framework of his order inevitably hemmed him in. As a man who had once sinned, but who kept his conscience all alive and painfully sensitive by the fretting of an unhealed wound, he might have been supposed safer within the line of virtue than if he had never sinned at all.

Thus we seem to see that, as regarded Hester Prynne, the whole seven years of outlaw and ignominy had been little other than a preparation for this very hour. But Arthur Dimmesdale!

346

Were such a man once more to fall, what plea could be urged in extenuation of his crime? None; unless it avail him somewhat that he was broken down by long and exquisite suffering; that his mind was darkened and confused by the very remorse which harrowed it; that, between fleeing as an avowed criminal, and remaining as a hypocrite, conscience might find it hard to strike the balance; that it was human to avoid the peril of death and infamy, and the inscrutable machinations of an enemy; that, finally, to this poor pilgrim, on his dreary and desert path, faint, sick, miserable, there appeared a glimpse of human affection and sympathy, a new life, and a true one, in exchange for the heavy doom which he was now expiating. And be the stern and sad truth spoken, that the breach which guilt has once made into the human soul is never, in this mortal state, repaired. It may be watched and guarded, so that the enemy shall not force his way again into the citadel, and might even in his subsequent assaults, select some other avenue, in preference to that where he had formerly succeeded. But there is still the ruined wall, and near it the stealthy tread of the foe that would win over again his unforgotten triumph.

The struggle, if there were one, need not be described. Let it suffice that the clergyman resolved to flee, and not alone.

"If in all these past seven years," thought he, "I could recall one instant of peace or hope, I would yet endure, for the sake of that earnest of Heaven's mercy. But now—since I am irrevocably doomed—wherefore should I not snatch the solace allowed to the condemned culprit before his execution? Or, if this be the path to a better life, as Hester would persuade me, I surely give up no fairer prospect by pursuing it! Neither can I any longer live without her companionship; so powerful is she to sustain—so tender to soothe! O Thou to whom I dare not lift mine eyes, wilt Thou yet pardon me?"

"Thou wilt go!" said Hester calmly, as he met her glance.

The decision once made, a glow of strange enjoyment threw its flickering brightness over the trouble of his breast. It was the exhilarating effect—upon a prisoner just escaped from the dungeon of his own heart—of breathing the wild, free atmosphere of an unredeemed, unchristianised, lawless region. His spirit rose, as it were, with a bound, and attained a nearer prospect of the sky, than throughout all the misery which had kept him grovelling on the earth. Of a deeply religious temperament, there was inevitably a tinge of the devotional in his mood.

"Do I feel joy again?" cried he, wondering at himself. "Methought the germ of it was dead in me! Oh, Hester, thou art my better angel! I seem to have flung myself—sick, sin-stained, and sorrow-blackened—down upon these forest leaves, and to have risen up all made anew, and with new powers to glorify Him that hath been merciful! This is already the better life! Why did we not find it sooner?"

"Let us not look back," answered Hester Prynne. "The past is gone! Wherefore should we linger upon it now? See! With this symbol I undo it all, and make it as if it had never been!"

So speaking, she undid the clasp that fastened the scarlet letter, and, taking it from her bosom, threw it to a distance among the withered leaves. The mystic token alighted on the hither verge of the stream. With a hand's-breadth further flight, it would have fallen into the water, and have given the little brook another woe to carry onward, besides the unintelligible tale which it still kept murmuring about. But there lay the embroidered letter, glittering like a lost jewel, which some ill-fated wanderer might pick up, and thenceforth be haunted by strange phantoms of guilt, sinkings of the heart, and unaccountable misfortune.

The stigma gone, Hester heaved a long, deep sigh, in which the burden of shame and anguish departed from her spirit. O exquisite relief! She had not known the weight until she felt the freedom! By another impulse, she took off the formal cap that confined her hair, and down it fell upon her shoulders, dark and rich, with at once a shadow and a light in its abundance, and imparting the charm of softness to her features. There played around her mouth, and beamed out of her eyes, a radiant and tender smile, that seemed gushing from the very heart of womanhood. A crimson flush was glowing on her cheek, that had been long so pale. Her sex, her youth, and the whole richness of her beauty, came back from what men call the irrevocable past, and clustered themselves with her maiden hope, and a happiness before unknown, within the magic circle of this hour. And, as if the gloom of the earth and sky had been but the effluence of these two mortal hearts, it vanished with their sorrow. All at once, as with a sudden smile of heaven, forth burst the sunshine, pouring a very flood into the obscure forest, gladdening each green leaf, transmuting the yellow fallen ones to gold, and gleaming adown the gray trunks of the solemn trees. The objects that had made a shadow hitherto, embodied the brightness now. The course of the little brook might be traced by its merry gleam afar into the wood's heart of mystery, which had become a mystery of joy.

Such was the sympathy of Nature—that wild, heathen Nature of the forest, never subjugated by human law, nor illumined by higher truth—with the bliss of these two spirits! Love, whether newly-born, or aroused from a death-like slumber, must always create a sunshine, filling the heart so full of radiance, that it overflows upon the outward world. Had the forest still kept its gloom, it would have been bright in Hester's eyes, and bright in Arthur Dimmesdale's!

Hester looked at him with a thrill of another joy.

"Thou must know Pearl!" said she. "Our little Pearl! Thou hast seen her—yes, I know it!—but thou wilt see her now with other eyes. She is a strange child! I hardly comprehend her! But thou wilt love her dearly, as I do, and wilt advise me how to deal with her!"

"Dost thou think the child will be glad to know me?" asked the minister, somewhat uneasily. "I have long shrunk from children, because they often show a distrust—a backwardness to be familiar with me. I have even been afraid of little Pearl!"

"Ah, that was sad!" answered the mother. "But she will love thee dearly, and thou her. She is not far off. I will call her. Pearl! Pearl!"

"I see the child," observed the minister. "Yonder she is, standing in a streak of sunshine, a good way off, on the other side of the brook. So thou thinkest the child will love me?"

Hester smiled, and again called to Pearl, who was visible at some distance, as the minister had described her, like a bright-apparelled vision in a sunbeam, which fell down upon her through an arch of boughs. The ray quivered to and fro, making her figure dim or distinct—now like a real child, now like a child's spirit—as the splendour went and came again. She heard her mother's voice, and approached slowly through the forest.

Pearl had not found the hour pass wearisomely while her mother sat talking with the clergyman. The great black forest—stern as it showed itself to those who brought the guilt and troubles of the world into its bosom—became the playmate of the lonely infant, as well as it knew how. Sombre as it was, it put on the kindest of its moods to welcome her. It offered her the partridge-berries, the growth of the preceding autumn, but ripening only in the spring, and now red as drops of blood upon the withered leaves. These Pearl gathered, and was pleased with their wild flavour. The small denizens of the wilderness hardly took pains to move out of her path. A partridge, indeed, with a brood of ten behind her, ran forward threateningly, but soon repented of her fierceness, and clucked to her young ones not to be afraid. A pigeon, alone on a low branch, allowed Pearl to come beneath, and uttered a sound as much of greeting as alarm. A squirrel, from the lofty depths of his domestic tree, chattered either in anger or merriment—for the squirrel is such a choleric and humorous little personage, that it is hard to distinguish between his moods—so he chattered at the child, and flung down a nut upon her head. It was a last year's nut, and already gnawed by his sharp tooth. A fox, startled from his sleep by her light footstep on the leaves, looked inquisitively at Pearl, as doubting whether it were better to steal off, or renew his nap on the same spot. A wolf, it is said—but here the tale has surely lapsed into the improbable—came up and smelt of Pearl's robe, and offered his savage head to be patted by her hand. The truth seems to be, however, that the mother-forest, and these wild things which it nourished, all recognised a kindred wilderness in the human child.

And she was gentler here than in the grassy-margined streets of the settlement, or in her mother's cottage. The flowers appeared to know it, and one and another whispered as she passed, "Adorn thyself with me, thou beautiful child, adorn thyself with me!"—and, to please them, Pearl gathered the violets, and anemones, and columbines, and some twigs of the freshest green, which the old trees held down before her eyes. With these she decorated her hair and her young waist, and became a nymph child, or an infant dryad, or whatever else was in closest sympathy with the antique wood. In such guise had Pearl adorned herself, when she heard her mother's voice, and came slowly back.

Slowly—for she saw the clergyman!

❧ 19 ❧

THE CHILD AT THE BROOKSIDE

"THOU WILT LOVE HER DEARLY," repeated Hester Prynne, as she and the minister sat watching little Pearl. "Dost thou not think her beautiful? And see with what natural skill she has made those simple flowers adorn her! Had she gathered pearls, and diamonds, and rubies in the wood, they could not have become her better! She is a splendid child! But I know whose brow she has!"

"Dost thou know, Hester," said Arthur Dimmesdale, with an unquiet smile, "that this dear child, tripping about always at thy side, hath caused me many an alarm? Methought—oh, Hester, what a thought is that, and how terrible to dread it!—that my own features were partly repeated in her face, and so strikingly that the world might see them! But she is mostly thine!"

"No, no! Not mostly!" answered the mother, with a tender smile. "A little longer, and thou needest not to be afraid to trace whose child she is. But how strangely beautiful she looks with those wild flowers in her hair! It is as if one of the fairies, whom we left in dear old England, had decked her out to meet us."

It was with a feeling which neither of them had ever before experienced, that they sat and watched Pearl's slow advance. In her was visible the tie that united them. She had been offered to the world, these seven past years, as the living hieroglyphic, in which was revealed the secret they so darkly sought to hide—all written in this symbol—all plainly manifest—had there been a prophet or magician skilled to read the character of flame! And Pearl was the oneness of their being. Be the foregone evil what it might, how could they doubt that their earthly lives and future destinies were conjoined when they beheld at once the material union, and the spiritual idea, in whom they met, and were to dwell immortally together; thoughts like these—and perhaps other thoughts, which they did not acknowledge or define—threw an awe about the child as she came onward.

"Let her see nothing strange—no passion or eagerness—in thy way of accosting her," whispered Hester. "Our Pearl is a fitful and fantastic little elf sometimes. Especially she is generally intolerant of emotion, when she does not fully comprehend the why and wherefore. But the child hath strong affections! She loves me, and will love thee!"

"Thou canst not think," said the minister, glancing aside at Hester Prynne, "how my heart dreads this interview, and yearns for it! But, in truth, as I already told thee, children are not readily won to be familiar with me. They will not climb my knee, nor prattle in my ear, nor answer to my smile, but stand apart, and eye me strangely. Even little babes, when I take them in my arms, weep bitterly. Yet Pearl, twice in her little lifetime, hath been kind to me! The first time—thou knowest it well! The last was when thou ledst her with thee to the house of yonder stern old Governor."

"And thou didst plead so bravely in her behalf and mine!" answered the mother. "I remember it; and so shall little Pearl. Fear nothing. She may be strange and shy at first, but will soon learn to love thee!"

By this time Pearl had reached the margin of the brook, and stood on the further side, gazing silently at Hester and the clergyman, who still sat together on the mossy tree-trunk waiting to receive her. Just where she had paused, the brook chanced to form a pool so smooth and quiet that it reflected a perfect image of her little figure, with all the brilliant picturesqueness of her beauty, in its adornment of flowers and wreathed foliage, but more refined and spiritualized than the reality. This image, so nearly identical with the living Pearl, seemed to communicate somewhat of its own shadowy and intangible quality to the child herself. It was strange, the way in which Pearl stood, looking so steadfastly at them through the dim medium of the forest gloom, herself, meanwhile, all glorified with a ray of sunshine, that was attracted thitherward as by a certain sympathy. In the brook beneath stood another child— another and the same—with likewise its ray of golden light. Hester felt herself, in some indistinct and tantalizing manner, estranged from Pearl, as if the child, in her lonely ramble through the forest, had strayed out of the sphere in which she and her mother dwelt together, and was now vainly seeking to return to it.

There were both truth and error in the impression; the child and mother were estranged, but through Hester's fault, not Pearl's. Since the latter rambled from her side, another inmate had been admitted within the circle of the mother's feelings, and so modified the aspect of them all, that Pearl, the returning wanderer, could not find her wonted place, and hardly knew where she was.

"I have a strange fancy," observed the sensitive minister, "that this brook is the boundary between two worlds, and that thou canst never meet thy Pearl again. Or is she an elfish spirit, who, as the legends of our childhood taught us, is forbidden to cross a running stream? Pray hasten her, for this delay has already imparted a tremor to my nerves."

"Come, dearest child!" said Hester encouragingly, and stretching out both her arms. "How slow thou art! When hast thou been so sluggish before now? Here is a friend of mine, who must be thy friend also. Thou wilt have twice as much love henceforward as thy mother alone could give thee! Leap across the brook and come to us. Thou canst leap like a young deer!"

Pearl, without responding in any manner to these honey-sweet expressions, remained on the other side of the brook. Now she fixed her bright wild eyes on her mother, now on the minister, and now included them both in the same glance, as if to detect and explain to herself the relation which they bore to one another. For some unaccountable reason, as Arthur Dimmesdale felt the child's eyes upon himself, his hand—with that gesture so habitual as to have become involuntary—stole over his heart. At length, assuming a singular air of authority, Pearl stretched out her hand, with the small forefinger extended, and pointing evidently towards her mother's breast. And beneath, in the mirror of the brook, there was the flower-girdled and sunny image of little Pearl, pointing her small forefinger too.

"Thou strange child! why dost thou not come to me?" exclaimed Hester.

Pearl still pointed with her forefinger, and a frown gathered on her brow—the more impressive from the childish, the almost baby-like aspect of the features that conveyed it. As her mother still kept beckoning to her, and arraying her face in a holiday suit of unaccustomed smiles, the child stamped her foot with a yet more imperious look and gesture. In the brook, again, was the fantastic beauty of the image, with its reflected frown, its pointed finger, and imperious gesture, giving emphasis to the aspect of little Pearl.

"Hasten, Pearl, or I shall be angry with thee!" cried Hester Prynne, who, however, inured to such behaviour on the elf-child's part at other seasons, was naturally anxious for a more seemly deportment now. "Leap across the brook, naughty child, and run hither! Else I must come to thee!"

But Pearl, not a whit startled at her mother's threats any more than mollified by her entreaties, now suddenly burst into a fit of passion, gesticulating violently, and throwing her small figure into the most extravagant contortions. She accompanied this wild outbreak with piercing shrieks, which the woods reverberated on all sides, so that, alone as she was in her childish and unreasonable wrath, it seemed as if a hidden multitude were lending her their sympathy and encouragement. Seen in the brook once more was the shadowy wrath of Pearl's image, crowned and girdled with flowers, but stamping its foot, wildly gesticulating, and, in the midst of all, still pointing its small forefinger at Hester's bosom.

"I see what ails the child," whispered Hester to the clergyman, and turning pale in spite of a strong effort to conceal her trouble and annoyance, "Children will not abide any, the slightest, change in the accustomed aspect of things that are daily before their eyes. Pearl misses something that she has always seen me wear!"

"I pray you," answered the minister, "if thou hast any means of pacifying the child, do it forthwith! Save it were the cankered wrath of an old witch like Mistress Hibbins," added he, attempting to smile, "I know nothing that I would not sooner encounter than this passion in a child. In Pearl's young beauty, as in the wrinkled witch, it has a preternatural effect. Pacify her if thou lovest me!"

Hester turned again towards Pearl with a crimson blush upon her cheek, a conscious glance aside clergyman, and then a heavy sigh, while, even before she had time to speak, the blush yielded to a deadly pallor.

"Pearl," said she sadly, "look down at thy feet! There!—before thee!—on the hither side of the brook!"

The child turned her eyes to the point indicated, and there lay the scarlet letter so close upon the margin of the stream that the gold embroidery was reflected in it.

"Bring it hither!" said Hester.

"Come thou and take it up!" answered Pearl.

"Was ever such a child!" observed Hester aside to the minister. "Oh, I have much to tell thee about her! But, in very truth, she is right as regards this hateful token. I must bear its torture yet a little longer—only a few days longer—until we shall have left this region, and look back hither as to a land which we have dreamed of. The forest cannot hide it! The mid-ocean shall take it from my hand, and swallow it up for ever!"

With these words she advanced to the margin of the brook, took up the scarlet letter, and fastened it again into her bosom. Hopefully, but a moment ago, as Hester had spoken of drowning it in the deep sea, there was a sense of inevitable doom upon her as she thus received back this deadly symbol from the hand of fate. She had flung it into infinite space! she had drawn an hour's free breath! and here again was the scarlet misery glittering on the old spot! So it ever is, whether thus typified or no, that an evil deed invests itself with the character of doom. Hester next gathered up the heavy tresses of her hair and confined them beneath her cap. As if there were a withering spell in the sad letter, her beauty, the warmth and richness of her womanhood, departed like fading sunshine, and a gray shadow seemed to fall across her.

When the dreary change was wrought, she extended her hand to Pearl.

"Dost thou know thy mother now, child?", asked she, reproachfully, but with a subdued tone. "Wilt thou come across the brook, and own thy mother, now that she has her shame upon her—now that she is sad?"

"Yes; now I will!" answered the child, bounding across the brook, and clasping Hester in her arms "Now thou art my mother indeed! and I am thy little Pearl!"

In a mood of tenderness that was not usual with her, she drew down her mother's head, and kissed her brow and both her cheeks. But then—by a kind of necessity that always impelled this child to alloy whatever comfort she might chance to give with a throb of anguish —Pearl put up her mouth and kissed the scarlet letter, too.

"That was not kind!" said Hester. "When thou hast shown me a little love, thou mockest me!"

"Why doth the minister sit yonder?" asked Pearl.

"He waits to welcome thee," replied her mother. "Come thou, and entreat his blessing! He loves thee, my little Pearl, and loves thy mother, too. Wilt thou not love him? Come he longs to greet thee!"

"Doth he love us?" said Pearl, looking up with acute intelligence into her mother's face. "Will he go back with us, hand in hand, we three together, into the town?"

"Not now, my child," answered Hester. "But in days to come he will walk hand in hand with us. We will have a home and fireside of our own; and thou shalt sit upon his knee; and he will teach thee many things, and love thee dearly. Thou wilt love him—wilt thou not?"

"And will he always keep his hand over his heart?" inquired Pearl.

"Foolish child, what a question is that!" exclaimed her mother.

"Come, and ask his blessing!"

But, whether influenced by the jealousy that seems instinctive with every petted child towards a dangerous rival, or from whatever caprice of her freakish nature, Pearl would show no favour to the clergyman. It was only by an exertion of force that her mother brought her up to him, hanging back, and manifesting her reluctance by odd grimaces; of which, ever since her babyhood, she had possessed a singular variety, and could transform her mobile physiognomy into a series of different aspects, with a new mischief in them, each and all. The minister— painfully embarrassed, but hoping that a kiss might prove a talisman to admit him into the child's kindlier regards—bent forward, and impressed one on her brow. Hereupon, Pearl broke away from her mother, and, running to the brook, stooped over it, and bathed her forehead, until the unwelcome kiss was quite washed off and diffused through a long lapse of the gliding water. She then remained apart, silently watching Hester and the clergyman; while they talked together and made such arrangements as were suggested by their new position and the purposes soon to be fulfilled.

And now this fateful interview had come to a close. The dell was to be left in solitude among its dark, old trees, which, with their multitudinous tongues, would whisper long of what had passed there, and no mortal be the wiser. And the melancholy brook would add this other tale to the mystery with which its little heart was already overburdened, and whereof it still kept up a murmuring babble, with not a whit more cheerfulness of tone than for ages heretofore.

✵ 2 0 ✵

THE MINISTER IN A MAZE

As THE MINISTER DEPARTED, in advance of Hester Prynne and little Pearl, he threw a backward glance, half expecting that he should discover only some faintly traced features or outline of the mother and the child, slowly fading into the twilight of the woods. So great a vicissitude in his life could not at once be received as real. But there was Hester, clad in her gray robe, still standing beside the tree trunk, which some blast had overthrown a long antiquity ago, and which time had ever since been covering with moss, so that these two fated ones, with earth's heaviest burden on them, might there sit down together, and find a single hour's rest and solace. And there was Pearl, too, lightly dancing from the margin of the brook—now that the intrusive third person was gone—and taking her old place by her mother's side. So the minister had not fallen asleep and dreamed!

In order to free his mind from this indistinctness and duplicity of impression, which vexed it with a strange disquietude, he recalled and more thoroughly defined the plans which Hester and himself had sketched for their departure. It had been determined between them that the Old World, with its crowds and cities, offered them a more eligible shelter and concealment than the wilds of New England or all America, with its alternatives of an Indian wigwam, or the few settlements of Europeans scattered thinly along the sea-board. Not to speak of the clergyman's health, so inadequate to sustain the hardships of a forest life, his native gifts, his culture, and his entire development would secure him a home only in the midst of civilization and refinement; the higher the state the more delicately adapted to it the man. In furtherance of this choice, it so happened that a ship lay in the harbour; one of those unquestionable cruisers, frequent at that day, which, without being absolutely outlaws of the deep, yet roamed over its surface with a remarkable irresponsibility of character. This vessel had recently arrived from the Spanish Main, and within three days' time would sail for Bristol. Hester Prynne—whose vocation, as a self-enlisted Sister of Charity, had brought her acquainted with the captain and crew—could take upon herself to secure the passage of two individuals and a child with all the secrecy which circumstances rendered more than desirable.

The minister had inquired of Hester, with no little interest, the precise time at which the vessel might be expected to depart. It would probably be on the fourth day from the present.

"This is most fortunate!" he had then said to himself. Now, why the Reverend Mr. Dimmesdale considered it so very fortunate we hesitate to reveal. Nevertheless—to hold nothing back from the reader—it was because, on the third day from the present, he was to preach the Election Sermon; and, as such an occasion formed an honourable epoch in the life of a New England Clergyman, he could not have chanced upon a more suitable mode and time of terminating his professional career. "At least, they shall say of me," thought this exemplary man, "that I leave no public duty unperformed or ill-performed!" Sad, indeed, that an introspection so profound and acute as this poor minister's should be so miserably deceived! We have had, and may still have, worse things to tell of him; but none, we apprehend, so pitiably weak; no evidence, at once so slight and irrefragable, of a subtle disease that had long since begun to eat into the real substance of his character. No man, for any considerable period, can wear one face to himself and another to the multitude, without finally getting bewildered as to which may be the true.

The excitement of Mr. Dimmesdale's feelings as he returned from his interview with Hester, lent him unaccustomed physical energy, and hurried him townward at a rapid pace. The pathway among the woods seemed wilder, more uncouth with its rude natural obstacles, and less trodden by the foot of man, than he remembered it on his outward journey. But he leaped across the plashy places, thrust himself through the clinging underbrush, climbed the ascent, plunged into the hollow, and overcame, in short, all the difficulties of the track, with an unweariable activity that astonished him. He could not but recall how feebly, and with what frequent pauses for breath he had toiled over the same ground, only two days before. As he drew near the town, he took an impression of change from the series of familiar objects that presented themselves. It seemed not yesterday, not one, not two, but many days, or even years ago, since he had quitted them. There, indeed, was each former trace of the street, as he remembered it, and all the peculiarities of the houses, with the due multitude of gable-peaks, and a weather-cock at every point where his memory suggested one. Not the less, however, came this importunately obtrusive sense of change. The same was true as regarded the acquaintances whom he met, and all the well-known shapes of human life, about the little town. They looked neither older nor younger now; the beards of the aged were no whiter, nor could the creeping babe of yesterday walk on his feet to-day; it was impossible to describe in what respect they differed from the individuals on whom he had so recently bestowed a parting glance; and yet the minister's deepest sense seemed to inform him of their mutability. A similar impression struck him most remarkably as he passed under the walls of his own church. The edifice had so very strange, and yet so familiar an aspect, that Mr. Dimmesdale's mind vibrated between two ideas; either that he had seen it only in a dream hitherto, or that he was merely dreaming about it now.

This phenomenon, in the various shapes which it assumed, indicated no external change, but so sudden and important a change in the spectator of the familiar scene, that the intervening space of a single day had operated on his consciousness like the lapse of years. The minister's own will, and Hester's will, and the fate that grew between them, had wrought this transformation. It was the same town as heretofore, but the same minister returned not from the forest. He might have said to the friends who greeted him—"I am not the man for whom you take me! I left him yonder in the forest, withdrawn into a secret dell, by a mossy tree trunk, and near a melancholy brook! Go, seek your minister, and see if his emaciated figure, his thin cheek, his white, heavy, pain-wrinkled brow, be not flung down there, like a cast-off garment!" His friends, no doubt, would still have insisted with him—"Thou art thyself the man!" but the error would have been their own, not his.

Before Mr. Dimmesdale reached home, his inner man gave him other evidences of a revolution in the sphere of thought and feeling. In truth, nothing short of a total change of dynasty and moral code, in that interior kingdom, was adequate to account for the impulses now communicated to the unfortunate and startled minister. At every step he was incited to do some strange, wild, wicked thing or other, with a sense that it would be at once involuntary and intentional, in spite of himself, yet growing out of a profounder self than that which opposed the impulse. For instance, he met one of his own deacons. The good old man addressed him with the paternal affection and patriarchal privilege which his venerable age, his upright and holy character, and his station in the church, entitled him to use and, conjoined with this, the deep, almost worshipping respect, which the minister's professional and private claims alike demanded. Never was there a more beautiful example of how the majesty of age and wisdom may comport with the obeisance and respect enjoined upon it, as from a lower social rank, and inferior order of endowment, towards a higher. Now, during a conversation of some two or three moments between the Reverend Mr. Dimmesdale and this excellent and hoary-bearded deacon, it was only by the most careful self-control that the former could refrain from uttering certain blasphemous suggestions that rose into his mind, respecting the communion-supper. He absolutely trembled and turned pale as ashes, lest his tongue should wag itself in utterance of these horrible matters, and plead his own consent for so doing, without his having fairly given it. And, even with this terror in his heart, he could hardly avoid laughing, to imagine how the sanctified old patriarchal deacon would have been petrified by his minister's impiety.

Again, another incident of the same nature. Hurrying along the street, the Reverend Mr. Dimmesdale encountered the eldest female member of his church, a most pious and exemplary old dame, poor, widowed, lonely, and with a heart as full of reminiscences about her dead husband and children, and her dead friends of long ago, as a burial-ground is full of storied gravestones. Yet all this, which would else have been such heavy sorrow, was made almost a solemn joy to her devout old soul, by religious consolations and the truths of Scripture, wherewith she had fed herself continually for more than thirty years. And since Mr. Dimmesdale had taken her in charge, the good grandam's chief earthly comfort—which, unless it had been likewise a heavenly comfort, could have been none at all—was to meet her pastor, whether casually, or of set purpose, and be refreshed with a word of warm, fragrant, heaven-breathing Gospel truth, from his beloved lips, into her dulled, but rapturously attentive ear. But, on this occasion, up to the moment of putting his lips to the old woman's ear, Mr. Dimmesdale, as the great enemy of souls would have it, could recall no text of Scripture, nor aught else, except a brief, pithy, and, as it then appeared to him, unanswerable argument against the immortality of the human soul. The instilment thereof into her mind would probably have caused this aged sister to drop down dead, at once, as by the effect of an intensely poisonous infusion. What he really did whisper, the minister could never afterwards recollect. There was, perhaps, a fortunate disorder in his utterance, which failed to impart any distinct idea to the good widows comprehension, or which Providence interpreted after a method of its own. Assuredly, as the minister looked back, he beheld an expression of divine gratitude and ecstasy that seemed like the shine of the celestial city on her face, so wrinkled and ashy pale.

Again, a third instance. After parting from the old church member, he met the youngest sister of them all. It was a maiden newly-won—and won by the Reverend Mr. Dimmesdale's own sermon, on the Sabbath after his vigil—to barter the transitory pleasures of the world for the heavenly hope that was to assume brighter substance as life grew dark around her, and which would gild the utter gloom with final glory. She was fair and pure as a lily that had bloomed in Paradise. The minister knew well that he was himself enshrined within the stainless sanctity of her heart, which hung its snowy curtains about his image, imparting to religion the warmth of love, and to love a religious purity. Satan, that afternoon, had surely led the poor young girl away from her mother's side, and thrown her into the pathway of this sorely tempted, or—shall we not rather say?—this lost and desperate man. As she drew nigh, the arch-fiend whispered him to condense into small compass, and drop into her tender bosom a germ of evil that would be sure to blossom darkly soon, and bear black fruit betimes. Such was his sense of power over this virgin soul, trusting him as she did, that the minister felt potent to blight all the field of innocence with but one wicked look, and develop all its opposite with but a word. So—with a mightier struggle than he had yet sustained—he held his Geneva cloak before his face, and hurried onward, making no sign of recognition, and leaving the young sister to digest his rudeness as she might. She ransacked her conscience—which was full of harmless little matters, like her pocket or her work-bag—and took herself to task, poor thing! for a thousand imaginary faults, and went about her household duties with swollen eyelids the next morning.

Before the minister had time to celebrate his victory over this last temptation, he was conscious of another impulse, more ludicrous, and almost as horrible. It was—we blush to tell it —it was to stop short in the road, and teach some very wicked words to a knot of little Puritan children who were playing there, and had but just begun to talk. Denying himself this freak, as unworthy of his cloth, he met a drunken seaman, one of the ship's crew from the Spanish Main. And here, since he had so valiantly forborne all other wickedness, poor Mr. Dimmesdale longed at least to shake hands with the tarry black-guard, and recreate himself with a few improper jests, such as dissolute sailors so abound with, and a volley of good, round, solid, satisfactory, and heaven-defying oaths! It was not so much a better principle, as partly his natural good taste, and still more his buckramed habit of clerical decorum, that carried him safely through the latter crisis.

"What is it that haunts and tempts me thus?" cried the minister to himself, at length, pausing in the street, and striking his hand against his forehead.

"Am I mad? or am I given over utterly to the fiend? Did I make a contract with him in the forest, and sign it with my blood? And does he now summon me to its fulfilment, by suggesting the performance of every wickedness which his most foul imagination can conceive?"

At the moment when the Reverend Mr. Dimmesdale thus communed with himself, and struck his forehead with his hand, old Mistress Hibbins, the reputed witch-lady, is said to have been passing by. She made a very grand appearance, having on a high head-dress, a rich gown of velvet, and a ruff done up with the famous yellow starch, of which Anne Turner, her especial friend, had taught her the secret, before this last good lady had been hanged for Sir Thomas Overbury's murder. Whether the witch had read the minister's thoughts or no, she came to a full stop, looked shrewdly into his face, smiled craftily, and—though little given to converse with clergymen—began a conversation.

"So, reverend sir, you have made a visit into the forest," observed the witch-lady, nodding her high head-dress at him. "The next time I pray you to allow me only a fair warning, and I shall be proud to bear you company. Without taking overmuch upon myself my good word will go far towards gaining any strange gentleman a fair reception from yonder potentate you wot of."

"I profess, madam," answered the clergyman, with a grave obeisance, such as the lady's rank demanded, and his own good breeding made imperative—"I profess, on my conscience and character, that I am utterly bewildered as touching the purport of your words! I went not into the forest to seek a potentate, neither do I, at any future time, design a visit thither, with a view to gaining the favour of such personage. My one sufficient object was to greet that pious friend of mine, the Apostle Eliot, and rejoice with him over the many precious souls he hath won from heathendom!"

"Ha, ha, ha!" cackled the old witch-lady, still nodding her high head-dress at the minister. "Well, well! we must needs talk thus in the daytime! You carry it off like an old hand! But at midnight, and in the forest, we shall have other talk together!"

She passed on with her aged stateliness, but often turning back her head and smiling at him, like one willing to recognise a secret intimacy of connexion.

"Have I then sold myself," thought the minister, "to the fiend whom, if men say true, this yellow-starched and velveted old hag has chosen for her prince and master?"

The wretched minister! He had made a bargain very like it! Tempted by a dream of happiness, he had yielded himself with deliberate choice, as he had never done before, to what he knew was deadly sin. And the infectious poison of that sin had been thus rapidly diffused throughout his moral system. It had stupefied all blessed impulses, and awakened into vivid life the whole brotherhood of bad ones. Scorn, bitterness, unprovoked malignity, gratuitous desire of ill, ridicule of whatever was good and holy, all awoke to tempt, even while they frightened him. And his encounter with old Mistress Hibbins, if it were a real incident, did but show its sympathy and fellowship with wicked mortals, and the world of perverted spirits.

He had by this time reached his dwelling on the edge of the burial ground, and, hastening up the stairs, took refuge in his study. The minister was glad to have reached this shelter, without first betraying himself to the world by any of those strange and wicked eccentricities to which he had been continually impelled while passing through the streets. He entered the accustomed room, and looked around him on its books, its windows, its fireplace, and the tapestried comfort of the walls, with the same perception of strangeness that had haunted him throughout his walk from the forest dell into the town and thitherward. Here he had studied and written; here gone through fast and vigil, and come forth half alive; here striven to pray; here borne a hundred thousand agonies! There was the Bible, in its rich old Hebrew, with Moses and the Prophets speaking to him, and God's voice through all.

There on the table, with the inky pen beside it, was an unfinished sermon, with a sentence broken in the midst, where his thoughts had ceased to gush out upon the page two days before. He knew that it was himself, the thin and white-cheeked minister, who had done and suffered these things, and written thus far into the Election Sermon! But he seemed to stand apart, and eye this former self with scornful pitying, but half-envious curiosity. That self was gone. Another man had returned out of the forest—a wiser one—with a knowledge of hidden mysteries which the simplicity of the former never could have reached. A bitter kind of knowledge that!

While occupied with these reflections, a knock came at the door of the study, and the minister said, "Come in!"—not wholly devoid of an idea that he might behold an evil spirit. And so he did! It was old Roger Chillingworth that entered. The minister stood white and speechless, with one hand on the Hebrew Scriptures, and the other spread upon his breast.

"Welcome home, reverend sir," said the physician "And how found you that godly man, the Apostle Eliot? But methinks, dear sir, you look pale, as if the travel through the wilderness had been too sore for you. Will not my aid be requisite to put you in heart and strength to preach your Election Sermon?"

"Nay, I think not so," rejoined the Reverend Mr. Dimmesdale. "My journey, and the sight of the holy Apostle yonder, and the free air which I have breathed have done me good, after so long confinement in my study. I think to need no more of your drugs, my kind physician, good though they be, and administered by a friendly hand."

All this time Roger Chillingworth was looking at the minister with the grave and intent regard of a physician towards his patient. But, in spite of this outward show, the latter was almost convinced of the old man's knowledge, or, at least, his confident suspicion, with respect to his own interview with Hester Prynne. The physician knew then that in the minister's regard he was no longer a trusted friend, but his bitterest enemy. So much being known, it would appear natural that a part of it should be expressed. It is singular, however, how long a time often passes before words embody things; and with what security two persons, who choose to avoid a certain subject, may approach its very verge, and retire without disturbing it. Thus the minister felt no apprehension that Roger Chillingworth would touch, in express words, upon the real position which they sustained towards one another. Yet did the physician, in his dark way, creep frightfully near the secret.

"Were it not better," said he, "that you use my poor skill tonight? Verily, dear sir, we must take pains to make you strong and vigorous for this occasion of the Election discourse. The people look for great things from you, apprehending that another year may come about and find their pastor gone."

"Yes, to another world," replied the minister with pious resignation. "Heaven grant it be a better one; for, in good sooth, I hardly think to tarry with my flock through the flitting seasons of another year! But touching your medicine, kind sir, in my present frame of body I need it not."

"I joy to hear it," answered the physician. "It may be that my remedies, so long administered in vain, begin now to take due effect. Happy man were I, and well deserving of New England's gratitude, could I achieve this cure!"

"I thank you from my heart, most watchful friend," said the Reverend Mr. Dimmesdale with a solemn smile. "I thank you, and can but requite your good deeds with my prayers."

"A good man's prayers are golden recompense!" rejoined old Roger Chillingworth, as he took his leave. "Yea, they are the current gold coin of the New Jerusalem, with the King's own mint mark on them!"

Left alone, the minister summoned a servant of the house, and requested food, which, being set before him, he ate with ravenous appetite. Then flinging the already written pages of the Election Sermon into the fire, he forthwith began another, which he wrote with such an impulsive flow of thought and emotion, that he fancied himself inspired; and only wondered that Heaven should see fit to transmit the grand and solemn music of its oracles through so foul an organ pipe as he. However, leaving that mystery to solve itself, or go unsolved for ever, he drove his task onward with earnest haste and ecstasy.

Thus the night fled away, as if it were a winged steed, and he careering on it; morning came, and peeped, blushing, through the curtains; and at last sunrise threw a golden beam into the study, and laid it right across the minister's bedazzled eyes. There he was, with the pen still between his fingers, and a vast, immeasurable tract of written space behind him!

❦ 21 ❦

THE NEW ENGLAND HOLIDAY

BETIMES IN THE morning of the day on which the new Governor was to receive his office at the hands of the people, Hester Prynne and little Pearl came into the market-place. It was already thronged with the craftsmen and other plebeian inhabitants of the town, in considerable numbers, among whom, likewise, were many rough figures, whose attire of deer-skins marked them as belonging to some of the forest settlements, which surrounded the little metropolis of the colony.

On this public holiday, as on all other occasions for seven years past, Hester was clad in a garment of coarse gray cloth. Not more by its hue than by some indescribable peculiarity in its fashion, it had the effect of making her fade personally out of sight and outline; while again the scarlet letter brought her back from this twilight indistinctness, and revealed her under the moral aspect of its own illumination. Her face, so long familiar to the townspeople, showed the marble quietude which they were accustomed to behold there. It was like a mask; or, rather like the frozen calmness of a dead woman's features; owing this dreary resemblance to the fact that Hester was actually dead, in respect to any claim of sympathy, and had departed out of the world with which she still seemed to mingle.

It might be, on this one day, that there was an expression unseen before, nor, indeed, vivid enough to be detected now; unless some preternaturally gifted observer should have first read the heart, and have afterwards sought a corresponding development in the countenance and mien. Such a spiritual seer might have conceived, that, after sustaining the gaze of the multitude through several miserable years as a necessity, a penance, and something which it was a stern religion to endure, she now, for one last time more, encountered it freely and voluntarily, in order to convert what had so long been agony into a kind of triumph. "Look your last on the scarlet letter and its wearer!"—the people's victim and lifelong bond-slave, as they fancied her, might say to them. "Yet a little while, and she will be beyond your reach! A few hours longer and the deep, mysterious ocean will quench and hide for ever the symbol which ye have caused to burn on her bosom!" Nor were it an inconsistency too improbable to be assigned to human nature, should we suppose a feeling of regret in Hester's mind, at the moment when she was about to win her freedom from the pain which had been thus deeply incorporated with her being. Might there not be an irresistible desire to quaff a last, long, breathless draught of the cup of wormwood and aloes, with which nearly all her years of womanhood had been perpetually flavoured. The wine of life, henceforth to be presented to her lips, must be indeed rich, delicious, and exhilarating, in its chased and golden beaker, or else leave an inevitable and weary languor, after the lees of bitterness wherewith she had been drugged, as with a cordial of intensest potency.

Pearl was decked out with airy gaiety. It would have been impossible to guess that this bright and sunny apparition owed its existence to the shape of gloomy gray; or that a fancy, at once so gorgeous and so delicate as must have been requisite to contrive the child's apparel, was the same that had achieved a task perhaps more difficult, in imparting so distinct a peculiarity to Hester's simple robe. The dress, so proper was it to little Pearl, seemed an effluence, or inevitable development and outward manifestation of her character, no more to be separated from her than the many-hued brilliancy from a butterfly's wing, or the painted glory from the leaf of a bright flower. As with these, so with the child; her garb was all of one idea with her nature. On this eventful day, moreover, there was a certain singular inquietude and excitement in her mood, resembling nothing so much as the shimmer of a diamond, that sparkles and flashes with the varied throbbings of the breast on which it is displayed. Children have always a sympathy in the agitations of those connected with them: always, especially, a sense of any trouble or impending revolution, of whatever kind, in domestic circumstances; and therefore Pearl, who was the gem on her mother's unquiet bosom, betrayed, by the very dance of her spirits, the emotions which none could detect in the marble passiveness of Hester's brow.

This effervescence made her flit with a bird-like movement, rather than walk by her mother's side.

She broke continually into shouts of a wild, inarticulate, and sometimes piercing music. When they reached the market-place, she became still more restless, on perceiving the stir and bustle that enlivened the spot; for it was usually more like the broad and lonesome green before a village meeting-house, than the centre of a town's business.

"Why, what is this, mother?" cried she. "Wherefore have all the people left their work to-day? Is it a play-day for the whole world? See, there is the blacksmith! He has washed his sooty face, and put on his Sabbath-day clothes, and looks as if he would gladly be merry, if any kind body would only teach him how! And there is Master Brackett, the old jailer, nodding and smiling at me. Why does he do so, mother?"

"He remembers thee a little babe, my child," answered Hester.

"He should not nod and smile at me, for all that—the black, grim, ugly-eyed old man!" said Pearl. "He may nod at thee, if he will; for thou art clad in gray, and wearest the scarlet letter. But see, mother, how many faces of strange people, and Indians among them, and sailors! What have they all come to do, here in the market-place?"

"They wait to see the procession pass," said Hester. "For the Governor and the magistrates are to go by, and the ministers, and all the great people and good people, with the music and the soldiers marching before them."

"And will the minister be there?" asked Pearl. "And will he hold out both his hands to me, as when thou ledst me to him from the brook-side?"

"He will be there, child," answered her mother, "but he will not greet thee to-day, nor must thou greet him."

"What a strange, sad man is he!" said the child, as if speaking partly to herself. "In the dark nighttime he calls us to him, and holds thy hand and mine, as when we stood with him on the scaffold yonder! And in the deep forest, where only the old trees can hear, and the strip of sky see it, he talks with thee, sitting on a heap of moss! And he kisses my forehead, too, so that the little brook would hardly wash it off! But, here, in the sunny day, and among all the people, he knows us not; nor must we know him! A strange, sad man is he, with his hand always over his heart!"

"Be quiet, Pearl—thou understandest not these things," said her mother. "Think not now of the minister, but look about thee, and see how cheery is everybody's face to-day. The children have come from their schools, and the grown people from their workshops and their fields, on purpose to be happy, for, to-day, a new man is beginning to rule over them; and so—as has been the custom of mankind ever since a nation was first gathered—they make merry and rejoice: as if a good and golden year were at length to pass over the poor old world!"

It was as Hester said, in regard to the unwonted jollity that brightened the faces of the people. Into this festal season of the year—as it already was, and continued to be during the greater part of two centuries—the Puritans compressed whatever mirth and public joy they deemed allowable to human infirmity; thereby so far dispelling the customary cloud, that, for the space of a single holiday, they appeared scarcely more grave than most other communities at a period of general affliction.

But we perhaps exaggerate the gray or sable tinge, which undoubtedly characterized the mood and manners of the age. The persons now in the market-place of Boston had not been born to an inheritance of Puritanic gloom. They were native Englishmen, whose fathers had lived in the sunny richness of the Elizabethan epoch; a time when the life of England, viewed as one great mass, would appear to have been as stately, magnificent, and joyous, as the world has ever witnessed. Had they followed their hereditary taste, the New England settlers would have illustrated all events of public importance by bonfires, banquets, pageantries, and processions. Nor would it have been impracticable, in the observance of majestic ceremonies, to combine mirthful recreation with solemnity, and give, as it were, a grotesque and brilliant embroidery to the great robe of state, which a nation, at such festivals, puts on. There was some shadow of an attempt of this kind in the mode of celebrating the day on which the political year of the colony commenced. The dim reflection of a remembered splendour, a colourless and manifold diluted repetition of what they had beheld in proud old London—we will not say at a royal coronation, but at a Lord Mayor's show—might be traced in the customs which our forefathers instituted, with reference to the annual installation of magistrates. The fathers and founders of the commonwealth—the statesman, the priest, and the soldier—seemed it a duty then to assume the outward state and majesty, which, in accordance with antique style, was looked upon as the proper garb of public and social eminence. All came forth to move in procession before the people's eye, and thus impart a needed dignity to the simple framework of a government so newly constructed.

Then, too, the people were countenanced, if not encouraged, in relaxing the severe and close application to their various modes of rugged industry, which at all other times, seemed of the same piece and material with their religion. Here, it is true, were none of the appliances which popular merriment would so readily have found in the England of Elizabeth's time, or that of James—no rude shows of a theatrical kind; no minstrel, with his harp and legendary ballad, nor gleeman with an ape dancing to his music; no juggler, with his tricks of mimic witchcraft; no Merry Andrew, to stir up the multitude with jests, perhaps a hundred years old, but still effective, by their appeals to the very broadest sources of mirthful sympathy. All such professors of the several branches of jocularity would have been sternly repressed, not only by the rigid discipline of law, but by the general sentiment which give law its vitality. Not the less, however, the great, honest face of the people smiled—grimly, perhaps, but widely too. Nor were sports wanting, such as the colonists had witnessed, and shared in, long ago, at the country fairs and on the village-greens of England; and which it was thought well to keep alive on this new soil, for the sake of the courage and manliness that were essential in them. Wrestling matches, in the different fashions of Cornwall and Devonshire, were seen here and there about the market-place; in one corner, there was a friendly bout at quarterstaff; and—what attracted most interest of all—on the platform of the pillory, already so noted in our pages, two masters of defence were commencing an exhibition with the buckler and broadsword. But, much to the disappointment of the crowd, this latter business was broken off by the interposition of the town beadle, who had no idea of permitting the majesty of the law to be violated by such an abuse of one of its consecrated places.

It may not be too much to affirm, on the whole, (the people being then in the first stages of joyless deportment, and the offspring of sires who had known how to be merry, in their day), that they would compare favourably, in point of holiday keeping, with their descendants, even at so long an interval as ourselves. Their immediate posterity, the generation next to the early emigrants, wore the blackest shade of Puritanism, and so darkened the national visage with it, that all the subsequent years have not sufficed to clear it up. We have yet to learn again the forgotten art of gaiety.

The picture of human life in the market-place, though its general tint was the sad gray, brown, or black of the English emigrants, was yet enlivened by some diversity of hue. A party of Indians—in their savage finery of curiously embroidered deerskin robes, wampum-belts, red and yellow ochre, and feathers, and armed with the bow and arrow and stone-headed spear—stood apart with countenances of inflexible gravity, beyond what even the Puritan aspect could attain. Nor, wild as were these painted barbarians, were they the wildest feature of the scene. This distinction could more justly be claimed by some mariners—a part of the crew of the vessel from the Spanish Main—who had come ashore to see the humours of Election Day. They were rough-looking desperadoes, with sun-blackened faces, and an immensity of beard; their wide short trousers were confined about the waist by belts, often clasped with a rough plate of gold, and sustaining always a long knife, and in some instances, a sword. From beneath their broad-brimmed hats of palm-leaf, gleamed eyes which, even in good-nature and merriment, had a kind of animal ferocity. They transgressed without fear or scruple, the rules of behaviour that were binding on all others: smoking tobacco under the beadle's very nose, although each whiff would have cost a townsman a shilling; and quaffing at their pleasure, draughts of wine or aqua-vitae from pocket flasks, which they freely tendered to the gaping crowd around them. It remarkably characterised the incomplete morality of the age, rigid as we call it, that a licence was allowed the seafaring class, not merely for their freaks on shore, but for far more desperate deeds on their proper element. The sailor of that day would go near to be arraigned as a pirate in our own. There could be little doubt, for instance, that this very ship's crew, though no unfavourable specimens of the nautical brotherhood, had been guilty, as we should phrase it, of depredations on the Spanish commerce, such as would have perilled all their necks in a modern court of justice.

But the sea in those old times heaved, swelled, and foamed very much at its own will, or subject only to the tempestuous wind, with hardly any attempts at regulation by human law. The buccaneer on the wave might relinquish his calling and become at once if he chose, a man of probity and piety on land; nor, even in the full career of his reckless life, was he regarded as a personage with whom it was disreputable to traffic or casually associate. Thus the Puritan elders in their black cloaks, starched bands, and steeple-crowned hats, smiled not unbenignantly at the clamour and rude deportment of these jolly seafaring men; and it excited neither surprise nor animadversion when so reputable a citizen as old Roger Chillingworth, the physician, was seen to enter the market-place in close and familiar talk with the commander of the questionable vessel.

The latter was by far the most showy and gallant figure, so far as apparel went, anywhere to be seen among the multitude. He wore a profusion of ribbons on his garment, and gold lace on his hat, which was also encircled by a gold chain, and surmounted with a feather. There was a sword at his side and a sword-cut on his forehead, which, by the arrangement of his hair, he seemed anxious rather to display than hide. A landsman could hardly have worn this garb and shown this face, and worn and shown them both with such a galliard air, without undergoing stern question before a magistrate, and probably incurring a fine or imprisonment, or perhaps an exhibition in the stocks. As regarded the shipmaster, however, all was looked upon as pertaining to the character, as to a fish his glistening scales.

After parting from the physician, the commander of the Bristol ship strolled idly through the market-place; until happening to approach the spot where Hester Prynne was standing, he appeared to recognise, and did not hesitate to address her. As was usually the case wherever Hester stood, a small vacant area—a sort of magic circle—had formed itself about her, into which, though the people were elbowing one another at a little distance, none ventured or felt disposed to intrude. It was a forcible type of the moral solitude in which the scarlet letter enveloped its fated wearer; partly by her own reserve, and partly by the instinctive, though no longer so unkindly, withdrawal of her fellow-creatures. Now, if never before, it answered a good purpose by enabling Hester and the seaman to speak together without risk of being overheard; and so changed was Hester Prynne's repute before the public, that the matron in town, most eminent for rigid morality, could not have held such intercourse with less result of scandal than herself.

"So, mistress," said the mariner, "I must bid the steward make ready one more berth than you bargained for! No fear of scurvy or ship fever this voyage. What with the ship's surgeon and this other doctor, our only danger will be from drug or pill; more by token, as there is a lot of apothecary's stuff aboard, which I traded for with a Spanish vessel."

"What mean you?" inquired Hester, startled more than she permitted to appear. "Have you another passenger?"

"Why, know you not," cried the shipmaster, "that this physician here—Chillingworth he calls himself—is minded to try my cabin-fare with you? Ay, ay, you must have known it; for he tells me he is of your party, and a close friend to the gentleman you spoke of—he that is in peril from these sour old Puritan rulers."

"They know each other well, indeed," replied Hester, with a mien of calmness, though in the utmost consternation. "They have long dwelt together."

Nothing further passed between the mariner and Hester Prynne. But at that instant she beheld old Roger Chillingworth himself, standing in the remotest corner of the market-place and smiling on her; a smile which—across the wide and bustling square, and through all the talk and laughter, and various thoughts, moods, and interests of the crowd—conveyed secret and fearful meaning.

❦ 22 ❦

THE PROCESSION

BEFORE HESTER PRYNNE could call together her thoughts, and consider what was practicable to be done in this new and startling aspect of affairs, the sound of military music was heard approaching along a contiguous street. It denoted the advance of the procession of magistrates and citizens on its way towards the meeting-house: where, in compliance with a custom thus early established, and ever since observed, the Reverend Mr. Dimmesdale was to deliver an Election Sermon.

Soon the head of the procession showed itself, with a slow and stately march, turning a corner, and making its way across the market-place. First came the music. It comprised a variety of instruments, perhaps imperfectly adapted to one another, and played with no great skill; but yet attaining the great object for which the harmony of drum and clarion addresses itself to the multitude—that of imparting a higher and more heroic air to the scene of life that passes before the eye. Little Pearl at first clapped her hands, but then lost for an instant the restless agitation that had kept her in a continual effervescence throughout the morning; she gazed silently, and seemed to be borne upward like a floating sea-bird on the long heaves and swells of sound. But she was brought back to her former mood by the shimmer of the sunshine on the weapons and bright armour of the military company, which followed after the music, and formed the honorary escort of the procession. This body of soldiery—which still sustains a corporate existence, and marches down from past ages with an ancient and honourable fame— was composed of no mercenary materials. Its ranks were filled with gentlemen who felt the stirrings of martial impulse, and sought to establish a kind of College of Arms, where, as in an association of Knights Templars, they might learn the science, and, so far as peaceful exercise would teach them, the practices of war. The high estimation then placed upon the military character might be seen in the lofty port of each individual member of the company. Some of them, indeed, by their services in the Low Countries and on other fields of European warfare, had fairly won their title to assume the name and pomp of soldiership. The entire array, moreover, clad in burnished steel, and with plumage nodding over their bright morions, had a brilliancy of effect which no modern display can aspire to equal.

And yet the men of civil eminence, who came immediately behind the military escort, were better worth a thoughtful observer's eye. Even in outward demeanour they showed a stamp of majesty that made the warrior's haughty stride look vulgar, if not absurd. It was an age when what we call talent had far less consideration than now, but the massive materials which produce stability and dignity of character a great deal more. The people possessed by hereditary right the quality of reverence, which, in their descendants, if it survive at all, exists in smaller proportion, and with a vastly diminished force in the selection and estimate of public men. The change may be for good or ill, and is partly, perhaps, for both. In that old day the English settler on these rude shores—having left king, nobles, and all degrees of awful rank behind, while still the faculty and necessity of reverence was strong in him—bestowed it on the white hair and venerable brow of age—on long-tried integrity—on solid wisdom and sad-coloured experience—on endowments of that grave and weighty order which gave the idea of permanence, and comes under the general definition of respectability. These primitive statesmen, therefore—Bradstreet, Endicott, Dudley, Bellingham, and their compeers—who were elevated to power by the early choice of the people, seem to have been not often brilliant, but distinguished by a ponderous sobriety, rather than activity of intellect. They had fortitude and self-reliance, and in time of difficulty or peril stood up for the welfare of the state like a line of cliffs against a tempestuous tide. The traits of character here indicated were well represented in the square cast of countenance and large physical development of the new colonial magistrates. So far as a demeanour of natural authority was concerned, the mother country need not have been ashamed to see these foremost men of an actual democracy adopted into the House of Peers, or make the Privy Council of the Sovereign.

Next in order to the magistrates came the young and eminently distinguished divine, from whose lips the religious discourse of the anniversary was expected. His was the profession at that era in which intellectual ability displayed itself far more than in political life; for—leaving a higher motive out of the question it offered inducements powerful enough in the almost worshipping respect of the community, to win the most aspiring ambition into its service. Even political power—as in the case of Increase Mather—was within the grasp of a successful priest.

It was the observation of those who beheld him now, that never, since Mr. Dimmesdale first set his foot on the New England shore, had he exhibited such energy as was seen in the gait and air with which he kept his pace in the procession. There was no feebleness of step as at other times; his frame was not bent, nor did his hand rest ominously upon his heart. Yet, if the clergyman were rightly viewed, his strength seemed not of the body. It might be spiritual and imparted to him by angelical ministrations. It might be the exhilaration of that potent cordial which is distilled only in the furnace-glow of earnest and long-continued thought. Or perchance his sensitive temperament was invigorated by the loud and piercing music that swelled heaven-ward, and uplifted him on its ascending wave. Nevertheless, so abstracted was his look, it might be questioned whether Mr. Dimmesdale even heard the music. There was his body, moving onward, and with an unaccustomed force. But where was his mind? Far and deep in its own region, busying itself, with preternatural activity, to marshal a procession of stately thoughts that were soon to issue thence; and so he saw nothing, heard nothing, knew nothing of what was around him; but the spiritual element took up the feeble frame and carried it along, unconscious of the burden, and converting it to spirit like itself. Men of uncommon intellect, who have grown morbid, possess this occasional power of mighty effort, into which they throw the life of many days and then are lifeless for as many more.

Hester Prynne, gazing steadfastly at the clergyman, felt a dreary influence come over her, but wherefore or whence she knew not, unless that he seemed so remote from her own sphere, and utterly beyond her reach. One glance of recognition she had imagined must needs pass between them. She thought of the dim forest, with its little dell of solitude, and love, and anguish, and the mossy tree-trunk, where, sitting hand-in-hand, they had mingled their sad and passionate talk with the melancholy murmur of the brook. How deeply had they known each other then! And was this the man? She hardly knew him now! He, moving proudly past, enveloped as it were, in the rich music, with the procession of majestic and venerable fathers; he, so unattainable in his worldly position, and still more so in that far vista of his unsympathizing thoughts, through which she now beheld him! Her spirit sank with the idea that all must have been a delusion, and that, vividly as she had dreamed it, there could be no real bond betwixt the clergyman and herself. And thus much of woman was there in Hester, that she could scarcely forgive him—least of all now, when the heavy footstep of their approaching Fate might be heard, nearer, nearer, nearer!—for being able so completely to withdraw himself from their mutual world—while she groped darkly, and stretched forth her cold hands, and found him not.

Pearl either saw and responded to her mother's feelings, or herself felt the remoteness and intangibility that had fallen around the minister. While the procession passed, the child was uneasy, fluttering up and down, like a bird on the point of taking flight. When the whole had gone by, she looked up into Hester's face—

"Mother," said she, "was that the same minister that kissed me by the brook?"

"Hold thy peace, dear little Pearl!" whispered her mother. "We must not always talk in the marketplace of what happens to us in the forest."

"I could not be sure that it was he—so strange he looked," continued the child. "Else I would have run to him, and bid him kiss me now, before all the people, even as he did yonder among the dark old trees. What would the minister have said, mother? Would he have clapped his hand over his heart, and scowled on me, and bid me begone?"

"What should he say, Pearl," answered Hester, "save that it was no time to kiss, and that kisses are not to be given in the market-place? Well for thee, foolish child, that thou didst not speak to him!"

Another shade of the same sentiment, in reference to Mr. Dimmesdale, was expressed by a person whose eccentricities—insanity, as we should term it—led her to do what few of the townspeople would have ventured on—to begin a conversation with the wearer of the scarlet letter in public. It was Mistress Hibbins, who, arrayed in great magnificence, with a triple ruff, a broidered stomacher, a gown of rich velvet, and a gold-headed cane, had come forth to see the procession. As this ancient lady had the renown (which subsequently cost her no less a price than her life) of being a principal actor in all the works of necromancy that were continually going forward, the crowd gave way before her, and seemed to fear the touch of her garment, as if it carried the plague among its gorgeous folds. Seen in conjunction with Hester Prynne— kindly as so many now felt towards the latter—the dread inspired by Mistress Hibbins had doubled, and caused a general movement from that part of the market-place in which the two women stood.

"Now, what mortal imagination could conceive it?" whispered the old lady confidentially to Hester. "Yonder divine man! That saint on earth, as the people uphold him to be, and as—I must needs say—he really looks! Who, now, that saw him pass in the procession, would think how little while it is since he went forth out of his study—chewing a Hebrew text of Scripture in his mouth, I warrant—to take an airing in the forest! Aha! we know what that means, Hester Prynne! But truly, forsooth, I find it hard to believe him the same man. Many a church member saw I, walking behind the music, that has danced in the same measure with me, when Somebody was fiddler, and, it might be, an Indian powwow or a Lapland wizard changing hands with us! That is but a trifle, when a woman knows the world. But this minister. Couldst thou surely tell, Hester, whether he was the same man that encountered thee on the forest path?"

"Madam, I know not of what you speak," answered Hester Prynne, feeling Mistress Hibbins to be of infirm mind; yet strangely startled and awe-stricken by the confidence with which she affirmed a personal connexion between so many persons (herself among them) and the Evil One. "It is not for me to talk lightly of a learned and pious minister of the Word, like the Reverend Mr. Dimmesdale."

"Fie, woman—fie!" cried the old lady, shaking her finger at Hester. "Dost thou think I have been to the forest so many times, and have yet no skill to judge who else has been there? Yea, though no leaf of the wild garlands which they wore while they danced be left in their hair! I know thee, Hester, for I behold the token. We may all see it in the sunshine! and it glows like a red flame in the dark. Thou wearest it openly, so there need be no question about that. But this minister! Let me tell thee in thine ear! When the Black Man sees one of his own servants, signed and sealed, so shy of owning to the bond as is the Reverend Mr. Dimmesdale, he hath a way of ordering matters so that the mark shall be disclosed, in open daylight, to the eyes of all the world! What is that the minister seeks to hide, with his hand always over his heart? Ha, Hester Prynne?"

"What is it, good Mistress Hibbins?" eagerly asked little Pearl.

"Hast thou seen it?"

"No matter, darling!" responded Mistress Hibbins, making Pearl a profound reverence. "Thou thyself wilt see it, one time or another. They say, child, thou art of the lineage of the Prince of Air! Wilt thou ride with me some fine night to see thy father? Then thou shalt know wherefore the minister keeps his hand over his heart!"

Laughing so shrilly that all the market-place could hear her, the weird old gentlewoman took her departure.

By this time the preliminary prayer had been offered in the meeting-house, and the accents of the Reverend Mr. Dimmesdale were heard commencing his discourse. An irresistible feeling kept Hester near the spot. As the sacred edifice was too much thronged to admit another auditor, she took up her position close beside the scaffold of the pillory. It was in sufficient proximity to bring the whole sermon to her ears, in the shape of an indistinct but varied murmur and flow of the minister's very peculiar voice.

This vocal organ was in itself a rich endowment, insomuch that a listener, comprehending nothing of the language in which the preacher spoke, might still have been swayed to and fro by the mere tone and cadence. Like all other music, it breathed passion and pathos, and emotions high or tender, in a tongue native to the human heart, wherever educated. Muffled as the sound was by its passage through the church walls, Hester Prynne listened with such intenseness, and sympathized so intimately, that the sermon had throughout a meaning for her, entirely apart from its indistinguishable words. These, perhaps, if more distinctly heard, might have been only a grosser medium, and have clogged the spiritual sense. Now she caught the low undertone, as of the wind sinking down to repose itself; then ascended with it, as it rose through progressive gradations of sweetness and power, until its volume seemed to envelop her with an atmosphere of awe and solemn grandeur. And yet, majestic as the voice sometimes became, there was for ever in it an essential character of plaintiveness. A loud or low expression of anguish—the whisper, or the shriek, as it might be conceived, of suffering humanity, that touched a sensibility in every bosom! At times this deep strain of pathos was all that could be heard, and scarcely heard sighing amid a desolate silence. But even when the minister's voice grew high and commanding—when it gushed irrepressibly upward—when it assumed its utmost breadth and power, so overfilling the church as to burst its way through the solid walls, and diffuse itself in the open air—still, if the auditor listened intently, and for the purpose, he could detect the same cry of pain. What was it? The complaint of a human heart, sorrow-laden, perchance guilty, telling its secret, whether of guilt or sorrow, to the great heart of mankind; beseeching its sympathy or forgiveness,—at every moment,—in each accent,—and never in vain! It was this profound and continual undertone that gave the clergyman his most appropriate power.

During all this time, Hester stood, statue-like, at the foot of the scaffold. If the minister's voice had not kept her there, there would, nevertheless, have been an inevitable magnetism in that spot, whence she dated the first hour of her life of ignominy. There was a sense within her —too ill-defined to be made a thought, but weighing heavily on her mind—that her whole orb of life, both before and after, was connected with this spot, as with the one point that gave it unity.

Little Pearl, meanwhile, had quitted her mother's side, and was playing at her own will about the market-place. She made the sombre crowd cheerful by her erratic and glistening ray, even as a bird of bright plumage illuminates a whole tree of dusky foliage by darting to and fro, half seen and half concealed amid the twilight of the clustering leaves. She had an undulating, but oftentimes a sharp and irregular movement. It indicated the restless vivacity of her spirit, which to-day was doubly indefatigable in its tip-toe dance, because it was played upon and vibrated with her mother's disquietude. Whenever Pearl saw anything to excite her ever active and wandering curiosity, she flew thitherward, and, as we might say, seized upon that man or thing as her own property, so far as she desired it, but without yielding the minutest degree of control over her motions in requital. The Puritans looked on, and, if they smiled, were none the less inclined to pronounce the child a demon offspring, from the indescribable charm of beauty and eccentricity that shone through her little figure, and sparkled with its activity. She ran and looked the wild Indian in the face, and he grew conscious of a nature wilder than his own. Thence, with native audacity, but still with a reserve as characteristic, she flew into the midst of a group of mariners, the swarthy-cheeked wild men of the ocean, as the Indians were of the land; and they gazed wonderingly and admiringly at Pearl, as if a flake of the sea-foam had taken the shape of a little maid, and were gifted with a soul of the sea-fire, that flashes beneath the prow in the night-time.

One of these seafaring men the shipmaster, indeed, who had spoken to Hester Prynne was so smitten with Pearl's aspect, that he attempted to lay hands upon her, with purpose to snatch a kiss. Finding it as impossible to touch her as to catch a humming-bird in the air, he took from his hat the gold chain that was twisted about it, and threw it to the child. Pearl immediately twined it around her neck and waist with such happy skill, that, once seen there, it became a part of her, and it was difficult to imagine her without it.

"Thy mother is yonder woman with the scarlet letter," said the seaman, "Wilt thou carry her a message from me?"

"If the message pleases me, I will," answered Pearl.

"Then tell her," rejoined he, "that I spake again with the black-a-visaged, hump shouldered old doctor, and he engages to bring his friend, the gentleman she wots of, aboard with him. So let thy mother take no thought, save for herself and thee. Wilt thou tell her this, thou witch-baby?"

"Mistress Hibbins says my father is the Prince of the Air!" cried Pearl, with a naughty smile. "If thou callest me that ill-name, I shall tell him of thee, and he will chase thy ship with a tempest!"

Pursuing a zigzag course across the marketplace, the child returned to her mother, and communicated what the mariner had said. Hester's strong, calm steadfastly-enduring spirit almost sank, at last, on beholding this dark and grim countenance of an inevitable doom, which at the moment when a passage seemed to open for the minister and herself out of their labyrinth of misery—showed itself with an unrelenting smile, right in the midst of their path.

With her mind harassed by the terrible perplexity in which the shipmaster's intelligence involved her, she was also subjected to another trial. There were many people present from the country round about, who had often heard of the scarlet letter, and to whom it had been made terrific by a hundred false or exaggerated rumours, but who had never beheld it with their own bodily eyes. These, after exhausting other modes of amusement, now thronged about Hester Prynne with rude and boorish intrusiveness. Unscrupulous as it was, however, it could not bring them nearer than a circuit of several yards. At that distance they accordingly stood, fixed there by the centrifugal force of the repugnance which the mystic symbol inspired. The whole gang of sailors, likewise, observing the press of spectators, and learning the purport of the scarlet letter, came and thrust their sunburnt and desperado-looking faces into the ring. Even the Indians were affected by a sort of cold shadow of the white man's curiosity and, gliding through the crowd, fastened their snake-like black eyes on Hester's bosom, conceiving, perhaps, that the wearer of this brilliantly embroidered badge must needs be a personage of high dignity among her people. Lastly, the inhabitants of the town (their own interest in this worn-out subject languidly reviving itself, by sympathy with what they saw others feel) lounged idly to the same quarter, and tormented Hester Prynne, perhaps more than all the rest, with their cool, well-acquainted gaze at her familiar shame. Hester saw and recognized the selfsame faces of that group of matrons, who had awaited her forthcoming from the prison-door seven years ago; all save one, the youngest and only compassionate among them, whose burial-robe she had since made. At the final hour, when she was so soon to fling aside the burning letter, it had strangely become the centre of more remark and excitement, and was thus made to sear her breast more painfully, than at any time since the first day she put it on.

While Hester stood in that magic circle of ignominy, where the cunning cruelty of her sentence seemed to have fixed her for ever, the admirable preacher was looking down from the sacred pulpit upon an audience whose very inmost spirits had yielded to his control. The sainted minister in the church! The woman of the scarlet letter in the marketplace! What imagination would have been irreverent enough to surmise that the same scorching stigma was on them both!

❧ 23 ❧

THE REVELATION OF THE SCARLET LETTER

THE ELOQUENT VOICE, on which the souls of the listening audience had been borne aloft as on the swelling waves of the sea, at length came to a pause. There was a momentary silence, profound as what should follow the utterance of oracles. Then ensued a murmur and half-hushed tumult, as if the auditors, released from the high spell that had transported them into the region of another's mind, were returning into themselves, with all their awe and wonder still heavy on them. In a moment more the crowd began to gush forth from the doors of the church. Now that there was an end, they needed more breath, more fit to support the gross and earthly life into which they relapsed, than that atmosphere which the preacher had converted into words of flame, and had burdened with the rich fragrance of his thought.

In the open air their rapture broke into speech. The street and the market-place absolutely babbled, from side to side, with applauses of the minister. His hearers could not rest until they had told one another of what each knew better than he could tell or hear.

According to their united testimony, never had man spoken in so wise, so high, and so holy a spirit, as he that spake this day; nor had inspiration ever breathed through mortal lips more evidently than it did through his. Its influence could be seen, as it were, descending upon him, and possessing him, and continually lifting him out of the written discourse that lay before him, and filling him with ideas that must have been as marvellous to himself as to his audience. His subject, it appeared, had been the relation between the Deity and the communities of mankind, with a special reference to the New England which they were here planting in the wilderness. And, as he drew towards the close, a spirit as of prophecy had come upon him, constraining him to its purpose as mightily as the old prophets of Israel were constrained, only with this difference, that, whereas the Jewish seers had denounced judgments and ruin on their country, it was his mission to foretell a high and glorious destiny for the newly gathered people of the Lord. But, throughout it all, and through the whole discourse, there had been a certain deep, sad undertone of pathos, which could not be interpreted otherwise than as the natural regret of one soon to pass away. Yes; their minister whom they so loved—and who so loved them all, that he could not depart heavenward without a sigh—had the foreboding of untimely death upon him, and would soon leave them in their tears. This idea of his transitory stay on

371

earth gave the last emphasis to the effect which the preacher had produced; it was as if an angel, in his passage to the skies, had shaken his bright wings over the people for an instant—at once a shadow and a splendour—and had shed down a shower of golden truths upon them.

Thus, there had come to the Reverend Mr. Dimmesdale—as to most men, in their various spheres, though seldom recognised until they see it far behind them—an epoch of life more brilliant and full of triumph than any previous one, or than any which could hereafter be. He stood, at this moment, on the very proudest eminence of superiority, to which the gifts or intellect, rich lore, prevailing eloquence, and a reputation of whitest sanctity, could exalt a clergyman in New England's earliest days, when the professional character was of itself a lofty pedestal. Such was the position which the minister occupied, as he bowed his head forward on the cushions of the pulpit at the close of his Election Sermon. Meanwhile Hester Prynne was standing beside the scaffold of the pillory, with the scarlet letter still burning on her breast!

Now was heard again the clamour of the music, and the measured tramp of the military escort issuing from the church door. The procession was to be marshalled thence to the town hall, where a solemn banquet would complete the ceremonies of the day.

Once more, therefore, the train of venerable and majestic fathers were seen moving through a broad pathway of the people, who drew back reverently, on either side, as the Governor and magistrates, the old and wise men, the holy ministers, and all that were eminent and renowned, advanced into the midst of them. When they were fairly in the marketplace, their presence was greeted by a shout. This—though doubtless it might acquire additional force and volume from the child-like loyalty which the age awarded to its rulers—was felt to be an irrepressible outburst of enthusiasm kindled in the auditors by that high strain of eloquence which was yet reverberating in their ears. Each felt the impulse in himself, and in the same breath, caught it from his neighbour. Within the church, it had hardly been kept down; beneath the sky it pealed upward to the zenith. There were human beings enough, and enough of highly wrought and symphonious feeling to produce that more impressive sound than the organ tones of the blast, or the thunder, or the roar of the sea; even that mighty swell of many voices, blended into one great voice by the universal impulse which makes likewise one vast heart out of the many. Never, from the soil of New England had gone up such a shout! Never, on New England soil had stood the man so honoured by his mortal brethren as the preacher!

How fared it with him, then? Were there not the brilliant particles of a halo in the air about his head? So etherealised by spirit as he was, and so apotheosised by worshipping admirers, did his footsteps, in the procession, really tread upon the dust of earth?

As the ranks of military men and civil fathers moved onward, all eyes were turned towards the point where the minister was seen to approach among them. The shout died into a murmur, as one portion of the crowd after another obtained a glimpse of him. How feeble and pale he looked, amid all his triumph! The energy—or say, rather, the inspiration which had held him up, until he should have delivered the sacred message that had brought its own strength along with it from heaven—was withdrawn, now that it had so faithfully performed its office. The glow, which they had just before beheld burning on his cheek, was extinguished, like a flame that sinks down hopelessly among the late decaying embers. It seemed hardly the face of a man alive, with such a death-like hue: it was hardly a man with life in him, that tottered on his path so nervously, yet tottered, and did not fall!

One of his clerical brethren—it was the venerable John Wilson—observing the state in which Mr. Dimmesdale was left by the retiring wave of intellect and sensibility, stepped forward hastily to offer his support. The minister tremulously, but decidedly, repelled the old man's arm. He still walked onward, if that movement could be so described, which rather resembled the wavering effort of an infant, with its mother's arms in view, outstretched to tempt him forward. And now, almost imperceptible as were the latter steps of his progress, he had come opposite the well-remembered and weather-darkened scaffold, where, long since, with all that dreary lapse of time between, Hester Prynne had encountered the world's ignominious stare. There stood Hester, holding little Pearl by the hand! And there was the scarlet letter on her breast! The minister here made a pause; although the music still played the stately and rejoicing march to which the procession moved. It summoned him onward—inward to the festival!—but here he made a pause.

Bellingham, for the last few moments, had kept an anxious eye upon him. He now left his own place in the procession, and advanced to give assistance judging, from Mr. Dimmesdale's aspect that he must otherwise inevitably fall. But there was something in the latter's expression that warned back the magistrate, although a man not readily obeying the vague intimations that pass from one spirit to another. The crowd, meanwhile, looked on with awe and wonder. This earthly faintness, was, in their view, only another phase of the minister's celestial strength; nor would it have seemed a miracle too high to be wrought for one so holy, had he ascended before their eyes, waxing dimmer and brighter, and fading at last into the light of heaven!

He turned towards the scaffold, and stretched forth his arms.

"Hester," said he, "come hither! Come, my little Pearl!"

It was a ghastly look with which he regarded them; but there was something at once tender and strangely triumphant in it. The child, with the bird-like motion, which was one of her characteristics, flew to him, and clasped her arms about his knees. Hester Prynne—slowly, as if impelled by inevitable fate, and against her strongest will—likewise drew near, but paused before she reached him. At this instant old Roger Chillingworth thrust himself through the crowd—or, perhaps, so dark, disturbed, and evil was his look, he rose up out of some nether region—to snatch back his victim from what he sought to do! Be that as it might, the old man rushed forward, and caught the minister by the arm.

"Madman, hold! what is your purpose?" whispered he. "Wave back that woman! Cast off this child! All shall be well! Do not blacken your fame, and perish in dishonour! I can yet save you! Would you bring infamy on your sacred profession?"

"Ha, tempter! Methinks thou art too late!" answered the minister, encountering his eye, fearfully, but firmly. "Thy power is not what it was! With God's help, I shall escape thee now!"

He again extended his hand to the woman of the scarlet letter.

"Hester Prynne," cried he, with a piercing earnestness, "in the name of Him, so terrible and so merciful, who gives me grace, at this last moment, to do what—for my own heavy sin and miserable agony—I withheld myself from doing seven years ago, come hither now, and twine thy strength about me! Thy strength, Hester; but let it be guided by the will which God hath granted me! This wretched and wronged old man is opposing it with all his might!—with all his own might, and the fiend's! Come, Hester—come! Support me up yonder scaffold."

The crowd was in a tumult. The men of rank and dignity, who stood more immediately around the clergyman, were so taken by surprise, and so perplexed as to the purport of what they saw—unable to receive the explanation which most readily presented itself, or to imagine any other—that they remained silent and inactive spectators of the judgement which Providence seemed about to work. They beheld the minister, leaning on Hester's shoulder, and supported by her arm around him, approach the scaffold, and ascend its steps; while still the little hand of the sin-born child was clasped in his. Old Roger Chillingworth followed, as one intimately connected with the drama of guilt and sorrow in which they had all been actors, and well entitled, therefore to be present at its closing scene.

"Hadst thou sought the whole earth over," said he looking darkly at the clergyman, "there was no one place so secret—no high place nor lowly place, where thou couldst have escaped me—save on this very scaffold!"

"Thanks be to Him who hath led me hither!" answered the minister.

Yet he trembled, and turned to Hester, with an expression of doubt and anxiety in his eyes, not the less evidently betrayed, that there was a feeble smile upon his lips.

"Is not this better," murmured he, "than what we dreamed of in the forest?"

"I know not! I know not!" she hurriedly replied. "Better? Yea; so we may both die, and little Pearl die with us!"

"For thee and Pearl, be it as God shall order," said the minister; "and God is merciful! Let me now do the will which He hath made plain before my sight. For, Hester, I am a dying man. So let me make haste to take my shame upon me!"

Partly supported by Hester Prynne, and holding one hand of little Pearl's, the Reverend Mr. Dimmesdale turned to the dignified and venerable rulers; to the holy ministers, who were his brethren; to the people, whose great heart was thoroughly appalled yet overflowing with tearful sympathy, as knowing that some deep life-matter—which, if full of sin, was full of anguish and repentance likewise—was now to be laid open to them. The sun, but little past its meridian, shone down upon the clergyman, and gave a distinctness to his figure, as he stood out from all the earth, to put in his plea of guilty at the bar of Eternal Justice.

"People of New England!" cried he, with a voice that rose over them, high, solemn, and majestic—yet had always a tremor through it, and sometimes a shriek, struggling up out of a fathomless depth of remorse and woe—"ye, that have loved me!—ye, that have deemed me holy!—behold me here, the one sinner of the world! At last—at last!—I stand upon the spot where, seven years since, I should have stood, here, with this woman, whose arm, more than the little strength wherewith I have crept hitherward, sustains me at this dreadful moment, from grovelling down upon my face! Lo, the scarlet letter which Hester wears! Ye have all shuddered at it! Wherever her walk hath been—wherever, so miserably burdened, she may have hoped to find repose—it hath cast a lurid gleam of awe and horrible repugnance round about her. But there stood one in the midst of you, at whose brand of sin and infamy ye have not shuddered!"

It seemed, at this point, as if the minister must leave the remainder of his secret undisclosed. But he fought back the bodily weakness—and, still more, the faintness of heart—that was striving for the mastery with him. He threw off all assistance, and stepped passionately forward a pace before the woman and the children.

"It was on him!" he continued, with a kind of fierceness; so determined was he to speak out the whole. "God's eye beheld it! The angels were for ever pointing at it! (The Devil knew it well, and fretted it continually with the touch of his burning finger!) But he hid it cunningly from men, and walked among you with the mien of a spirit, mournful, because so pure in a sinful world!—and sad, because he missed his heavenly kindred! Now, at the death-hour, he stands up before you! He bids you look again at Hester's scarlet letter! He tells you, that, with all its mysterious horror, it is but the shadow of what he bears on his own breast, and that even this, his own red stigma, is no more than the type of what has seared his inmost heart! Stand any here that question God's judgment on a sinner! Behold! Behold, a dreadful witness of it!"

With a convulsive motion, he tore away the ministerial band from before his breast. It was revealed! But it were irreverent to describe that revelation. For an instant, the gaze of the horror-stricken multitude was concentrated on the ghastly miracle; while the minister stood, with a flush of triumph in his face, as one who, in the crisis of acutest pain, had won a victory. Then, down he sank upon the scaffold! Hester partly raised him, and supported his head against her bosom. Old Roger Chillingworth knelt down beside him, with a blank, dull countenance, out of which the life seemed to have departed.

"Thou hast escaped me!" he repeated more than once. "Thou hast escaped me!"

"May God forgive thee!" said the minister. "Thou, too, hast deeply sinned!"

He withdrew his dying eyes from the old man, and fixed them on the woman and the child.

"My little Pearl," said he, feebly and there was a sweet and gentle smile over his face, as of a spirit sinking into deep repose; nay, now that the burden was removed, it seemed almost as if he would be sportive with the child—"dear little Pearl, wilt thou kiss me now? Thou wouldst not, yonder, in the forest! But now thou wilt?"

Pearl kissed his lips. A spell was broken. The great scene of grief, in which the wild infant bore a part had developed all her sympathies; and as her tears fell upon her father's cheek, they were the pledge that she would grow up amid human joy and sorrow, nor forever do battle with the world, but be a woman in it. Towards her mother, too, Pearl's errand as a messenger of anguish was fulfilled.

"Hester," said the clergyman, "farewell!"

"Shall we not meet again?" whispered she, bending her face down close to his. "Shall we not spend our immortal life together? Surely, surely, we have ransomed one another, with all this woe! Thou lookest far into eternity, with those bright dying eyes! Then tell me what thou seest!"

"Hush, Hester—hush!" said he, with tremulous solemnity. "The law we broke!—the sin here awfully revealed!—let these alone be in thy thoughts! I fear! I fear! It may be, that, when we forgot our God—when we violated our reverence each for the other's soul—it was thenceforth vain to hope that we could meet hereafter, in an everlasting and pure reunion. God knows; and He is merciful! He hath proved his mercy, most of all, in my afflictions. By giving me this burning torture to bear upon my breast! By sending yonder dark and terrible old man, to keep the torture always at red-heat! By bringing me hither, to die this death of triumphant ignominy before the people! Had either of these agonies been wanting, I had been lost for ever! Praised be His name! His will be done! Farewell!"

That final word came forth with the minister's expiring breath. The multitude, silent till then, broke out in a strange, deep voice of awe and wonder, which could not as yet find utterance, save in this murmur that rolled so heavily after the departed spirit.

✣ 24 ✣

CONCLUSION

AFTER MANY DAYS, when time sufficed for the people to arrange their thoughts in reference to the foregoing scene, there was more than one account of what had been witnessed on the scaffold.

Most of the spectators testified to having seen, on the breast of the unhappy minister, a SCARLET LETTER—the very semblance of that worn by Hester Prynne—imprinted in the flesh. As regarded its origin there were various explanations, all of which must necessarily have been conjectural. Some affirmed that the Reverend Mr. Dimmesdale, on the very day when Hester Prynne first wore her ignominious badge, had begun a course of penance—which he afterwards, in so many futile methods, followed out—by inflicting a hideous torture on himself. Others contended that the stigma had not been produced until a long time subsequent, when old Roger Chillingworth, being a potent necromancer, had caused it to appear, through the agency of magic and poisonous drugs. Others, again and those best able to appreciate the minister's peculiar sensibility, and the wonderful operation of his spirit upon the body— whispered their belief, that the awful symbol was the effect of the ever-active tooth of remorse, gnawing from the inmost heart outwardly, and at last manifesting Heaven's dreadful judgment by the visible presence of the letter. The reader may choose among these theories. We have thrown all the light we could acquire upon the portent, and would gladly, now that it has done its office, erase its deep print out of our own brain, where long meditation has fixed it in very undesirable distinctness.

It is singular, nevertheless, that certain persons, who were spectators of the whole scene, and professed never once to have removed their eyes from the Reverend Mr. Dimmesdale, denied that there was any mark whatever on his breast, more than on a new-born infant's. Neither, by their report, had his dying words acknowledged, nor even remotely implied, any—the slightest —connexion on his part, with the guilt for which Hester Prynne had so long worn the scarlet letter. According to these highly-respectable witnesses, the minister, conscious that he was dying—conscious, also, that the reverence of the multitude placed him already among saints and angels—had desired, by yielding up his breath in the arms of that fallen woman, to express to the world how utterly nugatory is the choicest of man's own righteousness. After exhausting life in his efforts for mankind's spiritual good, he had made the manner of his death a parable, in order to impress on his admirers the mighty and mournful lesson, that, in the view of Infinite Purity, we are sinners all alike. It was to teach them, that the holiest amongst us has but attained so far above his fellows as to discern more clearly the Mercy which looks down, and repudiate more utterly the phantom of human merit, which would look aspiringly upward. Without disputing a truth so momentous, we must be allowed to consider this version of Mr. Dimmesdale's story as only an instance of that stubborn fidelity with which a man's friends—and especially a clergyman's—will sometimes uphold his character, when proofs, clear as the mid-day sunshine on the scarlet letter, establish him a false and sin-stained creature of the dust.

The authority which we have chiefly followed—a manuscript of old date, drawn up from the verbal testimony of individuals, some of whom had known Hester Prynne, while others had heard the tale from contemporary witnesses fully confirms the view taken in the foregoing pages. Among many morals which press upon us from the poor minister's miserable experience, we put only this into a sentence:—"Be true! Be true! Be true! Show freely to the world, if not your worst, yet some trait whereby the worst may be inferred!"

Nothing was more remarkable than the change which took place, almost immediately after Mr. Dimmesdale's death, in the appearance and demeanour of the old man known as Roger Chillingworth. All his strength and energy—all his vital and intellectual force—seemed at once to desert him, insomuch that he positively withered up, shrivelled away and almost vanished from mortal sight, like an uprooted weed that lies wilting in the sun. This unhappy man had made the very principle of his life to consist in the pursuit and systematic exercise of revenge; and when, by its completest triumph consummation that evil principle was left with no further material to support it—when, in short, there was no more Devil's work on earth for him to do, it only remained for the unhumanised mortal to betake himself whither his master would find him tasks enough, and pay him his wages duly. But, to all these shadowy beings, so long our near acquaintances—as well Roger Chillingworth as his companions we would fain be merciful. It is a curious subject of observation and inquiry, whether hatred and love be not the same thing at bottom. Each, in its utmost development, supposes a high degree of intimacy and heart-knowledge; each renders one individual dependent for the food of his affections and spiritual fife upon another: each leaves the passionate lover, or the no less passionate hater, forlorn and desolate by the withdrawal of his subject. Philosophically considered, therefore, the two passions seem essentially the same, except that one happens to be seen in a celestial radiance, and the other in a dusky and lurid glow. In the spiritual world, the old physician and the minister—mutual victims as they have been—may, unawares, have found their earthly stock of hatred and antipathy transmuted into golden love.

Leaving this discussion apart, we have a matter of business to communicate to the reader. At old Roger Chillingworth's decease, (which took place within the year), and by his last will and testament, of which Governor Bellingham and the Reverend Mr. Wilson were executors, he bequeathed a very considerable amount of property, both here and in England to little Pearl, the daughter of Hester Prynne.

So Pearl—the elf child—the demon offspring, as some people up to that epoch persisted in considering her—became the richest heiress of her day in the New World. Not improbably this circumstance wrought a very material change in the public estimation; and had the mother and child remained here, little Pearl at a marriageable period of life might have mingled her wild blood with the lineage of the devoutest Puritan among them all. But, in no long time after the physician's death, the wearer of the scarlet letter disappeared, and Pearl along with her. For many years, though a vague report would now and then find its way across the sea—like a shapeless piece of driftwood tossed ashore with the initials of a name upon it—yet no tidings of

377

them unquestionably authentic were received. The story of the scarlet letter grew into a legend. Its spell, however, was still potent, and kept the scaffold awful where the poor minister had died, and likewise the cottage by the sea-shore where Hester Prynne had dwelt. Near this latter spot, one afternoon some children were at play, when they beheld a tall woman in a gray robe approach the cottage-door. In all those years it had never once been opened; but either she unlocked it or the decaying wood and iron yielded to her hand, or she glided shadow-like through these impediments—and, at all events, went in.

On the threshold she paused—turned partly round—for perchance the idea of entering alone and all so changed, the home of so intense a former life, was more dreary and desolate than even she could bear. But her hesitation was only for an instant, though long enough to display a scarlet letter on her breast.

And Hester Prynne had returned, and taken up her long-forsaken shame! But where was little Pearl? If still alive she must now have been in the flush and bloom of early womanhood. None knew—nor ever learned with the fulness of perfect certainty—whether the elf-child had gone thus untimely to a maiden grave; or whether her wild, rich nature had been softened and subdued and made capable of a woman's gentle happiness. But through the remainder of Hester's life there were indications that the recluse of the scarlet letter was the object of love and interest with some inhabitant of another land. Letters came, with armorial seals upon them, though of bearings unknown to English heraldry. In the cottage there were articles of comfort and luxury such as Hester never cared to use, but which only wealth could have purchased and affection have imagined for her. There were trifles too, little ornaments, beautiful tokens of a continual remembrance, that must have been wrought by delicate fingers at the impulse of a fond heart. And once Hester was seen embroidering a baby-garment with such a lavish richness of golden fancy as would have raised a public tumult had any infant thus apparelled, been shown to our sober-hued community.

In fine, the gossips of that day believed—and Mr. Surveyor Pue, who made investigations a century later, believed—and one of his recent successors in office, moreover, faithfully believes —that Pearl was not only alive, but married, and happy, and mindful of her mother; and that she would most joyfully have entertained that sad and lonely mother at her fireside.

But there was a more real life for Hester Prynne, here, in New England, than in that unknown region where Pearl had found a home. Here had been her sin; here, her sorrow; and here was yet to be her penitence. She had returned, therefore, and resumed—of her own free will, for not the sternest magistrate of that iron period would have imposed it—resumed the symbol of which we have related so dark a tale. Never afterwards did it quit her bosom. But, in the lapse of the toilsome, thoughtful, and self-devoted years that made up Hester's life, the scarlet letter ceased to be a stigma which attracted the world's scorn and bitterness, and became a type of something to be sorrowed over, and looked upon with awe, yet with reverence too. And, as Hester Prynne had no selfish ends, nor lived in any measure for her own profit and enjoyment, people brought all their sorrows and perplexities, and besought her counsel, as one who had herself gone through a mighty trouble. Women, more especially—in the continually recurring trials of wounded, wasted, wronged, misplaced, or erring and sinful passion—or with the dreary burden of a heart unyielded, because unvalued and unsought came to Hester's cottage, demanding why they were so wretched, and what the remedy! Hester comforted and counselled them, as best she might. She assured them, too, of her firm belief that, at some brighter period, when the world should have grown ripe for it, in Heaven's own time, a new truth would be revealed, in order to establish the whole relation between man and woman on a surer ground of mutual happiness. Earlier in life, Hester had vainly imagined that she herself might be the destined prophetess, but had long since recognised the impossibility that any mission of divine and mysterious truth should be confided to a woman stained with sin, bowed down with shame, or even burdened with a life-long sorrow. The angel and apostle of the coming revelation must be a woman, indeed, but lofty, pure, and beautiful, and wise; moreover, not through dusky grief, but the ethereal medium of joy; and showing how sacred love should make us happy, by the truest test of a life successful to such an end.

So said Hester Prynne, and glanced her sad eyes downward at the scarlet letter. And, after many, many years, a new grave was delved, near an old and sunken one, in that burial-ground beside which King's Chapel has since been built. It was near that old and sunken grave, yet with a space between, as if the dust of the two sleepers had no right to mingle. Yet one tombstone served for both. All around, there were monuments carved with armorial bearings; and on this simple slab of slate—as the curious investigator may still discern, and perplex himself with the purport—there appeared the semblance of an engraved escutcheon. It bore a device, a herald's wording of which may serve for a motto and brief description of our now concluded legend; so sombre is it, and relieved only by one ever-glowing point of light gloomier than the shadow:—

"ON A FIELD, SABLE, THE LETTER A, GULES"

THE HOUSE OF THE SEVEN GABLES

❦ I ❦

THE OLD PYNCHEON FAMILY

HALFWAY DOWN A BY-STREET of one of our New England towns stands a rusty wooden house, with seven acutely peaked gables, facing towards various points of the compass, and a huge, clustered chimney in the midst. The street is Pyncheon Street; the house is the old Pyncheon House; and an elm-tree, of wide circumference, rooted before the door, is familiar to every town-born child by the title of the Pyncheon Elm. On my occasional visits to the town aforesaid, I seldom failed to turn down Pyncheon Street, for the sake of passing through the shadow of these two antiquities,—the great elm-tree and the weather-beaten edifice.

The aspect of the venerable mansion has always affected me like a human countenance, bearing the traces not merely of outward storm and sunshine, but expressive also, of the long lapse of mortal life, and accompanying vicissitudes that have passed within. Were these to be worthily recounted, they would form a narrative of no small interest and instruction, and possessing, moreover, a certain remarkable unity, which might almost seem the result of artistic arrangement. But the story would include a chain of events extending over the better part of two centuries, and, written out with reasonable amplitude, would fill a bigger folio volume, or a longer series of duodecimos, than could prudently be appropriated to the annals of all New England during a similar period. It consequently becomes imperative to make short work with most of the traditionary lore of which the old Pyncheon House, otherwise known as the House of the Seven Gables, has been the theme. With a brief sketch, therefore, of the circumstances amid which the foundation of the house was laid, and a rapid glimpse at its quaint exterior, as it grew black in the prevalent east wind,—pointing, too, here and there, at some spot of more verdant mossiness on its roof and walls,—we shall commence the real action of our tale at an epoch not very remote from the present day. Still, there will be a connection with the long past —a reference to forgotten events and personages, and to manners, feelings, and opinions, almost or wholly obsolete—which, if adequately translated to the reader, would serve to illustrate how much of old material goes to make up the freshest novelty of human life. Hence, too, might be drawn a weighty lesson from the little-regarded truth, that the act of the passing generation is the germ which may and must produce good or evil fruit in a far-distant time; that, together with the seed of the merely temporary crop, which mortals term expediency, they inevitably sow the acorns of a more enduring growth, which may darkly overshadow their posterity.

The House of the Seven Gables, antique as it now looks, was not the first habitation erected by civilized man on precisely the same spot of ground. Pyncheon Street formerly bore the humbler appellation of Maule's Lane, from the name of the original occupant of the soil, before whose cottage-door it was a cow-path. A natural spring of soft and pleasant water—a rare treasure on the sea-girt peninsula where the Puritan settlement was made—had early induced Matthew Maule to build a hut, shaggy with thatch, at this point, although somewhat too remote from what was then the centre of the village. In the growth of the town, however, after some thirty or forty years, the site covered by this rude hovel had become exceedingly desirable in the eyes of a prominent and powerful personage, who asserted plausible claims to the proprietorship of this and a large adjacent tract of land, on the strength of a grant from the legislature. Colonel Pyncheon, the claimant, as we gather from whatever traits of him are preserved, was characterized by an iron energy of purpose. Matthew Maule, on the other hand, though an obscure man, was stubborn in the defence of what he considered his right; and, for several years, he succeeded in protecting the acre or two of earth which, with his own toil, he had hewn out of the primeval forest, to be his garden ground and homestead. No written record of this dispute is known to be in existence. Our acquaintance with the whole subject is derived chiefly from tradition. It would be bold, therefore, and possibly unjust, to venture a decisive opinion as to its merits; although it appears to have been at least a matter of doubt, whether Colonel Pyncheon's claim were not unduly stretched, in order to make it cover the small metes and bounds of Matthew Maule. What greatly strengthens such a suspicion is the fact that this controversy between two ill-matched antagonists—at a period, moreover, laud it as we may, when personal influence had far more weight than now—remained for years undecided, and came to a close only with the death of the party occupying the disputed soil. The mode of his death, too, affects the mind differently, in our day, from what it did a century and a half ago. It was a death that blasted with strange horror the humble name of the dweller in the cottage, and made it seem almost a religious act to drive the plough over the little area of his habitation, and obliterate his place and memory from among men.

Old Matthew Maule, in a word, was executed for the crime of witchcraft. He was one of the martyrs to that terrible delusion, which should teach us, among its other morals, that the influential classes, and those who take upon themselves to be leaders of the people, are fully liable to all the passionate error that has ever characterized the maddest mob. Clergymen, judges, statesmen,—the wisest, calmest, holiest persons of their day stood in the inner circle round about the gallows, loudest to applaud the work of blood, latest to confess themselves miserably deceived. If any one part of their proceedings can be said to deserve less blame than another, it was the singular indiscrimination with which they persecuted, not merely the poor and aged, as in former judicial massacres, but people of all ranks; their own equals, brethren, and wives. Amid the disorder of such various ruin, it is not strange that a man of inconsiderable note, like Maule, should have trodden the martyr's path to the hill of execution almost unremarked in the throng of his fellow sufferers. But, in after days, when the frenzy of that hideous epoch had subsided, it was remembered how loudly Colonel Pyncheon had joined in the general cry, to purge the land from witchcraft; nor did it fail to be whispered, that there was an invidious acrimony in the zeal with which he had sought the condemnation of Matthew Maule. It was well known that the victim had recognized the bitterness of personal enmity in his persecutor's conduct towards him, and that he declared himself hunted to death for his spoil. At the moment of execution—with the halter about his neck, and while Colonel Pyncheon sat on horseback, grimly gazing at the scene Maule had addressed him from the scaffold, and uttered a prophecy, of which history, as well as fireside tradition, has preserved the very words. "God," said the dying man, pointing his finger, with a ghastly look, at the undismayed countenance of his enemy,—"God will give him blood to drink!" After the reputed wizard's death, his humble homestead had fallen an easy spoil into Colonel Pyncheon's grasp. When it was understood, however, that the Colonel intended to erect a family mansion-spacious, ponderously framed of oaken timber, and calculated to endure for many generations of his posterity over the spot first covered by the log-built hut of Matthew Maule, there was much shaking of the head among the village gossips. Without absolutely expressing a doubt whether the stalwart Puritan had acted as a man of conscience and integrity throughout the proceedings which have been sketched, they, nevertheless, hinted that he was about to build his house over an unquiet grave. His home would include the home of the dead and buried wizard, and would thus afford the ghost of the latter a kind of privilege to haunt its new apartments, and the chambers into which future bridegrooms were to lead their brides, and where children of the Pyncheon blood were to be born. The terror and ugliness of Maule's crime, and the wretchedness of his punishment, would darken the freshly plastered walls, and infect them early with the scent of an old and melancholy house. Why, then,—while so much of the soil around him was bestrewn with the virgin forest leaves,—why should Colonel Pyncheon prefer a site that had already been accurst?

But the Puritan soldier and magistrate was not a man to be turned aside from his well-considered scheme, either by dread of the wizard's ghost, or by flimsy sentimentalities of any kind, however specious. Had he been told of a bad air, it might have moved him somewhat; but he was ready to encounter an evil spirit on his own ground. Endowed with commonsense, as massive and hard as blocks of granite, fastened together by stern rigidity of purpose, as with iron clamps, he followed out his original design, probably without so much as imagining an objection to it. On the score of delicacy, or any scrupulousness which a finer sensibility might have taught him, the Colonel, like most of his breed and generation, was impenetrable. He therefore dug his cellar, and laid the deep foundations of his mansion, on the square of earth whence Matthew Maule, forty years before, had first swept away the fallen leaves. It was a curious, and, as some people thought, an ominous fact, that, very soon after the workmen began their operations, the spring of water, above mentioned, entirely lost the deliciousness of its pristine quality. Whether its sources were disturbed by the depth of the new cellar, or whatever subtler cause might lurk at the bottom, it is certain that the water of Maule's Well, as it continued to be called, grew hard and brackish. Even such we find it now; and any old woman of the neighborhood will certify that it is productive of intestinal mischief to those who quench their thirst there.

The reader may deem it singular that the head carpenter of the new edifice was no other than the son of the very man from whose dead gripe the property of the soil had been wrested. Not improbably he was the best workman of his time; or, perhaps, the Colonel thought it expedient, or was impelled by some better feeling, thus openly to cast aside all animosity against the race of his fallen antagonist. Nor was it out of keeping with the general coarseness and matter-of-fact character of the age, that the son should be willing to earn an honest penny, or, rather, a weighty amount of sterling pounds, from the purse of his father's deadly enemy. At all events, Thomas Maule became the architect of the House of the Seven Gables, and performed his duty so faithfully that the timber framework fastened by his hands still holds together.

Thus the great house was built. Familiar as it stands in the writer's recollection,—for it has been an object of curiosity with him from boyhood, both as a specimen of the best and stateliest architecture of a longpast epoch, and as the scene of events more full of human interest, perhaps, than those of a gray feudal castle,—familiar as it stands, in its rusty old age, it is therefore only the more difficult to imagine the bright novelty with which it first caught the sunshine. The impression of its actual state, at this distance of a hundred and sixty years, darkens inevitably through the picture which we would fain give of its appearance on the morning when the Puritan magnate bade all the town to be his guests. A ceremony of consecration, festive as well as religious, was now to be performed. A prayer and discourse from the Rev. Mr. Higginson, and the outpouring of a psalm from the general throat of the community, was to be made acceptable to the grosser sense by ale, cider, wine, and brandy, in copious effusion, and, as some authorities aver, by an ox, roasted whole, or at least, by the weight and substance of an ox, in more manageable joints and sirloins. The carcass of a deer, shot within twenty miles, had supplied material for the vast circumference of a pasty. A codfish of sixty pounds, caught in the bay, had been dissolved into the rich liquid of a chowder. The chimney of the new house, in short, belching forth its kitchen smoke, impregnated the whole air with the scent of meats, fowls, and fishes, spicily concocted with odoriferous herbs, and onions in abundance. The mere smell of such festivity, making its way to everybody's nostrils, was at once an invitation and an appetite.

Maule's Lane, or Pyncheon Street, as it were now more decorous to call it, was thronged, at the appointed hour, as with a congregation on its way to church. All, as they approached, looked upward at the imposing edifice, which was henceforth to assume its rank among the habitations of mankind. There it rose, a little withdrawn from the line of the street, but in pride, not modesty. Its whole visible exterior was ornamented with quaint figures, conceived in the grotesqueness of a Gothic fancy, and drawn or stamped in the glittering plaster, composed of lime, pebbles, and bits of glass, with which the woodwork of the walls was overspread. On every side the seven gables pointed sharply towards the sky, and presented the aspect of a whole sisterhood of edifices, breathing through the spiracles of one great chimney. The many lattices, with their small, diamond-shaped panes, admitted the sunlight into hall and chamber, while, nevertheless, the second story, projecting far over the base, and itself retiring beneath the third, threw a shadowy and thoughtful gloom into the lower rooms. Carved globes of wood were affixed under the jutting stories. Little spiral rods of iron beautified each of the seven peaks. On the triangular portion of the gable, that fronted next the street, was a dial, put up that very morning, and on which the sun was still marking the passage of the first bright hour in a history that was not destined to be all so bright. All around were scattered shavings, chips, shingles, and broken halves of bricks; these, together with the lately turned earth, on which the grass had not begun to grow, contributed to the impression of strangeness and novelty proper to a house that had yet its place to make among men's daily interests.

The principal entrance, which had almost the breadth of a church-door, was in the angle between the two front gables, and was covered by an open porch, with benches beneath its shelter. Under this arched doorway, scraping their feet on the unworn threshold, now trod the clergymen, the elders, the magistrates, the deacons, and whatever of aristocracy there was in town or county. Thither, too, thronged the plebeian classes as freely as their betters, and in larger number. Just within the entrance, however, stood two serving-men, pointing some of the guests to the neighborhood of the kitchen and ushering others into the statelier rooms,— hospitable alike to all, but still with a scrutinizing regard to the high or low degree of each. Velvet garments sombre but rich, stiffly plaited ruffs and bands, embroidered gloves, venerable beards, the mien and countenance of authority, made it easy to distinguish the gentleman of worship, at that period, from the tradesman, with his plodding air, or the laborer, in his leathern jerkin, stealing awe-stricken into the house which he had perhaps helped to build.

One inauspicious circumstance there was, which awakened a hardly concealed displeasure in the breasts of a few of the more punctilious visitors. The founder of this stately mansion—a gentleman noted for the square and ponderous courtesy of his demeanor, ought surely to have stood in his own hall, and to have offered the first welcome to so many eminent personages as here presented themselves in honor of his solemn festival. He was as yet invisible; the most favored of the guests had not beheld him. This sluggishness on Colonel Pyncheon's part became still more unaccountable, when the second dignitary of the province made his appearance, and found no more ceremonious a reception. The lieutenant-governor, although his visit was one of the anticipated glories of the day, had alighted from his horse, and assisted his lady from her side-saddle, and crossed the Colonel's threshold, without other greeting than that of the principal domestic.

This person—a gray-headed man, of quiet and most respectful deportment—found it necessary to explain that his master still remained in his study, or private apartment; on entering which, an hour before, he had expressed a wish on no account to be disturbed.

"Do not you see, fellow," said the high-sheriff of the county, taking the servant aside, "that this is no less a man than the lieutenant-governor? Summon Colonel Pyncheon at once! I know that he received letters from England this morning; and, in the perusal and consideration of them, an hour may have passed away without his noticing it. But he will be ill-pleased, I judge, if you suffer him to neglect the courtesy due to one of our chief rulers, and who may be said to represent King William, in the absence of the governor himself. Call your master instantly."

"Nay, please your worship," answered the man, in much perplexity, but with a backwardness that strikingly indicated the hard and severe character of Colonel Pyncheon's domestic rule; "my master's orders were exceeding strict; and, as your worship knows, he permits of no discretion in the obedience of those who owe him service. Let who list open yonder door; I dare not, though the governor's own voice should bid me do it!"

"Pooh, pooh, master high sheriff!" cried the lieutenant-governor, who had overheard the foregoing discussion, and felt himself high enough in station to play a little with his dignity. "I will take the matter into my own hands. It is time that the good Colonel came forth to greet his friends; else we shall be apt to suspect that he has taken a sip too much of his Canary wine, in his extreme deliberation which cask it were best to broach in honor of the day! But since he is so much behindhand, I will give him a remembrancer myself!"

Accordingly, with such a tramp of his ponderous riding-boots as might of itself have been audible in the remotest of the seven gables, he advanced to the door, which the servant pointed out, and made its new panels reecho with a loud, free knock. Then, looking round, with a smile, to the spectators, he awaited a response. As none came, however, he knocked again, but with the same unsatisfactory result as at first. And now, being a trifle choleric in his temperament, the lieutenant-governor uplifted the heavy hilt of his sword, wherewith he so beat and banged upon the door, that, as some of the bystanders whispered, the racket might have disturbed the dead. Be that as it might, it seemed to produce no awakening effect on Colonel Pyncheon. When the sound subsided, the silence through the house was deep, dreary, and oppressive, notwithstanding that the tongues of many of the guests had already been loosened by a surreptitious cup or two of wine or spirits.

"Strange, forsooth!—very strange!" cried the lieutenant-governor, whose smile was changed to a frown. "But seeing that our host sets us the good example of forgetting ceremony, I shall likewise throw it aside, and make free to intrude on his privacy."

He tried the door, which yielded to his hand, and was flung wide open by a sudden gust of wind that passed, as with a loud sigh, from the outermost portal through all the passages and apartments of the new house. It rustled the silken garments of the ladies, and waved the long curls of the gentlemen's wigs, and shook the window-hangings and the curtains of the bedchambers; causing everywhere a singular stir, which yet was more like a hush. A shadow of awe and half-fearful anticipation—nobody knew wherefore, nor of what—had all at once fallen over the company.

They thronged, however, to the now open door, pressing the lieutenant-governor, in the eagerness of their curiosity, into the room in advance of them. At the first glimpse they beheld nothing extraordinary: a handsomely furnished room, of moderate size, somewhat darkened by curtains; books arranged on shelves; a large map on the wall, and likewise a portrait of Colonel Pyncheon, beneath which sat the original Colonel himself, in an oaken elbow-chair, with a pen in his hand. Letters, parchments, and blank sheets of paper were on the table before him. He appeared to gaze at the curious crowd, in front of which stood the lieutenant-governor; and there was a frown on his dark and massive countenance, as if sternly resentful of the boldness that had impelled them into his private retirement.

A little boy—the Colonel's grandchild, and the only human being that ever dared to be familiar with him—now made his way among the guests, and ran towards the seated figure; then pausing halfway, he began to shriek with terror. The company, tremulous as the leaves of a tree, when all are shaking together, drew nearer, and perceived that there was an unnatural distortion in the fixedness of Colonel Pyncheon's stare; that there was blood on his ruff, and that his hoary beard was saturated with it. It was too late to give assistance. The iron-hearted Puritan, the relentless persecutor, the grasping and strong-willed man was dead! Dead, in his new house! There is a tradition, only worth alluding to as lending a tinge of superstitious awe to a scene perhaps gloomy enough without it, that a voice spoke loudly among the guests, the tones of which were like those of old Matthew Maule, the executed wizard,—"God hath given him blood to drink!"

Thus early had that one guest,—the only guest who is certain, at one time or another, to find his way into every human dwelling,—thus early had Death stepped across the threshold of the House of the Seven Gables!

Colonel Pyncheon's sudden and mysterious end made a vast deal of noise in its day. There were many rumors, some of which have vaguely drifted down to the present time, how that appearances indicated violence; that there were the marks of fingers on his throat, and the print of a bloody hand on his plaited ruff; and that his peaked beard was dishevelled, as if it had been fiercely clutched and pulled. It was averred, likewise, that the lattice window, near the Colonel's chair, was open; and that, only a few minutes before the fatal occurrence, the figure of a man had been seen clambering over the garden fence, in the rear of the house. But it were folly to lay any stress on stories of this kind, which are sure to spring up around such an event as that now related, and which, as in the present case, sometimes prolong themselves for ages afterwards, like the toadstools that indicate where the fallen and buried trunk of a tree has long since mouldered into the earth. For our own part, we allow them just as little credence as to that other fable of the skeleton hand which the lieutenant-governor was said to have seen at the Colonel's throat, but which vanished away, as he advanced farther into the room. Certain it is, however, that there was a great consultation and dispute of doctors over the dead body. One,— John Swinnerton by name,—who appears to have been a man of eminence, upheld it, if we have rightly understood his terms of art, to be a case of apoplexy. His professional brethren, each for himself, adopted various hypotheses, more or less plausible, but all dressed out in a perplexing mystery of phrase, which, if it do not show a bewilderment of mind in these erudite physicians, certainly causes it in the unlearned peruser of their opinions. The coroner's jury sat upon the corpse, and, like sensible men, returned an unassailable verdict of "Sudden Death!"

It is indeed difficult to imagine that there could have been a serious suspicion of murder, or the slightest grounds for implicating any particular individual as the perpetrator. The rank, wealth, and eminent character of the deceased must have insured the strictest scrutiny into every ambiguous circumstance. As none such is on record, it is safe to assume that none existed. Tradition,—which sometimes brings down truth that history has let slip, but is oftener the wild babble of the time, such as was formerly spoken at the fireside and now congeals in newspapers,—tradition is responsible for all contrary averments. In Colonel Pyncheon's funeral sermon, which was printed, and is still extant, the Rev. Mr. Higginson enumerates, among the many felicities of his distinguished parishioner's earthly career, the happy seasonableness of his death. His duties all performed,—the highest prosperity attained,—his race and future generations fixed on a stable basis, and with a stately roof to shelter them for centuries to come, —what other upward step remained for this good man to take, save the final step from earth to the golden gate of heaven! The pious clergyman surely would not have uttered words like these had he in the least suspected that the Colonel had been thrust into the other world with the clutch of violence upon his throat.

The family of Colonel Pyncheon, at the epoch of his death, seemed destined to as fortunate a permanence as can anywise consist with the inherent instability of human affairs. It might fairly be anticipated that the progress of time would rather increase and ripen their prosperity, than wear away and destroy it. For, not only had his son and heir come into immediate enjoyment of a rich estate, but there was a claim through an Indian deed, confirmed by a subsequent grant of the General Court, to a vast and as yet unexplored and unmeasured tract of Eastern lands. These possessions—for as such they might almost certainly be reckoned—comprised the greater part of what is now known as Waldo County, in the state of Maine, and were more extensive than many a dukedom, or even a reigning prince's territory, on European soil. When the pathless forest that still covered this wild principality should give place—as it inevitably must, though perhaps not till ages hence—to the golden fertility of human culture, it would be the source of incalculable wealth to the Pyncheon blood. Had the Colonel survived only a few weeks longer, it is probable that his great political influence, and powerful connections at home and abroad, would have consummated all that was necessary to render the claim available. But, in spite of good Mr. Higginson's congratulatory eloquence, this appeared to be the one thing which Colonel Pyncheon, provident and sagacious as he was, had allowed to go at loose ends. So far as the prospective territory was concerned, he unquestionably died too soon. His son lacked not merely the father's eminent position, but the talent and force of character to achieve it: he could, therefore, effect nothing by dint of political interest; and the bare justice or legality of the claim was not so apparent, after the Colonel's decease, as it had been pronounced in his lifetime. Some connecting link had slipped out of the evidence, and could not anywhere be found.

Efforts, it is true, were made by the Pyncheons, not only then, but at various periods for nearly a hundred years afterwards, to obtain what they stubbornly persisted in deeming their right. But, in course of time, the territory was partly regranted to more favored individuals, and partly cleared and occupied by actual settlers. These last, if they ever heard of the Pyncheon title, would have laughed at the idea of any man's asserting a right—on the strength of mouldy parchments, signed with the faded autographs of governors and legislators long dead and forgotten—to the lands which they or their fathers had wrested from the wild hand of nature by their own sturdy toil. This impalpable claim, therefore, resulted in nothing more solid than to cherish, from generation to generation, an absurd delusion of family importance, which all along characterized the Pyncheons. It caused the poorest member of the race to feel as if he inherited a kind of nobility, and might yet come into the possession of princely wealth to support it. In the better specimens of the breed, this peculiarity threw an ideal grace over the hard material of human life, without stealing away any truly valuable quality. In the baser sort, its effect was to increase the liability to sluggishness and dependence, and induce the victim of a shadowy hope to remit all self-effort, while awaiting the realization of his dreams. Years and years after their claim had passed out of the public memory, the Pyncheons were accustomed to consult the Colonel's ancient map, which had been projected while Waldo County was still an unbroken wilderness. Where the old land surveyor had put down woods, lakes, and rivers, they marked out the cleared spaces, and dotted the villages and towns, and calculated the progressively increasing value of the territory, as if there were yet a prospect of its ultimately forming a princedom for themselves.

In almost every generation, nevertheless, there happened to be some one descendant of the family gifted with a portion of the hard, keen sense, and practical energy, that had so remarkably distinguished the original founder. His character, indeed, might be traced all the way down, as distinctly as if the Colonel himself, a little diluted, had been gifted with a sort of intermittent immortality on earth. At two or three epochs, when the fortunes of the family were low, this representative of hereditary qualities had made his appearance, and caused the traditionary gossips of the town to whisper among themselves, "Here is the old Pyncheon come again! Now the Seven Gables will be new-shingled!" From father to son, they clung to the ancestral house with singular tenacity of home attachment. For various reasons, however, and from impressions often too vaguely founded to be put on paper, the writer cherishes the belief that many, if not most, of the successive proprietors of this estate were troubled with doubts as to their moral right to hold it. Of their legal tenure there could be no question; but old Matthew Maule, it is to be feared, trode downward from his own age to a far later one, planting a heavy footstep, all the way, on the conscience of a Pyncheon. If so, we are left to dispose of the awful query, whether each inheritor of the property—conscious of wrong, and failing to rectify it— did not commit anew the great guilt of his ancestor, and incur all its original responsibilities. And supposing such to be the case, would it not be a far truer mode of expression to say of the Pyncheon family, that they inherited a great misfortune, than the reverse?

We have already hinted that it is not our purpose to trace down the history of the Pyncheon family, in its unbroken connection with the House of the Seven Gables; nor to show, as in a magic picture, how the rustiness and infirmity of age gathered over the venerable house itself. As regards its interior life, a large, dim looking-glass used to hang in one of the rooms, and was fabled to contain within its depths all the shapes that had ever been reflected there,—the old Colonel himself, and his many descendants, some in the garb of antique babyhood, and others in the bloom of feminine beauty or manly prime, or saddened with the wrinkles of frosty age. Had we the secret of that mirror, we would gladly sit down before it, and transfer its revelations to our page. But there was a story, for which it is difficult to conceive any foundation, that the posterity of Matthew Maule had some connection with the mystery of the looking-glass, and that, by what appears to have been a sort of mesmeric process, they could make its inner region all alive with the departed Pyncheons; not as they had shown themselves to the world, nor in their better and happier hours, but as doing over again some deed of sin, or in the crisis of life's bitterest sorrow. The popular imagination, indeed, long kept itself busy with the affair of the old Puritan Pyncheon and the wizard Maule; the curse which the latter flung from his scaffold was remembered, with the very important addition, that it had become a part of the Pyncheon inheritance. If one of the family did but gurgle in his throat, a bystander would be likely enough to whisper, between jest and earnest, "He has Maule's blood to drink!" The sudden death of a Pyncheon, about a hundred years ago, with circumstances very similar to what have been related of the Colonel's exit, was held as giving additional probability to the received opinion on this topic. It was considered, moreover, an ugly and ominous circumstance, that Colonel Pyncheon's picture—in obedience, it was said, to a provision of his will—remained affixed to the wall of the room in which he died. Those stern, immitigable features seemed to symbolize an evil influence, and so darkly to mingle the shadow of their presence with the sunshine of the passing hour, that no good thoughts or purposes could ever spring up and blossom there. To the thoughtful mind there will be no tinge of superstition in what we figuratively express, by affirming that the ghost of a dead progenitor—perhaps as a portion of his own punishment—is often doomed to become the Evil Genius of his family.

The Pyncheons, in brief, lived along, for the better part of two centuries, with perhaps less of outward vicissitude than has attended most other New England families during the same period of time. Possessing very distinctive traits of their own, they nevertheless took the general characteristics of the little community in which they dwelt; a town noted for its frugal, discreet, well-ordered, and home-loving inhabitants, as well as for the somewhat confined scope of its sympathies; but in which, be it said, there are odder individuals, and, now and then, stranger occurrences, than one meets with almost anywhere else. During the Revolution, the Pyncheon of that epoch, adopting the royal side, became a refugee; but repented, and made his reappearance, just at the point of time to preserve the House of the Seven Gables from confiscation. For the last seventy years the most noted event in the Pyncheon annals had been likewise the heaviest calamity that ever befell the race; no less than the violent death—for so it was adjudged—of one member of the family by the criminal act of another. Certain circumstances attending this fatal occurrence had brought the deed irresistibly home to a nephew of the deceased Pyncheon. The young man was tried and convicted of the crime; but either the circumstantial nature of the evidence, and possibly some lurking doubts in the breast of the executive, or, lastly—an argument of greater weight in a republic than it could have been under a monarchy,—the high respectability and political influence of the criminal's connections, had availed to mitigate his doom from death to perpetual imprisonment. This sad affair had chanced about thirty years before the action of our story commences. Latterly, there were rumors (which few believed, and only one or two felt greatly interested in) that this long-buried man was likely, for some reason or other, to be summoned forth from his living tomb.

It is essential to say a few words respecting the victim of this now almost forgotten murder. He was an old bachelor, and possessed of great wealth, in addition to the house and real estate which constituted what remained of the ancient Pyncheon property. Being of an eccentric and melancholy turn of mind, and greatly given to rummaging old records and hearkening to old traditions, he had brought himself, it is averred, to the conclusion that Matthew Maule, the wizard, had been foully wronged out of his homestead, if not out of his life. Such being the case, and he, the old bachelor, in possession of the ill-gotten spoil,—with the black stain of blood sunken deep into it, and still to be scented by conscientious nostrils,—the question occurred, whether it were not imperative upon him, even at this late hour, to make restitution to Maule's posterity. To a man living so much in the past, and so little in the present, as the secluded and antiquarian old bachelor, a century and a half seemed not so vast a period as to obviate the propriety of substituting right for wrong. It was the belief of those who knew him best, that he would positively have taken the very singular step of giving up the House of the Seven Gables to the representative of Matthew Maule, but for the unspeakable tumult which a suspicion of the old gentleman's project awakened among his Pyncheon relatives. Their exertions had the effect of suspending his purpose; but it was feared that he would perform, after death, by the operation of his last will, what he had so hardly been prevented from doing in his proper lifetime. But there is no one thing which men so rarely do, whatever the provocation or inducement, as to bequeath patrimonial property away from their own blood. They may love other individuals far better than their relatives,—they may even cherish dislike, or positive hatred, to the latter; but yet, in view of death, the strong prejudice of propinquity revives, and impels the testator to send down his estate in the line marked out by custom so immemorial that it looks like nature. In all the Pyncheons, this feeling had the energy of disease. It was too powerful for the conscientious scruples of the old bachelor; at whose death, accordingly, the mansion-house, together with most of his other riches, passed into the possession of his next legal representative.

This was a nephew, the cousin of the miserable young man who had been convicted of the uncle's murder. The new heir, up to the period of his accession, was reckoned rather a dissipated youth, but had at once reformed, and made himself an exceedingly respectable member of society. In fact, he showed more of the Pyncheon quality, and had won higher eminence in the world, than any of his race since the time of the original Puritan. Applying himself in earlier manhood to the study of the law, and having a natural tendency towards office, he had attained, many years ago, to a judicial situation in some inferior court, which gave him for life the very desirable and imposing title of judge. Later, he had engaged in politics, and served a part of two terms in Congress, besides making a considerable figure in both branches of the State legislature. Judge Pyncheon was unquestionably an honor to his race. He had built himself a country-seat within a few miles of his native town, and there spent such portions of his time as could be spared from public service in the display of every grace and virtue—as a newspaper phrased it, on the eve of an election—befitting the Christian, the good citizen, the horticulturist, and the gentleman.

There were few of the Pyncheons left to sun themselves in the glow of the Judge's prosperity. In respect to natural increase, the breed had not thriven; it appeared rather to be dying out. The only members of the family known to be extant were, first, the Judge himself, and a single surviving son, who was now travelling in Europe; next, the thirty years' prisoner, already alluded to, and a sister of the latter, who occupied, in an extremely retired manner, the House of the Seven Gables, in which she had a life-estate by the will of the old bachelor. She was understood to be wretchedly poor, and seemed to make it her choice to remain so; inasmuch as her affluent cousin, the Judge, had repeatedly offered her all the comforts of life, either in the old mansion or his own modern residence. The last and youngest Pyncheon was a little country-girl of seventeen, the daughter of another of the Judge's cousins, who had married a young woman of no family or property, and died early and in poor circumstances. His widow had recently taken another husband.

As for Matthew Maule's posterity, it was supposed now to be extinct. For a very long period after the witchcraft delusion, however, the Maules had continued to inhabit the town where their progenitor had suffered so unjust a death. To all appearance, they were a quiet, honest, well-meaning race of people, cherishing no malice against individuals or the public for the wrong which had been done them; or if, at their own fireside, they transmitted from father to child any hostile recollection of the wizard's fate and their lost patrimony, it was never acted upon, nor openly expressed. Nor would it have been singular had they ceased to remember that the House of the Seven Gables was resting its heavy framework on a foundation that was rightfully their own. There is something so massive, stable, and almost irresistibly imposing in the exterior presentment of established rank and great possessions, that their very existence seems to give them a right to exist; at least, so excellent a counterfeit of right, that few poor and humble men have moral force enough to question it, even in their secret minds. Such is the case now, after so many ancient prejudices have been overthrown; and it was far more so in ante-Revolutionary days, when the aristocracy could venture to be proud, and the low were content to be abased. Thus the Maules, at all events, kept their resentments within their own breasts. They were generally poverty-stricken; always plebeian and obscure; working with unsuccessful diligence at handicrafts; laboring on the wharves, or following the sea, as sailors before the mast; living here and there about the town, in hired tenements, and coming finally to the almshouse as the natural home of their old age. At last, after creeping, as it were, for such a length of time along the utmost verge of the opaque puddle of obscurity, they had taken that downright plunge which, sooner or later, is the destiny of all families, whether princely or plebeian. For thirty years past, neither town-record, nor gravestone, nor the directory, nor the knowledge or memory of man, bore any trace of Matthew Maule's descendants. His blood might possibly exist elsewhere; here, where its lowly current could be traced so far back, it had ceased to keep an onward course.

So long as any of the race were to be found, they had been marked out from other men—not strikingly, nor as with a sharp line, but with an effect that was felt rather than spoken of—by an hereditary character of reserve. Their companions, or those who endeavored to become such, grew conscious of a circle round about the Maules, within the sanctity or the spell of which, in spite of an exterior of sufficient frankness and good-fellowship, it was impossible for any man to step. It was this indefinable peculiarity, perhaps, that, by insulating them from human aid, kept them always so unfortunate in life. It certainly operated to prolong in their case, and to confirm to them as their only inheritance, those feelings of repugnance and superstitious terror with which the people of the town, even after awakening from their frenzy, continued to regard the memory of the reputed witches. The mantle, or rather the ragged cloak, of old Matthew Maule had fallen upon his children. They were half believed to inherit mysterious attributes; the family eye was said to possess strange power. Among other good-for-nothing properties and privileges, one was especially assigned them,—that of exercising an influence over people's dreams. The Pyncheons, if all stories were true, haughtily as they bore themselves in the noonday streets of their native town, were no better than bond-servants to these plebeian Maules, on entering the topsy-turvy commonwealth of sleep. Modern psychology, it may be, will endeavor to reduce these alleged necromancies within a system, instead of rejecting them as altogether fabulous.

A descriptive paragraph or two, treating of the seven-gabled mansion in its more recent aspect, will bring this preliminary chapter to a close. The street in which it upreared its venerable peaks has long ceased to be a fashionable quarter of the town; so that, though the old edifice was surrounded by habitations of modern date, they were mostly small, built entirely of wood, and typical of the most plodding uniformity of common life. Doubtless, however, the whole story of human existence may be latent in each of them, but with no picturesqueness, externally, that can attract the imagination or sympathy to seek it there. But as for the old structure of our story, its white-oak frame, and its boards, shingles, and crumbling plaster, and even the huge, clustered chimney in the midst, seemed to constitute only the least and meanest part of its reality. So much of mankind's varied experience had passed there,—so much had been suffered, and something, too, enjoyed,—that the very timbers were oozy, as with the moisture of a heart. It was itself like a great human heart, with a life of its own, and full of rich and sombre reminiscences.

The deep projection of the second story gave the house such a meditative look, that you could not pass it without the idea that it had secrets to keep, and an eventful history to moralize upon. In front, just on the edge of the unpaved sidewalk, grew the Pyncheon Elm, which, in reference to such trees as one usually meets with, might well be termed gigantic. It had been planted by a great-grandson of the first Pyncheon, and, though now four-score years of age, or perhaps nearer a hundred, was still in its strong and broad maturity, throwing its shadow from side to side of the street, overtopping the seven gables, and sweeping the whole black roof with its pendant foliage. It gave beauty to the old edifice, and seemed to make it a part of nature. The street having been widened about forty years ago, the front gable was now precisely on a line

393

with it. On either side extended a ruinous wooden fence of open lattice-work, through which could be seen a grassy yard, and, especially in the angles of the building, an enormous fertility of burdocks, with leaves, it is hardly an exaggeration to say, two or three feet long. Behind the house there appeared to be a garden, which undoubtedly had once been extensive, but was now infringed upon by other enclosures, or shut in by habitations and outbuildings that stood on another street. It would be an omission, trifling, indeed, but unpardonable, were we to forget the green moss that had long since gathered over the projections of the windows, and on the slopes of the roof nor must we fail to direct the reader's eye to a crop, not of weeds, but flower-shrubs, which were growing aloft in the air, not a great way from the chimney, in the nook between two of the gables. They were called Alice's Posies. The tradition was, that a certain Alice Pyncheon had flung up the seeds, in sport, and that the dust of the street and the decay of the roof gradually formed a kind of soil for them, out of which they grew, when Alice had long been in her grave. However the flowers might have come there, it was both sad and sweet to observe how Nature adopted to herself this desolate, decaying, gusty, rusty old house of the Pyncheon family; and how the ever-returning Summer did her best to gladden it with tender beauty, and grew melancholy in the effort.

There is one other feature, very essential to be noticed, but which, we greatly fear, may damage any picturesque and romantic impression which we have been willing to throw over our sketch of this respectable edifice. In the front gable, under the impending brow of the second story, and contiguous to the street, was a shop-door, divided horizontally in the midst, and with a window for its upper segment, such as is often seen in dwellings of a somewhat ancient date. This same shop-door had been a subject of no slight mortification to the present occupant of the august Pyncheon House, as well as to some of her predecessors. The matter is disagreeably delicate to handle; but, since the reader must needs be let into the secret, he will please to understand, that, about a century ago, the head of the Pyncheons found himself involved in serious financial difficulties. The fellow (gentleman, as he styled himself) can hardly have been other than a spurious interloper; for, instead of seeking office from the king or the royal governor, or urging his hereditary claim to Eastern lands, he bethought himself of no better avenue to wealth than by cutting a shop-door through the side of his ancestral residence. It was the custom of the time, indeed, for merchants to store their goods and transact business in their own dwellings. But there was something pitifully small in this old Pyncheon's mode of setting about his commercial operations; it was whispered, that, with his own hands, all beruffled as they were, he used to give change for a shilling, and would turn a half-penny twice over, to make sure that it was a good one. Beyond all question, he had the blood of a petty huckster in his veins, through whatever channel it may have found its way there.

Immediately on his death, the shop-door had been locked, bolted, and barred, and, down to the period of our story, had probably never once been opened. The old counter, shelves, and other fixtures of the little shop remained just as he had left them. It used to be affirmed, that the dead shop-keeper, in a white wig, a faded velvet coat, an apron at his waist, and his ruffles carefully turned back from his wrists, might be seen through the chinks of the shutters, any night of the year, ransacking his till, or poring over the dingy pages of his day-book. From the look of unutterable woe upon his face, it appeared to be his doom to spend eternity in a vain effort to make his accounts balance.

And now—in a very humble way, as will be seen—we proceed to open our narrative.

2

THE LITTLE SHOP-WINDOW

IT STILL LACKED HALF an hour of sunrise, when Miss Hepzibah Pyncheon—we will not say awoke, it being doubtful whether the poor lady had so much as closed her eyes during the brief night of midsummer—but, at all events, arose from her solitary pillow, and began what it would be mockery to term the adornment of her person. Far from us be the indecorum of assisting, even in imagination, at a maiden lady's toilet! Our story must therefore await Miss Hepzibah at the threshold of her chamber; only presuming, meanwhile, to note some of the heavy sighs that labored from her bosom, with little restraint as to their lugubrious depth and volume of sound, inasmuch as they could be audible to nobody save a disembodied listener like ourself. The Old Maid was alone in the old house. Alone, except for a certain respectable and orderly young man, an artist in the daguerreotype line, who, for about three months back, had been a lodger in a remote gable,—quite a house by itself, indeed,—with locks, bolts, and oaken bars on all the intervening doors. Inaudible, consequently, were poor Miss Hepzibah's gusty sighs. Inaudible the creaking joints of her stiffened knees, as she knelt down by the bedside. And inaudible, too, by mortal ear, but heard with all-comprehending love and pity in the farthest heaven, that almost agony of prayer—now whispered, now a groan, now a struggling silence—wherewith she besought the Divine assistance through the day! Evidently, this is to be a day of more than ordinary trial to Miss Hepzibah, who, for above a quarter of a century gone by, has dwelt in strict seclusion, taking no part in the business of life, and just as little in its intercourse and pleasures. Not with such fervor prays the torpid recluse, looking forward to the cold, sunless, stagnant calm of a day that is to be like innumerable yesterdays.

The maiden lady's devotions are concluded. Will she now issue forth over the threshold of our story? Not yet, by many moments. First, every drawer in the tall, old-fashioned bureau is to be opened, with difficulty, and with a succession of spasmodic jerks then, all must close again, with the same fidgety reluctance. There is a rustling of stiff silks; a tread of backward and forward footsteps to and fro across the chamber. We suspect Miss Hepzibah, moreover, of taking a step upward into a chair, in order to give heedful regard to her appearance on all sides, and at full length, in the oval, dingy-framed toilet-glass, that hangs above her table. Truly! well, indeed! who would have thought it! Is all this precious time to be lavished on the matutinal

395

repair and beautifying of an elderly person, who never goes abroad, whom nobody ever visits, and from whom, when she shall have done her utmost, it were the best charity to turn one's eyes another way?

Now she is almost ready. Let us pardon her one other pause; for it is given to the sole sentiment, or, we might better say,—heightened and rendered intense, as it has been, by sorrow and seclusion,—to the strong passion of her life. We heard the turning of a key in a small lock; she has opened a secret drawer of an escritoire, and is probably looking at a certain miniature, done in Malbone's most perfect style, and representing a face worthy of no less delicate a pencil. It was once our good fortune to see this picture. It is a likeness of a young man, in a silken dressing-gown of an old fashion, the soft richness of which is well adapted to the countenance of reverie, with its full, tender lips, and beautiful eyes, that seem to indicate not so much capacity of thought, as gentle and voluptuous emotion. Of the possessor of such features we shall have a right to ask nothing, except that he would take the rude world easily, and make himself happy in it. Can it have been an early lover of Miss Hepzibah? No; she never had a lover—poor thing, how could she?—nor ever knew, by her own experience, what love technically means. And yet, her undying faith and trust, her fresh remembrance, and continual devotedness towards the original of that miniature, have been the only substance for her heart to feed upon.

She seems to have put aside the miniature, and is standing again before the toilet-glass. There are tears to be wiped off. A few more footsteps to and fro; and here, at last,—with another pitiful sigh, like a gust of chill, damp wind out of a long-closed vault, the door of which has accidentally been set, ajar—here comes Miss Hepzibah Pyncheon! Forth she steps into the dusky, time-darkened passage; a tall figure, clad in black silk, with a long and shrunken waist, feeling her way towards the stairs like a near-sighted person, as in truth she is.

The sun, meanwhile, if not already above the horizon, was ascending nearer and nearer to its verge. A few clouds, floating high upward, caught some of the earliest light, and threw down its golden gleam on the windows of all the houses in the street, not forgetting the House of the Seven Gables, which—many such sunrises as it had witnessed—looked cheerfully at the present one. The reflected radiance served to show, pretty distinctly, the aspect and arrangement of the room which Hepzibah entered, after descending the stairs. It was a low-studded room, with a beam across the ceiling, panelled with dark wood, and having a large chimney-piece, set round with pictured tiles, but now closed by an iron fire-board, through which ran the funnel of a modern stove. There was a carpet on the floor, originally of rich texture, but so worn and faded in these latter years that its once brilliant figure had quite vanished into one indistinguishable hue. In the way of furniture, there were two tables: one, constructed with perplexing intricacy and exhibiting as many feet as a centipede; the other, most delicately wrought, with four long and slender legs, so apparently frail that it was almost incredible what a length of time the ancient tea-table had stood upon them. Half a dozen chairs stood about the room, straight and stiff, and so ingeniously contrived for the discomfort of the human person that they were irksome even to sight, and conveyed the ugliest possible idea of the state of society to which they could have been adapted. One exception there was, however, in a very antique elbow-chair, with a high back, carved elaborately in oak, and a roomy depth within its arms, that made up, by its spacious comprehensiveness, for the lack of any of those artistic curves which abound in a modern chair.

As for ornamental articles of furniture, we recollect but two, if such they may be called. One was a map of the Pyncheon territory at the eastward, not engraved, but the handiwork of some skilful old draughtsman, and grotesquely illuminated with pictures of Indians and wild beasts, among which was seen a lion; the natural history of the region being as little known as its geography, which was put down most fantastically awry. The other adornment was the portrait of old Colonel Pyncheon, at two thirds length, representing the stern features of a Puritanic-looking personage, in a skull-cap, with a laced band and a grizzly beard; holding a Bible with one hand, and in the other uplifting an iron sword-hilt. The latter object, being more successfully depicted by the artist, stood out in far greater prominence than the sacred volume. Face to face with this picture, on entering the apartment, Miss Hepzibah Pyncheon came to a pause; regarding it with a singular scowl, a strange contortion of the brow, which, by people who did not know her, would probably have been interpreted as an expression of bitter anger and ill-will. But it was no such thing. She, in fact, felt a reverence for the pictured visage, of which only a far-descended and time-stricken virgin could be susceptible; and this forbidding scowl was the innocent result of her near-sightedness, and an effort so to concentrate her powers of vision as to substitute a firm outline of the object instead of a vague one.

We must linger a moment on this unfortunate expression of poor Hepzibah's brow. Her scowl,—as the world, or such part of it as sometimes caught a transitory glimpse of her at the window, wickedly persisted in calling it,—her scowl had done Miss Hepzibah a very ill office, in establishing her character as an ill-tempered old maid; nor does it appear improbable that, by often gazing at herself in a dim looking-glass, and perpetually encountering her own frown with its ghostly sphere, she had been led to interpret the expression almost as unjustly as the world did. "How miserably cross I look!" she must often have whispered to herself; and ultimately have fancied herself so, by a sense of inevitable doom. But her heart never frowned. It was naturally tender, sensitive, and full of little tremors and palpitations; all of which weaknesses it retained, while her visage was growing so perversely stern, and even fierce. Nor had Hepzibah ever any hardihood, except what came from the very warmest nook in her affections.

All this time, however, we are loitering faintheartedly on the threshold of our story. In very truth, we have an invincible reluctance to disclose what Miss Hepzibah Pyncheon was about to do.

It has already been observed, that, in the basement story of the gable fronting on the street, an unworthy ancestor, nearly a century ago, had fitted up a shop. Ever since the old gentleman retired from trade, and fell asleep under his coffin-lid, not only the shop-door, but the inner arrangements, had been suffered to remain unchanged; while the dust of ages gathered inch-deep over the shelves and counter, and partly filled an old pair of scales, as if it were of value enough to be weighed. It treasured itself up, too, in the half-open till, where there still lingered a base sixpence, worth neither more nor less than the hereditary pride which had here been put to shame. Such had been the state and condition of the little shop in old Hepzibah's childhood, when she and her brother used to play at hide-and-seek in its forsaken precincts. So it had remained, until within a few days past.

But now, though the shop-window was still closely curtained from the public gaze, a remarkable change had taken place in its interior. The rich and heavy festoons of cobweb, which it had cost a long ancestral succession of spiders their life's labor to spin and weave, had been carefully brushed away from the ceiling. The counter, shelves, and floor had all been scoured, and the latter was overstrewn with fresh blue sand. The brown scales, too, had evidently undergone rigid discipline, in an unavailing effort to rub off the rust, which, alas! had eaten through and through their substance. Neither was the little old shop any longer empty of merchantable goods. A curious eye, privileged to take an account of stock and investigate behind the counter, would have discovered a barrel, yea, two or three barrels and half ditto,—one containing flour, another apples, and a third, perhaps, Indian meal. There was likewise a square box of pine-wood, full of soap in bars; also, another of the same size, in which were tallow candles, ten to the pound. A small stock of brown sugar, some white beans and split peas, and a few other commodities of low price, and such as are constantly in demand, made up the bulkier portion of the merchandise. It might have been taken for a ghostly or phantasmagoric reflection of the old shop-keeper Pyncheon's shabbily provided shelves, save that some of the articles were of a description and outward form which could hardly have been known in his day. For instance, there was a glass pickle-jar, filled with fragments of Gibraltar rock; not, indeed, splinters of the veritable stone foundation of the famous fortress, but bits of delectable candy, neatly done up in white paper. Jim Crow, moreover, was seen executing his world-renowned dance, in gingerbread. A party of leaden dragoons were galloping along one of the shelves, in equipments and uniform of modern cut; and there were some sugar figures, with no strong resemblance to the humanity of any epoch, but less unsatisfactorily representing our own fashions than those of a hundred years ago. Another phenomenon, still more strikingly modern, was a package of lucifer matches, which, in old times, would have been thought actually to borrow their instantaneous flame from the nether fires of Tophet.

In short, to bring the matter at once to a point, it was incontrovertibly evident that somebody had taken the shop and fixtures of the long-retired and forgotten Mr. Pyncheon, and was about to renew the enterprise of that departed worthy, with a different set of customers. Who could this bold adventurer be? And, of all places in the world, why had he chosen the House of the Seven Gables as the scene of his commercial speculations?

We return to the elderly maiden. She at length withdrew her eyes from the dark countenance of the Colonel's portrait, heaved a sigh,—indeed, her breast was a very cave of Aolus that morning,—and stept across the room on tiptoe, as is the customary gait of elderly women. Passing through an intervening passage, she opened a door that communicated with the shop, just now so elaborately described. Owing to the projection of the upper story—and still more to the thick shadow of the Pyncheon Elm, which stood almost directly in front of the gable—the twilight, here, was still as much akin to night as morning. Another heavy sigh from Miss Hepzibah! After a moment's pause on the threshold, peering towards the window with her near-sighted scowl, as if frowning down some bitter enemy, she suddenly projected herself into the shop. The haste, and, as it were, the galvanic impulse of the movement, were really quite startling.

Nervously—in a sort of frenzy, we might almost say—she began to busy herself in arranging some children's playthings, and other little wares, on the shelves and at the shop-window. In the aspect of this dark-arrayed, pale-faced, ladylike old figure there was a deeply tragic character that contrasted irreconcilably with the ludicrous pettiness of her employment. It seemed a queer anomaly, that so gaunt and dismal a personage should take a toy in hand; a miracle, that the toy did not vanish in her grasp; a miserably absurd idea, that she should go on perplexing her stiff and sombre intellect with the question how to tempt little boys into her premises! Yet such is undoubtedly her object. Now she places a gingerbread elephant against the window, but with so tremulous a touch that it tumbles upon the floor, with the dismemberment of three legs and its trunk; it has ceased to be an elephant, and has become a few bits of musty gingerbread. There, again, she has upset a tumbler of marbles, all of which roll different ways, and each individual marble, devil-directed, into the most difficult obscurity that it can find. Heaven help our poor old Hepzibah, and forgive us for taking a ludicrous view of her position! As her rigid and rusty frame goes down upon its hands and knees, in quest of the absconding marbles, we positively feel so much the more inclined to shed tears of sympathy, from the very fact that we must needs turn aside and laugh at her. For here,—and if we fail to impress it suitably upon the reader, it is our own fault, not that of the theme, here is one of the truest points of melancholy interest that occur in ordinary life. It was the final throe of what called itself old gentility. A lady—who had fed herself from childhood with the shadowy food of aristocratic reminiscences, and whose religion it was that a lady's hand soils itself irremediably by doing aught for bread,—this born lady, after sixty years of narrowing means, is fain to step down from her pedestal of imaginary rank. Poverty, treading closely at her heels for a lifetime, has come up with her at last. She must earn her own food, or starve! And we have stolen upon Miss Hepzibah Pyncheon, too irreverently, at the instant of time when the patrician lady is to be transformed into the plebeian woman.

In this republican country, amid the fluctuating waves of our social life, somebody is always at the drowning-point. The tragedy is enacted with as continual a repetition as that of a popular drama on a holiday, and, nevertheless, is felt as deeply, perhaps, as when an hereditary noble sinks below his order. More deeply; since, with us, rank is the grosser substance of wealth and a splendid establishment, and has no spiritual existence after the death of these, but dies hopelessly along with them. And, therefore, since we have been unfortunate enough to introduce our heroine at so inauspicious a juncture, we would entreat for a mood of due solemnity in the spectators of her fate. Let us behold, in poor Hepzibah, the immemorial, lady —two hundred years old, on this side of the water, and thrice as many on the other,—with her antique portraits, pedigrees, coats of arms, records and traditions, and her claim, as joint heiress, to that princely territory at the eastward, no longer a wilderness, but a populous fertility,—born, too, in Pyncheon Street, under the Pyncheon Elm, and in the Pyncheon House, where she has spent all her days,—reduced. Now, in that very house, to be the hucksteress of a cent-shop.

This business of setting up a petty shop is almost the only resource of women, in circumstances at all similar to those of our unfortunate recluse. With her near-sightedness, and those tremulous fingers of hers, at once inflexible and delicate, she could not be a seamstress; although her sampler, of fifty years gone by, exhibited some of the most recondite specimens of ornamental needlework. A school for little children had been often in her thoughts; and, at one time, she had begun a review of her early studies in the New England Primer, with a view to prepare herself for the office of instructress. But the love of children had never been quickened in Hepzibah's heart, and was now torpid, if not extinct; she watched the little people of the neighborhood from her chamber-window, and doubted whether she could tolerate a more intimate acquaintance with them. Besides, in our day, the very ABC has become a science greatly too abstruse to be any longer taught by pointing a pin from letter to letter. A modern child could teach old Hepzibah more than old Hepzibah could teach the child. So—with many a cold, deep heart-quake at the idea of at last coming into sordid contact with the world, from which she had so long kept aloof, while every added day of seclusion had rolled another stone against the cavern door of her hermitage—the poor thing bethought herself of the ancient shop-window, the rusty scales, and dusty till. She might have held back a little longer; but another circumstance, not yet hinted at, had somewhat hastened her decision. Her humble preparations, therefore, were duly made, and the enterprise was now to be commenced. Nor was she entitled to complain of any remarkable singularity in her fate; for, in the town of her nativity, we might point to several little shops of a similar description, some of them in houses as ancient as that of the Seven Gables; and one or two, it may be, where a decayed gentlewoman stands behind the counter, as grim an image of family pride as Miss Hepzibah Pyncheon herself.

It was overpoweringly ridiculous,—we must honestly confess it,—the deportment of the maiden lady while setting her shop in order for the public eye. She stole on tiptoe to the window, as cautiously as if she conceived some bloody-minded villain to be watching behind the elm-tree, with intent to take her life. Stretching out her long, lank arm, she put a paper of pearl-buttons, a jew's-harp, or whatever the small article might be, in its destined place, and straightway vanished back into the dusk, as if the world need never hope for another glimpse of her. It might have been fancied, indeed, that she expected to minister to the wants of the community unseen, like a disembodied divinity or enchantress, holding forth her bargains to the reverential and awe-stricken purchaser in an invisible hand. But Hepzibah had no such flattering dream. She was well aware that she must ultimately come forward, and stand revealed in her proper individuality; but, like other sensitive persons, she could not bear to be observed in the gradual process, and chose rather to flash forth on the world's astonished gaze at once.

The inevitable moment was not much longer to be delayed. The sunshine might now be seen stealing down the front of the opposite house, from the windows of which came a reflected gleam, struggling through the boughs of the elm-tree, and enlightening the interior of the shop more distinctly than heretofore. The town appeared to be waking up. A baker's cart had already rattled through the street, chasing away the latest vestige of night's sanctity with the jingle-jangle of its dissonant bells. A milkman was distributing the contents of his cans from door to door; and the harsh peal of a fisherman's conch shell was heard far off, around the corner. None of these tokens escaped Hepzibah's notice. The moment had arrived. To delay longer would be only to lengthen out her misery. Nothing remained, except to take down the bar from the shop-door, leaving the entrance free—more than free—welcome, as if all were household friends—to every passer-by, whose eyes might be attracted by the commodities at the window. This last act Hepzibah now performed, letting the bar fall with what smote upon her excited nerves as a most astounding clatter. Then—as if the only barrier betwixt herself and the world had been thrown down, and a flood of evil consequences would come tumbling through the gap—she fled into the inner parlor, threw herself into the ancestral elbow-chair, and wept.

Our miserable old Hepzibah! It is a heavy annoyance to a writer, who endeavors to represent nature, its various attitudes and circumstances, in a reasonably correct outline and true coloring, that so much of the mean and ludicrous should be hopelessly mixed up with the purest pathos which life anywhere supplies to him. What tragic dignity, for example, can be wrought into a scene like this! How can we elevate our history of retribution for the sin of long ago, when, as one of our most prominent figures, we are compelled to introduce—not a young and lovely woman, nor even the stately remains of beauty, storm-shattered by affliction—but a gaunt, sallow, rusty-jointed maiden, in a long-waisted silk gown, and with the strange horror of a turban on her head! Her visage is not even ugly. It is redeemed from insignificance only by the contraction of her eyebrows into a near-sighted scowl. And, finally, her great life-trial seems to be, that, after sixty years of idleness, she finds it convenient to earn comfortable bread by setting up a shop in a small way. Nevertheless, if we look through all the heroic fortunes of mankind, we shall find this same entanglement of something mean and trivial with whatever is noblest in joy or sorrow. Life is made up of marble and mud. And, without all the deeper trust in a comprehensive sympathy above us, we might hence be led to suspect the insult of a sneer, as well as an immitigable frown, on the iron countenance of fate. What is called poetic insight is the gift of discerning, in this sphere of strangely mingled elements, the beauty and the majesty which are compelled to assume a garb so sordid.

�＊ 3 ＊

THE FIRST CUSTOMER

MISS HEPZIBAH PYNCHEON sat in the oaken elbow-chair, with her hands over her face, giving way to that heavy down-sinking of the heart which most persons have experienced, when the image of hope itself seems ponderously moulded of lead, on the eve of an enterprise at once doubtful and momentous. She was suddenly startled by the tinkling alarum—high, sharp, and irregular—of a little bell. The maiden lady arose upon her feet, as pale as a ghost at cock-crow; for she was an enslaved spirit, and this the talisman to which she owed obedience. This little bell,—to speak in plainer terms,—being fastened over the shop-door, was so contrived as to vibrate by means of a steel spring, and thus convey notice to the inner regions of the house when any customer should cross the threshold. Its ugly and spiteful little din (heard now for the first time, perhaps, since Hepzibah's periwigged predecessor had retired from trade) at once set every nerve of her body in responsive and tumultuous vibration. The crisis was upon her! Her first customer was at the door!

Without giving herself time for a second thought, she rushed into the shop, pale, wild, desperate in gesture and expression, scowling portentously, and looking far better qualified to do fierce battle with a housebreaker than to stand smiling behind the counter, bartering small wares for a copper recompense. Any ordinary customer, indeed, would have turned his back and fled. And yet there was nothing fierce in Hepzibah's poor old heart; nor had she, at the moment, a single bitter thought against the world at large, or one individual man or woman. She wished them all well, but wished, too, that she herself were done with them, and in her quiet grave.

The applicant, by this time, stood within the doorway. Coming freshly, as he did, out of the morning light, he appeared to have brought some of its cheery influences into the shop along with him. It was a slender young man, not more than one or two and twenty years old, with rather a grave and thoughtful expression for his years, but likewise a springy alacrity and vigor. These qualities were not only perceptible, physically, in his make and motions, but made themselves felt almost immediately in his character. A brown beard, not too silken in its texture, fringed his chin, but as yet without completely hiding it; he wore a short mustache, too, and his dark, high-featured countenance looked all the better for these natural ornaments. As for his dress, it was of the simplest kind; a summer sack of cheap and ordinary material, thin checkered pantaloons, and a straw hat, by no means of the finest braid. Oak Hall might have supplied his entire equipment. He was chiefly marked as a gentleman—if such, indeed, he made any claim to be—by the rather remarkable whiteness and nicety of his clean linen.

He met the scowl of old Hepzibah without apparent alarm, as having heretofore encountered it and found it harmless.

"So, my dear Miss Pyncheon," said the daguerreotypist,—for it was that sole other occupant of the seven-gabled mansion,—"I am glad to see that you have not shrunk from your good purpose. I merely look in to offer my best wishes, and to ask if I can assist you any further in your preparations."

People in difficulty and distress, or in any manner at odds with the world, can endure a vast amount of harsh treatment, and perhaps be only the stronger for it; whereas they give way at once before the simplest expression of what they perceive to be genuine sympathy. So it proved with poor Hepzibah; for, when she saw the young man's smile,—looking so much the brighter on a thoughtful face,—and heard his kindly tone, she broke first into a hysteric giggle and then began to sob.

"Ah, Mr. Holgrave," cried she, as soon as she could speak, "I never can go through with it! Never, never, never! I wish I were dead, and in the old family tomb, with all my forefathers! With my father, and my mother, and my sister! Yes, and with my brother, who had far better find me there than here! The world is too chill and hard,—and I am too old, and too feeble, and too hopeless!"

"Oh, believe me, Miss Hepzibah," said the young man quietly, "these feelings will not trouble you any longer, after you are once fairly in the midst of your enterprise. They are unavoidable at this moment, standing, as you do, on the outer verge of your long seclusion, and peopling the world with ugly shapes, which you will soon find to be as unreal as the giants and ogres of a child's story-book. I find nothing so singular in life, as that everything appears to lose its substance the instant one actually grapples with it. So it will be with what you think so terrible."

"But I am a woman!" said Hepzibah piteously. "I was going to say, a lady,—but I consider that as past."

"Well; no matter if it be past!" answered the artist, a strange gleam of half-hidden sarcasm flashing through the kindliness of his manner. "Let it go! You are the better without it. I speak frankly, my dear Miss Pyncheon!—for are we not friends? I look upon this as one of the fortunate days of your life. It ends an epoch and begins one. Hitherto, the life-blood has been gradually chilling in your veins as you sat aloof, within your circle of gentility, while the rest of the world was fighting out its battle with one kind of necessity or another. Henceforth, you will at least have the sense of healthy and natural effort for a purpose, and of lending your strength be it great or small—to the united struggle of mankind. This is success,—all the success that anybody meets with!"

"It is natural enough, Mr. Holgrave, that you should have ideas like these," rejoined Hepzibah, drawing up her gaunt figure with slightly offended dignity. "You are a man, a young man, and brought up, I suppose, as almost everybody is nowadays, with a view to seeking your fortune. But I was born a lady, and have always lived one; no matter in what narrowness of means, always a lady."

"But I was not born a gentleman; neither have I lived like one," said Holgrave, slightly smiling; "so, my dear madam, you will hardly expect me to sympathize with sensibilities of this kind; though, unless I deceive myself, I have some imperfect comprehension of them. These names of gentleman and lady had a meaning, in the past history of the world, and conferred privileges, desirable or otherwise, on those entitled to bear them. In the present—and still more in the future condition of society-they imply, not privilege, but restriction!"

"These are new notions," said the old gentlewoman, shaking her head. "I shall never understand them; neither do I wish it."

"We will cease to speak of them, then," replied the artist, with a friendlier smile than his last one, "and I will leave you to feel whether it is not better to be a true woman than a lady. Do you really think, Miss Hepzibah, that any lady of your family has ever done a more heroic thing, since this house was built, than you are performing in it to-day? Never; and if the Pyncheons had always acted so nobly, I doubt whether an old wizard Maule's anathema, of which you told me once, would have had much weight with Providence against them."

"Ah!—no, no!" said Hepzibah, not displeased at this allusion to the sombre dignity of an inherited curse. "If old Maule's ghost, or a descendant of his, could see me behind the counter to-day, he would call it the fulfillment of his worst wishes. But I thank you for your kindness, Mr. Holgrave, and will do my utmost to be a good shop-keeper."

"Pray do" said Holgrave, "and let me have the pleasure of being your first customer. I am about taking a walk to the seashore, before going to my rooms, where I misuse Heaven's blessed sunshine by tracing out human features through its agency. A few of those biscuits, dipt in sea-water, will be just what I need for breakfast. What is the price of half a dozen?"

"Let me be a lady a moment longer," replied Hepzibah, with a manner of antique stateliness to which a melancholy smile lent a kind of grace. She put the biscuits into his hand, but rejected the compensation. "A Pyncheon must not, at all events under her forefathers' roof, receive money for a morsel of bread from her only friend!"

Holgrave took his departure, leaving her, for the moment, with spirits not quite so much depressed. Soon, however, they had subsided nearly to their former dead level. With a beating heart, she listened to the footsteps of early passengers, which now began to be frequent along the street. Once or twice they seemed to linger; these strangers, or neighbors, as the case might be, were looking at the display of toys and petty commodities in Hepzibah's shop-window. She was doubly tortured; in part, with a sense of overwhelming shame that strange and unloving eyes should have the privilege of gazing, and partly because the idea occurred to her, with ridiculous importunity, that the window was not arranged so skilfully, nor nearly to so much advantage, as it might have been. It seemed as if the whole fortune or failure of her shop might depend on the display of a different set of articles, or substituting a fairer apple for one which appeared to be specked. So she made the change, and straightway fancied that everything was spoiled by it; not recognizing that it was the nervousness of the juncture, and her own native squeamishness as an old maid, that wrought all the seeming mischief.

Anon, there was an encounter, just at the door-step, betwixt two laboring men, as their rough voices denoted them to be. After some slight talk about their own affairs, one of them chanced to notice the shop-window, and directed the other's attention to it.

"See here!" cried he; "what do you think of this? Trade seems to be looking up in Pyncheon Street!"

"Well, well, this is a sight, to be sure!" exclaimed the other. "In the old Pyncheon House, and underneath the Pyncheon Elm! Who would have thought it? Old Maid Pyncheon is setting up a cent-shop!"

"Will she make it go, think you, Dixey?" said his friend. "I don't call it a very good stand. There's another shop just round the corner."

"Make it go!" cried Dixey, with a most contemptuous expression, as if the very idea were impossible to be conceived. "Not a bit of it! Why, her face—I've seen it, for I dug her garden for her one year—her face is enough to frighten the Old Nick himself, if he had ever so great a mind to trade with her. People can't stand it, I tell you! She scowls dreadfully, reason or none, out of pure ugliness of temper."

"Well, that's not so much matter," remarked the other man. "These sour-tempered folks are mostly handy at business, and know pretty well what they are about. But, as you say, I don't think she'll do much. This business of keeping cent-shops is overdone, like all other kinds of trade, handicraft, and bodily labor. I know it, to my cost! My wife kept a cent-shop three months, and lost five dollars on her outlay."

"Poor business!" responded Dixey, in a tone as if he were shaking his head,—"poor business."

For some reason or other, not very easy to analyze, there had hardly been so bitter a pang in all her previous misery about the matter as what thrilled Hepzibah's heart on overhearing the above conversation. The testimony in regard to her scowl was frightfully important; it seemed to hold up her image wholly relieved from the false light of her self-partialities, and so hideous that she dared not look at it. She was absurdly hurt, moreover, by the slight and idle effect that her setting up shop—an event of such breathless interest to herself—appeared to have upon the public, of which these two men were the nearest representatives. A glance; a passing word or two; a coarse laugh; and she was doubtless forgotten before they turned the corner. They cared nothing for her dignity, and just as little for her degradation. Then, also, the augury of ill-success, uttered from the sure wisdom of experience, fell upon her half-dead hope like a clod into a grave. The man's wife had already tried the same experiment, and failed! How could the born lady—the recluse of half a lifetime, utterly unpractised in the world, at sixty years of age, —how could she ever dream of succeeding, when the hard, vulgar, keen, busy, hackneyed New England woman had lost five dollars on her little outlay! Success presented itself as an impossibility, and the hope of it as a wild hallucination.

Some malevolent spirit, doing his utmost to drive Hepzibah mad, unrolled before her imagination a kind of panorama, representing the great thoroughfare of a city all astir with customers. So many and so magnificent shops as there were! Groceries, toy-shops, drygoods stores, with their immense panes of plate-glass, their gorgeous fixtures, their vast and complete assortments of merchandise, in which fortunes had been invested; and those noble mirrors at the farther end of each establishment, doubling all this wealth by a brightly burnished vista of unrealities! On one side of the street this splendid bazaar, with a multitude of perfumed and glossy salesmen, smirking, smiling, bowing, and measuring out the goods. On the other, the dusky old House of the Seven Gables, with the antiquated shop-window under its projecting story, and Hepzibah herself, in a gown of rusty black silk, behind the counter, scowling at the world as it went by! This mighty contrast thrust itself forward as a fair expression of the odds against which she was to begin her struggle for a subsistence. Success? Preposterous! She would never think of it again! The house might just as well be buried in an eternal fog while all other houses had the sunshine on them; for not a foot would ever cross the threshold, nor a hand so much as try the door!

But, at this instant, the shop-bell, right over her head, tinkled as if it were bewitched. The old gentlewoman's heart seemed to be attached to the same steel spring, for it went through a series of sharp jerks, in unison with the sound. The door was thrust open, although no human form was perceptible on the other side of the half-window. Hepzibah, nevertheless, stood at a gaze, with her hands clasped, looking very much as if she had summoned up an evil spirit, and were afraid, yet resolved, to hazard the encounter.

"Heaven help me!" she groaned mentally. "Now is my hour of need!"

The door, which moved with difficulty on its creaking and rusty hinges, being forced quite open, a square and sturdy little urchin became apparent, with cheeks as red as an apple. He was clad rather shabbily (but, as it seemed, more owing to his mother's carelessness than his father's poverty), in a blue apron, very wide and short trousers, shoes somewhat out at the toes, and a chip hat, with the frizzles of his curly hair sticking through its crevices. A book and a small slate, under his arm, indicated that he was on his way to school. He stared at Hepzibah a moment, as an elder customer than himself would have been likely enough to do, not knowing what to make of the tragic attitude and queer scowl wherewith she regarded him.

"Well, child," said she, taking heart at sight of a personage so little formidable,—"well, my child, what did you wish for?"

"That Jim Crow there in the window," answered the urchin, holding out a cent, and pointing to the gingerbread figure that had attracted his notice, as he loitered along to school; "the one that has not a broken foot."

So Hepzibah put forth her lank arm, and, taking the effigy from the shop-window, delivered it to her first customer.

"No matter for the money," said she, giving him a little push towards the door; for her old gentility was contumaciously squeamish at sight of the copper coin, and, besides, it seemed such pitiful meanness to take the child's pocket-money in exchange for a bit of stale gingerbread. "No matter for the cent. You are welcome to Jim Crow."

The child, staring with round eyes at this instance of liberality, wholly unprecedented in his large experience of cent-shops, took the man of gingerbread, and quitted the premises. No sooner had he reached the sidewalk (little cannibal that he was!) than Jim Crow's head was in his mouth. As he had not been careful to shut the door, Hepzibah was at the pains of closing it after him, with a pettish ejaculation or two about the troublesomeness of young people, and particularly of small boys. She had just placed another representative of the renowned Jim Crow at the window, when again the shop-bell tinkled clamorously, and again the door being thrust open, with its characteristic jerk and jar, disclosed the same sturdy little urchin who, precisely two minutes ago, had made his exit. The crumbs and discoloration of the cannibal feast, as yet hardly consummated, were exceedingly visible about his mouth.

"What is it now, child?" asked the maiden lady rather impatiently; "did you come back to shut the door?"

"No," answered the urchin, pointing to the figure that had just been put up; "I want that other Jim Crow."

"Well, here it is for you," said Hepzibah, reaching it down; but recognizing that this pertinacious customer would not quit her on any other terms, so long as she had a gingerbread figure in her shop, she partly drew back her extended hand, "Where is the cent?"

The little boy had the cent ready, but, like a true-born Yankee, would have preferred the better bargain to the worse. Looking somewhat chagrined, he put the coin into Hepzibah's hand, and departed, sending the second Jim Crow in quest of the former one. The new shop-keeper dropped the first solid result of her commercial enterprise into the till. It was done! The sordid stain of that copper coin could never be washed away from her palm. The little schoolboy, aided by the impish figure of the negro dancer, had wrought an irreparable ruin. The structure of ancient aristocracy had been demolished by him, even as if his childish gripe had torn down the seven-gabled mansion. Now let Hepzibah turn the old Pyncheon portraits with their faces to the wall, and take the map of her Eastern territory to kindle the kitchen fire, and blow up the flame with the empty breath of her ancestral traditions! What had she to do with ancestry? Nothing; no more than with posterity! No lady, now, but simply Hepzibah Pyncheon, a forlorn old maid, and keeper of a cent-shop!

Nevertheless, even while she paraded these ideas somewhat ostentatiously through her mind, it is altogether surprising what a calmness had come over her. The anxiety and misgivings which had tormented her, whether asleep or in melancholy day-dreams, ever since her project began to take an aspect of solidity, had now vanished quite away. She felt the novelty of her position, indeed, but no longer with disturbance or affright. Now and then, there came a thrill of almost youthful enjoyment. It was the invigorating breath of a fresh outward atmosphere, after the long torpor and monotonous seclusion of her life. So wholesome is effort! So miraculous the strength that we do not know of! The healthiest glow that Hepzibah had known for years had come now in the dreaded crisis, when, for the first time, she had put forth her hand to help herself. The little circlet of the schoolboy's copper coin—dim and lustreless though it was, with the small services which it had been doing here and there about the world —had proved a talisman, fragrant with good, and deserving to be set in gold and worn next her heart. It was as potent, and perhaps endowed with the same kind of efficacy, as a galvanic ring! Hepzibah, at all events, was indebted to its subtile operation both in body and spirit; so much the more, as it inspired her with energy to get some breakfast, at which, still the better to keep up her courage, she allowed herself an extra spoonful in her infusion of black tea.

Her introductory day of shop-keeping did not run on, however, without many and serious interruptions of this mood of cheerful vigor. As a general rule, Providence seldom vouchsafes to mortals any more than just that degree of encouragement which suffices to keep them at a reasonably full exertion of their powers. In the case of our old gentlewoman, after the excitement of new effort had subsided, the despondency of her whole life threatened, ever and anon, to return. It was like the heavy mass of clouds which we may often see obscuring the sky, and making a gray twilight everywhere, until, towards nightfall, it yields temporarily to a glimpse of sunshine. But, always, the envious cloud strives to gather again across the streak of celestial azure.

Customers came in, as the forenoon advanced, but rather slowly; in some cases, too, it must be owned, with little satisfaction either to themselves or Miss Hepzibah; nor, on the whole, with an aggregate of very rich emolument to the till. A little girl, sent by her mother to match a skein of cotton thread, of a peculiar hue, took one that the near-sighted old lady pronounced extremely like, but soon came running back, with a blunt and cross message, that it would not do, and, besides, was very rotten! Then, there was a pale, care-wrinkled woman, not old but haggard, and already with streaks of gray among her hair, like silver ribbons; one of those women, naturally delicate, whom you at once recognize as worn to death by a brute—probably a drunken brute—of a husband, and at least nine children. She wanted a few pounds of flour, and offered the money, which the decayed gentlewoman silently rejected, and gave the poor soul better measure than if she had taken it. Shortly afterwards, a man in a blue cotton frock, much soiled, came in and bought a pipe, filling the whole shop, meanwhile, with the hot odor of strong drink, not only exhaled in the torrid atmosphere of his breath, but oozing out of his entire system, like an inflammable gas. It was impressed on Hepzibah's mind that this was the husband of the care-wrinkled woman. He asked for a paper of tobacco; and as she had neglected to provide herself with the article, her brutal customer dashed down his newly-bought pipe and left the shop, muttering some unintelligible words, which had the tone and bitterness of a curse. Hereupon Hepzibah threw up her eyes, unintentionally scowling in the face of Providence!

No less than five persons, during the forenoon, inquired for ginger-beer, or root-beer, or any drink of a similar brewage, and, obtaining nothing of the kind, went off in an exceedingly bad humor. Three of them left the door open, and the other two pulled it so spitefully in going out that the little bell played the very deuce with Hepzibah's nerves. A round, bustling, fire-ruddy housewife of the neighborhood burst breathless into the shop, fiercely demanding yeast; and when the poor gentlewoman, with her cold shyness of manner, gave her hot customer to understand that she did not keep the article, this very capable housewife took upon herself to administer a regular rebuke.

"A cent-shop, and no yeast!" quoth she; "That will never do! Who ever heard of such a thing? Your loaf will never rise, no more than mine will to-day. You had better shut up shop at once."

"Well," said Hepzibah, heaving a deep sigh, "perhaps I had!"

Several times, moreover, besides the above instance, her lady-like sensibilities were seriously infringed upon by the familiar, if not rude, tone with which people addressed her. They evidently considered themselves not merely her equals, but her patrons and superiors. Now, Hepzibah had unconsciously flattered herself with the idea that there would be a gleam or halo, of some kind or other, about her person, which would insure an obeisance to her sterling gentility, or, at least, a tacit recognition of it. On the other hand, nothing tortured her more intolerably than when this recognition was too prominently expressed. To one or two rather officious offers of sympathy, her responses were little short of acrimonious; and, we regret to say, Hepzibah was thrown into a positively unchristian state of mind by the suspicion that one of her customers was drawn to the shop, not by any real need of the article which she pretended to seek, but by a wicked wish to stare at her. The vulgar creature was determined to see for herself what sort of a figure a mildewed piece of aristocracy, after wasting all the bloom and much of the decline of her life apart from the world, would cut behind a counter. In this particular case, however mechanical and innocuous it might be at other times, Hepzibah's contortion of brow served her in good stead.

"I never was so frightened in my life!" said the curious customer, in describing the incident to one of her acquaintances. "She's a real old vixen, take my word of it! She says little, to be sure; but if you could only see the mischief in her eye!"

On the whole, therefore, her new experience led our decayed gentlewoman to very disagreeable conclusions as to the temper and manners of what she termed the lower classes, whom heretofore she had looked down upon with a gentle and pitying complaisance, as herself occupying a sphere of unquestionable superiority. But, unfortunately, she had likewise to struggle against a bitter emotion of a directly opposite kind: a sentiment of virulence, we mean, towards the idle aristocracy to which it had so recently been her pride to belong. When a lady, in a delicate and costly summer garb, with a floating veil and gracefully swaying gown, and, altogether, an ethereal lightness that made you look at her beautifully slippered feet, to see whether she trod on the dust or floated in the air,—when such a vision happened to pass through this retired street, leaving it tenderly and delusively fragrant with her passage, as if a bouquet of tea-roses had been borne along,—then again, it is to be feared, old Hepzibah's scowl could no longer vindicate itself entirely on the plea of near-sightedness.

"For what end," thought she, giving vent to that feeling of hostility which is the only real abasement of the poor in presence of the rich,—"for what good end, in the wisdom of Providence, does that woman live? Must the whole world toil, that the palms of her hands may be kept white and delicate?"

Then, ashamed and penitent, she hid her face.

"May God forgive me!" said she.

Doubtless, God did forgive her. But, taking the inward and outward history of the first half-day into consideration, Hepzibah began to fear that the shop would prove her ruin in a moral and religious point of view, without contributing very essentially towards even her temporal welfare.

❧ 4 ❧

A DAY BEHIND THE COUNTER

TOWARDS NOON, Hepzibah saw an elderly gentleman, large and portly, and of remarkably dignified demeanor, passing slowly along on the opposite side of the white and dusty street. On coming within the shadow of the Pyncheon Elm, he stopt, and (taking off his hat, meanwhile, to wipe the perspiration from his brow) seemed to scrutinize, with especial interest, the dilapidated and rusty-visaged House of the Seven Gables. He himself, in a very different style, was as well worth looking at as the house. No better model need be sought, nor could have been found, of a very high order of respectability, which, by some indescribable magic, not merely expressed itself in his looks and gestures, but even governed the fashion of his garments, and rendered them all proper and essential to the man. Without appearing to differ, in any tangible way, from other people's clothes, there was yet a wide and rich gravity about them that must have been a characteristic of the wearer, since it could not be defined as pertaining either to the cut or material. His gold-headed cane, too,—a serviceable staff, of dark polished wood,—had similar traits, and, had it chosen to take a walk by itself, would have been recognized anywhere as a tolerably adequate representative of its master. This character— which showed itself so strikingly in everything about him, and the effect of which we seek to convey to the reader—went no deeper than his station, habits of life, and external circumstances. One perceived him to be a personage of marked influence and authority; and, especially, you could feel just as certain that he was opulent as if he had exhibited his bank account, or as if you had seen him touching the twigs of the Pyncheon Elm, and, Midas-like, transmuting them to gold.

In his youth, he had probably been considered a handsome man; at his present age, his brow was too heavy, his temples too bare, his remaining hair too gray, his eye too cold, his lips too closely compressed, to bear any relation to mere personal beauty. He would have made a good and massive portrait; better now, perhaps, than at any previous period of his life, although his look might grow positively harsh in the process of being fixed upon the canvas. The artist would have found it desirable to study his face, and prove its capacity for varied expression; to darken it with a frown,—to kindle it up with a smile.

While the elderly gentleman stood looking at the Pyncheon House, both the frown and the smile passed successively over his countenance. His eye rested on the shop-window, and putting up a pair of gold-bowed spectacles, which he held in his hand, he minutely surveyed Hepzibah's little arrangement of toys and commodities. At first it seemed not to please him,— nay, to cause him exceeding displeasure,—and yet, the very next moment, he smiled. While the latter expression was yet on his lips, he caught a glimpse of Hepzibah, who had involuntarily bent forward to the window; and then the smile changed from acrid and disagreeable to the sunniest complacency and benevolence. He bowed, with a happy mixture of dignity and courteous kindliness, and pursued his way.

"There he is!" said Hepzibah to herself, gulping down a very bitter emotion, and, since she could not rid herself of it, trying to drive it back into her heart. "What does he think of it, I wonder? Does it please him? Ah! he is looking back!"

The gentleman had paused in the street, and turned himself half about, still with his eyes fixed on the shop-window. In fact, he wheeled wholly round, and commenced a step or two, as if designing to enter the shop; but, as it chanced, his purpose was anticipated by Hepzibah's first customer, the little cannibal of Jim Crow, who, staring up at the window, was irresistibly attracted by an elephant of gingerbread. What a grand appetite had this small urchin!—Two Jim Crows immediately after breakfast!—and now an elephant, as a preliminary whet before dinner. By the time this latter purchase was completed, the elderly gentleman had resumed his way, and turned the street corner.

"Take it as you like, Cousin Jaffrey," muttered the maiden lady, as she drew back, after cautiously thrusting out her head, and looking up and down the street,—"Take it as you like! You have seen my little shop-window. Well!—what have you to say?—is not the Pyncheon House my own, while I'm alive?"

After this incident, Hepzibah retreated to the back parlor, where she at first caught up a half-finished stocking, and began knitting at it with nervous and irregular jerks; but quickly finding herself at odds with the stitches, she threw it aside, and walked hurriedly about the room. At length she paused before the portrait of the stern old Puritan, her ancestor, and the founder of the house. In one sense, this picture had almost faded into the canvas, and hidden itself behind the duskiness of age; in another, she could not but fancy that it had been growing more prominent and strikingly expressive, ever since her earliest familiarity with it as a child. For, while the physical outline and substance were darkening away from the beholder's eye, the bold, hard, and, at the same time, indirect character of the man seemed to be brought out in a kind of spiritual relief. Such an effect may occasionally be observed in pictures of antique date. They acquire a look which an artist (if he have anything like the complacency of artists nowadays) would never dream of presenting to a patron as his own characteristic expression, but which, nevertheless, we at once recognize as reflecting the unlovely truth of a human soul. In such cases, the painter's deep conception of his subject's inward traits has wrought itself into the essence of the picture, and is seen after the superficial coloring has been rubbed off by time.

While gazing at the portrait, Hepzibah trembled under its eye. Her hereditary reverence made her afraid to judge the character of the original so harshly as a perception of the truth compelled her to do. But still she gazed, because the face of the picture enabled her—at least, she fancied so—to read more accurately, and to a greater depth, the face which she had just seen in the street.

"This is the very man!" murmured she to herself. "Let Jaffrey Pyncheon smile as he will, there is that look beneath! Put on him a skull-cap, and a band, and a black cloak, and a Bible in one hand and a sword in the other,—then let Jaffrey smile as he might,—nobody would doubt that it was the old Pyncheon come again. He has proved himself the very man to build up a new house! Perhaps, too, to draw down a new curse!"

Thus did Hepzibah bewilder herself with these fantasies of the old time. She had dwelt too much alone,—too long in the Pyncheon House,—until her very brain was impregnated with the dry-rot of its timbers. She needed a walk along the noonday street to keep her sane.

By the spell of contrast, another portrait rose up before her, painted with more daring flattery than any artist would have ventured upon, but yet so delicately touched that the likeness remained perfect. Malbone's miniature, though from the same original, was far inferior to Hepzibah's air-drawn picture, at which affection and sorrowful remembrance wrought together. Soft, mildly, and cheerfully contemplative, with full, red lips, just on the verge of a smile, which the eyes seemed to herald by a gentle kindling-up of their orbs! Feminine traits, moulded inseparably with those of the other sex! The miniature, likewise, had this last peculiarity; so that you inevitably thought of the original as resembling his mother, and she a lovely and lovable woman, with perhaps some beautiful infirmity of character, that made it all the pleasanter to know and easier to love her.

"Yes," thought Hepzibah, with grief of which it was only the more tolerable portion that welled up from her heart to her eyelids, "they persecuted his mother in him! He never was a Pyncheon!"

But here the shop-bell rang; it was like a sound from a remote distance,—so far had Hepzibah descended into the sepulchral depths of her reminiscences. On entering the shop, she found an old man there, a humble resident of Pyncheon Street, and whom, for a great many years past, she had suffered to be a kind of familiar of the house. He was an immemorial personage, who seemed always to have had a white head and wrinkles, and never to have possessed but a single tooth, and that a half-decayed one, in the front of the upper jaw. Well advanced as Hepzibah was, she could not remember when Uncle Venner, as the neighborhood called him, had not gone up and down the street, stooping a little and drawing his feet heavily over the gravel or pavement. But still there was something tough and vigorous about him, that not only kept him in daily breath, but enabled him to fill a place which would else have been vacant in the apparently crowded world. To go of errands with his slow and shuffling gait, which made you doubt how he ever was to arrive anywhere; to saw a small household's foot or two of firewood, or knock to pieces an old barrel, or split up a pine board for kindling-stuff; in summer, to dig the few yards of garden ground appertaining to a low-rented tenement, and share the produce of his labor at the halves; in winter, to shovel away the snow from the sidewalk, or open paths to the woodshed, or along the clothes-line; such were some of the essential offices which Uncle Venner performed among at least a score of families. Within that circle, he claimed the same sort of privilege, and probably felt as much warmth of interest, as a clergyman does in the range of his parishioners. Not that he laid claim to the tithe pig; but, as an analogous mode of reverence, he went his rounds, every morning, to gather up the crumbs of the table and overflowings of the dinner-pot, as food for a pig of his own.

In his younger days—for, after all, there was a dim tradition that he had been, not young, but younger—Uncle Venner was commonly regarded as rather deficient, than otherwise, in his wits. In truth he had virtually pleaded guilty to the charge, by scarcely aiming at such success as other men seek, and by taking only that humble and modest part in the intercourse of life which belongs to the alleged deficiency. But now, in his extreme old age,—whether it were that his long and hard experience had actually brightened him, or that his decaying judgment rendered him less capable of fairly measuring himself,—the venerable man made pretensions to no little wisdom, and really enjoyed the credit of it. There was likewise, at times, a vein of something like poetry in him; it was the moss or wall-flower of his mind in its small dilapidation, and gave a charm to what might have been vulgar and commonplace in his earlier and middle life. Hepzibah had a regard for him, because his name was ancient in the town and had formerly been respectable. It was a still better reason for awarding him a species of familiar reverence that Uncle Venner was himself the most ancient existence, whether of man or thing, in Pyncheon Street, except the House of the Seven Gables, and perhaps the elm that overshadowed it.

This patriarch now presented himself before Hepzibah, clad in an old blue coat, which had a fashionable air, and must have accrued to him from the cast-off wardrobe of some dashing clerk. As for his trousers, they were of tow-cloth, very short in the legs, and bagging down strangely in the rear, but yet having a suitableness to his figure which his other garment entirely lacked. His hat had relation to no other part of his dress, and but very little to the head that wore it. Thus Uncle Venner was a miscellaneous old gentleman, partly himself, but, in good measure, somebody else; patched together, too, of different epochs; an epitome of times and fashions.

"So, you have really begun trade," said he,—"really begun trade! Well, I'm glad to see it. Young people should never live idle in the world, nor old ones neither, unless when the rheumatize gets hold of them. It has given me warning already; and in two or three years longer, I shall think of putting aside business and retiring to my farm. That's yonder,—the great brick house, you know,—the workhouse, most folks call it; but I mean to do my work first, and go there to be idle and enjoy myself. And I'm glad to see you beginning to do your work, Miss Hepzibah!"

"Thank you, Uncle Venner" said Hepzibah, smiling; for she always felt kindly towards the simple and talkative old man. Had he been an old woman, she might probably have repelled the freedom, which she now took in good part. "It is time for me to begin work, indeed! Or, to speak the truth, I have just begun when I ought to be giving it up."

"Oh, never say that, Miss Hepzibah!" answered the old man. "You are a young woman yet. Why, I hardly thought myself younger than I am now, it seems so little while ago since I used to see you playing about the door of the old house, quite a small child! Oftener, though, you used to be sitting at the threshold, and looking gravely into the street; for you had always a grave kind of way with you,—a grown-up air, when you were only the height of my knee. It seems as if I saw you now; and your grandfather with his red cloak, and his white wig, and his cocked hat, and his cane, coming out of the house, and stepping so grandly up the street! Those old gentlemen that grew up before the Revolution used to put on grand airs. In my young days, the great man of the town was commonly called King; and his wife, not Queen to be sure, but Lady. Nowadays, a man would not dare to be called King; and if he feels himself a little above common folks, he only stoops so much the lower to them. I met your cousin, the Judge, ten minutes ago; and, in my old tow-cloth trousers, as you see, the Judge raised his hat to me, I do believe! At any rate, the Judge bowed and smiled!"

"Yes," said Hepzibah, with something bitter stealing unawares into her tone; "my cousin Jaffrey is thought to have a very pleasant smile!"

"And so he has" replied Uncle Venner. "And that's rather remarkable in a Pyncheon; for, begging your pardon, Miss Hepzibah, they never had the name of being an easy and agreeable set of folks. There was no getting close to them. But Now, Miss Hepzibah, if an old man may be bold to ask, why don't Judge Pyncheon, with his great means, step forward, and tell his cousin to shut up her little shop at once? It's for your credit to be doing something, but it's not for the Judge's credit to let you!"

"We won't talk of this, if you please, Uncle Venner," said Hepzibah coldly. "I ought to say, however, that, if I choose to earn bread for myself, it is not Judge Pyncheon's fault. Neither will he deserve the blame," added she more kindly, remembering Uncle Venner's privileges of age and humble familiarity, "if I should, by and by, find it convenient to retire with you to your farm."

"And it's no bad place, either, that farm of mine!" cried the old man cheerily, as if there were something positively delightful in the prospect. "No bad place is the great brick farm-house, especially for them that will find a good many old cronies there, as will be my case. I quite long to be among them, sometimes, of the winter evenings; for it is but dull business for a lonesome elderly man, like me, to be nodding, by the hour together, with no company but his air-tight stove. Summer or winter, there's a great deal to be said in favor of my farm! And, take it in the autumn, what can be pleasanter than to spend a whole day on the sunny side of a barn or a wood-pile, chatting with somebody as old as one's self; or, perhaps, idling away the time with a natural-born simpleton, who knows how to be idle, because even our busy Yankees never have found out how to put him to any use? Upon my word, Miss Hepzibah, I doubt whether I've ever been so comfortable as I mean to be at my farm, which most folks call the workhouse. But you,—you're a young woman yet,—you never need go there! Something still better will turn up for you. I'm sure of it!"

Hepzibah fancied that there was something peculiar in her venerable friend's look and tone; insomuch, that she gazed into his face with considerable earnestness, endeavoring to discover what secret meaning, if any, might be lurking there. Individuals whose affairs have reached an utterly desperate crisis almost invariably keep themselves alive with hopes, so much the more airily magnificent as they have the less of solid matter within their grasp whereof to mould any judicious and moderate expectation of good. Thus, all the while Hepzibah was perfecting the scheme of her little shop, she had cherished an unacknowledged idea that some harlequin trick of fortune would intervene in her favor. For example, an uncle—who had sailed for India fifty years before, and never been heard of since—might yet return, and adopt her to be the comfort of his very extreme and decrepit age, and adorn her with pearls, diamonds, and Oriental shawls and turbans, and make her the ultimate heiress of his unreckonable riches. Or the member of Parliament, now at the head of the English branch of the family,—with which the elder stock, on this side of the Atlantic, had held little or no intercourse for the last two centuries,—this eminent gentleman might invite Hepzibah to quit the ruinous House of the Seven Gables, and come over to dwell with her kindred at Pyncheon Hall. But, for reasons the most imperative, she could not yield to his request. It was more probable, therefore, that the descendants of a Pyncheon who had emigrated to Virginia, in some past generation, and became a great planter there,—hearing of Hepzibah's destitution, and impelled by the splendid generosity of character with which their Virginian mixture must have enriched the New England blood,—would send her a remittance of a thousand dollars, with a hint of repeating the favor annually. Or,—and, surely, anything so undeniably just could not be beyond the limits of reasonable anticipation,—the great claim to the heritage of Waldo County might finally be decided in favor of the Pyncheons; so that, instead of keeping a cent-shop, Hepzibah would build a palace, and look down from its highest tower on hill, dale, forest, field, and town, as her own share of the ancestral territory.

These were some of the fantasies which she had long dreamed about; and, aided by these, Uncle Venner's casual attempt at encouragement kindled a strange festal glory in the poor, bare, melancholy chambers of her brain, as if that inner world were suddenly lighted up with gas. But either he knew nothing of her castles in the air,—as how should he?—or else her earnest scowl disturbed his recollection, as it might a more courageous man's. Instead of pursuing any weightier topic, Uncle Venner was pleased to favor Hepzibah with some sage counsel in her shop-keeping capacity.

"Give no credit!"—these were some of his golden maxims,—"Never take paper-money.

Look well to your change! Ring the silver on the four-pound weight! Shove back all English half-pence and base copper tokens, such as are very plenty about town! At your leisure hours, knit children's woollen socks and mittens! Brew your own yeast, and make your own ginger-beer!"

And while Hepzibah was doing her utmost to digest the hard little pellets of his already uttered wisdom, he gave vent to his final, and what he declared to be his all-important advice, as follows:—

"Put on a bright face for your customers, and smile pleasantly as you hand them what they ask for! A stale article, if you dip it in a good, warm, sunny smile, will go off better than a fresh one that you've scowled upon."

To this last apothegm poor Hepzibah responded with a sigh so deep and heavy that it almost rustled Uncle Venner quite away, like a withered leaf,—as he was,—before an autumnal gale. Recovering himself, however, he bent forward, and, with a good deal of feeling in his ancient visage, beckoned her nearer to him.

"When do you expect him home?" whispered he.

"Whom do you mean?" asked Hepzibah, turning pale.

"Ah!—You don't love to talk about it," said Uncle Venner. "Well, well! we'll say no more, though there's word of it all over town. I remember him, Miss Hepzibah, before he could run alone!"

During the remainder of the day, poor Hepzibah acquitted herself even less creditably, as a shop-keeper, than in her earlier efforts. She appeared to be walking in a dream; or, more truly, the vivid life and reality assumed by her emotions made all outward occurrences unsubstantial, like the teasing phantasms of a half-conscious slumber. She still responded, mechanically, to the frequent summons of the shop-bell, and, at the demand of her customers, went prying with vague eyes about the shop, proffering them one article after another, and thrusting aside—perversely, as most of them supposed—the identical thing they asked for. There is sad confusion, indeed, when the spirit thus flits away into the past, or into the more awful future, or, in any manner, steps across the spaceless boundary betwixt its own region and the actual world; where the body remains to guide itself as best it may, with little more than the mechanism of animal life. It is like death, without death's quiet privilege,—its freedom from mortal care. Worst of all, when the actual duties are comprised in such petty details as now vexed the brooding soul of the old gentlewoman. As the animosity of fate would have it, there was a great influx of custom in the course of the afternoon. Hepzibah blundered to and fro about her small place of business, committing the most unheard-of errors: now stringing up twelve, and now seven, tallow-candles, instead of ten to the pound; selling ginger for Scotch snuff, pins for needles, and needles for pins; misreckoning her change, sometimes to the public detriment, and much oftener to her own; and thus she went on, doing her utmost to bring chaos back again, until, at the close of the day's labor, to her inexplicable astonishment, she found the money-drawer almost destitute of coin. After all her painful traffic, the whole proceeds were perhaps half a dozen coppers, and a questionable ninepence which ultimately proved to be copper likewise.

At this price, or at whatever price, she rejoiced that the day had reached its end. Never before had she had such a sense of the intolerable length of time that creeps between dawn and sunset, and of the miserable irksomeness of having aught to do, and of the better wisdom that it would be to lie down at once, in sullen resignation, and let life, and its toils and vexations, trample over one's prostrate body as they may! Hepzibah's final operation was with the little devourer of Jim Crow and the elephant, who now proposed to eat a camel. In her bewilderment, she offered him first a wooden dragoon, and next a handful of marbles; neither of which being adapted to his else omnivorous appetite, she hastily held out her whole remaining stock of natural history in gingerbread, and huddled the small customer out of the shop. She then muffled the bell in an unfinished stocking, and put up the oaken bar across the door.

During the latter process, an omnibus came to a stand-still under the branches of the elm-tree. Hepzibah's heart was in her mouth. Remote and dusky, and with no sunshine on all the intervening space, was that region of the Past whence her only guest might be expected to arrive! Was she to meet him now?

Somebody, at all events, was passing from the farthest interior of the omnibus towards its entrance. A gentleman alighted; but it was only to offer his hand to a young girl whose slender figure, nowise needing such assistance, now lightly descended the steps, and made an airy little jump from the final one to the sidewalk. She rewarded her cavalier with a smile, the cheery glow of which was seen reflected on his own face as he reentered the vehicle. The girl then turned towards the House of the Seven Gables, to the door of which, meanwhile,—not the shop-door, but the antique portal,—the omnibus-man had carried a light trunk and a bandbox. First giving a sharp rap of the old iron knocker, he left his passenger and her luggage at the door-step, and departed.

"Who can it be?" thought Hepzibah, who had been screwing her visual organs into the acutest focus of which they were capable. "The girl must have mistaken the house." She stole softly into the hall, and, herself invisible, gazed through the dusty side-lights of the portal at the young, blooming, and very cheerful face which presented itself for admittance into the gloomy old mansion. It was a face to which almost any door would have opened of its own accord.

The young girl, so fresh, so unconventional, and yet so orderly and obedient to common rules, as you at once recognized her to be, was widely in contrast, at that moment, with everything about her. The sordid and ugly luxuriance of gigantic weeds that grew in the angle of the house, and the heavy projection that overshadowed her, and the time-worn framework of the door,—none of these things belonged to her sphere. But, even as a ray of sunshine, fall into what dismal place it may, instantaneously creates for itself a propriety in being there, so did it seem altogether fit that the girl should be standing at the threshold. It was no less evidently proper that the door should swing open to admit her. The maiden lady herself, sternly inhospitable in her first purposes, soon began to feel that the door ought to be shoved back, and the rusty key be turned in the reluctant lock.

"Can it be Phoebe?" questioned she within herself. "It must be little Phoebe; for it can be nobody else,—and there is a look of her father about her, too! But what does she want here? And how like a country cousin, to come down upon a poor body in this way, without so much as a day's notice, or asking whether she would be welcome! Well; she must have a night's lodging, I suppose; and to-morrow the child shall go back to her mother."

Phoebe, it must be understood, was that one little offshoot of the Pyncheon race to whom we have already referred, as a native of a rural part of New England, where the old fashions and feelings of relationship are still partially kept up. In her own circle, it was regarded as by no means improper for kinsfolk to visit one another without invitation, or preliminary and ceremonious warning. Yet, in consideration of Miss Hepzibah's recluse way of life, a letter had actually been written and despatched, conveying information of Phoebe's projected visit. This epistle, for three or four days past, had been in the pocket of the penny-postman, who, happening to have no other business in Pyncheon Street, had not yet made it convenient to call at the House of the Seven Gables.

"No—she can stay only one night," said Hepzibah, unbolting the door. "If Clifford were to find her here, it might disturb him!"

5

MAY AND NOVEMBER

PHOEBE PYNCHEON SLEPT, on the night of her arrival, in a chamber that looked down on the garden of the old house. It fronted towards the east, so that at a very seasonable hour a glow of crimson light came flooding through the window, and bathed the dingy ceiling and paper-hangings in its own hue. There were curtains to Phoebe's bed; a dark, antique canopy, and ponderous festoons of a stuff which had been rich, and even magnificent, in its time; but which now brooded over the girl like a cloud, making a night in that one corner, while elsewhere it was beginning to be day. The morning light, however, soon stole into the aperture at the foot of the bed, betwixt those faded curtains. Finding the new guest there,—with a bloom on her cheeks like the morning's own, and a gentle stir of departing slumber in her limbs, as when an early breeze moves the foliage,—the dawn kissed her brow. It was the caress which a dewy maiden—such as the Dawn is, immortally—gives to her sleeping sister, partly from the impulse of irresistible fondness, and partly as a pretty hint that it is time now to unclose her eyes.

At the touch of those lips of light, Phoebe quietly awoke, and, for a moment, did not recognize where she was, nor how those heavy curtains chanced to be festooned around her. Nothing, indeed, was absolutely plain to her, except that it was now early morning, and that, whatever might happen next, it was proper, first of all, to get up and say her prayers. She was the more inclined to devotion from the grim aspect of the chamber and its furniture, especially the tall, stiff chairs; one of which stood close by her bedside, and looked as if some old-fashioned personage had been sitting there all night, and had vanished only just in season to escape discovery.

When Phoebe was quite dressed, she peeped out of the window, and saw a rosebush in the garden. Being a very tall one, and of luxuriant growth, it had been propped up against the side of the house, and was literally covered with a rare and very beautiful species of white rose. A large portion of them, as the girl afterwards discovered, had blight or mildew at their hearts; but, viewed at a fair distance, the whole rosebush looked as if it had been brought from Eden that very summer, together with the mould in which it grew. The truth was, nevertheless, that it had been planted by Alice Pyncheon,—she was Phoebe's great-great-grand-aunt,—in soil which, reckoning only its cultivation as a garden-plat, was now unctuous with nearly two hundred years of vegetable decay. Growing as they did, however, out of the old earth, the flowers still sent a fresh and sweet incense up to their Creator; nor could it have been the less pure and acceptable because Phoebe's young breath mingled with it, as the fragrance floated past the window. Hastening down the creaking and carpetless staircase, she found her way into the garden, gathered some of the most perfect of the roses, and brought them to her chamber.

Little Phoebe was one of those persons who possess, as their exclusive patrimony, the gift of practical arrangement. It is a kind of natural magic that enables these favored ones to bring out the hidden capabilities of things around them; and particularly to give a look of comfort and habitableness to any place which, for however brief a period, may happen to be their home. A wild hut of underbrush, tossed together by wayfarers through the primitive forest, would acquire the home aspect by one night's lodging of such a woman, and would retain it long after her quiet figure had disappeared into the surrounding shade. No less a portion of such homely witchcraft was requisite to reclaim, as it were, Phoebe's waste, cheerless, and dusky chamber, which had been untenanted so long—except by spiders, and mice, and rats, and ghosts—that it was all overgrown with the desolation which watches to obliterate every trace of man's happier hours. What was precisely Phoebe's process we find it impossible to say. She appeared to have no preliminary design, but gave a touch here and another there; brought some articles of furniture to light and dragged others into the shadow; looped up or let down a window-curtain; and, in the course of half an hour, had fully succeeded in throwing a kindly and hospitable smile over the apartment. No longer ago than the night before, it had resembled nothing so much as the old maid's heart; for there was neither sunshine nor household fire in one nor the other, and, save for ghosts and ghostly reminiscences, not a guest, for many years gone by, had entered the heart or the chamber.

There was still another peculiarity of this inscrutable charm. The bedchamber, no doubt, was a chamber of very great and varied experience, as a scene of human life: the joy of bridal nights had throbbed itself away here; new immortals had first drawn earthly breath here; and here old people had died. But—whether it were the white roses, or whatever the subtile influence might be—a person of delicate instinct would have known at once that it was now a maiden's bedchamber, and had been purified of all former evil and sorrow by her sweet breath and happy thoughts. Her dreams of the past night, being such cheerful ones, had exorcised the gloom, and now haunted the chamber in its stead.

After arranging matters to her satisfaction, Phoebe emerged from her chamber, with a purpose to descend again into the garden. Besides the rosebush, she had observed several other species of flowers growing there in a wilderness of neglect, and obstructing one another's development (as is often the parallel case in human society) by their uneducated entanglement and confusion. At the head of the stairs, however, she met Hepzibah, who, it being still early, invited her into a room which she would probably have called her boudoir, had her education embraced any such French phrase. It was strewn about with a few old books, and a work-basket, and a dusty writing-desk; and had, on one side, a large black article of furniture, of very strange appearance, which the old gentlewoman told Phoebe was a harpsichord. It looked more like a coffin than anything else; and, indeed,—not having been played upon, or opened, for years,—there must have been a vast deal of dead music in it, stifled for want of air. Human finger was hardly known to have touched its chords since the days of Alice Pyncheon, who had learned the sweet accomplishment of melody in Europe.

Hepzibah bade her young guest sit down, and, herself taking a chair near by, looked as earnestly at Phoebe's trim little figure as if she expected to see right into its springs and motive secrets.

"Cousin Phoebe," said she, at last, "I really can't see my way clear to keep you with me."

These words, however, had not the inhospitable bluntness with which they may strike the reader; for the two relatives, in a talk before bedtime, had arrived at a certain degree of mutual understanding. Hepzibah knew enough to enable her to appreciate the circumstances (resulting from the second marriage of the girl's mother) which made it desirable for Phoebe to establish herself in another home. Nor did she misinterpret Phoebe's character, and the genial activity pervading it,—one of the most valuable traits of the true New England woman,—which had impelled her forth, as might be said, to seek her fortune, but with a self-respecting purpose to confer as much benefit as she could anywise receive. As one of her nearest kindred, she had naturally betaken herself to Hepzibah, with no idea of forcing herself on her cousin's protection, but only for a visit of a week or two, which might be indefinitely extended, should it prove for the happiness of both.

To Hepzibah's blunt observation, therefore, Phoebe replied as frankly, and more cheerfully.

"Dear cousin, I cannot tell how it will be," said she. "But I really think we may suit one another much better than you suppose."

"You are a nice girl,—I see it plainly," continued Hepzibah; "and it is not any question as to that point which makes me hesitate. But, Phoebe, this house of mine is but a melancholy place for a young person to be in. It lets in the wind and rain, and the snow, too, in the garret and upper chambers, in winter-time, but it never lets in the sunshine. And as for myself, you see what I am,—a dismal and lonesome old woman (for I begin to call myself old, Phoebe), whose temper, I am afraid, is none of the best, and whose spirits are as bad as can be! I cannot make your life pleasant, Cousin Phoebe, neither can I so much as give you bread to eat."

"You will find me a cheerful little body" answered Phoebe, smiling, and yet with a kind of gentle dignity, "and I mean to earn my bread. You know I have not been brought up a Pyncheon. A girl learns many things in a New England village."

"Ah! Phoebe," said Hepzibah, sighing, "your knowledge would do but little for you here! And then it is a wretched thought that you should fling away your young days in a place like this. Those cheeks would not be so rosy after a month or two. Look at my face!" and, indeed, the contrast was very striking,—"you see how pale I am! It is my idea that the dust and continual decay of these old houses are unwholesome for the lungs."

"There is the garden,—the flowers to be taken care of," observed Phoebe. "I should keep myself healthy with exercise in the open air."

"And, after all, child," exclaimed Hepzibah, suddenly rising, as if to dismiss the subject, "it is not for me to say who shall be a guest or inhabitant of the old Pyncheon House. Its master is coming."

"Do you mean Judge Pyncheon?" asked Phoebe in surprise.

"Judge Pyncheon!" answered her cousin angrily. "He will hardly cross the threshold while I live! No, no! But, Phoebe, you shall see the face of him I speak of."

She went in quest of the miniature already described, and returned with it in her hand. Giving it to Phoebe, she watched her features narrowly, and with a certain jealousy as to the mode in which the girl would show herself affected by the picture.

"How do you like the face?" asked Hepzibah.

"It is handsome!—it is very beautiful!" said Phoebe admiringly. "It is as sweet a face as a man's can be, or ought to be. It has something of a child's expression,—and yet not childish,—only one feels so very kindly towards him! He ought never to suffer anything. One would bear much for the sake of sparing him toil or sorrow. Who is it, Cousin Hepzibah?"

"Did you never hear," whispered her cousin, bending towards her, "of Clifford Pyncheon?"

"Never. I thought there were no Pyncheons left, except yourself and our cousin Jaffrey," answered Phoebe. "And yet I seem to have heard the name of Clifford Pyncheon. Yes!—from my father or my mother; but has he not been a long while dead?"

"Well, well, child, perhaps he has!" said Hepzibah with a sad, hollow laugh; "but, in old houses like this, you know, dead people are very apt to come back again! We shall see. And, Cousin Phoebe, since, after all that I have said, your courage does not fail you, we will not part so soon. You are welcome, my child, for the present, to such a home as your kinswoman can offer you."

With this measured, but not exactly cold assurance of a hospitable purpose, Hepzibah kissed her cheek.

They now went below stairs, where Phoebe—not so much assuming the office as attracting it to herself, by the magnetism of innate fitness—took the most active part in preparing breakfast. The mistress of the house, meanwhile, as is usual with persons of her stiff and unmalleable cast, stood mostly aside; willing to lend her aid, yet conscious that her natural inaptitude would be likely to impede the business in hand. Phoebe and the fire that boiled the teakettle were equally bright, cheerful, and efficient, in their respective offices. Hepzibah gazed forth from her habitual sluggishness, the necessary result of long solitude, as from another sphere. She could not help being interested, however, and even amused, at the readiness with which her new inmate adapted herself to the circumstances, and brought the house, moreover, and all its rusty old appliances, into a suitableness for her purposes. Whatever she did, too, was done without conscious effort, and with frequent outbreaks of song, which were exceedingly pleasant to the ear. This natural tunefulness made Phoebe seem like a bird in a shadowy tree; or conveyed the idea that the stream of life warbled through her heart as a brook sometimes warbles through a pleasant little dell. It betokened the cheeriness of an active temperament, finding joy in its activity, and, therefore, rendering it beautiful; it was a New England trait,—the stern old stuff of Puritanism with a gold thread in the web.

Hepzibah brought out some old silver spoons with the family crest upon them, and a china tea-set painted over with grotesque figures of man, bird, and beast, in as grotesque a landscape. These pictured people were odd humorists, in a world of their own,—a world of vivid brilliancy, so far as color went, and still unfaded, although the teapot and small cups were as ancient as the custom itself of tea-drinking.

"Your great-great-great-great-grandmother had these cups, when she was married," said Hepzibah to Phoebe. "She was a Davenport, of a good family. They were almost the first teacups ever seen in the colony; and if one of them were to be broken, my heart would break with it. But it is nonsense to speak so about a brittle teacup, when I remember what my heart has gone through without breaking."

The cups—not having been used, perhaps, since Hepzibah's youth—had contracted no small burden of dust, which Phoebe washed away with so much care and delicacy as to satisfy even the proprietor of this invaluable china.

"What a nice little housewife you are!" exclaimed the latter, smiling, and at the same time frowning so prodigiously that the smile was sunshine under a thunder-cloud. "Do you do other things as well? Are you as good at your book as you are at washing teacups?"

"Not quite, I am afraid," said Phoebe, laughing at the form of Hepzibah's question. "But I was schoolmistress for the little children in our district last summer, and might have been so still."

"Ah! 'tis all very well!" observed the maiden lady, drawing herself up. "But these things must have come to you with your mother's blood. I never knew a Pyncheon that had any turn for them."

It is very queer, but not the less true, that people are generally quite as vain, or even more so, of their deficiencies than of their available gifts; as was Hepzibah of this native inapplicability, so to speak, of the Pyncheons to any useful purpose. She regarded it as an hereditary trait; and so, perhaps, it was, but unfortunately a morbid one, such as is often generated in families that remain long above the surface of society.

Before they left the breakfast-table, the shop-bell rang sharply, and Hepzibah set down the remnant of her final cup of tea, with a look of sallow despair that was truly piteous to behold. In cases of distasteful occupation, the second day is generally worse than the first. We return to the rack with all the soreness of the preceding torture in our limbs. At all events, Hepzibah had fully satisfied herself of the impossibility of ever becoming wonted to this peevishly obstreperous little bell. Ring as often as it might, the sound always smote upon her nervous system rudely and suddenly. And especially now, while, with her crested teaspoons and antique china, she was flattering herself with ideas of gentility, she felt an unspeakable disinclination to confront a customer.

"Do not trouble yourself, dear cousin!" cried Phoebe, starting lightly up. "I am shop-keeper to-day."

"You, child!" exclaimed Hepzibah. "What can a little country girl know of such matters?"

"Oh, I have done all the shopping for the family at our village store," said Phoebe. "And I have had a table at a fancy fair, and made better sales than anybody. These things are not to be learnt; they depend upon a knack that comes, I suppose," added she, smiling, "with one's mother's blood. You shall see that I am as nice a little saleswoman as I am a housewife!"

The old gentlewoman stole behind Phoebe, and peeped from the passageway into the shop, to note how she would manage her undertaking. It was a case of some intricacy. A very ancient woman, in a white short gown and a green petticoat, with a string of gold beads about her neck, and what looked like a nightcap on her head, had brought a quantity of yarn to barter for the commodities of the shop. She was probably the very last person in town who still kept the time-honored spinning-wheel in constant revolution. It was worth while to hear the croaking and hollow tones of the old lady, and the pleasant voice of Phoebe, mingling in one twisted thread of talk; and still better to contrast their figures,—so light and bloomy,—so decrepit and dusky,—with only the counter betwixt them, in one sense, but more than threescore years, in another. As for the bargain, it was wrinkled slyness and craft pitted against native truth and sagacity.

"Was not that well done?" asked Phoebe, laughing, when the customer was gone.

"Nicely done, indeed, child!" answered Hepzibah. "I could not have gone through with it nearly so well. As you say, it must be a knack that belongs to you on the mother's side."

It is a very genuine admiration, that with which persons too shy or too awkward to take a due part in the bustling world regard the real actors in life's stirring scenes; so genuine, in fact, that the former are usually fain to make it palatable to their self-love, by assuming that these active and forcible qualities are incompatible with others, which they choose to deem higher and more important. Thus, Hepzibah was well content to acknowledge Phoebe's vastly superior gifts as a shop-keeper'—she listened, with compliant ear, to her suggestion of various methods whereby the influx of trade might be increased, and rendered profitable, without a hazardous outlay of capital. She consented that the village maiden should manufacture yeast, both liquid and in cakes; and should brew a certain kind of beer, nectareous to the palate, and of rare stomachic virtues; and, moreover, should bake and exhibit for sale some little spice-cakes, which whosoever tasted would longingly desire to taste again. All such proofs of a ready mind and skilful handiwork were highly acceptable to the aristocratic hucksteress, so long as she could murmur to herself with a grim smile, and a half-natural sigh, and a sentiment of mixed wonder, pity, and growing affection:—

"What a nice little body she is! If she only could be a lady; too—but that's impossible! Phoebe is no Pyncheon. She takes everything from her mother!"

As to Phoebe's not being a lady, or whether she were a lady or no, it was a point, perhaps, difficult to decide, but which could hardly have come up for judgment at all in any fair and healthy mind. Out of New England, it would be impossible to meet with a person combining so many ladylike attributes with so many others that form no necessary (if compatible) part of the character. She shocked no canon of taste; she was admirably in keeping with herself, and never jarred against surrounding circumstances. Her figure, to be sure,—so small as to be almost childlike, and so elastic that motion seemed as easy or easier to it than rest, would hardly have suited one's idea of a countess. Neither did her face—with the brown ringlets on either side, and the slightly piquant nose, and the wholesome bloom, and the clear shade of tan, and the half dozen freckles, friendly remembrances of the April sun and breeze—precisely give us a right to call her beautiful. But there was both lustre and depth in her eyes. She was very pretty; as graceful as a bird, and graceful much in the same way; as pleasant about the house as a gleam of sunshine falling on the floor through a shadow of twinkling leaves, or as a ray of firelight that dances on the wall while evening is drawing nigh. Instead of discussing her claim to rank among ladies, it would be preferable to regard Phoebe as the example of feminine grace and availability combined, in a state of society, if there were any such, where ladies did not exist. There it should be woman's office to move in the midst of practical affairs, and to gild them all, the very homeliest,—were it even the scouring of pots and kettles,—with an atmosphere of loveliness and joy.

Such was the sphere of Phoebe. To find the born and educated lady, on the other hand, we need look no farther than Hepzibah, our forlorn old maid, in her rustling and rusty silks, with her deeply cherished and ridiculous consciousness of long descent, her shadowy claims to princely territory, and, in the way of accomplishment, her recollections, it may be, of having formerly thrummed on a harpsichord, and walked a minuet, and worked an antique tapestry-stitch on her sampler. It was a fair parallel between new Plebeianism and old Gentility.

It really seemed as if the battered visage of the House of the Seven Gables, black and heavy-browed as it still certainly looked, must have shown a kind of cheerfulness glimmering through its dusky windows as Phoebe passed to and fro in the interior. Otherwise, it is impossible to explain how the people of the neighborhood so soon became aware of the girl's presence. There was a great run of custom, setting steadily in, from about ten o' clock until towards noon,—relaxing, somewhat, at dinner-time, but recommencing in the afternoon, and, finally, dying away a half an hour or so before the long day's sunset. One of the stanchest patrons was little Ned Higgins, the devourer of Jim Crow and the elephant, who to-day signalized his omnivorous prowess by swallowing two dromedaries and a locomotive. Phoebe laughed, as she summed up her aggregate of sales upon the slate; while Hepzibah, first drawing on a pair of silk gloves, reckoned over the sordid accumulation of copper coin, not without silver intermixed, that had jingled into the till.

"We must renew our stock, Cousin Hepzibah!" cried the little saleswoman. "The gingerbread figures are all gone, and so are those Dutch wooden milkmaids, and most of our other playthings. There has been constant inquiry for cheap raisins, and a great cry for whistles, and trumpets, and jew's-harps; and at least a dozen little boys have asked for molasses-candy. And we must contrive to get a peck of russet apples, late in the season as it is. But, dear cousin, what an enormous heap of copper! Positively a copper mountain!"

"Well done! well done! well done!" quoth Uncle Venner, who had taken occasion to shuffle in and out of the shop several times in the course of the day. "Here's a girl that will never end her days at my farm! Bless my eyes, what a brisk little soul!"

"Yes, Phoebe is a nice girl!" said Hepzibah, with a scowl of austere approbation. "But, Uncle Venner, you have known the family a great many years. Can you tell me whether there ever was a Pyncheon whom she takes after?"

"I don't believe there ever was," answered the venerable man. "At any rate, it never was my luck to see her like among them, nor, for that matter, anywhere else. I've seen a great deal of the world, not only in people's kitchens and back-yards but at the street-corners, and on the wharves, and in other places where my business calls me; and I'm free to say, Miss Hepzibah, that I never knew a human creature do her work so much like one of God's angels as this child Phoebe does!"

Uncle Venner's eulogium, if it appear rather too high-strained for the person and occasion, had, nevertheless, a sense in which it was both subtle and true. There was a spiritual quality in Phoebe's activity. The life of the long and busy day—spent in occupations that might so easily have taken a squalid and ugly aspect—had been made pleasant, and even lovely, by the spontaneous grace with which these homely duties seemed to bloom out of her character; so that labor, while she dealt with it, had the easy and flexible charm of play. Angels do not toil, but let their good works grow out of them; and so did Phoebe.

The two relatives—the young maid and the old one—found time before nightfall, in the intervals of trade, to make rapid advances towards affection and confidence. A recluse, like Hepzibah, usually displays remarkable frankness, and at least temporary affability, on being absolutely cornered, and brought to the point of personal intercourse; like the angel whom Jacob wrestled with, she is ready to bless you when once overcome.

The old gentlewoman took a dreary and proud satisfaction in leading Phoebe from room to room of the house, and recounting the traditions with which, as we may say, the walls were lugubriously frescoed. She showed the indentations made by the lieutenant-governor's sword-hilt in the door-panels of the apartment where old Colonel Pyncheon, a dead host, had received his affrighted visitors with an awful frown. The dusky terror of that frown, Hepzibah observed, was thought to be lingering ever since in the passageway. She bade Phoebe step into one of the tall chairs, and inspect the ancient map of the Pyncheon territory at the eastward. In a tract of land on which she laid her finger, there existed a silver mine, the locality of which was precisely pointed out in some memoranda of Colonel Pyncheon himself, but only to be made known when the family claim should be recognized by government. Thus it was for the interest of all New England that the Pyncheons should have justice done them. She told, too, how that there was undoubtedly an immense treasure of English guineas hidden somewhere about the house, or in the cellar, or possibly in the garden.

"If you should happen to find it, Phoebe," said Hepzibah, glancing aside at her with a grim yet kindly smile, "we will tie up the shop-bell for good and all!"

"Yes, dear cousin," answered Phoebe; "but, in the mean time, I hear somebody ringing it!"

When the customer was gone, Hepzibah talked rather vaguely, and at great length, about a certain Alice Pyncheon, who had been exceedingly beautiful and accomplished in her lifetime, a hundred years ago. The fragrance of her rich and delightful character still lingered about the place where she had lived, as a dried rose-bud scents the drawer where it has withered and perished. This lovely Alice had met with some great and mysterious calamity, and had grown thin and white, and gradually faded out of the world. But, even now, she was supposed to haunt the House of the Seven Gables, and, a great many times,—especially when one of the Pyncheons was to die,—she had been heard playing sadly and beautifully on the harpsichord. One of these tunes, just as it had sounded from her spiritual touch, had been written down by an amateur of music; it was so exquisitely mournful that nobody, to this day, could bear to hear it played, unless when a great sorrow had made them know the still profounder sweetness of it.

"Was it the same harpsichord that you showed me?" inquired Phoebe.

"The very same," said Hepzibah. "It was Alice Pyncheon's harpsichord. When I was learning music, my father would never let me open it. So, as I could only play on my teacher's instrument, I have forgotten all my music long ago."

Leaving these antique themes, the old lady began to talk about the daguerreotypist, whom, as he seemed to be a well-meaning and orderly young man, and in narrow circumstances, she had permitted to take up his residence in one of the seven gables. But, on seeing more of Mr. Holgrave, she hardly knew what to make of him. He had the strangest companions imaginable; men with long beards, and dressed in linen blouses, and other such new-fangled and ill-fitting garments; reformers, temperance lecturers, and all manner of cross-looking philanthropists; community-men, and come-outers, as Hepzibah believed, who acknowledged no law, and ate no solid food, but lived on the scent of other people's cookery, and turned up their noses at the fare. As for the daguerreotypist, she had read a paragraph in a penny paper, the other day, accusing him of making a speech full of wild and disorganizing matter, at a meeting of his banditti-like associates. For her own part, she had reason to believe that he practised animal magnetism, and, if such things were in fashion nowadays, should be apt to suspect him of studying the Black Art up there in his lonesome chamber.

"But, dear cousin," said Phoebe, "if the young man is so dangerous, why do you let him stay? If he does nothing worse, he may set the house on fire!"

"Why, sometimes," answered Hepzibah, "I have seriously made it a question, whether I ought not to send him away. But, with all his oddities, he is a quiet kind of a person, and has such a way of taking hold of one's mind, that, without exactly liking him (for I don't know enough of the young man), I should be sorry to lose sight of him entirely. A woman clings to slight acquaintances when she lives so much alone as I do."

"But if Mr. Holgrave is a lawless person!" remonstrated Phoebe, a part of whose essence it was to keep within the limits of law.

"Oh!" said Hepzibah carelessly,—for, formal as she was, still, in her life's experience, she had gnashed her teeth against human law,—"I suppose he has a law of his own!"

❦ 6 ❧

MAULE'S WELL

AFTER AN EARLY TEA, the little country-girl strayed into the garden. The enclosure had formerly been very extensive, but was now contracted within small compass, and hemmed about, partly by high wooden fences, and partly by the outbuildings of houses that stood on another street. In its centre was a grass-plat, surrounding a ruinous little structure, which showed just enough of its original design to indicate that it had once been a summer-house. A hop-vine, springing from last year's root, was beginning to clamber over it, but would be long in covering the roof with its green mantle. Three of the seven gables either fronted or looked sideways, with a dark solemnity of aspect, down into the garden.

The black, rich soil had fed itself with the decay of a long period of time; such as fallen leaves, the petals of flowers, and the stalks and seed—vessels of vagrant and lawless plants, more useful after their death than ever while flaunting in the sun. The evil of these departed years would naturally have sprung up again, in such rank weeds (symbolic of the transmitted vices of society) as are always prone to root themselves about human dwellings. Phoebe saw, however, that their growth must have been checked by a degree of careful labor, bestowed daily and systematically on the garden. The white double rosebush had evidently been propped up anew against the house since the commencement of the season; and a pear-tree and three damson-trees, which, except a row of currant-bushes, constituted the only varieties of fruit, bore marks of the recent amputation of several superfluous or defective limbs. There were also a few species of antique and hereditary flowers, in no very flourishing condition, but scrupulously weeded; as if some person, either out of love or curiosity, had been anxious to bring them to such perfection as they were capable of attaining. The remainder of the garden presented a well-selected assortment of esculent vegetables, in a praiseworthy state of advancement. Summer squashes almost in their golden blossom; cucumbers, now evincing a tendency to spread away from the main stock, and ramble far and wide; two or three rows of string-beans and as many more that were about to festoon themselves on poles; tomatoes, occupying a site so sheltered and sunny that the plants were already gigantic, and promised an early and abundant harvest.

Phoebe wondered whose care and toil it could have been that had planted these vegetables,

423

and kept the soil so clean and orderly. Not surely her cousin Hepzibah's, who had no taste nor spirits for the lady-like employment of cultivating flowers, and—with her recluse habits, and tendency to shelter herself within the dismal shadow of the house—would hardly have come forth under the speck of open sky to weed and hoe among the fraternity of beans and squashes.

It being her first day of complete estrangement from rural objects, Phoebe found an unexpected charm in this little nook of grass, and foliage, and aristocratic flowers, and plebeian vegetables. The eye of Heaven seemed to look down into it pleasantly, and with a peculiar smile, as if glad to perceive that nature, elsewhere overwhelmed, and driven out of the dusty town, had here been able to retain a breathing-place. The spot acquired a somewhat wilder grace, and yet a very gentle one, from the fact that a pair of robins had built their nest in the pear-tree, and were making themselves exceedingly busy and happy in the dark intricacy of its boughs. Bees, too,—strange to say,—had thought it worth their while to come hither, possibly from the range of hives beside some farm-house miles away. How many aerial voyages might they have made, in quest of honey, or honey-laden, betwixt dawn and sunset! Yet, late as it now was, there still arose a pleasant hum out of one or two of the squash-blossoms, in the depths of which these bees were plying their golden labor. There was one other object in the garden which Nature might fairly claim as her inalienable property, in spite of whatever man could do to render it his own. This was a fountain, set round with a rim of old mossy stones, and paved, in its bed, with what appeared to be a sort of mosaic-work of variously colored pebbles. The play and slight agitation of the water, in its upward gush, wrought magically with these variegated pebbles, and made a continually shifting apparition of quaint figures, vanishing too suddenly to be definable. Thence, swelling over the rim of moss-grown stones, the water stole away under the fence, through what we regret to call a gutter, rather than a channel. Nor must we forget to mention a hen-coop of very reverend antiquity that stood in the farther corner of the garden, not a great way from the fountain. It now contained only Chanticleer, his two wives, and a solitary chicken. All of them were pure specimens of a breed which had been transmitted down as an heirloom in the Pyncheon family, and were said, while in their prime, to have attained almost the size of turkeys, and, on the score of delicate flesh, to be fit for a prince's table. In proof of the authenticity of this legendary renown, Hepzibah could have exhibited the shell of a great egg, which an ostrich need hardly have been ashamed of. Be that as it might, the hens were now scarcely larger than pigeons, and had a queer, rusty, withered aspect, and a gouty kind of movement, and a sleepy and melancholy tone throughout all the variations of their clucking and cackling. It was evident that the race had degenerated, like many a noble race besides, in consequence of too strict a watchfulness to keep it pure. These feathered people had existed too long in their distinct variety; a fact of which the present representatives, judging by their lugubrious deportment, seemed to be aware. They kept themselves alive, unquestionably, and laid now and then an egg, and hatched a chicken; not for any pleasure of their own, but that the world might not absolutely lose what had once been so admirable a breed of fowls. The distinguishing mark of the hens was a crest of lamentably scanty growth, in these latter days, but so oddly and wickedly analogous to Hepzibah's turban, that Phoebe—to the poignant distress of her conscience, but inevitably—was led to fancy a general resemblance betwixt these forlorn bipeds and her respectable relative.

The girl ran into the house to get some crumbs of bread, cold potatoes, and other such scraps as were suitable to the accommodating appetite of fowls. Returning, she gave a peculiar call, which they seemed to recognize. The chicken crept through the pales of the coop and ran, with some show of liveliness, to her feet; while Chanticleer and the ladies of his household regarded her with queer, sidelong glances, and then croaked one to another, as if communicating their sage opinions of her character. So wise, as well as antique, was their aspect, as to give color to the idea, not merely that they were the descendants of a time-honored race, but that they had existed, in their individual capacity, ever since the House of the Seven Gables was founded, and were somehow mixed up with its destiny. They were a species of tutelary sprite, or Banshee; although winged and feathered differently from most other guardian angels.

"Here, you odd little chicken!" said Phoebe; "here are some nice crumbs for you!"

The chicken, hereupon, though almost as venerable in appearance as its mother—possessing, indeed, the whole antiquity of its progenitors in miniature,—mustered vivacity enough to flutter upward and alight on Phoebe's shoulder.

"That little fowl pays you a high compliment!" said a voice behind Phoebe.

Turning quickly, she was surprised at sight of a young man, who had found access into the garden by a door opening out of another gable than that whence she had emerged. He held a hoe in his hand, and, while Phoebe was gone in quest of the crumbs, had begun to busy himself with drawing up fresh earth about the roots of the tomatoes.

"The chicken really treats you like an old acquaintance," continued he in a quiet way, while a smile made his face pleasanter than Phoebe at first fancied it. "Those venerable personages in the coop, too, seem very affably disposed. You are lucky to be in their good graces so soon! They have known me much longer, but never honor me with any familiarity, though hardly a day passes without my bringing them food. Miss Hepzibah, I suppose, will interweave the fact with her other traditions, and set it down that the fowls know you to be a Pyncheon!"

"The secret is," said Phoebe, smiling, "that I have learned how to talk with hens and chickens."

"Ah, but these hens," answered the young man,—"these hens of aristocratic lineage would scorn to understand the vulgar language of a barn-yard fowl. I prefer to think—and so would Miss Hepzibah—that they recognize the family tone. For you are a Pyncheon?"

"My name is Phoebe Pyncheon," said the girl, with a manner of some reserve; for she was aware that her new acquaintance could be no other than the daguerreotypist, of whose lawless propensities the old maid had given her a disagreeable idea. "I did not know that my cousin Hepzibah's garden was under another person's care."

"Yes," said Holgrave, "I dig, and hoe, and weed, in this black old earth, for the sake of refreshing myself with what little nature and simplicity may be left in it, after men have so long sown and reaped here. I turn up the earth by way of pastime. My sober occupation, so far as I have any, is with a lighter material. In short, I make pictures out of sunshine; and, not to be too much dazzled with my own trade, I have prevailed with Miss Hepzibah to let me lodge in one of these dusky gables. It is like a bandage over one's eyes, to come into it. But would you like to see a specimen of my productions?"

"A daguerreotype likeness, do you mean?" asked Phoebe with less reserve; for, in spite of prejudice, her own youthfulness sprang forward to meet his. "I don't much like pictures of that sort,—they are so hard and stern; besides dodging away from the eye, and trying to escape altogether. They are conscious of looking very unamiable, I suppose, and therefore hate to be seen."

"If you would permit me," said the artist, looking at Phoebe, "I should like to try whether the daguerreotype can bring out disagreeable traits on a perfectly amiable face. But there certainly is truth in what you have said. Most of my likenesses do look unamiable; but the very sufficient reason, I fancy, is, because the originals are so. There is a wonderful insight in Heaven's broad and simple sunshine. While we give it credit only for depicting the merest surface, it actually brings out the secret character with a truth that no painter would ever venture upon, even could he detect it. There is, at least, no flattery in my humble line of art.

Now, here is a likeness which I have taken over and over again, and still with no better result. Yet the original wears, to common eyes, a very different expression. It would gratify me to have your judgment on this character."

He exhibited a daguerreotype miniature in a morocco case. Phoebe merely glanced at it, and gave it back.

"I know the face," she replied; "for its stern eye has been following me about all day. It is my Puritan ancestor, who hangs yonder in the parlor. To be sure, you have found some way of copying the portrait without its black velvet cap and gray beard, and have given him a modern coat and satin cravat, instead of his cloak and band. I don't think him improved by your alterations."

"You would have seen other differences had you looked a little longer," said Holgrave, laughing, yet apparently much struck. "I can assure you that this is a modern face, and one which you will very probably meet. Now, the remarkable point is, that the original wears, to the world's eye,—and, for aught I know, to his most intimate friends,—an exceedingly pleasant countenance, indicative of benevolence, openness of heart, sunny good-humor, and other praiseworthy qualities of that cast. The sun, as you see, tells quite another story, and will not be coaxed out of it, after half a dozen patient attempts on my part. Here we have the man, sly, subtle, hard, imperious, and, withal, cold as ice. Look at that eye! Would you like to be at its mercy? At that mouth! Could it ever smile? And yet, if you could only see the benign smile of the original! It is so much the more unfortunate, as he is a public character of some eminence, and the likeness was intended to be engraved."

"Well, I don't wish to see it any more," observed Phoebe, turning away her eyes. "It is certainly very like the old portrait. But my cousin Hepzibah has another picture,—a miniature. If the original is still in the world, I think he might defy the sun to make him look stern and hard."

"You have seen that picture, then!" exclaimed the artist, with an expression of much interest. "I never did, but have a great curiosity to do so. And you judge favorably of the face?"

"There never was a sweeter one," said Phoebe. "It is almost too soft and gentle for a man's."

"Is there nothing wild in the eye?" continued Holgrave, so earnestly that it embarrassed Phoebe, as did also the quiet freedom with which he presumed on their so recent acquaintance. "Is there nothing dark or sinister anywhere? Could you not conceive the original to have been guilty of a great crime?"

"It is nonsense," said Phoebe a little impatiently, "for us to talk about a picture which you have never seen. You mistake it for some other. A crime, indeed! Since you are a friend of my cousin Hepzibah's, you should ask her to show you the picture."

"It will suit my purpose still better to see the original," replied the daguerreotypist coolly. "As to his character, we need not discuss its points; they have already been settled by a competent tribunal, or one which called itself competent. But, stay! Do not go yet, if you please! I have a proposition to make you."

Phoebe was on the point of retreating, but turned back, with some hesitation; for she did not exactly comprehend his manner, although, on better observation, its feature seemed rather to be lack of ceremony than any approach to offensive rudeness. There was an odd kind of authority, too, in what he now proceeded to say, rather as if the garden were his own than a place to which he was admitted merely by Hepzibah's courtesy.

"If agreeable to you," he observed, "it would give me pleasure to turn over these flowers, and those ancient and respectable fowls, to your care. Coming fresh from country air and occupations, you will soon feel the need of some such out-of-door employment. My own sphere does not so much lie among flowers. You can trim and tend them, therefore, as you please; and

I will ask only the least trifle of a blossom, now and then, in exchange for all the good, honest kitchen vegetables with which I propose to enrich Miss Hepzibah's table. So we will be fellow-laborers, somewhat on the community system."

Silently, and rather surprised at her own compliance, Phoebe accordingly betook herself to weeding a flower-bed, but busied herself still more with cogitations respecting this young man, with whom she so unexpectedly found herself on terms approaching to familiarity. She did not altogether like him. His character perplexed the little country-girl, as it might a more practised observer; for, while the tone of his conversation had generally been playful, the impression left on her mind was that of gravity, and, except as his youth modified it, almost sternness. She rebelled, as it were, against a certain magnetic element in the artist's nature, which he exercised towards her, possibly without being conscious of it.

After a little while, the twilight, deepened by the shadows of the fruit-trees and the surrounding buildings, threw an obscurity over the garden.

"There," said Holgrave, "it is time to give over work! That last stroke of the hoe has cut off a beanstalk. Good-night, Miss Phoebe Pyncheon! Any bright day, if you will put one of those rosebuds in your hair, and come to my rooms in Central Street, I will seize the purest ray of sunshine, and make a picture of the flower and its wearer." He retired towards his own solitary gable, but turned his head, on reaching the door, and called to Phoebe, with a tone which certainly had laughter in it, yet which seemed to be more than half in earnest.

"Be careful not to drink at Maule's well!" said he. "Neither drink nor bathe your face in it!"

"Maule's well!" answered Phoebe. "Is that it with the rim of mossy stones? I have no thought of drinking there,—but why not?"

"Oh," rejoined the daguerreotypist, "because, like an old lady's cup of tea, it is water bewitched!"

He vanished; and Phoebe, lingering a moment, saw a glimmering light, and then the steady beam of a lamp, in a chamber of the gable. On returning into Hepzibah's apartment of the house, she found the low-studded parlor so dim and dusky that her eyes could not penetrate the interior. She was indistinctly aware, however, that the gaunt figure of the old gentlewoman was sitting in one of the straight-backed chairs, a little withdrawn from the window, the faint gleam of which showed the blanched paleness of her cheek, turned sideways towards a corner.

"Shall I light a lamp, Cousin Hepzibah?" she asked.

"Do, if you please, my dear child," answered Hepzibah. "But put it on the table in the corner of the passage. My eyes are weak; and I can seldom bear the lamplight on them."

What an instrument is the human voice! How wonderfully responsive to every emotion of the human soul! In Hepzibah's tone, at that moment, there was a certain rich depth and moisture, as if the words, commonplace as they were, had been steeped in the warmth of her heart. Again, while lighting the lamp in the kitchen, Phoebe fancied that her cousin spoke to her.

"In a moment, cousin!" answered the girl. "These matches just glimmer, and go out."

But, instead of a response from Hepzibah, she seemed to hear the murmur of an unknown voice. It was strangely indistinct, however, and less like articulate words than an unshaped sound, such as would be the utterance of feeling and sympathy, rather than of the intellect. So vague was it, that its impression or echo in Phoebe's mind was that of unreality. She concluded that she must have mistaken some other sound for that of the human voice; or else that it was altogether in her fancy.

She set the lighted lamp in the passage, and again entered the parlor. Hepzibah's form, though its sable outline mingled with the dusk, was now less imperfectly visible. In the remoter parts of the room, however, its walls being so ill adapted to reflect light, there was nearly the same obscurity as before.

"Cousin," said Phoebe, "did you speak to me just now?"

"No, child!" replied Hepzibah.

Fewer words than before, but with the same mysterious music in them! Mellow, melancholy, yet not mournful, the tone seemed to gush up out of the deep well of Hepzibah's heart, all steeped in its profoundest emotion. There was a tremor in it, too, that—as all strong feeling is electric—partly communicated itself to Phoebe. The girl sat silently for a moment. But soon, her senses being very acute, she became conscious of an irregular respiration in an obscure corner of the room. Her physical organization, moreover, being at once delicate and healthy, gave her a perception, operating with almost the effect of a spiritual medium, that somebody was near at hand.

"My dear cousin," asked she, overcoming an indefinable reluctance, "is there not some one in the room with us?"

"Phoebe, my dear little girl," said Hepzibah, after a moment's pause, "you were up betimes, and have been busy all day. Pray go to bed; for I am sure you must need rest. I will sit in the parlor awhile, and collect my thoughts. It has been my custom for more years, child, than you have lived!" While thus dismissing her, the maiden lady stept forward, kissed Phoebe, and pressed her to her heart, which beat against the girl's bosom with a strong, high, and tumultuous swell. How came there to be so much love in this desolate old heart, that it could afford to well over thus abundantly?

"Goodnight, cousin," said Phoebe, strangely affected by Hepzibah's manner. "If you begin to love me, I am glad!"

She retired to her chamber, but did not soon fall asleep, nor then very profoundly. At some uncertain period in the depths of night, and, as it were, through the thin veil of a dream, she was conscious of a footstep mounting the stairs heavily, but not with force and decision. The voice of Hepzibah, with a hush through it, was going up along with the footsteps; and, again, responsive to her cousin's voice, Phoebe heard that strange, vague murmur, which might be likened to an indistinct shadow of human utterance.

7

THE GUEST

WHEN PHOEBE AWOKE,—WHICH she did with the early twittering of the conjugal couple of robins in the pear-tree,—she heard movements below stairs, and, hastening down, found Hepzibah already in the kitchen. She stood by a window, holding a book in close contiguity to her nose, as if with the hope of gaining an olfactory acquaintance with its contents, since her imperfect vision made it not very easy to read them. If any volume could have manifested its essential wisdom in the mode suggested, it would certainly have been the one now in Hepzibah's hand; and the kitchen, in such an event, would forthwith have streamed with the fragrance of venison, turkeys, capons, larded partridges, puddings, cakes, and Christmas pies, in all manner of elaborate mixture and concoction. It was a cookery book, full of innumerable old fashions of English dishes, and illustrated with engravings, which represented the arrangements of the table at such banquets as it might have befitted a nobleman to give in the great hall of his castle. And, amid these rich and potent devices of the culinary art (not one of which, probably, had been tested, within the memory of any man's grandfather), poor Hepzibah was seeking for some nimble little titbit, which, with what skill she had, and such materials as were at hand, she might toss up for breakfast.

Soon, with a deep sigh, she put aside the savory volume, and inquired of Phoebe whether old Speckle, as she called one of the hens, had laid an egg the preceding day. Phoebe ran to see, but returned without the expected treasure in her hand. At that instant, however, the blast of a fish-dealer's conch was heard, announcing his approach along the street. With energetic raps at the shop-window, Hepzibah summoned the man in, and made purchase of what he warranted as the finest mackerel in his cart, and as fat a one as ever he felt with his finger so early in the season. Requesting Phoebe to roast some coffee,—which she casually observed was the real Mocha, and so long kept that each of the small berries ought to be worth its weight in gold,— the maiden lady heaped fuel into the vast receptacle of the ancient fireplace in such quantity as soon to drive the lingering dusk out of the kitchen. The country-girl, willing to give her utmost assistance, proposed to make an Indian cake, after her mother's peculiar method, of easy manufacture, and which she could vouch for as possessing a richness, and, if rightly prepared,

NATHANIEL HAWTHORNE

a delicacy, unequalled by any other mode of breakfast-cake. Hepzibah gladly assenting, the kitchen was soon the scene of savory preparation. Perchance, amid their proper element of smoke, which eddied forth from the ill-constructed chimney, the ghosts of departed cook-maids looked wonderingly on, or peeped down the great breadth of the flue, despising the simplicity of the projected meal, yet ineffectually pining to thrust their shadowy hands into each inchoate dish. The half-starved rats, at any rate, stole visibly out of their hiding-places, and sat on their hind-legs, snuffing the fumy atmosphere, and wistfully awaiting an opportunity to nibble.

Hepzibah had no natural turn for cookery, and, to say the truth, had fairly incurred her present meagreness by often choosing to go without her dinner rather than be attendant on the rotation of the spit, or ebullition of the pot. Her zeal over the fire, therefore, was quite an heroic test of sentiment. It was touching, and positively worthy of tears (if Phoebe, the only spectator, except the rats and ghosts aforesaid, had not been better employed than in shedding them), to see her rake out a bed of fresh and glowing coals, and proceed to broil the mackerel. Her usually pale cheeks were all ablaze with heat and hurry. She watched the fish with as much tender care and minuteness of attention as if,—we know not how to express it otherwise,—as if her own heart were on the gridiron, and her immortal happiness were involved in its being done precisely to a turn!

Life, within doors, has few pleasanter prospects than a neatly arranged and well-provisioned breakfast-table. We come to it freshly, in the dewy youth of the day, and when our spiritual and sensual elements are in better accord than at a later period; so that the material delights of the morning meal are capable of being fully enjoyed, without any very grievous reproaches, whether gastric or conscientious, for yielding even a trifle overmuch to the animal department of our nature. The thoughts, too, that run around the ring of familiar guests have a piquancy and mirthfulness, and oftentimes a vivid truth, which more rarely find their way into the elaborate intercourse of dinner. Hepzibah's small and ancient table, supported on its slender and graceful legs, and covered with a cloth of the richest damask, looked worthy to be the scene and centre of one of the cheerfullest of parties. The vapor of the broiled fish arose like incense from the shrine of a barbarian idol, while the fragrance of the Mocha might have gratified the nostrils of a tutelary Lar, or whatever power has scope over a modern breakfast-table. Phoebe's Indian cakes were the sweetest offering of all,—in their hue befitting the rustic altars of the innocent and golden age,—or, so brightly yellow were they, resembling some of the bread which was changed to glistening gold when Midas tried to eat it. The butter must not be forgotten,—butter which Phoebe herself had churned, in her own rural home, and brought it to her cousin as a propitiatory gift,—smelling of clover-blossoms, and diffusing the charm of pastoral scenery through the dark-panelled parlor. All this, with the quaint gorgeousness of the old china cups and saucers, and the crested spoons, and a silver cream-jug (Hepzibah's only other article of plate, and shaped like the rudest porringer), set out a board at which the stateliest of old Colonel Pyncheon's guests need not have scorned to take his place. But the Puritan's face scowled down out of the picture, as if nothing on the table pleased his appetite.

By way of contributing what grace she could, Phoebe gathered some roses and a few other flowers, possessing either scent or beauty, and arranged them in a glass pitcher, which, having long ago lost its handle, was so much the fitter for a flower-vase. The early sunshine—as fresh as that which peeped into Eve's bower while she and Adam sat at breakfast there—came twinkling through the branches of the pear-tree, and fell quite across the table. All was now ready. There were chairs and plates for three. A chair and plate for Hepzibah,—the same for Phoebe,—but what other guest did her cousin look for?

Throughout this preparation there had been a constant tremor in Hepzibah's frame; an agitation so powerful that Phoebe could see the quivering of her gaunt shadow, as thrown by the firelight on the kitchen wall, or by the sunshine on the parlor floor. Its manifestations were so various, and agreed so little with one another, that the girl knew not what to make of it. Sometimes it seemed an ecstasy of delight and happiness. At such moments, Hepzibah would fling out her arms, and infold Phoebe in them, and kiss her cheek as tenderly as ever her mother had; she appeared to do so by an inevitable impulse, and as if her bosom were oppressed with tenderness, of which she must needs pour out a little, in order to gain breathing-room. The next moment, without any visible cause for the change, her unwonted joy shrank back, appalled, as it were, and clothed itself in mourning; or it ran and hid itself, so to speak, in the dungeon of her heart, where it had long lain chained, while a cold, spectral sorrow took the place of the imprisoned joy, that was afraid to be enfranchised,—a sorrow as black as that was bright. She often broke into a little, nervous, hysteric laugh, more touching than any tears could be; and forthwith, as if to try which was the most touching, a gush of tears would follow; or perhaps the laughter and tears came both at once, and surrounded our poor Hepzibah, in a moral sense, with a kind of pale, dim rainbow. Towards Phoebe, as we have said, she was affectionate,—far tenderer than ever before, in their brief acquaintance, except for that one kiss on the preceding night,—yet with a continually recurring pettishness and irritability. She would speak sharply to her; then, throwing aside all the starched reserve of her ordinary manner, ask pardon, and the next instant renew the just-forgiven injury.

At last, when their mutual labor was all finished, she took Phoebe's hand in her own trembling one.

"Bear with me, my dear child," she cried; "for truly my heart is full to the brim! Bear with me; for I love you, Phoebe, though I speak so roughly. Think nothing of it, dearest child! By and by, I shall be kind, and only kind!"

"My dearest cousin, cannot you tell me what has happened?" asked Phoebe, with a sunny and tearful sympathy. "What is it that moves you so?"

"Hush! hush! He is coming!" whispered Hepzibah, hastily wiping her eyes. "Let him see you first, Phoebe; for you are young and rosy, and cannot help letting a smile break out whether or no. He always liked bright faces! And mine is old now, and the tears are hardly dry on it. He never could abide tears. There; draw the curtain a little, so that the shadow may fall across his side of the table! But let there be a good deal of sunshine, too; for he never was fond of gloom, as some people are. He has had but little sunshine in his life,—poor Clifford,—and, oh, what a black shadow. Poor, poor Clifford!"

Thus murmuring in an undertone, as if speaking rather to her own heart than to Phoebe, the old gentlewoman stepped on tiptoe about the room, making such arrangements as suggested themselves at the crisis.

Meanwhile there was a step in the passage-way, above stairs. Phoebe recognized it as the same which had passed upward, as through her dream, in the night-time. The approaching guest, whoever it might be, appeared to pause at the head of the staircase; he paused twice or thrice in the descent; he paused again at the foot. Each time, the delay seemed to be without purpose, but rather from a forgetfulness of the purpose which had set him in motion, or as if the person's feet came involuntarily to a stand-still because the motive-power was too feeble to sustain his progress. Finally, he made a long pause at the threshold of the parlor. He took hold of the knob of the door; then loosened his grasp without opening it. Hepzibah, her hands convulsively clasped, stood gazing at the entrance.

"Dear Cousin Hepzibah, pray don't look so!" said Phoebe, trembling; for her cousin's emotion, and this mysteriously reluctant step, made her feel as if a ghost were coming into the room. "You really frighten me! Is something awful going to happen?"

"Hush!" whispered Hepzibah. "Be cheerful! whatever may happen, be nothing but cheerful!"

The final pause at the threshold proved so long, that Hepzibah, unable to endure the suspense, rushed forward, threw open the door, and led in the stranger by the hand. At the first glance, Phoebe saw an elderly personage, in an old-fashioned dressing-gown of faded damask, and wearing his gray or almost white hair of an unusual length. It quite overshadowed his forehead, except when he thrust it back, and stared vaguely about the room. After a very brief inspection of his face, it was easy to conceive that his footstep must necessarily be such an one as that which, slowly and with as indefinite an aim as a child's first journey across a floor, had just brought him hitherward. Yet there were no tokens that his physical strength might not have sufficed for a free and determined gait. It was the spirit of the man that could not walk. The expression of his countenance—while, notwithstanding it had the light of reason in it—seemed to waver, and glimmer, and nearly to die away, and feebly to recover itself again. It was like a flame which we see twinkling among half-extinguished embers; we gaze at it more intently than if it were a positive blaze, gushing vividly upward,—more intently, but with a certain impatience, as if it ought either to kindle itself into satisfactory splendor, or be at once extinguished.

For an instant after entering the room, the guest stood still, retaining Hepzibah's hand instinctively, as a child does that of the grown person who guides it. He saw Phoebe, however, and caught an illumination from her youthful and pleasant aspect, which, indeed, threw a cheerfulness about the parlor, like the circle of reflected brilliancy around the glass vase of flowers that was standing in the sunshine. He made a salutation, or, to speak nearer the truth, an ill-defined, abortive attempt at curtsy. Imperfect as it was, however, it conveyed an idea, or, at least, gave a hint, of indescribable grace, such as no practised art of external manners could have attained. It was too slight to seize upon at the instant; yet, as recollected afterwards, seemed to transfigure the whole man.

"Dear Clifford," said Hepzibah, in the tone with which one soothes a wayward infant, "this is our cousin Phoebe,—little Phoebe Pyncheon,—Arthur's only child, you know. She has come from the country to stay with us awhile; for our old house has grown to be very lonely now."

"Phoebe—Phoebe Pyncheon?—Phoebe?" repeated the guest, with a strange, sluggish, ill-defined utterance. "Arthur's child! Ah, I forget! No matter. She is very welcome!"

"Come, dear Clifford, take this chair," said Hepzibah, leading him to his place. "Pray, Phoebe, lower the curtain a very little more. Now let us begin breakfast."

The guest seated himself in the place assigned him, and looked strangely around. He was evidently trying to grapple with the present scene, and bring it home to his mind with a more satisfactory distinctness. He desired to be certain, at least, that he was here, in the low-studded, cross-beamed, oaken-panelled parlor, and not in some other spot, which had stereotyped itself into his senses. But the effort was too great to be sustained with more than a fragmentary success. Continually, as we may express it, he faded away out of his place; or, in other words, his mind and consciousness took their departure, leaving his wasted, gray, and melancholy figure—a substantial emptiness, a material ghost—to occupy his seat at table. Again, after a blank moment, there would be a flickering taper-gleam in his eyeballs. It betokened that his spiritual part had returned, and was doing its best to kindle the heart's household fire, and light up intellectual lamps in the dark and ruinous mansion, where it was doomed to be a forlorn inhabitant.

At one of these moments of less torpid, yet still imperfect animation, Phoebe became convinced of what she had at first rejected as too extravagant and startling an idea. She saw that the person before her must have been the original of the beautiful miniature in her cousin Hepzibah's possession. Indeed, with a feminine eye for costume, she had at once identified the damask dressing-gown, which enveloped him, as the same in figure, material, and fashion, with that so elaborately represented in the picture. This old, faded garment, with all its pristine brilliancy extinct, seemed, in some indescribable way, to translate the wearer's untold misfortune, and make it perceptible to the beholder's eye. It was the better to be discerned, by this exterior type, how worn and old were the soul's more immediate garments; that form and countenance, the beauty and grace of which had almost transcended the skill of the most exquisite of artists. It could the more adequately be known that the soul of the man must have suffered some miserable wrong, from its earthly experience. There he seemed to sit, with a dim veil of decay and ruin betwixt him and the world, but through which, at flitting intervals, might be caught the same expression, so refined, so softly imaginative, which Malbone—venturing a happy touch, with suspended breath—had imparted to the miniature! There had been something so innately characteristic in this look, that all the dusky years, and the burden of unfit calamity which had fallen upon him, did not suffice utterly to destroy it.

Hepzibah had now poured out a cup of deliciously fragrant coffee, and presented it to her guest. As his eyes met hers, he seemed bewildered and disquieted.

"Is this you, Hepzibah?" he murmured sadly; then, more apart, and perhaps unconscious that he was overheard, "How changed! how changed! And is she angry with me? Why does she bend her brow so?"

Poor Hepzibah! It was that wretched scowl which time and her near-sightedness, and the fret of inward discomfort, had rendered so habitual that any vehemence of mood invariably evoked it. But at the indistinct murmur of his words her whole face grew tender, and even lovely, with sorrowful affection; the harshness of her features disappeared, as it were, behind the warm and misty glow.

"Angry!" she repeated; "angry with you, Clifford!"

Her tone, as she uttered the exclamation, had a plaintive and really exquisite melody thrilling through it, yet without subduing a certain something which an obtuse auditor might still have mistaken for asperity. It was as if some transcendent musician should draw a soul-thrilling sweetness out of a cracked instrument, which makes its physical imperfection heard in the midst of ethereal harmony,—so deep was the sensibility that found an organ in Hepzibah's voice!

"There is nothing but love here, Clifford," she added,—"nothing but love! You are at home!"

The guest responded to her tone by a smile, which did not half light up his face. Feeble as it was, however, and gone in a moment, it had a charm of wonderful beauty. It was followed by a coarser expression; or one that had the effect of coarseness on the fine mould and outline of his countenance, because there was nothing intellectual to temper it. It was a look of appetite. He ate food with what might almost be termed voracity; and seemed to forget himself, Hepzibah, the young girl, and everything else around him, in the sensual enjoyment which the bountifully spread table afforded. In his natural system, though high-wrought and delicately refined, a sensibility to the delights of the palate was probably inherent. It would have been kept in check, however, and even converted into an accomplishment, and one of the thousand modes of intellectual culture, had his more ethereal characteristics retained their vigor. But as it existed now, the effect was painful and made Phoebe droop her eyes.

In a little while the guest became sensible of the fragrance of the yet untasted coffee. He quaffed it eagerly. The subtle essence acted on him like a charmed draught, and caused the opaque substance of his animal being to grow transparent, or, at least, translucent; so that a spiritual gleam was transmitted through it, with a clearer lustre than hitherto.

"More, more!" he cried, with nervous haste in his utterance, as if anxious to retain his grasp of what sought to escape him. "This is what I need! Give me more!"

Under this delicate and powerful influence he sat more erect, and looked out from his eyes with a glance that took note of what it rested on. It was not so much that his expression grew more intellectual; this, though it had its share, was not the most peculiar effect. Neither was what we call the moral nature so forcibly awakened as to present itself in remarkable prominence. But a certain fine temper of being was now not brought out in full relief, but changeably and imperfectly betrayed, of which it was the function to deal with all beautiful and enjoyable things. In a character where it should exist as the chief attribute, it would bestow on its possessor an exquisite taste, and an enviable susceptibility of happiness. Beauty would be his life; his aspirations would all tend toward it; and, allowing his frame and physical organs to be in consonance, his own developments would likewise be beautiful. Such a man should have nothing to do with sorrow; nothing with strife; nothing with the martyrdom which, in an infinite variety of shapes, awaits those who have the heart, and will, and conscience, to fight a battle with the world. To these heroic tempers, such martyrdom is the richest meed in the world's gift. To the individual before us, it could only be a grief, intense in due proportion with the severity of the infliction. He had no right to be a martyr; and, beholding him so fit to be happy and so feeble for all other purposes, a generous, strong, and noble spirit would, methinks, have been ready to sacrifice what little enjoyment it might have planned for itself,—it would have flung down the hopes, so paltry in its regard,—if thereby the wintry blasts of our rude sphere might come tempered to such a man.

Not to speak it harshly or scornfully, it seemed Clifford's nature to be a Sybarite. It was perceptible, even there, in the dark old parlor, in the inevitable polarity with which his eyes were attracted towards the quivering play of sunbeams through the shadowy foliage. It was seen in his appreciating notice of the vase of flowers, the scent of which he inhaled with a zest almost peculiar to a physical organization so refined that spiritual ingredients are moulded in with it. It was betrayed in the unconscious smile with which he regarded Phoebe, whose fresh and maidenly figure was both sunshine and flowers,—their essence, in a prettier and more agreeable mode of manifestation. Not less evident was this love and necessity for the Beautiful, in the instinctive caution with which, even so soon, his eyes turned away from his hostess, and wandered to any quarter rather than come back. It was Hepzibah's misfortune,—not Clifford's fault. How could he,—so yellow as she was, so wrinkled, so sad of mien, with that odd uncouthness of a turban on her head, and that most perverse of scowls contorting her brow,—how could he love to gaze at her? But, did he owe her no affection for so much as she had silently given? He owed her nothing. A nature like Clifford's can contract no debts of that kind. It is—we say it without censure, nor in diminution of the claim which it indefeasibly possesses on beings of another mould—it is always selfish in its essence; and we must give it leave to be so, and heap up our heroic and disinterested love upon it so much the more, without a recompense. Poor Hepzibah knew this truth, or, at least, acted on the instinct of it. So long estranged from what was lovely as Clifford had been, she rejoiced—rejoiced, though with a present sigh, and a secret purpose to shed tears in her own chamber that he had brighter objects now before his eyes than her aged and uncomely features. They never possessed a charm; and if they had, the canker of her grief for him would long since have destroyed it.

The guest leaned back in his chair. Mingled in his countenance with a dreamy delight, there was a troubled look of effort and unrest. He was seeking to make himself more fully sensible of the scene around him; or, perhaps, dreading it to be a dream, or a play of imagination, was vexing the fair moment with a struggle for some added brilliancy and more durable illusion.

"How pleasant!—How delightful!" he murmured, but not as if addressing any one. "Will it last? How balmy the atmosphere through that open window! An open window! How beautiful that play of sunshine! Those flowers, how very fragrant! That young girl's face, how cheerful, how blooming!—a flower with the dew on it, and sunbeams in the dew-drops! Ah! this must be all a dream! A dream! A dream! But it has quite hidden the four stone walls!"

Then his face darkened, as if the shadow of a cavern or a dungeon had come over it; there was no more light in its expression than might have come through the iron grates of a prison-window—still lessening, too, as if he were sinking farther into the depths. Phoebe (being of that quickness and activity of temperament that she seldom long refrained from taking a part, and generally a good one, in what was going forward) now felt herself moved to address the stranger.

"Here is a new kind of rose, which I found this morning in the garden," said she, choosing a small crimson one from among the flowers in the vase. "There will be but five or six on the bush this season. This is the most perfect of them all; not a speck of blight or mildew in it. And how sweet it is!—sweet like no other rose! One can never forget that scent!"

"Ah!—let me see!—let me hold it!" cried the guest, eagerly seizing the flower, which, by the spell peculiar to remembered odors, brought innumerable associations along with the fragrance that it exhaled. "Thank you! This has done me good. I remember how I used to prize this flower,—long ago, I suppose, very long ago!—or was it only yesterday? It makes me feel young again! Am I young? Either this remembrance is singularly distinct, or this consciousness strangely dim! But how kind of the fair young girl! Thank you! Thank you!"

The favorable excitement derived from this little crimson rose afforded Clifford the brightest moment which he enjoyed at the breakfast-table. It might have lasted longer, but that his eyes happened, soon afterwards, to rest on the face of the old Puritan, who, out of his dingy frame and lustreless canvas, was looking down on the scene like a ghost, and a most ill-tempered and ungenial one. The guest made an impatient gesture of the hand, and addressed Hepzibah with what might easily be recognized as the licensed irritability of a petted member of the family.

"Hepzibah!—Hepzibah!" cried he with no little force and distinctness, "why do you keep that odious picture on the wall? Yes, yes!—that is precisely your taste! I have told you, a thousand times, that it was the evil genius of the house!—my evil genius particularly! Take it down, at once!"

"Dear Clifford," said Hepzibah sadly, "you know it cannot be!"

"Then, at all events," continued he, still speaking with some energy, "pray cover it with a crimson curtain, broad enough to hang in folds, and with a golden border and tassels. I cannot bear it! It must not stare me in the face!"

"Yes, dear Clifford, the picture shall be covered," said Hepzibah soothingly. "There is a crimson curtain in a trunk above stairs,—a little faded and moth-eaten, I'm afraid,—but Phoebe and I will do wonders with it."

"This very day, remember" said he; and then added, in a low, self-communing voice, "Why should we live in this dismal house at all? Why not go to the South of France?—to Italy?—Paris, Naples, Venice, Rome? Hepzibah will say we have not the means. A droll idea that!"

He smiled to himself, and threw a glance of fine sarcastic meaning towards Hepzibah.

But the several moods of feeling, faintly as they were marked, through which he had passed, occurring in so brief an interval of time, had evidently wearied the stranger. He was probably accustomed to a sad monotony of life, not so much flowing in a stream, however sluggish, as stagnating in a pool around his feet. A slumberous veil diffused itself over his countenance, and had an effect, morally speaking, on its naturally delicate and elegant outline, like that which a brooding mist, with no sunshine in it, throws over the features of a landscape. He appeared to become grosser,—almost cloddish. If aught of interest or beauty—even ruined beauty—had heretofore been visible in this man, the beholder might now begin to doubt it, and to accuse his own imagination of deluding him with whatever grace had flickered over that visage, and whatever exquisite lustre had gleamed in those filmy eyes.

Before he had quite sunken away, however, the sharp and peevish tinkle of the shop-bell made itself audible. Striking most disagreeably on Clifford's auditory organs and the characteristic sensibility of his nerves, it caused him to start upright out of his chair.

"Good heavens, Hepzibah! what horrible disturbance have we now in the house?" cried he, wreaking his resentful impatience—as a matter of course, and a custom of old—on the one person in the world that loved him. "I have never heard such a hateful clamor! Why do you permit it? In the name of all dissonance, what can it be?"

It was very remarkable into what prominent relief—even as if a dim picture should leap suddenly from its canvas—Clifford's character was thrown by this apparently trifling annoyance. The secret was, that an individual of his temper can always be pricked more acutely through his sense of the beautiful and harmonious than through his heart. It is even possible—for similar cases have often happened—that if Clifford, in his foregoing life, had enjoyed the means of cultivating his taste to its utmost perfectibility, that subtile attribute might, before this period, have completely eaten out or filed away his affections. Shall we venture to pronounce, therefore, that his long and black calamity may not have had a redeeming drop of mercy at the bottom?

"Dear Clifford, I wish I could keep the sound from your ears," said Hepzibah, patiently, but reddening with a painful suffusion of shame. "It is very disagreeable even to me. But, do you know, Clifford, I have something to tell you? This ugly noise,—pray run, Phoebe, and see who is there!—this naughty little tinkle is nothing but our shop-bell!"

"Shop-bell!" repeated Clifford, with a bewildered stare.

"Yes, our shop-bell," said Hepzibah, a certain natural dignity, mingled with deep emotion, now asserting itself in her manner. "For you must know, dearest Clifford, that we are very poor. And there was no other resource, but either to accept assistance from a hand that I would push aside (and so would you!) were it to offer bread when we were dying for it,—no help, save from him, or else to earn our subsistence with my own hands! Alone, I might have been content to starve. But you were to be given back to me! Do you think, then, dear Clifford," added she, with a wretched smile, "that I have brought an irretrievable disgrace on the old house, by opening a little shop in the front gable? Our great-great-grandfather did the same, when there was far less need! Are you ashamed of me?"

"Shame! Disgrace! Do you speak these words to me, Hepzibah?" said Clifford,—not angrily, however; for when a man's spirit has been thoroughly crushed, he may be peevish at small offences, but never resentful of great ones. So he spoke with only a grieved emotion. "It was not kind to say so, Hepzibah! What shame can befall me now?"

And then the unnerved man—he that had been born for enjoyment, but had met a doom so very wretched—burst into a woman's passion of tears. It was but of brief continuance, however; soon leaving him in a quiescent, and, to judge by his countenance, not an uncomfortable state. From this mood, too, he partially rallied for an instant, and looked at Hepzibah with a smile, the keen, half-derisory purport of which was a puzzle to her.

"Are we so very poor, Hepzibah?" said he.

Finally, his chair being deep and softly cushioned, Clifford fell asleep. Hearing the more regular rise and fall of his breath (which, however, even then, instead of being strong and full, had a feeble kind of tremor, corresponding with the lack of vigor in his character),—hearing these tokens of settled slumber, Hepzibah seized the opportunity to peruse his face more attentively than she had yet dared to do. Her heart melted away in tears; her profoundest spirit sent forth a moaning voice, low, gentle, but inexpressibly sad. In this depth of grief and pity she felt that there was no irreverence in gazing at his altered, aged, faded, ruined face. But no sooner was she a little relieved than her conscience smote her for gazing curiously at him, now that he was so changed; and, turning hastily away, Hepzibah let down the curtain over the sunny window, and left Clifford to slumber there.

𝒮 8 𝒮

THE PYNCHEON OF TO-DAY

PHOEBE, on entering the shop, beheld there the already familiar face of the little devourer—if we can reckon his mighty deeds aright—of Jim Crow, the elephant, the camel, the dromedaries, and the locomotive. Having expended his private fortune, on the two preceding days, in the purchase of the above unheard-of luxuries, the young gentleman's present errand was on the part of his mother, in quest of three eggs and half a pound of raisins. These articles Phoebe accordingly supplied, and, as a mark of gratitude for his previous patronage, and a slight super-added morsel after breakfast, put likewise into his hand a whale! The great fish, reversing his experience with the prophet of Nineveh, immediately began his progress down the same red pathway of fate whither so varied a caravan had preceded him. This remarkable urchin, in truth, was the very emblem of old Father Time, both in respect of his all-devouring appetite for men and things, and because he, as well as Time, after ingulfing thus much of creation, looked almost as youthful as if he had been just that moment made.

After partly closing the door, the child turned back, and mumbled something to Phoebe, which, as the whale was but half disposed of, she could not perfectly understand.

"What did you say, my little fellow?" asked she.

"Mother wants to know" repeated Ned Higgins more distinctly, "how Old Maid Pyncheon's brother does? Folks say he has got home."

"My cousin Hepzibah's brother?" exclaimed Phoebe, surprised at this sudden explanation of the relationship between Hepzibah and her guest. "Her brother! And where can he have been?"

The little boy only put his thumb to his broad snub-nose, with that look of shrewdness which a child, spending much of his time in the street, so soon learns to throw over his features, however unintelligent in themselves. Then as Phoebe continued to gaze at him, without answering his mother's message, he took his departure.

As the child went down the steps, a gentleman ascended them, and made his entrance into the shop. It was the portly, and, had it possessed the advantage of a little more height, would have been the stately figure of a man considerably in the decline of life, dressed in a black suit of some thin stuff, resembling broadcloth as closely as possible. A gold-headed cane, of rare

438

Oriental wood, added materially to the high respectability of his aspect, as did also a neckcloth of the utmost snowy purity, and the conscientious polish of his boots. His dark, square countenance, with its almost shaggy depth of eyebrows, was naturally impressive, and would, perhaps, have been rather stern, had not the gentleman considerately taken upon himself to mitigate the harsh effect by a look of exceeding good-humor and benevolence. Owing, however, to a somewhat massive accumulation of animal substance about the lower region of his face, the look was, perhaps, unctuous rather than spiritual, and had, so to speak, a kind of fleshly effulgence, not altogether so satisfactory as he doubtless intended it to be. A susceptible observer, at any rate, might have regarded it as affording very little evidence of the general benignity of soul whereof it purported to be the outward reflection. And if the observer chanced to be ill-natured, as well as acute and susceptible, he would probably suspect that the smile on the gentleman's face was a good deal akin to the shine on his boots, and that each must have cost him and his boot-black, respectively, a good deal of hard labor to bring out and preserve them.

As the stranger entered the little shop, where the projection of the second story and the thick foliage of the elm-tree, as well as the commodities at the window, created a sort of gray medium, his smile grew as intense as if he had set his heart on counteracting the whole gloom of the atmosphere (besides any moral gloom pertaining to Hepzibah and her inmates) by the unassisted light of his countenance. On perceiving a young rose-bud of a girl, instead of the gaunt presence of the old maid, a look of surprise was manifest. He at first knit his brows; then smiled with more unctuous benignity than ever.

"Ah, I see how it is!" said he in a deep voice,—a voice which, had it come from the throat of an uncultivated man, would have been gruff, but, by dint of careful training, was now sufficiently agreeable,—"I was not aware that Miss Hepzibah Pyncheon had commenced business under such favorable auspices. You are her assistant, I suppose?"

"I certainly am," answered Phoebe, and added, with a little air of lady-like assumption (for, civil as the gentleman was, he evidently took her to be a young person serving for wages), "I am a cousin of Miss Hepzibah, on a visit to her."

"Her cousin?—and from the country? Pray pardon me, then," said the gentleman, bowing and smiling, as Phoebe never had been bowed to nor smiled on before; "in that case, we must be better acquainted; for, unless I am sadly mistaken, you are my own little kinswoman likewise! Let me see,—Mary?—Dolly?—Phoebe?—yes, Phoebe is the name! Is it possible that you are Phoebe Pyncheon, only child of my dear cousin and classmate, Arthur? Ah, I see your father now, about your mouth! Yes, yes! we must be better acquainted! I am your kinsman, my dear. Surely you must have heard of Judge Pyncheon?"

As Phoebe curtsied in reply, the Judge bent forward, with the pardonable and even praiseworthy purpose—considering the nearness of blood and the difference of age—of bestowing on his young relative a kiss of acknowledged kindred and natural affection. Unfortunately (without design, or only with such instinctive design as gives no account of itself to the intellect) Phoebe, just at the critical moment, drew back; so that her highly respectable kinsman, with his body bent over the counter and his lips protruded, was betrayed into the rather absurd predicament of kissing the empty air. It was a modern parallel to the case of Ixion embracing a cloud, and was so much the more ridiculous as the Judge prided himself on eschewing all airy matter, and never mistaking a shadow for a substance. The truth was,—and it is Phoebe's only excuse,—that, although Judge Pyncheon's glowing benignity might not be absolutely unpleasant to the feminine beholder, with the width of a street, or even an ordinary-sized room, interposed between, yet it became quite too intense, when this dark, full-fed physiognomy (so roughly bearded, too, that no razor could ever make it smooth) sought to bring itself into actual contact with the object of its regards. The man, the sex, somehow or other, was entirely too prominent in the Judge's demonstrations of that sort. Phoebe's eyes sank, and, without knowing why, she felt herself blushing deeply under his look. Yet she had been kissed before, and without any particular squeamishness, by perhaps half a dozen different cousins, younger as well as older than this dark-browned, grisly-bearded, white-neck-clothed, and unctuously-benevolent Judge! Then, why not by him?

On raising her eyes, Phoebe was startled by the change in Judge Pyncheon's face. It was quite as striking, allowing for the difference of scale, as that betwixt a landscape under a broad sunshine and just before a thunder-storm; not that it had the passionate intensity of the latter aspect, but was cold, hard, immitigable, like a day-long brooding cloud.

"Dear me! what is to be done now?" thought the country-girl to herself. "He looks as if there were nothing softer in him than a rock, nor milder than the east wind! I meant no harm! Since he is really my cousin, I would have let him kiss me, if I could!"

Then, all at once, it struck Phoebe that this very Judge Pyncheon was the original of the miniature which the daguerreotypist had shown her in the garden, and that the hard, stern, relentless look, now on his face, was the same that the sun had so inflexibly persisted in bringing out. Was it, therefore, no momentary mood, but, however skillfully concealed, the settled temper of his life? And not merely so, but was it hereditary in him, and transmitted down, as a precious heirloom, from that bearded ancestor, in whose picture both the expression and, to a singular degree, the features of the modern Judge were shown as by a kind of prophecy? A deeper philosopher than Phoebe might have found something very terrible in this idea. It implied that the weaknesses and defects, the bad passions, the mean tendencies, and the moral diseases which lead to crime are handed down from one generation to another, by a far surer process of transmission than human law has been able to establish in respect to the riches and honors which it seeks to entail upon posterity.

But, as it happened, scarcely had Phoebe's eyes rested again on the Judge's countenance than all its ugly sternness vanished; and she found herself quite overpowered by the sultry, dog-day heat, as it were, of benevolence, which this excellent man diffused out of his great heart into the surrounding atmosphere,—very much like a serpent, which, as a preliminary to fascination, is said to fill the air with his peculiar odor.

"I like that, Cousin Phoebe!" cried he, with an emphatic nod of approbation. "I like it much, my little cousin! You are a good child, and know how to take care of yourself. A young girl—especially if she be a very pretty one—can never be too chary of her lips."

"Indeed, sir," said Phoebe, trying to laugh the matter off, "I did not mean to be unkind."

Nevertheless, whether or no it were entirely owing to the inauspicious commencement of their acquaintance, she still acted under a certain reserve, which was by no means customary to her frank and genial nature. The fantasy would not quit her, that the original Puritan, of whom she had heard so many sombre traditions,—the progenitor of the whole race of New England Pyncheons, the founder of the House of the Seven Gables, and who had died so strangely in it,—had now stept into the shop. In these days of off-hand equipment, the matter was easily enough arranged. On his arrival from the other world, he had merely found it necessary to spend a quarter of an hour at a barber's, who had trimmed down the Puritan's full beard into a pair of grizzled whiskers, then, patronizing a ready-made clothing establishment, he had exchanged his velvet doublet and sable cloak, with the richly worked band under his chin, for a white collar and cravat, coat, vest, and pantaloons; and lastly, putting aside his steel-hilted broadsword to take up a gold-headed cane, the Colonel Pyncheon of two centuries ago steps forward as the Judge of the passing moment!

Of course, Phoebe was far too sensible a girl to entertain this idea in any other way than as matter for a smile. Possibly, also, could the two personages have stood together before her eye, many points of difference would have been perceptible, and perhaps only a general resemblance. The long lapse of intervening years, in a climate so unlike that which had fostered the ancestral Englishman, must inevitably have wrought important changes in the physical system of his descendant. The Judge's volume of muscle could hardly be the same as the Colonel's; there was undoubtedly less beef in him. Though looked upon as a weighty man among his contemporaries in respect of animal substance, and as favored with a remarkable degree of fundamental development, well adapting him for the judicial bench, we conceive that the modern Judge Pyncheon, if weighed in the same balance with his ancestor, would have required at least an old-fashioned fifty-six to keep the scale in equilibrio. Then the Judge's face had lost the ruddy English hue that showed its warmth through all the duskiness of the Colonel's weather-beaten cheek, and had taken a sallow shade, the established complexion of his countrymen. If we mistake not, moreover, a certain quality of nervousness had become more or less manifest, even in so solid a specimen of Puritan descent as the gentleman now under discussion. As one of its effects, it bestowed on his countenance a quicker mobility than the old Englishman's had possessed, and keener vivacity, but at the expense of a sturdier something, on which these acute endowments seemed to act like dissolving acids. This process, for aught we know, may belong to the great system of human progress, which, with every ascending footstep, as it diminishes the necessity for animal force, may be destined gradually to spiritualize us, by refining away our grosser attributes of body. If so, Judge Pyncheon could endure a century or two more of such refinement as well as most other men.

The similarity, intellectual and moral, between the Judge and his ancestor appears to have been at least as strong as the resemblance of mien and feature would afford reason to anticipate. In old Colonel Pyncheon's funeral discourse the clergyman absolutely canonized his deceased parishioner, and opening, as it were, a vista through the roof of the church, and thence through the firmament above, showed him seated, harp in hand, among the crowned choristers of the spiritual world. On his tombstone, too, the record is highly eulogistic; nor does history, so far as he holds a place upon its page, assail the consistency and uprightness of his character. So also, as regards the Judge Pyncheon of to-day, neither clergyman, nor legal critic, nor inscriber of tombstones, nor historian of general or local politics, would venture a word against this eminent person's sincerity as a Christian, or respectability as a man, or integrity as a judge, or courage and faithfulness as the often-tried representative of his political party. But, besides these cold, formal, and empty words of the chisel that inscribes, the voice that speaks, and the pen that writes, for the public eye and for distant time,—and which inevitably lose much of their truth and freedom by the fatal consciousness of so doing,—there were traditions about the ancestor, and private diurnal gossip about the Judge, remarkably accordant in their testimony. It is often instructive to take the woman's, the private and domestic, view of a public man; nor can anything be more curious than the vast discrepancy between portraits intended for engraving and the pencil-sketches that pass from hand to hand behind the original's back.

For example: tradition affirmed that the Puritan had been greedy of wealth; the Judge, too, with all the show of liberal expenditure, was said to be as close-fisted as if his gripe were of iron. The ancestor had clothed himself in a grim assumption of kindliness, a rough heartiness of word and manner, which most people took to be the genuine warmth of nature, making its way through the thick and inflexible hide of a manly character. His descendant, in compliance with the requirements of a nicer age, had etherealized this rude benevolence into that broad benignity of smile wherewith he shone like a noonday sun along the streets, or glowed like a household fire in the drawing-rooms of his private acquaintance. The Puritan— if not belied by some singular stories, murmured, even at this day, under the narrator's breath—had fallen into certain transgressions to which men of his great animal development, whatever their faith or principles, must continue liable, until they put off impurity, along with the gross earthly substance that involves it. We must not stain our page with any contemporary scandal, to a similar purport, that may have been whispered against the Judge. The Puritan, again, an autocrat in his own household, had worn out three wives, and, merely by the remorseless weight and hardness of his character in the conjugal relation, had sent them, one after another, broken-hearted, to their graves. Here the parallel, in some sort, fails. The Judge had wedded but a single wife, and lost her in the third or fourth year of their marriage. There was a fable, however,—for such we choose to consider it, though, not impossibly, typical of Judge Pyncheon's marital deportment,—that the lady got her death-blow in the honeymoon, and never smiled again, because her husband compelled her to serve him with coffee every morning at his bedside, in token of fealty to her liege-lord and master.

But it is too fruitful a subject, this of hereditary resemblances,—the frequent recurrence of which, in a direct line, is truly unaccountable, when we consider how large an accumulation of ancestry lies behind every man at the distance of one or two centuries. We shall only add, therefore, that the Puritan—so, at least, says chimney-corner tradition, which often preserves traits of character with marvellous fidelity—was bold, imperious, relentless, crafty; laying his purposes deep, and following them out with an inveteracy of pursuit that knew neither rest nor conscience; trampling on the weak, and, when essential to his ends, doing his utmost to beat down the strong. Whether the Judge in any degree resembled him, the further progress of our narrative may show.

Scarcely any of the items in the above-drawn parallel occurred to Phoebe, whose country birth and residence, in truth, had left her pitifully ignorant of most of the family traditions, which lingered, like cobwebs and incrustations of smoke, about the rooms and chimney-corners of the House of the Seven Gables. Yet there was a circumstance, very trifling in itself, which impressed her with an odd degree of horror. She had heard of the anathema flung by Maule, the executed wizard, against Colonel Pyncheon and his posterity,—that God would give them blood to drink,—and likewise of the popular notion, that this miraculous blood might now and then be heard gurgling in their throats. The latter scandal—as became a person of sense, and, more especially, a member of the Pyncheon family—Phoebe had set down for the absurdity which it unquestionably was. But ancient superstitions, after being steeped in human hearts and embodied in human breath, and passing from lip to ear in manifold repetition, through a series of generations, become imbued with an effect of homely truth. The smoke of the domestic hearth has scented them through and through. By long transmission among household facts, they grow to look like them, and have such a familiar way of making themselves at home that their influence is usually greater than we suspect. Thus it happened, that when Phoebe heard a certain noise in Judge Pyncheon's throat,—rather habitual with him, not altogether voluntary, yet indicative of nothing, unless it were a slight bronchial complaint, or, as some people hinted, an apoplectic symptom,—when the girl heard this queer and awkward ingurgitation (which the writer never did hear, and therefore cannot describe), she very foolishly started, and clasped her hands.

Of course, it was exceedingly ridiculous in Phoebe to be discomposed by such a trifle, and still more unpardonable to show her discomposure to the individual most concerned in it. But the incident chimed in so oddly with her previous fancies about the Colonel and the Judge, that, for the moment, it seemed quite to mingle their identity.

"What is the matter with you, young woman?" said Judge Pyncheon, giving her one of his harsh looks. "Are you afraid of anything?"

"Oh, nothing, sir—nothing in the world!" answered Phoebe, with a little laugh of vexation at herself. "But perhaps you wish to speak with my cousin Hepzibah. Shall I call her?"

"Stay a moment, if you please," said the Judge, again beaming sunshine out of his face. "You seem to be a little nervous this morning. The town air, Cousin Phoebe, does not agree with your good, wholesome country habits. Or has anything happened to disturb you?— anything remarkable in Cousin Hepzibah's family?— An arrival, eh? I thought so! No wonder you are out of sorts, my little cousin. To be an inmate with such a guest may well startle an innocent young girl!"

"You quite puzzle me, sir," replied Phoebe, gazing inquiringly at the Judge. "There is no frightful guest in the house, but only a poor, gentle, childlike man, whom I believe to be Cousin Hepzibah's brother. I am afraid (but you, sir, will know better than I) that he is not quite in his sound senses; but so mild and quiet he seems to be, that a mother might trust her baby with him; and I think he would play with the baby as if he were only a few years older than itself. He startle me!—Oh, no indeed!"

"I rejoice to hear so favorable and so ingenuous an account of my cousin Clifford," said the benevolent Judge. "Many years ago, when we were boys and young men together, I had a great affection for him, and still feel a tender interest in all his concerns. You say, Cousin Phoebe, he appears to be weak minded. Heaven grant him at least enough of intellect to repent of his past sins!"

"Nobody, I fancy," observed Phoebe, "can have fewer to repent of."

"And is it possible, my dear," rejoined the Judge, with a commiserating look, "that you have never heard of Clifford Pyncheon?—that you know nothing of his history? Well, it is all right; and your mother has shown a very proper regard for the good name of the family with which she connected herself. Believe the best you can of this unfortunate person, and hope the best! It is a rule which Christians should always follow, in their judgments of one another; and especially is it right and wise among near relatives, whose characters have necessarily a degree of mutual dependence. But is Clifford in the parlor? I will just step in and see."

"Perhaps, sir, I had better call my cousin Hepzibah," said Phoebe; hardly knowing, however, whether she ought to obstruct the entrance of so affectionate a kinsman into the private regions of the house. "Her brother seemed to be just falling asleep after breakfast; and I am sure she would not like him to be disturbed. Pray, sir, let me give her notice!"

But the Judge showed a singular determination to enter unannounced; and as Phoebe, with the vivacity of a person whose movements unconsciously answer to her thoughts, had stepped towards the door, he used little or no ceremony in putting her aside.

"No, no, Miss Phoebe!" said Judge Pyncheon in a voice as deep as a thunder-growl, and with a frown as black as the cloud whence it issues. "Stay you here! I know the house, and know my cousin Hepzibah, and know her brother Clifford likewise.—nor need my little country cousin put herself to the trouble of announcing me!"—in these latter words, by the bye, there were symptoms of a change from his sudden harshness into his previous benignity of manner. "I am at home here, Phoebe, you must recollect, and you are the stranger. I will just step in, therefore, and see for myself how Clifford is, and assure him and Hepzibah of my kindly feelings and best wishes. It is right, at this juncture, that they should both hear from my own lips how much I desire to serve them. Ha! here is Hepzibah herself!"

Such was the case. The vibrations of the Judge's voice had reached the old gentlewoman in the parlor, where she sat, with face averted, waiting on her brother's slumber. She now issued forth, as would appear, to defend the entrance, looking, we must needs say, amazingly like the dragon which, in fairy tales, is wont to be the guardian over an enchanted beauty. The habitual scowl of her brow was undeniably too fierce, at this moment, to pass itself off on the innocent score of near-sightedness; and it was bent on Judge Pyncheon in a way that seemed to confound, if not alarm him, so inadequately had he estimated the moral force of a deeply grounded antipathy. She made a repelling gesture with her hand, and stood a perfect picture of prohibition, at full length, in the dark frame of the doorway. But we must betray Hepzibah's secret, and confess that the native timorousness of her character even now developed itself in a quick tremor, which, to her own perception, set each of her joints at variance with its fellows.

Possibly, the Judge was aware how little true hardihood lay behind Hepzibah's formidable front. At any rate, being a gentleman of steady nerves, he soon recovered himself, and failed not to approach his cousin with outstretched hand; adopting the sensible precaution, however, to cover his advance with a smile, so broad and sultry, that, had it been only half as warm as it looked, a trellis of grapes might at once have turned purple under its summer-like exposure. It may have been his purpose, indeed, to melt poor Hepzibah on the spot, as if she were a figure of yellow wax.

"Hepzibah, my beloved cousin, I am rejoiced!" exclaimed the Judge most emphatically. "Now, at length, you have something to live for. Yes, and all of us, let me say, your friends and kindred, have more to live for than we had yesterday. I have lost no time in hastening to offer any assistance in my power towards making Clifford comfortable. He belongs to us all. I know how much he requires,—how much he used to require,—with his delicate taste, and his love of the beautiful. Anything in my house,—pictures, books, wine, luxuries of the table,—he may command them all! It would afford me most heartfelt gratification to see him! Shall I step in, this moment?"

"No," replied Hepzibah, her voice quivering too painfully to allow of many words. "He cannot see visitors!"

"A visitor, my dear cousin!—do you call me so?" cried the Judge, whose sensibility, it seems, was hurt by the coldness of the phrase. "Nay, then, let me be Clifford's host, and your own likewise. Come at once to my house. The country air, and all the conveniences,—I may say luxuries,—that I have gathered about me, will do wonders for him. And you and I, dear Hepzibah, will consult together, and watch together, and labor together, to make our dear Clifford happy. Come! why should we make more words about what is both a duty and a pleasure on my part? Come to me at once!"

On hearing these so hospitable offers, and such generous recognition of the claims of kindred, Phoebe felt very much in the mood of running up to Judge Pyncheon, and giving him, of her own accord, the kiss from which she had so recently shrunk away. It was quite otherwise with Hepzibah; the Judge's smile seemed to operate on her acerbity of heart like sunshine upon vinegar, making it ten times sourer than ever.

"Clifford," said she,—still too agitated to utter more than an abrupt sentence,—"Clifford has a home here!"

"May Heaven forgive you, Hepzibah," said Judge Pyncheon,—reverently lifting his eyes towards that high court of equity to which he appealed,—"if you suffer any ancient prejudice or animosity to weigh with you in this matter. I stand here with an open heart, willing and anxious to receive yourself and Clifford into it. Do not refuse my good offices,—my earnest propositions for your welfare! They are such, in all respects, as it behooves your nearest kinsman to make. It will be a heavy responsibility, cousin, if you confine your brother to this dismal house and stifled air, when the delightful freedom of my country-seat is at his command."

"It would never suit Clifford," said Hepzibah, as briefly as before.

"Woman!" broke forth the Judge, giving way to his resentment, "what is the meaning of all this? Have you other resources? Nay, I suspected as much! Take care, Hepzibah, take care!

Clifford is on the brink of as black a ruin as ever befell him yet! But why do I talk with you, woman as you are? Make way!—I must see Clifford!"

Hepzibah spread out her gaunt figure across the door, and seemed really to increase in bulk; looking the more terrible, also, because there was so much terror and agitation in her heart. But Judge Pyncheon's evident purpose of forcing a passage was interrupted by a voice from the inner room; a weak, tremulous, wailing voice, indicating helpless alarm, with no more energy for self-defence than belongs to a frightened infant.

"Hepzibah, Hepzibah!" cried the voice; "go down on your knees to him! Kiss his feet! Entreat him not to come in! Oh, let him have mercy on me! Mercy! mercy!"

For the instant, it appeared doubtful whether it were not the Judge's resolute purpose to set Hepzibah aside, and step across the threshold into the parlor, whence issued that broken and miserable murmur of entreaty. It was not pity that restrained him, for, at the first sound of the enfeebled voice, a red fire kindled in his eyes, and he made a quick pace forward, with something inexpressibly fierce and grim darkening forth, as it were, out of the whole man. To know Judge Pyncheon was to see him at that moment. After such a revelation, let him smile with what sultriness he would, he could much sooner turn grapes purple, or pumpkins yellow, than melt the iron-branded impression out of the beholder's memory. And it rendered his aspect not the less, but more frightful, that it seemed not to express wrath or hatred, but a certain hot fellness of purpose, which annihilated everything but itself.

Yet, after all, are we not slandering an excellent and amiable man? Look at the Judge now! He is apparently conscious of having erred, in too energetically pressing his deeds of loving-kindness on persons unable to appreciate them. He will await their better mood, and hold himself as ready to assist them then as at this moment. As he draws back from the door, an all-comprehensive benignity blazes from his visage, indicating that he gathers Hepzibah, little Phoebe, and the invisible Clifford, all three, together with the whole world besides, into his immense heart, and gives them a warm bath in its flood of affection.

"You do me great wrong, dear Cousin Hepzibah!" said he, first kindly offering her his hand, and then drawing on his glove preparatory to departure. "Very great wrong! But I forgive it, and will study to make you think better of me. Of course, our poor Clifford being in so unhappy a state of mind, I cannot think of urging an interview at present. But I shall watch over his welfare as if he were my own beloved brother; nor do I at all despair, my dear cousin, of constraining both him and you to acknowledge your injustice. When that shall happen, I desire no other revenge than your acceptance of the best offices in my power to do you."

With a bow to Hepzibah, and a degree of paternal benevolence in his parting nod to Phoebe, the Judge left the shop, and went smiling along the street. As is customary with the rich, when they aim at the honors of a republic, he apologized, as it were, to the people, for his wealth, prosperity, and elevated station, by a free and hearty manner towards those who knew him; putting off the more of his dignity in due proportion with the humbleness of the man whom he saluted, and thereby proving a haughty consciousness of his advantages as irrefragably as if he had marched forth preceded by a troop of lackeys to clear the way. On this particular forenoon, so excessive was the warmth of Judge Pyncheon's kindly aspect, that (such, at least, was the rumor about town) an extra passage of the water-carts was found essential, in order to lay the dust occasioned by so much extra sunshine!

No sooner had he disappeared than Hepzibah grew deadly white, and, staggering towards Phoebe, let her head fall on the young girl's shoulder.

"O Phoebe!" murmured she, "that man has been the horror of my life! Shall I never, never have the courage,—will my voice never cease from trembling long enough to let me tell him what he is?"

"Is he so very wicked?" asked Phoebe. "Yet his offers were surely kind!"

"Do not speak of them,—he has a heart of iron!" rejoined Hepzibah. "Go, now, and talk to Clifford! Amuse and keep him quiet! It would disturb him wretchedly to see me so agitated as I am. There, go, dear child, and I will try to look after the shop."

Phoebe went accordingly, but perplexed herself, meanwhile, with queries as to the purport of the scene which she had just witnessed, and also whether judges, clergymen, and other characters of that eminent stamp and respectability, could really, in any single instance, be otherwise than just and upright men. A doubt of this nature has a most disturbing influence, and, if shown to be a fact, comes with fearful and startling effect on minds of the trim, orderly, and limit-loving class, in which we find our little country-girl. Dispositions more boldly speculative may derive a stern enjoyment from the discovery, since there must be evil in the world, that a high man is as likely to grasp his share of it as a low one. A wider scope of view, and a deeper insight, may see rank, dignity, and station, all proved illusory, so far as regards their claim to human reverence, and yet not feel as if the universe were thereby tumbled headlong into chaos. But Phoebe, in order to keep the universe in its old place, was fain to smother, in some degree, her own intuitions as to Judge Pyncheon's character. And as for her cousin's testimony in disparagement of it, she concluded that Hepzibah's judgment was embittered by one of those family feuds which render hatred the more deadly by the dead and corrupted love that they intermingle with its native poison.

❧ 9 ❧

CLIFFORD AND PHOEBE

TRULY WAS THERE SOMETHING HIGH, generous, and noble in the native composition of our poor old Hepzibah! Or else,—and it was quite as probably the case,—she had been enriched by poverty, developed by sorrow, elevated by the strong and solitary affection of her life, and thus endowed with heroism, which never could have characterized her in what are called happier circumstances. Through dreary years Hepzibah had looked forward—for the most part despairingly, never with any confidence of hope, but always with the feeling that it was her brightest possibility—to the very position in which she now found herself. In her own behalf, she had asked nothing of Providence but the opportunity of devoting herself to this brother, whom she had so loved,—so admired for what he was, or might have been,—and to whom she had kept her faith, alone of all the world, wholly, unfalteringly, at every instant, and throughout life. And here, in his late decline, the lost one had come back out of his long and strange misfortune, and was thrown on her sympathy, as it seemed, not merely for the bread of his physical existence, but for everything that should keep him morally alive. She had responded to the call. She had come forward,—our poor, gaunt Hepzibah, in her rusty silks, with her rigid joints, and the sad perversity of her scowl,—ready to do her utmost; and with affection enough, if that were all, to do a hundred times as much! There could be few more tearful sights,—and Heaven forgive us if a smile insist on mingling with our conception of it!—few sights with truer pathos in them, than Hepzibah presented on that first afternoon.

How patiently did she endeavor to wrap Clifford up in her great, warm love, and make it all the world to him, so that he should retain no torturing sense of the coldness and dreariness without! Her little efforts to amuse him! How pitiful, yet magnanimous, they were!

Remembering his early love of poetry and fiction, she unlocked a bookcase, and took down several books that had been excellent reading in their day. There was a volume of Pope, with the Rape of the Lock in it, and another of the Tatler, and an odd one of Dryden's Miscellanies, all with tarnished gilding on their covers, and thoughts of tarnished brilliancy inside. They had no success with Clifford. These, and all such writers of society, whose new works glow like the rich texture of a just-woven carpet, must be content to relinquish their charm, for every reader, after an age or two, and could hardly be supposed to retain any portion of it for a mind that

447

had utterly lost its estimate of modes and manners. Hepzibah then took up Rasselas, and began to read of the Happy Valley, with a vague idea that some secret of a contented life had there been elaborated, which might at least serve Clifford and herself for this one day. But the Happy Valley had a cloud over it. Hepzibah troubled her auditor, moreover, by innumerable sins of emphasis, which he seemed to detect, without any reference to the meaning; nor, in fact, did he appear to take much note of the sense of what she read, but evidently felt the tedium of the lecture, without harvesting its profit. His sister's voice, too, naturally harsh, had, in the course of her sorrowful lifetime, contracted a kind of croak, which, when it once gets into the human throat, is as ineradicable as sin. In both sexes, occasionally, this lifelong croak, accompanying each word of joy or sorrow, is one of the symptoms of a settled melancholy; and wherever it occurs, the whole history of misfortune is conveyed in its slightest accent. The effect is as if the voice had been dyed black; or,—if we must use a more moderate simile,—this miserable croak, running through all the variations of the voice, is like a black silken thread, on which the crystal beads of speech are strung, and whence they take their hue. Such voices have put on mourning for dead hopes; and they ought to die and be buried along with them!

Discerning that Clifford was not gladdened by her efforts, Hepzibah searched about the house for the means of more exhilarating pastime. At one time, her eyes chanced to rest on Alice Pyncheon's harpsichord. It was a moment of great peril; for,—despite the traditionary awe that had gathered over this instrument of music, and the dirges which spiritual fingers were said to play on it,—the devoted sister had solemn thoughts of thrumming on its chords for Clifford's benefit, and accompanying the performance with her voice. Poor Clifford! Poor Hepzibah! Poor harpsichord! All three would have been miserable together. By some good agency,—possibly, by the unrecognized interposition of the long-buried Alice herself,—the threatening calamity was averted.

But the worst of all—the hardest stroke of fate for Hepzibah to endure, and perhaps for Clifford, too was his invincible distaste for her appearance. Her features, never the most agreeable, and now harsh with age and grief, and resentment against the world for his sake; her dress, and especially her turban; the queer and quaint manners, which had unconsciously grown upon her in solitude,—such being the poor gentlewoman's outward characteristics, it is no great marvel, although the mournfullest of pities, that the instinctive lover of the Beautiful was fain to turn away his eyes. There was no help for it. It would be the latest impulse to die within him. In his last extremity, the expiring breath stealing faintly through Clifford's lips, he would doubtless press Hepzibah's hand, in fervent recognition of all her lavished love, and close his eyes,—but not so much to die, as to be constrained to look no longer on her face! Poor Hepzibah! She took counsel with herself what might be done, and thought of putting ribbons on her turban; but, by the instant rush of several guardian angels, was withheld from an experiment that could hardly have proved less than fatal to the beloved object of her anxiety.

To be brief, besides Hepzibah's disadvantages of person, there was an uncouthness pervading all her deeds; a clumsy something, that could but ill adapt itself for use, and not at all for ornament. She was a grief to Clifford, and she knew it. In this extremity, the antiquated virgin turned to Phoebe. No grovelling jealousy was in her heart. Had it pleased Heaven to crown the heroic fidelity of her life by making her personally the medium of Clifford's happiness, it would have rewarded her for all the past, by a joy with no bright tints, indeed, but deep and true, and worth a thousand gayer ecstasies. This could not be. She therefore turned to Phoebe, and resigned the task into the young girl's hands. The latter took it up cheerfully, as she did everything, but with no sense of a mission to perform, and succeeding all the better for that same simplicity.

By the involuntary effect of a genial temperament, Phoebe soon grew to be absolutely essential to the daily comfort, if not the daily life, of her two forlorn companions. The grime and sordidness of the House of the Seven Gables seemed to have vanished since her appearance there; the gnawing tooth of the dry-rot was stayed among the old timbers of its skeleton frame; the dust had ceased to settle down so densely, from the antique ceilings, upon the floors and furniture of the rooms below,—or, at any rate, there was a little housewife, as light-footed as the breeze that sweeps a garden walk, gliding hither and thither to brush it all away. The shadows of gloomy events that haunted the else lonely and desolate apartments; the heavy, breathless scent which death had left in more than one of the bedchambers, ever since his visits of long ago,—these were less powerful than the purifying influence scattered throughout the atmosphere of the household by the presence of one youthful, fresh, and thoroughly wholesome heart. There was no morbidness in Phoebe; if there had been, the old Pyncheon House was the very locality to ripen it into incurable disease. But now her spirit resembled, in its potency, a minute quantity of ottar of rose in one of Hepzibah's huge, iron-bound trunks, diffusing its fragrance through the various articles of linen and wrought-lace, kerchiefs, caps, stockings, folded dresses, gloves, and whatever else was treasured there. As every article in the great trunk was the sweeter for the rose-scent, so did all the thoughts and emotions of Hepzibah and Clifford, sombre as they might seem, acquire a subtle attribute of happiness from Phoebe's intermixture with them. Her activity of body, intellect, and heart impelled her continually to perform the ordinary little toils that offered themselves around her, and to think the thought proper for the moment, and to sympathize,—now with the twittering gayety of the robins in the pear-tree, and now to such a depth as she could with Hepzibah's dark anxiety, or the vague moan of her brother. This facile adaptation was at once the symptom of perfect health and its best preservative.

A nature like Phoebe's has invariably its due influence, but is seldom regarded with due honor. Its spiritual force, however, may be partially estimated by the fact of her having found a place for herself, amid circumstances so stern as those which surrounded the mistress of the house; and also by the effect which she produced on a character of so much more mass than her own. For the gaunt, bony frame and limbs of Hepzibah, as compared with the tiny lightsomeness of Phoebe's figure, were perhaps in some fit proportion with the moral weight and substance, respectively, of the woman and the girl.

To the guest,—to Hepzibah's brother,—or Cousin Clifford, as Phoebe now began to call him, —she was especially necessary. Not that he could ever be said to converse with her, or often manifest, in any other very definite mode, his sense of a charm in her society. But if she were a long while absent he became pettish and nervously restless, pacing the room to and fro with the uncertainty that characterized all his movements; or else would sit broodingly in his great chair, resting his head on his hands, and evincing life only by an electric sparkle of ill-humor, whenever Hepzibah endeavored to arouse him. Phoebe's presence, and the contiguity of her fresh life to his blighted one, was usually all that he required. Indeed, such was the native gush and play of her spirit, that she was seldom perfectly quiet and undemonstrative, any more than a fountain ever ceases to dimple and warble with its flow. She possessed the gift of song, and that, too, so naturally, that you would as little think of inquiring whence she had caught it, or what master had taught her, as of asking the same questions about a bird, in whose small strain of music we recognize the voice of the Creator as distinctly as in the loudest accents of his thunder. So long as Phoebe sang, she might stray at her own will about the house. Clifford was content, whether the sweet, airy homeliness of her tones came down from the upper chambers, or along the passageway from the shop, or was sprinkled through the foliage of the pear-tree, inward from the garden, with the twinkling sunbeams. He would sit quietly, with a gentle pleasure gleaming over his face, brighter now, and now a little dimmer, as the song happened to float near him, or was more remotely heard. It pleased him best, however, when she sat on a low footstool at his knee.

It is perhaps remarkable, considering her temperament, that Phoebe oftener chose a strain of pathos than of gayety. But the young and happy are not ill pleased to temper their life with a transparent shadow. The deepest pathos of Phoebe's voice and song, moreover, came sifted through the golden texture of a cheery spirit, and was somehow so interfused with the quality thence acquired, that one's heart felt all the lighter for having wept at it. Broad mirth, in the sacred presence of dark misfortune, would have jarred harshly and irreverently with the solemn symphony that rolled its undertone through Hepzibah's and her brother's life. Therefore, it was well that Phoebe so often chose sad themes, and not amiss that they ceased to be so sad while she was singing them.

Becoming habituated to her companionship, Clifford readily showed how capable of imbibing pleasant tints and gleams of cheerful light from all quarters his nature must originally have been. He grew youthful while she sat by him. A beauty,—not precisely real, even in its utmost manifestation, and which a painter would have watched long to seize and fix upon his canvas, and, after all, in vain,—beauty, nevertheless, that was not a mere dream, would sometimes play upon and illuminate his face. It did more than to illuminate; it transfigured him with an expression that could only be interpreted as the glow of an exquisite and happy spirit. That gray hair, and those furrows,—with their record of infinite sorrow so deeply written across his brow, and so compressed, as with a futile effort to crowd in all the tale, that the whole inscription was made illegible,—these, for the moment, vanished. An eye at once tender and acute might have beheld in the man some shadow of what he was meant to be. Anon, as age came stealing, like a sad twilight, back over his figure, you would have felt tempted to hold an argument with Destiny, and affirm, that either this being should not have been made mortal, or mortal existence should have been tempered to his qualities. There seemed no necessity for his having drawn breath at all; the world never wanted him; but, as he had breathed, it ought always to have been the balmiest of summer air. The same perplexity will invariably haunt us with regard to natures that tend to feed exclusively upon the Beautiful, let their earthly fate be as lenient as it may.

Phoebe, it is probable, had but a very imperfect comprehension of the character over which she had thrown so beneficent a spell. Nor was it necessary. The fire upon the hearth can gladden a whole semicircle of faces round about it, but need not know the individuality of one among them all. Indeed, there was something too fine and delicate in Clifford's traits to be perfectly appreciated by one whose sphere lay so much in the Actual as Phoebe's did. For Clifford, however, the reality, and simplicity, and thorough homeliness of the girl's nature were as powerful a charm as any that she possessed. Beauty, it is true, and beauty almost perfect in its own style, was indispensable. Had Phoebe been coarse in feature, shaped clumsily, of a harsh voice, and uncouthly mannered, she might have been rich with all good gifts, beneath this unfortunate exterior, and still, so long as she wore the guise of woman, she would have shocked Clifford, and depressed him by her lack of beauty. But nothing more beautiful— nothing prettier, at least—was ever made than Phoebe. And, therefore, to this man,—whose whole poor and impalpable enjoyment of existence heretofore, and until both his heart and fancy died within him, had been a dream,—whose images of women had more and more lost their warmth and substance, and been frozen, like the pictures of secluded artists, into the chillest ideality,—to him, this little figure of the cheeriest household life was just what he required to bring him back into the breathing world. Persons who have wandered, or been expelled, out of the common track of things, even were it for a better system, desire nothing so much as to be led back. They shiver in their loneliness, be it on a mountain-top or in a dungeon.

Now, Phoebe's presence made a home about her,—that very sphere which the outcast, the prisoner, the potentate,—the wretch beneath mankind, the wretch aside from it, or the wretch above it,—instinctively pines after,—a home! She was real! Holding her hand, you felt something; a tender something; a substance, and a warm one: and so long as you should feel its grasp, soft as it was, you might be certain that your place was good in the whole sympathetic chain of human nature. The world was no longer a delusion.

By looking a little further in this direction, we might suggest an explanation of an often-suggested mystery. Why are poets so apt to choose their mates, not for any similarity of poetic endowment, but for qualities which might make the happiness of the rudest handicraftsman as well as that of the ideal craftsman of the spirit? Because, probably, at his highest elevation, the poet needs no human intercourse; but he finds it dreary to descend, and be a stranger.

There was something very beautiful in the relation that grew up between this pair, so closely and constantly linked together, yet with such a waste of gloomy and mysterious years from his birthday to hers. On Clifford's part it was the feeling of a man naturally endowed with the liveliest sensibility to feminine influence, but who had never quaffed the cup of passionate love, and knew that it was now too late. He knew it, with the instinctive delicacy that had survived his intellectual decay. Thus, his sentiment for Phoebe, without being paternal, was not less chaste than if she had been his daughter. He was a man, it is true, and recognized her as a woman. She was his only representative of womankind. He took unfailing note of every charm that appertained to her sex, and saw the ripeness of her lips, and the virginal development of her bosom. All her little womanly ways, budding out of her like blossoms on a young fruit-tree, had their effect on him, and sometimes caused his very heart to tingle with the keenest thrills of pleasure. At such moments,—for the effect was seldom more than momentary,—the half-torpid man would be full of harmonious life, just as a long-silent harp is full of sound, when the musician's fingers sweep across it. But, after all, it seemed rather a perception, or a sympathy, than a sentiment belonging to himself as an individual. He read Phoebe as he would a sweet and simple story; he listened to her as if she were a verse of household poetry, which God, in requital of his bleak and dismal lot, had permitted some angel, that most pitied him, to warble through the house. She was not an actual fact for him, but the interpretation of all that he lacked on earth brought warmly home to his conception; so that this mere symbol, or life-like picture, had almost the comfort of reality.

But we strive in vain to put the idea into words. No adequate expression of the beauty and profound pathos with which it impresses us is attainable. This being, made only for happiness, and heretofore so miserably failing to be happy,—his tendencies so hideously thwarted, that, some unknown time ago, the delicate springs of his character, never morally or intellectually strong, had given way, and he was now imbecile,—this poor, forlorn voyager from the Islands of the Blest, in a frail bark, on a tempestuous sea, had been flung, by the last mountain-wave of his shipwreck, into a quiet harbor. There, as he lay more than half lifeless on the strand, the fragrance of an earthly rose-bud had come to his nostrils, and, as odors will, had summoned up reminiscences or visions of all the living and breathing beauty amid which he should have had his home. With his native susceptibility of happy influences, he inhales the slight, ethereal rapture into his soul, and expires!

And how did Phoebe regard Clifford? The girl's was not one of those natures which are most attracted by what is strange and exceptional in human character. The path which would best have suited her was the well-worn track of ordinary life; the companions in whom she would most have delighted were such as one encounters at every turn. The mystery which enveloped Clifford, so far as it affected her at all, was an annoyance, rather than the piquant charm which many women might have found in it. Still, her native kindliness was brought strongly into play, not by what was darkly picturesque in his situation, nor so much, even, by the finer graces of his character, as by the simple appeal of a heart so forlorn as his to one so full of genuine sympathy as hers. She gave him an affectionate regard, because he needed so much love, and seemed to have received so little. With a ready tact, the result of ever-active and wholesome sensibility, she discerned what was good for him, and did it. Whatever was morbid in his mind and experience she ignored; and thereby kept their intercourse healthy, by the incautious, but, as it were, heaven-directed freedom of her whole conduct. The sick in mind, and, perhaps, in body, are rendered more darkly and hopelessly so by the manifold reflection of their disease, mirrored back from all quarters in the deportment of those about them; they are compelled to inhale the poison of their own breath, in infinite repetition. But Phoebe afforded her poor patient a supply of purer air. She impregnated it, too, not with a wild-flower scent,—for wildness was no trait of hers,—but with the perfume of garden-roses, pinks, and other blossoms of much sweetness, which nature and man have consented together in making grow from summer to summer, and from century to century. Such a flower was Phoebe in her relation with Clifford, and such the delight that he inhaled from her.

Yet, it must be said, her petals sometimes drooped a little, in consequence of the heavy atmosphere about her. She grew more thoughtful than heretofore. Looking aside at Clifford's face, and seeing the dim, unsatisfactory elegance and the intellect almost quenched, she would try to inquire what had been his life. Was he always thus? Had this veil been over him from his birth?—this veil, under which far more of his spirit was hidden than revealed, and through which he so imperfectly discerned the actual world,—or was its gray texture woven of some dark calamity? Phoebe loved no riddles, and would have been glad to escape the perplexity of this one. Nevertheless, there was so far a good result of her meditations on Clifford's character, that, when her involuntary conjectures, together with the tendency of every strange circumstance to tell its own story, had gradually taught her the fact, it had no terrible effect upon her. Let the world have done him what vast wrong it might, she knew Cousin Clifford too well—or fancied so—ever to shudder at the touch of his thin, delicate fingers.

Within a few days after the appearance of this remarkable inmate, the routine of life had established itself with a good deal of uniformity in the old house of our narrative. In the morning, very shortly after breakfast, it was Clifford's custom to fall asleep in his chair; nor, unless accidentally disturbed, would he emerge from a dense cloud of slumber or the thinner mists that flitted to and fro, until well towards noonday. These hours of drowsihead were the season of the old gentlewoman's attendance on her brother, while Phoebe took charge of the shop; an arrangement which the public speedily understood, and evinced their decided preference of the younger shopwoman by the multiplicity of their calls during her administration of affairs. Dinner over, Hepzibah took her knitting-work,—a long stocking of gray yarn, for her brother's winter wear,—and with a sigh, and a scowl of affectionate farewell to Clifford, and a gesture enjoining watchfulness on Phoebe, went to take her seat behind the counter. It was now the young girl's turn to be the nurse,—the guardian, the playmate,—or whatever is the fitter phrase,—of the gray-haired man.

❧ 10 ❧

THE PYNCHEON GARDEN

CLIFFORD, except for Phoebe's More active instigation would ordinarily have yielded to the torpor which had crept through all his modes of being, and which sluggishly counselled him to sit in his morning chair till eventide. But the girl seldom failed to propose a removal to the garden, where Uncle Venner and the daguerreotypist had made such repairs on the roof of the ruinous arbor, or summer-house, that it was now a sufficient shelter from sunshine and casual showers. The hop-vine, too, had begun to grow luxuriantly over the sides of the little edifice, and made an interior of verdant seclusion, with innumerable peeps and glimpses into the wider solitude of the garden.

Here, sometimes, in this green play-place of flickering light, Phoebe read to Clifford. Her acquaintance, the artist, who appeared to have a literary turn, had supplied her with works of fiction, in pamphlet form,—and a few volumes of poetry, in altogether a different style and taste from those which Hepzibah selected for his amusement. Small thanks were due to the books, however, if the girl's readings were in any degree more successful than her elderly cousin's. Phoebe's voice had always a pretty music in it, and could either enliven Clifford by its sparkle and gayety of tone, or soothe him by a continued flow of pebbly and brook-like cadences. But the fictions—in which the country-girl, unused to works of that nature, often became deeply absorbed—interested her strange auditor very little, or not at all. Pictures of life, scenes of passion or sentiment, wit, humor, and pathos, were all thrown away, or worse than thrown away, on Clifford; either because he lacked an experience by which to test their truth, or because his own griefs were a touch-stone of reality that few feigned emotions could withstand. When Phoebe broke into a peal of merry laughter at what she read, he would now and then laugh for sympathy, but oftener respond with a troubled, questioning look. If a tear—a maiden's sunshiny tear over imaginary woe—dropped upon some melancholy page, Clifford either took it as a token of actual calamity, or else grew peevish, and angrily motioned her to close the volume. And wisely too! Is not the world sad enough, in genuine earnest, without making a pastime of mock sorrows?

With poetry it was rather better. He delighted in the swell and subsidence of the rhythm, and the happily recurring rhyme. Nor was Clifford incapable of feeling the sentiment of poetry,

453

—not, perhaps, where it was highest or deepest, but where it was most flitting and ethereal. It was impossible to foretell in what exquisite verse the awakening spell might lurk; but, on raising her eyes from the page to Clifford's face, Phoebe would be made aware, by the light breaking through it, that a more delicate intelligence than her own had caught a lambent flame from what she read. One glow of this kind, however, was often the precursor of gloom for many hours afterward; because, when the glow left him, he seemed conscious of a missing sense and power, and groped about for them, as if a blind man should go seeking his lost eyesight.

It pleased him more, and was better for his inward welfare, that Phoebe should talk, and make passing occurrences vivid to his mind by her accompanying description and remarks. The life of the garden offered topics enough for such discourse as suited Clifford best. He never failed to inquire what flowers had bloomed since yesterday. His feeling for flowers was very exquisite, and seemed not so much a taste as an emotion; he was fond of sitting with one in his hand, intently observing it, and looking from its petals into Phoebe's face, as if the garden flower were the sister of the household maiden. Not merely was there a delight in the flower's perfume, or pleasure in its beautiful form, and the delicacy or brightness of its hue; but Clifford's enjoyment was accompanied with a perception of life, character, and individuality, that made him love these blossoms of the garden, as if they were endowed with sentiment and intelligence. This affection and sympathy for flowers is almost exclusively a woman's trait. Men, if endowed with it by nature, soon lose, forget, and learn to despise it, in their contact with coarser things than flowers. Clifford, too, had long forgotten it; but found it again now, as he slowly revived from the chill torpor of his life.

It is wonderful how many pleasant incidents continually came to pass in that secluded garden-spot when once Phoebe had set herself to look for them. She had seen or heard a bee there, on the first day of her acquaintance with the place. And often,—almost continually, indeed,—since then, the bees kept coming thither, Heaven knows why, or by what pertinacious desire, for far-fetched sweets, when, no doubt, there were broad clover-fields, and all kinds of garden growth, much nearer home than this. Thither the bees came, however, and plunged into the squash-blossoms, as if there were no other squash-vines within a long day's flight, or as if the soil of Hepzibah's garden gave its productions just the very quality which these laborious little wizards wanted, in order to impart the Hymettus odor to their whole hive of New England honey. When Clifford heard their sunny, buzzing murmur, in the heart of the great yellow blossoms, he looked about him with a joyful sense of warmth, and blue sky, and green grass, and of God's free air in the whole height from earth to heaven. After all, there need be no question why the bees came to that one green nook in the dusty town. God sent them thither to gladden our poor Clifford. They brought the rich summer with them, in requital of a little honey.

When the bean-vines began to flower on the poles, there was one particular variety which bore a vivid scarlet blossom. The daguerreotypist had found these beans in a garret, over one of the seven gables, treasured up in an old chest of drawers by some horticultural Pyncheon of days gone by, who doubtless meant to sow them the next summer, but was himself first sown in Death's garden-ground. By way of testing whether there were still a living germ in such ancient seeds, Holgrave had planted some of them; and the result of his experiment was a splendid row of bean-vines, clambering, early, to the full height of the poles, and arraying them, from top to bottom, in a spiral profusion of red blossoms. And, ever since the unfolding of the first bud, a multitude of humming-birds had been attracted thither. At times, it seemed as if for every one of the hundred blossoms there was one of these tiniest fowls of the air,—a thumb's bigness of burnished plumage, hovering and vibrating about the bean-poles. It was with indescribable interest, and even more than childish delight, that Clifford watched the humming-birds. He used to thrust his head softly out of the arbor to see them the better; all the while, too, motioning Phoebe to be quiet, and snatching glimpses of the smile upon her face, so as to heap his enjoyment up the higher with her sympathy. He had not merely grown young;—he was a child again.

Hepzibah, whenever she happened to witness one of these fits of miniature enthusiasm, would shake her head, with a strange mingling of the mother and sister, and of pleasure and sadness, in her aspect. She said that it had always been thus with Clifford when the humming-birds came,—always, from his babyhood,—and that his delight in them had been one of the earliest tokens by which he showed his love for beautiful things. And it was a wonderful coincidence, the good lady thought, that the artist should have planted these scarlet-flowering beans—which the humming-birds sought far and wide, and which had not grown in the Pyncheon garden before for forty years—on the very summer of Clifford's return.

Then would the tears stand in poor Hepzibah's eyes, or overflow them with a too abundant gush, so that she was fain to betake herself into some corner, lest Clifford should espy her agitation. Indeed, all the enjoyments of this period were provocative of tears. Coming so late as it did, it was a kind of Indian summer, with a mist in its balmiest sunshine, and decay and death in its gaudiest delight. The more Clifford seemed to taste the happiness of a child, the sadder was the difference to be recognized. With a mysterious and terrible Past, which had annihilated his memory, and a blank Future before him, he had only this visionary and impalpable Now, which, if you once look closely at it, is nothing. He himself, as was perceptible by many symptoms, lay darkly behind his pleasure, and knew it to be a baby-play, which he was to toy and trifle with, instead of thoroughly believing. Clifford saw, it may be, in the mirror of his deeper consciousness, that he was an example and representative of that great class of people whom an inexplicable Providence is continually putting at cross-purposes with the world: breaking what seems its own promise in their nature; withholding their proper food, and setting poison before them for a banquet; and thus—when it might so easily, as one would think, have been adjusted otherwise—making their existence a strangeness, a solitude, and torment. All his life long, he had been learning how to be wretched, as one learns a foreign tongue; and now, with the lesson thoroughly by heart, he could with difficulty comprehend his little airy happiness. Frequently there was a dim shadow of doubt in his eyes. "Take my hand, Phoebe," he would say, "and pinch it hard with your little fingers! Give me a rose, that I may press its thorns, and prove myself awake by the sharp touch of pain!" Evidently, he desired this prick of a trifling anguish, in order to assure himself, by that quality which he best knew to be real, that the garden, and the seven weather-beaten gables, and Hepzibah's scowl, and Phoebe's smile, were real likewise. Without this signet in his flesh, he could have attributed no more substance to them than to the empty confusion of imaginary scenes with which he had fed his spirit, until even that poor sustenance was exhausted.

The author needs great faith in his reader's sympathy; else he must hesitate to give details so minute, and incidents apparently so trifling, as are essential to make up the idea of this garden-life. It was the Eden of a thunder-smitten Adam, who had fled for refuge thither out of the same dreary and perilous wilderness into which the original Adam was expelled.

One of the available means of amusement, of which Phoebe made the most in Clifford's behalf, was that feathered society, the hens, a breed of whom, as we have already said, was an immemorial heirloom in the Pyncheon family. In compliance with a whim of Clifford, as it troubled him to see them in confinement, they had been set at liberty, and now roamed at will about the garden; doing some little mischief, but hindered from escape by buildings on three sides, and the difficult peaks of a wooden fence on the other. They spent much of their abundant leisure on the margin of Maule's well, which was haunted by a kind of snail, evidently a titbit to their palates; and the brackish water itself, however nauseous to the rest of the world, was so greatly esteemed by these fowls, that they might be seen tasting, turning up their heads, and smacking their bills, with precisely the air of wine-bibbers round a probationary cask. Their generally quiet, yet often brisk, and constantly diversified talk, one to another, or sometimes in soliloquy,—as they scratched worms out of the rich, black soil, or pecked at such plants as suited their taste,—had such a domestic tone, that it was almost a wonder why you could not establish a regular interchange of ideas about household matters, human and gallinaceous. All hens are well worth studying for the piquancy and rich variety of their manners; but by no possibility can there have been other fowls of such odd appearance and deportment as these ancestral ones. They probably embodied the traditionary peculiarities of their whole line of progenitors, derived through an unbroken succession of eggs; or else this individual Chanticleer and his two wives had grown to be humorists, and a little crack-brained withal, on account of their solitary way of life, and out of sympathy for Hepzibah, their lady-patroness.

Queer, indeed, they looked! Chanticleer himself, though stalking on two stilt-like legs, with the dignity of interminable descent in all his gestures, was hardly bigger than an ordinary partridge; his two wives were about the size of quails; and as for the one chicken, it looked small enough to be still in the egg, and, at the same time, sufficiently old, withered, wizened, and experienced, to have been founder of the antiquated race. Instead of being the youngest of the family, it rather seemed to have aggregated into itself the ages, not only of these living specimens of the breed, but of all its forefathers and foremothers, whose united excellences and oddities were squeezed into its little body. Its mother evidently regarded it as the one chicken of the world, and as necessary, in fact, to the world's continuance, or, at any rate, to the equilibrium of the present system of affairs, whether in church or state. No lesser sense of the infant fowl's importance could have justified, even in a mother's eyes, the perseverance with which she watched over its safety, ruffling her small person to twice its proper size, and flying in everybody's face that so much as looked towards her hopeful progeny. No lower estimate could have vindicated the indefatigable zeal with which she scratched, and her unscrupulousness in digging up the choicest flower or vegetable, for the sake of the fat earthworm at its root. Her nervous cluck, when the chicken happened to be hidden in the long grass or under the squash-leaves; her gentle croak of satisfaction, while sure of it beneath her wing; her note of ill-concealed fear and obstreperous defiance, when she saw her arch-enemy, a neighbor's cat, on the top of the high fence,—one or other of these sounds was to be heard at almost every moment of the day. By degrees, the observer came to feel nearly as much interest in this chicken of illustrious race as the mother-hen did.

Phoebe, after getting well acquainted with the old hen, was sometimes permitted to take the chicken in her hand, which was quite capable of grasping its cubic inch or two of body. While she curiously examined its hereditary marks,—the peculiar speckle of its plumage, the funny tuft on its head, and a knob on each of its legs,—the little biped, as she insisted, kept giving her a sagacious wink. The daguerreotypist once whispered her that these marks betokened the oddities of the Pyncheon family, and that the chicken itself was a symbol of the life of the old house, embodying its interpretation, likewise, although an unintelligible one, as such clews generally are. It was a feathered riddle; a mystery hatched out of an egg, and just as mysterious as if the egg had been addle!

The second of Chanticleer's two wives, ever since Phoebe's arrival, had been in a state of heavy despondency, caused, as it afterwards appeared, by her inability to lay an egg. One day, however, by her self-important gait, the sideways turn of her head, and the cock of her eye, as she pried into one and another nook of the garden,—croaking to herself, all the while, with inexpressible complacency,—it was made evident that this identical hen, much as mankind undervalued her, carried something about her person the worth of which was not to be estimated either in gold or precious stones. Shortly after, there was a prodigious cackling and gratulation of Chanticleer and all his family, including the wizened chicken, who appeared to understand the matter quite as well as did his sire, his mother, or his aunt. That afternoon Phoebe found a diminutive egg,—not in the regular nest, it was far too precious to be trusted there,—but cunningly hidden under the currant-bushes, on some dry stalks of last year's grass. Hepzibah, on learning the fact, took possession of the egg and appropriated it to Clifford's breakfast, on account of a certain delicacy of flavor, for which, as she affirmed, these eggs had always been famous. Thus unscrupulously did the old gentlewoman sacrifice the continuance, perhaps, of an ancient feathered race, with no better end than to supply her brother with a dainty that hardly filled the bowl of a tea-spoon! It must have been in reference to this outrage that Chanticleer, the next day, accompanied by the bereaved mother of the egg, took his post in front of Phoebe and Clifford, and delivered himself of a harangue that might have proved as long as his own pedigree, but for a fit of merriment on Phoebe's part. Hereupon, the offended fowl stalked away on his long stilts, and utterly withdrew his notice from Phoebe and the rest of human nature, until she made her peace with an offering of spice-cake, which, next to snails, was the delicacy most in favor with his aristocratic taste.

We linger too long, no doubt, beside this paltry rivulet of life that flowed through the garden of the Pyncheon House. But we deem it pardonable to record these mean incidents and poor delights, because they proved so greatly to Clifford's benefit. They had the earth-smell in them, and contributed to give him health and substance. Some of his occupations wrought less desirably upon him. He had a singular propensity, for example, to hang over Maule's well, and look at the constantly shifting phantasmagoria of figures produced by the agitation of the water over the mosaic-work of colored pebbles at the bottom. He said that faces looked upward to him there,—beautiful faces, arrayed in bewitching smiles,—each momentary face so fair and rosy, and every smile so sunny, that he felt wronged at its departure, until the same flitting witchcraft made a new one. But sometimes he would suddenly cry out, "The dark face gazes at me!" and be miserable the whole day afterwards. Phoebe, when she hung over the fountain by Clifford's side, could see nothing of all this,—neither the beauty nor the ugliness,—but only the colored pebbles, looking as if the gush of the waters shook and disarranged them. And the dark face, that so troubled Clifford, was no more than the shadow thrown from a branch of one of the damson-trees, and breaking the inner light of Maule's well. The truth was, however, that his fancy—reviving faster than his will and judgment, and always stronger than they—created shapes of loveliness that were symbolic of his native character, and now and then a stern and dreadful shape that typified his fate.

On Sundays, after Phoebe had been at church,—for the girl had a church-going conscience, and would hardly have been at ease had she missed either prayer, singing, sermon, or benediction,—after church-time, therefore, there was, ordinarily, a sober little festival in the garden. In addition to Clifford, Hepzibah, and Phoebe, two guests made up the company. One was the artist Holgrave, who, in spite of his consociation with reformers, and his other queer and questionable traits, continued to hold an elevated place in Hepzibah's regard. The other, we are almost ashamed to say, was the venerable Uncle Venner, in a clean shirt, and a broadcloth coat, more respectable than his ordinary wear, inasmuch as it was neatly patched on each elbow, and might be called an entire garment, except for a slight inequality in the length of its skirts. Clifford, on several occasions, had seemed to enjoy the old man's intercourse, for the sake of his mellow, cheerful vein, which was like the sweet flavor of a frost-bitten apple, such as one picks up under the tree in December. A man at the very lowest point of the social scale was easier and more agreeable for the fallen gentleman to encounter than a person at any of the intermediate degrees; and, moreover, as Clifford's young manhood had been lost, he was fond of feeling himself comparatively youthful, now, in apposition with the patriarchal age of Uncle Venner. In fact, it was sometimes observable that Clifford half wilfully hid from himself the consciousness of being stricken in years, and cherished visions of an earthly future still before him; visions, however, too indistinctly drawn to be followed by disappointment—though, doubtless, by depression—when any casual incident or recollection made him sensible of the withered leaf.

So this oddly composed little social party used to assemble under the ruinous arbor. Hepzibah—stately as ever at heart, and yielding not an inch of her old gentility, but resting upon it so much the more, as justifying a princess-like condescension—exhibited a not ungraceful hospitality. She talked kindly to the vagrant artist, and took sage counsel—lady as she was—with the wood-sawyer, the messenger of everybody's petty errands, the patched philosopher. And Uncle Venner, who had studied the world at street-corners, and other posts equally well adapted for just observation, was as ready to give out his wisdom as a town-pump to give water.

"Miss Hepzibah, ma'am," said he once, after they had all been cheerful together, "I really enjoy these quiet little meetings of a Sabbath afternoon. They are very much like what I expect to have after I retire to my farm!"

"Uncle Venner" observed Clifford in a drowsy, inward tone, "is always talking about his farm. But I have a better scheme for him, by and by. We shall see!"

"Ah, Mr. Clifford Pyncheon!" said the man of patches, "you may scheme for me as much as you please; but I'm not going to give up this one scheme of my own, even if I never bring it really to pass. It does seem to me that men make a wonderful mistake in trying to heap up property upon property. If I had done so, I should feel as if Providence was not bound to take care of me; and, at all events, the city wouldn't be! I'm one of those people who think that infinity is big enough for us all—and eternity long enough."

"Why, so they are, Uncle Venner," remarked Phoebe after a pause; for she had been trying to fathom the profundity and appositeness of this concluding apothegm. "But for this short life of ours, one would like a house and a moderate garden-spot of one's own."

"It appears to me," said the daguerreotypist, smiling, "that Uncle Venner has the principles of Fourier at the bottom of his wisdom; only they have not quite so much distinctness in his mind as in that of the systematizing Frenchman."

"Come, Phoebe," said Hepzibah, "it is time to bring the currants."

And then, while the yellow richness of the declining sunshine still fell into the open space of the garden, Phoebe brought out a loaf of bread and a china bowl of currants, freshly gathered from the bushes, and crushed with sugar. These, with water,—but not from the fountain of ill omen, close at hand,—constituted all the entertainment. Meanwhile, Holgrave took some pains to establish an intercourse with Clifford, actuated, it might seem, entirely by an impulse of kindliness, in order that the present hour might be cheerfuller than most which the poor recluse had spent, or was destined yet to spend. Nevertheless, in the artist's deep, thoughtful, all-observant eyes, there was, now and then, an expression, not sinister, but questionable; as if he had some other interest in the scene than a stranger, a youthful and unconnected adventurer, might be supposed to have. With great mobility of outward mood, however, he applied himself to the task of enlivening the party; and with so much success, that even dark-hued Hepzibah threw off one tint of melancholy, and made what shift she could with the remaining portion. Phoebe said to herself,—"How pleasant he can be!" As for Uncle Venner, as a mark of friendship and approbation, he readily consented to afford the young man his countenance in the way of his profession,—not metaphorically, be it understood, but literally, by allowing a daguerreotype of his face, so familiar to the town, to be exhibited at the entrance of Holgrave's studio.

Clifford, as the company partook of their little banquet, grew to be the gayest of them all. Either it was one of those up-quivering flashes of the spirit, to which minds in an abnormal state are liable, or else the artist had subtly touched some chord that made musical vibration. Indeed, what with the pleasant summer evening, and the sympathy of this little circle of not unkindly souls, it was perhaps natural that a character so susceptible as Clifford's should become animated, and show itself readily responsive to what was said around him. But he gave out his own thoughts, likewise, with an airy and fanciful glow; so that they glistened, as it were, through the arbor, and made their escape among the interstices of the foliage. He had been as cheerful, no doubt, while alone with Phoebe, but never with such tokens of acute, although partial intelligence.

But, as the sunlight left the peaks of the Seven Gables, so did the excitement fade out of Clifford's eyes. He gazed vaguely and mournfully about him, as if he missed something precious, and missed it the more drearily for not knowing precisely what it was.

"I want my happiness!" at last he murmured hoarsely and indistinctly, hardly shaping out the words. "Many, many years have I waited for it! It is late! It is late! I want my happiness!"

Alas, poor Clifford! You are old, and worn with troubles that ought never to have befallen you. You are partly crazy and partly imbecile; a ruin, a failure, as almost everybody is,—though some in less degree, or less perceptibly, than their fellows. Fate has no happiness in store for you; unless your quiet home in the old family residence with the faithful Hepzibah, and your long summer afternoons with Phoebe, and these Sabbath festivals with Uncle Venner and the daguerreotypist, deserve to be called happiness! Why not? If not the thing itself, it is marvellously like it, and the more so for that ethereal and intangible quality which causes it all to vanish at too close an introspection. Take it, therefore, while you may. Murmur not,— question not,—but make the most of it!

THE ARCHED WINDOW

FROM THE INERTNESS, or what we may term the vegetative character, of his ordinary mood, Clifford would perhaps have been content to spend one day after another, interminably,—or, at least, throughout the summer-time,—in just the kind of life described in the preceding pages. Fancying, however, that it might be for his benefit occasionally to diversify the scene, Phoebe sometimes suggested that he should look out upon the life of the street. For this purpose, they used to mount the staircase together, to the second story of the house, where, at the termination of a wide entry, there was an arched window, of uncommonly large dimensions, shaded by a pair of curtains. It opened above the porch, where there had formerly been a balcony, the balustrade of which had long since gone to decay, and been removed. At this arched window, throwing it open, but keeping himself in comparative obscurity by means of the curtain, Clifford had an opportunity of witnessing such a portion of the great world's movement as might be supposed to roll through one of the retired streets of a not very populous city. But he and Phoebe made a sight as well worth seeing as any that the city could exhibit. The pale, gray, childish, aged, melancholy, yet often simply cheerful, and sometimes delicately intelligent aspect of Clifford, peering from behind the faded crimson of the curtain,—watching the monotony of every-day occurrences with a kind of inconsequential interest and earnestness, and, at every petty throb of his sensibility, turning for sympathy to the eyes of the bright young girl!

If once he were fairly seated at the window, even Pyncheon Street would hardly be so dull and lonely but that, somewhere or other along its extent, Clifford might discover matter to occupy his eye, and titillate, if not engross, his observation. Things familiar to the youngest child that had begun its outlook at existence seemed strange to him. A cab; an omnibus, with its populous interior, dropping here and there a passenger, and picking up another, and thus typifying that vast rolling vehicle, the world, the end of whose journey is everywhere and nowhere; these objects he followed eagerly with his eyes, but forgot them before the dust raised by the horses and wheels had settled along their track. As regarded novelties (among which cabs and omnibuses were to be reckoned), his mind appeared to have lost its proper gripe and retentiveness. Twice or thrice, for example, during the sunny hours of the day, a water-cart went along by the Pyncheon House, leaving a broad wake of moistened earth, instead of the white dust that had risen at a lady's lightest footfall; it was like a summer shower, which the city authorities had caught and tamed, and compelled it into the commonest routine of their convenience. With the water-cart Clifford could never grow familiar; it always affected him with just the same surprise as at first. His mind took an apparently sharp impression from it, but lost the recollection of this perambulatory shower, before its next reappearance, as completely as did the street itself, along which the heat so quickly strewed white dust again. It was the same with the railroad. Clifford could hear the obstreperous howl of the steam-devil, and, by leaning a little way from the arched window, could catch a glimpse of the trains of cars, flashing a brief transit across the extremity of the street. The idea of terrible energy thus forced upon him was new at every recurrence, and seemed to affect him as disagreeably, and with almost as much surprise, the hundredth time as the first.

Nothing gives a sadder sense of decay than this loss or suspension of the power to deal with unaccustomed things, and to keep up with the swiftness of the passing moment. It can merely be a suspended animation; for, were the power actually to perish, there would be little use of immortality. We are less than ghosts, for the time being, whenever this calamity befalls us.

Clifford was indeed the most inveterate of conservatives. All the antique fashions of the street were dear to him; even such as were characterized by a rudeness that would naturally have annoyed his fastidious senses. He loved the old rumbling and jolting carts, the former track of which he still found in his long-buried remembrance, as the observer of to-day finds the wheel-tracks of ancient vehicles in Herculaneum. The butcher's cart, with its snowy canopy, was an acceptable object; so was the fish-cart, heralded by its horn; so, likewise, was the countryman's cart of vegetables, plodding from door to door, with long pauses of the patient horse, while his owner drove a trade in turnips, carrots, summer-squashes, string-beans, green peas, and new potatoes, with half the housewives of the neighborhood. The baker's cart, with the harsh music of its bells, had a pleasant effect on Clifford, because, as few things else did, it jingled the very dissonance of yore. One afternoon a scissor-grinder chanced to set his wheel a-going under the Pyncheon Elm, and just in front of the arched window. Children came running with their mothers' scissors, or the carving-knife, or the paternal razor, or anything else that lacked an edge (except, indeed, poor Clifford's wits), that the grinder might apply the article to his magic wheel, and give it back as good as new. Round went the busily revolving machinery, kept in motion by the scissor-grinder's foot, and wore away the hard steel against the hard stone, whence issued an intense and spiteful prolongation of a hiss as fierce as those emitted by Satan and his compeers in Pandemonium, though squeezed into smaller compass. It was an ugly, little, venomous serpent of a noise, as ever did petty violence to human ears. But Clifford listened with rapturous delight. The sound, however disagreeable, had very brisk life in it, and, together with the circle of curious children watching the revolutions of the wheel, appeared to give him a more vivid sense of active, bustling, and sunshiny existence than he had attained in almost any other way. Nevertheless, its charm lay chiefly in the past; for the scissor-grinder's wheel had hissed in his childish ears.

He sometimes made doleful complaint that there were no stage-coaches nowadays. And he asked in an injured tone what had become of all those old square-topped chaises, with wings sticking out on either side, that used to be drawn by a plough-horse, and driven by a farmer's wife and daughter, peddling whortle-berries and blackberries about the town. Their disappearance made him doubt, he said, whether the berries had not left off growing in the broad pastures and along the shady country lanes.

But anything that appealed to the sense of beauty, in however humble a way, did not require to be recommended by these old associations. This was observable when one of those Italian boys (who are rather a modern feature of our streets) came along with his barrel-organ, and stopped under the wide and cool shadows of the elm. With his quick professional eye he took note of the two faces watching him from the arched window, and, opening his instrument, began to scatter its melodies abroad. He had a monkey on his shoulder, dressed in a Highland plaid; and, to complete the sum of splendid attractions wherewith he presented himself to the public, there was a company of little figures, whose sphere and habitation was in the mahogany case of his organ, and whose principle of life was the music which the Italian made it his business to grind out. In all their variety of occupation,—the cobbler, the blacksmith, the soldier, the lady with her fan, the toper with his bottle, the milk-maid sitting by her cow—this fortunate little society might truly be said to enjoy a harmonious existence, and to make life literally a dance. The Italian turned a crank; and, behold! every one of these small individuals started into the most curious vivacity. The cobbler wrought upon a shoe; the blacksmith hammered his iron, the soldier waved his glittering blade; the lady raised a tiny breeze with her fan; the jolly toper swigged lustily at his bottle; a scholar opened his book with eager thirst for knowledge, and turned his head to and fro along the page; the milkmaid energetically drained her cow; and a miser counted gold into his strong-box,—all at the same turning of a crank. Yes; and, moved by the self-same impulse, a lover saluted his mistress on her lips! Possibly some cynic, at once merry and bitter, had desired to signify, in this pantomimic scene, that we mortals, whatever our business or amusement,—however serious, however trifling,—all dance to one identical tune, and, in spite of our ridiculous activity, bring nothing finally to pass. For the most remarkable aspect of the affair was, that, at the cessation of the music, everybody was petrified at once, from the most extravagant life into a dead torpor. Neither was the cobbler's shoe finished, nor the blacksmith's iron shaped out; nor was there a drop less of brandy in the toper's bottle, nor a drop more of milk in the milkmaid's pail, nor one additional coin in the miser's strong-box, nor was the scholar a page deeper in his book. All were precisely in the same condition as before they made themselves so ridiculous by their haste to toil, to enjoy, to accumulate gold, and to become wise. Saddest of all, moreover, the lover was none the happier for the maiden's granted kiss! But, rather than swallow this last too acrid ingredient, we reject the whole moral of the show.

The monkey, meanwhile, with a thick tail curling out into preposterous prolixity from beneath his tartans, took his station at the Italian's feet. He turned a wrinkled and abominable little visage to every passer-by, and to the circle of children that soon gathered round, and to Hepzibah's shop-door, and upward to the arched window, whence Phoebe and Clifford were looking down. Every moment, also, he took off his Highland bonnet, and performed a bow and scrape. Sometimes, moreover, he made personal application to individuals, holding out his small black palm, and otherwise plainly signifying his excessive desire for whatever filthy lucre might happen to be in anybody's pocket. The mean and low, yet strangely man-like expression of his wilted countenance; the prying and crafty glance, that showed him ready to gripe at every miserable advantage; his enormous tail (too enormous to be decently concealed under his gabardine), and the deviltry of nature which it betokened,—take this monkey just as he was, in short, and you could desire no better image of the Mammon of copper coin, symbolizing the grossest form of the love of money. Neither was there any possibility of satisfying the covetous little devil. Phoebe threw down a whole handful of cents, which he picked up with joyless eagerness, handed them over to the Italian for safekeeping, and immediately recommenced a series of pantomimic petitions for more.

Doubtless, more than one New-Englander—or, let him be of what country he might, it is as likely to be the case—passed by, and threw a look at the monkey, and went on, without imagining how nearly his own moral condition was here exemplified. Clifford, however, was a being of another order. He had taken childish delight in the music, and smiled, too, at the figures which it set in motion. But, after looking awhile at the long-tailed imp, he was so shocked by his horrible ugliness, spiritual as well as physical, that he actually began to shed tears; a weakness which men of merely delicate endowments, and destitute of the fiercer, deeper, and more tragic power of laughter, can hardly avoid, when the worst and meanest aspect of life happens to be presented to them.

Pyncheon Street was sometimes enlivened by spectacles of more imposing pretensions than the above, and which brought the multitude along with them. With a shivering repugnance at the idea of personal contact with the world, a powerful impulse still seized on Clifford, whenever the rush and roar of the human tide grew strongly audible to him. This was made evident, one day, when a political procession, with hundreds of flaunting banners, and drums, fifes, clarions, and cymbals, reverberating between the rows of buildings, marched all through town, and trailed its length of trampling footsteps, and most infrequent uproar, past the ordinarily quiet House of the Seven Gables. As a mere object of sight, nothing is more deficient in picturesque features than a procession seen in its passage through narrow streets. The spectator feels it to be fool's play, when he can distinguish the tedious commonplace of each man's visage, with the perspiration and weary self-importance on it, and the very cut of his pantaloons, and the stiffness or laxity of his shirt-collar, and the dust on the back of his black coat. In order to become majestic, it should be viewed from some vantage point, as it rolls its slow and long array through the centre of a wide plain, or the stateliest public square of a city; for then, by its remoteness, it melts all the petty personalities, of which it is made up, into one broad mass of existence,—one great life,—one collected body of mankind, with a vast, homogeneous spirit animating it. But, on the other hand, if an impressible person, standing alone over the brink of one of these processions, should behold it, not in its atoms, but in its aggregate,—as a mighty river of life, massive in its tide, and black with mystery, and, out of its depths, calling to the kindred depth within him,—then the contiguity would add to the effect. It might so fascinate him that he would hardly be restrained from plunging into the surging stream of human sympathies.

So it proved with Clifford. He shuddered; he grew pale; he threw an appealing look at Hepzibah and Phoebe, who were with him at the window. They comprehended nothing of his emotions, and supposed him merely disturbed by the unaccustomed tumult. At last, with tremulous limbs, he started up, set his foot on the window-sill, and in an instant more would have been in the unguarded balcony. As it was, the whole procession might have seen him, a wild, haggard figure, his gray locks floating in the wind that waved their banners; a lonely being, estranged from his race, but now feeling himself man again, by virtue of the irrepressible instinct that possessed him. Had Clifford attained the balcony, he would probably have leaped into the street; but whether impelled by the species of terror that sometimes urges its victim over the very precipice which he shrinks from, or by a natural magnetism, tending towards the great centre of humanity, it were not easy to decide. Both impulses might have wrought on him at once.

But his companions, affrighted by his gesture,—which was that of a man hurried away in spite of himself,—seized Clifford's garment and held him back. Hepzibah shrieked. Phoebe, to whom all extravagance was a horror, burst into sobs and tears.

"Clifford, Clifford! are you crazy?" cried his sister.

"I hardly know, Hepzibah," said Clifford, drawing a long breath. "Fear nothing,—it is over now,—but had I taken that plunge, and survived it, methinks it would have made me another man!"

Possibly, in some sense, Clifford may have been right. He needed a shock; or perhaps he required to take a deep, deep plunge into the ocean of human life, and to sink down and be covered by its profoundness, and then to emerge, sobered, invigorated, restored to the world and to himself. Perhaps again, he required nothing less than the great final remedy—death!

A similar yearning to renew the broken links of brotherhood with his kind sometimes showed itself in a milder form; and once it was made beautiful by the religion that lay even deeper than itself. In the incident now to be sketched, there was a touching recognition, on Clifford's part, of God's care and love towards him,—towards this poor, forsaken man, who, if any mortal could, might have been pardoned for regarding himself as thrown aside, forgotten, and left to be the sport of some fiend, whose playfulness was an ecstasy of mischief.

It was the Sabbath morning; one of those bright, calm Sabbaths, with its own hallowed atmosphere, when Heaven seems to diffuse itself over the earth's face in a solemn smile, no less sweet than solemn. On such a Sabbath morn, were we pure enough to be its medium, we should be conscious of the earth's natural worship ascending through our frames, on whatever spot of ground we stood. The church-bells, with various tones, but all in harmony, were calling out and responding to one another,—"It is the Sabbath!—The Sabbath!—Yea; the Sabbath!"— and over the whole city the bells scattered the blessed sounds, now slowly, now with livelier joy, now one bell alone, now all the bells together, crying earnestly,—"It is the Sabbath!"—and flinging their accents afar off, to melt into the air and pervade it with the holy word. The air with God's sweetest and tenderest sunshine in it, was meet for mankind to breathe into their hearts, and send it forth again as the utterance of prayer.

Clifford sat at the window with Hepzibah, watching the neighbors as they stepped into the street. All of them, however unspiritual on other days, were transfigured by the Sabbath influence; so that their very garments—whether it were an old man's decent coat well brushed for the thousandth time, or a little boy's first sack and trousers finished yesterday by his mother's needle—had somewhat of the quality of ascension-robes. Forth, likewise, from the portal of the old house stepped Phoebe, putting up her small green sunshade, and throwing upward a glance and smile of parting kindness to the faces at the arched window. In her aspect there was a familiar gladness, and a holiness that you could play with, and yet reverence it as much as ever. She was like a prayer, offered up in the homeliest beauty of one's mother-tongue. Fresh was Phoebe, moreover, and airy and sweet in her apparel; as if nothing that she wore— neither her gown, nor her small straw bonnet, nor her little kerchief, any more than her snowy stockings—had ever been put on before; or, if worn, were all the fresher for it, and with a fragrance as if they had lain among the rosebuds.

The girl waved her hand to Hepzibah and Clifford, and went up the street; a religion in herself, warm, simple, true, with a substance that could walk on earth, and a spirit that was capable of heaven.

"Hepzibah," asked Clifford, after watching Phoebe to the corner, "do you never go to church?"

"No, Clifford!" she replied,—"not these many, many years!"

"Were I to be there," he rejoined, "it seems to me that I could pray once more, when so many human souls were praying all around me!"

She looked into Clifford's face, and beheld there a soft natural effusion; for his heart gushed out, as it were, and ran over at his eyes, in delightful reverence for God, and kindly affection for his human brethren. The emotion communicated itself to Hepzibah. She yearned to take him by the hand, and go and kneel down, they two together,—both so long separate from the world, and, as she now recognized, scarcely friends with Him above,—to kneel down among the people, and be reconciled to God and man at once.

"Dear brother," said she earnestly, "let us go! We belong nowhere. We have not a foot of space in any church to kneel upon; but let us go to some place of worship, even if we stand in the broad aisle. Poor and forsaken as we are, some pew-door will be opened to us!"

So Hepzibah and her brother made themselves, ready—as ready as they could in the best of their old-fashioned garments, which had hung on pegs, or been laid away in trunks, so long that the dampness and mouldy smell of the past was on them,—made themselves ready, in their faded bettermost, to go to church. They descended the staircase together,—gaunt, sallow Hepzibah, and pale, emaciated, age-stricken Clifford! They pulled open the front door, and stepped across the threshold, and felt, both of them, as if they were standing in the presence of the whole world, and with mankind's great and terrible eye on them alone. The eye of their Father seemed to be withdrawn, and gave them no encouragement. The warm sunny air of the street made them shiver. Their hearts quaked within them at the idea of taking one step farther.

"It cannot be, Hepzibah!—it is too late," said Clifford with deep sadness. "We are ghosts! We have no right among human beings,—no right anywhere but in this old house, which has a curse on it, and which, therefore, we are doomed to haunt! And, besides," he continued, with a fastidious sensibility, inalienably characteristic of the man, "it would not be fit nor beautiful to go! It is an ugly thought that I should be frightful to my fellow-beings, and that children would cling to their mothers' gowns at sight of me!"

They shrank back into the dusky passage-way, and closed the door. But, going up the staircase again, they found the whole interior of the house tenfold more dismal, and the air closer and heavier, for the glimpse and breath of freedom which they had just snatched. They could not flee; their jailer had but left the door ajar in mockery, and stood behind it to watch them stealing out. At the threshold, they felt his pitiless gripe upon them. For, what other dungeon is so dark as one's own heart! What jailer so inexorable as one's self!

But it would be no fair picture of Clifford's state of mind were we to represent him as continually or prevailingly wretched. On the contrary, there was no other man in the city, we are bold to affirm, of so much as half his years, who enjoyed so many lightsome and griefless moments as himself. He had no burden of care upon him; there were none of those questions and contingencies with the future to be settled which wear away all other lives, and render them not worth having by the very process of providing for their support. In this respect he was a child,—a child for the whole term of his existence, be it long or short. Indeed, his life seemed to be standing still at a period little in advance of childhood, and to cluster all his reminiscences about that epoch; just as, after the torpor of a heavy blow, the sufferer's reviving consciousness goes back to a moment considerably behind the accident that stupefied him. He sometimes told Phoebe and Hepzibah his dreams, in which he invariably played the part of a child, or a very young man. So vivid were they, in his relation of them, that he once held a dispute with his sister as to the particular figure or print of a chintz morning-dress which he had seen their mother wear, in the dream of the preceding night. Hepzibah, piquing herself on a woman's accuracy in such matters, held it to be slightly different from what Clifford described; but, producing the very gown from an old trunk, it proved to be identical with his remembrance of it. Had Clifford, every time that he emerged out of dreams so lifelike, undergone the torture of transformation from a boy into an old and broken man, the daily recurrence of the shock would have been too much to bear. It would have caused an acute agony to thrill from the morning twilight, all the day through, until bedtime; and even then would have mingled a dull, inscrutable pain and pallid hue of misfortune with the visionary bloom and adolescence of his slumber. But the nightly moonshine interwove itself with the morning mist, and enveloped him as in a robe, which he hugged about his person, and seldom let realities pierce through; he was not often quite awake, but slept open-eyed, and perhaps fancied himself most dreaming then.

Thus, lingering always so near his childhood, he had sympathies with children, and kept his heart the fresher thereby, like a reservoir into which rivulets were pouring not far from the fountain-head. Though prevented, by a subtle sense of propriety, from desiring to associate with them, he loved few things better than to look out of the arched window and see a little girl driving her hoop along the sidewalk, or schoolboys at a game of ball. Their voices, also, were very pleasant to him, heard at a distance, all swarming and intermingling together as flies do in a sunny room.

Clifford would, doubtless, have been glad to share their sports. One afternoon he was seized with an irresistible desire to blow soap-bubbles; an amusement, as Hepzibah told Phoebe apart, that had been a favorite one with her brother when they were both children. Behold him, therefore, at the arched window, with an earthen pipe in his mouth! Behold him, with his gray hair, and a wan, unreal smile over his countenance, where still hovered a beautiful grace, which his worst enemy must have acknowledged to be spiritual and immortal, since it had survived so long! Behold him, scattering airy spheres abroad from the window into the street! Little impalpable worlds were those soap-bubbles, with the big world depicted, in hues bright as imagination, on the nothing of their surface. It was curious to see how the passers-by regarded these brilliant fantasies, as they came floating down, and made the dull atmosphere imaginative about them. Some stopped to gaze, and perhaps, carried a pleasant recollection of the bubbles onward as far as the street-corner; some looked angrily upward, as if poor Clifford wronged them by setting an image of beauty afloat so near their dusty pathway. A great many put out their fingers or their walking-sticks to touch, withal; and were perversely gratified, no doubt, when the bubble, with all its pictured earth and sky scene, vanished as if it had never been.

At length, just as an elderly gentleman of very dignified presence happened to be passing, a large bubble sailed majestically down, and burst right against his nose! He looked up,—at first with a stern, keen glance, which penetrated at once into the obscurity behind the arched window,—then with a smile which might be conceived as diffusing a dog-day sultriness for the space of several yards about him.

"Aha, Cousin Clifford!" cried Judge Pyncheon. "What! Still blowing soap-bubbles!"

The tone seemed as if meant to be kind and soothing, but yet had a bitterness of sarcasm in it. As for Clifford, an absolute palsy of fear came over him. Apart from any definite cause of dread which his past experience might have given him, he felt that native and original horror of the excellent Judge which is proper to a weak, delicate, and apprehensive character in the presence of massive strength. Strength is incomprehensible by weakness, and, therefore, the more terrible. There is no greater bugbear than a strong-willed relative in the circle of his own connections.

THE DAGUERREOTYPIST

IT MUST NOT BE SUPPOSED that the life of a personage naturally so active as Phoebe could be wholly confined within the precincts of the old Pyncheon House. Clifford's demands upon her time were usually satisfied, in those long days, considerably earlier than sunset. Quiet as his daily existence seemed, it nevertheless drained all the resources by which he lived. It was not physical exercise that overwearied him,—for except that he sometimes wrought a little with a hoe, or paced the garden-walk, or, in rainy weather, traversed a large unoccupied room,—it was his tendency to remain only too quiescent, as regarded any toil of the limbs and muscles. But, either there was a smouldering fire within him that consumed his vital energy, or the monotony that would have dragged itself with benumbing effect over a mind differently situated was no monotony to Clifford. Possibly, he was in a state of second growth and recovery, and was constantly assimilating nutriment for his spirit and intellect from sights, sounds, and events which passed as a perfect void to persons more practised with the world. As all is activity and vicissitude to the new mind of a child, so might it be, likewise, to a mind that had undergone a kind of new creation, after its long-suspended life.

Be the cause what it might, Clifford commonly retired to rest, thoroughly exhausted, while the sunbeams were still melting through his window-curtains, or were thrown with late lustre on the chamber wall. And while he thus slept early, as other children do, and dreamed of childhood, Phoebe was free to follow her own tastes for the remainder of the day and evening.

This was a freedom essential to the health even of a character so little susceptible of morbid influences as that of Phoebe. The old house, as we have already said, had both the dry-rot and the damp-rot in its walls; it was not good to breathe no other atmosphere than that. Hepzibah, though she had her valuable and redeeming traits, had grown to be a kind of lunatic by imprisoning herself so long in one place, with no other company than a single series of ideas, and but one affection, and one bitter sense of wrong. Clifford, the reader may perhaps imagine, was too inert to operate morally on his fellow-creatures, however intimate and exclusive their relations with him. But the sympathy or magnetism among human beings is more subtile and universal than we think; it exists, indeed, among different classes of organized life, and vibrates from one to another. A flower, for instance, as Phoebe herself observed, always began to droop

467

sooner in Clifford's hand, or Hepzibah's, than in her own; and by the same law, converting her whole daily life into a flower fragrance for these two sickly spirits, the blooming girl must inevitably droop and fade much sooner than if worn on a younger and happier breast. Unless she had now and then indulged her brisk impulses, and breathed rural air in a suburban walk, or ocean breezes along the shore,—had occasionally obeyed the impulse of Nature, in New England girls, by attending a metaphysical or philosophical lecture, or viewing a seven-mile panorama, or listening to a concert,—had gone shopping about the city, ransacking entire depots of splendid merchandise, and bringing home a ribbon,—had employed, likewise, a little time to read the Bible in her chamber, and had stolen a little more to think of her mother and her native place—unless for such moral medicines as the above, we should soon have beheld our poor Phoebe grow thin and put on a bleached, unwholesome aspect, and assume strange, shy ways, prophetic of old-maidenhood and a cheerless future.

Even as it was, a change grew visible; a change partly to be regretted, although whatever charm it infringed upon was repaired by another, perhaps more precious. She was not so constantly gay, but had her moods of thought, which Clifford, on the whole, liked better than her former phase of unmingled cheerfulness; because now she understood him better and more delicately, and sometimes even interpreted him to himself. Her eyes looked larger, and darker, and deeper; so deep, at some silent moments, that they seemed like Artesian wells, down, down, into the infinite. She was less girlish than when we first beheld her alighting from the omnibus; less girlish, but more a woman.

The only youthful mind with which Phoebe had an opportunity of frequent intercourse was that of the daguerreotypist. Inevitably, by the pressure of the seclusion about them, they had been brought into habits of some familiarity. Had they met under different circumstances, neither of these young persons would have been likely to bestow much thought upon the other, unless, indeed, their extreme dissimilarity should have proved a principle of mutual attraction. Both, it is true, were characters proper to New England life, and possessing a common ground, therefore, in their more external developments; but as unlike, in their respective interiors, as if their native climes had been at world-wide distance. During the early part of their acquaintance, Phoebe had held back rather more than was customary with her frank and simple manners from Holgrave's not very marked advances. Nor was she yet satisfied that she knew him well, although they almost daily met and talked together, in a kind, friendly, and what seemed to be a familiar way.

The artist, in a desultory manner, had imparted to Phoebe something of his history. Young as he was, and had his career terminated at the point already attained, there had been enough of incident to fill, very creditably, an autobiographic volume. A romance on the plan of Gil Blas, adapted to American society and manners, would cease to be a romance. The experience of many individuals among us, who think it hardly worth the telling, would equal the vicissitudes of the Spaniard's earlier life; while their ultimate success, or the point whither they tend, may be incomparably higher than any that a novelist would imagine for his hero. Holgrave, as he told Phoebe somewhat proudly, could not boast of his origin, unless as being exceedingly humble, nor of his education, except that it had been the scantiest possible, and obtained by a few winter-months' attendance at a district school. Left early to his own guidance, he had begun to be self-dependent while yet a boy; and it was a condition aptly suited to his natural force of will. Though now but twenty-two years old (lacking some months, which are years in such a life), he had already been, first, a country schoolmaster; next, a salesman in a country store; and, either at the same time or afterwards, the political editor of a country newspaper. He had subsequently travelled New England and the Middle States, as a peddler, in the employment of a Connecticut manufactory of cologne-water and other essences. In an episodical way he had studied and practised dentistry, and with very flattering success, especially in many of the factory-towns along our inland streams. As a supernumerary official, of some kind or other, aboard a packet-ship, he had visited Europe, and found means, before his return, to see Italy, and part of France and Germany. At a later period he had spent some months in a community of Fourierists. Still more recently he had been a public lecturer on Mesmerism, for which science (as he assured Phoebe, and, indeed, satisfactorily proved, by putting Chanticleer, who happened to be scratching near by, to sleep) he had very remarkable endowments.

His present phase, as a daguerreotypist, was of no more importance in his own view, nor likely to be more permanent, than any of the preceding ones. It had been taken up with the careless alacrity of an adventurer, who had his bread to earn. It would be thrown aside as carelessly, whenever he should choose to earn his bread by some other equally digressive means. But what was most remarkable, and, perhaps, showed a more than common poise in the young man, was the fact that, amid all these personal vicissitudes, he had never lost his identity. Homeless as he had been,—continually changing his whereabout, and, therefore, responsible neither to public opinion nor to individuals,—putting off one exterior, and snatching up another, to be soon shifted for a third,—he had never violated the innermost man, but had carried his conscience along with him. It was impossible to know Holgrave without recognizing this to be the fact. Hepzibah had seen it. Phoebe soon saw it likewise, and gave him the sort of confidence which such a certainty inspires. She was startled, however, and sometimes repelled,—not by any doubt of his integrity to whatever law he acknowledged, but by a sense that his law differed from her own. He made her uneasy, and seemed to unsettle everything around her, by his lack of reverence for what was fixed, unless, at a moment's warning, it could establish its right to hold its ground.

Then, moreover, she scarcely thought him affectionate in his nature. He was too calm and cool an observer. Phoebe felt his eye, often; his heart, seldom or never. He took a certain kind of interest in Hepzibah and her brother, and Phoebe herself. He studied them attentively, and allowed no slightest circumstance of their individualities to escape him. He was ready to do them whatever good he might; but, after all, he never exactly made common cause with them, nor gave any reliable evidence that he loved them better in proportion as he knew them more. In his relations with them, he seemed to be in quest of mental food, not heart-sustenance. Phoebe could not conceive what interested him so much in her friends and herself, intellectually, since he cared nothing for them, or, comparatively, so little, as objects of human affection.

Always, in his interviews with Phoebe, the artist made especial inquiry as to the welfare of Clifford, whom, except at the Sunday festival, he seldom saw.

"Does he still seem happy?" he asked one day.

"As happy as a child," answered Phoebe; "but—like a child, too—very easily disturbed."

"How disturbed?" inquired Holgrave. "By things without, or by thoughts within?"

"I cannot see his thoughts! How should I?" replied Phoebe with simple piquancy. "Very often his humor changes without any reason that can be guessed at, just as a cloud comes over the sun. Lately, since I have begun to know him better, I feel it to be not quite right to look closely into his moods. He has had such a great sorrow, that his heart is made all solemn and sacred by it. When he is cheerful,—when the sun shines into his mind,—then I venture to peep in, just as far as the light reaches, but no further. It is holy ground where the shadow falls!"

"How prettily you express this sentiment!" said the artist. "I can understand the feeling, without possessing it. Had I your opportunities, no scruples would prevent me from fathoming Clifford to the full depth of my plummet-line!"

"How strange that you should wish it!" remarked Phoebe involuntarily. "What is Cousin Clifford to you?"

"Oh, nothing,—of course, nothing!" answered Holgrave with a smile. "Only this is such an odd and incomprehensible world! The more I look at it, the more it puzzles me, and I begin to suspect that a man's bewilderment is the measure of his wisdom. Men and women, and children, too, are such strange creatures, that one never can be certain that he really knows them; nor ever guess what they have been from what he sees them to be now. Judge Pyncheon! Clifford! What a complex riddle—a complexity of complexities—do they present! It requires intuitive sympathy, like a young girl's, to solve it. A mere observer, like myself (who never have any intuitions, and am, at best, only subtile and acute), is pretty certain to go astray."

The artist now turned the conversation to themes less dark than that which they had touched upon. Phoebe and he were young together; nor had Holgrave, in his premature experience of life, wasted entirely that beautiful spirit of youth, which, gushing forth from one small heart and fancy, may diffuse itself over the universe, making it all as bright as on the first day of creation. Man's own youth is the world's youth; at least, he feels as if it were, and imagines that the earth's granite substance is something not yet hardened, and which he can mould into whatever shape he likes. So it was with Holgrave. He could talk sagely about the world's old age, but never actually believed what he said; he was a young man still, and therefore looked upon the world—that gray-bearded and wrinkled profligate, decrepit, without being venerable—as a tender stripling, capable of being improved into all that it ought to be, but scarcely yet had shown the remotest promise of becoming. He had that sense, or inward prophecy,—which a young man had better never have been born than not to have, and a mature man had better die at once than utterly to relinquish,—that we are not doomed to creep on forever in the old bad way, but that, this very now, there are the harbingers abroad of a golden era, to be accomplished in his own lifetime. It seemed to Holgrave,—as doubtless it has seemed to the hopeful of every century since the epoch of Adam's grandchildren,—that in this age, more than ever before, the moss-grown and rotten Past is to be torn down, and lifeless institutions to be thrust out of the way, and their dead corpses buried, and everything to begin anew.

As to the main point,—may we never live to doubt it!—as to the better centuries that are coming, the artist was surely right. His error lay in supposing that this age, more than any past or future one, is destined to see the tattered garments of Antiquity exchanged for a new suit, instead of gradually renewing themselves by patchwork; in applying his own little life-span as the measure of an interminable achievement; and, more than all, in fancying that it mattered anything to the great end in view whether he himself should contend for it or against it. Yet it was well for him to think so. This enthusiasm, infusing itself through the calmness of his character, and thus taking an aspect of settled thought and wisdom, would serve to keep his youth pure, and make his aspirations high. And when, with the years settling down more weightily upon him, his early faith should be modified by inevitable experience, it would be with no harsh and sudden revolution of his sentiments. He would still have faith in man's brightening destiny, and perhaps love him all the better, as he should recognize his helplessness in his own behalf; and the haughty faith, with which he began life, would be well bartered for a far humbler one at its close, in discerning that man's best directed effort accomplishes a kind of dream, while God is the sole worker of realities.

Holgrave had read very little, and that little in passing through the thoroughfare of life, where the mystic language of his books was necessarily mixed up with the babble of the multitude, so that both one and the other were apt to lose any sense that might have been properly their own. He considered himself a thinker, and was certainly of a thoughtful turn, but, with his own path to discover, had perhaps hardly yet reached the point where an educated man begins to think. The true value of his character lay in that deep consciousness of inward strength, which made all his past vicissitudes seem merely like a change of garments; in that enthusiasm, so quiet that he scarcely knew of its existence, but which gave a warmth to everything that he laid his hand on; in that personal ambition, hidden—from his own as well as other eyes—among his more generous impulses, but in which lurked a certain efficacy, that might solidify him from a theorist into the champion of some practicable cause. Altogether in his culture and want of culture,—in his crude, wild, and misty philosophy, and the practical experience that counteracted some of its tendencies; in his magnanimous zeal for man's welfare, and his recklessness of whatever the ages had established in man's behalf; in his faith, and in his infidelity; in what he had, and in what he lacked,—the artist might fitly enough stand forth as the representative of many compeers in his native land.

His career it would be difficult to prefigure. There appeared to be qualities in Holgrave, such as, in a country where everything is free to the hand that can grasp it, could hardly fail to put some of the world's prizes within his reach. But these matters are delightfully uncertain. At almost every step in life, we meet with young men of just about Holgrave's age, for whom we anticipate wonderful things, but of whom, even after much and careful inquiry, we never happen to hear another word. The effervescence of youth and passion, and the fresh gloss of the intellect and imagination, endow them with a false brilliancy, which makes fools of themselves and other people. Like certain chintzes, calicoes, and ginghams, they show finely in their first newness, but cannot stand the sun and rain, and assume a very sober aspect after washing-day.

But our business is with Holgrave as we find him on this particular afternoon, and in the arbor of the Pyncheon garden. In that point of view, it was a pleasant sight to behold this young man, with so much faith in himself, and so fair an appearance of admirable powers,—so little harmed, too, by the many tests that had tried his metal,—it was pleasant to see him in his kindly intercourse with Phoebe. Her thought had scarcely done him justice when it pronounced him cold; or, if so, he had grown warmer now. Without such purpose on her part, and unconsciously on his, she made the House of the Seven Gables like a home to him, and the garden a familiar precinct. With the insight on which he prided himself, he fancied that he could look through Phoebe, and all around her, and could read her off like a page of a child's story-book. But these transparent natures are often deceptive in their depth; those pebbles at the bottom of the fountain are farther from us than we think. Thus the artist, whatever he might judge of Phoebe's capacity, was beguiled, by some silent charm of hers, to talk freely of what he dreamed of doing in the world. He poured himself out as to another self. Very possibly, he forgot Phoebe while he talked to her, and was moved only by the inevitable tendency of thought, when rendered sympathetic by enthusiasm and emotion, to flow into the first safe reservoir which it finds. But, had you peeped at them through the chinks of the garden-fence, the young man's earnestness and heightened color might have led you to suppose that he was making love to the young girl!

At length, something was said by Holgrave that made it apposite for Phoebe to inquire what had first brought him acquainted with her cousin Hepzibah, and why he now chose to lodge in the desolate old Pyncheon House. Without directly answering her, he turned from the Future, which had heretofore been the theme of his discourse, and began to speak of the influences of the Past. One subject, indeed, is but the reverberation of the other.

"Shall we never, never get rid of this Past?" cried he, keeping up the earnest tone of his preceding conversation. "It lies upon the Present like a giant's dead body In fact, the case is just as if a young giant were compelled to waste all his strength in carrying about the corpse of the old giant, his grandfather, who died a long while ago, and only needs to be decently buried. Just think a moment, and it will startle you to see what slaves we are to bygone times,—to Death, if we give the matter the right word!"

"But I do not see it," observed Phoebe.

"For example, then," continued Holgrave: "a dead man, if he happens to have made a will, disposes of wealth no longer his own; or, if he die intestate, it is distributed in accordance with the notions of men much longer dead than he. A dead man sits on all our judgment-seats; and living judges do but search out and repeat his decisions. We read in dead men's books! We laugh at dead men's jokes, and cry at dead men's pathos! We are sick of dead men's diseases, physical and moral, and die of the same remedies with which dead doctors killed their patients! We worship the living Deity according to dead men's forms and creeds. Whatever we seek to do, of our own free motion, a dead man's icy hand obstructs us! Turn our eyes to what point we may, a dead man's white, immitigable face encounters them, and freezes our very heart! And we must be dead ourselves before we can begin to have our proper influence on our own world, which will then be no longer our world, but the world of another generation, with which we shall have no shadow of a right to interfere. I ought to have said, too, that we live in dead men's houses; as, for instance, in this of the Seven Gables!"

"And why not," said Phoebe, "so long as we can be comfortable in them?"

"But we shall live to see the day, I trust," went on the artist, "when no man shall build his house for posterity. Why should he? He might just as reasonably order a durable suit of clothes, —leather, or guttapercha, or whatever else lasts longest,—so that his great-grandchildren should have the benefit of them, and cut precisely the same figure in the world that he himself does. If each generation were allowed and expected to build its own houses, that single change, comparatively unimportant in itself, would imply almost every reform which society is now suffering for. I doubt whether even our public edifices—our capitols, state-houses, court-houses, city-hall, and churches,—ought to be built of such permanent materials as stone or brick. It were better that they should crumble to ruin once in twenty years, or thereabouts, as a hint to the people to examine into and reform the institutions which they symbolize."

"How you hate everything old!" said Phoebe in dismay. "It makes me dizzy to think of such a shifting world!"

"I certainly love nothing mouldy," answered Holgrave. "Now, this old Pyncheon House! Is it a wholesome place to live in, with its black shingles, and the green moss that shows how damp they are?—its dark, low-studded rooms—its grime and sordidness, which are the crystallization on its walls of the human breath, that has been drawn and exhaled here in discontent and anguish? The house ought to be purified with fire,—purified till only its ashes remain!"

"Then why do you live in it?" asked Phoebe, a little piqued.

"Oh, I am pursuing my studies here; not in books, however," replied Holgrave. "The house, in my view, is expressive of that odious and abominable Past, with all its bad influences, against which I have just been declaiming. I dwell in it for a while, that I may know the better how to hate it. By the bye, did you ever hear the story of Maule, the wizard, and what happened between him and your immeasurably great-grandfather?"

"Yes, indeed!" said Phoebe; "I heard it long ago, from my father, and two or three times from my cousin Hepzibah, in the month that I have been here. She seems to think that all the calamities of the Pyncheons began from that quarrel with the wizard, as you call him. And you, Mr. Holgrave look as if you thought so too! How singular that you should believe what is so very absurd, when you reject many things that are a great deal worthier of credit!"

"I do believe it," said the artist seriously; "not as a superstition, however, but as proved by unquestionable facts, and as exemplifying a theory. Now, see: under those seven gables, at which we now look up,—and which old Colonel Pyncheon meant to be the house of his descendants, in prosperity and happiness, down to an epoch far beyond the present,—under that roof, through a portion of three centuries, there has been perpetual remorse of conscience, a constantly defeated hope, strife amongst kindred, various misery, a strange form of death, dark suspicion, unspeakable disgrace,—all, or most of which calamity I have the means of tracing to the old Puritan's inordinate desire to plant and endow a family. To plant a family! This idea is at the bottom of most of the wrong and mischief which men do. The truth is, that, once in every half-century, at longest, a family should be merged into the great, obscure mass of humanity, and forget all about its ancestors. Human blood, in order to keep its freshness, should run in hidden streams, as the water of an aqueduct is conveyed in subterranean pipes. In the family existence of these Pyncheons, for instance,—forgive me Phoebe, but I cannot think of you as one of them,—in their brief New England pedigree, there has been time enough to infect them all with one kind of lunacy or another."

"You speak very unceremoniously of my kindred," said Phoebe, debating with herself whether she ought to take offence.

"I speak true thoughts to a true mind!" answered Holgrave, with a vehemence which Phoebe had not before witnessed in him. "The truth is as I say! Furthermore, the original perpetrator and father of this mischief appears to have perpetuated himself, and still walks the street,—at least, his very image, in mind and body,—with the fairest prospect of transmitting to posterity as rich and as wretched an inheritance as he has received! Do you remember the daguerreotype, and its resemblance to the old portrait?"

"How strangely in earnest you are!" exclaimed Phoebe, looking at him with surprise and perplexity; half alarmed and partly inclined to laugh. "You talk of the lunacy of the Pyncheons; is it contagious?"

"I understand you!" said the artist, coloring and laughing. "I believe I am a little mad. This subject has taken hold of my mind with the strangest tenacity of clutch since I have lodged in yonder old gable. As one method of throwing it off, I have put an incident of the Pyncheon family history, with which I happen to be acquainted, into the form of a legend, and mean to publish it in a magazine."

"Do you write for the magazines?" inquired Phoebe.

"Is it possible you did not know it?" cried Holgrave. "Well, such is literary fame! Yes. Miss Phoebe Pyncheon, among the multitude of my marvellous gifts I have that of writing stories; and my name has figured, I can assure you, on the covers of Graham and Godey, making as respectable an appearance, for aught I could see, as any of the canonized bead-roll with which it was associated. In the humorous line, I am thought to have a very pretty way with me; and as for pathos, I am as provocative of tears as an onion. But shall I read you my story?"

"Yes, if it is not very long," said Phoebe,—and added laughingly,—"nor very dull."

As this latter point was one which the daguerreotypist could not decide for himself, he forthwith produced his roll of manuscript, and, while the late sunbeams gilded the seven gables, began to read.

❧ 13 ❧

ALICE PYNCHEON

THERE WAS A MESSAGE BROUGHT, one day, from the worshipful Gervayse Pyncheon to young Matthew Maule, the carpenter, desiring his immediate presence at the House of the Seven Gables.

"And what does your master want with me?" said the carpenter to Mr. Pyncheon's black servant. "Does the house need any repair? Well it may, by this time; and no blame to my father who built it, neither! I was reading the old Colonel's tombstone, no longer ago than last Sabbath; and, reckoning from that date, the house has stood seven-and-thirty years. No wonder if there should be a job to do on the roof."

"Don't know what massa wants," answered Scipio. "The house is a berry good house, and old Colonel Pyncheon think so too, I reckon;—else why the old man haunt it so, and frighten a poor nigga, As he does?"

"Well, well, friend Scipio; let your master know that I'm coming," said the carpenter with a laugh. "For a fair, workmanlike job, he'll find me his man. And so the house is haunted, is it? It will take a tighter workman than I am to keep the spirits out of the Seven Gables. Even if the Colonel would be quiet," he added, muttering to himself, "my old grandfather, the wizard, will be pretty sure to stick to the Pyncheons as long as their walls hold together."

"What's that you mutter to yourself, Matthew Maule?" asked Scipio. "And what for do you look so black at me?"

"No matter, darky," said the carpenter. "Do you think nobody is to look black but yourself? Go tell your master I'm coming; and if you happen to see Mistress Alice, his daughter, give Matthew Maule's humble respects to her. She has brought a fair face from Italy,—fair, and gentle, and proud,—has that same Alice Pyncheon!"

"He talk of Mistress Alice!" cried Scipio, as he returned from his errand. "The low carpenter-man! He no business so much as to look at her a great way off!"

This young Matthew Maule, the carpenter, it must be observed, was a person little understood, and not very generally liked, in the town where he resided; not that anything could be alleged against his integrity, or his skill and diligence in the handicraft which he

474

exercised. The aversion (as it might justly be called) with which many persons regarded him was partly the result of his own character and deportment, and partly an inheritance.

He was the grandson of a former Matthew Maule, one of the early settlers of the town, and who had been a famous and terrible wizard in his day. This old reprobate was one of the sufferers when Cotton Mather, and his brother ministers, and the learned judges, and other wise men, and Sir William Phipps, the sagacious governor, made such laudable efforts to weaken the great enemy of souls, by sending a multitude of his adherents up the rocky pathway of Gallows Hill. Since those days, no doubt, it had grown to be suspected that, in consequence of an unfortunate overdoing of a work praiseworthy in itself, the proceedings against the witches had proved far less acceptable to the Beneficent Father than to that very Arch Enemy whom they were intended to distress and utterly overwhelm. It is not the less certain, however, that awe and terror brooded over the memories of those who died for this horrible crime of witchcraft. Their graves, in the crevices of the rocks, were supposed to be incapable of retaining the occupants who had been so hastily thrust into them. Old Matthew Maule, especially, was known to have as little hesitation or difficulty in rising out of his grave as an ordinary man in getting out of bed, and was as often seen at midnight as living people at noonday. This pestilent wizard (in whom his just punishment seemed to have wrought no manner of amendment) had an inveterate habit of haunting a certain mansion, styled the House of the Seven Gables, against the owner of which he pretended to hold an unsettled claim for ground-rent. The ghost, it appears,—with the pertinacity which was one of his distinguishing characteristics while alive,—insisted that he was the rightful proprietor of the site upon which the house stood. His terms were, that either the aforesaid ground-rent, from the day when the cellar began to be dug, should be paid down, or the mansion itself given up; else he, the ghostly creditor, would have his finger in all the affairs of the Pyncheons, and make everything go wrong with them, though it should be a thousand years after his death. It was a wild story, perhaps, but seemed not altogether so incredible to those who could remember what an inflexibly obstinate old fellow this wizard Maule had been.

Now, the wizard's grandson, the young Matthew Maule of our story, was popularly supposed to have inherited some of his ancestor's questionable traits. It is wonderful how many absurdities were promulgated in reference to the young man. He was fabled, for example, to have a strange power of getting into people's dreams, and regulating matters there according to his own fancy, pretty much like the stage-manager of a theatre. There was a great deal of talk among the neighbors, particularly the petticoated ones, about what they called the witchcraft of Maule's eye. Some said that he could look into people's minds; others, that, by the marvellous power of this eye, he could draw people into his own mind, or send them, if he pleased, to do errands to his grandfather, in the spiritual world; others, again, that it was what is termed an Evil Eye, and possessed the valuable faculty of blighting corn, and drying children into mummies with the heartburn. But, after all, what worked most to the young carpenter's disadvantage was, first, the reserve and sternness of his natural disposition, and next, the fact of his not being a church-communicant, and the suspicion of his holding heretical tenets in matters of religion and polity.

After receiving Mr. Pyncheon's message, the carpenter merely tarried to finish a small job, which he happened to have in hand, and then took his way towards the House of the Seven Gables. This noted edifice, though its style might be getting a little out of fashion, was still as respectable a family residence as that of any gentleman in town. The present owner, Gervayse Pyncheon, was said to have contracted a dislike to the house, in consequence of a shock to his sensibility, in early childhood, from the sudden death of his grandfather. In the very act of running to climb Colonel Pyncheon's knee, the boy had discovered the old Puritan to be a corpse. On arriving at manhood, Mr. Pyncheon had visited England, where he married a lady of fortune, and had subsequently spent many years, partly in the mother country, and partly in various cities on the continent of Europe. During this period, the family mansion had been consigned to the charge of a kinsman, who was allowed to make it his home for the time being, in consideration of keeping the premises in thorough repair. So faithfully had this contract been fulfilled, that now, as the carpenter approached the house, his practised eye could detect nothing to criticise in its condition. The peaks of the seven gables rose up sharply; the shingled roof looked thoroughly water-tight; and the glittering plaster-work entirely covered the exterior walls, and sparkled in the October sun, as if it had been new only a week ago.

The house had that pleasant aspect of life which is like the cheery expression of comfortable activity in the human countenance. You could see, at once, that there was the stir of a large family within it. A huge load of oak-wood was passing through the gateway, towards the outbuildings in the rear; the fat cook—or probably it might be the housekeeper—stood at the side door, bargaining for some turkeys and poultry which a countryman had brought for sale. Now and then a maid-servant, neatly dressed, and now the shining sable face of a slave, might be seen bustling across the windows, in the lower part of the house. At an open window of a room in the second story, hanging over some pots of beautiful and delicate flowers,—exotics, but which had never known a more genial sunshine than that of the New England autumn,— was the figure of a young lady, an exotic, like the flowers, and beautiful and delicate as they. Her presence imparted an indescribable grace and faint witchery to the whole edifice. In other respects, it was a substantial, jolly-looking mansion, and seemed fit to be the residence of a patriarch, who might establish his own headquarters in the front gable and assign one of the remainder to each of his six children, while the great chimney in the centre should symbolize the old fellow's hospitable heart, which kept them all warm, and made a great whole of the seven smaller ones.

There was a vertical sundial on the front gable; and as the carpenter passed beneath it, he looked up and noted the hour.

"Three o'clock!" said he to himself. "My father told me that dial was put up only an hour before the old Colonel's death. How truly it has kept time these seven-and-thirty years past! The shadow creeps and creeps, and is always looking over the shoulder of the sunshine!"

It might have befitted a craftsman, like Matthew Maule, on being sent for to a gentleman's house, to go to the back door, where servants and work-people were usually admitted; or at least to the side entrance, where the better class of tradesmen made application. But the carpenter had a great deal of pride and stiffness in his nature; and, at this moment, moreover, his heart was bitter with the sense of hereditary wrong, because he considered the great Pyncheon House to be standing on soil which should have been his own. On this very site, beside a spring of delicious water, his grandfather had felled the pine-trees and built a cottage, in which children had been born to him; and it was only from a dead man's stiffened fingers that Colonel Pyncheon had wrested away the title-deeds. So young Maule went straight to the principal entrance, beneath a portal of carved oak, and gave such a peal of the iron knocker that you would have imagined the stern old wizard himself to be standing at the threshold.

Black Scipio answered the summons in a prodigious, hurry; but showed the whites of his eyes in amazement on beholding only the carpenter.

"Lord-a-mercy, what a great man he be, this carpenter fellow!" mumbled Scipio, down in his throat. "Anybody think he beat on the door with his biggest hammer!"

"Here I am!" said Maule sternly. "Show me the way to your master's parlor."

As he stept into the house, a note of sweet and melancholy music thrilled and vibrated along the passage-way, proceeding from one of the rooms above stairs. It was the harpsichord which Alice Pyncheon had brought with her from beyond the sea. The fair Alice bestowed most of her maiden leisure between flowers and music, although the former were apt to droop, and the melodies were often sad. She was of foreign education, and could not take kindly to the New England modes of life, in which nothing beautiful had ever been developed.

As Mr. Pyncheon had been impatiently awaiting Maule's arrival, black Scipio, of course, lost no time in ushering the carpenter into his master's presence. The room in which this gentleman sat was a parlor of moderate size, looking out upon the garden of the house, and having its windows partly shadowed by the foliage of fruit-trees. It was Mr. Pyncheon's peculiar apartment, and was provided with furniture, in an elegant and costly style, principally from Paris; the floor (which was unusual at that day) being covered with a carpet, so skillfully and richly wrought that it seemed to glow as with living flowers. In one corner stood a marble woman, to whom her own beauty was the sole and sufficient garment. Some pictures—that looked old, and had a mellow tinge diffused through all their artful splendor—hung on the walls. Near the fireplace was a large and very beautiful cabinet of ebony, inlaid with ivory; a piece of antique furniture, which Mr. Pyncheon had bought in Venice, and which he used as the treasure-place for medals, ancient coins, and whatever small and valuable curiosities he had picked up on his travels. Through all this variety of decoration, however, the room showed its original characteristics; its low stud, its cross-beam, its chimney-piece, with the old-fashioned Dutch tiles; so that it was the emblem of a mind industriously stored with foreign ideas, and elaborated into artificial refinement, but neither larger, nor, in its proper self, more elegant than before.

There were two objects that appeared rather out of place in this very handsomely furnished room. One was a large map, or surveyor's plan, of a tract of land, which looked as if it had been drawn a good many years ago, and was now dingy with smoke, and soiled, here and there, with the touch of fingers. The other was a portrait of a stern old man, in a Puritan garb, painted roughly, but with a bold effect, and a remarkably strong expression of character.

At a small table, before a fire of English sea-coal, sat Mr. Pyncheon, sipping coffee, which had grown to be a very favorite beverage with him in France. He was a middle-aged and really handsome man, with a wig flowing down upon his shoulders; his coat was of blue velvet, with lace on the borders and at the button-holes; and the firelight glistened on the spacious breadth of his waistcoat, which was flowered all over with gold. On the entrance of Scipio, ushering in the carpenter, Mr. Pyncheon turned partly round, but resumed his former position, and proceeded deliberately to finish his cup of coffee, without immediate notice of the guest whom he had summoned to his presence. It was not that he intended any rudeness or improper neglect,—which, indeed, he would have blushed to be guilty of,—but it never occurred to him that a person in Maule's station had a claim on his courtesy, or would trouble himself about it one way or the other.

The carpenter, however, stepped at once to the hearth, and turned himself about, so as to look Mr. Pyncheon in the face.

"You sent for me," said he. "Be pleased to explain your business, that I may go back to my own affairs."

"Ah! excuse me," said Mr. Pyncheon quietly. "I did not mean to tax your time without a recompense. Your name, I think, is Maule,—Thomas or Matthew Maule,—a son or grandson of the builder of this house?"

"Matthew Maule," replied the carpenter,—"son of him who built the house,—grandson of the rightful proprietor of the soil."

"I know the dispute to which you allude," observed Mr. Pyncheon with undisturbed equanimity. "I am well aware that my grandfather was compelled to resort to a suit at law, in

477

order to establish his claim to the foundation-site of this edifice. We will not, if you please, renew the discussion. The matter was settled at the time, and by the competent authorities,—equitably, it is to be presumed,—and, at all events, irrevocably. Yet, singularly enough, there is an incidental reference to this very subject in what I am now about to say to you. And this same inveterate grudge,—excuse me, I mean no offence,—this irritability, which you have just shown, is not entirely aside from the matter."

"If you can find anything for your purpose, Mr. Pyncheon," said the carpenter, "in a man's natural resentment for the wrongs done to his blood, you are welcome to it."

"I take you at your word, Goodman Maule," said the owner of the Seven Gables, with a smile, "and will proceed to suggest a mode in which your hereditary resentments—justifiable or otherwise—may have had a bearing on my affairs. You have heard, I suppose, that the Pyncheon family, ever since my grandfather's days, have been prosecuting a still unsettled claim to a very large extent of territory at the Eastward?"

"Often," replied Maule,—and it is said that a smile came over his face,—"very often,—from my father!"

"This claim," continued Mr. Pyncheon, after pausing a moment, as if to consider what the carpenter's smile might mean, "appeared to be on the very verge of a settlement and full allowance, at the period of my grandfather's decease. It was well known, to those in his confidence, that he anticipated neither difficulty nor delay. Now, Colonel Pyncheon, I need hardly say, was a practical man, well acquainted with public and private business, and not at all the person to cherish ill-founded hopes, or to attempt the following out of an impracticable scheme. It is obvious to conclude, therefore, that he had grounds, not apparent to his heirs, for his confident anticipation of success in the matter of this Eastern claim. In a word, I believe,—and my legal advisers coincide in the belief, which, moreover, is authorized, to a certain extent, by the family traditions,—that my grandfather was in possession of some deed, or other document, essential to this claim, but which has since disappeared."

"Very likely," said Matthew Maule,—and again, it is said, there was a dark smile on his face, —"but what can a poor carpenter have to do with the grand affairs of the Pyncheon family?"

"Perhaps nothing," returned Mr. Pyncheon, "possibly much!"

Here ensued a great many words between Matthew Maule and the proprietor of the Seven Gables, on the subject which the latter had thus broached. It seems (although Mr. Pyncheon had some hesitation in referring to stories so exceedingly absurd in their aspect) that the popular belief pointed to some mysterious connection and dependence, existing between the family of the Maules and these vast unrealized possessions of the Pyncheons. It was an ordinary saying that the old wizard, hanged though he was, had obtained the best end of the bargain in his contest with Colonel Pyncheon; inasmuch as he had got possession of the great Eastern claim, in exchange for an acre or two of garden-ground. A very aged woman, recently dead, had often used the metaphorical expression, in her fireside talk, that miles and miles of the Pyncheon lands had been shovelled into Maule's grave; which, by the bye, was but a very shallow nook, between two rocks, near the summit of Gallows Hill. Again, when the lawyers were making inquiry for the missing document, it was a by-word that it would never be found, unless in the wizard's skeleton hand. So much weight had the shrewd lawyers assigned to these fables, that (but Mr. Pyncheon did not see fit to inform the carpenter of the fact) they had secretly caused the wizard's grave to be searched. Nothing was discovered, however, except that, unaccountably, the right hand of the skeleton was gone.

Now, what was unquestionably important, a portion of these popular rumors could be traced, though rather doubtfully and indistinctly, to chance words and obscure hints of the executed wizard's son, and the father of this present Matthew Maule. And here Mr. Pyncheon could bring an item of his own personal evidence into play. Though but a child at the time, he either remembered or fancied that Matthew's father had had some job to perform on the day before, or possibly the very morning of the Colonel's decease, in the private room where he and the carpenter were at this moment talking. Certain papers belonging to Colonel Pyncheon, as his grandson distinctly recollected, had been spread out on the table.

Matthew Maule understood the insinuated suspicion.

"My father," he said,—but still there was that dark smile, making a riddle of his countenance,—"my father was an honester man than the bloody old Colonel! Not to get his rights back again would he have carried off one of those papers!"

"I shall not bandy words with you," observed the foreign-bred Mr. Pyncheon, with haughty composure. "Nor will it become me to resent any rudeness towards either my grandfather or myself. A gentleman, before seeking intercourse with a person of your station and habits, will first consider whether the urgency of the end may compensate for the disagreeableness of the means. It does so in the present instance."

He then renewed the conversation, and made great pecuniary offers to the carpenter, in case the latter should give information leading to the discovery of the lost document, and the consequent success of the Eastern claim. For a long time Matthew Maule is said to have turned a cold ear to these propositions. At last, however, with a strange kind of laugh, he inquired whether Mr. Pyncheon would make over to him the old wizard's homestead-ground, together with the House of the Seven Gables, now standing on it, in requital of the documentary evidence so urgently required.

The wild, chimney-corner legend (which, without copying all its extravagances, my narrative essentially follows) here gives an account of some very strange behavior on the part of Colonel Pyncheon's portrait. This picture, it must be understood, was supposed to be so intimately connected with the fate of the house, and so magically built into its walls, that, if once it should be removed, that very instant the whole edifice would come thundering down in a heap of dusty ruin. All through the foregoing conversation between Mr. Pyncheon and the carpenter, the portrait had been frowning, clenching its fist, and giving many such proofs of excessive discomposure, but without attracting the notice of either of the two colloquists. And finally, at Matthew Maule's audacious suggestion of a transfer of the seven-gabled structure, the ghostly portrait is averred to have lost all patience, and to have shown itself on the point of descending bodily from its frame. But such incredible incidents are merely to be mentioned aside.

"Give up this house!" exclaimed Mr. Pyncheon, in amazement at the proposal. "Were I to do so, my grandfather would not rest quiet in his grave!"

"He never has, if all stories are true," remarked the carpenter composedly. "But that matter concerns his grandson more than it does Matthew Maule. I have no other terms to propose."

Impossible as he at first thought it to comply with Maule's conditions, still, on a second glance, Mr. Pyncheon was of opinion that they might at least be made matter of discussion. He himself had no personal attachment for the house, nor any pleasant associations connected with his childish residence in it. On the contrary, after seven-and-thirty years, the presence of his dead grandfather seemed still to pervade it, as on that morning when the affrighted boy had beheld him, with so ghastly an aspect, stiffening in his chair. His long abode in foreign parts, moreover, and familiarity with many of the castles and ancestral halls of England, and the marble palaces of Italy, had caused him to look contemptuously at the House of the Seven Gables, whether in point of splendor or convenience. It was a mansion exceedingly inadequate to the style of living which it would be incumbent on Mr. Pyncheon to support, after realizing his territorial rights. His steward might deign to occupy it, but never, certainly, the great landed proprietor himself. In the event of success, indeed, it was his purpose to return to England; nor, to say the truth, would he recently have quitted that more congenial home, had not his own fortune, as well as his deceased wife's, begun to give symptoms of exhaustion. The Eastern claim once fairly settled, and put upon the firm basis of actual possession, Mr. Pyncheon's property—to be measured by miles, not acres—would be worth an earldom, and would reasonably entitle him to solicit, or enable him to purchase, that elevated dignity from the British monarch. Lord Pyncheon!—or the Earl of Waldo!—how could such a magnate be expected to contract his grandeur within the pitiful compass of seven shingled gables?

In short, on an enlarged view of the business, the carpenter's terms appeared so ridiculously easy that Mr. Pyncheon could scarcely forbear laughing in his face. He was quite ashamed, after the foregoing reflections, to propose any diminution of so moderate a recompense for the immense service to be rendered.

"I consent to your proposition, Maule!" cried he. "Put me in possession of the document essential to establish my rights, and the House of the Seven Gables is your own!"

According to some versions of the story, a regular contract to the above effect was drawn up by a lawyer, and signed and sealed in the presence of witnesses. Others say that Matthew Maule was contented with a private written agreement, in which Mr. Pyncheon pledged his honor and integrity to the fulfillment of the terms concluded upon. The gentleman then ordered wine, which he and the carpenter drank together, in confirmation of their bargain. During the whole preceding discussion and subsequent formalities, the old Puritan's portrait seems to have persisted in its shadowy gestures of disapproval; but without effect, except that, as Mr. Pyncheon set down the emptied glass, he thought he beheld his grandfather frown.

"This sherry is too potent a wine for me; it has affected my brain already," he observed, after a somewhat startled look at the picture. "On returning to Europe, I shall confine myself to the more delicate vintages of Italy and France, the best of which will not bear transportation."

"My Lord Pyncheon may drink what wine he will, and wherever he pleases," replied the carpenter, as if he had been privy to Mr. Pyncheon's ambitious projects. "But first, sir, if you desire tidings of this lost document, I must crave the favor of a little talk with your fair daughter Alice."

"You are mad, Maule!" exclaimed Mr. Pyncheon haughtily; and now, at last, there was anger mixed up with his pride. "What can my daughter have to do with a business like this?"

Indeed, at this new demand on the carpenter's part, the proprietor of the Seven Gables was even more thunder-struck than at the cool proposition to surrender his house. There was, at least, an assignable motive for the first stipulation; there appeared to be none whatever for the last. Nevertheless, Matthew Maule sturdily insisted on the young lady being summoned, and even gave her father to understand, in a mysterious kind of explanation,—which made the matter considerably darker than it looked before,—that the only chance of acquiring the requisite knowledge was through the clear, crystal medium of a pure and virgin intelligence, like that of the fair Alice. Not to encumber our story with Mr. Pyncheon's scruples, whether of conscience, pride, or fatherly affection, he at length ordered his daughter to be called. He well knew that she was in her chamber, and engaged in no occupation that could not readily be laid aside; for, as it happened, ever since Alice's name had been spoken, both her father and the carpenter had heard the sad and sweet music of her harpsichord, and the airier melancholy of her accompanying voice.

So Alice Pyncheon was summoned, and appeared. A portrait of this young lady, painted by a Venetian artist, and left by her father in England, is said to have fallen into the hands of the present Duke of Devonshire, and to be now preserved at Chatsworth; not on account of any associations with the original, but for its value as a picture, and the high character of beauty in the countenance. If ever there was a lady born, and set apart from the world's vulgar mass by a certain gentle and cold stateliness, it was this very Alice Pyncheon. Yet there was the womanly mixture in her; the tenderness, or, at least, the tender capabilities. For the sake of that redeeming quality, a man of generous nature would have forgiven all her pride, and have been content, almost, to lie down in her path, and let Alice set her slender foot upon his heart. All that he would have required was simply the acknowledgment that he was indeed a man, and a fellow-being, moulded of the same elements as she.

As Alice came into the room, her eyes fell upon the carpenter, who was standing near its centre, clad in green woollen jacket, a pair of loose breeches, open at the knees, and with a long pocket for his rule, the end of which protruded; it was as proper a mark of the artisan's calling as Mr. Pyncheon's full-dress sword of that gentleman's aristocratic pretensions. A glow of artistic approval brightened over Alice Pyncheon's face; she was struck with admiration— which she made no attempt to conceal—of the remarkable comeliness, strength, and energy of Maule's figure. But that admiring glance (which most other men, perhaps, would have cherished as a sweet recollection all through life) the carpenter never forgave. It must have been the devil himself that made Maule so subtile in his preception.

"Does the girl look at me as if I were a brute beast?" thought he, setting his teeth. "She shall know whether I have a human spirit; and the worse for her, if it prove stronger than her own!"

"My father, you sent for me," said Alice, in her sweet and harp-like voice. "But, if you have business with this young man, pray let me go again. You know I do not love this room, in spite of that Claude, with which you try to bring back sunny recollections."

"Stay a moment, young lady, if you please!" said Matthew Maule. "My business with your father is over. With yourself, it is now to begin!"

Alice looked towards her father, in surprise and inquiry.

"Yes, Alice," said Mr. Pyncheon, with some disturbance and confusion. "This young man— his name is Matthew Maule—professes, so far as I can understand him, to be able to discover, through your means, a certain paper or parchment, which was missing long before your birth. The importance of the document in question renders it advisable to neglect no possible, even if improbable, method of regaining it. You will therefore oblige me, my dear Alice, by answering this person's inquiries, and complying with his lawful and reasonable requests, so far as they may appear to have the aforesaid object in view. As I shall remain in the room, you need apprehend no rude nor unbecoming deportment, on the young man's part; and, at your slightest wish, of course, the investigation, or whatever we may call it, shall immediately be broken off."

"Mistress Alice Pyncheon," remarked Matthew Maule, with the utmost deference, but yet a half-hidden sarcasm in his look and tone, "will no doubt feel herself quite safe in her father's presence, and under his all-sufficient protection."

"I certainly shall entertain no manner of apprehension, with my father at hand," said Alice with maidenly dignity. "Neither do I conceive that a lady, while true to herself, can have aught to fear from whomsoever, or in any circumstances!"

Poor Alice! By what unhappy impulse did she thus put herself at once on terms of defiance against a strength which she could not estimate?

"Then, Mistress Alice," said Matthew Maule, handing a chair,—gracefully enough, for a craftsman, "will it please you only to sit down, and do me the favor (though altogether beyond a poor carpenter's deserts) to fix your eyes on mine!"

Alice complied, She was very proud. Setting aside all advantages of rank, this fair girl deemed herself conscious of a power—combined of beauty, high, unsullied purity, and the preservative force of womanhood—that could make her sphere impenetrable, unless betrayed by treachery within. She instinctively knew, it may be, that some sinister or evil potency was now striving to pass her barriers; nor would she decline the contest. So Alice put woman's might against man's might; a match not often equal on the part of woman.

Her father meanwhile had turned away, and seemed absorbed in the contemplation of a landscape by Claude, where a shadowy and sun-streaked vista penetrated so remotely into an ancient wood, that it would have been no wonder if his fancy had lost itself in the picture's bewildering depths. But, in truth, the picture was no more to him at that moment than the blank wall against which it hung. His mind was haunted with the many and strange tales which he had heard, attributing mysterious if not supernatural endowments to these Maules, as well the grandson here present as his two immediate ancestors. Mr. Pyncheon's long residence abroad, and intercourse with men of wit and fashion,—courtiers, worldlings, and free-thinkers, —had done much towards obliterating the grim Puritan superstitions, which no man of New England birth at that early period could entirely escape. But, on the other hand, had not a whole community believed Maule's grandfather to be a wizard? Had not the crime been proved? Had not the wizard died for it? Had he not bequeathed a legacy of hatred against the Pyncheons to this only grandson, who, as it appeared, was now about to exercise a subtle influence over the daughter of his enemy's house? Might not this influence be the same that was called witchcraft?

Turning half around, he caught a glimpse of Maule's figure in the looking-glass. At some paces from Alice, with his arms uplifted in the air, the carpenter made a gesture as if directing downward a slow, ponderous, and invisible weight upon the maiden.

"Stay, Maule!" exclaimed Mr. Pyncheon, stepping forward. "I forbid your proceeding further!"

"Pray, my dear father, do not interrupt the young man," said Alice, without changing her position. "His efforts, I assure you, will prove very harmless."

Again Mr. Pyncheon turned his eyes towards the Claude. It was then his daughter's will, in opposition to his own, that the experiment should be fully tried. Henceforth, therefore, he did but consent, not urge it. And was it not for her sake far more than for his own that he desired its success? That lost parchment once restored, the beautiful Alice Pyncheon, with the rich dowry which he could then bestow, might wed an English duke or a German reigning-prince, instead of some New England clergyman or lawyer! At the thought, the ambitious father almost consented, in his heart, that, if the devil's power were needed to the accomplishment of this great object, Maule might evoke him. Alice's own purity would be her safeguard.

With his mind full of imaginary magnificence, Mr. Pyncheon heard a half-uttered exclamation from his daughter. It was very faint and low; so indistinct that there seemed but half a will to shape out the words, and too undefined a purport to be intelligible. Yet it was a call for help!—his conscience never doubted it;—and, little more than a whisper to his ear, it was a dismal shriek, and long reechoed so, in the region round his heart! But this time the father did not turn.

After a further interval, Maule spoke.

"Behold your daughter," said he.

Mr. Pyncheon came hastily forward. The carpenter was standing erect in front of Alice's chair, and pointing his finger towards the maiden with an expression of triumphant power, the limits of which could not be defined, as, indeed, its scope stretched vaguely towards the unseen and the infinite. Alice sat in an attitude of profound repose, with the long brown lashes drooping over her eyes.

"There she is!" said the carpenter. "Speak to her!"

"Alice! My daughter!" exclaimed Mr. Pyncheon. "My own Alice!"

She did not stir.

"Louder!" said Maule, smiling.

"Alice! Awake!" cried her father. "It troubles me to see you thus! Awake!"

He spoke loudly, with terror in his voice, and close to that delicate ear which had always been so sensitive to every discord. But the sound evidently reached her not. It is indescribable what a sense of remote, dim, unattainable distance betwixt himself and Alice was impressed on the father by this impossibility of reaching her with his voice.

"Best touch her!" said Matthew Maule "Shake the girl, and roughly, too! My hands are hardened with too much use of axe, saw, and plane,—else I might help you!"

Mr. Pyncheon took her hand, and pressed it with the earnestness of startled emotion. He kissed her, with so great a heart-throb in the kiss, that he thought she must needs feel it. Then, in a gust of anger at her insensibility, he shook her maiden form with a violence which, the next moment, it affrighted him to remember. He withdrew his encircling arms, and Alice—whose figure, though flexible, had been wholly impassive—relapsed into the same attitude as before these attempts to arouse her. Maule having shifted his position, her face was turned towards him slightly, but with what seemed to be a reference of her very slumber to his guidance.

Then it was a strange sight to behold how the man of conventionalities shook the powder out of his periwig; how the reserved and stately gentleman forgot his dignity; how the gold-embroidered waistcoat flickered and glistened in the firelight with the convulsion of rage, terror, and sorrow in the human heart that was beating under it.

"Villain!" cried Mr. Pyncheon, shaking his clenched fist at Maule. "You and the fiend together have robbed me of my daughter. Give her back, spawn of the old wizard, or you shall climb Gallows Hill in your grandfather's footsteps!"

"Softly, Mr. Pyncheon!" said the carpenter with scornful composure. "Softly, an' it please your worship, else you will spoil those rich lace-ruffles at your wrists! Is it my crime if you have sold your daughter for the mere hope of getting a sheet of yellow parchment into your clutch? There sits Mistress Alice quietly asleep. Now let Matthew Maule try whether she be as proud as the carpenter found her awhile since."

He spoke, and Alice responded, with a soft, subdued, inward acquiescence, and a bending of her form towards him, like the flame of a torch when it indicates a gentle draught of air. He beckoned with his hand, and, rising from her chair,—blindly, but undoubtingly, as tending to her sure and inevitable centre,—the proud Alice approached him. He waved her back, and, retreating, Alice sank again into her seat.

"She is mine!" said Matthew Maule. "Mine, by the right of the strongest spirit!"

In the further progress of the legend, there is a long, grotesque, and occasionally awe-striking account of the carpenter's incantations (if so they are to be called), with a view of discovering the lost document. It appears to have been his object to convert the mind of Alice into a kind of telescopic medium, through which Mr. Pyncheon and himself might obtain a glimpse into the spiritual world. He succeeded, accordingly, in holding an imperfect sort of intercourse, at one remove, with the departed personages in whose custody the so much valued secret had been carried beyond the precincts of earth. During her trance, Alice described three figures as being present to her spiritualized perception. One was an aged, dignified, stern-looking gentleman, clad as for a solemn festival in grave and costly attire, but with a great blood-stain on his richly wrought band; the second, an aged man, meanly dressed, with a dark and malign countenance, and a broken halter about his neck; the third, a person not so advanced in life as the former two, but beyond the middle age, wearing a coarse woollen tunic and leather breeches, and with a carpenter's rule sticking out of his side pocket. These three visionary characters possessed a mutual knowledge of the missing document. One of them, in truth,—it was he with the blood-stain on his band,—seemed, unless his gestures were misunderstood, to hold the parchment in his immediate keeping, but was prevented by his two partners in the mystery from disburdening himself of the trust. Finally, when he showed a purpose of shouting forth the secret loudly enough to be heard from his own sphere into that of mortals, his companions struggled with him, and pressed their hands over his mouth; and forthwith—whether that he were choked by it, or that the secret itself was of a crimson hue—there was a fresh flow of blood upon his band. Upon this, the two meanly dressed figures mocked and jeered at the much-abashed old dignitary, and pointed their fingers at the stain.

At this juncture, Maule turned to Mr. Pyncheon.

"It will never be allowed," said he. "The custody of this secret, that would so enrich his heirs, makes part of your grandfather's retribution. He must choke with it until it is no longer of any value. And keep you the House of the Seven Gables! It is too dear bought an inheritance, and too heavy with the curse upon it, to be shifted yet awhile from the Colonel's posterity."

Mr. Pyncheon tried to speak, but—what with fear and passion—could make only a gurgling murmur in his throat. The carpenter smiled.

"Aha, worshipful sir!—so you have old Maule's blood to drink!" said he jeeringly.

"Fiend in man's shape! why dost thou keep dominion over my child?" cried Mr. Pyncheon, when his choked utterance could make way. "Give me back my daughter. Then go thy ways; and may we never meet again!"

"Your daughter!" said Matthew Maule. "Why, she is fairly mine! Nevertheless, not to be too hard with fair Mistress Alice, I will leave her in your keeping; but I do not warrant you that she shall never have occasion to remember Maule, the carpenter."

He waved his hands with an upward motion; and, after a few repetitions of similar gestures, the beautiful Alice Pyncheon awoke from her strange trance. She awoke without the slightest recollection of her visionary experience; but as one losing herself in a momentary reverie, and returning to the consciousness of actual life, in almost as brief an interval as the down-sinking flame of the hearth should quiver again up the chimney. On recognizing Matthew Maule, she assumed an air of somewhat cold but gentle dignity, the rather, as there was a certain peculiar smile on the carpenter's visage that stirred the native pride of the fair Alice. So ended, for that time, the quest for the lost title-deed of the Pyncheon territory at the Eastward; nor, though often subsequently renewed, has it ever yet befallen a Pyncheon to set his eye upon that parchment.

But, alas for the beautiful, the gentle, yet too haughty Alice! A power that she little dreamed of had laid its grasp upon her maiden soul. A will, most unlike her own, constrained her to do its grotesque and fantastic bidding. Her father as it proved, had martyred his poor child to an inordinate desire for measuring his land by miles instead of acres. And, therefore, while Alice Pyncheon lived, she was Maule's slave, in a bondage more humiliating, a thousand-fold, than that which binds its chain around the body. Seated by his humble fireside, Maule had but to wave his hand; and, wherever the proud lady chanced to be,—whether in her chamber, or entertaining her father's stately guests, or worshipping at church,—whatever her place or occupation, her spirit passed from beneath her own control, and bowed itself to Maule. "Alice, laugh!"—the carpenter, beside his hearth, would say; or perhaps intensely will it, without a spoken word. And, even were it prayer-time, or at a funeral, Alice must break into wild laughter. "Alice, be sad!"—and, at the instant, down would come her tears, quenching all the mirth of those around her like sudden rain upon a bonfire. "Alice, dance."—and dance she would, not in such court-like measures as she had learned abroad, but some high-paced jig, or hop-skip rigadoon, befitting the brisk lasses at a rustic merry-making. It seemed to be Maule's impulse, not to ruin Alice, nor to visit her with any black or gigantic mischief, which would have crowned her sorrows with the grace of tragedy, but to wreak a low, ungenerous scorn upon her. Thus all the dignity of life was lost. She felt herself too much abased, and longed to change natures with some worm!

One evening, at a bridal party (but not her own; for, so lost from self-control, she would have deemed it sin to marry), poor Alice was beckoned forth by her unseen despot, and constrained, in her gossamer white dress and satin slippers, to hasten along the street to the mean dwelling of a laboring-man. There was laughter and good cheer within; for Matthew Maule, that night, was to wed the laborer's daughter, and had summoned proud Alice Pyncheon to wait upon his bride. And so she did; and when the twain were one, Alice awoke out of her enchanted sleep. Yet, no longer proud,—humbly, and with a smile all steeped in sadness,—she kissed Maule's wife, and went her way. It was an inclement night; the southeast wind drove the mingled snow and rain into her thinly sheltered bosom; her satin slippers were wet through and through, as she trod the muddy sidewalks. The next day a cold; soon, a settled cough; anon, a hectic cheek, a wasted form, that sat beside the harpsichord, and filled the house with music! Music in which a strain of the heavenly choristers was echoed! Oh; joy! For Alice had borne her last humiliation! Oh, greater joy! For Alice was penitent of her one earthly sin, and proud no more!

The Pyncheons made a great funeral for Alice. The kith and kin were there, and the whole respectability of the town besides. But, last in the procession, came Matthew Maule, gnashing his teeth, as if he would have bitten his own heart in twain,—the darkest and wofullest man that ever walked behind a corpse! He meant to humble Alice, not to kill her; but he had taken a woman's delicate soul into his rude gripe, to play with—and she was dead!

❧ 14 ❧

PHOEBE'S GOOD-BYE

HOLGRAVE, plunging into his tale with the energy and absorption natural to a young author, had given a good deal of action to the parts capable of being developed and exemplified in that manner. He now observed that a certain remarkable drowsiness (wholly unlike that with which the reader possibly feels himself affected) had been flung over the senses of his auditress. It was the effect, unquestionably, of the mystic gesticulations by which he had sought to bring bodily before Phoebe's perception the figure of the mesmerizing carpenter. With the lids drooping over her eyes,—now lifted for an instant, and drawn down again as with leaden weights,—she leaned slightly towards him, and seemed almost to regulate her breath by his. Holgrave gazed at her, as he rolled up his manuscript, and recognized an incipient stage of that curious psychological condition which, as he had himself told Phoebe, he possessed more than an ordinary faculty of producing. A veil was beginning to be muffled about her, in which she could behold only him, and live only in his thoughts and emotions. His glance, as he fastened it on the young girl, grew involuntarily more concentrated; in his attitude there was the consciousness of power, investing his hardly mature figure with a dignity that did not belong to its physical manifestation. It was evident, that, with but one wave of his hand and a corresponding effort of his will, he could complete his mastery over Phoebe's yet free and virgin spirit: he could establish an influence over this good, pure, and simple child, as dangerous, and perhaps as disastrous, as that which the carpenter of his legend had acquired and exercised over the ill-fated Alice.

To a disposition like Holgrave's, at once speculative and active, there is no temptation so great as the opportunity of acquiring empire over the human spirit; nor any idea more seductive to a young man than to become the arbiter of a young girl's destiny. Let us, therefore, —whatever his defects of nature and education, and in spite of his scorn for creeds and institutions,—concede to the daguerreotypist the rare and high quality of reverence for another's individuality. Let us allow him integrity, also, forever after to be confided in; since he forbade himself to twine that one link more which might have rendered his spell over Phoebe indissoluble.

He made a slight gesture upward with his hand.

"You really mortify me, my dear Miss Phoebe!" he exclaimed, smiling half-sarcastically at her. "My poor story, it is but too evident, will never do for Godey or Graham! Only think of your falling asleep at what I hoped the newspaper critics would pronounce a most brilliant, powerful, imaginative, pathetic, and original winding up! Well, the manuscript must serve to light lamps with;—if, indeed, being so imbued with my gentle dulness, it is any longer capable of flame!"

"Me asleep! How can you say so?" answered Phoebe, as unconscious of the crisis through which she had passed as an infant of the precipice to the verge of which it has rolled. "No, no! I consider myself as having been very attentive; and, though I don't remember the incidents quite distinctly, yet I have an impression of a vast deal of trouble and calamity,—so, no doubt, the story will prove exceedingly attractive."

By this time the sun had gone down, and was tinting the clouds towards the zenith with those bright hues which are not seen there until some time after sunset, and when the horizon has quite lost its richer brilliancy. The moon, too, which had long been climbing overhead, and unobtrusively melting its disk into the azure,—like an ambitious demagogue, who hides his aspiring purpose by assuming the prevalent hue of popular sentiment,—now began to shine out, broad and oval, in its middle pathway. These silvery beams were already powerful enough to change the character of the lingering daylight. They softened and embellished the aspect of the old house; although the shadows fell deeper into the angles of its many gables, and lay brooding under the projecting story, and within the half-open door. With the lapse of every moment, the garden grew more picturesque; the fruit-trees, shrubbery, and flower-bushes had a dark obscurity among them. The commonplace characteristics—which, at noontide, it seemed to have taken a century of sordid life to accumulate—were now transfigured by a charm of romance. A hundred mysterious years were whispering among the leaves, whenever the slight sea-breeze found its way thither and stirred them. Through the foliage that roofed the little summer-house the moonlight flickered to and fro, and fell silvery white on the dark floor, the table, and the circular bench, with a continual shift and play, according as the chinks and wayward crevices among the twigs admitted or shut out the glimmer.

So sweetly cool was the atmosphere, after all the feverish day, that the summer eve might be fancied as sprinkling dews and liquid moonlight, with a dash of icy temper in them, out of a silver vase. Here and there, a few drops of this freshness were scattered on a human heart, and gave it youth again, and sympathy with the eternal youth of nature. The artist chanced to be one on whom the reviving influence fell. It made him feel—what he sometimes almost forgot, thrust so early as he had been into the rude struggle of man with man—how youthful he still was.

"It seems to me," he observed, "that I never watched the coming of so beautiful an eve, and never felt anything so very much like happiness as at this moment. After all, what a good world we live in! How good, and beautiful! How young it is, too, with nothing really rotten or age-worn in it! This old house, for example, which sometimes has positively oppressed my breath with its smell of decaying timber! And this garden, where the black mould always clings to my spade, as if I were a sexton delving in a graveyard! Could I keep the feeling that now possesses me, the garden would every day be virgin soil, with the earth's first freshness in the flavor of its beans and squashes; and the house!—it would be like a bower in Eden, blossoming with the earliest roses that God ever made. Moonlight, and the sentiment in man's heart responsive to it, are the greatest of renovators and reformers. And all other reform and renovation, I suppose, will prove to be no better than moonshine!"

"I have been happier than I am now; at least, much gayer," said Phoebe thoughtfully. "Yet I am sensible of a great charm in this brightening moonlight; and I love to watch how the day, tired as it is, lags away reluctantly, and hates to be called yesterday so soon. I never cared much about moonlight before. What is there, I wonder, so beautiful in it, to-night?"

"And you have never felt it before?" inquired the artist, looking earnestly at the girl through the twilight.

"Never," answered Phoebe; "and life does not look the same, now that I have felt it so. It seems as if I had looked at everything, hitherto, in broad daylight, or else in the ruddy light of a cheerful fire, glimmering and dancing through a room. Ah, poor me!" she added, with a half-melancholy laugh. "I shall never be so merry as before I knew Cousin Hepzibah and poor Cousin Clifford. I have grown a great deal older, in this little time. Older, and, I hope, wiser, and,—not exactly sadder,—but, certainly, with not half so much lightness in my spirits! I have given them my sunshine, and have been glad to give it; but, of course, I cannot both give and keep it. They are welcome, notwithstanding!"

"You have lost nothing, Phoebe, worth keeping, nor which it was possible to keep," said Holgrave after a pause. "Our first youth is of no value; for we are never conscious of it until after it is gone. But sometimes—always, I suspect, unless one is exceedingly unfortunate—there comes a sense of second youth, gushing out of the heart's joy at being in love; or, possibly, it may come to crown some other grand festival in life, if any other such there be. This bemoaning of one's self (as you do now) over the first, careless, shallow gayety of youth departed, and this profound happiness at youth regained,—so much deeper and richer than that we lost,—are essential to the soul's development. In some cases, the two states come almost simultaneously, and mingle the sadness and the rapture in one mysterious emotion."

"I hardly think I understand you," said Phoebe.

"No wonder," replied Holgrave, smiling; "for I have told you a secret which I hardly began to know before I found myself giving it utterance. Remember it, however; and when the truth becomes clear to you, then think of this moonlight scene!"

"It is entirely moonlight now, except only a little flush of faint crimson, upward from the west, between those buildings," remarked Phoebe. "I must go in. Cousin Hepzibah is not quick at figures, and will give herself a headache over the day's accounts, unless I help her."

But Holgrave detained her a little longer.

"Miss Hepzibah tells me," observed he, "that you return to the country in a few days."

"Yes, but only for a little while," answered Phoebe; "for I look upon this as my present home. I go to make a few arrangements, and to take a more deliberate leave of my mother and friends. It is pleasant to live where one is much desired and very useful; and I think I may have the satisfaction of feeling myself so here."

"You surely may, and more than you imagine," said the artist. "Whatever health, comfort, and natural life exists in the house is embodied in your person. These blessings came along with you, and will vanish when you leave the threshold. Miss Hepzibah, by secluding herself from society, has lost all true relation with it, and is, in fact, dead; although she galvanizes herself into a semblance of life, and stands behind her counter, afflicting the world with a greatly-to-be-deprecated scowl. Your poor cousin Clifford is another dead and long-buried person, on whom the governor and council have wrought a necromantic miracle. I should not wonder if he were to crumble away, some morning, after you are gone, and nothing be seen of him more, except a heap of dust. Miss Hepzibah, at any rate, will lose what little flexibility she has. They both exist by you."

"I should be very sorry to think so," answered Phoebe gravely. "But it is true that my small abilities were precisely what they needed; and I have a real interest in their welfare,—an odd kind of motherly sentiment,—which I wish you would not laugh at! And let me tell you frankly, Mr. Holgrave, I am sometimes puzzled to know whether you wish them well or ill."

"Undoubtedly," said the daguerreotypist, "I do feel an interest in this antiquated, poverty-stricken old maiden lady, and this degraded and shattered gentleman,—this abortive lover of the beautiful. A kindly interest, too, helpless old children that they are! But you have no conception what a different kind of heart mine is from your own. It is not my impulse, as regards these two individuals, either to help or hinder; but to look on, to analyze, to explain matters to myself, and to comprehend the drama which, for almost two hundred years, has been dragging its slow length over the ground where you and I now tread. If permitted to witness the close, I doubt not to derive a moral satisfaction from it, go matters how they may. There is a conviction within me that the end draws nigh. But, though Providence sent you hither to help, and sends me only as a privileged and meet spectator, I pledge myself to lend these unfortunate beings whatever aid I can!"

"I wish you would speak more plainly," cried Phoebe, perplexed and displeased; "and, above all, that you would feel more like a Christian and a human being! How is it possible to see people in distress without desiring, more than anything else, to help and comfort them? You talk as if this old house were a theatre; and you seem to look at Hepzibah's and Clifford's misfortunes, and those of generations before them, as a tragedy, such as I have seen acted in the hall of a country hotel, only the present one appears to be played exclusively for your amusement. I do not like this. The play costs the performers too much, and the audience is too cold-hearted."

"You are severe," said Holgrave, compelled to recognize a degree of truth in the piquant sketch of his own mood.

"And then," continued Phoebe, "what can you mean by your conviction, which you tell me of, that the end is drawing near? Do you know of any new trouble hanging over my poor relatives? If so, tell me at once, and I will not leave them!"

"Forgive me, Phoebe!" said the daguerreotypist, holding out his hand, to which the girl was constrained to yield her own. "I am somewhat of a mystic, it must be confessed. The tendency is in my blood, together with the faculty of mesmerism, which might have brought me to Gallows Hill, in the good old times of witchcraft. Believe me, if I were really aware of any secret, the disclosure of which would benefit your friends,—who are my own friends, likewise,—you should learn it before we part. But I have no such knowledge."

"You hold something back!" said Phoebe.

"Nothing,—no secrets but my own," answered Holgrave. "I can perceive, indeed, that Judge Pyncheon still keeps his eye on Clifford, in whose ruin he had so large a share. His motives and intentions, however are a mystery to me. He is a determined and relentless man, with the genuine character of an inquisitor; and had he any object to gain by putting Clifford to the rack, I verily believe that he would wrench his joints from their sockets, in order to accomplish it. But, so wealthy and eminent as he is,—so powerful in his own strength, and in the support of society on all sides,—what can Judge Pyncheon have to hope or fear from the imbecile, branded, half-torpid Clifford?"

"Yet," urged Phoebe, "you did speak as if misfortune were impending!"

"Oh, that was because I am morbid!" replied the artist. "My mind has a twist aside, like almost everybody's mind, except your own. Moreover, it is so strange to find myself an inmate of this old Pyncheon House, and sitting in this old garden—(hark, how Maule's well is murmuring!)—that, were it only for this one circumstance, I cannot help fancying that Destiny is arranging its fifth act for a catastrophe."

"There!" cried Phoebe with renewed vexation; for she was by nature as hostile to mystery as the sunshine to a dark corner. "You puzzle me more than ever!"

"Then let us part friends!" said Holgrave, pressing her hand. "Or, if not friends, let us part before you entirely hate me. You, who love everybody else in the world!"

"Good-by, then," said Phoebe frankly. "I do not mean to be angry a great while, and should be sorry to have you think so. There has Cousin Hepzibah been standing in the shadow of the doorway, this quarter of an hour past! She thinks I stay too long in the damp garden. So, good-night, and good-by."

On the second morning thereafter, Phoebe might have been seen, in her straw bonnet, with a shawl on one arm and a little carpet-bag on the other, bidding adieu to Hepzibah and Cousin Clifford. She was to take a seat in the next train of cars, which would transport her to within half a dozen miles of her country village.

The tears were in Phoebe's eyes; a smile, dewy with affectionate regret, was glimmering around her pleasant mouth. She wondered how it came to pass, that her life of a few weeks, here in this heavy-hearted old mansion, had taken such hold of her, and so melted into her associations, as now to seem a more important centre-point of remembrance than all which had gone before. How had Hepzibah—grim, silent, and irresponsive to her overflow of cordial sentiment—contrived to win so much love? And Clifford,—in his abortive decay, with the mystery of fearful crime upon him, and the close prison-atmosphere yet lurking in his breath,—how had he transformed himself into the simplest child, whom Phoebe felt bound to watch over, and be, as it were, the providence of his unconsidered hours! Everything, at that instant of farewell, stood out prominently to her view. Look where she would, lay her hand on what she might, the object responded to her consciousness, as if a moist human heart were in it.

She peeped from the window into the garden, and felt herself more regretful at leaving this spot of black earth, vitiated with such an age-long growth of weeds, than joyful at the idea of again scenting her pine forests and fresh clover-fields. She called Chanticleer, his two wives, and the venerable chicken, and threw them some crumbs of bread from the breakfast-table. These being hastily gobbled up, the chicken spread its wings, and alighted close by Phoebe on the window-sill, where it looked gravely into her face and vented its emotions in a croak. Phoebe bade it be a good old chicken during her absence, and promised to bring it a little bag of buckwheat.

"Ah, Phoebe!" remarked Hepzibah, "you do not smile so naturally as when you came to us! Then, the smile chose to shine out; now, you choose it should. It is well that you are going back, for a little while, into your native air. There has been too much weight on your spirits. The house is too gloomy and lonesome; the shop is full of vexations; and as for me, I have no faculty of making things look brighter than they are. Dear Clifford has been your only comfort!"

"Come hither, Phoebe," suddenly cried her cousin Clifford, who had said very little all the morning. "Close!—closer!—and look me in the face!"

Phoebe put one of her small hands on each elbow of his chair, and leaned her face towards him, so that he might peruse it as carefully as he would. It is probable that the latent emotions of this parting hour had revived, in some degree, his bedimmed and enfeebled faculties. At any rate, Phoebe soon felt that, if not the profound insight of a seer, yet a more than feminine delicacy of appreciation, was making her heart the subject of its regard. A moment before, she had known nothing which she would have sought to hide. Now, as if some secret were hinted to her own consciousness through the medium of another's perception, she was fain to let her eyelids droop beneath Clifford's gaze. A blush, too,—the redder, because she strove hard to keep it down,—ascended bigger and higher, in a tide of fitful progress, until even her brow was all suffused with it.

"It is enough, Phoebe," said Clifford, with a melancholy smile. "When I first saw you, you were the prettiest little maiden in the world; and now you have deepened into beauty. Girlhood has passed into womanhood; the bud is a bloom! Go, now—I feel lonelier than I did."

Phoebe took leave of the desolate couple, and passed through the shop, twinkling her eyelids to shake off a dew-drop; for—considering how brief her absence was to be, and therefore the folly of being cast down about it—she would not so far acknowledge her tears as to dry them with her handkerchief. On the doorstep, she met the little urchin whose marvellous feats of gastronomy have been recorded in the earlier pages of our narrative. She took from the window some specimen or other of natural history,—her eyes being too dim with moisture to inform her accurately whether it was a rabbit or a hippopotamus,—put it into the child's hand as a parting gift, and went her way. Old Uncle Venner was just coming out of his door, with a wood-horse and saw on his shoulder; and, trudging along the street, he scrupled not to keep company with Phoebe, so far as their paths lay together; nor, in spite of his patched coat and rusty beaver, and the curious fashion of his tow-cloth trousers, could she find it in her heart to outwalk him.

"We shall miss you, next Sabbath afternoon," observed the street philosopher. "It is unaccountable how little while it takes some folks to grow just as natural to a man as his own breath; and, begging your pardon, Miss Phoebe (though there can be no offence in an old man's saying it), that's just what you've grown to me! My years have been a great many, and your life is but just beginning; and yet, you are somehow as familiar to me as if I had found you at my mother's door, and you had blossomed, like a running vine, all along my pathway since. Come back soon, or I shall be gone to my farm; for I begin to find these wood-sawing jobs a little too tough for my back-ache."

"Very soon, Uncle Venner," replied Phoebe.

"And let it be all the sooner, Phoebe, for the sake of those poor souls yonder," continued her companion. "They can never do without you, now,—never, Phoebe; never—no more than if one of God's angels had been living with them, and making their dismal house pleasant and comfortable! Don't it seem to you they'd be in a sad case, if, some pleasant summer morning like this, the angel should spread his wings, and fly to the place he came from? Well, just so they feel, now that you're going home by the railroad! They can't bear it, Miss Phoebe; so be sure to come back!"

"I am no angel, Uncle Venner," said Phoebe, smiling, as she offered him her hand at the street-corner. "But, I suppose, people never feel so much like angels as when they are doing what little good they may. So I shall certainly come back!"

Thus parted the old man and the rosy girl; and Phoebe took the wings of the morning, and was soon flitting almost as rapidly away as if endowed with the aerial locomotion of the angels to whom Uncle Venner had so graciously compared her.

15

THE SCOWL AND SMILE

SEVERAL DAYS PASSED over the Seven Gables, heavily and drearily enough. In fact (not to attribute the whole gloom of sky and earth to the one inauspicious circumstance of Phoebe's departure), an easterly storm had set in, and indefatigably apply itself to the task of making the black roof and walls of the old house look more cheerless than ever before. Yet was the outside not half so cheerless as the interior. Poor Clifford was cut off, at once, from all his scanty resources of enjoyment. Phoebe was not there; nor did the sunshine fall upon the floor. The garden, with its muddy walks, and the chill, dripping foliage of its summer-house, was an image to be shuddered at. Nothing flourished in the cold, moist, pitiless atmosphere, drifting with the brackish scud of sea-breezes, except the moss along the joints of the shingle-roof, and the great bunch of weeds, that had lately been suffering from drought, in the angle between the two front gables.

As for Hepzibah, she seemed not merely possessed with the east wind, but to be, in her very person, only another phase of this gray and sullen spell of weather; the East-Wind itself, grim and disconsolate, in a rusty black silk gown, and with a turban of cloud-wreaths on its head. The custom of the shop fell off, because a story got abroad that she soured her small beer and other damageable commodities, by scowling on them. It is, perhaps, true that the public had something reasonably to complain of in her deportment; but towards Clifford she was neither ill-tempered nor unkind, nor felt less warmth of heart than always, had it been possible to make it reach him. The inutility of her best efforts, however, palsied the poor old gentlewoman. She could do little else than sit silently in a corner of the room, when the wet pear-tree branches, sweeping across the small windows, created a noonday dusk, which Hepzibah unconsciously darkened with her woe-begone aspect. It was no fault of Hepzibah's. Everything—even the old chairs and tables, that had known what weather was for three or four such lifetimes as her own —looked as damp and chill as if the present were their worst experience. The picture of the Puritan Colonel shivered on the wall. The house itself shivered, from every attic of its seven gables down to the great kitchen fireplace, which served all the better as an emblem of the mansion's heart, because, though built for warmth, it was now so comfortless and empty.

Hepzibah attempted to enliven matters by a fire in the parlor. But the storm demon kept watch above, and, whenever a flame was kindled, drove the smoke back again, choking the chimney's sooty throat with its own breath. Nevertheless, during four days of this miserable storm, Clifford wrapt himself in an old cloak, and occupied his customary chair. On the morning of the fifth, when summoned to breakfast, he responded only by a broken-hearted murmur, expressive of a determination not to leave his bed. His sister made no attempt to change his purpose. In fact, entirely as she loved him, Hepzibah could hardly have borne any longer the wretched duty—so impracticable by her few and rigid faculties—of seeking pastime for a still sensitive, but ruined mind, critical and fastidious, without force or volition. It was at least something short of positive despair, that to-day she might sit shivering alone, and not suffer continually a new grief, and unreasonable pang of remorse, at every fitful sigh of her fellow sufferer.

But Clifford, it seemed, though he did not make his appearance below stairs, had, after all, bestirred himself in quest of amusement. In the course of the forenoon, Hepzibah heard a note of music, which (there being no other tuneful contrivance in the House of the Seven Gables) she knew must proceed from Alice Pyncheon's harpsichord. She was aware that Clifford, in his youth, had possessed a cultivated taste for music, and a considerable degree of skill in its practice. It was difficult, however, to conceive of his retaining an accomplishment to which daily exercise is so essential, in the measure indicated by the sweet, airy, and delicate, though most melancholy strain, that now stole upon her ear. Nor was it less marvellous that the long-silent instrument should be capable of so much melody. Hepzibah involuntarily thought of the ghostly harmonies, prelusive of death in the family, which were attributed to the legendary Alice. But it was, perhaps, proof of the agency of other than spiritual fingers, that, after a few touches, the chords seemed to snap asunder with their own vibrations, and the music ceased.

But a harsher sound succeeded to the mysterious notes; nor was the easterly day fated to pass without an event sufficient in itself to poison, for Hepzibah and Clifford, the balmiest air that ever brought the humming-birds along with it. The final echoes of Alice Pyncheon's performance (or Clifford's, if his we must consider it) were driven away by no less vulgar a dissonance than the ringing of the shop-bell. A foot was heard scraping itself on the threshold, and thence somewhat ponderously stepping on the floor. Hepzibah delayed a moment, while muffling herself in a faded shawl, which had been her defensive armor in a forty years' warfare against the east wind. A characteristic sound, however,—neither a cough nor a hem, but a kind of rumbling and reverberating spasm in somebody's capacious depth of chest;—impelled her to hurry forward, with that aspect of fierce faint-heartedness so common to women in cases of perilous emergency. Few of her sex, on such occasions, have ever looked so terrible as our poor scowling Hepzibah. But the visitor quietly closed the shop-door behind him, stood up his umbrella against the counter, and turned a visage of composed benignity, to meet the alarm and anger which his appearance had excited.

Hepzibah's presentiment had not deceived her. It was no other than Judge Pyncheon, who, after in vain trying the front door, had now effected his entrance into the shop.

"How do you do, Cousin Hepzibah?—and how does this most inclement weather affect our poor Clifford?" began the Judge; and wonderful it seemed, indeed, that the easterly storm was not put to shame, or, at any rate, a little mollified, by the genial benevolence of his smile. "I could not rest without calling to ask, once more, whether I can in any manner promote his comfort, or your own."

"You can do nothing," said Hepzibah, controlling her agitation as well as she could. "I devote myself to Clifford. He has every comfort which his situation admits of."

"But allow me to suggest, dear cousin," rejoined the Judge, "you err,—in all affection and kindness, no doubt, and with the very best intentions,—but you do err, nevertheless, in keeping your brother so secluded. Why insulate him thus from all sympathy and kindness? Clifford, alas! has had too much of solitude. Now let him try society,—the society, that is to say, of kindred and old friends. Let me, for instance, but see Clifford, and I will answer for the good effect of the interview."

"You cannot see him," answered Hepzibah. "Clifford has kept his bed since yesterday."

"What! How! Is he ill?" exclaimed Judge Pyncheon, starting with what seemed to be angry alarm; for the very frown of the old Puritan darkened through the room as he spoke. "Nay, then, I must and will see him! What if he should die?"

"He is in no danger of death," said Hepzibah,—and added, with bitterness that she could repress no longer, "none; unless he shall be persecuted to death, now, by the same man who long ago attempted it!"

"Cousin Hepzibah," said the Judge, with an impressive earnestness of manner, which grew even to tearful pathos as he proceeded, "is it possible that you do not perceive how unjust, how unkind, how unchristian, is this constant, this long-continued bitterness against me, for a part which I was constrained by duty and conscience, by the force of law, and at my own peril, to act? What did I do, in detriment to Clifford, which it was possible to leave undone? How could you, his sister,—if, for your never-ending sorrow, as it has been for mine, you had known what I did,—have, shown greater tenderness? And do you think, cousin, that it has cost me no pang? —that it has left no anguish in my bosom, from that day to this, amidst all the prosperity with which Heaven has blessed me?—or that I do not now rejoice, when it is deemed consistent with the dues of public justice and the welfare of society that this dear kinsman, this early friend, this nature so delicately and beautifully constituted,—so unfortunate, let us pronounce him, and forbear to say, so guilty,—that our own Clifford, in fine, should be given back to life, and its possibilities of enjoyment? Ah, you little know me, Cousin Hepzibah! You little know this heart! It now throbs at the thought of meeting him! There lives not the human being (except yourself,—and you not more than I) who has shed so many tears for Clifford's calamity. You behold some of them now. There is none who would so delight to promote his happiness! Try me, Hepzibah!—try me, Cousin!—try the man whom you have treated as your enemy and Clifford's!—try Jaffrey Pyncheon, and you shall find him true, to the heart's core!"

"In the name of Heaven," cried Hepzibah, provoked only to intenser indignation by this outgush of the inestimable tenderness of a stern nature,—"in God's name, whom you insult, and whose power I could almost question, since he hears you utter so many false words without palsying your tongue,—give over, I beseech you, this loathsome pretence of affection for your victim! You hate him! Say so, like a man! You cherish, at this moment, some black purpose against him in your heart! Speak it out, at once!—or, if you hope so to promote it better, hide it till you can triumph in its success! But never speak again of your love for my poor brother. I cannot bear it! It will drive me beyond a woman's decency! It will drive me mad! Forbear! Not another word! It will make me spurn you!"

For once, Hepzibah's wrath had given her courage. She had spoken. But, after all, was this unconquerable distrust of Judge Pyncheon's integrity, and this utter denial, apparently, of his claim to stand in the ring of human sympathies,—were they founded in any just perception of his character, or merely the offspring of a woman's unreasonable prejudice, deduced from nothing?

The Judge, beyond all question, was a man of eminent respectability. The church acknowledged it; the state acknowledged it. It was denied by nobody. In all the very extensive sphere of those who knew him, whether in his public or private capacities, there was not an individual—except Hepzibah, and some lawless mystic, like the daguerreotypist, and, possibly, a few political opponents—who would have dreamed of seriously disputing his claim to a high and honorable place in the world's regard. Nor (we must do him the further justice to say) did Judge Pyncheon himself, probably, entertain many or very frequent doubts, that his enviable reputation accorded with his deserts. His conscience, therefore, usually considered the surest witness to a man's integrity,—his conscience, unless it might be for the little space of five minutes in the twenty-four hours, or, now and then, some black day in the whole year's circle, —his conscience bore an accordant testimony with the world's laudatory voice. And yet, strong as this evidence may seem to be, we should hesitate to peril our own conscience on the assertion, that the Judge and the consenting world were right, and that poor Hepzibah with her solitary prejudice was wrong. Hidden from mankind,—forgotten by himself, or buried so deeply under a sculptured and ornamented pile of ostentatious deeds that his daily life could take no note of it,—there may have lurked some evil and unsightly thing. Nay, we could almost venture to say, further, that a daily guilt might have been acted by him, continually renewed, and reddening forth afresh, like the miraculous blood-stain of a murder, without his necessarily and at every moment being aware of it.

Men of strong minds, great force of character, and a hard texture of the sensibilities, are very capable of falling into mistakes of this kind. They are ordinarily men to whom forms are of paramount importance. Their field of action lies among the external phenomena of life. They possess vast ability in grasping, and arranging, and appropriating to themselves, the big, heavy, solid unrealities, such as gold, landed estate, offices of trust and emolument, and public honors. With these materials, and with deeds of goodly aspect, done in the public eye, an individual of this class builds up, as it were, a tall and stately edifice, which, in the view of other people, and ultimately in his own view, is no other than the man's character, or the man himself. Behold, therefore, a palace! Its splendid halls and suites of spacious apartments are floored with a mosaic-work of costly marbles; its windows, the whole height of each room, admit the sunshine through the most transparent of plate-glass; its high cornices are gilded, and its ceilings gorgeously painted; and a lofty dome—through which, from the central pavement, you may gaze up to the sky, as with no obstructing medium between—surmounts the whole. With what fairer and nobler emblem could any man desire to shadow forth his character? Ah! but in some low and obscure nook,—some narrow closet on the ground-floor, shut, locked and bolted, and the key flung away,—or beneath the marble pavement, in a stagnant water-puddle, with the richest pattern of mosaic-work above,—may lie a corpse, half decayed, and still decaying, and diffusing its death-scent all through the palace! The inhabitant will not be conscious of it, for it has long been his daily breath! Neither will the visitors, for they smell only the rich odors which the master sedulously scatters through the palace, and the incense which they bring, and delight to burn before him! Now and then, perchance, comes in a seer, before whose sadly gifted eye the whole structure melts into thin air, leaving only the hidden nook, the bolted closet, with the cobwebs festooned over its forgotten door, or the deadly hole under the pavement, and the decaying corpse within. Here, then, we are to seek the true emblem of the man's character, and of the deed that gives whatever reality it possesses to his life. And, beneath the show of a marble palace, that pool of stagnant water, foul with many impurities, and, perhaps, tinged with blood,—that secret abomination, above which, possibly, he may say his prayers, without remembering it,—is this man's miserable soul!

To apply this train of remark somewhat more closely to Judge Pyncheon. We might say (without in the least imputing crime to a personage of his eminent respectability) that there was enough of splendid rubbish in his life to cover up and paralyze a more active and subtile conscience than the Judge was ever troubled with. The purity of his judicial character, while on the bench; the faithfulness of his public service in subsequent capacities; his devotedness to his party, and the rigid consistency with which he had adhered to its principles, or, at all events, kept pace with its organized movements; his remarkable zeal as president of a Bible society; his unimpeachable integrity as treasurer of a widow's and orphan's fund; his benefits to horticulture, by producing two much esteemed varieties of the pear and to agriculture, through the agency of the famous Pyncheon bull; the cleanliness of his moral deportment, for a great many years past; the severity with which he had frowned upon, and finally cast off, an expensive and dissipated son, delaying forgiveness until within the final quarter of an hour of the young man's life; his prayers at morning and eventide, and graces at meal-time; his efforts in furtherance of the temperance cause; his confining himself, since the last attack of the gout, to five diurnal glasses of old sherry wine; the snowy whiteness of his linen, the polish of his boots, the handsomeness of his gold-headed cane, the square and roomy fashion of his coat, and the fineness of its material, and, in general, the studied propriety of his dress and equipment; the scrupulousness with which he paid public notice, in the street, by a bow, a lifting of the hat, a nod, or a motion of the hand, to all and sundry of his acquaintances, rich or poor; the smile of broad benevolence wherewith he made it a point to gladden the whole world,—what room could possibly be found for darker traits in a portrait made up of lineaments like these? This proper face was what he beheld in the looking-glass. This admirably arranged life was what he was conscious of in the progress of every day. Then might not he claim to be its result and sum, and say to himself and the community, "Behold Judge Pyncheon there"?

And allowing that, many, many years ago, in his early and reckless youth, he had committed some one wrong act,—or that, even now, the inevitable force of circumstances should occasionally make him do one questionable deed among a thousand praiseworthy, or, at least, blameless ones,—would you characterize the Judge by that one necessary deed, and that half-forgotten act, and let it overshadow the fair aspect of a lifetime? What is there so ponderous in evil, that a thumb's bigness of it should outweigh the mass of things not evil which were heaped into the other scale! This scale and balance system is a favorite one with people of Judge Pyncheon's brotherhood. A hard, cold man, thus unfortunately situated, seldom or never looking inward, and resolutely taking his idea of himself from what purports to be his image as reflected in the mirror of public opinion, can scarcely arrive at true self-knowledge, except through loss of property and reputation. Sickness will not always help him do it; not always the death-hour!

But our affair now is with Judge Pyncheon as he stood confronting the fierce outbreak of Hepzibah's wrath. Without premeditation, to her own surprise, and indeed terror, she had given vent, for once, to the inveteracy of her resentment, cherished against this kinsman for thirty years.

Thus far the Judge's countenance had expressed mild forbearance,—grave and almost gentle deprecation of his cousin's unbecoming violence,—free and Christian-like forgiveness of the wrong inflicted by her words. But when those words were irrevocably spoken, his look assumed sternness, the sense of power, and immitigable resolve; and this with so natural and imperceptible a change, that it seemed as if the iron man had stood there from the first, and the meek man not at all. The effect was as when the light, vapory clouds, with their soft coloring, suddenly vanish from the stony brow of a precipitous mountain, and leave there the frown which you at once feel to be eternal. Hepzibah almost adopted the insane belief that it was her old Puritan ancestor, and not the modern Judge, on whom she had just been wreaking the bitterness of her heart. Never did a man show stronger proof of the lineage attributed to him than Judge Pyncheon, at this crisis, by his unmistakable resemblance to the picture in the inner room.

"Cousin Hepzibah," said he very calmly, "it is time to have done with this."

"With all my heart!" answered she. "Then, why do you persecute us any longer? Leave poor Clifford and me in peace. Neither of us desires anything better!"

"It is my purpose to see Clifford before I leave this house," continued the Judge. "Do not act like a madwoman, Hepzibah! I am his only friend, and an all-powerful one. Has it never occurred to you,—are you so blind as not to have seen,—that, without not merely my consent, but my efforts, my representations, the exertion of my whole influence, political, official, personal, Clifford would never have been what you call free? Did you think his release a triumph over me? Not so, my good cousin; not so, by any means! The furthest possible from that! No; but it was the accomplishment of a purpose long entertained on my part. I set him free!"

"You!" answered Hepzibah. "I never will believe it! He owed his dungeon to you; his freedom to God's providence!"

"I set him free!" reaffirmed Judge Pyncheon, with the calmest composure. "And I came hither now to decide whether he shall retain his freedom. It will depend upon himself. For this purpose, I must see him."

"Never!—it would drive him mad!" exclaimed Hepzibah, but with an irresoluteness sufficiently perceptible to the keen eye of the Judge; for, without the slightest faith in his good intentions, she knew not whether there was most to dread in yielding or resistance. "And why should you wish to see this wretched, broken man, who retains hardly a fraction of his intellect, and will hide even that from an eye which has no love in it?"

"He shall see love enough in mine, if that be all!" said the Judge, with well-grounded confidence in the benignity of his aspect. "But, Cousin Hepzibah, you confess a great deal, and very much to the purpose. Now, listen, and I will frankly explain my reasons for insisting on this interview. At the death, thirty years since, of our uncle Jaffrey, it was found,—I know not whether the circumstance ever attracted much of your attention, among the sadder interests that clustered round that event,—but it was found that his visible estate, of every kind, fell far short of any estimate ever made of it. He was supposed to be immensely rich. Nobody doubted that he stood among the weightiest men of his day. It was one of his eccentricities, however,—and not altogether a folly, neither,—to conceal the amount of his property by making distant and foreign investments, perhaps under other names than his own, and by various means, familiar enough to capitalists, but unnecessary here to be specified. By Uncle Jaffrey's last will and testament, as you are aware, his entire property was bequeathed to me, with the single exception of a life interest to yourself in this old family mansion, and the strip of patrimonial estate remaining attached to it."

"And do you seek to deprive us of that?" asked Hepzibah, unable to restrain her bitter contempt. "Is this your price for ceasing to persecute poor Clifford?"

"Certainly not, my dear cousin!" answered the Judge, smiling benevolently. "On the contrary, as you must do me the justice to own, I have constantly expressed my readiness to double or treble your resources, whenever you should make up your mind to accept any kindness of that nature at the hands of your kinsman. No, no! But here lies the gist of the matter. Of my uncle's unquestionably great estate, as I have said, not the half—no, not one third, as I am fully convinced—was apparent after his death. Now, I have the best possible reasons for believing that your brother Clifford can give me a clew to the recovery of the remainder."

"Clifford!—Clifford know of any hidden wealth? Clifford have it in his power to make you

497

rich?" cried the old gentlewoman, affected with a sense of something like ridicule at the idea. "Impossible! You deceive yourself! It is really a thing to laugh at!"

"It is as certain as that I stand here!" said Judge Pyncheon, striking his gold-headed cane on the floor, and at the same time stamping his foot, as if to express his conviction the more forcibly by the whole emphasis of his substantial person. "Clifford told me so himself!"

"No, no!" exclaimed Hepzibah incredulously. "You are dreaming, Cousin Jaffrey."

"I do not belong to the dreaming class of men," said the Judge quietly. "Some months before my uncle's death, Clifford boasted to me of the possession of the secret of incalculable wealth. His purpose was to taunt me, and excite my curiosity. I know it well. But, from a pretty distinct recollection of the particulars of our conversation, I am thoroughly convinced that there was truth in what he said. Clifford, at this moment, if he chooses,—and choose he must!—can inform me where to find the schedule, the documents, the evidences, in whatever shape they exist, of the vast amount of Uncle Jaffrey's missing property. He has the secret. His boast was no idle word. It had a directness, an emphasis, a particularity, that showed a backbone of solid meaning within the mystery of his expression."

"But what could have been Clifford's object," asked Hepzibah, "in concealing it so long?"

"It was one of the bad impulses of our fallen nature," replied the Judge, turning up his eyes. "He looked upon me as his enemy. He considered me as the cause of his overwhelming disgrace, his imminent peril of death, his irretrievable ruin. There was no great probability, therefore, of his volunteering information, out of his dungeon, that should elevate me still higher on the ladder of prosperity. But the moment has now come when he must give up his secret."

"And what if he should refuse?" inquired Hepzibah. "Or,—as I steadfastly believe,—what if he has no knowledge of this wealth?"

"My dear cousin," said Judge Pyncheon, with a quietude which he had the power of making more formidable than any violence, "since your brother's return, I have taken the precaution (a highly proper one in the near kinsman and natural guardian of an individual so situated) to have his deportment and habits constantly and carefully overlooked. Your neighbors have been eye-witnesses to whatever has passed in the garden. The butcher, the baker, the fish-monger, some of the customers of your shop, and many a prying old woman, have told me several of the secrets of your interior. A still larger circle—I myself, among the rest —can testify to his extravagances at the arched window. Thousands beheld him, a week or two ago, on the point of flinging himself thence into the street. From all this testimony, I am led to apprehend—reluctantly, and with deep grief—that Clifford's misfortunes have so affected his intellect, never very strong, that he cannot safely remain at large. The alternative, you must be aware,—and its adoption will depend entirely on the decision which I am now about to make, —the alternative is his confinement, probably for the remainder of his life, in a public asylum for persons in his unfortunate state of mind."

"You cannot mean it!" shrieked Hepzibah.

"Should my cousin Clifford," continued Judge Pyncheon, wholly undisturbed, "from mere malice, and hatred of one whose interests ought naturally to be dear to him,—a mode of passion that, as often as any other, indicates mental disease,—should he refuse me the information so important to myself, and which he assuredly possesses, I shall consider it the one needed jot of evidence to satisfy my mind of his insanity. And, once sure of the course pointed out by conscience, you know me too well, Cousin Hepzibah, to entertain a doubt that I shall pursue it."

"O Jaffrey,—Cousin Jaffrey," cried Hepzibah mournfully, not passionately, "it is you that are diseased in mind, not Clifford! You have forgotten that a woman was your mother!—that you have had sisters, brothers, children of your own!—or that there ever was affection between man and man, or pity from one man to another, in this miserable world! Else, how could you have dreamed of this? You are not young, Cousin Jaffrey!—no, nor middle-aged,—but already an old man! The hair is white upon your head! How many years have you to live? Are you not rich enough for that little time? Shall you be hungry,—shall you lack clothes, or a roof to shelter you, —between this point and the grave? No! but, with the half of what you now possess, you could revel in costly food and wines, and build a house twice as splendid as you now inhabit, and make a far greater show to the world,—and yet leave riches to your only son, to make him bless the hour of your death! Then, why should you do this cruel, cruel thing?—so mad a thing, that I know not whether to call it wicked! Alas, Cousin Jaffrey, this hard and grasping spirit has run in our blood these two hundred years. You are but doing over again, in another shape, what your ancestor before you did, and sending down to your posterity the curse inherited from him!"

"Talk sense, Hepzibah, for Heaven's sake!" exclaimed the Judge, with the impatience natural to a reasonable man, on hearing anything so utterly absurd as the above, in a discussion about matters of business. "I have told you my determination. I am not apt to change. Clifford must give up his secret, or take the consequences. And let him decide quickly; for I have several affairs to attend to this morning, and an important dinner engagement with some political friends."

"Clifford has no secret!" answered Hepzibah. "And God will not let you do the thing you meditate!"

"We shall see," said the unmoved Judge. "Meanwhile, choose whether you will summon Clifford, and allow this business to be amicably settled by an interview between two kinsmen, or drive me to harsher measures, which I should be most happy to feel myself justified in avoiding. The responsibility is altogether on your part."

"You are stronger than I," said Hepzibah, after a brief consideration; "and you have no pity in your strength! Clifford is not now insane; but the interview which you insist upon may go far to make him so. Nevertheless, knowing you as I do, I believe it to be my best course to allow you to judge for yourself as to the improbability of his possessing any valuable secret. I will call Clifford. Be merciful in your dealings with him!—be far more merciful than your heart bids you be!—for God is looking at you, Jaffrey Pyncheon!"

The Judge followed his cousin from the shop, where the foregoing conversation had passed, into the parlor, and flung himself heavily into the great ancestral chair. Many a former Pyncheon had found repose in its capacious arms: rosy children, after their sports; young men, dreamy with love; grown men, weary with cares; old men, burdened with winters,—they had mused, and slumbered, and departed to a yet profounder sleep. It had been a long tradition, though a doubtful one, that this was the very chair, seated in which the earliest of the Judge's New England forefathers—he whose picture still hung upon the wall—had given a dead man's silent and stern reception to the throng of distinguished guests. From that hour of evil omen until the present, it may be,—though we know not the secret of his heart,—but it may be that no wearier and sadder man had ever sunk into the chair than this same Judge Pyncheon, whom we have just beheld so immitigably hard and resolute. Surely, it must have been at no slight cost that he had thus fortified his soul with iron. Such calmness is a mightier effort than the violence of weaker men. And there was yet a heavy task for him to do. Was it a little matter—a trifle to be prepared for in a single moment, and to be rested from in another moment,—that he must now, after thirty years, encounter a kinsman risen from a living tomb, and wrench a secret from him, or else consign him to a living tomb again?

"Did you speak?" asked Hepzibah, looking in from the threshold of the parlor; for she imagined that the Judge had uttered some sound which she was anxious to interpret as a relenting impulse. "I thought you called me back."

"No, no" gruffly answered Judge Pyncheon with a harsh frown, while his brow grew almost a black purple, in the shadow of the room. "Why should I call you back? Time flies! Bid Clifford come to me!"

The Judge had taken his watch from his vest pocket and now held it in his hand, measuring the interval which was to ensue before the appearance of Clifford.

𝕾 16 𝕼

CLIFFORD'S CHAMBER

NEVER HAD the old house appeared so dismal to poor Hepzibah as when she departed on that wretched errand. There was a strange aspect in it. As she trode along the foot-worn passages, and opened one crazy door after another, and ascended the creaking staircase, she gazed wistfully and fearfully around. It would have been no marvel, to her excited mind, if, behind or beside her, there had been the rustle of dead people's garments, or pale visages awaiting her on the landing-place above. Her nerves were set all ajar by the scene of passion and terror through which she had just struggled. Her colloquy with Judge Pyncheon, who so perfectly represented the person and attributes of the founder of the family, had called back the dreary past. It weighed upon her heart. Whatever she had heard, from legendary aunts and grandmothers, concerning the good or evil fortunes of the Pyncheons,—stories which had heretofore been kept warm in her remembrance by the chimney-corner glow that was associated with them,—now recurred to her, sombre, ghastly, cold, like most passages of family history, when brooded over in melancholy mood. The whole seemed little else but a series of calamity, reproducing itself in successive generations, with one general hue, and varying in little, save the outline. But Hepzibah now felt as if the Judge, and Clifford, and herself,—they three together,—were on the point of adding another incident to the annals of the house, with a bolder relief of wrong and sorrow, which would cause it to stand out from all the rest. Thus it is that the grief of the passing moment takes upon itself an individuality, and a character of climax, which it is destined to lose after a while, and to fade into the dark gray tissue common to the grave or glad events of many years ago. It is but for a moment, comparatively, that anything looks strange or startling,—a truth that has the bitter and the sweet in it.

But Hepzibah could not rid herself of the sense of something unprecedented at that instant passing and soon to be accomplished. Her nerves were in a shake. Instinctively she paused before the arched window, and looked out upon the street, in order to seize its permanent objects with her mental grasp, and thus to steady herself from the reel and vibration which affected her more immediate sphere. It brought her up, as we may say, with a kind of shock, when she beheld everything under the same appearance as the day before, and numberless preceding days, except for the difference between sunshine and sullen storm. Her eyes travelled along the street, from doorstep to doorstep, noting the wet sidewalks, with here and there a puddle in hollows that had been imperceptible until filled with water. She screwed her dim optics to their acutest point, in the hope of making out, with greater distinctness, a certain window, where she half saw, half guessed, that a tailor's seamstress was sitting at her work. Hepzibah flung herself upon that unknown woman's companionship, even thus far off. Then she was attracted by a chaise rapidly passing, and watched its moist and glistening top, and its splashing wheels, until it had turned the corner, and refused to carry any further her idly trifling, because appalled and overburdened, mind. When the vehicle had disappeared, she allowed herself still another loitering moment; for the patched figure of good Uncle Venner was now visible, coming slowly from the head of the street downward, with a rheumatic limp, because the east wind had got into his joints. Hepzibah wished that he would pass yet more slowly, and befriend her shivering solitude a little longer. Anything that would take her out of the grievous present, and interpose human beings betwixt herself and what was nearest to her, —whatever would defer for an instant the inevitable errand on which she was bound,—all such impediments were welcome. Next to the lightest heart, the heaviest is apt to be most playful.

Hepzibah had little hardihood for her own proper pain, and far less for what she must inflict on Clifford. Of so slight a nature, and so shattered by his previous calamities, it could not well be short of utter ruin to bring him face to face with the hard, relentless man who had been his evil destiny through life. Even had there been no bitter recollections, nor any hostile interest now at stake between them, the mere natural repugnance of the more sensitive system to the massive, weighty, and unimpressible one, must, in itself, have been disastrous to the former. It would be like flinging a porcelain vase, with already a crack in it, against a granite column. Never before had Hepzibah so adequately estimated the powerful character of her cousin Jaffrey,—powerful by intellect, energy of will, the long habit of acting among men, and, as she believed, by his unscrupulous pursuit of selfish ends through evil means. It did but increase the difficulty that Judge Pyncheon was under a delusion as to the secret which he supposed Clifford to possess. Men of his strength of purpose and customary sagacity, if they chance to adopt a mistaken opinion in practical matters, so wedge it and fasten it among things known to be true, that to wrench it out of their minds is hardly less difficult than pulling up an oak. Thus, as the Judge required an impossibility of Clifford, the latter, as he could not perform it, must needs perish. For what, in the grasp of a man like this, was to become of Clifford's soft poetic nature, that never should have had a task more stubborn than to set a life of beautiful enjoyment to the flow and rhythm of musical cadences! Indeed, what had become of it already? Broken! Blighted! All but annihilated! Soon to be wholly so!

For a moment, the thought crossed Hepzibah's mind, whether Clifford might not really have such knowledge of their deceased uncle's vanished estate as the Judge imputed to him. She remembered some vague intimations, on her brother's part, which—if the supposition were not essentially preposterous—might have been so interpreted. There had been schemes of travel and residence abroad, day-dreams of brilliant life at home, and splendid castles in the air, which it would have required boundless wealth to build and realize. Had this wealth been in her power, how gladly would Hepzibah have bestowed it all upon her iron-hearted kinsman, to buy for Clifford the freedom and seclusion of the desolate old house! But she believed that her brother's schemes were as destitute of actual substance and purpose as a child's pictures of its future life, while sitting in a little chair by its mother's knee. Clifford had none but shadowy gold at his command; and it was not the stuff to satisfy Judge Pyncheon!

Was there no help in their extremity? It seemed strange that there should be none, with a city round about her. It would be so easy to throw up the window, and send forth a shriek, at the strange agony of which everybody would come hastening to the rescue, well understanding it to be the cry of a human soul, at some dreadful crisis! But how wild, how almost laughable, the fatality,—and yet how continually it comes to pass, thought Hepzibah, in this dull delirium of a world,—that whosoever, and with however kindly a purpose, should come to help, they would be sure to help the strongest side! Might and wrong combined, like iron magnetized, are endowed with irresistible attraction. There would be Judge Pyncheon,—a person eminent in the public view, of high station and great wealth, a philanthropist, a member of Congress and of the church, and intimately associated with whatever else bestows good name,—so imposing, in these advantageous lights, that Hepzibah herself could hardly help shrinking from her own conclusions as to his hollow integrity. The Judge, on one side! And who, on the other? The guilty Clifford! Once a byword! Now, an indistinctly remembered ignominy!

Nevertheless, in spite of this perception that the Judge would draw all human aid to his own behalf, Hepzibah was so unaccustomed to act for herself, that the least word of counsel would have swayed her to any mode of action. Little Phoebe Pyncheon would at once have lighted up the whole scene, if not by any available suggestion, yet simply by the warm vivacity of her character. The idea of the artist occurred to Hepzibah. Young and unknown, mere vagrant adventurer as he was, she had been conscious of a force in Holgrave which might well adapt him to be the champion of a crisis. With this thought in her mind, she unbolted a door, cobwebbed and long disused, but which had served as a former medium of communication between her own part of the house and the gable where the wandering daguerreotypist had now established his temporary home. He was not there. A book, face downward, on the table, a roll of manuscript, a half-written sheet, a newspaper, some tools of his present occupation, and several rejected daguerreotypes, conveyed an impression as if he were close at hand. But, at this period of the day, as Hepzibah might have anticipated, the artist was at his public rooms. With an impulse of idle curiosity, that flickered among her heavy thoughts, she looked at one of the daguerreotypes, and beheld Judge Pyncheon frowning at her. Fate stared her in the face. She turned back from her fruitless quest, with a heartsinking sense of disappointment. In all her years of seclusion, she had never felt, as now, what it was to be alone. It seemed as if the house stood in a desert, or, by some spell, was made invisible to those who dwelt around, or passed beside it; so that any mode of misfortune, miserable accident, or crime might happen in it without the possibility of aid. In her grief and wounded pride, Hepzibah had spent her life in divesting herself of friends; she had wilfully cast off the support which God has ordained his creatures to need from one another; and it was now her punishment, that Clifford and herself would fall the easier victims to their kindred enemy.

Returning to the arched window, she lifted her eyes,—scowling, poor, dim-sighted Hepzibah, in the face of Heaven!—and strove hard to send up a prayer through the dense gray pavement of clouds. Those mists had gathered, as if to symbolize a great, brooding mass of human trouble, doubt, confusion, and chill indifference, between earth and the better regions. Her faith was too weak; the prayer too heavy to be thus uplifted. It fell back, a lump of lead, upon her heart. It smote her with the wretched conviction that Providence intermeddled not in these petty wrongs of one individual to his fellow, nor had any balm for these little agonies of a solitary soul; but shed its justice, and its mercy, in a broad, sunlike sweep, over half the universe at once. Its vastness made it nothing. But Hepzibah did not see that, just as there comes a warm sunbeam into every cottage window, so comes a lovebeam of God's care and pity for every separate need.

At last, finding no other pretext for deferring the torture that she was to inflict on Clifford,— her reluctance to which was the true cause of her loitering at the window, her search for the artist, and even her abortive prayer,—dreading, also, to hear the stern voice of Judge Pyncheon from below stairs, chiding her delay,—she crept slowly, a pale, grief-stricken figure, a dismal shape of woman, with almost torpid limbs, slowly to her brother's door, and knocked!

There was no reply.

And how should there have been? Her hand, tremulous with the shrinking purpose which directed it, had smitten so feebly against the door that the sound could hardly have gone inward. She knocked again. Still no response! Nor was it to be wondered at. She had struck with the entire force of her heart's vibration, communicating, by some subtle magnetism, her own terror to the summons. Clifford would turn his face to the pillow, and cover his head beneath the bedclothes, like a startled child at midnight. She knocked a third time, three regular strokes, gentle, but perfectly distinct, and with meaning in them; for, modulate it with what cautious art we will, the hand cannot help playing some tune of what we feel upon the senseless wood.

Clifford returned no answer.

"Clifford! Dear brother!" said Hepzibah. "Shall I come in?"

A silence.

Two or three times, and more, Hepzibah repeated his name, without result; till, thinking her brother's sleep unwontedly profound, she undid the door, and entering, found the chamber vacant. How could he have come forth, and when, without her knowledge? Was it possible that, in spite of the stormy day, and worn out with the irksomeness within doors he had betaken himself to his customary haunt in the garden, and was now shivering under the cheerless shelter of the summer-house? She hastily threw up a window, thrust forth her turbaned head and the half of her gaunt figure, and searched the whole garden through, as completely as her dim vision would allow. She could see the interior of the summer-house, and its circular seat, kept moist by the droppings of the roof. It had no occupant. Clifford was not thereabouts; unless, indeed, he had crept for concealment (as, for a moment, Hepzibah fancied might be the case) into a great, wet mass of tangled and broad-leaved shadow, where the squash-vines were clambering tumultuously upon an old wooden framework, set casually aslant against the fence. This could not be, however; he was not there; for, while Hepzibah was looking, a strange grimalkin stole forth from the very spot, and picked his way across the garden. Twice he paused to snuff the air, and then anew directed his course towards the parlor window. Whether it was only on account of the stealthy, prying manner common to the race, or that this cat seemed to have more than ordinary mischief in his thoughts, the old gentlewoman, in spite of her much perplexity, felt an impulse to drive the animal away, and accordingly flung down a window stick. The cat stared up at her, like a detected thief or murderer, and, the next instant, took to flight. No other living creature was visible in the garden. Chanticleer and his family had either not left their roost, disheartened by the interminable rain, or had done the next wisest thing, by seasonably returning to it. Hepzibah closed the window.

But where was Clifford? Could it be that, aware of the presence of his Evil Destiny, he had crept silently down the staircase, while the Judge and Hepzibah stood talking in the shop, and had softly undone the fastenings of the outer door, and made his escape into the street? With that thought, she seemed to behold his gray, wrinkled, yet childlike aspect, in the old-fashioned garments which he wore about the house; a figure such as one sometimes imagines himself to be, with the world's eye upon him, in a troubled dream. This figure of her wretched brother would go wandering through the city, attracting all eyes, and everybody's wonder and repugnance, like a ghost, the more to be shuddered at because visible at noontide. To incur the ridicule of the younger crowd, that knew him not,—the harsher scorn and indignation of a few old men, who might recall his once familiar features! To be the sport of boys, who, when old enough to run about the streets, have no more reverence for what is beautiful and holy, nor pity for what is sad,—no more sense of sacred misery, sanctifying the human shape in which it embodies itself,—than if Satan were the father of them all! Goaded by their taunts, their loud, shrill cries, and cruel laughter,—insulted by the filth of the public ways, which they would fling upon him,—or, as it might well be, distracted by the mere strangeness of his situation, though nobody should afflict him with so much as a thoughtless word,—what wonder if Clifford were to break into some wild extravagance which was certain to be interpreted as lunacy? Thus Judge Pyncheon's fiendish scheme would be ready accomplished to his hands!

Then Hepzibah reflected that the town was almost completely water-girdled. The wharves stretched out towards the centre of the harbor, and, in this inclement weather, were deserted by the ordinary throng of merchants, laborers, and sea-faring men; each wharf a solitude, with the vessels moored stem and stern, along its misty length. Should her brother's aimless footsteps stray thitherward, and he but bend, one moment, over the deep, black tide, would he not bethink himself that here was the sure refuge within his reach, and that, with a single step, or the slightest overbalance of his body, he might be forever beyond his kinsman's gripe? Oh, the temptation! To make of his ponderous sorrow a security! To sink, with its leaden weight upon him, and never rise again!

The horror of this last conception was too much for Hepzibah. Even Jaffrey Pyncheon must help her now She hastened down the staircase, shrieking as she went.

"Clifford is gone!" she cried. "I cannot find my brother. Help, Jaffrey Pyncheon! Some harm will happen to him!"

She threw open the parlor-door. But, what with the shade of branches across the windows, and the smoke-blackened ceiling, and the dark oak-panelling of the walls, there was hardly so much daylight in the room that Hepzibah's imperfect sight could accurately distinguish the Judge's figure. She was certain, however, that she saw him sitting in the ancestral arm-chair, near the centre of the floor, with his face somewhat averted, and looking towards a window. So firm and quiet is the nervous system of such men as Judge Pyncheon, that he had perhaps stirred not more than once since her departure, but, in the hard composure of his temperament, retained the position into which accident had thrown him.

"I tell you, Jaffrey," cried Hepzibah impatiently, as she turned from the parlor-door to search other rooms, "my brother is not in his chamber! You must help me seek him!"

But Judge Pyncheon was not the man to let himself be startled from an easy-chair with haste ill-befitting either the dignity of his character or his broad personal basis, by the alarm of an hysteric woman. Yet, considering his own interest in the matter, he might have bestirred himself with a little more alacrity.

"Do you hear me, Jaffrey Pyncheon?" screamed Hepzibah, as she again approached the parlor-door, after an ineffectual search elsewhere. "Clifford is gone."

At this instant, on the threshold of the parlor, emerging from within, appeared Clifford himself! His face was preternaturally pale; so deadly white, indeed, that, through all the glimmering indistinctness of the passageway, Hepzibah could discern his features, as if a light fell on them alone. Their vivid and wild expression seemed likewise sufficient to illuminate them; it was an expression of scorn and mockery, coinciding with the emotions indicated by his gesture. As Clifford stood on the threshold, partly turning back, he pointed his finger within the parlor, and shook it slowly as though he would have summoned, not Hepzibah alone, but the whole world, to gaze at some object inconceivably ridiculous. This action, so ill-timed and extravagant,—accompanied, too, with a look that showed more like joy than any other kind of excitement,—compelled Hepzibah to dread that her stern kinsman's ominous visit had driven her poor brother to absolute insanity. Nor could she otherwise account for the Judge's quiescent mood than by supposing him craftily on the watch, while Clifford developed these symptoms of a distracted mind.

"Be quiet, Clifford!" whispered his sister, raising her hand to impress caution. "Oh, for Heaven's sake, be quiet!"

"Let him be quiet! What can he do better?" answered Clifford, with a still wilder gesture, pointing into the room which he had just quitted. "As for us, Hepzibah, we can dance now!— we can sing, laugh, play, do what we will! The weight is gone, Hepzibah! It is gone off this weary old world, and we may be as light-hearted as little Phoebe herself."

And, in accordance with his words, he began to laugh, still pointing his finger at the object, invisible to Hepzibah, within the parlor. She was seized with a sudden intuition of some horrible thing. She thrust herself past Clifford, and disappeared into the room; but almost immediately returned, with a cry choking in her throat. Gazing at her brother with an affrighted glance of inquiry, she beheld him all in a tremor and a quake, from head to foot, while, amid these commoted elements of passion or alarm, still flickered his gusty mirth.

"My God! what is to become of us?" gasped Hepzibah.

"Come!" said Clifford in a tone of brief decision, most unlike what was usual with him. "We stay here too long! Let us leave the old house to our cousin Jaffrey! He will take good care of it!"

Hepzibah now noticed that Clifford had on a cloak,—a garment of long ago,—in which he had constantly muffled himself during these days of easterly storm. He beckoned with his hand, and intimated, so far as she could comprehend him, his purpose that they should go together from the house. There are chaotic, blind, or drunken moments, in the lives of persons who lack real force of character,—moments of test, in which courage would most assert itself,— but where these individuals, if left to themselves, stagger aimlessly along, or follow implicitly whatever guidance may befall them, even if it be a child's. No matter how preposterous or insane, a purpose is a Godsend to them. Hepzibah had reached this point. Unaccustomed to action or responsibility,—full of horror at what she had seen, and afraid to inquire, or almost to imagine, how it had come to pass,—affrighted at the fatality which seemed to pursue her brother,—stupefied by the dim, thick, stifling atmosphere of dread which filled the house as with a death-smell, and obliterated all definiteness of thought,—she yielded without a question, and on the instant, to the will which Clifford expressed. For herself, she was like a person in a dream, when the will always sleeps. Clifford, ordinarily so destitute of this faculty, had found it in the tension of the crisis.

"Why do you delay so?" cried he sharply. "Put on your cloak and hood, or whatever it pleases you to wear! No matter what; you cannot look beautiful nor brilliant, my poor Hepzibah! Take your purse, with money in it, and come along!"

Hepzibah obeyed these instructions, as if nothing else were to be done or thought of. She began to wonder, it is true, why she did not wake up, and at what still more intolerable pitch of dizzy trouble her spirit would struggle out of the maze, and make her conscious that nothing of all this had actually happened. Of course it was not real; no such black, easterly day as this had yet begun to be; Judge Pyncheon had not talked with, her. Clifford had not laughed, pointed, beckoned her away with him; but she had merely been afflicted—as lonely sleepers often are— with a great deal of unreasonable misery, in a morning dream!

"Now—now—I shall certainly awake!" thought Hepzibah, as she went to and fro, making her little preparations. "I can bear it no longer I must wake up now!"

But it came not, that awakening moment! It came not, even when, just before they left the house, Clifford stole to the parlor-door, and made a parting obeisance to the sole occupant of the room.

"What an absurd figure the old fellow cuts now!" whispered he to Hepzibah. "Just when he fancied he had me completely under his thumb! Come, come; make haste! or he will start up, like Giant Despair in pursuit of Christian and Hopeful, and catch us yet!"

As they passed into the street, Clifford directed Hepzibah's attention to something on one of the posts of the front door. It was merely the initials of his own name, which, with somewhat of his characteristic grace about the forms of the letters, he had cut there when a boy. The brother and sister departed, and left Judge Pyncheon sitting in the old home of his forefathers, all by himself; so heavy and lumpish that we can liken him to nothing better than a defunct nightmare, which had perished in the midst of its wickedness, and left its flabby corpse on the breast of the tormented one, to be gotten rid of as it might!

ᏚᏒ 17 ᏒᏚ

THE FLIGHT OF TWO OWLS

SUMMER AS IT WAS, the east wind set poor Hepzibah's few remaining teeth chattering in her head, as she and Clifford faced it, on their way up Pyncheon Street, and towards the centre of the town. Not merely was it the shiver which this pitiless blast brought to her frame (although her feet and hands, especially, had never seemed so death-a-cold as now), but there was a moral sensation, mingling itself with the physical chill, and causing her to shake more in spirit than in body. The world's broad, bleak atmosphere was all so comfortless! Such, indeed, is the impression which it makes on every new adventurer, even if he plunge into it while the warmest tide of life is bubbling through his veins. What, then, must it have been to Hepzibah and Clifford,—so time-stricken as they were, yet so like children in their inexperience,—as they left the doorstep, and passed from beneath the wide shelter of the Pyncheon Elm! They were wandering all abroad, on precisely such a pilgrimage as a child often meditates, to the world's end, with perhaps a sixpence and a biscuit in his pocket. In Hepzibah's mind, there was the wretched consciousness of being adrift. She had lost the faculty of self-guidance; but, in view of the difficulties around her, felt it hardly worth an effort to regain it, and was, moreover, incapable of making one.

As they proceeded on their strange expedition, she now and then cast a look sidelong at Clifford, and could not but observe that he was possessed and swayed by a powerful excitement. It was this, indeed, that gave him the control which he had at once, and so irresistibly, established over his movements. It not a little resembled the exhilaration of wine. Or, it might more fancifully be compared to a joyous piece of music, played with wild vivacity, but upon a disordered instrument. As the cracked jarring note might always be heard, and as it jarred loudest amidst the loftiest exultation of the melody, so was there a continual quake through Clifford, causing him most to quiver while he wore a triumphant smile, and seemed almost under a necessity to skip in his gait.

They met few people abroad, even on passing from the retired neighborhood of the House of the Seven Gables into what was ordinarily the more thronged and busier portion of the town. Glistening sidewalks, with little pools of rain, here and there, along their unequal surface; umbrellas displayed ostentatiously in the shop-windows, as if the life of trade had concentrated

508

itself in that one article; wet leaves of the horse-chestnut or elm-trees, torn off untimely by the blast and scattered along the public way; an unsightly, accumulation of mud in the middle of the street, which perversely grew the more unclean for its long and laborious washing,—these were the more definable points of a very sombre picture. In the way of movement and human life, there was the hasty rattle of a cab or coach, its driver protected by a waterproof cap over his head and shoulders; the forlorn figure of an old man, who seemed to have crept out of some subterranean sewer, and was stooping along the kennel, and poking the wet rubbish with a stick, in quest of rusty nails; a merchant or two, at the door of the post-office, together with an editor and a miscellaneous politician, awaiting a dilatory mail; a few visages of retired sea-captains at the window of an insurance office, looking out vacantly at the vacant street, blaspheming at the weather, and fretting at the dearth as well of public news as local gossip. What a treasure-trove to these venerable quidnuncs, could they have guessed the secret which Hepzibah and Clifford were carrying along with them! But their two figures attracted hardly so much notice as that of a young girl, who passed at the same instant, and happened to raise her skirt a trifle too high above her ankles. Had it been a sunny and cheerful day, they could hardly have gone through the streets without making themselves obnoxious to remark. Now, probably, they were felt to be in keeping with the dismal and bitter weather, and therefore did not stand out in strong relief, as if the sun were shining on them, but melted into the gray gloom and were forgotten as soon as gone.

Poor Hepzibah! Could she have understood this fact, it would have brought her some little comfort; for, to all her other troubles,—strange to say!—there was added the womanish and old-maiden-like misery arising from a sense of unseemliness in her attire. Thus, she was fain to shrink deeper into herself, as it were, as if in the hope of making people suppose that here was only a cloak and hood, threadbare and woefully faded, taking an airing in the midst of the storm, without any wearer!

As they went on, the feeling of indistinctness and unreality kept dimly hovering round about her, and so diffusing itself into her system that one of her hands was hardly palpable to the touch of the other. Any certainty would have been preferable to this. She whispered to herself, again and again, "Am I awake?—Am I awake?" and sometimes exposed her face to the chill spatter of the wind, for the sake of its rude assurance that she was. Whether it was Clifford's purpose, or only chance, had led them thither, they now found themselves passing beneath the arched entrance of a large structure of gray stone. Within, there was a spacious breadth, and an airy height from floor to roof, now partially filled with smoke and steam, which eddied voluminously upward and formed a mimic cloud-region over their heads. A train of cars was just ready for a start; the locomotive was fretting and fuming, like a steed impatient for a headlong rush; and the bell rang out its hasty peal, so well expressing the brief summons which life vouchsafes to us in its hurried career. Without question or delay,—with the irresistible decision, if not rather to be called recklessness, which had so strangely taken possession of him, and through him of Hepzibah,—Clifford impelled her towards the cars, and assisted her to enter. The signal was given; the engine puffed forth its short, quick breaths; the train began its movement; and, along with a hundred other passengers, these two unwonted travellers sped onward like the wind.

At last, therefore, and after so long estrangement from everything that the world acted or enjoyed, they had been drawn into the great current of human life, and were swept away with it, as by the suction of fate itself.

Still haunted with the idea that not one of the past incidents, inclusive of Judge Pyncheon's visit, could be real, the recluse of the Seven Gables murmured in her brother's ear,—

"Clifford! Clifford! Is not this a dream?"

"A dream, Hepzibah!" repeated he, almost laughing in her face. "On the contrary, I have never been awake before!"

Meanwhile, looking from the window, they could see the world racing past them. At one moment, they were rattling through a solitude; the next, a village had grown up around them; a few breaths more, and it had vanished, as if swallowed by an earthquake. The spires of meeting-houses seemed set adrift from their foundations; the broad-based hills glided away. Everything was unfixed from its age-long rest, and moving at whirlwind speed in a direction opposite to their own.

Within the car there was the usual interior life of the railroad, offering little to the observation of other passengers, but full of novelty for this pair of strangely enfranchised prisoners. It was novelty enough, indeed, that there were fifty human beings in close relation with them, under one long and narrow roof, and drawn onward by the same mighty influence that had taken their two selves into its grasp. It seemed marvellous how all these people could remain so quietly in their seats, while so much noisy strength was at work in their behalf. Some, with tickets in their hats (long travellers these, before whom lay a hundred miles of railroad), had plunged into the English scenery and adventures of pamphlet novels, and were keeping company with dukes and earls. Others, whose briefer span forbade their devoting themselves to studies so abstruse, beguiled the little tedium of the way with penny-papers. A party of girls, and one young man, on opposite sides of the car, found huge amusement in a game of ball. They tossed it to and fro, with peals of laughter that might be measured by mile-lengths; for, faster than the nimble ball could fly, the merry players fled unconsciously along, leaving the trail of their mirth afar behind, and ending their game under another sky than had witnessed its commencement. Boys, with apples, cakes, candy, and rolls of variously tinctured lozenges,— merchandise that reminded Hepzibah of her deserted shop,—appeared at each momentary stopping-place, doing up their business in a hurry, or breaking it short off, lest the market should ravish them away with it. New people continually entered. Old acquaintances—for such they soon grew to be, in this rapid current of affairs—continually departed. Here and there, amid the rumble and the tumult, sat one asleep. Sleep; sport; business; graver or lighter study; and the common and inevitable movement onward! It was life itself!

Clifford's naturally poignant sympathies were all aroused. He caught the color of what was passing about him, and threw it back more vividly than he received it, but mixed, nevertheless, with a lurid and portentous hue. Hepzibah, on the other hand, felt herself more apart from human kind than even in the seclusion which she had just quitted.

"You are not happy, Hepzibah!" said Clifford apart, in a tone of approach. "You are thinking of that dismal old house, and of Cousin Jaffrey"—here came the quake through him,—"and of Cousin Jaffrey sitting there, all by himself! Take my advice,—follow my example,—and let such things slip aside. Here we are, in the world, Hepzibah!—in the midst of life!—in the throng of our fellow beings! Let you and I be happy! As happy as that youth and those pretty girls, at their game of ball!"

"Happy—" thought Hepzibah, bitterly conscious, at the word, of her dull and heavy heart, with the frozen pain in it,—"happy. He is mad already; and, if I could once feel myself broad awake, I should go mad too!"

If a fixed idea be madness, she was perhaps not remote from it. Fast and far as they had rattled and clattered along the iron track, they might just as well, as regarded Hepzibah's mental images, have been passing up and down Pyncheon Street. With miles and miles of varied scenery between, there was no scene for her save the seven old gable-peaks, with their moss, and the tuft of weeds in one of the angles, and the shop-window, and a customer shaking the door, and compelling the little bell to jingle fiercely, but without disturbing Judge

Pyncheon! This one old house was everywhere! It transported its great, lumbering bulk with more than railroad speed, and set itself phlegmatically down on whatever spot she glanced at. The quality of Hepzibah's mind was too unmalleable to take new impressions so readily as Clifford's. He had a winged nature; she was rather of the vegetable kind, and could hardly be kept long alive, if drawn up by the roots. Thus it happened that the relation heretofore existing between her brother and herself was changed. At home, she was his guardian; here, Clifford had become hers, and seemed to comprehend whatever belonged to their new position with a singular rapidity of intelligence. He had been startled into manhood and intellectual vigor; or, at least, into a condition that resembled them, though it might be both diseased and transitory.

The conductor now applied for their tickets; and Clifford, who had made himself the purse-bearer, put a bank-note into his hand, as he had observed others do.

"For the lady and yourself?" asked the conductor. "And how far?"

"As far as that will carry us," said Clifford. "It is no great matter. We are riding for pleasure merely."

"You choose a strange day for it, sir!" remarked a gimlet-eyed old gentleman on the other side of the car, looking at Clifford and his companion, as if curious to make them out. "The best chance of pleasure, in an easterly rain, I take it, is in a man's own house, with a nice little fire in the chimney."

"I cannot precisely agree with you," said Clifford, courteously bowing to the old gentleman, and at once taking up the clew of conversation which the latter had proffered. "It had just occurred to me, on the contrary, that this admirable invention of the railroad—with the vast and inevitable improvements to be looked for, both as to speed and convenience—is destined to do away with those stale ideas of home and fireside, and substitute something better."

"In the name of common-sense," asked the old gentleman rather testily, "what can be better for a man than his own parlor and chimney-corner?"

"These things have not the merit which many good people attribute to them," replied Clifford. "They may be said, in few and pithy words, to have ill served a poor purpose. My impression is, that our wonderfully increased and still increasing facilities of locomotion are destined to bring us around again to the nomadic state. You are aware, my dear sir,—you must have observed it in your own experience,—that all human progress is in a circle; or, to use a more accurate and beautiful figure, in an ascending spiral curve. While we fancy ourselves going straight forward, and attaining, at every step, an entirely new position of affairs, we do actually return to something long ago tried and abandoned, but which we now find etherealized, refined, and perfected to its ideal. The past is but a coarse and sensual prophecy of the present and the future. To apply this truth to the topic now under discussion. In the early epochs of our race, men dwelt in temporary huts, of bowers of branches, as easily constructed as a bird's-nest, and which they built,—if it should be called building, when such sweet homes of a summer solstice rather grew than were made with hands,—which Nature, we will say, assisted them to rear where fruit abounded, where fish and game were plentiful, or, most especially, where the sense of beauty was to be gratified by a lovelier shade than elsewhere, and a more exquisite arrangement of lake, wood, and hill. This life possessed a charm which, ever since man quitted it, has vanished from existence. And it typified something better than itself. It had its drawbacks; such as hunger and thirst, inclement weather, hot sunshine, and weary and foot-blistering marches over barren and ugly tracts, that lay between the sites desirable for their fertility and beauty. But in our ascending spiral, we escape all this. These railroads—could but the whistle be made musical, and the rumble and the jar got rid of—are positively the greatest blessing that the ages have wrought out for us. They give us wings; they annihilate the toil and dust of pilgrimage; they spiritualize travel! Transition being so facile, what can be any man's inducement to tarry in one spot? Why, therefore, should he build a more cumbrous habitation than can readily be carried off with him? Why should he make himself a prisoner for life in brick, and stone, and old worm-eaten timber, when he may just as easily dwell, in one sense, nowhere,—in a better sense, wherever the fit and beautiful shall offer him a home?"

Clifford's countenance glowed, as he divulged this theory; a youthful character shone out from within, converting the wrinkles and pallid duskiness of age into an almost transparent mask. The merry girls let their ball drop upon the floor, and gazed at him. They said to themselves, perhaps, that, before his hair was gray and the crow's-feet tracked his temples, this now decaying man must have stamped the impress of his features on many a woman's heart. But, alas! no woman's eye had seen his face while it was beautiful.

"I should scarcely call it an improved state of things," observed Clifford's new acquaintance, "to live everywhere and nowhere!"

"Would you not?" exclaimed Clifford, with singular energy. "It is as clear to me as sunshine, —were there any in the sky,—that the greatest possible stumbling-blocks in the path of human happiness and improvement are these heaps of bricks and stones, consolidated with mortar, or hewn timber, fastened together with spike-nails, which men painfully contrive for their own torment, and call them house and home! The soul needs air; a wide sweep and frequent change of it. Morbid influences, in a thousand-fold variety, gather about hearths, and pollute the life of households. There is no such unwholesome atmosphere as that of an old home, rendered poisonous by one's defunct forefathers and relatives. I speak of what I know. There is a certain house within my familiar recollection,—one of those peaked-gable (there are seven of them), projecting-storied edifices, such as you occasionally see in our older towns,—a rusty, crazy, creaky, dry-rotted, dingy, dark, and miserable old dungeon, with an arched window over the porch, and a little shop-door on one side, and a great, melancholy elm before it! Now, sir, whenever my thoughts recur to this seven-gabled mansion (the fact is so very curious that I must needs mention it), immediately I have a vision or image of an elderly man, of remarkably stern countenance, sitting in an oaken elbow-chair, dead, stone-dead, with an ugly flow of blood upon his shirt-bosom! Dead, but with open eyes! He taints the whole house, as I remember it. I could never flourish there, nor be happy, nor do nor enjoy what God meant me to do and enjoy."

His face darkened, and seemed to contract, and shrivel itself up, and wither into age.

"Never, sir!" he repeated. "I could never draw cheerful breath there!"

"I should think not," said the old gentleman, eyeing Clifford earnestly, and rather apprehensively. "I should conceive not, sir, with that notion in your head!"

"Surely not," continued Clifford; "and it were a relief to me if that house could be torn down, or burnt up, and so the earth be rid of it, and grass be sown abundantly over its foundation. Not that I should ever visit its site again! for, sir, the farther I get away from it, the more does the joy, the lightsome freshness, the heart-leap, the intellectual dance, the youth, in short,—yes, my youth, my youth!—the more does it come back to me. No longer ago than this morning, I was old. I remember looking in the glass, and wondering at my own gray hair, and the wrinkles, many and deep, right across my brow, and the furrows down my cheeks, and the prodigious trampling of crow's-feet about my temples! It was too soon! I could not bear it! Age had no right to come! I had not lived! But now do I look old? If so, my aspect belies me strangely; for—a great weight being off my mind—I feel in the very heyday of my youth, with the world and my best days before me!"

"I trust you may find it so," said the old gentleman, who seemed rather embarrassed, and desirous of avoiding the observation which Clifford's wild talk drew on them both. "You have my best wishes for it."

"For Heaven's sake, dear Clifford, be quiet!" whispered his sister. "They think you mad."

"Be quiet yourself, Hepzibah!" returned her brother. "No matter what they think! I am not mad. For the first time in thirty years my thoughts gush up and find words ready for them. I must talk, and I will!"

He turned again towards the old gentleman, and renewed the conversation.

"Yes, my dear sir," said he, "it is my firm belief and hope that these terms of roof and hearth-stone, which have so long been held to embody something sacred, are soon to pass out of men's daily use, and be forgotten. Just imagine, for a moment, how much of human evil will crumble away, with this one change! What we call real estate—the solid ground to build a house on—is the broad foundation on which nearly all the guilt of this world rests. A man will commit almost any wrong,—he will heap up an immense pile of wickedness, as hard as granite, and which will weigh as heavily upon his soul, to eternal ages,—only to build a great, gloomy, dark-chambered mansion, for himself to die in, and for his posterity to be miserable in. He lays his own dead corpse beneath the underpinning, as one may say, and hangs his frowning picture on the wall, and, after thus converting himself into an evil destiny, expects his remotest great-grandchildren to be happy there. I do not speak wildly. I have just such a house in my mind's eye!"

"Then, sir," said the old gentleman, getting anxious to drop the subject, "you are not to blame for leaving it."

"Within the lifetime of the child already born," Clifford went on, "all this will be done away. The world is growing too ethereal and spiritual to bear these enormities a great while longer. To me, though, for a considerable period of time, I have lived chiefly in retirement, and know less of such things than most men,—even to me, the harbingers of a better era are unmistakable. Mesmerism, now! Will that effect nothing, think you, towards purging away the grossness out of human life?"

"All a humbug!" growled the old gentleman.

"These rapping spirits, that little Phoebe told us of, the other day," said Clifford,—"what are these but the messengers of the spiritual world, knocking at the door of substance? And it shall be flung wide open!"

"A humbug, again!" cried the old gentleman, growing more and more testy at these glimpses of Clifford's metaphysics. "I should like to rap with a good stick on the empty pates of the dolts who circulate such nonsense!"

"Then there is electricity,—the demon, the angel, the mighty physical power, the all-pervading intelligence!" exclaimed Clifford. "Is that a humbug, too? Is it a fact—or have I dreamt it—that, by means of electricity, the world of matter has become a great nerve, vibrating thousands of miles in a breathless point of time? Rather, the round globe is a vast head, a brain, instinct with intelligence! Or, shall we say, it is itself a thought, nothing but thought, and no longer the substance which we deemed it!"

"If you mean the telegraph," said the old gentleman, glancing his eye toward its wire, alongside the rail-track, "it is an excellent thing,—that is, of course, if the speculators in cotton and politics don't get possession of it. A great thing, indeed, sir, particularly as regards the detection of bank-robbers and murderers."

"I don't quite like it, in that point of view," replied Clifford. "A bank-robber, and what you call a murderer, likewise, has his rights, which men of enlightened humanity and conscience should regard in so much the more liberal spirit, because the bulk of society is prone to controvert their existence. An almost spiritual medium, like the electric telegraph, should be consecrated to high, deep, joyful, and holy missions. Lovers, day by day—hour by hour, if so often moved to do it,—might send their heart-throbs from Maine to Florida, with some such words as these 'I love you forever!'—'My heart runs over with love!'—'I love you more than I can!' and, again, at the next message 'I have lived an hour longer, and love you twice as much!' Or, when a good man has departed, his distant friend should be conscious of an electric thrill, as from the world of happy spirits, telling him 'Your dear friend is in bliss!' Or, to an absent husband, should come tidings thus 'An immortal being, of whom you are the father, has this moment come from God!' and immediately its little voice would seem to have reached so far, and to be echoing in his heart. But for these poor rogues, the bank-robbers,—who, after all, are about as honest as nine people in ten, except that they disregard certain formalities, and prefer to transact business at midnight rather than 'Change-hours,—and for these murderers, as you phrase it, who are often excusable in the motives of their deed, and deserve to be ranked among public benefactors, if we consider only its result,—for unfortunate individuals like these, I really cannot applaud the enlistment of an immaterial and miraculous power in the universal world-hunt at their heels!"

"You can't, hey?" cried the old gentleman, with a hard look.

"Positively, no!" answered Clifford. "It puts them too miserably at disadvantage. For example, sir, in a dark, low, cross-beamed, panelled room of an old house, let us suppose a dead man, sitting in an arm-chair, with a blood-stain on his shirt-bosom,—and let us add to our hypothesis another man, issuing from the house, which he feels to be over-filled with the dead man's presence,—and let us lastly imagine him fleeing, Heaven knows whither, at the speed of a hurricane, by railroad! Now, sir, if the fugitive alight in some distant town, and find all the people babbling about that self-same dead man, whom he has fled so far to avoid the sight and thought of, will you not allow that his natural rights have been infringed? He has been deprived of his city of refuge, and, in my humble opinion, has suffered infinite wrong!"

"You are a strange man; Sir!" said the old gentleman, bringing his gimlet-eye to a point on Clifford, as if determined to bore right into him. "I can't see through you!"

"No, I'll be bound you can't!" cried Clifford, laughing. "And yet, my dear sir, I am as transparent as the water of Maule's well! But come, Hepzibah! We have flown far enough for once. Let us alight, as the birds do, and perch ourselves on the nearest twig, and consult wither we shall fly next!"

Just then, as it happened, the train reached a solitary way-station. Taking advantage of the brief pause, Clifford left the car, and drew Hepzibah along with him. A moment afterwards, the train—with all the life of its interior, amid which Clifford had made himself so conspicuous an object—was gliding away in the distance, and rapidly lessening to a point which, in another moment, vanished. The world had fled away from these two wanderers. They gazed drearily about them. At a little distance stood a wooden church, black with age, and in a dismal state of ruin and decay, with broken windows, a great rift through the main body of the edifice, and a rafter dangling from the top of the square tower. Farther off was a farm-house, in the old style, as venerably black as the church, with a roof sloping downward from the three-story peak, to within a man's height of the ground. It seemed uninhabited. There were the relics of a wood-pile, indeed, near the door, but with grass sprouting up among the chips and scattered logs. The small rain-drops came down aslant; the wind was not turbulent, but sullen, and full of chilly moisture.

Clifford shivered from head to foot. The wild effervescence of his mood—which had so readily supplied thoughts, fantasies, and a strange aptitude of words, and impelled him to talk from the mere necessity of giving vent to this bubbling-up gush of ideas had entirely subsided. A powerful excitement had given him energy and vivacity. Its operation over, he forthwith began to sink.

"You must take the lead now, Hepzibah!" murmured he, with a torpid and reluctant utterance. "Do with me as you will!" She knelt down upon the platform where they were standing and lifted her clasped hands to the sky. The dull, gray weight of clouds made it invisible; but it was no hour for disbelief,—no juncture this to question that there was a sky above, and an Almighty Father looking from it!

"O God!"—ejaculated poor, gaunt Hepzibah,—then paused a moment, to consider what her prayer should be,—"O God,—our Father,—are we not thy children? Have mercy on us!"

❧ 18 ❧

GOVERNOR PYNCHEON

JUDGE PYNCHEON, while his two relatives have fled away with such ill-considered haste, still sits in the old parlor, keeping house, as the familiar phrase is, in the absence of its ordinary occupants. To him, and to the venerable House of the Seven Gables, does our story now betake itself, like an owl, bewildered in the daylight, and hastening back to his hollow tree.

The Judge has not shifted his position for a long while now. He has not stirred hand or foot, nor withdrawn his eyes so much as a hair's-breadth from their fixed gaze towards the corner of the room, since the footsteps of Hepzibah and Clifford creaked along the passage, and the outer door was closed cautiously behind their exit. He holds his watch in his left hand, but clutched in such a manner that you cannot see the dial-plate. How profound a fit of meditation! Or, supposing him asleep, how infantile a quietude of conscience, and what wholesome order in the gastric region, are betokened by slumber so entirely undisturbed with starts, cramp, twitches, muttered dreamtalk, trumpet-blasts through the nasal organ, or any slightest irregularity of breath! You must hold your own breath, to satisfy yourself whether he breathes at all. It is quite inaudible. You hear the ticking of his watch; his breath you do not hear. A most refreshing slumber, doubtless! And yet, the Judge cannot be asleep. His eyes are open! A veteran politician, such as he, would never fall asleep with wide-open eyes, lest some enemy or mischief-maker, taking him thus at unawares, should peep through these windows into his consciousness, and make strange discoveries among the reminiscences, projects, hopes, apprehensions, weaknesses, and strong points, which he has heretofore shared with nobody. A cautious man is proverbially said to sleep with one eye open. That may be wisdom. But not with both; for this were heedlessness! No, no! Judge Pyncheon cannot be asleep.

It is odd, however, that a gentleman so burdened with engagements,—and noted, too, for punctuality,—should linger thus in an old lonely mansion, which he has never seemed very fond of visiting. The oaken chair, to be sure, may tempt him with its roominess. It is, indeed, a spacious, and, allowing for the rude age that fashioned it, a moderately easy seat, with capacity enough, at all events, and offering no restraint to the Judge's breadth of beam. A bigger man might find ample accommodation in it. His ancestor, now pictured upon the wall, with all his English beef about him, used hardly to present a front extending from elbow to elbow of this chair, or a base that would cover its whole cushion. But there are better chairs than this,—mahogany, black walnut, rosewood, spring-seated and damask-cushioned, with varied slopes, and innumerable artifices to make them easy, and obviate the irksomeness of too tame an ease,—a score of such might be at Judge Pyncheon's service. Yes! in a score of drawing-rooms he would be more than welcome. Mamma would advance to meet him, with outstretched hand; the virgin daughter, elderly as he has now got to be,—an old widower, as he smilingly describes himself,—would shake up the cushion for the Judge, and do her pretty utmost to make him comfortable. For the Judge is a prosperous man. He cherishes his schemes, moreover, like other people, and reasonably brighter than most others; or did so, at least, as he lay abed this morning, in an agreeable half-drowse, planning the business of the day, and speculating on the probabilities of the next fifteen years. With his firm health, and the little inroad that age has made upon him, fifteen years or twenty—yes, or perhaps five-and-twenty!—are no more than he may fairly call his own. Five-and-twenty years for the enjoyment of his real estate in town and country, his railroad, bank, and insurance shares, his United States stock,—his wealth, in short, however invested, now in possession, or soon to be acquired; together with the public honors that have fallen upon him, and the weightier ones that are yet to fall! It is good! It is excellent! It is enough!

Still lingering in the old chair! If the Judge has a little time to throw away, why does not he visit the insurance office, as is his frequent custom, and sit awhile in one of their leathern-cushioned arm-chairs, listening to the gossip of the day, and dropping some deeply designed chance-word, which will be certain to become the gossip of to-morrow. And have not the bank directors a meeting at which it was the Judge's purpose to be present, and his office to preside? Indeed they have; and the hour is noted on a card, which is, or ought to be, in Judge Pyncheon's right vest-pocket. Let him go thither, and loll at ease upon his moneybags! He has lounged long enough in the old chair!

This was to have been such a busy day. In the first place, the interview with Clifford. Half an hour, by the Judge's reckoning, was to suffice for that; it would probably be less, but—taking into consideration that Hepzibah was first to be dealt with, and that these women are apt to make many words where a few would do much better—it might be safest to allow half an hour. Half an hour? Why, Judge, it is already two hours, by your own undeviatingly accurate chronometer. Glance your eye down at it and see! Ah; he will not give himself the trouble either to bend his head, or elevate his hand, so as to bring the faithful time-keeper within his range of vision! Time, all at once, appears to have become a matter of no moment with the Judge!

And has he forgotten all the other items of his memoranda? Clifford's affair arranged, he was to meet a State Street broker, who has undertaken to procure a heavy percentage, and the best of paper, for a few loose thousands which the Judge happens to have by him, uninvested. The wrinkled note-shaver will have taken his railroad trip in vain. Half an hour later, in the street next to this, there was to be an auction of real estate, including a portion of the old Pyncheon property, originally belonging to Maule's garden ground. It has been alienated from the Pyncheons these four-score years; but the Judge had kept it in his eye, and had set his heart on reannexing it to the small demesne still left around the Seven Gables; and now, during this odd fit of oblivion, the fatal hammer must have fallen, and transferred our ancient patrimony to some alien possessor. Possibly, indeed, the sale may have been postponed till fairer weather. If so, will the Judge make it convenient to be present, and favor the auctioneer with his bid, On the proximate occasion?

The next affair was to buy a horse for his own driving. The one heretofore his favorite stumbled, this very morning, on the road to town, and must be at once discarded. Judge Pyncheon's neck is too precious to be risked on such a contingency as a stumbling steed.

Should all the above business be seasonably got through with, he might attend the meeting of a charitable society; the very name of which, however, in the multiplicity of his benevolence, is quite forgotten; so that this engagement may pass unfulfilled, and no great harm done. And if he have time, amid the press of more urgent matters, he must take measures for the renewal of Mrs. Pyncheon's tombstone, which, the sexton tells him, has fallen on its marble face, and is cracked quite in twain. She was a praiseworthy woman enough, thinks the Judge, in spite of her nervousness, and the tears that she was so oozy with, and her foolish behavior about the coffee; and as she took her departure so seasonably, he will not grudge the second tombstone. It is better, at least, than if she had never needed any! The next item on his list was to give orders for some fruit-trees, of a rare variety, to be deliverable at his country-seat in the ensuing autumn. Yes, buy them, by all means; and may the peaches be luscious in your mouth, Judge Pyncheon! After this comes something more important. A committee of his political party has besought him for a hundred or two of dollars, in addition to his previous disbursements, towards carrying on the fall campaign. The Judge is a patriot; the fate of the country is staked on the November election; and besides, as will be shadowed forth in another paragraph, he has no trifling stake of his own in the same great game. He will do what the committee asks; nay, he will be liberal beyond their expectations; they shall have a check for five hundred dollars, and more anon, if it be needed. What next? A decayed widow, whose husband was Judge Pyncheon's early friend, has laid her case of destitution before him, in a very moving letter. She and her fair daughter have scarcely bread to eat. He partly intends to call on her to-day,—perhaps so—perhaps not,—accordingly as he may happen to have leisure, and a small bank-note.

Another business, which, however, he puts no great weight on (it is well, you know, to be heedful, but not over-anxious, as respects one's personal health),—another business, then, was to consult his family physician. About what, for Heaven's sake? Why, it is rather difficult to describe the symptoms. A mere dimness of sight and dizziness of brain, was it?—or disagreeable choking, or stifling, or gurgling, or bubbling, in the region of the thorax, as the anatomists say?—or was it a pretty severe throbbing and kicking of the heart, rather creditable to him than otherwise, as showing that the organ had not been left out of the Judge's physical contrivance? No matter what it was. The doctor probably would smile at the statement of such trifles to his professional ear; the Judge would smile in his turn; and meeting one another's eyes, they would enjoy a hearty laugh together! But a fig for medical advice. The Judge will never need it.

Pray, pray, Judge Pyncheon, look at your watch, Now! What—not a glance! It is within ten minutes of the dinner hour! It surely cannot have slipped your memory that the dinner of to-day is to be the most important, in its consequences, of all the dinners you ever ate. Yes, precisely the most important; although, in the course of your somewhat eminent career, you have been placed high towards the head of the table, at splendid banquets, and have poured out your festive eloquence to ears yet echoing with Webster's mighty organ-tones. No public dinner this, however. It is merely a gathering of some dozen or so of friends from several districts of the State; men of distinguished character and influence, assembling, almost casually, at the house of a common friend, likewise distinguished, who will make them welcome to a little better than his ordinary fare. Nothing in the way of French cookery, but an excellent dinner, nevertheless. Real turtle, we understand, and salmon, tautog, canvas-backs, pig, English mutton, good roast beef, or dainties of that serious kind, fit for substantial country gentlemen, as these honorable persons mostly are. The delicacies of the season, in short, and flavored by a brand of old Madeira which has been the pride of many seasons. It is the Juno brand; a glorious wine, fragrant, and full of gentle might; a bottled-up happiness, put by for use; a golden liquid, worth more than liquid gold; so rare and admirable, that veteran wine-bibbers count it among their epochs to have tasted it! It drives away the heart-ache, and substitutes no head-ache! Could the Judge but quaff a glass, it might enable him to shake off the unaccountable lethargy which (for the ten intervening minutes, and five to boot, are already past) has made him such a laggard at this momentous dinner. It would all but revive a dead man! Would you like to sip it now, Judge Pyncheon?

Alas, this dinner. Have you really forgotten its true object? Then let us whisper it, that you may start at once out of the oaken chair, which really seems to be enchanted, like the one in Comus, or that in which Moll Pitcher imprisoned your own grandfather. But ambition is a talisman more powerful than witchcraft. Start up, then, and, hurrying through the streets, burst in upon the company, that they may begin before the fish is spoiled! They wait for you; and it is little for your interest that they should wait. These gentlemen—need you be told it?—have assembled, not without purpose, from every quarter of the State. They are practised politicians, every man of them, and skilled to adjust those preliminary measures which steal from the people, without its knowledge, the power of choosing its own rulers. The popular voice, at the next gubernatorial election, though loud as thunder, will be really but an echo of what these gentlemen shall speak, under their breath, at your friend's festive board. They meet to decide upon their candidate. This little knot of subtle schemers will control the convention, and, through it, dictate to the party. And what worthier candidate,—more wise and learned, more noted for philanthropic liberality, truer to safe principles, tried oftener by public trusts, more spotless in private character, with a larger stake in the common welfare, and deeper grounded, by hereditary descent, in the faith and practice of the Puritans,—what man can be presented for the suffrage of the people, so eminently combining all these claims to the chief-rulership as Judge Pyncheon here before us?

Make haste, then! Do your part! The meed for which you have toiled, and fought, and climbed, and crept, is ready for your grasp! Be present at this dinner!—drink a glass or two of that noble wine!—make your pledges in as low a whisper as you will!—and you rise up from table virtually governor of the glorious old State! Governor Pyncheon of Massachusetts!

And is there no potent and exhilarating cordial in a certainty like this? It has been the grand purpose of half your lifetime to obtain it. Now, when there needs little more than to signify your acceptance, why do you sit so lumpishly in your great-great-grandfather's oaken chair, as if preferring it to the gubernatorial one? We have all heard of King Log; but, in these jostling times, one of that royal kindred will hardly win the race for an elective chief-magistracy.

Well; it is absolutely too late for dinner! Turtle, salmon, tautog, woodcock, boiled turkey, South-Down mutton, pig, roast-beef, have vanished, or exist only in fragments, with lukewarm potatoes, and gravies crusted over with cold fat. The Judge, had he done nothing else, would have achieved wonders with his knife and fork. It was he, you know, of whom it used to be said, in reference to his ogre-like appetite, that his Creator made him a great animal, but that the dinner-hour made him a great beast. Persons of his large sensual endowments must claim indulgence, at their feeding-time. But, for once, the Judge is entirely too late for dinner! Too late, we fear, even to join the party at their wine! The guests are warm and merry; they have given up the Judge; and, concluding that the Free-Soilers have him, they will fix upon another candidate. Were our friend now to stalk in among them, with that wide-open stare, at once wild and stolid, his ungenial presence would be apt to change their cheer. Neither would it be seemly in Judge Pyncheon, generally so scrupulous in his attire, to show himself at a dinner-table with that crimson stain upon his shirt-bosom. By the bye, how came it there? It is an ugly sight, at any rate; and the wisest way for the Judge is to button his coat closely over his breast, and, taking his horse and chaise from the livery stable, to make all speed to his own house.

There, after a glass of brandy and water, and a mutton-chop, a beefsteak, a broiled fowl, or some such hasty little dinner and supper all in one, he had better spend the evening by the fireside. He must toast his slippers a long while, in order to get rid of the chilliness which the air of this vile old house has sent curdling through his veins.

Up, therefore, Judge Pyncheon, up! You have lost a day. But to-morrow will be here anon. Will you rise, betimes, and make the most of it? To-morrow. To-morrow! To-morrow. We, that are alive, may rise betimes to-morrow. As for him that has died to-day, his morrow will be the resurrection morn.

Meanwhile the twilight is glooming upward out of the corners of the room. The shadows of the tall furniture grow deeper, and at first become more definite; then, spreading wider, they lose their distinctness of outline in the dark gray tide of oblivion, as it were, that creeps slowly over the various objects, and the one human figure sitting in the midst of them. The gloom has not entered from without; it has brooded here all day, and now, taking its own inevitable time, will possess itself of everything. The Judge's face, indeed, rigid and singularly white, refuses to melt into this universal solvent. Fainter and fainter grows the light. It is as if another double-handful of darkness had been scattered through the air. Now it is no longer gray, but sable. There is still a faint appearance at the window; neither a glow, nor a gleam, nor a glimmer,—any phrase of light would express something far brighter than this doubtful perception, or sense, rather, that there is a window there. Has it yet vanished? No!—yes!—not quite! And there is still the swarthy whiteness,—we shall venture to marry these ill-agreeing words,—the swarthy whiteness of Judge Pyncheon's face. The features are all gone: there is only the paleness of them left. And how looks it now? There is no window! There is no face! An infinite, inscrutable blackness has annihilated sight! Where is our universe? All crumbled away from us; and we, adrift in chaos, may hearken to the gusts of homeless wind, that go sighing and murmuring about in quest of what was once a world!

Is there no other sound? One other, and a fearful one. It is the ticking of the Judge's watch, which, ever since Hepzibah left the room in search of Clifford, he has been holding in his hand. Be the cause what it may, this little, quiet, never-ceasing throb of Time's pulse, repeating its small strokes with such busy regularity, in Judge Pyncheon's motionless hand, has an effect of terror, which we do not find in any other accompaniment of the scene.

But, listen! That puff of the breeze was louder. It had a tone unlike the dreary and sullen one which has bemoaned itself, and afflicted all mankind with miserable sympathy, for five days past. The wind has veered about! It now comes boisterously from the northwest, and, taking hold of the aged framework of the Seven Gables, gives it a shake, like a wrestler that would try strength with his antagonist. Another and another sturdy tussle with the blast! The old house creaks again, and makes a vociferous but somewhat unintelligible bellowing in its sooty throat (the big flue, we mean, of its wide chimney), partly in complaint at the rude wind, but rather, as befits their century and a half of hostile intimacy, in tough defiance. A rumbling kind of a bluster roars behind the fire-board. A door has slammed above stairs. A window, perhaps, has been left open, or else is driven in by an unruly gust. It is not to be conceived, before-hand, what wonderful wind-instruments are these old timber mansions, and how haunted with the strangest noises, which immediately begin to sing, and sigh, and sob, and shriek,—and to smite with sledge-hammers, airy but ponderous, in some distant chamber,—and to tread along the entries as with stately footsteps, and rustle up and down the staircase, as with silks miraculously stiff,—whenever the gale catches the house with a window open, and gets fairly into it. Would that we were not an attendant spirit here! It is too awful! This clamor of the wind through the lonely house; the Judge's quietude, as he sits invisible; and that pertinacious ticking of his watch!

As regards Judge Pyncheon's invisibility, however, that matter will soon be remedied. The northwest wind has swept the sky clear. The window is distinctly seen. Through its panes, moreover, we dimly catch the sweep of the dark, clustering foliage outside, fluttering with a constant irregularity of movement, and letting in a peep of starlight, now here, now there. Oftener than any other object, these glimpses illuminate the Judge's face. But here comes more effectual light. Observe that silvery dance upon the upper branches of the pear-tree, and now a little lower, and now on the whole mass of boughs, while, through their shifting intricacies, the moonbeams fall aslant into the room. They play over the Judge's figure and show that he has not stirred throughout the hours of darkness. They follow the shadows, in changeful sport, across his unchanging features. They gleam upon his watch. His grasp conceals the dial-plate, —but we know that the faithful hands have met; for one of the city clocks tells midnight.

A man of sturdy understanding, like Judge Pyncheon, cares no more for twelve o'clock at night than for the corresponding hour of noon. However just the parallel drawn, in some of the preceding pages, between his Puritan ancestor and himself, it fails in this point. The Pyncheon of two centuries ago, in common with most of his contemporaries, professed his full belief in spiritual ministrations, although reckoning them chiefly of a malignant character. The Pyncheon of to-night, who sits in yonder arm-chair, believes in no such nonsense. Such, at least, was his creed, some few hours since. His hair will not bristle, therefore, at the stories which—in times when chimney-corners had benches in them, where old people sat poking into the ashes of the past, and raking out traditions like live coals—used to be told about this very room of his ancestral house. In fact, these tales are too absurd to bristle even childhood's hair. What sense, meaning, or moral, for example, such as even ghost-stories should be susceptible of, can be traced in the ridiculous legend, that, at midnight, all the dead Pyncheons are bound to assemble in this parlor? And, pray, for what? Why, to see whether the portrait of their ancestor still keeps its place upon the wall, in compliance with his testamentary directions! Is it worth while to come out of their graves for that?

We are tempted to make a little sport with the idea. Ghost-stories are hardly to be treated seriously any longer. The family-party of the defunct Pyncheons, we presume, goes off in this wise.

First comes the ancestor himself, in his black cloak, steeple-hat, and trunk-breeches, girt about the waist with a leathern belt, in which hangs his steel-hilted sword; he has a long staff in his hand, such as gentlemen in advanced life used to carry, as much for the dignity of the thing as for the support to be derived from it. He looks up at the portrait; a thing of no substance, gazing at its own painted image! All is safe. The picture is still there. The purpose of his brain has been kept sacred thus long after the man himself has sprouted up in graveyard grass. See! he lifts his ineffectual hand, and tries the frame. All safe! But is that a smile?—is it not, rather a frown of deadly import, that darkens over the shadow of his features? The stout Colonel is dissatisfied! So decided is his look of discontent as to impart additional distinctness to his features; through which, nevertheless, the moonlight passes, and flickers on the wall beyond. Something has strangely vexed the ancestor! With a grim shake of the head, he turns away. Here come other Pyncheons, the whole tribe, in their half a dozen generations, jostling and elbowing one another, to reach the picture. We behold aged men and grandames, a clergyman with the Puritanic stiffness still in his garb and mien, and a red-coated officer of the old French war; and there comes the shop-keeping Pyncheon of a century ago, with the ruffles turned back from his wrists; and there the periwigged and brocaded gentleman of the artist's legend, with the beautiful and pensive Alice, who brings no pride out of her virgin grave. All try the picture-frame. What do these ghostly people seek? A mother lifts her child, that his little hands may touch it! There is evidently a mystery about the picture, that perplexes these poor Pyncheons when they ought to be at rest. In a corner, meanwhile, stands the figure of an elderly man, in a leathern jerkin and breeches, with a carpenter's rule sticking out of his side pocket; he points his finger at the bearded Colonel and his descendants, nodding, jeering, mocking, and finally bursting into obstreperous, though inaudible laughter.

Indulging our fancy in this freak, we have partly lost the power of restraint and guidance. We distinguish an unlooked-for figure in our visionary scene. Among those ancestral people there is a young man, dressed in the very fashion of to-day: he wears a dark frock-coat, almost destitute of skirts, gray pantaloons, gaiter boots of patent leather, and has a finely wrought gold chain across his breast, and a little silver-headed whalebone stick in his hand. Were we to meet this figure at noonday, we should greet him as young Jaffrey Pyncheon, the Judge's only surviving child, who has been spending the last two years in foreign travel. If still in life, how comes his shadow hither? If dead, what a misfortune! The old Pyncheon property, together with the great estate acquired by the young man's father, would devolve on whom? On poor, foolish Clifford, gaunt Hepzibah, and rustic little Phoebe! But another and a greater marvel greets us! Can we believe our eyes? A stout, elderly gentleman has made his appearance; he has an aspect of eminent respectability, wears a black coat and pantaloons, of roomy width, and might be pronounced scrupulously neat in his attire, but for a broad crimson stain across his snowy neckcloth and down his shirt-bosom. Is it the Judge, or no? How can it be Judge Pyncheon? We discern his figure, as plainly as the flickering moonbeams can show us anything, still seated in the oaken chair! Be the apparition whose it may, it advances to the picture, seems to seize the frame, tries to peep behind it, and turns away, with a frown as black as the ancestral one.

The fantastic scene just hinted at must by no means be considered as forming an actual portion of our story. We were betrayed into this brief extravagance by the quiver of the moonbeams; they dance hand-in-hand with shadows, and are reflected in the looking-glass, which, you are aware, is always a kind of window or doorway into the spiritual world. We needed relief, moreover, from our too long and exclusive contemplation of that figure in the chair. This wild wind, too, has tossed our thoughts into strange confusion, but without tearing them away from their one determined centre. Yonder leaden Judge sits immovably upon our soul. Will he never stir again? We shall go mad unless he stirs! You may the better estimate his quietude by the fearlessness of a little mouse, which sits on its hind legs, in a streak of moonlight, close by Judge Pyncheon's foot, and seems to meditate a journey of exploration over this great black bulk. Ha! what has startled the nimble little mouse? It is the visage of grimalkin, outside of the window, where he appears to have posted himself for a deliberate watch. This grimalkin has a very ugly look. Is it a cat watching for a mouse, or the devil for a human soul? Would we could scare him from the window!

Thank Heaven, the night is well-nigh past! The moonbeams have no longer so silvery a gleam, nor contrast so strongly with the blackness of the shadows among which they fall. They are paler now; the shadows look gray, not black. The boisterous wind is hushed. What is the hour? Ah! the watch has at last ceased to tick; for the Judge's forgetful fingers neglected to wind it up, as usual, at ten o'clock, being half an hour or so before his ordinary bedtime,—and it has run down, for the first time in five years. But the great world-clock of Time still keeps its beat. The dreary night—for, oh, how dreary seems its haunted waste, behind us!—gives place to a fresh, transparent, cloudless morn. Blessed, blessed radiance! The daybeam—even what little of it finds its way into this always dusky parlor—seems part of the universal benediction, annulling evil, and rendering all goodness possible, and happiness attainable. Will Judge Pyncheon now rise up from his chair? Will he go forth, and receive the early sunbeams on his brow? Will he begin this new day,—which God has smiled upon, and blessed, and given to mankind,—will he begin it with better purposes than the many that have been spent amiss? Or are all the deep-laid schemes of yesterday as stubborn in his heart, and as busy in his brain, as ever?

In this latter case, there is much to do. Will the Judge still insist with Hepzibah on the interview with Clifford? Will he buy a safe, elderly gentleman's horse? Will he persuade the purchaser of the old Pyncheon property to relinquish the bargain in his favor? Will he see his family physician, and obtain a medicine that shall preserve him, to be an honor and blessing to his race, until the utmost term of patriarchal longevity? Will Judge Pyncheon, above all, make due apologies to that company of honorable friends, and satisfy them that his absence from the festive board was unavoidable, and so fully retrieve himself in their good opinion that he shall yet be Governor of Massachusetts? And all these great purposes accomplished, will he walk the streets again, with that dog-day smile of elaborate benevolence, sultry enough to tempt flies to come and buzz in it? Or will he, after the tomb-like seclusion of the past day and night, go forth a humbled and repentant man, sorrowful, gentle, seeking no profit, shrinking from worldly honor, hardly daring to love God, but bold to love his fellow man, and to do him what good he may? Will he bear about with him,—no odious grin of feigned benignity, insolent in its pretence, and loathsome in its falsehood,—but the tender sadness of a contrite heart, broken, at last, beneath its own weight of sin? For it is our belief, whatever show of honor he may have piled upon it, that there was heavy sin at the base of this man's being.

Rise up, Judge Pyncheon! The morning sunshine glimmers through the foliage, and, beautiful and holy as it is, shuns not to kindle up your face. Rise up, thou subtle, worldly, selfish, iron-hearted hypocrite, and make thy choice whether still to be subtle, worldly, selfish, iron-hearted, and hypocritical, or to tear these sins out of thy nature, though they bring the lifeblood with them! The Avenger is upon thee! Rise up, before it be too late!

What! Thou art not stirred by this last appeal? No, not a jot! And there we see a fly,—one of your common house-flies, such as are always buzzing on the window-pane,—which has smelt out Governor Pyncheon, and alights, now on his forehead, now on his chin, and now, Heaven help us! is creeping over the bridge of his nose, towards the would-be chief-magistrate's wide-open eyes! Canst thou not brush the fly away? Art thou too sluggish? Thou man, that hadst so many busy projects yesterday! Art thou too weak, that wast so powerful? Not brush away a fly? Nay, then, we give thee up!

And hark! the shop-bell rings. After hours like these latter ones, through which we have borne our heavy tale, it is good to be made sensible that there is a living world, and that even this old, lonely mansion retains some manner of connection with it. We breathe more freely, emerging from Judge Pyncheon's presence into the street before the Seven Gables.

✣ 19 ✣

ALICE'S POSIES

UNCLE VENNER, trundling a wheelbarrow, was the earliest person stirring in the neighborhood the day after the storm.

Pyncheon Street, in front of the House of the Seven Gables, was a far pleasanter scene than a by-lane, confined by shabby fences, and bordered with wooden dwellings of the meaner class, could reasonably be expected to present. Nature made sweet amends, that morning, for the five unkindly days which had preceded it. It would have been enough to live for, merely to look up at the wide benediction of the sky, or as much of it as was visible between the houses, genial once more with sunshine. Every object was agreeable, whether to be gazed at in the breadth, or examined more minutely. Such, for example, were the well-washed pebbles and gravel of the sidewalk; even the sky-reflecting pools in the centre of the street; and the grass, now freshly verdant, that crept along the base of the fences, on the other side of which, if one peeped over, was seen the multifarious growth of gardens. Vegetable productions, of whatever kind, seemed more than negatively happy, in the juicy warmth and abundance of their life. The Pyncheon Elm, throughout its great circumference, was all alive, and full of the morning sun and a sweet-tempered little breeze, which lingered within this verdant sphere, and set a thousand leafy tongues a-whispering all at once. This aged tree appeared to have suffered nothing from the gale. It had kept its boughs unshattered, and its full complement of leaves; and the whole in perfect verdure, except a single branch, that, by the earlier change with which the elm-tree sometimes prophesies the autumn, had been transmuted to bright gold. It was like the golden branch that gained Aeneas and the Sibyl admittance into Hades.

This one mystic branch hung down before the main entrance of the Seven Gables, so nigh the ground that any passer-by might have stood on tiptoe and plucked it off. Presented at the door, it would have been a symbol of his right to enter, and be made acquainted with all the secrets of the house. So little faith is due to external appearance, that there was really an inviting aspect over the venerable edifice, conveying an idea that its history must be a decorous and happy one, and such as would be delightful for a fireside tale. Its windows gleamed cheerfully in the slanting sunlight. The lines and tufts of green moss, here and there, seemed pledges of familiarity and sisterhood with Nature; as if this human dwelling-place, being of such old date, had established its prescriptive title among primeval oaks and whatever other objects, by virtue of their long continuance, have acquired a gracious right to be. A person of imaginative temperament, while passing by the house, would turn, once and again, and peruse it well: its many peaks, consenting together in the clustered chimney; the deep projection over its basement-story; the arched window, imparting a look, if not of grandeur, yet of antique gentility, to the broken portal over which it opened; the luxuriance of gigantic burdocks, near the threshold; he would note all these characteristics, and be conscious of something deeper than he saw. He would conceive the mansion to have been the residence of the stubborn old Puritan, Integrity, who, dying in some forgotten generation, had left a blessing in all its rooms and chambers, the efficacy of which was to be seen in the religion, honesty, moderate competence, or upright poverty and solid happiness, of his descendants, to this day.

One object, above all others, would take root in the imaginative observer's memory. It was the great tuft of flowers,—weeds, you would have called them, only a week ago,—the tuft of crimson-spotted flowers, in the angle between the two front gables. The old people used to give them the name of Alice's Posies, in remembrance of fair Alice Pyncheon, who was believed to have brought their seeds from Italy. They were flaunting in rich beauty and full bloom to-day, and seemed, as it were, a mystic expression that something within the house was consummated.

It was but little after sunrise, when Uncle Venner made his appearance, as aforesaid, impelling a wheelbarrow along the street. He was going his matutinal rounds to collect cabbage-leaves, turnip-tops, potato-skins, and the miscellaneous refuse of the dinner-pot, which the thrifty housewives of the neighborhood were accustomed to put aside, as fit only to feed a pig. Uncle Venner's pig was fed entirely, and kept in prime order, on these eleemosynary contributions; insomuch that the patched philosopher used to promise that, before retiring to his farm, he would make a feast of the portly grunter, and invite all his neighbors to partake of the joints and spare-ribs which they had helped to fatten. Miss Hepzibah Pyncheon's housekeeping had so greatly improved, since Clifford became a member of the family, that her share of the banquet would have been no lean one; and Uncle Venner, accordingly, was a good deal disappointed not to find the large earthen pan, full of fragmentary eatables, that ordinarily awaited his coming at the back doorstep of the Seven Gables.

"I never knew Miss Hepzibah so forgetful before," said the patriarch to himself. "She must have had a dinner yesterday,—no question of that! She always has one, nowadays. So where's the pot-liquor and potato-skins, I ask? Shall I knock, and see if she's stirring yet? No, no,—'t won't do! If little Phoebe was about the house, I should not mind knocking; but Miss Hepzibah, likely as not, would scowl down at me out of the window, and look cross, even if she felt pleasantly. So, I'll come back at noon."

With these reflections, the old man was shutting the gate of the little back-yard. Creaking on its hinges, however, like every other gate and door about the premises, the sound reached the ears of the occupant of the northern gable, one of the windows of which had a side-view towards the gate.

"Good-morning, Uncle Venner!" said the daguerreotypist, leaning out of the window. "Do you hear nobody stirring?"

"Not a soul," said the man of patches. "But that's no wonder. 'Tis barely half an hour past sunrise, yet. But I'm really glad to see you, Mr. Holgrave! There's a strange, lonesome look about this side of the house; so that my heart misgave me, somehow or other, and I felt as if there was nobody alive in it. The front of the house looks a good deal cheerier; and Alice's Posies are blooming there beautifully; and if I were a young man, Mr. Holgrave, my sweetheart should have one of those flowers in her bosom, though I risked my neck climbing for it! Well, and did the wind keep you awake last night?"

"It did, indeed!" answered the artist, smiling. "If I were a believer in ghosts,—and I don't quite know whether I am or not,—I should have concluded that all the old Pyncheons were running riot in the lower rooms, especially in Miss Hepzibah's part of the house. But it is very quiet now."

"Yes, Miss Hepzibah will be apt to over-sleep herself, after being disturbed, all night, with the racket," said Uncle Venner. "But it would be odd, now, wouldn't it, if the Judge had taken both his cousins into the country along with him? I saw him go into the shop yesterday."

"At what hour?" inquired Holgrave.

"Oh, along in the forenoon," said the old man. "Well, well! I must go my rounds, and so must my wheelbarrow. But I'll be back here at dinner-time; for my pig likes a dinner as well as a breakfast. No meal-time, and no sort of victuals, ever seems to come amiss to my pig. Good morning to you! And, Mr. Holgrave, if I were a young man, like you, I'd get one of Alice's Posies, and keep it in water till Phoebe comes back."

"I have heard," said the daguerreotypist, as he drew in his head, "that the water of Maule's well suits those flowers best."

Here the conversation ceased, and Uncle Venner went on his way. For half an hour longer, nothing disturbed the repose of the Seven Gables; nor was there any visitor, except a carrier-boy, who, as he passed the front doorstep, threw down one of his newspapers; for Hepzibah, of late, had regularly taken it in. After a while, there came a fat woman, making prodigious speed, and stumbling as she ran up the steps of the shop-door. Her face glowed with fire-heat, and, it being a pretty warm morning, she bubbled and hissed, as it were, as if all a-fry with chimney-warmth, and summer-warmth, and the warmth of her own corpulent velocity. She tried the shop-door; it was fast. She tried it again, with so angry a jar that the bell tinkled angrily back at her.

"The deuce take Old Maid Pyncheon!" muttered the irascible housewife. "Think of her pretending to set up a cent-shop, and then lying abed till noon! These are what she calls gentlefolk's airs, I suppose! But I'll either start her ladyship, or break the door down!"

She shook it accordingly, and the bell, having a spiteful little temper of its own, rang obstreperously, making its remonstrances heard,—not, indeed, by the ears for which they were intended,—but by a good lady on the opposite side of the street. She opened the window, and addressed the impatient applicant.

"You'll find nobody there, Mrs. Gubbins."

"But I must and will find somebody here!" cried Mrs. Gubbins, inflicting another outrage on the bell. "I want a half-pound of pork, to fry some first-rate flounders for Mr. Gubbins's breakfast; and, lady or not, Old Maid Pyncheon shall get up and serve me with it!"

"But do hear reason, Mrs. Gubbins!" responded the lady opposite. "She, and her brother too, have both gone to their cousin's, Judge Pyncheon's at his country-seat. There's not a soul in the house, but that young daguerreotype-man that sleeps in the north gable. I saw old Hepzibah and Clifford go away yesterday; and a queer couple of ducks they were, paddling through the mud-puddles! They're gone, I'll assure you."

"And how do you know they're gone to the Judge's?" asked Mrs. Gubbins. "He's a rich man; and there's been a quarrel between him and Hepzibah this many a day, because he won't give her a living. That's the main reason of her setting up a cent-shop."

"I know that well enough," said the neighbor. "But they're gone,—that's one thing certain. And who but a blood relation, that couldn't help himself, I ask you, would take in that awful-tempered old maid, and that dreadful Clifford? That's it, you may be sure."

Mrs. Gubbins took her departure, still brimming over with hot wrath against the absent Hepzibah. For another half-hour, or, perhaps, considerably more, there was almost as much quiet on the outside of the house as within. The elm, however, made a pleasant, cheerful, sunny sigh, responsive to the breeze that was elsewhere imperceptible; a swarm of insects buzzed merrily under its drooping shadow, and became specks of light whenever they darted into the sunshine; a locust sang, once or twice, in some inscrutable seclusion of the tree; and a solitary little bird, with plumage of pale gold, came and hovered about Alice's Posies.

At last our small acquaintance, Ned Higgins, trudged up the street, on his way to school; and happening, for the first time in a fortnight, to be the possessor of a cent, he could by no means get past the shop-door of the Seven Gables. But it would not open. Again and again, however, and half a dozen other agains, with the inexorable pertinacity of a child intent upon some object important to itself, did he renew his efforts for admittance. He had, doubtless, set his heart upon an elephant; or, possibly, with Hamlet, he meant to eat a crocodile. In response to his more violent attacks, the bell gave, now and then, a moderate tinkle, but could not be stirred into clamor by any exertion of the little fellow's childish and tiptoe strength. Holding by the door-handle, he peeped through a crevice of the curtain, and saw that the inner door, communicating with the passage towards the parlor, was closed.

"Miss Pyncheon!" screamed the child, rapping on the window-pane, "I want an elephant!"

There being no answer to several repetitions of the summons, Ned began to grow impatient; and his little pot of passion quickly boiling over, he picked up a stone, with a naughty purpose to fling it through the window; at the same time blubbering and sputtering with wrath. A man —one of two who happened to be passing by—caught the urchin's arm.

"What's the trouble, old gentleman?" he asked.

"I want old Hepzibah, or Phoebe, or any of them!" answered Ned, sobbing. "They won't open the door; and I can't get my elephant!"

"Go to school, you little scamp!" said the man. "There's another cent-shop round the corner. 'T is very strange, Dixey," added he to his companion, "what's become of all these Pyncheon's! Smith, the livery-stable keeper, tells me Judge Pyncheon put his horse up yesterday, to stand till after dinner, and has not taken him away yet. And one of the Judge's hired men has been in, this morning, to make inquiry about him. He's a kind of person, they say, that seldom breaks his habits, or stays out o' nights."

"Oh, he'll turn up safe enough!" said Dixey. "And as for Old Maid Pyncheon, take my word for it, she has run in debt, and gone off from her creditors. I foretold, you remember, the first morning she set up shop, that her devilish scowl would frighten away customers. They couldn't stand it!"

"I never thought she'd make it go," remarked his friend. "This business of cent-shops is overdone among the women-folks. My wife tried it, and lost five dollars on her outlay!"

"Poor business!" said Dixey, shaking his head. "Poor business!"

In the course of the morning, there were various other attempts to open a communication with the supposed inhabitants of this silent and impenetrable mansion. The man of root-beer came, in his neatly painted wagon, with a couple of dozen full bottles, to be exchanged for empty ones; the baker, with a lot of crackers which Hepzibah had ordered for her retail custom; the butcher, with a nice titbit which he fancied she would be eager to secure for Clifford. Had any observer of these proceedings been aware of the fearful secret hidden within the house, it would have affected him with a singular shape and modification of horror, to see the current of human life making this small eddy hereabouts,—whirling sticks, straws and all such trifles, round and round, right over the black depth where a dead corpse lay unseen!

The butcher was so much in earnest with his sweetbread of lamb, or whatever the dainty might be, that he tried every accessible door of the Seven Gables, and at length came round again to the shop, where he ordinarily found admittance.

"It's a nice article, and I know the old lady would jump at it," said he to himself. "She can't be gone away! In fifteen years that I have driven my cart through Pyncheon Street, I've never known her to be away from home; though often enough, to be sure, a man might knock all day without bringing her to the door. But that was when she'd only herself to provide for."

Peeping through the same crevice of the curtain where, only a little while before, the urchin of elephantine appetite had peeped, the butcher beheld the inner door, not closed, as the child had seen it, but ajar, and almost wide open. However it might have happened, it was the fact. Through the passage-way there was a dark vista into the lighter but still obscure interior of the parlor. It appeared to the butcher that he could pretty clearly discern what seemed to be the stalwart legs, clad in black pantaloons, of a man sitting in a large oaken chair, the back of which concealed all the remainder of his figure. This contemptuous tranquillity on the part of an occupant of the house, in response to the butcher's indefatigable efforts to attract notice, so piqued the man of flesh that he determined to withdraw.

"So," thought he, "there sits Old Maid Pyncheon's bloody brother, while I've been giving myself all this trouble! Why, if a hog hadn't more manners, I'd stick him! I call it demeaning a man's business to trade with such people; and from this time forth, if they want a sausage or an ounce of liver, they shall run after the cart for it!"

He tossed the titbit angrily into his cart, and drove off in a pet.

Not a great while afterwards there was a sound of music turning the corner and approaching down the street, with several intervals of silence, and then a renewed and nearer outbreak of brisk melody. A mob of children was seen moving onward, or stopping, in unison with the sound, which appeared to proceed from the centre of the throng; so that they were loosely bound together by slender strains of harmony, and drawn along captive; with ever and anon an accession of some little fellow in an apron and straw-hat, capering forth from door or gateway. Arriving under the shadow of the Pyncheon Elm, it proved to be the Italian boy, who, with his monkey and show of puppets, had once before played his hurdy-gurdy beneath the arched window. The pleasant face of Phoebe—and doubtless, too, the liberal recompense which she had flung him—still dwelt in his remembrance. His expressive features kindled up, as he recognized the spot where this trifling incident of his erratic life had chanced. He entered the neglected yard (now wilder than ever, with its growth of hog-weed and burdock), stationed himself on the doorstep of the main entrance, and, opening his show-box, began to play. Each individual of the automatic community forthwith set to work, according to his or her proper vocation: the monkey, taking off his Highland bonnet, bowed and scraped to the by-standers most obsequiously, with ever an observant eye to pick up a stray cent; and the young foreigner himself, as he turned the crank of his machine, glanced upward to the arched window, expectant of a presence that would make his music the livelier and sweeter. The throng of children stood near; some on the sidewalk; some within the yard; two or three establishing themselves on the very door-step; and one squatting on the threshold. Meanwhile, the locust kept singing in the great old Pyncheon Elm.

"I don't hear anybody in the house," said one of the children to another. "The monkey won't pick up anything here."

"There is somebody at home," affirmed the urchin on the threshold. "I heard a step!"

Still the young Italian's eye turned sidelong upward; and it really seemed as if the touch of genuine, though slight and almost playful, emotion communicated a juicier sweetness to the dry, mechanical process of his minstrelsy. These wanderers are readily responsive to any natural kindness—be it no more than a smile, or a word itself not understood, but only a warmth in it—which befalls them on the roadside of life. They remember these things, because they are the little enchantments which, for the instant,—for the space that reflects a landscape in a soap-bubble,—build up a home about them. Therefore, the Italian boy would not be discouraged by the heavy silence with which the old house seemed resolute to clog the vivacity of his instrument. He persisted in his melodious appeals; he still looked upward, trusting that his dark, alien countenance would soon be brightened by Phoebe's sunny aspect. Neither could he be willing to depart without again beholding Clifford, whose sensibility, like Phoebe's smile, had talked a kind of heart's language to the foreigner. He repeated all his music over and over again, until his auditors were getting weary. So were the little wooden people in his show-box, and the monkey most of all. There was no response, save the singing of the locust.

"No children live in this house," said a schoolboy, at last. "Nobody lives here but an old maid and an old man. You'll get nothing here! Why don't you go along?"

"You fool, you, why do you tell him?" whispered a shrewd little Yankee, caring nothing for the music, but a good deal for the cheap rate at which it was had. "Let him play as he likes! If there's nobody to pay him, that's his own lookout!"

Once more, however, the Italian ran over his round of melodies. To the common observer— who could understand nothing of the case, except the music and the sunshine on the hither side of the door—it might have been amusing to watch the pertinacity of the street-performer. Will he succeed at last? Will that stubborn door be suddenly flung open? Will a group of joyous children, the young ones of the house, come dancing, shouting, laughing, into the open air, and cluster round the show-box, looking with eager merriment at the puppets, and tossing each a copper for long-tailed Mammon, the monkey, to pick up?

But to us, who know the inner heart of the Seven Gables as well as its exterior face, there is a ghastly effect in this repetition of light popular tunes at its door-step. It would be an ugly business, indeed, if Judge Pyncheon (who would not have cared a fig for Paganini's fiddle in his most harmonious mood) should make his appearance at the door, with a bloody shirt-bosom, and a grim frown on his swarthily white visage, and motion the foreign vagabond away! Was ever before such a grinding out of jigs and waltzes, where nobody was in the cue to dance? Yes, very often. This contrast, or intermingling of tragedy with mirth, happens daily, hourly, momently. The gloomy and desolate old house, deserted of life, and with awful Death sitting sternly in its solitude, was the emblem of many a human heart, which, nevertheless, is compelled to hear the thrill and echo of the world's gayety around it.

Before the conclusion of the Italian's performance, a couple of men happened to be passing, On their way to dinner. "I say, you young French fellow!" called out one of them,—"come away from that doorstep, and go somewhere else with your nonsense! The Pyncheon family live there; and they are in great trouble, just about this time. They don't feel musical to-day. It is reported all over town that Judge Pyncheon, who owns the house, has been murdered; and the city marshal is going to look into the matter. So be off with you, at once!"

As the Italian shouldered his hurdy-gurdy, he saw on the doorstep a card, which had been covered, all the morning, by the newspaper that the carrier had flung upon it, but was now shuffled into sight. He picked it up, and perceiving something written in pencil, gave it to the man to read. In fact, it was an engraved card of Judge Pyncheon's with certain pencilled memoranda on the back, referring to various businesses which it had been his purpose to transact during the preceding day. It formed a prospective epitome of the day's history; only that affairs had not turned out altogether in accordance with the programme. The card must have been lost from the Judge's vest-pocket in his preliminary attempt to gain access by the main entrance of the house. Though well soaked with rain, it was still partially legible.

"Look here; Dixey!" cried the man. "This has something to do with Judge Pyncheon. See!—here's his name printed on it; and here, I suppose, is some of his handwriting."

"Let's go to the city marshal with it!" said Dixey. "It may give him just the clew he wants. After all," whispered he in his companion's ear, "it would be no wonder if the Judge has gone into that door and never come out again! A certain cousin of his may have been at his old tricks. And Old Maid Pyncheon having got herself in debt by the cent-shop,—and the Judge's pocket-book being well filled,—and bad blood amongst them already! Put all these things together and see what they make!"

"Hush, hush!" whispered the other. "It seems like a sin to be the first to speak of such a thing. But I think, with you, that we had better go to the city marshal."

"Yes, yes!" said Dixey. "Well!—I always said there was something devilish in that woman's scowl!"

The men wheeled about, accordingly, and retraced their steps up the street. The Italian, also, made the best of his way off, with a parting glance up at the arched window. As for the children, they took to their heels, with one accord, and scampered as if some giant or ogre were in pursuit, until, at a good distance from the house, they stopped as suddenly and simultaneously as they had set out. Their susceptible nerves took an indefinite alarm from what they had overheard. Looking back at the grotesque peaks and shadowy angles of the old mansion, they fancied a gloom diffused about it which no brightness of the sunshine could dispel. An imaginary Hepzibah scowled and shook her finger at them, from several windows at the same moment. An imaginary Clifford—for (and it would have deeply wounded him to know it) he had always been a horror to these small people—stood behind the unreal Hepzibah, making awful gestures, in a faded dressing-gown. Children are even more apt, if possible, than grown people, to catch the contagion of a panic terror. For the rest of the day, the more timid went whole streets about, for the sake of avoiding the Seven Gables; while the bolder signalized their hardihood by challenging their comrades to race past the mansion at full speed.

It could not have been more than half an hour after the disappearance of the Italian boy, with his unseasonable melodies, when a cab drove down the street. It stopped beneath the Pyncheon Elm; the cabman took a trunk, a canvas bag, and a bandbox, from the top of his vehicle, and deposited them on the doorstep of the old house; a straw bonnet, and then the pretty figure of a young girl, came into view from the interior of the cab. It was Phoebe! Though not altogether so blooming as when she first tripped into our story,—for, in the few intervening weeks, her experiences had made her graver, more womanly, and deeper-eyed, in token of a heart that had begun to suspect its depths,—still there was the quiet glow of natural sunshine over her. Neither had she forfeited her proper gift of making things look real, rather than fantastic, within her sphere. Yet we feel it to be a questionable venture, even for Phoebe, at this juncture, to cross the threshold of the Seven Gables. Is her healthful presence potent enough to chase away the crowd of pale, hideous, and sinful phantoms, that have gained admittance there since her departure? Or will she, likewise, fade, sicken, sadden, and grow into deformity, and be only another pallid phantom, to glide noiselessly up and down the stairs, and affright children as she pauses at the window?

At least, we would gladly forewarn the unsuspecting girl that there is nothing in human shape or substance to receive her, unless it be the figure of Judge Pyncheon, who—wretched spectacle that he is, and frightful in our remembrance, since our night-long vigil with him!—still keeps his place in the oaken chair.

Phoebe first tried the shop-door. It did not yield to her hand; and the white curtain, drawn across the window which formed the upper section of the door, struck her quick perceptive faculty as something unusual. Without making another effort to enter here, she betook herself to the great portal, under the arched window. Finding it fastened, she knocked. A reverberation came from the emptiness within. She knocked again, and a third time; and, listening intently, fancied that the floor creaked, as if Hepzibah were coming, with her ordinary tiptoe movement, to admit her. But so dead a silence ensued upon this imaginary sound, that she began to question whether she might not have mistaken the house, familiar as she thought herself with its exterior.

Her notice was now attracted by a child's voice, at some distance. It appeared to call her name. Looking in the direction whence it proceeded, Phoebe saw little Ned Higgins, a good way down the street, stamping, shaking his head violently, making deprecatory gestures with both hands, and shouting to her at mouth-wide screech.

"No, no, Phoebe!" he screamed. "Don't you go in! There's something wicked there! Don't—don't—don't go in!"

But, as the little personage could not be induced to approach near enough to explain himself, Phoebe concluded that he had been frightened, on some of his visits to the shop, by her cousin Hepzibah; for the good lady's manifestations, in truth, ran about an equal chance of scaring children out of their wits, or compelling them to unseemly laughter. Still, she felt the more, for this incident, how unaccountably silent and impenetrable the house had become. As her next resort, Phoebe made her way into the garden, where on so warm and bright a day as the present, she had little doubt of finding Clifford, and perhaps Hepzibah also, idling away the noontide in the shadow of the arbor. Immediately on her entering the garden gate, the family of hens half ran, half flew to meet her; while a strange grimalkin, which was prowling under the parlor window, took to his heels, clambered hastily over the fence, and vanished. The arbor was vacant, and its floor, table, and circular bench were still damp, and bestrewn with twigs and the disarray of the past storm. The growth of the garden seemed to have got quite out of bounds; the weeds had taken advantage of Phoebe's absence, and the long-continued rain, to run rampant over the flowers and kitchen-vegetables. Maule's well had overflowed its stone border, and made a pool of formidable breadth in that corner of the garden.

The impression of the whole scene was that of a spot where no human foot had left its print for many preceding days,—probably not since Phoebe's departure,—for she saw a side-comb of her own under the table of the arbor, where it must have fallen on the last afternoon when she and Clifford sat there.

The girl knew that her two relatives were capable of far greater oddities than that of shutting themselves up in their old house, as they appeared now to have done. Nevertheless, with indistinct misgivings of something amiss, and apprehensions to which she could not give shape, she approached the door that formed the customary communication between the house and garden. It was secured within, like the two which she had already tried. She knocked, however; and immediately, as if the application had been expected, the door was drawn open, by a considerable exertion of some unseen person's strength, not wide, but far enough to afford her a sidelong entrance. As Hepzibah, in order not to expose herself to inspection from without, invariably opened a door in this manner, Phoebe necessarily concluded that it was her cousin who now admitted her.

Without hesitation, therefore, she stepped across the threshold, and had no sooner entered than the door closed behind her.

❧ 20 ❧

THE FLOWER OF EDEN

PHOEBE, coming so suddenly from the sunny daylight, was altogether bedimmed in such density of shadow as lurked in most of the passages of the old house. She was not at first aware by whom she had been admitted. Before her eyes had adapted themselves to the obscurity, a hand grasped her own with a firm but gentle and warm pressure, thus imparting a welcome which caused her heart to leap and thrill with an indefinable shiver of enjoyment. She felt herself drawn along, not towards the parlor, but into a large and unoccupied apartment, which had formerly been the grand reception-room of the Seven Gables. The sunshine came freely into all the uncurtained windows of this room, and fell upon the dusty floor; so that Phoebe now clearly saw—what, indeed, had been no secret, after the encounter of a warm hand with hers—that it was not Hepzibah nor Clifford, but Holgrave, to whom she owed her reception. The subtile, intuitive communication, or, rather, the vague and formless impression of something to be told, had made her yield unresistingly to his impulse. Without taking away her hand, she looked eagerly in his face, not quick to forebode evil, but unavoidably conscious that the state of the family had changed since her departure, and therefore anxious for an explanation.

The artist looked paler than ordinary; there was a thoughtful and severe contraction of his forehead, tracing a deep, vertical line between the eyebrows. His smile, however, was full of genuine warmth, and had in it a joy, by far the most vivid expression that Phoebe had ever witnessed, shining out of the New England reserve with which Holgrave habitually masked whatever lay near his heart. It was the look wherewith a man, brooding alone over some fearful object, in a dreary forest or illimitable desert, would recognize the familiar aspect of his dearest friend, bringing up all the peaceful ideas that belong to home, and the gentle current of every-day affairs. And yet, as he felt the necessity of responding to her look of inquiry, the smile disappeared.

"I ought not to rejoice that you have come, Phoebe," said he. "We meet at a strange moment!"

"What has happened!" she exclaimed. "Why is the house so deserted? Where are Hepzibah and Clifford?"

"Gone! I cannot imagine where they are!" answered Holgrave. "We are alone in the house!"

"Hepzibah and Clifford gone?" cried Phoebe. "It is not possible! And why have you brought me into this room, instead of the parlor? Ah, something terrible has happened! I must run and see!"

"No, no, Phoebe!" said Holgrave holding her back. "It is as I have told you. They are gone, and I know not whither. A terrible event has, indeed happened, but not to them, nor, as I undoubtingly believe, through any agency of theirs. If I read your character rightly, Phoebe," he continued, fixing his eyes on hers with stern anxiety, intermixed with tenderness, "gentle as you are, and seeming to have your sphere among common things, you yet possess remarkable strength. You have wonderful poise, and a faculty which, when tested, will prove itself capable of dealing with matters that fall far out of the ordinary rule."

"Oh, no, I am very weak!" replied Phoebe, trembling. "But tell me what has happened!"

"You are strong!" persisted Holgrave. "You must be both strong and wise; for I am all astray, and need your counsel. It may be you can suggest the one right thing to do!"

"Tell me!—tell me!" said Phoebe, all in a tremble. "It oppresses,—it terrifies me,—this mystery! Anything else I can bear!"

The artist hesitated. Notwithstanding what he had just said, and most sincerely, in regard to the self-balancing power with which Phoebe impressed him, it still seemed almost wicked to bring the awful secret of yesterday to her knowledge. It was like dragging a hideous shape of death into the cleanly and cheerful space before a household fire, where it would present all the uglier aspect, amid the decorousness of everything about it. Yet it could not be concealed from her; she must needs know it.

"Phoebe," said he, "do you remember this?" He put into her hand a daguerreotype; the same that he had shown her at their first interview in the garden, and which so strikingly brought out the hard and relentless traits of the original.

"What has this to do with Hepzibah and Clifford?" asked Phoebe, with impatient surprise that Holgrave should so trifle with her at such a moment. "It is Judge Pyncheon! You have shown it to me before!"

"But here is the same face, taken within this half-hour" said the artist, presenting her with another miniature. "I had just finished it when I heard you at the door."

"This is death!" shuddered Phoebe, turning very pale. "Judge Pyncheon dead!"

"Such as there represented," said Holgrave, "he sits in the next room. The Judge is dead, and Clifford and Hepzibah have vanished! I know no more. All beyond is conjecture. On returning to my solitary chamber, last evening, I noticed no light, either in the parlor, or Hepzibah's room, or Clifford's; no stir nor footstep about the house. This morning, there was the same death-like quiet. From my window, I overheard the testimony of a neighbor, that your relatives were seen leaving the house in the midst of yesterday's storm. A rumor reached me, too, of Judge Pyncheon being missed. A feeling which I cannot describe—an indefinite sense of some catastrophe, or consummation—impelled me to make my way into this part of the house, where I discovered what you see. As a point of evidence that may be useful to Clifford, and also as a memorial valuable to myself,—for, Phoebe, there are hereditary reasons that connect me strangely with that man's fate,—I used the means at my disposal to preserve this pictorial record of Judge Pyncheon's death."

Even in her agitation, Phoebe could not help remarking the calmness of Holgrave's demeanor. He appeared, it is true, to feel the whole awfulness of the Judge's death, yet had received the fact into his mind without any mixture of surprise, but as an event preordained, happening inevitably, and so fitting itself into past occurrences that it could almost have been prophesied.

"Why have you not thrown open the doors, and called in witnesses?" inquired she with a painful shudder. "It is terrible to be here alone!"

"But Clifford!" suggested the artist. "Clifford and Hepzibah! We must consider what is best to be done in their behalf. It is a wretched fatality that they should have disappeared! Their flight will throw the worst coloring over this event of which it is susceptible. Yet how easy is the explanation, to those who know them! Bewildered and terror-stricken by the similarity of this death to a former one, which was attended with such disastrous consequences to Clifford, they have had no idea but of removing themselves from the scene. How miserably unfortunate! Had Hepzibah but shrieked aloud,—had Clifford flung wide the door, and proclaimed Judge Pyncheon's death,—it would have been, however awful in itself, an event fruitful of good consequences to them. As I view it, it would have gone far towards obliterating the black stain on Clifford's character."

"And how," asked Phoebe, "could any good come from what is so very dreadful?"

"Because," said the artist, "if the matter can be fairly considered and candidly interpreted, it must be evident that Judge Pyncheon could not have come unfairly to his end. This mode of death had been an idiosyncrasy with his family, for generations past; not often occurring, indeed, but, when it does occur, usually attacking individuals about the Judge's time of life, and generally in the tension of some mental crisis, or, perhaps, in an access of wrath. Old Maule's prophecy was probably founded on a knowledge of this physical predisposition in the Pyncheon race. Now, there is a minute and almost exact similarity in the appearances connected with the death that occurred yesterday and those recorded of the death of Clifford's uncle thirty years ago. It is true, there was a certain arrangement of circumstances, unnecessary to be recounted, which made it possible nay, as men look at these things, probable, or even certain—that old Jaffrey Pyncheon came to a violent death, and by Clifford's hands."

"Whence came those circumstances?" exclaimed Phoebe. "He being innocent, as we know him to be!"

"They were arranged," said Holgrave,—"at least such has long been my conviction,—they were arranged after the uncle's death, and before it was made public, by the man who sits in yonder parlor. His own death, so like that former one, yet attended by none of those suspicious circumstances, seems the stroke of God upon him, at once a punishment for his wickedness, and making plain the innocence of Clifford. But this flight,—it distorts everything! He may be in concealment, near at hand. Could we but bring him back before the discovery of the Judge's death, the evil might be rectified."

"We must not hide this thing a moment longer!" said Phoebe. "It is dreadful to keep it so closely in our hearts. Clifford is innocent. God will make it manifest! Let us throw open the doors, and call all the neighborhood to see the truth!"

"You are right, Phoebe," rejoined Holgrave. "Doubtless you are right."

Yet the artist did not feel the horror, which was proper to Phoebe's sweet and order-loving character, at thus finding herself at issue with society, and brought in contact with an event that transcended ordinary rules. Neither was he in haste, like her, to betake himself within the precincts of common life. On the contrary, he gathered a wild enjoyment,—as it were, a flower of strange beauty, growing in a desolate spot, and blossoming in the wind,—such a flower of momentary happiness he gathered from his present position. It separated Phoebe and himself from the world, and bound them to each other, by their exclusive knowledge of Judge Pyncheon's mysterious death, and the counsel which they were forced to hold respecting it. The secret, so long as it should continue such, kept them within the circle of a spell, a solitude in the midst of men, a remoteness as entire as that of an island in mid-ocean; once divulged, the ocean would flow betwixt them, standing on its widely sundered shores. Meanwhile, all the circumstances of their situation seemed to draw them together; they were like two children who go hand in hand, pressing closely to one another's side, through a shadow-haunted passage. The image of awful Death, which filled the house, held them united by his stiffened grasp.

These influences hastened the development of emotions that might not otherwise have flowered so. Possibly, indeed, it had been Holgrave's purpose to let them die in their undeveloped germs. "Why do we delay so?" asked Phoebe. "This secret takes away my breath! Let us throw open the doors!"

"In all our lives there can never come another moment like this!" said Holgrave. "Phoebe, is it all terror?—nothing but terror? Are you conscious of no joy, as I am, that has made this the only point of life worth living for?"

"It seems a sin," replied Phoebe, trembling, "to think of joy at such a time!"

"Could you but know, Phoebe, how it was with me the hour before you came!" exclaimed the artist. "A dark, cold, miserable hour! The presence of yonder dead man threw a great black shadow over everything; he made the universe, so far as my perception could reach, a scene of guilt and of retribution more dreadful than the guilt. The sense of it took away my youth. I never hoped to feel young again! The world looked strange, wild, evil, hostile; my past life, so lonesome and dreary; my future, a shapeless gloom, which I must mould into gloomy shapes! But, Phoebe, you crossed the threshold; and hope, warmth, and joy came in with you! The black moment became at once a blissful one. It must not pass without the spoken word. I love you!"

"How can you love a simple girl like me?" asked Phoebe, compelled by his earnestness to speak. "You have many, many thoughts, with which I should try in vain to sympathize. And I, —I, too,—I have tendencies with which you would sympathize as little. That is less matter. But I have not scope enough to make you happy."

"You are my only possibility of happiness!" answered Holgrave. "I have no faith in it, except as you bestow it on me!"

"And then—I am afraid!" continued Phoebe, shrinking towards Holgrave, even while she told him so frankly the doubts with which he affected her. "You will lead me out of my own quiet path. You will make me strive to follow you where it is pathless. I cannot do so. It is not my nature. I shall sink down and perish!"

"Ah, Phoebe!" exclaimed Holgrave, with almost a sigh, and a smile that was burdened with thought.

"It will be far otherwise than as you forebode. The world owes all its onward impulses to men ill at ease. The happy man inevitably confines himself within ancient limits. I have a presentiment that, hereafter, it will be my lot to set out trees, to make fences,—perhaps, even, in due time, to build a house for another generation,—in a word, to conform myself to laws and the peaceful practice of society. Your poise will be more powerful than any oscillating tendency of mine."

"I would not have it so!" said Phoebe earnestly.

"Do you love me?" asked Holgrave. "If we love one another, the moment has room for nothing more. Let us pause upon it, and be satisfied. Do you love me, Phoebe?"

"You look into my heart," said she, letting her eyes drop. "You know I love you!"

And it was in this hour, so full of doubt and awe, that the one miracle was wrought, without which every human existence is a blank. The bliss which makes all things true, beautiful, and holy shone around this youth and maiden. They were conscious of nothing sad nor old. They transfigured the earth, and made it Eden again, and themselves the two first dwellers in it. The dead man, so close beside them, was forgotten. At such a crisis, there is no death; for immortality is revealed anew, and embraces everything in its hallowed atmosphere.

But how soon the heavy earth-dream settled down again!

"Hark!" whispered Phoebe. "Somebody is at the street door!"

"Now let us meet the world!" said Holgrave. "No doubt, the rumor of Judge Pyncheon's visit to this house, and the flight of Hepzibah and Clifford, is about to lead to the investigation of the premises. We have no way but to meet it. Let us open the door at once."

But, to their surprise, before they could reach the street door,—even before they quitted the room in which the foregoing interview had passed,—they heard footsteps in the farther passage. The door, therefore, which they supposed to be securely locked,—which Holgrave, indeed, had seen to be so, and at which Phoebe had vainly tried to enter,—must have been opened from without. The sound of footsteps was not harsh, bold, decided, and intrusive, as the gait of strangers would naturally be, making authoritative entrance into a dwelling where they knew themselves unwelcome. It was feeble, as of persons either weak or weary; there was the mingled murmur of two voices, familiar to both the listeners.

"Can it be?" whispered Holgrave.

"It is they!" answered Phoebe. "Thank God!—thank God!"

And then, as if in sympathy with Phoebe's whispered ejaculation, they heard Hepzibah's voice more distinctly.

"Thank God, my brother, we are at home!"

"Well!—Yes!—thank God!" responded Clifford. "A dreary home, Hepzibah! But you have done well to bring me hither! Stay! That parlor door is open. I cannot pass by it! Let me go and rest me in the arbor, where I used,—oh, very long ago, it seems to me, after what has befallen us,—where I used to be so happy with little Phoebe!"

But the house was not altogether so dreary as Clifford imagined it. They had not made many steps,—in truth, they were lingering in the entry, with the listlessness of an accomplished purpose, uncertain what to do next,—when Phoebe ran to meet them. On beholding her, Hepzibah burst into tears. With all her might, she had staggered onward beneath the burden of grief and responsibility, until now that it was safe to fling it down. Indeed, she had not energy to fling it down, but had ceased to uphold it, and suffered it to press her to the earth. Clifford appeared the stronger of the two.

"It is our own little Phoebe!—Ah! and Holgrave with, her" exclaimed he, with a glance of keen and delicate insight, and a smile, beautiful, kind, but melancholy. "I thought of you both, as we came down the street, and beheld Alice's Posies in full bloom. And so the flower of Eden has bloomed, likewise, in this old, darksome house to-day."

❧ 21 ❧

THE DEPARTURE

THE SUDDEN DEATH of so prominent a member of the social world as the Honorable Judge Jaffrey Pyncheon created a sensation (at least, in the circles more immediately connected with the deceased) which had hardly quite subsided in a fortnight.

It may be remarked, however, that, of all the events which constitute a person's biography, there is scarcely one—none, certainly, of anything like a similar importance—to which the world so easily reconciles itself as to his death. In most other cases and contingencies, the individual is present among us, mixed up with the daily revolution of affairs, and affording a definite point for observation. At his decease, there is only a vacancy, and a momentary eddy,— very small, as compared with the apparent magnitude of the ingurgitated object,—and a bubble or two, ascending out of the black depth and bursting at the surface. As regarded Judge Pyncheon, it seemed probable, at first blush, that the mode of his final departure might give him a larger and longer posthumous vogue than ordinarily attends the memory of a distinguished man. But when it came to be understood, on the highest professional authority, that the event was a natural, and—except for some unimportant particulars, denoting a slight idiosyncrasy—by no means an unusual form of death, the public, with its customary alacrity, proceeded to forget that he had ever lived. In short, the honorable Judge was beginning to be a stale subject before half the country newspapers had found time to put their columns in mourning, and publish his exceedingly eulogistic obituary.

Nevertheless, creeping darkly through the places which this excellent person had haunted in his lifetime, there was a hidden stream of private talk, such as it would have shocked all decency to speak loudly at the street-corners. It is very singular, how the fact of a man's death often seems to give people a truer idea of his character, whether for good or evil, than they have ever possessed while he was living and acting among them. Death is so genuine a fact that it excludes falsehood, or betrays its emptiness; it is a touchstone that proves the gold, and dishonors the baser metal. Could the departed, whoever he may be, return in a week after his decease, he would almost invariably find himself at a higher or lower point than he had formerly occupied, on the scale of public appreciation. But the talk, or scandal, to which we now allude, had reference to matters of no less old a date than the supposed murder, thirty or forty years ago, of the late Judge Pyncheon's uncle. The medical opinion with regard to his own recent and regretted decease had almost entirely obviated the idea that a murder was committed in the former case. Yet, as the record showed, there were circumstances irrefragably indicating that some person had gained access to old Jaffrey Pyncheon's private apartments, at or near the moment of his death. His desk and private drawers, in a room contiguous to his bedchamber, had been ransacked; money and valuable articles were missing; there was a bloody hand-print on the old man's linen; and, by a powerfully welded chain of deductive evidence, the guilt of the robbery and apparent murder had been fixed on Clifford, then residing with his uncle in the House of the Seven Gables.

Whencesoever originating, there now arose a theory that undertook so to account for these circumstances as to exclude the idea of Clifford's agency. Many persons affirmed that the history and elucidation of the facts, long so mysterious, had been obtained by the daguerreotypist from one of those mesmerical seers who, nowadays, so strangely perplex the aspect of human affairs, and put everybody's natural vision to the blush, by the marvels which they see with their eyes shut.

According to this version of the story, Judge Pyncheon, exemplary as we have portrayed him in our narrative, was, in his youth, an apparently irreclaimable scapegrace. The brutish, the animal instincts, as is often the case, had been developed earlier than the intellectual qualities, and the force of character, for which he was afterwards remarkable. He had shown himself wild, dissipated, addicted to low pleasures, little short of ruffianly in his propensities, and recklessly expensive, with no other resources than the bounty of his uncle. This course of conduct had alienated the old bachelor's affection, once strongly fixed upon him. Now it is averred,—but whether on authority available in a court of justice, we do not pretend to have investigated,—that the young man was tempted by the devil, one night, to search his uncle's private drawers, to which he had unsuspected means of access. While thus criminally occupied, he was startled by the opening of the chamber-door. There stood old Jaffrey Pyncheon, in his nightclothes! The surprise of such a discovery, his agitation, alarm, and horror, brought on the crisis of a disorder to which the old bachelor had an hereditary liability; he seemed to choke with blood, and fell upon the floor, striking his temple a heavy blow against the corner of a table. What was to be done? The old man was surely dead! Assistance would come too late! What a misfortune, indeed, should it come too soon, since his reviving consciousness would bring the recollection of the ignominious offence which he had beheld his nephew in the very act of committing!

But he never did revive. With the cool hardihood that always pertained to him, the young man continued his search of the drawers, and found a will, of recent date, in favor of Clifford,— which he destroyed,—and an older one, in his own favor, which he suffered to remain. But before retiring, Jaffrey bethought himself of the evidence, in these ransacked drawers, that some one had visited the chamber with sinister purposes. Suspicion, unless averted, might fix upon the real offender. In the very presence of the dead man, therefore, he laid a scheme that should free himself at the expense of Clifford, his rival, for whose character he had at once a contempt and a repugnance. It is not probable, be it said, that he acted with any set purpose of involving Clifford in a charge of murder. Knowing that his uncle did not die by violence, it may not have occurred to him, in the hurry of the crisis, that such an inference might be drawn. But, when the affair took this darker aspect, Jaffrey's previous steps had already pledged him to those which remained. So craftily had he arranged the circumstances, that, at Clifford's trial, his cousin hardly found it necessary to swear to anything false, but only to withhold the one decisive explanation, by refraining to state what he had himself done and witnessed.

Thus Jaffrey Pyncheon's inward criminality, as regarded Clifford, was, indeed, black and damnable; while its mere outward show and positive commission was the smallest that could possibly consist with so great a sin. This is just the sort of guilt that a man of eminent respectability finds it easiest to dispose of. It was suffered to fade out of sight or be reckoned a venial matter, in the Honorable Judge Pyncheon's long subsequent survey of his own life. He shuffled it aside, among the forgotten and forgiven frailties of his youth, and seldom thought of it again.

We leave the Judge to his repose. He could not be styled fortunate at the hour of death. Unknowingly, he was a childless man, while striving to add more wealth to his only child's inheritance. Hardly a week after his decease, one of the Cunard steamers brought intelligence of the death, by cholera, of Judge Pyncheon's son, just at the point of embarkation for his native land. By this misfortune Clifford became rich; so did Hepzibah; so did our little village maiden, and, through her, that sworn foe of wealth and all manner of conservatism,—the wild reformer, —Holgrave!

It was now far too late in Clifford's life for the good opinion of society to be worth the trouble and anguish of a formal vindication. What he needed was the love of a very few; not the admiration, or even the respect, of the unknown many. The latter might probably have been won for him, had those on whom the guardianship of his welfare had fallen deemed it advisable to expose Clifford to a miserable resuscitation of past ideas, when the condition of whatever comfort he might expect lay in the calm of forgetfulness. After such wrong as he had suffered, there is no reparation. The pitiable mockery of it, which the world might have been ready enough to offer, coming so long after the agony had done its utmost work, would have been fit only to provoke bitterer laughter than poor Clifford was ever capable of. It is a truth (and it would be a very sad one but for the higher hopes which it suggests) that no great mistake, whether acted or endured, in our mortal sphere, is ever really set right. Time, the continual vicissitude of circumstances, and the invariable inopportunity of death, render it impossible. If, after long lapse of years, the right seems to be in our power, we find no niche to set it in. The better remedy is for the sufferer to pass on, and leave what he once thought his irreparable ruin far behind him.

The shock of Judge Pyncheon's death had a permanently invigorating and ultimately beneficial effect on Clifford. That strong and ponderous man had been Clifford's nightmare. There was no free breath to be drawn, within the sphere of so malevolent an influence. The first effect of freedom, as we have witnessed in Clifford's aimless flight, was a tremulous exhilaration. Subsiding from it, he did not sink into his former intellectual apathy. He never, it is true, attained to nearly the full measure of what might have been his faculties. But he recovered enough of them partially to light up his character, to display some outline of the marvellous grace that was abortive in it, and to make him the object of no less deep, although less melancholy interest than heretofore. He was evidently happy. Could we pause to give another picture of his daily life, with all the appliances now at command to gratify his instinct for the Beautiful, the garden scenes, that seemed so sweet to him, would look mean and trivial in comparison.

Very soon after their change of fortune, Clifford, Hepzibah, and little Phoebe, with the approval of the artist, concluded to remove from the dismal old House of the Seven Gables, and take up their abode, for the present, at the elegant country-seat of the late Judge Pyncheon. Chanticleer and his family had already been transported thither, where the two hens had forthwith begun an indefatigable process of egg-laying, with an evident design, as a matter of duty and conscience, to continue their illustrious breed under better auspices than for a century past. On the day set for their departure, the principal personages of our story, including good Uncle Venner, were assembled in the parlor.

"The country-house is certainly a very fine one, so far as the plan goes," observed Holgrave, as the party were discussing their future arrangements. "But I wonder that the late Judge—being so opulent, and with a reasonable prospect of transmitting his wealth to descendants of his own—should not have felt the propriety of embodying so excellent a piece of domestic architecture in stone, rather than in wood. Then, every generation of the family might have altered the interior, to suit its own taste and convenience; while the exterior, through the lapse of years, might have been adding venerableness to its original beauty, and thus giving that impression of permanence which I consider essential to the happiness of any one moment."

"Why," cried Phoebe, gazing into the artist's face with infinite amazement, "how wonderfully your ideas are changed! A house of stone, indeed! It is but two or three weeks ago that you seemed to wish people to live in something as fragile and temporary as a bird's-nest!"

"Ah, Phoebe, I told you how it would be!" said the artist, with a half-melancholy laugh. "You find me a conservative already! Little did I think ever to become one. It is especially unpardonable in this dwelling of so much hereditary misfortune, and under the eye of yonder portrait of a model conservative, who, in that very character, rendered himself so long the evil destiny of his race."

"That picture!" said Clifford, seeming to shrink from its stern glance. "Whenever I look at it, there is an old dreamy recollection haunting me, but keeping just beyond the grasp of my mind. Wealth, it seems to say!—boundless wealth!—unimaginable wealth! I could fancy that, when I was a child, or a youth, that portrait had spoken, and told me a rich secret, or had held forth its hand, with the written record of hidden opulence. But those old matters are so dim with me, nowadays! What could this dream have been?"

"Perhaps I can recall it," answered Holgrave. "See! There are a hundred chances to one that no person, unacquainted with the secret, would ever touch this spring."

"A secret spring!" cried Clifford. "Ah, I remember now! I did discover it, one summer afternoon, when I was idling and dreaming about the house, long, long ago. But the mystery escapes me."

The artist put his finger on the contrivance to which he had referred. In former days, the effect would probably have been to cause the picture to start forward. But, in so long a period of concealment, the machinery had been eaten through with rust; so that at Holgrave's pressure, the portrait, frame and all, tumbled suddenly from its position, and lay face downward on the floor. A recess in the wall was thus brought to light, in which lay an object so covered with a century's dust that it could not immediately be recognized as a folded sheet of parchment. Holgrave opened it, and displayed an ancient deed, signed with the hieroglyphics of several Indian sagamores, and conveying to Colonel Pyncheon and his heirs, forever, a vast extent of territory at the Eastward.

"This is the very parchment, the attempt to recover which cost the beautiful Alice Pyncheon her happiness and life," said the artist, alluding to his legend. "It is what the Pyncheons sought in vain, while it was valuable; and now that they find the treasure, it has long been worthless."

"Poor Cousin Jaffrey! This is what deceived him," exclaimed Hepzibah. "When they were young together, Clifford probably made a kind of fairy-tale of this discovery. He was always dreaming hither and thither about the house, and lighting up its dark corners with beautiful stories. And poor Jaffrey, who took hold of everything as if it were real, thought my brother had found out his uncle's wealth. He died with this delusion in his mind!"

"But," said Phoebe, apart to Holgrave, "how came you to know the secret?"

"My dearest Phoebe," said Holgrave, "how will it please you to assume the name of Maule? As for the secret, it is the only inheritance that has come down to me from my ancestors. You should have known sooner (only that I was afraid of frightening you away) that, in this long drama of wrong and retribution, I represent the old wizard, and am probably as much a wizard as ever he was. The son of the executed Matthew Maule, while building this house, took the opportunity to construct that recess, and hide away the Indian deed, on which depended the immense land-claim of the Pyncheons. Thus they bartered their eastern territory for Maule's garden-ground."

"And now" said Uncle Venner "I suppose their whole claim is not worth one man's share in my farm yonder!"

"Uncle Venner," cried Phoebe, taking the patched philosopher's hand, "you must never talk any more about your farm! You shall never go there, as long as you live! There is a cottage in our new garden,—the prettiest little yellowish-brown cottage you ever saw; and the sweetest-looking place, for it looks just as if it were made of gingerbread,—and we are going to fit it up and furnish it, on purpose for you. And you shall do nothing but what you choose, and shall be as happy as the day is long, and shall keep Cousin Clifford in spirits with the wisdom and pleasantness which is always dropping from your lips!"

"Ah! my dear child," quoth good Uncle Venner, quite overcome, "if you were to speak to a young man as you do to an old one, his chance of keeping his heart another minute would not be worth one of the buttons on my waistcoat! And—soul alive!—that great sigh, which you made me heave, has burst off the very last of them! But, never mind! It was the happiest sigh I ever did heave; and it seems as if I must have drawn in a gulp of heavenly breath, to make it with. Well, well, Miss Phoebe! They'll miss me in the gardens hereabouts, and round by the back doors; and Pyncheon Street, I'm afraid, will hardly look the same without old Uncle Venner, who remembers it with a mowing field on one side, and the garden of the Seven Gables on the other. But either I must go to your country-seat, or you must come to my farm,—that's one of two things certain; and I leave you to choose which!"

"Oh, come with us, by all means, Uncle Venner!" said Clifford, who had a remarkable enjoyment of the old man's mellow, quiet, and simple spirit. "I want you always to be within five minutes, saunter of my chair. You are the only philosopher I ever knew of whose wisdom has not a drop of bitter essence at the bottom!"

"Dear me!" cried Uncle Venner, beginning partly to realize what manner of man he was. "And yet folks used to set me down among the simple ones, in my younger days! But I suppose I am like a Roxbury russet,—a great deal the better, the longer I can be kept. Yes; and my words of wisdom, that you and Phoebe tell me of, are like the golden dandelions, which never grow in the hot months, but may be seen glistening among the withered grass, and under the dry leaves, sometimes as late as December. And you are welcome, friends, to my mess of dandelions, if there were twice as many!"

A plain, but handsome, dark-green barouche had now drawn up in front of the ruinous portal of the old mansion-house. The party came forth, and (with the exception of good Uncle Venner, who was to follow in a few days) proceeded to take their places. They were chatting and laughing very pleasantly together; and—as proves to be often the case, at moments when we ought to palpitate with sensibility—Clifford and Hepzibah bade a final farewell to the abode of their forefathers, with hardly more emotion than if they had made it their arrangement to return thither at tea-time. Several children were drawn to the spot by so unusual a spectacle as the barouche and pair of gray horses. Recognizing little Ned Higgins among them, Hepzibah put her hand into her pocket, and presented the urchin, her earliest and staunchest customer, with silver enough to people the Domdaniel cavern of his interior with as various a procession of quadrupeds as passed into the ark.

Two men were passing, just as the barouche drove off.

"Well, Dixey," said one of them, "what do you think of this? My wife kept a cent-shop three months, and lost five dollars on her outlay. Old Maid Pyncheon has been in trade just about as long, and rides off in her carriage with a couple of hundred thousand,—reckoning her share, and Clifford's, and Phoebe's,—and some say twice as much! If you choose to call it luck, it is all very well; but if we are to take it as the will of Providence, why, I can't exactly fathom it!"

"Pretty good business!" quoth the sagacious Dixey,—"pretty good business!"

Maule's well, all this time, though left in solitude, was throwing up a succession of kaleidoscopic pictures, in which a gifted eye might have seen foreshadowed the coming fortunes of Hepzibah and Clifford, and the descendant of the legendary wizard, and the village maiden, over whom he had thrown love's web of sorcery. The Pyncheon Elm, moreover, with what foliage the September gale had spared to it, whispered unintelligible prophecies. And wise Uncle Venner, passing slowly from the ruinous porch, seemed to hear a strain of music, and fancied that sweet Alice Pyncheon—after witnessing these deeds, this bygone woe and this present happiness, of her kindred mortals—had given one farewell touch of a spirit's joy upon her harpsichord, as she floated heavenward from the HOUSE OF THE SEVEN GABLES!

Made in the USA
Monee, IL
30 January 2021